BLUE INK REVIEW

Journey into Darkness: A Story in Four Parts
J. Arthur Moore
(Reviewed: August, 2014)

Originally published in four separate volumes, J. Arthur Moore's chronicle of a young Arkansas boy's experiences on both sides of the Civil War battle lines gains emotional power as a single long tale.

At the outset of the tale, ten-year-old Duane Kinkade's father enlists in the Confederate army, and when raiders kill the boy's mother, he is left on his own. His search for his father takes Duane into battle at Shiloh, where he's wounded then rescued by a Union doctor. The fact that the boy moves from Confederate to Union forces in this section and those that follow seems improbable, but Moore's work is otherwise so well researched that readers will believe it was possible.

Duane's shifting perspective underscores war's dreadful toll on all combatants. The boy is blinded while serving with the Confederacy at Gettysburg. Back with the Union in the final section, he endures the deaths of two friends, just kids like himself.

"War does thin's ta ya," Duane says in a passage characteristic both of Moore's less-than-subtle use of dialect and the novel's fundamental power. "It makes ya kill when ya really ain't wantin' naturely ta do it. It's a horror ya cain't b'lieve really happens." Moore's central point, that war is hell and everyone longs for peace, is underscored in a poignant scene where a Federal band, playing within earshot of the Confederate army encamped across the river, begins with John Brown's Body but also plays Dixie; as it closes with Home Sweet Home, "tears ran unchecked down the cheeks of a hundred thousand [sic] men and boys."

Heartfelt and affecting, written in plain prose that suits its young protagonist, this sad story poignantly drives home the human cost of war.

Blue Ink Heads-Up: This would be an excellent resource for middle-school American history classes, giving a boy's-eye view of the Civil War and reminding students that kids their own age were caught up in active duty during the war. The solid research and gripping battle scenes will engage adult Civil War buffs.

Also available in hardcover and ebook.

JOURNEY INTO DARKNESS
a story in four parts
Written by J. Arthur Moore

The novel is written in four parts at the request of a young friend on behalf of young readers who do not like thick books

Journey Into Darkness has been recognized by the Mom's Choice Award For excellence in young adult/historic fiction/book series

musicians from the 150th anniversary of Antietam

JOURNEY INTO DARKNESS

3rd edition – Color Copyright © 2019 by J. Arthur Moore
3rd edition B&W Copyright © 2018 by J. Arthur Moore
2nd edition – color Copyright © 2015 by J. Arthur Moore
original copyright © 2014 by J. Arthur Moore
originally published in a four-book series
On the Eve of Conflict–2013
On the Eve of Conflict (2nd Edition) – 2017
On the Eve of Conflict (3rd Edition) – 2018
Up from Corinth – 2011
Up from Corinth(2nd Edition) – 2017
Up from Corinth (3rd Edition) – 2018
Across the Valley to Darkness – 2013
Across the Valley to Darkness(2nd Edition) – 2017
Across the Valley to Darkness (3rd Edition) – 2018
Toward the End of the Search – 2013
Toward the End of the Search (2nd Edition) – 2017
Toward the End of the Search (3rd Edition) – 2018
All rights reserved.

ISBN: 978-621-434-049-1 (softcover)
978-621-434-050-7 (hardcover)
978-621-434-051-4 (eBook)
978-1-952874-07-9 (kindle)

This is a work of historic fiction. As a blend of fact and fiction, the names, characters, places, and incidents either are the product of the author's imagination or are references to actual persons, events, and locales, blended within the context of the story, through research.
Copyright © 2020 J. Arthur Moore

Printed in New York by:

⬛OMNIBOOK Co.

OMNIBOOK CO.
99 Wall Street, Suite 118
New York, NY 10005
USA
+1 866-216-9965
www.omnibookcompany.com
For e-book purchase: Kindle on Amazon, Barnes and Noble
Wholesale purchase: Ingram (615) 793-5000, Baker & Taylor (800) 775-1800
Book purchase: Amazon.com, Barnes & Noble, and www.omnibookcompany.com
Omnibook titles may be purchased in bulk for educational, business, fund-raising, or sales promotional use.
For more information please e-mail info@omnibookcompany.com

Designed by: Gian Carlo Tan

Dedication

Journey Into Darkness is dedicated in His love and in friendship to Charley French, David Rowland, Richie Christman, Matthew Oswald, and Christopher Oswald who helped to bring the story to life by becoming a part of the story through their images as the characters in the story. It is also dedicated to all, young and old, who pick up the book and join Duane Kinkade in his experiences encountered during the Civil War and in so doing take their own journeys through America's Civil War history.

Author's notes

Journey Into Darkness was begun nearly fifty years ago. It was finally written during the 1980's, beginning in the fall of 1984, at the request of Charley French, one of several campers who heard the story while on camping trips with the author. Learning the original story had not been worked on for some time, he offered to represent the main character if the author would continue to work on the story. So for him and others who have enjoyed the telling of *Journey Into Darkness* that first book was written.

Another camper, Michael Flanagan, suggested the format of the story. On behalf of the many young readers who did not like thick books, he felt several smaller books would be more appropriate. Therefore the story of *Journey Into Darkness* was told in a series of four books.

The first of these books to be published was *Up From Corinth*, the second in the series, but the first to be written. Published in July 2011, it was followed by the balance of the series in the spring of 2013. In the spring of 2014, with the writing and the publishing of *Blake's Story, Revenge and Forgiveness*, it was decided, in the interest of cost and those who wanted the complete story, to publish the complete novel as a single book. As this was in progress, it was decided to publish another book, written during the academic year of 82-83, *Summer of Two Worlds*. Thus all three books, originally available in manuscript form only, came out in the spring of 2014. The photography for *Blake's Story* had not been completed, so a second edition was planned to be released in full color. As this was being done, it was decided to re-release **Journey** in full color as well. As a result, a second edition of **Journey** was published in full color. In the process, portions of the novel were rewritten to take into account new material brought to the author's attention. This third edition adds a choice between a black and white version or the color version as a money-saving option along with some updates, as all books are moved to a more focused final publisher, Omnibooks Company.

The Photography

All photography is by the author. Duane Kinkade is represented by Charley French; Jamie Fowler is represented by Richie Christman; Johnny Applebee is represented by David Rowland; Tod Gardner is represented by Matthew Oswald; and Jonah Christopher is represented by Christopher Oswald. All youngsters were participants in camping programs directed by the author.

Character photo sessions were taken at Valley Forge National Park, The Episcopal Academy Devon Campus, Warwick County Park Chester County, Colonial Pennsylvania Plantation at Ridley Creek State Park – all in Chester and Delaware Counties in Pennsylvania. Additional photography was taken at the Colonial Pennsylvania Plantation Civil War encampment 1987, 150th anniversary events at Antietam and Chancellorsville.

Acknowledgements

This book is made possible by the tireless and dedicated work of KC Normanns who worked tirelessly to create the first edition of Journey, first as a 4-book series and later as a novel in four parts, while at Xlibris, and has been key to bringing my books to life in full color at LitFire Publishing after she made the move to the publisher, and to putting together packages to support the marketing and publishing of both current books, Blake's Story, Revenge and Forgiveness and Journey Into Darkness, in full color. Patrick Grayson has been the leader on the production side and gone out of his way to trouble shoot and direct the progress of publication and the processes for support elements such as web site and Facebook. This three way team has succeeded with the help of excellent design team support as well as the management team with which each works.

Continuing this work has been the efforts of Sophia Myers who picked up the leadership role for Journey Into Darkness final evolution through the publication process and Noel Brock who has become the go to person for website content development and management, and their respective teams. Finally, Eric Armstrong saw to it that the copyright documents were acquired from the U.S. Copyright Office and final best images were placed in the maps section of the print master.

This Black and White special edition is made possible through the efforts of Andy Sullivan and his support teams at Omnibook Company. Countless hours on the phone and in coordination with his design team have been dedicated to developing the 3rd edition of the 4-book series, and now the publishing of the 4-part novel, providing a complete choice of formats at a lower retail price as opposed to the 4-part novel in full color.

For all this and for these people, I am truly grateful.

This is the house where *Journey Into Darkness, Summer of Two Worlds*, Heir to Balmawr, and many other works were written back in the years 1976 through 1990, as it looked when the author lived there. It is currently abandoned in possession of a bank.

CONTENTS

REFERENCES

J. Arthur Moore

ON THE EVE OF
Conflict

The Beginning of The Story
Book 1 of JOURNEY INTO DARKNESS

JOURNEY INTO DARKNESS

a story in four parts

part 1

On the Eve of Conflict

part 2

Up From Corinth

part 3

Across the Valley to Darkness

part 4

Toward the End of the Search

the beginning of the story

JOURNEY INTO DARKNESS

written by
J. Arthur Moore

Dedication

On the Eve of Conflict is dedicated in His love and in friendship to Charley French and Richie Christman, each of whom has helped by becoming forever a part of the story through the photographic material, and to all who have enjoyed its telling and shared in the adventure of its creation.

Duane Kinkade

Jamie Fowler

The head of the ax hung momentarily suspended in the air before it was drawn forcefully downward. As it struck the chunk of tree round with a loud crack, the grain collapsed and the cord wood flew apart. The ax blade bit into the chopping stump and there it stayed. The man paused to wipe the sweat from his eyebrows with the back of his hand, while the boy bent to gather up the pieces of wood from where they had fallen about the wood yard.

Andrew Kinkade was a man of enthusiastic energy. Nearing his thirty- fourth birthday, he was small in stature with unexpected strength from years of work on the farm and, in earlier years, at the store the family once owned. He picked up his plain, light-colored shirt from where it lay across the rough, wooden saw horse and wiped the wood chips from his arms and head before shaking the shirt out and slipping it on. He watched his son stack the last of the wood while he tucked in his shirt tail and pulled on his suspender straps.

"Son, what ya say we call this done fer now 'n head off fishin fer a bit?" The man paused with his thumbs hooked in the waistband of his trousers. Duane tossed the last of the pieces onto the stack of split wood. "Sure, Pa," the boy responded. "I'm ready fer it. My feet'll like ta hang in the water 'n cool off." He parked himself on the stack of wood to catch his breath. "Hey, Pounder!" he called.

The large tan and white head of his long-haired mixed-breed dog raised itself from behind the scattering of unsplit rounds beyond the chopping block. The large mouth opened wide in a lazy yawn, then he shook his head to dislodge a bothersome fly. Dark eyes met dark eyes as the dog awaited his young master's expected command.

"Com 'ere, boy." The boy slapped his thigh lightly. "Ya wanna go fishin?" Slowly the dog stretched, then pushed himself to his feet. Shuffling around the scattered wood chunks, he worked his way to where the boy waited and sank into a seated position by his side, resting his muzzle in the boy's lap. The ten-year-old boy gently stroked his friend's neck and scratched him under the ears. Duane was of slight build and somewhat short in stature. Pounder, while still a pup, not yet a year old, stood fully as tall as the boy and outweighed him by an extra ten pounds. They were the best of friends, inseparable from the day they met in a back alley of the nearby town of Bendton. Lifting his head, Pounder reached out to lick the side of the boy's face, in complete agreement with the fishing idea. The pass of the large tongue from under the chin, up the cheek, and across the ear, tickled; and Duane drew back, jumping to his feet.

Mr. Kinkade spoke, "Why don't you two find us some worms whilst I see 'bout gittin the poles from the barn."

"Okay," the boy called, already on his way toward the treeshaded end of the garden. "Meet ya at the rocks near the lane ta the creek."

Pounder followed as the two ran off to search the garden's edge and nearby rocks. Duane's bare feet padded across the yard, sending up small clouds of dust. Sweat streaked the boy's tanned flesh, staining the waistband of his trousers and darkening the edges of his suspender straps. Dust quickly attached itself in a thin coating to the moisture of his skin from the waist up.

The dog ran ahead and began to pick at the small rocks, digging gingerly with his paws. As Duane joined him, he rolled one over, then sat to watch the boy inspect for worms. A quick grab captured one single creature as it began to burrow into the dirt. The search continued. Pounder turned over the stones, then dug into the soft soil of the garden while Duane caught what few worms could be uncovered. A short time later Mr. Kinkade approached with poles and an old coffee tin which they used for carrying bait.

"Got eny?" the man asked.

"Seven," his son replied.

"Thet'll do." The boy stood to share his prizes. "Here." His father held out the can and the worms were safely deposited. A handful of dirt was added and the nail-punched lid was secured.

Pounder observed that preparations were complete, so he started ahead to tend to the serious business of hunting rabbits along the way. As the dog raced off ahead, the man handed his son his pole and they turned to follow. The pole was a green willow branch with a length of string from the general store and a regular store-bought hook. The dog's excited bark signaled a chase was on. Duane smiled to himself, for he knew the rabbit would win in the end.

The boy and his father followed the worn lane between the garden and the corn field until it passed around a small knoll and into a stand of pine trees. They took their time and ambled slowly along. The boy paused to watch a squirrel bound across the pine needles and disappear into a tree. The man stopped to witness the wonder his son had for creatures. They moved on, the boy taking the lead.

"Pa," Duane spoke without turning. "Ya think ther's gonna be a war?"

"I dunno, Son." They both continued to walk on. "Ther's a lot a talk. I really think there might."

Nothing more was said for several minutes. Sunlight shone in a bright splotch ahead where the woodland gave way to an open meadow.

"Ya gonna go if there is?" the boy asked.

"I hafta do what's right by you 'n yer ma 'n by this land. So I s'pose so."

The sudden brightness enveloped the two as they entered the meadow. Shading their eyes against the glare, they paused a moment to get used to the light, then moved on. The land sloped in a gentle downhill roll, until it bottomed out at a broad meandering creek which coursed its way across the heart of the grassland. The spring grass was knee-high with splashes of color from wild flowers and the deep purple of thistles in bloom. As the man and the boy approached the water's edge, the dog came splashing through the shallows along the shore to join them. Bounding up the embankment, he paused to shake the water from his long coat and for a brief moment was lost in a mist that sparkled in a fine dusty glitter of sunlight. The three then headed downstream to a deep pool of quiet water shaded by a large, gnarled oak tree. There they settled down for the serious business of fishing.

Mr. Kinkade found his regular place at the base of the tree where he sat with his back against its trunk. Once comfortable, he began to bait his hook and drop it in. Duane nestled into a favorite position among the rocks along the bank. Pounder lay on the grass nearby, head on front paws, where he could quietly survey the boy's progress, keep a watchful eye on their surroundings, and doze when he felt bored.

An uneventful hour slipped by. Nothing much was said. The fish weren't biting. It was a time of quiet peace. Small sparrows chirped and flitted about in the grass along the creek's bank. A black water snake slithered along the water's surface to crawl out on a large rock near the far bank and sun itself in the warmth of the afternoon. Dragon flies hovered above the water near the tall grass in the shallows. Water spiders danced in interlacing rings on its surface. Duane left his pole propped in the rocks and concentrated on a search among the stones for salamanders and crawfish. His father slipped into a quiet nap, dozing where he sat. Pounder lay motionless except for his eyes. They followed every move the boy made.

Suddenly there was a loud splash as Mr. Kinkade's line came to life and the pole was dragged into the water. Andrew awoke with a start, in time to see the dog spring to his feet and leap into the water after the fishing pole. Duane turned to see what the sudden commotion was about and saw his father standing on the creek bank, watching Pounder chase after the fishing pole.

Snatching the base of the pole, the dog struggled with his prize, working his way backwards toward the embankment. A large catfish splashed about on the end of the line, fighting against being pulled ashore. The man leaned down to take the incoming pole as his son hurried closer to be part of the excitement. The pole came within reach when the fish made a sudden dive beside a large underwater rock. The line snagged. Andrew took the pole and pulled while the dog scrambled up the bank to stand by the boy and supervise. Suddenly the line snapped and the contest was ended.

"Almost, Pa," Duane commented.

Pounder took time to shake off the water and the boy hurried backwards, raising his hand to shield himself from the spray.

His father smiled at the sight. "Guess fishin's done fer now," he observed. Glancing skyward, he continued, "Git'n on t'wards supper. Time ta be headin in."

"Soon's I fetch m' pole 'n the bait can." Duane retrieved the things from their place along the bank, then joined his father.

As before, the dog ran ahead. The boy and his father followed. Laughing together about the story they would tell his ma about the one that got away, they headed toward the wooded path and disappeared into the shadows.

*   *   *

As the first rays of sunlight raced out of the east, the early morning mists were scattered, revealing the glistening trees and the freshly plowed fertile fields throughout the valley, nestled in the Ozark Hill region in northwestern Arkansas. Tucked along the southern end of the valley was the bustling little village of Bendton, with the glow of the morning sun glinting off the belfry of its little church. About five miles north, and set in a small glen on the hillside, just back from a dirt lane, was the little farm, full of the early morning sounds and sights generated by the coming of a new spring day.

Whiffs of smoke rising from the cabin's chimney suggested that breakfast was being prepared. The wood-frame cabin was small. It had only three rooms – a main one for dining and living and two tiny bedrooms. The outhouse stood about ten yards out the back door, just to the side of the wood yard. The farmyard area was scattered with cackling hens, and from a fencepost somewhere in the barnyard a rooster raised its morning call. From the barn came the sounds of a lowing cow, a horse's whinny, and the clatter of a pail. The morning chores were underway. The barn, like the house, was of wood construction and small in size. It contained but a few tools and some livestock. The hay was stacked in a grain yard beside the structure. A small flat-bed wagon was kept outside the board fence that surrounded the barn yard. The old wood-plank gate sagged from use and age. Missing shingles from the roof showed dark holes near the ridge of the steep slope.

Laura Kinkade, a small, slip of a woman in her thirties, with her dark hair pinned up in a bun on the back of her head, emerged from the cabin wearing a dark plain dress and an apron. She called toward the barn, "Dee! you git yerself an yer pa in here an warshed up fer brekfist fer it gits cold! An mind ya use both hands when ya bring the milk this time! I want 'nough in the dipper ta bottle taday."

"Yeh, Ma," replied the boy indifferently, as he stepped from the barn into the early morning brightness.

He paused briefly, squinting his eyes against the glare. His pa joined him a moment later and the two stood at the barn door for a minute. Pounder lay along the wall beside the open door. He stood as the two emerged and padded silently to the boy's side.

"Ya take the milk ta yer Ma, Dee, 'n mind what she says 'bout usin' two hands. I'll turn the calf in with her ma 'n be right along."

"Sure, Pa," affirmed the boy as he started for the house.

The dog kept pace alongside as the boy crossed the yard to the house. Duane set the milk on the porch while he went around to the side of the house where the pump and water trough were. Pounder stopped at the corner of the structure to watch while the boy washed his hands and face in the trough. Then with eyes shut tight against the water dripping from his hair, Duane reached blindly for the towel that hung on the pump handle. The dog sat down to wait. Duane's father arrived from the barn just in time to catch the towel as the back of the boy's hand brushed against it, sending it sliding from the pump handle toward the ground.

"If you'd only larn ta open yer eyes, I wouldn't haf ta play at rescuer like this." He smiled as he handed Duane the towel.

The boy dried his face and hands, and flicked the towel across the top of the pump. Pushing his brown hair back out of his eyes, he headed back toward the porch where he picked up the milk, mounted the steps, and entered the main room. The dog followed as far as the steps. There he plopped down with a thud to nap while the family ate.

The tantalizing smell of hot cakes filled the room. Duane placed the milk on the table and went over to the stove to watch the bubbles pop as the batter grew and burst on the griddle.

"If'n ya don't set yerself down ta the table, yer not gonna git nothin ta eat." The words came with a smile as the boy's mother flipped the cakes and he went to his seat.

"Call yer Pa, Dee," Mrs. Kinkade instructed without turning from the stove.

"No need ta, Son," her husband remarked as he entered the cabin and hung his coat on its peg beside the door. "Smelled them hotcakes clear outside 'n figured I'd best hurry if'n I was ta git some 'fer Dee ate 'em all." They sat down to breakfast and the man said grace. Then as they ate, he discussed the plans for the day.

"Dee," his father instructed, "I want ya ta fill the woodbox fer yer Ma 'n have a bucket a water in here fer her. I've ta go ta town ta git what groc'ries 'n supplies I kin, 'n I figure ya kin be a help. So soon's brekfist is don, ya git ta be doin them chores so's ta be ready when I am."

"You bet, Pa!" exclaimed the boy.

The thought of going to town excited Duane so that he forgot to open his mouth as he attempted to take in a forkful of hotcake dripping with molasses. He quickly looked to see if his Pa had noticed. After all a grown boy of ten doesn't usually miss his mouth when it comes to getting in food. He knew his Ma hadn't noticed, cause she would have said something immediately.

"Is there enythin I kin git ya while I'm ta town, Laura?" the man asked his wife.

"I'll give ya a list a what I need. Git what's there."

When he was finished with breakfast, Mr. Kinkade pushed his plate back, stretched his arms at his side, and settled back in his chair, folding them across his chest. He stared thoughtfully at the ceiling for a moment, then turned toward his son who was wiping up his plate with a last bit of hotcake.

"On my way, Pa," Duane said as he gulped it down and hurriedly scraped his chair back from the table.

The boy skipped out the door to do as he had been instructed, grabbing the water bucket en route as he passed the drain board.

"Come on, Pounder," he called as he went. "We're goin ta town taday." The dog jumped up to follow.

Mr. Kinkade followed along a short time later to hitch the team to the wagon. Within the quarter hour they were up in the wagon seat and ready to roll. The dog centered himself in the wagon bed, just behind the seat where he could peer ahead between the man and his son or survey the countryside as it rolled past.

"When shall I 'spect ya back?" Mrs. Kinkade asked.

"We ought ta be back sometime late aftanoon," her husband replied.

"Take good care a yerselfs, now. 'N don't go findin no trouble," she called after them as they left the farm yard and headed for the road. It wasn't that she expected them to get into trouble. It was just something more to say before they were gone, leaving her no one to talk to until they returned.

The sun was all the way up, now, and shining clear in the bright blue morning sky. As the horses ambled along, Duane couldn't help but to notice how sweet the air smelled and how carefree and unconcerned the jackrabbit feeding along the roadside seemed to be. The boy turned to observe the dog tense at the sight of the animal and reached out to calm him with a gentle stroking of the massive head. Then, resting his hand on the soft coat of the dog's back, he wondered what it would be like if there were to be a war as he had heard there might. There had been talk for a long time of secession, yet that hadn't happened. There might be a lot of excitement. But for now, war was just talk. He gazed into his friend's brown eyes, smiled, then went back to scanning the countryside.

An hour passed as the wagon rumbled the country roads, rolling up its small cloud of dust, which caught in the morning breeze and drifted into nothing.

They approached the village of Bendton. The outskirts consisted of small farms with their frame buildings along the road and the fields stretching away on either side. Then they passed small clapboard homes, each on an acre or so of ground. Some had barns out back for a horse and a cow and maybe a few chickens, and some didn't. But all had little narrow shanties, each with its halo of aroma. In the center of the town were the hotel and saloons with their squared, weathered wood fronts, the shops, a bank, and, on the northern outskirts of town, the small church, which doubled as a schoolhouse during the week. The town cemetery crowned a small hill further to the northwest. Most structures were of wood construction. Some were stone or a clay brick.

But something wasn't right. Almost everyone in the little town was at the newspaper office. Mr. Kinkade halted the rig in front of the shop to hear what was going on and why all the excitement.

"So they fin'ly done it," commented one of the men.

"But are ya sure it's true?" asked a second.

"Here's proof in black 'n white. See fer yerself," replied the first.

"I didn't think they had 'tin 'em," observed a third.

"Will some'n please tell me what's up?" Duane's pa inquired. Some turned to notice him.

"Ain't ya heard, Andy? Abe Lincoln's done declared war!" was the answer. "Some a our men fired at a Fort Sumter off East som'eres 'n Lincoln got mad."

Laughter rippled through the crowd. Pounder joined in with a sharp bark.

"Dee, ya best go look up Jamie. I've some un'spected business here ta tend ta," ordered the boy's father.

"But, Pa..."

"No but's 'bout it. Now take off."

The boy climbed down from the wagon as his dog jumped from the side to follow. Mr. Kinkade watched his son start down the street, kicking at the dirt and small stones to vent his anger, while his dog accompanied him quietly at his side. A worried sadness showed in a half smile. Duane walked toward the brick building near the center of town. It was the Marshal's office. His friend, Jamie, was Marshal Jonathan Fowler's son.

"Doggone it," Duane muttered to himself as he approached the office structure, "Why is't thet I always have ta be treated like a kid.

Why can't I listen ta growd-up talk sometimes." He paused at the porch steps outside.

Pounder stopped and, with a soft whine of inquiry, looked up at his young master.

"It's okay, boy. Ya stay outside on the porch." He pointed to the shadowed wall near the door.

The dog bounded up to the wooden walk, crossed to his regular spot, then dropped quietly. Resting his muzzle on his forepaws, he followed the boy with his eyes, as he climbed the steps and entered the office.

"Hey, Jamie!" he greeted, "are we really at war now?"

But the office seemed empty. Then a head full of curly, black hair popped up from behind the marshal's desk and large brown eyes peered at him across the paper-littered writing surface. "Hi, Dee," the cheerful voice greeted.

"What ya doin?" Duane paused for his eyes to adjust to the dim interior light.

"Dropped some papers," the boy explained as he stood up, then perched himself on the corner of the desktop. "War?" he continued. "So I hear." He shuffled through the papers as Duane crossed the room and dropped himself into the marshal's wooden, swivel chair.

"They need all the men they kin git. Nigh onta ever'one in town who thinks he kin fight has already signed up. Pa says he's gonna stay back ta defend 'gainst raiders. They seem ta be hittin closer, now."

"Raiders?" Duane was whirling himself around in circles. Snagging the desk with his toe, he halted his movement. Then leaning back, he propped his boots on the desktop to listen.

"Yeah, groups a outlaws has bin raidin 'n burnin farms 'n small towns ta the north. Pa says they git closer ev'ry week." Jamie laid the papers in the middle of the desk as he hopped down and walked over toward a bookcase by the wall.

"I hope he's wrong." Duane spun the chair to follow his friend's movement. "Hey, when da the recruits leave?"

"They're s'posed ta head east on the riverboat out a Ozark come the end a the month," came Jamie's reply. He reached beside the case for a broom.

"How long ya think the war'll last?" Duane pushed the chair back, rocking on its spring.

"Most people say it'll be over in six weeks." Jamie leaned on the broom. "But I think they're wrong. Say, is yer Pa gonna sign up?"

"I dunno." The chair flopped forward. "I guess so."

"Hey, gimme a hand here." Jamie suddenly realized he wasn't getting any work done. "You straighten up the papers on Pa's desk whilst I finish sweepin the floor."

"Yeah, okay." The boy spun the chair to face the desk, and the two of them set to work straightening up the office. Jamie swept the floor, directing the dirt under the cabinet in the corner. Duane divided the papers on the desk into two neat piles, one with pictures and the other without.

*   *   *

It was the edge of evening when the wagon turned off the road and onto the lane into the farm. The western sky was a brilliant flame color while a silver disk with a broken edge shown in the black-blue eastern sky. The cabin with its yellow squares of light was an inviting sight. The boy and his father, hungry from the trip, would soon sit down to supper.

*   *   *

The fire leapt merrily on the hearth. The supper dishes had been washed and put away, and the evening chores were done. Mr. Kinkade was sitting in his favorite chair and staring into the fire. His wife rocked slowly in her high-backed, wooden rocker, quietly darning socks for her husband. Duane lay on the rug in front of the hearth, drawing pictures on wrapping paper with pieces of charcoal. Pounder lay napping, close to his side.

The man did not take his eyes off the fire as he addressed his wife. "Laura." He paused. "Ya know the South is secedin ta become the Confederacy. Well I heard taday thet fightin broke out in South Carolina 'n Lincoln declared war." He stopped and turned toward her. "I signed up taday ta help defend Arkansas if she should come ta be attacked."

The boy dropped his piece of charcoal and looked up at his father. Even though he had expected his pa to sign up, the reality that he had actually done so came as a shock to him. His mother stood up and, laying her darning aside, walked over to where her husband sat. Tears welled up in her eyes and dampened her cheeks. He reached up and clasped her hands in his, then pulled here into his lap. The dog merely opened his eyes to watch, though sensed the boy was upset and tensed to move if the boy should.

"Oh, Andy!" she cried and buried her face in his arms. He stroked her hair gently as he held her close and tried hard not to cry.

Duane felt a sudden emptiness in the pit of his stomach. He left his drawings and slipped out to the porch. His cheeks glistened wet as he looked out toward the shadow that was the barn and up toward the broken moon. His mouth quivered and he began to shake all over. The dog slipped silently to his side where he sat and watched the troubled face of the boy he loved. Grasping a post at the edge of the porch, Duane held tightly as he stood sobbing silently, the tears streaking his face. Suddenly the boy ran from the porch toward the haystack beside the barn. He threw himself down, buried his face in his arms, and cried out his heartache to the hay. He lay there a long time asking God why there had to be a war and why his father had to go. Pounder followed to lie by his side and lick the tears from his face. Duane caressed the soft head, then wrapped his arm around the thickly coated neck in an affectionate embrace and buried his face in its softness. The tears flowed as Pounder whined his concern for his grieving master. Finally the boy calmed down enough to notice that someone was approaching.

"Dee?" his father spoke gently.

Duane rolled over onto his back and gazed at his pa. Mr. Kinkade sat down beside him and the boy crawled closer to his father and lay his head in the security of his pa's lap. For a few minutes neither spoke.

"Pa," the boy began, "why do ya have ta go? Cain't they fight without ya?"

"Son, if ev'ry father thought they could fight without him, the South wouldn't stand a chance." He held his son affectionately, caressing his shoulders as he hugged him close.

They sat there quietly as the sky slowly rotated over their heads. Strong arms wrapped the boy gently and held him close, hoping to God that he would be coming back after the war. Duane looked at his father and saw the hurt and the worry that he was feeling as he gazed intently at his home. The man's eyes turned to his son.

"Ain't it time ya git ta bed? Yer ma'll wonder where ya got ta."

"Ain't tired, Pa. I couldn't sleep now nohow."

His father stood up bringing Duane to his feet by his shoulders. The dog rose to his feet and watched. Grasping the boy's right shoulder firmly, the man turned his son in the direction of the lane. Pounder eased himself to a seated position and watched them go. They strolled slowly down the dirt and gravel pathway and across the meadows to their favorite fishing hole. Dark silhouettes of trees against the starlit sky seemed to float overhead as they passed along the ground between them.

Ma watched them from the doorway as they drifted through the moonlight, growing smaller in the distance. She understood, and turned to the hearth to keep the fire going and to await their return. Pounder, too, understood. He returned to the house where he lay down at the top of the steps to await their return.

The glistening silvery meadow smelled sweet in the night air as father and son walked quietly side by side.

"Pa, what's war like?"

"I dunno, Son. I've neve been in one b'fore. I s'pose it's bloody 'n tirin 'n prob'ly som'thin cruel. I fig'r when men go ta war, they fergit the enemy is people jest like them."

They continued on quietly for a time. Passing through the stand of silent pines, they came upon the meadow. They went on until they reached the darkened shape that was the oak, and there they stopped. The water rippled and gurgled along, interrupted every once in a while by a flash and a splash as a catfish broke across the surface.

Duane watched in silence as he relaxed against the sturdy figure who stood behind him. His pa absentmindedly rubbed his son's arms against the chill night air.

"When the war's over, Dee, we'll come down here afta the big one out there. Next time he won't steal my pole."

They both smiled at the memory.

The two stood there a long time, like statues in the night. It was a special feeling, a need each had to be close to the other, knowing full well there was much to do before the parting, and there was a distinct possibility they would never see each other once his father left. An owl hooted in the distance. Crickets sang in the grass. The need passed. The two turned and started back toward the house.

The dog stood as his master and the man crossed the yard toward the house, then preceded them inside. Mrs. Kinkade was darning socks when they arrived, and laid her work aside as the two entered the cabin.

"Night, Pa," Dee whispered after they had closed the door for the night. He went to his ma and kissed her lightly on the cheek. "Night, Ma."

Pounder followed the boy into his room. The boy's room was small and sparsely furnished – his bed, a wardrobe, and a chair. As he kicked off his boots and changed into his nightshirt, he could hear his parents banking the fire for the night. The lamp light dimmed and went out. Tossing his clothes in a heap on the chair, Duane climbed into bed and sat with his knees tucked up under his chin.

The dog raised himself halfway onto the bed and pushed his muzzle under Duane's wrist. The boy stroked the muzzle and face, then tossled his ears gently with both hands.

"I love ya, Pounder," he said softly. The dog whined his own love for the boy. "Go ta bed, now, boy."

The large shadowy form slipped from the bed and curled itself into a comfortable position across the doorway.

Faint moonlight drifted in the window, casting a glow on the room. Duane sat there, his mind reeling, but blurred. He was tired. Pulling up the quilt, the boy settled down into the bed, closed his eyes, and drifted into sleep.

* * *

The sun stood high in a cloud-streaked sky. Before the afternoon was done, there would be a shower. The air was still and stuffy. The spring planting had been finished and the first shoots were showing, and buds were exploding into leaf as the trees awakened to the ending of April. Two and a half weeks had passed since the trip into town. The time was near for Andrew Kinkade to leave for the war which was fast brewing and would break as surely as the April storm building in the air.

The man stopped working out the weeds in the ground between the corn rows. For ten years he had worked the farm. As a lad of seventeen he had worked on a riverboat out of Ozark. Having met Laura Blankenfield on a trip up from Little Rock, they eventually married and set up a store in Ozark. Looking for something further from the city filth, the Kinkades moved their business to Bendton. Duane was born in October of 1850. His parents decided to sell the store and take up farming. They liked being outdoors and felt farming would be a healthier way of life for Duane to grow up with.

Resting on his hoe handle, the worried man watched his son at work partway down the field. Barefoot and stripped to his waist against the sun's heat, Duane chopped expertly into the ground, separating the weeds from the earth. Sweat and dirt streaked his tanned and dirt-dusted body. A feeling of sadness washed through the father's mind and he longed to hold his son, to protect him, and to forget all about leaving for a war. A whisper of a breeze stirred his hair. He pondered the chore of preparing Duane to take over while he was gone. The war would be over by winter, but it still meant that the boy and his mother would have to harvest the crops and prepare the farm for winter while he was gone. And the idea did occur to him that he might not return. But it was a ridiculous thought and was dismissed from mind.

The clouds were billowing rapidly in rising mounds of white and grey and black. A few large drops of water fell, raising small dust clouds over dark, damp stains in the field's dirt.

"Dee," his father called, "storm's 'bout ta break. Time ta head fer the barn."

"Comin, Pa."

A flash of lightning chased the clouds across the sun, followed by rumbles of thunder and darkening skies. The storm broke as Duane caught up to his father.

"Storm's here, Pa." The boy reached his arm around his father's waist and felt the security of the strong, taut body, streaked with sweat, dust, and rain. This man, his pa, he was his tower of strength and his protection against the world. The downpour drenched the boy's hair and his trousers and he felt the clamminess of both plastered against his skin. He looked at his father's worried face, then leaned momentarily against the strong figure. A hand on his shoulder assured him his father sensed his feelings.

Once in the shelter of the barn, the tools were set by the door, then the man stood in the opening and watched the storm. Duane felt a drop of water strike the back of his shoulder and looked up toward the hole in the roof as a glare of light silhouetted it sharply for a split second and died out with an explosive crash. He joined his father, watching the wind drive sheets of water, and the explosive fireworks light up the world around them in dancing and ghostly visions.

A large form raced across the yard from somewhere beyond the garden as Pounder dashed toward the protection of the porch.

"Here, boy!" Duane called.

The dog changed direction mid-stride and flew into the barn. The boy and his father laughed as the drenched beast shook himself vigorously, then rolled in the dirt of the straw-strewn floor.

"Pa, I'm not ticklish taday."

Andrew's worried thoughts fell aside for the moment. "Is that a statement 'r a challenge?"

"A challenge."

The man reached down and lifted his son off the floor. Pounder jumped to his feet and started barking in playful, sharp yelps. Holding the boy around the waist with his left arm, Andrew ran the fingers of his free hand down Duane's ribs. The boy squirmed, but with both hands free, attacked his father's waist and ribs with merciless fingers. The sudden movement threw them off balance and they fell onto the strawstrewn ground. The dog danced in circles around the two. Tumbling about like a couple of puppies, they wore each other down, proving each to the other that he wasn't ticklish, each fending off the other's attack.

"Okay, Pa," Duane puffed, "I'm ticklish." They stopped, the man lying on his stomach; the boy having rolled to his knees to the side; the dog dropping to an alert crouch, ready to spring if the moment was right. There was a pause for each to catch his breath. Duane sat back on his heels. "Pa, when da ya leave?" he broke the quiet.

"End a the week, Son."

Andrew rolled over onto his back and Duane dropped down to lie close beside him. Pounder relaxed and lay down.

"What did I tell ya 'bout helpin yer Ma while I'm gone?"

"Do my chores 's usual, mend the fence...'n the barn roof, 'n tend the crops 'n animals."

The storm died and the evening sun slanted its brightness through the cracks in the barn boards, casting patterns of light across the floor. Bars of light danced against the rain and dirtstreaked flesh of his pa's chest, face, and arms, as Duane sat up and laughed at the sight.

"Ya sure do look like sumthin, Pa. Like maybe Jamie's Pa got ya locked up."

"Maybe since the sun's back, we should finish thet piece a corn 'fer we stop ta supper." He pushed himself to his feet and started toward the glare of the doorway. Taking up his hoe from its place by the door, he stopped to await the boy.

"Comin, Pa." Duane scrambled to his feet. "Jest waitin ta be sure ya meant it."

As they returned to the field and continued to work the weeds from the rows, Pounder again took off to romp in the woods. An hour had passed when the two finally finished. Wearily they approached the barn, left their tools inside the door, and continued around to the pump to wash up.

Mrs. Kinkade greeted them from the doorway of the cabin. "I 'spect ya'll see ta gittin all thet dust 'n dirt off afer comin in. I put yer shirts on the pump." She waited until they disappeared around the corner of the building, then turned back into the house.

The boy and his father took turns pumping and splashing water over each other's bodies. A cake of soap on the edge of the water trough helped with the more stubborn dirt, ground into hands and elbows. Duane dried his head and arms briskly; then tossing the towel to his father, pulled on his collarless, homespun shirt. Andrew did the same, leaving the towel spread on the pump handle to dry.

As they ascended the steps, Duane paused to call toward the wood lot. "Pounder! Come!"

There was a distant crashing as the dog burst into view and bounded toward the house. His coat was plastered with wet and mud where he had wallowed in the bottom land near the creek.

"Whoa, now," the boy warned. "Ya cain't come in all a mess like thet! Go warsh up." He pointed toward the brook down the lane toward the road.

Pounder ambled off in the direction indicated.

Laura turned from the table as the two padded into the room. "Ya both must've been soaked in thet downpour. How fer did ya git?" she inquired.

"We done the sweet corn," Duane reported as he settled himself into his chair. "But we watched the storm from the barn."

His mother placed hot biscuits on the table as they all drew up their chairs. A plate of beef and a dish of garden beans and potatoes were already waiting.

They bowed their heads as his pa asked the blessing. "Dear Lord, bless this food we're 'bout ta eat 'n give us strength fer the hard times ahead. Amen."

"Andy, how much more da ya have ta do?" the woman asked as they helped themselves to the food.

"Afta supper, Dee 'n I'll walk the farm 'n go over ev'rythin ta be sure it's in order."

They ate quietly for several minutes before the man continued.

"We'll leave fer town tamorra mornin. We kin get what we'll need 'n make eny final 'rangements fer the summer items 'n fall sale a crops. The company forms up at two past noon. Ther'll be a parade 'n we'll camp east a town fer the night. Ya kin spend the night at Sally Rigg's boardin house 'n I'll see ya agin Saturday early 'fer we leave."

Duane finished a biscuit and drained his milk. "Pa, could I stay with ya tamorra night?"

"I'll check with Lieutenant Stanley. It should be okay. Da ya mind, Laura?"

"No. Thet's fine." She took the dishes to the drainboard.

The man and his son left the room. Pounder was waiting on the porch. He was wet, but clean of mud.

The woman turned to watch them stroll to the barn. The sun was nearing the western horizon. In another hour it would dip below for the night. A sudden surge of emotion and apprehension forced tears to her eyes. Wiping them away with the backs of her hands, she wondered, why did this war have to come? When he leaves he may never return. For another moment Laura stood watching, until her menfolk and the dog disappeared within the barn.

"Oh, God!" she prayed softly, "please, keep him safe. Bring him back ta us. We need him. We love him." She brushed new tears from her eyes, then returned to the table to finish clearing away the meal and its dishes.

Duane and his father walked through the barn looking to each tool and piece of equipment. Now and then they would stop while the man studied a harness or a corner, silently committing these moments with his son and these everyday sights to his memory – bidding a quiet farewell as though he might never see them again. Pounder sat in the doorway, a quiet sentinel, and watched the movement within. The sun had set and the twilight was fading as the three walked across the yard and up the steps to the front porch. They paused briefly, framed in the light of the open doorway, and watched together as the last rays of light faded from the western sky.

*　　*　　*

The wagon stood near the porch. The team was hitched and stood uneasy, waiting to be on the way. Duane knelt by his dog just outside the door, with his father's new uniform and blankets tied in a bundle, resting on the floorboards near his feet.

"Ya look afta thin's whilst we're gone. Ya hear, now, Pounder."

He stroked the head and neck, and scratched behind the ears. The dog sat quietly panting. He yawned, then licked the side of the boy's face in acknowledgment.

"Good, boy. Ya stay here now." He stood and looked to see if preparations were almost complete.

His ma had a basket of food on the table and was tucking a cloth over the contents. His pa came from the bedroom with the shotgun and a pack of cartridges and percussion caps in hand.

"Laura, you 'r Dee may need this while I'm away. Ya neve' know what people might do in times like these." He hung the gun on the pegs over the fireplace and placed the cartridges and caps on the mantle. "Guess we're ready."

Duane picked up the bundle and climbed into the back of the wagon. His mother took the basket from the table. Andrew reached for his wife's arm and they walked out the door, closing it behind them. He helped her onto the wagon seat, then, climbing up beside her, took up the reins, and clucked the horses into motion. Pounder stood watching from the porch as the wagon rattled across the farmyard toward the dirt road beyond. There it paused while the man took one last look back at his home place. A thickness in his throat made it hard to swallow and moisture blurred his vision. Fighting back his emotions, Andrew started the horses again. The wagon rattled onward, leaving the farm behind, lost in a trailing cloud of dust.

*   *   *

The warmth of the morning sun radiated through the white canvass of the tent. As the drum beat the Reveille, its cadence intruded on the man's dreams. He woke with a start, wondering at first what he was doing sleeping on the ground. Pushing off the rough wool blanket, he remembered, then looked to the figure sleeping beside him. Raising himself on his elbow, Andrew watched his son, still lost in a world of dreams. He smiled. How it hurt inside to know he would not see him until the Fall. The boy stirred. His father reached over and shook his shoulder gently.

"Dee, wake up."

"Huh?" He opened his eyes, squinting sleepily in a daze of half consciousness.

Mr. Kinkade wrapped him in his arms and pulled him close, tickling him through the blanket. The boy squirmed and struggled to free his arms, and struck back.

"Thet was a sneaky way ta do, Pa!"

"Don't matter, Son," he resisted the counterattack. "It got ya awake."

The attack was short-lived as the man hugged his son close and the boy squeezed back.

"Up 'n dress," Mr. Kinkade instructed. "They feed ya diff'rnt here then yer Ma does ta home."

Untangling themselves from the blankets, the two took the clothing that had been folded on their boots to serve as a pillow. Pulling on trousers and shirts, they jammed their feet into their boots, then sat up and finished dressing.

Duane briefly studied the man in his new uniform, then crawled through the tent flap. "Come on, Pa, I'm hungry."

He stepped out into the bustle of the camp with his father close behind. Men were headed toward the mess tent, some still tucking in shirttails as they went.

"Dee, this way." Andrew pressed his son's arm to guide him in the right direction.

The cook tent was set near the center of the small camp. Nearly fifty youths and men gathered in line to take a tin plate, cup, and fork, then file past the cook table. Biscuits, ham, grits, and coffee were the morning fare. Once the plates were filled, each member of the troop found a place of his choosing to sit and eat. Duane and his father chose the tongue of a nearby wagon – the man settling on the main beam while his son perched on the crosstree.

Quiet conversation and a leisurely breakfast were interrupted with a new commotion as families joined their men folk. Laura found Andrew and their son and joined them at the wagon.

"How'd ya sleep?" she asked, leaning against the wagon's wheel.

"Real good," Duane responded.

"Not bad," his father added, "but I'd rather be ta home." He finished a biscuit and sipped from his cup.

Duane chewed on a piece of ham. It was good to be together, all three of them. He became aware of the noise about them, of other families, of camp smoke, of horses. There was a feeling of family in a military encampment which signaled the separation of families.

The previous day's parade had been a fine showing of what the small town could do as a send-off for its men folk.

A small band rendered the occasion musical and was joined by the crowd in a rousing rendition of DIXIE. The church women had fashioned a company flag and presented it to Captain Bellet. Little bundles of tailoring needs had been put together for each soldier, and food packets of baked goods and some cooked meat were given for the journey to Ozark. There were no weapons. During the last two weeks, most wives and mothers had fashioned a uniform of sorts for their men folk. Each consisted of a light- blue pair of trousers and a light, butternut brown shirt. More equipment was expected when the company reached the larger encampment at Ozark.

Morning drifted aimlessly along as the company's officers kept busy with meetings and organizational arrangements. The afternoon was spent learning drills and movements. Food supplies were loaded for the horses and the troops. Extra camp equipment and blankets were packed. The evening was spent with family and friends. As darkness deepened, the recruits drifted toward their tents.

Duane and his mother stood at the edge of the camp and watched their man walk off to its midst. They waved one last time as he disappeared into the cluster of humanity. The two stood close together for several minutes, then turned to walk back through town to Sally Riggs' place.

Saturday dawned clear and cool. The camp was up with the sun. By the time the town folk were stirring, the camp had been taken down and the wagons were being loaded. The company prepared for an early departure in order to cover the twenty-three miles to Ozark by nightfall. Family and friends began to gather shortly after seven in the morning. Within the hour the company was fully packed and formed up for the march south. Loud cheering, last instructions from wives and mothers, and a plentiful mixing of tears sent them on their way. Many watched and waved for another quarter hour until the company disappeared over the last visible hill. A cloud of road dust hung on the hill's crest, then drifted away on the morning breeze.

Duane stood in the road with his mother, oblivious of all other people, aware only that a great aching emptiness hurt within his chest. He loved his father so much, and this grief he felt within was almost more than he could bear. Silent tears stung his eyes. He felt a drop of moisture on his wrist and suddenly realized his mother, too, was hurting. The boy slipped his arm around his mother's waist and she pulled him close in a loving embrace of common need and a mutual sense of deep loss. It was just the two of them now. Together they would survive this season of separation.

*　*　*

It was early afternoon as the wagon rattled across the small wooden bridge which spanned the brook that cut across the lane leading from the road to the farmyard. An extra horse was tied behind as its owner, Jamie Fowler, rode in the wagon bed with his friend, Duane. Eager barking echoed across the meadowland as Pounder bounded through the grass toward the inbound rig.

"Hey, Pounder!" the boy called.

"He sure has growd since I last saw him," Jamie observed.

"We'll git off here, Ma," Duane stated.

Laura slowed the team as the two boys jumped to the ground. They ran to meet an excited Pounder. The wagon moved on toward the house. The dog gathered himself midstride to leap at the boy and the two went down, rolling playfully in the grass. Mrs. Kinkade tied the team at the porch for the boys to help unload and put away. She proceeded with opening up the house and starting preparations for supper. The dog and the boys, having officially greeted one another, followed across the grass toward the house.

Knowing how hard the first days would be for her son and herself, Laura had invited Jamie to spend a week with them. His mother agreed it would be good for both families. Jonathan would be busy helping his town to adjust to the loss of its men folk, and she and her daughters would be busy with the women's aid group preparing clothing and other supplies to send to the army. At ten years of age, Jamie was the youngest of three children. He could be a help to his mother and sisters, but the week away would be good for him as well as for his friend, Duane. The two had been close friends their entire lives as their families had known each other since the earlier years when the Kinkades had the general store. Jamie was the taller of the two and slightly heavier while Duane was the elder by six months.

"Race ya ta the wagon," Jamie challenged.

"Yer on!"

They broke into a fast run. The dog charged ahead, then slowed to keep pace. All three arrived together, though Jamie was the first to touch the spoke of the large rear wooden wheel. After catching their breath the boys began to carry the contents of the wagon into the house.

"Where d'ya want these, Mrs. Kinkade?" asked Jamie.

"Put ev'rythin' ta the table," she replied. "I'll take care a them while you two tend the team."

After the wagon was unloaded, Duane led the team to the barnyard fence. The three horses were turned loose in the enclosure. Harnesses were taken in and hung on their pegs within the barn. Jamie's saddle and bridle were carried in and laid across the wooden rail of a box stall. Pounder was like a shadow. He followed each movement close at the boys' heels.

Dust particles danced in the beam of sunlight which intruded through the hole in the barn's roof.

"Thet's some hole ya got up there," Jamie observed.

"Yeah," Duane acknowledged. "Pa says I need ta mend it whilst he's gone."

"Dee!" the voice called from the house.

The three hurried outside. "Yeah, Ma," he responded.

"I need fresh water 'n firewood," she stated.

"Okay!"

"I'll git the wood while yer fetchin water," Jamie offered.

"It's ov'r ther," Duane pointed. He turned to the house with the dog at his side.

* * *

The afternoon was spent catching up on chores and tending to the livestock. Following supper, the boys sat on the edge of the porch flooring and visited. Pounder lay napping close at Duane's side. Mrs. Kinkade cleaned up inside. When she finished she joined the boys outside, settling down at the top of the steps.

The three talked quietly for nearly an hour – Jamie sharing news of his family, Laura asking after his family's health and recent events in town, the boys speaking of plans for adventure, Mrs. Kinkade speaking of chores which should be included in their activity. Evening wore on and dusk came. The sun settled below the horizon and its light faded.

"Time fer bed," Mrs. Kinkade observed.

The four arose and stretched tired muscles. Pounder hopped down from the porch and trotted off toward the side yard for a drink from the water trough and a last run. The boys waited for him to return while Duane's mother banked the wood stove. The dog returned. The cabin door was closed for the night.

"Night, Ma." The boy kissed his mother's cheek and they embraced, each to reassure the other that it would be all right.

"Night, Son." She waited for the boys to turn in before she blew out the lamp and went to bed.

Jamie and Duane changed into night shirts, laying their clothes across the chair. Pounder settled across the doorway while the boys climbed into bed.

"Kinda tight fit," Jamie commented.

"Ya don't push me ta the floor 'n I'll not push you," Duane promised.

They settled down beneath the quilt, Jamie pulling his arms close to take as little space as possible, and Duane hanging part way out the side of the bed near the dog. A warm dampness licked at the back of his hand. His fingers searched for the soft chin and scratched gently.

"Dee?" Jamie whispered.

"Yea?" came the reply.

"How 'bout goin fishin tamorra?"

"Sounds good by me."
"Night."
"Night."

*   *   *

The early days of the week drifted leisurely, one into the next. Duane and Jamie tended the daily chores and worked the fields. Mrs. Kinkade was busy in the garden when not occupied with house chores or making a new uniform for her husband.

The fishing trip of the first afternoon fizzled as the fish wouldn't bite. So the boys stripped off their clothing and went swimming instead. Pounder, too, enjoyed the swim. He joined them in their play with eager energy. However, when they were busy with chores, he either watched lazily from a comfortable vantage point or set out on an adventure of his own.

Mid-week continued to be bright and clear, yet cooler than the first two days. Morning chores were done and all had just finished breakfast when Duane spoke up.

"Ma, kin me 'n Jamie ride up ta Old Justin's place? It's a nice day fer ridin 'n we haven't seen him yet this spring."

Mrs. Kinkade was just gathering dishes from the table. "I reckon thet'd be all right. I'll give ya some a yest'rday's bread ta take ta him."

The boys helped to clear the table.

"'Fore ya go," Laura continued, "fetch up the laundry tub 'n extra water. 'N bring yer dirty clothes so's I kin warsh whilst yer gone."

"Yes'm," Duane replied.

The two hurried to do as asked. Meanwhile, Mrs. Kinkade wrapped a loaf of bread in a flour sack and tied a piece of line around the top to hang it from the saddle. Outside, the metallic clatter heralded the movement of the wash tub from its peg on the side of the house to the front porch. After a period of quiet while away at the pump, the boys came clambering up the steps with two buckets of water. They placed them on the floor, just inside the door. Mrs. Kinkade handed Duane the sack as she kissed him lightly on the cheek.

"You all be careful, now," she said. "We will," Jamie assured.

"See ya by suppertime," Duane added.

The two walked to the barn with the dog dancing excitedly alongside. Mrs. Kinkade filled a large kettle and placed it on the stove. Glancing out the door for any sign of activity, she crossed to the bedroom and gathered the dirty clothing from the chair, the floor, and the bedpost. Returning to the main room she stepped out onto the porch and deposited the collection in the empty tub. She remained waiting for the boys to finish saddling their horses and to start on their way. The horses had been led from the barnyard and tied at the fence rail. They were ready except for tightening the cinch straps. With final adjustments completed, stirrups were dropped and the horses untied and turned toward the house. The boys mounted and rode first to the porch.

"We'll be goin now, Ma," Duane stated.

"Ya both look afta each other," she smiled. "Pounder, ya see they keep safe, ya hear."

A sharp bark acknowledged the instruction.

Mrs. Kinkade watched as the boys reined their mounts toward the front lane and the dog raced ahead. Pounder splashed through the brook as the horses clopped across the bridge deck. He raced on to the road where he sat and waited to see which way his master would turn. The riders turned north and disappeared around a small hill. The woman turned back into the house to check the water heating on the stove.

Justin Pierce's place was about six and a half miles up the road. He lived alone, a bearded bachelor of fifty-some years. Periodically he would stop at the Kinkade farm to visit, and always he would show up to help with the harvest.

Duane and his father always helped Justin when his crops were ready for harvest. On occasion he would join them and ride into town for staple goods or other supplies. Yet, for the most part, he was a loner and kept to himself.

The boys were in no hurry. They enjoyed letting the horses amble along at a slow walk while Pounder departed on small scouting trips to chase a rabbit or follow a scent. There were several small farms along the way and twice they waved at a distant figure, busy in the fields. Grasshoppers flitted about the tall grass. Butterflies and bees busied themselves on wildflower blossoms. An occasional bird filled the air with song in harmony with the constant waves of vibrant noise from the katydids. They paused at a bubbling stream for the horses to drink and to quench their own thirsts, then rode on. As they neared the end of the journey, they came upon a quarter-mile stretch of straight road.

"Race ya ta thet hill crest," Jamie challenged.

"The horses 'r tired," Duane observed.

"It's not but a short run," the younger boy offered.

"Okay," Duane accepted. "Go!"

Pounder was startled by the sudden charge into a dead run and bolted into motion alongside. Then something caught his ear and he suddenly cut in front of the racing pair. Jamie's horse turned to avoid the dog as Duane reined his mount to the side to prevent a collision. The younger boy, caught completely unaware, went flying from his saddle. He struck the ground hard and rolled wildly through the grass. The reins hung free and the horse stopped to graze. Duane brought his horse up short, dropping his reins as he jumped to the ground.

He approached the still figure, lying unconscious in the tall grass, already tended to by the soft whines of the dog who lay at his side washing the dirt from his face with gentle passes of the large tongue.

The dark curly hair was a tangle of dirt and weeds, grass and wildflower. Streaks of red and ground-in dirt marred the side of the boy's face. His clothing was stained with brown and green, the soft red of sparse bleeding, and was torn in several places.

Duane knelt beside his friend. He was breathing. There was no significant sign of serious injury. But he lay so still and quiet-like.

"Why, Pounder?" he inquired of the dog. "Why'd ya cut us off 'n git Jamie hurt?"

The dog responded by taking gentle hold of his master's hand and tugging lightly. He let go and started to walk away. Duane was puzzled and did not move. The dog repeated his request.

"Ya want me ta folla?" The boy stood.

Pounder ran ahead toward the hill, but avoided the road. Duane followed. Climbing the hill, the dog stopped just below the crest and lay down. The boy approached cautiously. Suddenly he heard it – gunfire and shouting, and another noise he could not distinguish. Stealthily he crept to the hilltop and peered at the scene beyond.

Justin's place lay a half mile ahead. The boy could barely make out a group of riders in a frenzy of shouting and shooting, working their horses in small circles. The other sound, he observed, was the roar of flames as they consumed the structures of the small farm. A panic of fear surged through the boy's stomach and he felt a rising sickness. He had to do something before there was a chance of being discovered.

The two hurried back to Jamie. Duane dropped beside his friend and called frantically, "Jamie! Jamie! Wake up!" He shook a shoulder. "Jamie! Ya okay?"

Slowly, the boy began to stir. "Ohhh," he moaned softly. He opened his eyes and stared at Duane. "What happened? I hurt all ov'r."

"Yer horse threw ya," Duane answered. "Enythin broke?"

"Can't feel nothin," Jamie responded. "Dunno yet." He tried to sit up. "Ev'rythin seems ta work." He rose into a seated position.

"We gotta git outa here," Duane's voice was urgent. "There's raiders ahead. They're burnin Justin's place."

Jamie's brown eyes clouded briefly with pain. He caught a quick breath to keep from crying out, then relaxed.

"What hurt?" his friend asked.

"Ev'rythin." He continued to work himself to his hands and knees, then with help from Duane, he pushed himself to his feet. "I think I'm jest banged 'n bruised. Nothin seems broke."

"Kin ya ride?"

"Yeah."

The dog started ahead, circling through the meadow around the hill, heading toward a stand of trees. Duane helped his friend onto his horse, then mounted his own. The two followed. By the time they arrived at a safe spot to view the destruction, the raiders had departed. The sound of galloping hoof beats faded northward leaving the crackling fire and silence. Cautiously the boys rode into the farmyard. What livestock remained had been slaughtered. The buildings were reduced to crackling embers and white smoke. There was no sign of Mr. Pierce.

"We gotta warn the others," Duane stated.

"I gotta tell Pa," Jamie added.

Pounder searched about the wrecked farm, following and exploring scents which were new and confusing. Finally he sorted out what he was looking for and followed it down the lane a short distance. He would know these raiders if they came again. Suddenly he turned and ran barking toward the trees on the far side of the yard as a single figure leading a horse came into view.

"It's okay, boy!" Duane called. "Mr. Pierce! Over here!"

The man recognized the boys and hurried to where they waited. He was unhurt, but very angry.

"Ya okay?" Jamie called.

"Damn right, I'm okay!" he called. "They was here when I come up 'n I knew this weren't the time ta face em." As he approached, he noticed Jamie's disheveled appearance. "What happened ta you, boy?"

"My dog caused his horse ta throw 'im. He was tryin ta warn us so's we wouldn't git caught."

Pounder returned to sit near Duane's foot.

"Mighty smart dog, Dee." Justin gathered the reins and mounted his horse. "This the same pup I saw last fall?"

"The same."

"Sure did a heap a growin." He guided the horse to turn and face the destruction.

"Kin we do enythin ta help?" Jamie asked.

"Don't appear nothin's left," the old man stated. "We best head fer town 'n warn folks along the way." He reined his mount toward the road.

The small party turned to follow and began the trip homeward. They rode much of the way at an easy walk since the boys' horses had not had a chance to rest. Warning was given at each farm along the way. Upon arriving home, the three sat down at the kitchen table and gave a full report to Mrs. Kinkade. Mr. Pierce was invited to spend the night. He would go on to town to report to the marshal. Jamie would stay on as originally arranged and the family would ride into town on Saturday.

Laura took the shotgun down and removed two cartridges from their pack. Each barrel was loaded and tamped and the gun was returned to its place. Two caps were removed from their tin and placed conveniently on the mantle.

*   *   *

An overcast sky gave a dingy cast to the afternoon air. The little brook bubbled noisily along its course through the meadow. Pounder lay on the wooden planks that spanned the water and watched the barefoot boys, stripped of their shirts, gathering up stones from the stream bed.

"How deep ya think we kin make this water?" Jamie inquired as he dumped his armful onto the pile already begun on the brook's embankment.

"It should come as high as the bank," Duane believed. They had selected the lower edge of a quiet pool as their dam site. Here the brook was narrow and the embankment was about two feet high on either side. For a half hour they had been gathering stones from along the stream's bed and piled them near the selected work site.

"Guess this oughta be 'nough," Duane observed.

"I'll hand em ta ya," his friend offered.

Construction began. The first stones were passed from the pile and placed in the water. As the cut was filled with the collection of stone, the boys noted with disappointment that the water just passed through the pile.

"It's not holdin much a enythin," Jamie complained.

"Maybe the stones aren't big 'nough," Duane suggested.

"Dee, here's a real big one out here in the grass."

Hidden amidst the wildflowers, Jamie had discovered a large rock, bigger than any they had found as yet. It measured nearly three feet from end to end. Using a shovel they had brought from the barn, the two struggled to remove the rock from the ground. Pounder came to help dig. He worked on one side while the boys worked on the other. Finally it was loosened. Even so, it was so large as to require the shovel as a lever and the combined weight of both boys to pry it from the ground. With much effort, they rolled it to the edge of the bank and toppled it into the water. It fell with a loud crunch, wedging itself among the smaller stones. Yet, still, the water did not rise.

The dog stood on the far bank and watched as the boys finally exhausted their supply of building material.

"Why not shovel dirt 'n clay from the bank into the stones?" Jamie suggested.

"Worth a try," Duane agreed.

Part of the bank was cut away from below the construction site and the dirt shoveled behind the stone work.

"It's workin," Duane observed.

The water began to rise. Then, as the pressure grew from the rising water, the dirt began to wash away.

"Darn, thet's not workin neither," Jamie complained.

The dog started digging along the top of the bank, sending dirt, grass, and weeds into the water's flow.

"Look," Jamie pointed, "the grass is helpin ta hold the dirt."

Duane cut small chunks of sod from the meadow grasses. He passed them to Jamie who, in turn, dumped them upside-down onto the stones. It worked. The structure began to hold water.

The two worked at a feverish pace until the stone and sod construction was well over a foot in height.

"Look's good, Jamie," the older boy commented.

"Let's see how deep it gits," the other suggested.

The two boys and the dog gathered on the bank, just upstream from their project, and sat to watch for results.

Distant thunder rumbled in the sky. Jamie rubbed absentmindedly at the scabbed-over scratches on his cheek from the accident of two days back. Duane brushed the dirt from his hands onto his trousers. The water continued to rise as their structure continued to hold. A sudden rush of air chilled their naked backs and the boys shivered in its coolness. Raindrops splashed on their shoulders and dampened their hair as they fell, too, on the brook's surface, sending ever-widening rings wavering outward. Pounder shook his head.

Lightning danced across the sky and thunder crashed.

"Guess we'd best head in," Jamie suggested.

"Let's wait a bit 'n see how our dam works," Duane protested.

The air hummed, then split with a blinding flash and an explosive crash as a bolt of lightning struck a tree on the hill out near the road. The storm burst upon them in a heavy deluge and each was instantly drenched through.

"Let's go!" Jamie screamed.

The boys grabbed their shirts from where they lay on the bridge and fled to the protection of the porch with the dog right on their heels. Duane's mother met them at the door.

"Don't ya two have 'nough sense ta come in fer it rains!" she exclaimed. "Ya'll ketch yer death in this. An look at you, Pounder. Yer bad as these boys here!" She shook her head. "Ya strip outa them wet thin's right here, then wrap up in some'thin dry by the fire."

While Jamie and Duane peeled off their wet trousers and johns, Mrs. Kinkade rummaged through a blanket chest for two flannel bed sheets. She shook them open and wrapped one around each naked child as he entered the room, and herded him over by the hearth.

"You wait!" she ordered as the dog started through the door.

Pounder sat, forlorn and dripping, while she went in search of an old worn blanket. She returned instead with a worn towel and an armful of flour sacks. Pounder stood and shook himself.

"Com'on in," she called. "Git ther' by the fire," she pointed. Throwing the towel to Duane, his mother explained, "Dee, lay this out fer yer dog, then rub him down with these flour sacks." She tossed the sacks to Jamie.

Duane worked with the sheet draped over his shoulders and managed to direct his dog to lie down on the towel. Meanwhile, his mother stirred up the fire and added three more sticks to fuel it. While Jamie passed the sacks to Duane, Laura closed the door against the storm and took a seat on the floor between the boys. She used the edge of Jamie's sheet and vigorously rubbed the moisture from his hair while her son used the sacks to dry his dog. When she was satisfied that Jamie's head was sufficiently dry, she went to work on her son's. Neither boy protested. She was gentle, and the warmth of the fire felt good as it warmed the sheets and dried their skin. Pounder rolled over on his back to enjoy his drying rubdown, then shifted to his belly, resting his chin on his forepaws. The damp sacks were tossed into a pile on the hearthstone where the fire's heat began to steam the dampness from them.

Thin wisps of vapor drifted from the fabric as well as from the dog's coat. Outside, the storm howled and buffeted the roof. Lightning flashed and thunder crashed. Laura rubbed the sheet against Duane's arms and back. There was a peace wrapped in the comfort of the sheet and the warmth of the fire.

There was a security in his mother's presence and the boy leaned back into her arms. She held him tenderly, folding her arms around this precious son and holding him close. Jamie snuggled up close on her other side and she took him also into her embrace. As she sat there holding the two boys close and felt their sense of security and that moment of peace and the presence of love and trust, as she stared with the two of them and the dog at the flames dancing merrily and in comforting warmth, as she sat there and listened to the violence of the storm outside; she was struck with the irony in the quiet security they had at this moment in contrast to the uncertain and unknowing absence of her husband. Somewhere there was a war unfolding. It seemed so unreal! God, how she missed him!

"Ma?" Duane gazed blankly beyond the flames to some distant place in his mind.

"Yes, Son."

"Do ya miss Pa?"

She held him closer and touched her chin to the top of his head. "I miss yer Pa very much, Dee. I miss him so much thet it aches me inside."

There was a moment of quiet. Even the storm was beginning to subside so that the crackle of the fire dominated the mind.

"I love ya, Ma."

"I love ya, too, Dee." Tears stung the woman's eyes. A sudden thickness filled her throat. She wanted to cry, but fought instead to control her emotion.

"Mrs. Kinkade?"

"Yes, Jamie," she rasped, her voice broken by her feelings.

"If'n ya was my Ma, I'd love ya, too."

She smiled. "Thank ya, Jamie." The emotion passed to a sense of humor tickling in her train of thought. "Ya boys best be thinkin a gittin inta a change a clothes ta do the chores. I'm gonna git started with som'thin ta eat."

Duane rolled forward and sprawled on the floor beside Pounder. Jamie crawled into the rocking chair and tucked his knees in close to his chin. Mrs. Kinkade pushed herself to her feet and turned toward the stove. The storm had dwindled to a soft drizzle and the woman wandered to the door to look out across the fields.

"Dee, Jamie, come look!" she called as she stepped out onto the porch.

The boys and the dog rushed to the doorway to see what the excitement was about.

"I neve seen the front meada flooded so," Laura remarked.

Duane dropped a corner of the sheet to free his arm and pointed to a spot below the bridge. "Look!" he exclaimed. "Our dam musta worked! See the hole where the water falls away?" The others looked and acknowledged. "Thet's where we built the dam this aftanoon."

"Yeah," agreed Jamie. "With the storm 'n all, it musta got more water 'n it could let through."

The flow of water boiled over the top of the stones and the edges of the embankment to either side, backing over twenty feet into the field beyond either bank of the brook. The clouds passed and a brightness of late afternoon sun flooded the yard as the drizzle faded to nothing. No more was said as the boys and Pounder turned back through the door toward the bedroom. Mrs. Kinkade picked up the wet clothing from its pile on the floorboards and stepped to the edge of the porch to ring it out. Then she, too disappeared into the house.

*   *   *

At week's end, the wagon was hitched up and the farm was left in the care of the dog. The trip to town was uneventful, yet informative. Laura arranged to have a daguerreotype made of her and Duane. The small photographic image was enclosed in a closing frame to be sent with their letters to Andrew. The first mail had arrived and included a letter which had been hastily written and posted in Ozark. It was brief, stating the man's love for his family and providing information on how their letters should be sent. The company's immediate destination was Little Rock. There it would become part of the larger force already engaged in training and outfitting in preparation for assignment as needed.

The afternoon was spent at the Fowler's. For the children it was a time of play, mostly hide-and-seek.

Their parents spoke of the war and of the threat caused by marauding raiders who were entering the northwestern part of the state from western Missouri. Perhaps it would be best for the Kinkades to bring their livestock and move in with one of the families on the edge of town. But Laura didn't want that just yet. She and her son had to take care of the place for Andrew. They would, however, keep the option open should the danger reach a crisis.

The boy and his mother retired to the boarding house for the night. They each wrote a letter to Private Andrew Kinkade. The following morning the picture and the letters were wrapped in a small paper packet and posted at the stage depot to go with the mail destined for the army camps at Little Rock. It was Sunday, so they attended services at the community church and departed toward home after dinner.

Weeks dragged into months. The season slipped into summer. The crops grew. The boy and his dog wandered the hills, went swimming, maintained the little dam which began to improve in effectiveness as silt and debris from summer storms built up behind the stonework.

Periodically Jamie spent a few days or he and his father would stop on their way to visit the outlying farms. From time to time the Kinkades would spend a day or two in town. The chores were done, the crops were cared for, socks were mended, letters were written. The mail traveled slowly and erratically, but gradually Duane and his mother learned of his father's life in the army. There was also news of the opening battles of a war which was expected to be over by the autumn harvest.

On May 6, 1861, Arkansas adopted an Ordinance of Secession and the Confederate Congress recognized the existence of war between the United States and the Confederate States.

As Spring gave way to Summer, preparations increased in intensity. States of the Confederacy seized properties, stores, fortifications, and remaining troops from the Federals. To the west, competition was underway to gain control of the Indian Territory. Officers were appointed and troops were prepared. The advancing season saw increased activity in naval engagements and some skirmishes along the coast and in the East. July saw an accelerating pace of skirmishes and engagements of troops in Missouri and northwestern Arkansas as troops fought for control of Missouri. By mid month the Union had assembled an army and was advancing toward Manassas, Virginia. Throughout the third week, Confederate forces were also massing along Bull Run near Manassas.

As July drew to a close, the boy and his mother had heard of the battle at Manassas and had become aware of a general realization that the war would not be as quickly decided as had once been thought. Word came that a brigade of state troops under a General Pearce was joining with a General McCulloch with more Arkansas troops and troops from Missouri, en route to engage the Union forces near Springfield. It was unclear as to the whereabouts of the company from Bendton.

*   *   *

The dog padded through the open door into the kitchen and plopped noisily beside the table. Laura listened as she worked at the stove, for the footsteps that followed behind. Duane walked carefully to the table where he set the dipper of milk from the morning's chores. The air sizzled with the fragrance of eggs frying. The boy approached the stove to glance into the skillet and to be near his ma.

"Smells good," he observed.

She tousled his hair affectionately. "Almost done."

He turned to a nearby shelf and took down a glass pitcher. Returning to the table, he emptied the milk into the container.

"Ma?" Duane began as he poured the milk.

"Yes?" She didn't turn from the stove.

"Afta brekfist, me 'n Pounder wanta ride over ta the Pryor's farm 'n see if they's heard enythin 'bout the Bendton Company from their sons." He turned and set the empty container on the drain board.

"There's chores ta be doin round here this mornin." She set the platter of eggs and cornbread on the table. "Wait till afta noon. Remember yer Pa said the gate ta the barnyard needs fixin as does the hole in the roof." She reached her hand behind his head and pulled him gently along. "Now sit up ta yer brekfist fer it gits cold."

They sat to the table and Duane said grace. As they ate, they spoke of plans to get help for the harvest and prepare for winter. It had become obvious that the war was not ending, but expanding. Duane shared some of his cornbread with the dog that kept an expectant eye out for anything that might come his way, on purpose or accidental. A piece of egg which slipped from the fork was caught mid-air before reaching the floor.

When Duane had finished, he took his dishes to the drain board. A dusty stray beam of sunlight drifting in through the window fell on the plate, highlighting the glazed pattern. The boy's gaze fell on the pattern and he followed it absentmindedly with his finger. Having slowly passed the finger over the eggy surface, he turned it up and stared at the yellow slime.

Mrs. Kinkade finished her coffee and returned the empty cup to its saucer. She turned to watch her son's play as Pounder stood, stretched and walked to his side. After a minute, she broke the silence.

"The work ain't gittin done of itself."

"Yeah, Ma." He offered the finger to his dog who eagerly licked it clean.

"Dee!"

"It were dirty," the boy alibied as he turned quickly toward the door and darted out.

Duane flashed through the air with the dog flying on ahead as he flew off the porch to the ground, avoiding all three steps. His dark hair whipped about in the breeze of flight. Landing squarely on bare feet, he stopped short and glanced at the rough blue sky spattered recklessly with white puffs of cottonlike clouds. The morning light sparkled in his brown eyes as his line of sight fell to the roof line of the barn, that squat structure with its weathered coat of paint and the hole in the middle of the roof where the wind had blown off the shingles in a late winter storm. The boy stood in the middle of the yard for a moment with his hands in his pockets and stared at that hole.

A sharp barking reminded him that the dog was ready for some kind of adventure.

"Hey, Pounder. Come 'ere, boy." The dog hurried back from the shadow of the barn and the boy knelt to give him a rough rubbing on his neck.

Duane stood and slowly approached the barn doors which stood slightly ajar. Pounder followed as the boy inserted the toes of his foot in the crack between the two doors and pulled one open just enough to squeeze through. He stood inside the door with his hands jammed back into his pockets, and gazed at the hole from the underside. Pounder eased himself into a sitting position and waited. Then the boy led and the dog followed as the two surveyed the barn's interior with an eye for likely spots in which there might be some shingles. Along the wall to the right were three box stalls, empty as the stock was out to pasture, with bridles hanging from the corner posts and two saddles on wooden horses in front. Near the back door was a heap of wood scraps. In the back of the barn to the left were two standing stalls. Along the left wall were the feed bins and the stacked sacks of grain. Also along that wall were the harnesses, a work bench, and tools racked on the wall. Cabinets and shelves were along the front wall. In the center of the floor was a pile of hay, while some barrels, crates, and tools lay scattered about the rest of the floor space.

Duane strolled over to the scrap pile near the back door and investigated it with a kick. Pounder dug hesitantly, not knowing what was wanted. Perhaps there were some shingles if he looked. Glancing about for something to sit on while he searched through the wood scraps, he spied a small empty crate near the box stalls. Approaching it, he stepped gingerly on the top edge of one side to turn the opening toward him, carefully hooked an inside corner with a toe, and swung it into the air toward the scrap pile. Pounder, who was still pawing through the debris, barked sharply and jumped to the side as the crate bounced near his side. The boy finished positioning the seat, withdrew his hands from his pockets, and sat down to sort. One by one he picked up the wood pieces and chucked them behind him, and would have succeeded in scattering the pile, except that the dog kept picking them up and fetching them to the boy's side. But there were no shingles. Placing chin in hand, Duane sat there and stared at Pounder. The dog cocked his head to the side and stared back.

"Nothin here, boy. Guess the roof'll hafta wait." After a moment, he stood up, thrusting his hands into his pockets, and called, "Come on, Pounder. We'll take one last look fer quittin."

They walked first along the box stalls, looking into each as they passed. Approaching the pile of hay in the middle, they kicked and pawed it into oblivion. Still no shingles. It really didn't matter. He wasn't in any mood to climb up onto the roof. Maybe he could fix the gate first and do the roof another time. The two reached the door. Duane pushed it open with his foot and they passed outside to survey the fence.

Shuffling first to a position about ten feet from the gate, Duane squatted in the dirt with both elbows on his knees, his chin in his hands, and his head tilted slightly to one side. The dog dropped down beside him to wait. From this vantage point they watched the sagging gate, almost as though they expected it to tell them why it sagged. Suddenly the boy saw why. The rope – running from the tall post to which the gate was hinged, to the outer end of the gate – was broken, causing the end to rest on the ground. All he had to do to fix it was to find a piece of rope with which to replace the broken one.

The dog whined as if to say, how much longer before we can do something interesting?

"This won't take long, boy." The boy stroked his friend's heavy coat. "Ya jest lay here a bit. I'll say when it's done."

Pounder yawned, then lay on his belly to watch and wait. The boy thought a bit longer. After a moment's concentration he recalled a coil of line hanging on the far side of the barn. Using this, he first secured one end to the end of the gate, then took the other and climbed the fence to tie it to the top of the post. But one problem presented itself. The gate was too heavy to lift from where he was working so that he could tie the rope to the post. Surveying the problem from where he stood, it became evident that he would have to prop the fence up somehow. Some scraps of wood solved the problem and shortly afterwards the gate swung freely.

Gee, that sure was easy, he thought. He looked back toward the barn roof and studied it thoughtfully for about five seconds. Then tossing the wood blocks aside, Duane shrugged his shoulders in a the-heck-with-it way and turned down the back lane toward the back meadow where the fishing hole was.

"Come on, Pounder. Let's go."

The dog jumped up to follow and they quickly disappeared beyond the tall crop in the corn field.

The sun winked quietly on the cool rippling water as the boy and the dog ran across the sloping meadow toward the deep pool in the creek near the shadow of the oak tree. Duane dropped down in the hot sunlight at the pool's edge. Pounder ran splashing into the shallows where the rocks were. The day felt warm and the water looked inviting. The grass was cool and felt good against his bare arms. A fish broke the surface nearby as if to say, come on in; and the boy watched him play within the depths of the dark pool. Soon he found that he was staring at himself in his reflection on the surface of the water, so he made a few faces until one satisfied him. Rolling over onto his back, Duane stared at the blue, white-splashed sky and felt the sun dance on his face. Gee it felt warm. Maybe he'd take a short dip.

Springing to his feet, the boy quickly scattered his clothes on the ground around him and, with a quick step, leaped into the pool. The moment of impact snapped and he felt himself suspended momentarily beneath the water before he broke through into the air. The coolness was great. So for the next two hours he became a fish and explored the water's depths, just missed getting eaten by a coon, had a near brush with a fisherman, was saved from numerous imaginary disasters when his dog splashed out to the rescue, and lost all track of time.

Darkening skies interrupted his images of adventure and he decided it was time to head for home. A sudden breeze kicked up and a dampness invaded the air. Thunder rumbled in the distance and an occasional flash sparked the clouds. The rain began as Duane touched the shore and it occurred to the boy that it might be just as much fun to run about and soak up the wet drops. The dog climbed out on the bank beside him and shook vigorously to rid himself of excess water. Duane closed his eyes tight and laughed as the spray struck his body and his face. He could feel rivulets of moisture running down his neck and back, arms and legs. A light rush of air chilled the skin and sent shivers through the boy's body. Slipping on his johns, Duane picked up the remainder of his clothing and carried it as he struck out toward the house at a slow and easy walk. Pounder followed at his side, stopping every now and then to shake off the extra moisture of the rainfall.

The storm quit as quickly as it had begun. By the time the boy and his dog crossed into the farmyard, the sun was breaking clear and sparkling about the damp yard. A quiet settled on the farm and the boy paused to feel it. Pounder took the opportunity to roll in the grass while Duane pulled on his trousers, slipped into his shirt, and wiped the dirt from his feet before starting toward the porch. He had been gone longer than he had planned. It was well past midday. As he straightened up, the boy caught the sound of horses, several of them, rushing up the road approaching the farm. The dog stopped mid-roll and jumped to his feet, barking wildly. In the air was a faint hint of that scent from an earlier experience.

Like a flash Duane was on the porch and in the house. The dog followed on his heels, barking wildly, hackles raised.

"Ma! Ma! Raiders!"

Mrs. Kinkade gazed at her son in momentary disbelief before moving toward the hearth to get the shotgun. Pulling back both hammers, she placed the caps on their nipples, then carefully lowered the hammers to rest on them. With fear and determination she crossed the threshold to meet whoever was coming, on the porch and with barrel leveled. Her dark cotton dress blew slightly in the breeze of late afternoon. She stood firm with face set and eyes dark and angry.

"Ya stay back, ya hear now!" she instructed her son.

Duane nodded to her back but said nothing. Remaining in the cabin, he knelt beside the dog and restrained him from charging through the open door.

Seven men rode full tilt into the farm yard with guns drawn. Their horses were lathered from hard riding and they themselves were matted with dirt and sweat. Reining to a halt facing the woman, they said nothing, only laughed when she told them to get out. Several shots rang out as she flew backwards against the wall and slumped to the floor. They looked at one another and roared with laughter, then proceeded to pick out targets throughout the yard until they had emptied their guns. Turning their attention to the barn, they started gathering whatever they could take.

The cackling hens scattered about the flying hooves of the prancing horses. Frantic squawking added to a sense of fear and confusion as individual raiders dismounted, grabbed the birds by the neck, and swiftly executed them. Dead poultry was passed to mounted members of the band who tied them to leather thongs hanging on their saddles. Two of the group used their ropes and horses to tear down fencing and to pull the wagon over on its side.

Busy at killing and destroying, the raiders did not notice the boy with glazed eyes of disbelief. He remained motionless within the house, frozen by fear and shock, while the commotion unfolded outside. His grasp slipped and the dog broke free. Pounder dashed wildly through the door, gathered the power within every muscle of motion to spring from the porch at the closest rider. The startled killer reached for his revolver. Before it was clear of the holster, the heavy bulk of wild fury struck the man carrying him to the ground. Instinctively the dog sank his teeth into the unprotected throat. An eruption of blood bathed the dog and man with a red flow of death, as the two struck the ground and rolled in the damp earth. The impact broke the deathgrip. The dog rolled free of the corpse, momentarily disoriented.

Still in a daze, Duane stood in the open door, staring at the floundering dog. He turned and saw the crumpled body beside the door. The boy moved mechanically slow, to stand by his mother's side, to stare at the unreal. Then it struck him. "Ma? Ma!" he screamed as he dropped beside her, blinded by bitter tears. The shotgun rested in lifeless hands.

As some of the riders turned in reaction to their fallen comrade and the sudden scream, the blood-splattered dog regained his footing and the boy took the gun to stand and face his enemies.

"Hey! Over here!" one called.

They turned, caught off guard, to face a bloodied beast and the screaming boy with shotgun leveled at them. His face was tear-streaked, but his eyes were dry with a crazed look about them.

"You killed her!" he cried. "Murderers! Damn ya ta Hell!"

The voice shrieked uncontrollably as his thumbs pulled back the twin hammers.

The remaining six grabbed for their guns as the boy's piece spoke loudly twice. But the revolvers were empty. One grabbed his leg and doubled up in pain as his horse screamed and reared, twisting wide-eyed, struck by part of the blast. A second rider was blown to the ground, struck through the chest with the full force of the charge.

Three of those remaining drew saddle rifles as the dog raced across the yard and leaped once more to the attack. Shots rang out. A boot caught the dog on the side of the head. As Pounder flipped sideways in mid-flight, the boy flew back against the porch post. The dog's body hit the dirt and tumbled toward the corner of the porch. The gun slipped from Duane's grip and fell down the steps as his head exploded in pain. A burning sensation invaded his chest and blackness clouded his consciousness as he collapsed forward, falling from the wooden floor into the rain-wet grass.

Reddish dampness soaked the boy's dark hair and washed down the side of the pale face, collecting into a pool in the dirt. A widening red seeped through the fabric of the shirt as it flowed from a hole near the side of his chest. The small body lay still and deathlike in its pooling blood.

Quickly the riders sheathed their rifles and wheeled their horses around toward the barn. The haystack was fired. Brands of burning stalk were used to ignite the barn. A burning brand of wood was thrown through the open door of the cabin as the remaining raiders hastened to depart toward the road. Galloping hooves faded down the lane as flames crackled from the barn and the burning haystack.

Dampness still hung on the late afternoon air from the earlier shower, and the sun glistened brightly on its journey approaching the horizon. The crickets chattered noisily from the undergrowth. The horses, the cow and her calf wandered in from the back pastureland. They stopped to graze by the garden. An eerie silence hung about the farm, broken by crickets, crackling flames, and contented munching of the large animals.

Stunned, but unhurt, the dog whined in pain as he slowly pushed himself to his feet. His nose caught the scent of fire in the cabin as he hopped awkwardly onto the porch and limped in the direction of the door. Retrieving the torch from within, he emerged from the room with the burning wood clamped in his teeth. Pounder paused briefly, dazed and uncertain, then walked to the edge of the flooring and dropped it in the grass.

The dog turned to the still form that was his master. He licked the blood from the pale face. The skin was warm. He whined his plea for some response, some movement. There was none. Pounder lay down beside his helpless friend, resting his muzzle protectively on a bloodied hand. There he remained until dusk.

The evening light began to fade as the sun dipped below the horizon and a deep blue-black began to reach across the heavens from the east. Pounder had not moved from the boy. There had been no change, no movement, for nearly four hours. The barn was gone. Only wisps of white smoke and a glow of read embers marked where it had stood. The livestock had moved to the front meadow near the brook. In the darkness of nightfall, a broken moon cast its dim glow on the countryside and dark forms of the horses and cattle revealed where they had settled down for the night's sleep.

The dark canopy with its twinkling vastness was complete. Quiet sounds of night, the tree toads and crickets, wrapped the silence of death and destruction. The soft light of the moon caressed the bodies that lay in the farmyard and about the porch of the cabin. The dog stirred.

Whining softly, he nudged the small form beside him, pleading for the boy to wake up. Still, no response. Pounder sat up and howled mournfully at the moon. The ghostly cry echoed in the night air. Finally, the dog stood, made one last attempt to rouse his master, then walked off across the yard out the front lane. Crossing the wooden bridge, he broke into a loping run as he faded into the night along the road to Bendton.

*   *   *

The white clapboard house stood behind a low picket fence on a side street near the eastern end of town. In the fading light and long shadows of a moon nearing the end of its night's passing, a dark shape padded across the weedy grass of the side yard and sprung upon the porch.

Scratching at the door and barking wildly, Pounder sought to get the attention of Duane's friend, Jamie. When the door creaked open, it was the boy's father who peered out at the dog with blood-crusted coat, barking wildly with a mixture of mournful and pleading whines.

"What's there, Pa?" the boy called from his bedroom door within.

"It's yer friend's dog, 'n he's all bloodied," the father replied. "Fetch a lamp, Son."

The man took the dog into the kitchen where Jamie lit a lamp. His mother, a tall thin woman, joined them there, her long dark hair flowing in her movement.

"What's happened?" she asked.

"Dunno," her husband answered. "Jest found him at the door."

"Where's he hurt?" Katherine wondered as she prodded the dog in search of his wounds.

"He's not," Jonathan observed, his face twisted by a sudden horrible thought. "Oh my God!" he exclaimed. "It's the family!"

"What?" his wife didn't follow.

"Raiders?" Jamie whispered the question, afraid of the answer.

"Yes," his father confirmed. "Jamie, git Doc Porter. Tell him ta meet me here soon's he kin, thet we're goin ta the Kinkade place. I'll saddle the horses. Katherine, go over ta the saloon an wake Charley. Tell him what's up 'n ta git some riders an meet me at the Kinkade's."

Jamie ran off in his nightshirt to find the doctor. The girls, awakened by the flurry of activity, joined their parents to find out what was happening. Pounder was left in their care while the marshal and his wife quickly dressed and prepared to depart. Jonathan brought the horses around as Jamie returned to report that the doctor was on his way.

"Kin I come?" the boy asked.

"Not now," the man replied. "Wait here an look ta the dog while we first find out what's out there."

Jamie accepted his father's decision, wanting very much to know what had happened, yet knowing it could be dangerous. Doc Porter arrived on horseback, his medical supplies stowed in his saddlebags. Mrs. Fowler had returned to report that Charley would be along within the hour with as much help as he could find.

The night was at its blackest – in the last hour before dawn would begin to lighten the eastern horizon. The three riders were ready to depart. Pounder barked wildly, protesting at being left behind. The door closed behind them as Doc and the Fowlers mounted their horses and headed at a gallop out the familiar country road.

Dawn had brightened the morning horizon as clattering hooves crossed the bridge and entered the killing ground. The three reined their horses to a stop at the corner of the dwelling and gazed horror-stricken at the scene before them.

"Oh, dear God," the woman gasped.

They quickly dismounted and hurried to the boy and his mother. Doc knew at a glance that Laura was dead. He turned his attention to the boy as Mrs. Fowler knelt by the woman and her husband stood with the horses, studying the death and destruction, trying to comprehend why a man could be so heartless.

Daryll Porter was an experienced doctor on the downhill end of his fifties. Straight black hair had an abundant mix of white. He was a large man, over six feet in height, and still physically trim from constant activity in a demanding practice. On his knees beside the still figure, he gently searched for an indication of life. The boy's skin was warm to the touch, but pale from loss of blood. A faint pulse was evident on the side of his neck.

"Dee's alive," Doc reported as he continued to search gently to find the extent of his wounds.

"Laura's dead," Mrs. Fowler stated as she caressed the side of her friend's face. The tears came and she could not hold them back.

"I guessed as much," Doc observed. "What about the others, Jon?"

The marshal turned to check on the two who lay in the yard. After shoving at each body with a toe, he replied, "They're both quite dead, Doc. An even if they weren't, I'd 'ave finished 'em." There was bitterness in his voice. He returned to stand by the doctor. "How bad?" he asked.

"I'm not sure." He looked up at the woman. "Kate, could ya see if the table is clear inside so Jon 'n me kin bring the boy in?"

Mrs. Fowler stood, still staring at the dead woman. She forced herself to turn away and to enter the house.

"Take his feet, Jon, an try ta keep him flat out."

The two men carefully slipped their arms under the small, still form and eased him from the ground. They carried him inside and placed him on the wooden surface of the table. Katherine took the water bucket from the floor near the drain board and left to refill it with fresh water. Doc Porter began to work on his young patient while the marshal went out to fetch his medical supplies.

The boy's shirt was cut away and the pieces tossed to the floor. An ominous hole was found beneath the fabric and crusting blood. Torn flesh was embedded with fragments of bone and shredded muscle tissue.

"Looks real bad," the marshal observed as he stood by to help.

"It surely is," Doc agreed. "But luck may be on the boy's side." He continued to look further in search of wounds.

"How d' ya mean?" the woman asked as she poured some water into a basin.

"It don't look like there's damage inside." His examination finished, he looked up to give instructions. "Jon, find a sheet and rip it inta bandage strips. Kate, ya help me here."

As the two worked over the boy and the marshal prepared bandages, riders arrived in the yard. Mr. Fowler finished ripping down the sheet before stepping out to organize a pursuit. The boy was bathed and the wound was cleaned out. Chips of bone, dirt, and pieces of fabric were picked from the torn tissue. The bullet had ripped between two ribs, shattering bone and tearing flesh. One rib was splintered, another broken, and two more were cracked.

The marshal returned. "Ramsey 'n Jensen 'r stayin on ta take care a thin's outside," he reported. "Charley 'n me 'r takin the rest ta see if we kin track the skunks 'n clean 'em out. See ya when we git back." He was gone.

Galloping hoofbeats faded as Doc and Kate continued their work.

"What's important," Porter explained as they worked, "is thet these ribs not be moved til they heal. Otherwise they kin rupture a lung. Then it's all over." New bleeding continued as he worked and had to be constantly sponged out with a cloth.

"Hold this fer me while I find my sewin thin's."

A packet of sinew thread and sewing needles was taken from the bag and one of the needles was prepared with a length of the line. The open flesh was pulled together to cover the wound, then carefully sewn shut. Some bleeding continued to seep around the stitching. The work was covered with a dressing. All was wrapped tightly with bandage strips and tied securely to help hold the wound closed and to keep the ribs in place.

The head wound was a deep trench, cut through the scalp, high on the left side. It, too, was cleaned, stitched, and wrapped. Scraps of board were brought in from the barnyard fence and placed between the mattress and rope spring on the boy's bed to firm it up and protect the ribs. When the bed had been prepared and the boy had been dressed in a clean pair of johns, he was carefully moved to his room for the long vigil of care and healing that would follow.

Outside, the two men who had remained had righted the wagon which had survived the fire, brought in the horses, and rigged temporary harnessing with the rope which they cut from the gate. The dead woman's body had been wrapped in a flannel sheet and placed in the wagon. The others had been loaded and covered with a blanket. Mrs. Fowler had bundled up some of Laura's clothing to send along for burial garments. The two left with instructions to ask Sally Riggs to come out and bring the younger Fowler children. Laureen, the eldest, could stay to look after the needs of the boarding house if she needed.

The wagon rattled out of the yard toward town. Doc and Kate cleaned up the operating theater and returned it to use as a kitchen once more. The medical bag was packed and set aside on a pantry shelf. Then the woman began to prepare a pot of soup while the man started a fire in the stove and prepared another in the fireplace should it be needed in the evening.

Duane lay unconscious. He had not moved in the course of the surgery nor stirred since he had been tucked into bed. The pale face rested on the clean pillow. White bandages about his head had reddened at the wound with new bleeding. The quilt covering showed an almost imperceptible rise and fall of slow, shallow breathing. The eyes closed, the face without expression; the small body lay committed to the course of time and healing, in the care of friends who loved him.

*　　*　　*

By the end of the day, Mrs. Riggs, the children, and the dog arrived at the farm. Pounder went directly to the bedroom to find his master, as all who were present checked in on his condition. The dog whined, beseeching the boy to acknowledge him. Doc assured the dog that he would be all right and patted him gently on the head. Pounder sat down by the chair to watch until all had left the room. Then he settled on the floor across the door and began his vigil.

It was decided that Mrs. Riggs would stay on and care for Duane. Her husband was also away to the war and the boarding house had few patrons. Jamie could stay and help with chores and as needed. The wagon had been outfitted with harness and tack from the livery stable.

It would be kept beside the house and the gear stored under canvass in the wagon bed. The team and livestock could forage in the meadows. Mrs. Fowler and her daughter would go home. She and the two girls would take turns tending to needs at the boarding house and at the Fowler house. Doc Porter and the marshal would check in periodically. As soon as Duane was strong enough, he would be moved into a room at the boarding house and live with Mrs. Riggs. The Kinkade house would be closed up until such time as Andrew returned from the war and could take charge of his family's affairs.

All except Jamie and Mrs. Riggs departed the following morning. They kept their vigil in the days that followed – changing the bandages each day and trying to force some broth or tea between stilled lips so that the boy's strength could be maintained and some nourishment might help the healing. Attempts to feed the dog or to get him to move were fruitless. He drank some water and occasionally nibbled a scrap of food, but otherwise remained in his place near his friend.

Infection set in by the second day and damp cloths wrung from a basin of cold water were used to fight a stubborn fever. Duane began to stir as his condition worsened and he became delirious. Jamie and Mrs. Riggs took turns staying by his side around the clock during the crisis. Continual feeding of broth and tea helped to keep the boy from weakening. After two frightening days, the puss cleared from the wound, the fever broke, and the boy calmed. He settled into a relaxed sleep which lasted another day and a half.

Finally, nearly a week following that day of fire, Duane began to waken. Pounder barked joyously and bathed his master's face with his tongue. The woman quickly put an end to such behavior as she and Jamie rejoiced in the boy's recovery. There were tears of joy followed by a time of grief as Duane recalled what had happened. He was told of his mother's burial in the church yard shortly after the killing and of what was known about the raiders – the two he and Pounder had killed and the failed attempt to track them down. He in turn related the story of what had taken place that day.

The pace of his healing quickened. But it was the end of the second week before he was permitted out of bed. Several more days passed before he could remain up any length of time. During that week the bandages came off the head wound and the stitching was cut away and removed from his skin. The outside had healed, but the ribs had a ways to go. They were to be kept wrapped for at least three more weeks.

Late in the third week, it was decided that Duane was strong enough for the move to town. The house was closed up and all personal possessions were packed and loaded into the wagon, including the boy's bed. Doc came out to tend the boy on the move and to be sure he could safely stand the trip. Duane was assisted into the wagon and settled into his bed where he was to remain on his back during the course of the journey. He found it extremely painful and spent much of his effort fighting tears. The dog sat in the wagon bed beside him and the doctor rode seated on a trunk by the bed. Their presence was a comfort.

The trip was long and arduous. By the time they arrived at Riggs's Boarding House, Duane was exhausted. He was moved into a back room above the kitchen. The bed had been freshly made and the room cleaned for his coming. Doc Porter carried the boy up the back steps from the kitchen and helped him change into his night shirt. Pounder stayed close by and followed every detail of settling in. Duane was tucked into bed and a light meal of thin soup and a glass of milk was carried up on a tray. He ate slowly while Jamie brought his clothing and personal things to be stowed in the wardrobe. The bed was taken apart and stored in the barn. The wagon and team were turned over to the livery stable for care.

It had been a hard day. When all had finally left the room, the dog went to the bed to check on his friend. He nuzzled the hand that lay on the bed covers and was rewarded by a gentle stroking of his nose and a weak good night. Pounder settled on the floor across the door. Duane lay staring out the window at the sky beyond. Quiet tears of loss and loneliness slid down his cheeks. He closed his eyes and allowed exhaustion to take over as he drifted into dreamless sleep.

*　　*　　*

It was early the following morning. Duane had finished his breakfast which Mrs. Riggs had brought up on a tray. Pounder had been a great help as he ate half the food. The boy really wasn't very hungry. He settled back against the pillow, too weak to lift the tray from his lap to the bedside table. The dog settled on the floor beside the bed. He was busy getting up the last crumbs from the floor. The boy had closed his eyes and was drifting off to sleep. Light footsteps bounced up the back steps and down the hall to the bedroom. Duane opened his eyes to find Jamie standing in the door.

"Ya awake?" his friend asked.

"Yeah," Duane replied. "Could ya move this tray fer me?"

"Sure." The dog looked up as Jamie entered the room. "Pa sent these letters fer ya." He handed them to the patient as he lifted the tray to the table. "They're from yer Pa. Been here a while, but ya bin too sick."

Jamie settled in a small wooden rocker with upholstered seat and back panels, while Duane stared at the letters. Tears came to his eyes without warning and slid down his cheeks. The writings were addressed to his ma and him. The younger boy swallowed hard to force a painful lump from his throat. Pounder wandered over to sit beside the rocker and pushed his muzzle under an idle hand.

"Hi, fella," Jamie greeted hoarsely. "Ya want some attention, huh."

The dog woofed softly and the boy stroked the massive head. Pounder rested his chin on Jamie's knee and enjoyed the attention. Duane finally wiped his eyes with his shirt sleeve and opened the letters. He read silently for several minutes while Jamie attended to Pounder.

"Eny news?" Jamie asked as Duane let his hand fall and rested the letters on the bedcovers.

"Pa's bin assigned ta the 13th Arkansas under a Colonel James Tappan. They're s'posed ta be on the way ta places along the Mississippi. He's not sure where. There's bin some sickness in camp. He's a corporal now. Last month there was a battle north a here in Springfield, Missouri. Thet's 'bout it."

"Who won the battle?"

The dog's eyes followed the speakers.

"We did." He carefully folded the letters and slipped them under his pillow. "I'll read em agin later," Duane explained. He turned his eyes to his friend. "What's gonna happen ta the farm? This is September already. It's time ta harvest."

"Pa'll take care a thin's. He's already talkin ta friends 'bout goin out next week ta git the crops in."

Duane closed his eyes. For a moment, no more was said. A tear slipped free. His lips quivered. When he opened his eyes, they were wet. His voice cracked as he spoke. "It jest don't seem real."

"Hey," Jamie broke in. "Ya need yer rest." As he stood, so did the dog. "I'll take this tray down 'n stop back near mid day." Jamie reached for the tray.

"Okay," Duane smiled weakly. "See ya then."

Pounder followed the boy to the door. There he settled on the floor as Jamie waved to his friend and departed. Duane reached under the pillow for the letters and read through the first a second time. He was tired, emotionally worn out. Resting the letters at his side, he closed his eyes and slipped into a tired slumber.

*　　*　　*

Summer drifted into Fall. Mrs. Riggs and Jamie were Duane's constant companions. She tended him as his mother would have, but as a friend. Jamie became like a brother. As the days passed, the recovery progressed and the boy was able to spend some minutes, then hours, in the rocking chair. Finally, he could move about the house and enjoy spending hours in the kitchen where he could be closer to the day's activity. He wrote to his father to tell him of the raid and his mother's death. The boys would visit for hours; then, when Duane was able to sit up, play at checkers or cards. On some days Jamie brought a copy of the newspaper and they would spread it across the kitchen table to read the news of the war. As his strength improved, Duane helped Mrs. Riggs about the kitchen. Pounder had claimed an approved spot in the corner near the back stairway. He was not permitted in the rest of the dwelling as long as there were boarders. He did, however, consent to taking walks with Jamie while Duane remained behind in the kitchen.

In the weeks that followed, Duane was permitted to leave the house for short walks. The boys wandered to the Marshal's Office, the newspaper office, for a walk about the streets, and finally, to the cemetery, where he wept by his mother's grave. Some days, when their friends were out swimming in the broad creek near the edge of town, Duane would sit on the bank and Jamie would join the others in the water. Rainy days were usually spent in the comfort of the boarding house kitchen.

The leaves turned. The days shortened. The weather became grey and chilled. Autumn advanced toward Winter. Late September saw action to the north in Lexington, Missouri. As October passed, so, too, did Duane's eleventh birthday. It was a day of particular loneliness. No one knew of its significance. Those who did – those who mattered – were absent. The boy kept its importance to himself. Early November saw battle at Belmont, Missouri, across the Mississippi from Columbus, Kentucky. According to his pa's last letter, the 13th was to be in that area as part of a buildup of fortifications into western Kentucky.

*   *   *

The snow fell softly and silently that Christmas. Duane stood gazing out the window into the woodlot and watched as it thickened on the tree limbs, fence rails, and firewood. A speck of red flitted along a fence post, then onto wood chips in the yard. The cardinal looked for the bread crumbs Mrs. Riggs had thrown out that morning.

The smells and sounds of Christmas dinner being prepared trespassed on his thoughts, and he felt a sudden sense of sadness. This was his first Christmas alone.

"I'm goin afta wood fer the stove," Duane called as he grabbed his coat. He dashed out the door without waiting for an answer. Pounder followed at his heels.

The boy paused on the back porch so as not to frighten the bird, and ordered the dog to sit quietly. He tried to concentrate on the movement of red and the falling snow and to push his sadness out of his mind. The cardinal flew off into a tree and chirped brightly at the boy. Then the thoughts and memories flooded back into his mind and overwhelmed him. Duane sat on the snowy steps and sobbed quietly. The dog rested a consoling chin on the boy's leg.

"Why, God! Why did it haf ta be! Why? Why?"

Mrs. Riggs turned from the stove and sensed the boy's sadness. She checked out the window and saw him, lonely and crying, huddled on the back steps, his dog close at his side, with snow crusting on his clothes and the animal's back. She opened the door and called softly.

"Dee, git yerself 'n yer dog in here afor ya ketch yer death. Come in an git warm." There was a soft understanding for his sadness in her voice.

The boy rose from the steps, went into the warm kitchen and the waiting arms of the landlady. Pounder followed to his corner near the stairway and sat, watching the boy. The two stood there a long moment, the boy crying out his anguish, and the kind woman wishing she could comfort him.

*   *   *

There were no letters and little news through the winter. Much of the army had gone into a long camp. It was the afternoon of the last day of February when Mrs. Riggs called from the back door.

"Dee!" her voice carried in the chill air. "There's a letter here fer ya from somewhere in Mississippi. Jamie thinks it's from yer pa."

Duane, who had been gathering wood for the supper cooking, dropped everything and raced for the kitchen door in his hurried excitement to read the letter. Pounder looked up from his corner, awakened from his nap by the banging door.

"Where?" he asked breathlessly.

"It's right here. Slow down fer ya hurt yerself."

Snatching the letter from her hand, he grabbed a bread knife and tore open the cover paper.

"Dee!" But she decided not to say anything more.

Not bothering to remove his coat, the boy fell into a chair and spread his letter on the table.

> *February 2, 1862*
> *My dearest Laura and Dee,*
>
> *I'm sorry I didn't get to write since November last. Federal troops under General Grant attacked our camps at Belmont, Missouri. The fighting was fierce and involved Yankee gunboats, artillery, infantry. Losses were heavy, but we finally drove them off. I got a battlefield promotion to sergeant.*
> *I received your letter of July, but any that may have followed haven't reached me yet. Were you able to get the crops in all right and do you have enough for the winter? Did you have a good Christmas and holiday season? I missed you both very much.*
> *There's been a lot of sickness through the camp. I was laid up about three weeks. Things seem to be going all right*

here. We're a little short on everything but we're making do.

We're going on to Tennessee. That same Yankee general, Grant, has been making things hot up there. His forces have been threatening Fort Henry. We're going in to lend support.

I love you both very much and sure do miss you. Sure hope this war is over soon.

Your devoted husband and father,

Andrew Kinkade
Sergeant, 13th Arkansas

PS – Laura, the socks got holes in the holes now. We're hoping to pick off a Union supply train on our way and get us some new clothes.

Duane looked at the letter a long time. His eyes began to burn and an uncontrollable tear fell onto the paper. Mrs. Riggs noticed the sudden quiet and hurt that enveloped the boy as he read his letter.

"Is som'thin wrong, Dee?" she ventured.

"He don't know," he answered without turning. "He neve got my letter! He ain't knowin Ma's dead!" Duane turned to her and she saw the awful hurt in his eyes.

Carefully he folded the letter and tucked it into his shirt. He wiped a shirt sleeve across his eyes.

"I best git thet wood now," he said listlessly and shuffled out the door.

Mrs. Riggs watched him from the window as the gusty grey wind whipped about him. The dog lowered his head to his paws and watched for the boy's return. Slowly and deliberately, Duane picked up each piece of wood and placed it in his left arm. Leaving the shelter of the shed, he again crossed the grey world of wind that was the back yard of the boarding house and entered into the warmth of the kitchen.

Dumping the wood in its box, he hung his coat on its peg by the door.

"I'm goin ta my room fer a while."

"I'll call ya when supper's on," Mrs. Riggs acknowledged softly.

She turned to the table to finish preparing the meat for the oven. As Duane mounted the kitchen stairway, went to his room and closed the door, the dog followed. Inside the room, Pounder settled in his corner and watched his young master.

Kicking his boots under the chair, the boy flopped down on his stomach across the bed with his feet dangling over one side and his hands and head over the other. He stared at the floor and his eyes followed the cracks in the floorboards until they blurred into the same daze of nothingness that his mind was in. Everything was nothing. He felt like an ant looking down at the floor from miles away.

Duane forced his eyes to focus, bringing him back to reality. Rolling over on his back he looked up toward the ceiling. It, too, seemed to back away from him and again he felt small and inconspicuous. Time became eternity and he lay there for a long time in a state of nothingness. Gradually he again began to think.

He reached into his shirt and withdrew the letter. Slowly opening it up, he gazed at the lines. A sudden urge took hold of him – an urge to find his father. It surged throughout his body giving him new energy and filling him with excitement. The ceiling no longer looked so high nor the floor so far down.

He looked at the letter again. "We're on our way to Tennessee... Fort Henry."

Suddenly Duane knew just exactly what he was going to do. A military wagon train expected through day after tomorrow was probably headed for Ozark. If he could sneak into one of the wagons and get to Ozark, he would try to find William Kearney, captain of the sternwheeler, Ozark Queen, whom he knew from earlier visits with his pa. Maybe he could get the captain to take him along on his next trip down the Arkansas and on south to Vicksburg. Once there, he might be able to get in with a unit headed north.

The dog sensed the boy's excitement. Pounding his tail on the floor, he shared his enthusiasm as he followed the preparations with his eyes.

Taking two blankets from the drawer in the wardrobe, Duane rolled a change of clothes into them and tied the bundle tightly together. This he tucked carefully into a corner of the cabinet so that it would be ready when the chance came for him to leave. He thought a minute as to what to do about food. Some leftovers wrapped in a paper would solve the problem. He lay down again and in his mind he saw his trip and imagined how it would be when he found his pa in Tennessee.

The boy passed the remainder of the afternoon in his dream world until it was shattered by the woman's voice calling him to supper. Snapping back to the present, Duane grabbed his boots from under the chair and stuffed his feet into them. He and the dog were out the door and halfway to the stairs when he remembered the letter. Rushing back to the room, he carefully refolded it, then placed it in the rope holding his bundle together, while Pounder stood waiting in the doorway.

"Comb yer hair, an wash yer hands," Mrs. Riggs ordered when Duane bounced down the stairs and into the kitchen. "An I'd appreciate it if ya'd bring the rolls with ya when ya come ta the table." Her tone was kinder.

The rest sure did him good, she thought as she carried the tray of vegetables into the dining room. Pounder settled in his corner to enjoy his dish of table scraps.

"Taylor," Mrs. Riggs asked a long-term boarder as she set things on the table, "would ya do me the honors a carvin tanight?"

"Of course, Sally. Have ya heard eny news from Joseph?"

"Not since last month. But Dee got a letter taday from his pa."

"Someone call?" Duane asked entering with the rolls.

"What did ya hear from yer pa?" the man asked.

The boy set the rolls on the table by Mrs. Riggs, then took his seat partway down the side. "Pa's letter was a might slow ta gittin here. He sent it the beginnin a the month. But he says Gen'ral Grant's afta Fort Henry 'n thet he's afta Gen'ral Grant. He also said his socks got holes in the holes…"

A burst of laughter followed, interrupting after the last comment. "…'n thet they plan ta git new clothes off'n the first Yankee supply train they come across."

"Reverend, will ya ask the blessin," the landlady requested. They bowed their heads in silence.

"Father God, look down on us as we are gathered here to partake of this food. Bless those who are absent from our midst and bring them safely home. Amen."

The room filled with conversation — each told of his day's events and they discussed the war.

The reverend, who always ate supper at the boarding house, spoke up. "Sally, ya set a mighty fine meal."

"Reverend, ya always say thet an I thank ya fer the compliment."

"Mr. Andrews," she turned to one of the guests, "I understand yer leavin us tamorra. We sure enjoyed yer stayin here."

"I rather enjoyed it maself," he commented. "I'll always know where ta stay wheneve I'm in these parts agin."

"Boy, ya said yer pa was headed fer Tennessee?" another guest asked. "Do ya know what part a Tennessee he's headed fer?"

"No sir," Duane replied. "He jest said Tennessee."

"Did he way where'bouts in Mississippi he was 'r what unit he was with?"

"He didn't say enythin 'bout thet at all. The letter was posted from Mississippi."

"Hol on a minute," Taylor cut in. "Ya got an awful lot a questions, mister. Unhealthy questions at thet. Why the sudden inter'st in the boy's pa?"

"Jest curious."

"Well ya keep yer curiosity ta yerself. We don't care ta discuss the where'bouts of ar relatives with strangers."

As conversation shifted and the minutes passed, Duane sensed that this stranger was staring at him. The man was well dressed. Yet it occurred to the boy that there was something familiar about him. By meal's end, he had become very uncomfortable and wanted to get away quickly.

Back in the kitchen he asked, "Is it all right ta go ta Jamie's fer a bit? Me 'n Pounder need ta git out some."

"Sure, Dee," the woman smiled. "Don't be long."

He took down his coat and hat and wrapped a scarf to tie the hat against the wind. Mrs. Riggs left the room to bring more leftovers from the table while the boy and his dog headed through the hall toward the front door. As they stepped out into the storm and headed for the Fowler house, he sensed that someone was following. They were nearing the Marshal's Office when Pounder suddenly stopped. An ominous growl rumbled deep in his throat.

The dog turned, muscles taught, ready to break into a run. Duane restrained him as he turned to see what caused such behavior. The stranger stood, ghostlike in the swirling snow, a revolver in his hand.

Pounder erupted into a frenzy of barking and struggled to break free. As the stranger leveled the gun's barrel at the dog and pulled back the hammer, the boy knew and released the fury of the dog. This was one of the raiders and he had recognized the boy.

Gunshots roared – two, so close together to seem as one. The man flew backwards, sprawling in the snow as the mighty dog yelped and collapsed in mid-flight. Crimson red splattered the snow where the stranger fell, and puddled out from the great furry form which lay still near the boy.

"Nooo!" he cried as he fell in the snow beside his friend.

Footsteps approached from behind. He glanced up to see Marshal Fowler approaching, gun drawn, smoke wisping from the barrel. The boy buried his face in the warm fur of the strong neck. Uncontrolled sobbing wracked the small body as he wept bitterly and his insides felt wretched with pain and grief. The marshal checked the stranger, then holstered his gun. He returned to kneel beside the boy.

A small crowd began to gather. Mrs. Riggs spotted the boy on the street and came running.

"Oh, no!" she shrieked. "Not Dee!"

Jonathan stood and caught her. "It aint the boy, Sally. It's his dog."

"Oh, God!" she cried. "Why must you hurt him so." The man sought to comfort her as she wept on his shoulder.

Someone had gone for the doctor and he approached the subdued crowd. A few began to turn away. He saw the boy on the ground, the dog, the blood. Doc Porter knelt beside them and put an arm across the boy's shoulder.

"Dee, let me git a look," he spoke softly. The sobbing boy shook his head. "Come on," the man pleaded. "I can't help if ya don't let me have a look."

He eased the boy off the dog.

"Ow!" Duane cried as he grabbed his chest and collapsed in the snow.

"Quick, Jon!" the doctor caught the boy in his arms, "help me get him into yer office." As they lifted him from the ground he continued. "Sally, cover thet dog 'n keep him warm till I git back."

A spectator offered a coat and the woman knelt by the dog while Duane was carried to the warmth of the building. He was carefully eased onto the desk. Wincing with pain, he heaved a long sigh of relief once he was down. The tears continued.

"I'm okay, Doc," he sobbed. "It jest hurts ta move." Again the tears overflowed. "Why did he hafta kill Pounder?"

"We don't know thet he did," the doctor spoke softly. "Ya stay here with the marshal while I go see."

The two men exchanged nods of understanding as the one left and the other remained with the boy. After what seemed forever, Mrs. Riggs opened the door and entered the warmth of the room.

There were tears in her eyes and joy on her face. "Yer dog's alive, Dee!" she beamed. "They're takin him ta Doc's office 'n ya kin see him there in a hour."

Disbelief and joy lit the boy's face. Tears came with the smile and broken sobs of emotional relief as the woman embraced him to reassure him that all would be well. Even Jonathan's eyes glistened wet as he spoke.

"Sally, ya take the boy home 'n mind he don't strain his self any more. After he's warmed up, ya go ta Doc's, he'll wanta check him out, too." The marshal helped the boy to his feet. "I'll tend thin's here."

The boy moved slowly to avoid the pain in his chest as the two moved toward the door. When they had gone, Marshal Fowler reached his coat and hat from their pegs, then he, too, departed to attend to the stranger in the street.

*   *   *

It had been Duane's intention to tell Jamie of his plans that stormy night and to arrange for him to keep Pounder during his absence. As it turned out, he never spoke to his friend. Pounder's wound was serious but not likely to be fatal. He had been shot through the neck, suffering torn muscle tissue and loss of blood. Duane had strained the area of his injury – pulling tissue and bone, but without serious damage. It would be painful for several days.

Pounder was very weak when the boy saw him that night. He whined painfully and tried to lick the boy's hand. The dog was unable to lift his head or move his body. A bandage was wrapped about his neck and he lay motionless on his side. Tears of joy slid down the boy's face as he knelt beside his friend and gently caressed his head.

In bed that night he pondered the wisdom of his earlier decision. Pounder needed him now. The next day was spent with the dog at Doc Porter's office. Pounder slept for much of the time, but as he had kept his vigil by the boy, so now the boy kept his vigil by his dog. Jamie joined him and he learned that the military train had been delayed by the storm. Duane decided not to tell the other boy of his plan but to wait and see how his dog recovered.

Within a few days, Pounder was strong enough to move home again. A comfortable place was prepared in the corner of the kitchen and there he was to stay during the balance of his recovery. The bedroom felt empty without the dog's presence in his corner, and Duane lay awake at night thinking of Pounder and contemplating his decision.

The military wagons passed through a week late. Duane decided to go. His dog was much stronger and could get along without him.

*　　*　　*

Duane excused himself from breakfast to take some table scraps to the dog. While everyone else lingered in the dining room, the boy set a plate of scraps for the dog, then searched for some leftovers for himself. The pantry contained a piece of cooked beef from the previous night, and a tray on the table contained some extra biscuits from breakfast. A piece of wrapping paper was taken from a storage drawer and an empty flour sack from a closet shelf. Duane wrapped the food and packed it in the sack, then set it out on the back porch.

Making a hurried trip to his room, he returned with the bundle, checking to see if the kitchen was empty before he slipped across the room and out the back door. Grabbing the food pack en route, he crossed to the wood shed where he stowed his gear in preparation for his departure. To make it look good, he returned with an armful of wood. But no one was in the kitchen.

Returning once more to his room, the boy took paper and pencil and wrote a note for Mrs. Riggs. He told her he had gone to find his pa and asked if she could take care of Pounder.

If that wasn't possible, Jamie would probably do it. He folded the paper to lay it down, but paused as he remembered something else. Writing once more, he added his thanks for all she had done and closed it with his love. The note was left on the pillow. It was time to go.

Duane returned to the kitchen and settled on his knees beside his dog.

"Pounder, I'm goin away. Ya gotta stay here 'n be real good. Ya gotta git well, too, 'n be strong fer when I git back. I dunno how long I'll be gone, but I am comin back." He hugged the furry bulk gently so as not to hurt his wound, then kissed him on his muzzle. "I love ya, Pounder," he whispered as the tears slid down his face. The dog licked at the salty drops as he returned his love for the boy. "I'm gonna miss ya som'thin fierce." Another tear escaped and he quickly wiped it away.

Duane stood slowly. As he reached down his coat and hat, he looked once more at Pounder. Their eyes met. Sudden emotion rushed through the boy. His eyes blurred and his throat tightened thick and painful. He wanted so much to cry.

Pounder knew. It showed in his eyes. He had to go now or he wouldn't be able to make himself do it.

It was clear outside. After slipping on the coat and cramming his hat on his head, Duane stuffed his scarf and a pair of gloves into his pockets. He turned to the back door.

"I'm goin ta Jamie's," he called as he hurried out the door and pulled it shut before Mrs. Riggs could respond.

Once outside, Duane went directly to the wood shed, gathered his gear, then headed toward the livery barn where the wagons had been gathered. It was still too early for people to be about or businesses to open. Even so, the boy followed the back alleys to avoid being seen and approached the livery from behind the corral fencing.

Activity was concentrated around two wagons which were being loaded with extra sacks of grain. The teams had already been hitched and stood ready to depart. Several supply wagons, parked alongside the barn, were temporarily unattended. Duane chose one of these, worked his way along the fencing, and approached the back end of the wagon. The bed was filled with crates of stores and supplies, and covered over with a canvass. The boy lifted a corner of the cover in search of open space within. He safely swung his gear over the tail of the wagon and dropped it into a narrow slot between the sideboards and a crate. With his hands free, he pushed at barrels and boxes until he was able to create a space large enough to crawl into. Voices approached from in front of the barn.

"Sergeant Winters," someone called. "Git yer men ta their wagons and prepare ta move out."

"Yes, sir," a gruff voice responded.

Grabbing the tail boards with both hands, Duane shoved off from the ground and hauled himself over the edge. Squirming down into the tight space he had created, the boy pushed the cover back over the end boards.

The wagon rocked sideways as the troopers climbed to the seat. There was an organized commotion as the troops were assembled and preparations were completed to move out. It seemed an hour, but it was only a matter of minutes before the orders ran down the line and the train of wagons began to move.

For a moment Duane felt a strong urge to abandon his plan. He loved Pounder and hated to leave him. There was Jamie's close friendship. He knew Mrs. Riggs would worry and he didn't want to hurt her. He did love her and knew she loved him. But he missed his pa. He wanted so much to be with him and to feel secure in his presence. The pangs of indecision hurt.

The wagon lurched into motion and rocked him against a crate. It was too late now. He was on his way. He was committed.

Suddenly he felt very lonely.

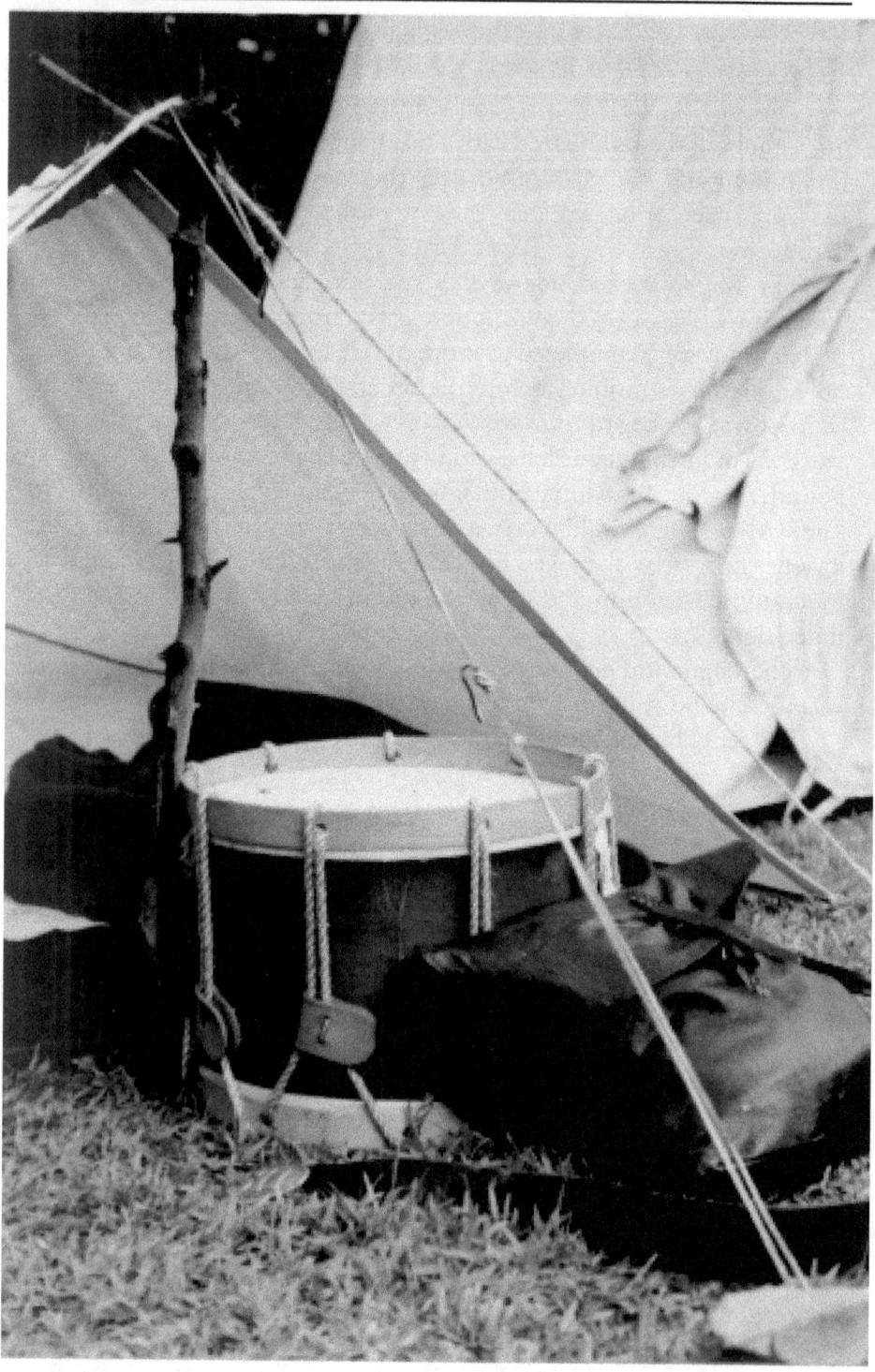

EPILOGUE

It was getting on toward dark when the wagon finally ceased its bumpy monotony. The day was wintry cold, yet beads of sweat dampened the boy's whole body as he fought the pain in his chest, aggravated by the long and rough ride. Duane grew tense and listened cautiously as orders passed among the troops to pull the wagons together for the night.

"Sergeant Winters, take yer wagon under the trees there 'long with the rest a the supply wagons." The slow movement of the officer's horse could be heard as the voice traveled up the road. "Sergeant Reilly, set the company street 'long the east side a the road." The orders grew faint as the lieutenant rode back to the front of the column.

One more short ride and the wagon came to a final rest.

"Hey, Kelly! Gimme a hand with these horses," the driver called.

Duane watched for his chance to crawl out of the wagon unnoticed. Looking out from under the canvass, he could see in the dim evening light, the organized commotion as the camp was established. He heard the jingle of trace chains and the clatter of cross-trees as the team was unhitched and the wagon's tongue was allowed to drop to the ground with a thunk. Everyone was occupied, either with the placement of the wagons or the setup of tent canvass.

With painful slowness Duane worked himself free of his cramped quarters. He managed to crawl up and lay along top the tailboards where he was able to drag his gear up and over their edge. Dropping his bedroll to the ground below, he rolled off the hard rail and let himself fall to the snow-covered grass. There he collapsed to hands and knees to grit his teeth and allow the pain to subside before moving further. He pondered how he was going to leave the camp without being caught. The boy collected his gear and stood up, keeping close to the darkness of the wagon and its shadows.

He shook within as an authoritative voice startled him from behind. "Boy, what ya think yer doin here?" But before Duane could respond, "Go on 'n run 'long now. This ain't no kid's playin place." Without further comment, the soldier disappeared into the routine of the camp.

Glancing about him, Duane took his bearings and found himself on the outskirts of Ozark. The town itself was a few hundred yards beyond the worm fence that struck out perpendicular to the road, just ahead of the wagon. The boy carefully eased his gear over a shoulder. Then circling around the horse lines, Duane turned in the direction of town. Following the edge of the field near the roadside, he walked along slowly, keeping to the tree shadows and trying to conserve his energy. Already exhausted from the ride and the pain, he held to the knowledge that the riverboat docking area was less than a mile ahead. Hopefully the Ozark Queen would be there and Captain Kearney would still be her skipper.

"Sergeant!" The boy overheard the conversation as he passed the edge of the tent street. "Lieutenant Reynolds will take charge."

"Yes, Sir," the man acknowledged.

The captain continued. "I'm on my way ta see the rive' boat is ready ta take us on come mornin. Ya help the lieutenant by seein the cook wagon is open 'n runnin supper. I 'spect ta be back near seven."

The two exchanged sharp salutes, then the captain wheeled his horse and galloped toward the town. Duane moved on, satisfied to know that the riverboat was to be there.

*　　*　　*

Dimly lit windows cast an eerie glow and a multitude of mysterious shadows about the streets along the waterfront. There was a great deal of pedestrian activity in the early evening hours as stevedores and sailors wandered from one bar or card game to another, or gathered in small knots to pass the latest gossip before drifting on to some rented room for the night. Apart from the movement of nightlife in the streets, the boat landing wharfs were a silent maze of freight and shipping goods, some having recently arrived and some waiting to be loaded aboard a freight or packet boat. Many small skiffs and sailing boats bobbed in the water near the landing. The only large vessel was tied up port side to the freight wharf. It was the stern-wheeler, Ozark Queen.

A few lamps were lit on each of her decks along the outer cabin walls nearest the forward stairs and ladders. Illumination glowed through the windows of the engine room, the pilot house, a few cabins, and crew's quarters. No activity was evident on board since most of the crew had gone ashore for the evening. The river's water lapped gently under the boat's bow and against its stilled paddles. A murmur of distant and indistinct voices hung on the evening air, highlighted by an occasional raucous outburst of laughter or profanity. Otherwise, the waterfront was quiet. A horse snorted its boredom. The single steed was tied to a post near the gangplank to the boat. In the shadows of the main deck, two men were absorbed in animated conversation, their whispers barely audible to a quiet observer.

Duane watched from his hiding place perched on a flour barrel on the shadow side of a wall of crates. He had approached the vessel under cover of the waterfront clutter and had seen the captain's horse tied at the gangway. Thinking it best to await the officer's departure, the boy had crept as close as he dared to try and overhear the conversation. He had also confirmed for himself that this was the Queen and the other man with the captain was the boat's skipper, William Kearney. While Duane waited on the barrel, he nibbled on the beef and biscuits in the flour sack.

Captain Kearney was a slender figure, just shy of six feet in height. He cut a crisp appearance in his tailored blue uniform and short-billed cap with polished black visor. Long sideburns and a neatly trimmed mustache added an authoritative dignity to his character.

"No, Captain," Kearney was saying, "I'm glad ta help anytime." The voices rose and fell on the chilled evening breeze, and the aroma of his pipe smoke scented the night air. "Now to your men. They won't have it easy by any means. Ya say ya've seventy-five?"

"Yeah, an' nearly a dozen supply wagons 'n twenty-eight horses."

The two turned toward the ship's bow.

"Thet'll make thin's awfully crowded," remarked Kearney. "They'll have all this deck. But as ya see, much a the inner space is taken by the engine boilers 'n gear drive. There's storage 'n some cabin space up front. But once ya put yer wagons on the side decks 'n yer horses in the storeroom spaces, ya'll not have much space left. Yer enlisted men stay to the main deck. Yer officers kin use cabins aft on the passenger deck. We do have some passengers in the forward cabins. We also haf ta pick up a small company a soldiers an supplies at Pine Bluff." They arrived at the main staircase and started up. "Let's go up an I'll show ya what's fer yer use."

"Fine," the Confederate officer replied. Captain Masters was an experienced soldier, tall, clean-shaven, and busy fidgeting with a handful of papers. Folding the papers into one hand, he continued as the two reached the top step, "We'll come aboard afta daybreak. Thet way we'll have good light ta put up the horses an git the wagons on board."

The two men became lost to the boy in the silence of the vessel's shadows. Duane consumed the last of the food while he waited. It was several minutes before he was able to discern their presence when they finally emerged from the dark recesses of the engine room on the main deck.

"By the way, Captain," the skipper had begun, "there are a few rules I hold to. No one's ta be on the pilot house deck or in the boiler room 'cept my crew."

They started down the rampway toward the planking of the wharf. Masters paused to separate the papers in his hand as he spoke.

"Thet's reasonable ta be expected, 'n I'll see ta it." He offered a sheaf of papers to Kearney. "Here's yer set a my orders 'n official paperwork. I'll have my train here come an hour afta sunup."

"See ya then," the ship's skipper shook hands, then stuffed the papers in a side pocket of his coat. He waited on the slope of the ramp while the army officer tucked his papers in a breast pocket on his way toward his horse. Kearney's pipe had gone out some time ago. As he watched the other man's departure, he knocked the ashes from the bowl and slipped the cold pipe into the pocket with the papers.

Releasing the reins from the hitching post ring, Captain Masters mounted easily then turned his horse toward the shadowed streets which would take him from the town. As the horse's snow-muffled footsteps faded and the Queen's captain turned from the wharf, Duane stepped hesitantly from the shadows. "Captain Kearney, Sir," he called, unsure of the reception he might receive.

The captain stopped at the sound of the vaguely familiar voice and turned to observe the slight figure standing at the edge of the shadows.

"What is it, Boy? Don't I know you?" He screwed up his face in an attempt to see what he could not see in the dark of the night. "Come up here in the light so's I kin make ya out better."

Duane approached the man. It had been nearly four years since his pa had brought him to the big city and he wasn't sure the captain would know him. He certainly did not know the captain except by association with distant memories.

"I do know ya. But I can't say as it's been recent." He reached out as the boy approached and placed a calloused hand under the boy's chin to turn his face to a better light.

"Why yer Andy Kinkade's boy, ain't ya?"

"Yes, Sir."

The same hand shifted to a shoulder to draw the boy toward the deck of the boat. "Come on aboard 'n tell me what brings ya lookin fer me."

"How'd ya know?" the boy asked as he walked with the man up the gangway.

"Ya wouldn't a asked fer me by name, fer one thin," the skipper began. He paused as they reached the deck of the Queen, and turned the boy to face him squarely. With both hands on the boy's shoulders and the deck lamplight on his own face, he continued. "Fer 'nother thin, ya wouldn't be here in the first place 'n ya wouldn't be packin a bedroll." There was a brief pause, but the boy looked him square in the face and the captain saw in those brown eyes a lonely determination and pain.

"How are ya called?"

"I'm called Dee. My given name is Duane." He shifted his bedroll to ease the strain on his ribs.

"Ya wanna come up ta my cabin 'n tell me why yer here? It's a mite cold out 'n ya kin sit a spell while I've a cup a coffee."

"Okay."

Captain Kearney started toward a forward stairway. Duane followed at his side. As they mounted the steps, the pain from the day's travels rose once more in his consciousness and the boy was forced to stop and rest before continuing at a much slower pace.

"What's wrong with ya, Boy?" a concerned Kearney asked.

"Nothin, Sir."

"What da ya mean nothin?" the captain reached to relieve the boy of his gear. His hand was brushed aside. "It's plain ta see thet som'thin's hurtin ya. Now give me yer gear 'n ya kin say yer story when we're inside."

Reluctantly Duane allowed the man to take his burden for the remainder of the climb to the top deck. The two entered the warmth of the captain's quarters and closed the door against the winter chill.

Duane's gear was parked on the floor near the door as Kearney offered him a chair on his way to the coffee pot on the stove.

"Take the chair at my desk, Dee. It's firm and should be good fer yer back." He poured a cup of coffee, then turned toward a large wooden rocker beside a small table.

"It's not my back, Sir," Duane returned as he settled into the swivel oak chair.

"Then tell me why yer here," he leaned back and sipped from the cup. "Why are ya painin so, Dee?"

"I need yer help, Captain." The boy rested his head against the back of the chair and closed his eyes a moment as he gave in to his exhaustion.

"Are ya okay, Son?" The boy nodded without comment. "Want somethin hot ta drink? There's hot cocoa in the galley."

"Yeah," Duane acknowledged. "Thet sure would go good. I'm awful cold inside 'n tired."

"I'll be right back."

William Kearney set his cup on the table as he rose from the chair to cross the room to the door. " Ya kin look about while I'm out. Won't take long."

The boy opened his eyes at the sound of the door latch, took a deep breath, and rolled his head to the side to glance about the cabin. It was comfortably furnished and finished in fine woods. A small bookcase contained several leather-bound volumes, some finished in gilt trim. A painting on the wall depicted two sternwheelers belching smoke and cutting water in a river race. Some papers lay scattered on the writing surface of the open roll-top desk. The many pigeon holes were like little treasure troves with aging papers and a myriad of oddments. The door latch clicked as the man reentered carrying a small enameled teapot, steaming at the spout, and a tin cup. Somewhat rested, Duane sat up in the chair as the captain pushed the door shut, crossed to the desk, and poured the boy a cup of steaming cocoa. Duane sipped the refreshing warmth. Kearney heated the contents of his own cup before returning to the rocker.

"Better?" the man asked.

"Yeh," the boy confirmed.

The captain held his cup with both hands just under his lips.

"Tell me, Dee, why is't yer here."

There was a moment of quiet while Duane drained his cup, then set it on the desk. "Well, Sir," he began, "I'm lookin ta find my Pa. He left fer the war last spring. Last I heard from him, he was goin ta Fort Henry. But he ain't got my letters fer months. He don't know Ma's dead."

"What!" Kearney sat forward. "Yer ma's dead?"

"Kilt last summer by raiders."

"Thet how come ya be ta hurtin?"

"Yeah. I was shot 'n left fer dead. Taday's ride in the wagon was pretty rough an made it hurt agin."

"What ride in the wagon? Tell ya what. Start ta the beginnin 'n I'll try ta sort this all out."

The two sat for another half hour while the boy's story unfolded and the man's many questions were answered, bringing into focus the reasons for and the nature of the quest that Duane was attempting to undertake.

"I'm not sure I agree with what yer wantin ta do, Dee." The man pulled at his chin thoughtfully. "I kin see why." He stood to refill his cup. "There's more cocoa in thet pot. Help yerself."

They drank in silence.

"Kin ya help me, Captain Kearney?" Duane finished the last of his beverage as he awaited a response.

The captain turned from the stove and crossed the room to his bunk against the wall. The boy swung the chair about to face him. "Tell ya what." The man leaned against the end rail. "Thet train ya came with is comin aboard at daylight on its way east. We'll be workin down rive' all the way ta Vicksburg. Thet's where they'll ketch the railroad fer whereve' they end up goin."

"How long's it take ta git there?"

"Depends on many thin's, like weather, currents, stops 'long the way. Reckon we should make it in six 'r seven days. I'll take ya 'long 'n think on it durin the trip. If'n I decide so, I'll help ya git on yer way. But if not, ya come back up rive' with me 'n I see's ya git back ta Bendton. Ya gotta promise ya'll do as I think best."

"I promise."

"Then 'tis settled. Ya'll put up in my cabin fer the trip. I'll git a spare bed from one a the passenger cabins tamorra. Ya'll use mine fer tanight."

Kearney moved to collect Duane's gear as the boy spoke.

"Yes, Sir, but then they'll think I'm a sissy 'r thet I'm special 'r som'thin."

"Ya are special, Dee. I'm sure they'll understand if we explain the circumstances. Besides, whose ta give a dam. They don't even know ya rode with em." A sudden idea occurred to the captain and a sly smile creased at the corners of his mouth. "I jest put ya on as my cabin boy. Yer an official part a the crew. First thin come mornin, we'll fit ya up official lookin, uniform 'n all."

"Okay," the boy pushed to his feet. "Guess I'm awful tired."

The man separated the blankets from the food sack, untied the roll, and shook them open. Duane's extra clothing and a bundle of letters fell to the floor. They were scooped up and tossed onto a small wooden chair with the food sack, and the blankets were folded and laid at the foot of the bed.

"Throw yer clothes on thet same chair," the captain instructed as he turned down the bedcovers, "an climb in against the wall. There's plenty a room fer the two of us."

Duane crossed to the extra chair and stripped to his johns. As he removed his shirt, Kearney observed the scar on the side of his chest.

"How bad did they git ya?" he asked as he helped the boy up over the side of the wooden front.

"Couple a ribs 'n a piece a my head. But Pounder 'n me took two a them."

"Pounder?" he eased the boy to the back of the mattress as he pulled the covers up to his chin.

"My dog." Duane snuggled into a ball between the cold sheets.

"Yeah. I fergot." He pushed the pillow under the boy's head. "I've several thin's ta tend ta fer I turn in. Ya sleep good now."

"Yes, Sir, Captain. Thanks."

William Kearney left the boy and crossed to his desk. Pulling the pipe and papers from his pocket, he put the pipe aside and spread the papers on the clutter of the writing surface. There he settled with a fresh cup of coffee to work with his papers. A half hour passed before he checked the fire in the stove, set aside his work, and considered turning in. Checking on the boy, he found him sleeping soundly with an arm hanging over the front edge of the bed and the covers kicked partway off.

The man smiled affectionately as he pulled them back over the boy's shoulders. Lifting the blankets he had laid across the foot of the bunk, Captain Kearney turned down the lamp and settled in the wooden rocker for the night.

*   *   *

The grand commotion of a busy port reverberated in the early morning air. Bosses shouted orders. Winches creaked. Horses whinnied and hooves clattered on wooden planking. Men groaned under heavy loads. Crates grated against ramp and deck. Soldiers, deck hands, and dock workers were busy loading the wagons and other cargo, and leading horses to their temporary stabling. On board the Queen Captain Kearney supervised the placement of all that boarded his vessel. Captain Masters directed activity on the wharf.

Leaning over the railing of the top deck, Duane had a clear view of the activity below. He looked smartly dressed in the cabin boy uniform that Kearney had dug out of a wooden chest in the storage locker. Breakfast had been early, before the morning sun had begun to lighten the eastern sky. The boy had been introduced to some of his chores just after he was awakened when he was asked to clear pots and cups to the galley and return with fresh coffee. He also helped to set and clear the breakfast meal. The crew was on board at daybreak. Dock workers arrived shortly thereafter and began loading an assortment of cargo from the dock's clutter. Captain Masters was as good as his word. The troop train arrived an hour after sunup and activity quickened to a fever pitch.

While the boy watched, teams were unhitched and led on board. Wagons were broken down as tongue and cross trees were removed from their brackets and loaded into the wagon beds. A dozen men bent their backs to the wheels and frames as they rolled them up the loading ramp and positioned them on the deck. Once spotted, wheels were blocked and ropes run through to secure them in their places. Some wagons had to be lifted on board by winch and derrick beam to be placed on the far side of the deck. Duane felt an excitement tingle from within as he watched the scene beneath him. He was surprised as he watched the soldiers about their work and realized many didn't have a regular uniform. Grey trousers were mixed with brown, blue, and black. They wore shirts of all colors and styles. Some had vests. Jackets, too, varied in style and color. Some were uniform, but many were not. He could smell the damp of the river, the hint of sweat and horses. Mingling, too, was the smell of wood smoke as the boilers were brought to pressure in readiness to set the paddle wheel into motion. Overhead was the whoosh of black smoke rolling from the stack. And somewhere was the hiss as surplus steam pressure escaped.

Activity subsided. The dock had been cleared of wagons and much of the assortment of freight. A new crowd had appeared as a score of young boys gathered to watch the activity of the departing steamboat. Footsteps approached on the forward stairsteps. Duane turned to see Captain Kearney appear from the lower deck, pipe in mouth, and a thin curl of smoke drifting behind his back.

"We goin now?" the boy asked.

"Shortly," the man replied as he took the pipe from his teeth. "Come on up ta the wheelhouse while we prepare ta cast off."

The boy followed the man up the last stairway to the wheelhouse deck. Once inside the glass-enclosed structure, Captain Kearney drew gently on the pipe as he approached the speaker tubes.

"Carney!" he hollered into a pipe.

"Aye, Captain?" a deep voice echoed back from below.

"Ya ready down there?"

"We're ready, Sir."

"Stand by. About five yet."

"Aye, Sir."

"Dee," he turned to the boy and pointed the pipe stem to a large flat table with long pigeon holes in series beneath. "See if thet's the chart a this part a the river."

"How kin I tell?' the boy asked, crossing to the table.

"Ya'll see the name Ozark in large letters near the center."

While the boy checked the chart, the captain reached overhead and pulled the wooden grip on the whistle cord. A loud shrieking told all the Ozark Queen was about to cast off.

"Yes, Sir," Duane replied. "This says Ozark in the middle."

"Thanks," Kearney acknowledged as he stepped to the door.

The boy followed and watched from the doorway as the captain went to the rail to call to the deck hands and the Confederate captain.

"Captain Masters, are ya all secure down there?"

"Yes, Sir, Mr. Kearney," the officer replied from below.

"Linesmen, cast yer lines fore an aft. Keep them kids clear a the edge." He hurried back in and called on the speaking tube as he slipped the keeper ropes from the two sides of the wheel. "Carney, give me ahead slow."

"Aye, Sir," the voice replied.

Again the whistle shrieked as the vessel began to vibrate with a new sound and the drive beams pushed the great paddle wheel into motion. A movement caught the boy's eye as a young man in his early twenties moved to a small platform in the starboard railing in front of the pilot house. Duane became aware of a slow gliding movement as the captain turned the wheel and the town with its waterfront began to slip away. They were moving. Suddenly the boy's senses closed down. Everything was shut out as a muffled silence and an empty loneliness enveloped him and his immediate surroundings seemed to become strangely distant. The panic of his uncertain future passed as he sensed once more the aroma of the captain's pipe and could hear again the slow pulsing of the engine's machinery, the rush of the smoke from the twin stacks, and the creaking of the pilot wheel.

"Who's thet outside?" Duane asked.

"James Wyatt," Kearney replied. "He's watchin the river. Sometimes when we git ta tricky water we hafta measure an some'n will stand there an call the mark. He'll be in shortly. He's my cub pilot, learnin ta steer this craft. Once we're underway, he'll take the wheel."

Duane walked to a portside window where he looked back at the receding town as it dwindled into the distance. Warm sunlight flooded through the windows, glistening in the glass and sparkling off polished wood and brass fixtures.

"It seems quiet up here in a strange way," the boy observed.

"Now as we're on our way," the man suggested, "ya kin go on down 'n look about. I'll not be needin ya fer a hour 'r so."

"Okay," Duane agreed.

He walked out into bright sunlight, but was surprised by the chill of the moving air. Descending toward the main deck, he found the protection offered by the overhanging deck structure cut the draft and its chill. The lower decks were awash with activity as passengers strolled the upper deck and the soldiers lounged about on the cargo deck. Some stood to watch the passing shore line. Others settled on deck, cargo crates, against wagon wheel or cabin wall – to card game, a small conversation, or a tune on harmonica or guitar. A routine began to settle about the boat. Duane wandered through the small knots of soldiers until he found a spot he liked. Climbing onto a wagon seat, he settled to listen as a small group of soldiers shared their rendition of THE BONNIE BLUE FLAG.

A musically entertaining half hour drifted by before a card game exploded into angry words as a sore loser vented his anger.

"Come on, Sammy. Ya lost the hand fair 'n square an ya know it. Either shut up an play 'r go cool off." The voice bore the impatience of one tired of the same sore loser from previous experience.

"Yer all a pack a cheats!" The man jumped to his feet and threw a hand of cards in the face of the nearest soldier. He stormed away from the game and approached the group near Duane.

"Why don't ya shut up yer cat yowlin. Ya make a barnyard sound pretty." Insults fell of calloused listeners.

"Sergeant Winters," one suggested, "yer known ta be a sore loser. So go fer a walk 'n cool down."

As the angry figure turned to leave, his eyes fell on the boy perched on the wagon seat. "What's a snivlin brat like you sittin 'round in thet monkey suit fer?" His scowling voice grated and Duane cringed within. "Git down from there 'n git outta my sight. Else I jest might throw ya over the side." He moved menacingly toward the wagon.

One young red-head, fresh from the farm, stepped forward to confront the grizzled sergeant. "Ya best cool down, Sarg, 'er I'm gonna…"

"What!" the older man bellowed. "Yer way outta line, Soldier!" Before anyone realized what was happening, he reached up, grabbed Duane by the coat, and lifted him bodily from the wagon seat. The boy felt fear paralyze him from within and his desire to cry out remained silenced. "If I choose ta drop this monkey inta the river," he held the frightened boy up for all to see, "then I'll do it."

The red-head continued. "It might be I'm a farm boy, but I'm bigger 'n you. Ya best put thet boy down 'r I'll tear ya limb from limb!"

"Sergeant!" another voice challenged from the nearby stairs. "Ya harm a hair on my cabin boy 'n ya'll die right here on this river! Put him down!"

Duane felt himself lowered to firm footing on the boat's deck.

"Thanks," he barely whispered as the large hands released him.

"Mister!" Kearney continued, "I dunno what yer problem is, but this here boy's seen more hell then you have."

"No," Duane protested as the captain approached.

"They're gonna hear it, Dee," he placed a protective hand on the boy's shoulder as he stood beside him. "Ya've no shame." Nearby soldier's looked up to listen. "Dee's here on a search fer his pa. He's already been in combat with murderin raiders who kilt his ma an left him fer dead, too. He 'n his dog kilt two a them. Now he's done his piece a this war. Ya let him be. Save yer anger fer the enemy."

Silence. The sergeant jammed his hands into his pockets and walked away, his head bent low in shame. He passed from sight beyond the wagons. Kearney spoke quietly to the boy and they turned to climb the ladder toward the upper deck. The soldiers watched them go before exchanging surprised glances and entering into respectful talk about what they had just witnessed.

The day drifted on as the riverboat continued its journey downriver. Wild country and some scattered farmland extended as far as the eye could see along either side of the river. Late in the evening Duane descended from his supper chores to settle on the grand staircase at the front of the Queen and watch the gathering darkness of the eastern sky. Quiet conversation, music, and the soft strands of YELLOW ROSE drifted in the chill air to mingle with the throbbing of the boat's engines and the swoosh of billowing smoke and churning paddle.

A bearded figure approached from the port side and stopped to stand near the boy.

"Boy," he began with embarrassment. "Kin ya eve find it ta fergive me." He looked out toward the river. "I neve meant no harm. Sometimes I do bad thin's when I git mad at a person." He paused in awkward silence, then turned and his eyes met the boy's. They were dark with a hint of blue and a glistening of emotion. Duane knew he was sincere and his heart reached out to the man. The sergeant continued, "I ask ta be yer friend."

They searched each others eyes in silence and read into the depths of souls in pain. The boy smiled sadly. "My name's Dee. What's yers?"

"Sammy Winters, sergeant, Confederate Army."

"Hey, Sergeant Sammy Winters, I'm watchin the stars come. Ya wanna set here with me? I neve seen a river sky go ta night b'fer."

"Thet'd be good," the man responded.

He walked around to ascend the steps and settle on the broad tread beside the boy. They fell into a soft conversation, their voices lost in the mingled sounds of the evening. Night crept on, the velvet black reached out of the east and across the heavens, and a broken moon joined a million bits of light to cast a ghostly glow on a ribbon of river, the two figures seated on the grand staircase, and the vessel journeying onward in the night.

*   *   *

In the days that followed, Duane spent all his spare time mingling with the company of soldiers on the cargo deck. His story was quickly known to them and they accepted him with respect. There were a few who withheld their friendship, but most enjoyed his presence. Sergeant Winters became his unofficial guardian and was mellowed through his companionship with the boy. He watched for Duane to arrive on deck and was inseparable until Duane departed to undertake the duties of his position. There was little to do but talk, play cards, or share song and music; except when it came one's turn to clean the temporary stables, feed the horses, or help with meal preparations.

The boredom of routine was broken late on the second day when the Queen approached the small port at Pine Bluff. The shrill cry of the boat's whistle pierced the afternoon air to alert the populace of her coming. Duane watched with the sergeant at his side. The boy was perched on a wagon wheel for a better view; the man leaned against the corner of the wagon's bed. It had been an unusually warm day. Their clothing was clammy from perspiration so they had unbuttoned their shirts, pulled out the tails, and folded up their sleeves.

As the boat neared the wharf, boys swimming in the river stopped to watch. How refreshing the water must feel, Duane thought as he watched. Some climbed a tree on the shoreline to wave and shout to the boat's crew. Others swam out to meet her. On board the Ozark Queen, the deck was chaotic with commotion as the crew prepared to dock. Some of the crew stood by to throw mooring lines to shore hands standing ready on the wharf. Others prepared to run out the gangplank. As naked swimmers approached the vessel, some of the soldiers and the deck hands reached to haul them from the water. An air of enthusiastic excitement grew in the movement of the boys scrambling on board and the preparations for docking. The lively chatter of bragging rights from the first to reach the deck and all who dared to take the challenge mixed with the shouting of orders, the heartbeat of the engine room, the whinnies of startled horses, shouted conversations, and the rush of water rolling from under the vessel's bow. Some of the new arrivals sat on the edge of the deck with their feet dangling in the rough splash of the wake. Others visited with members of the crew known from previous stops or stood poised to return to the river as the boat neared the wharf, or hung in the water clinging to the edge of the shallow hull.

Captain Kearney's orders rang from overhead. "Ya deckhands git them boys on deck ta haul their feet in 'n them in the water ta swim clear. We're comin in now!"

Duane watched as those in the water shoved off to swim clear and head for the shallows beyond the wharf. But one toeheaded ten-year-old slipped as he tried to push off.

"Sammy!" Duane pointed to the water, "thet boy's in trouble!"

"Hold on!" Winters called. "I'll haul ya out!"

A look of helpless horror froze on the youngster's face as he slipped along the boat's hull toward the stern and the menacing motion of the paddle wheel.

The sergeant hurried along the edge of the deck, trying frantically to catch up to the figure in the water. Duane jumped down from his perch on the wagon wheel and dashed toward the engine room.

"Carney! Stop the wheel!" he screamed in panic. "A kid's caught in the water!"

The noise of the pistons driving the rockers and beams which powered the wheel, thundered about him as he entered the dark cavity of machinery. The engineer could not hear the boy, but sensed the urgency of his actions. Dumping the steam pressure with an explosive hissing, Carney threw the reverse lever and returned steam to ease the moving beams to a stop. The returning pressure had to be increased slowly or the machinery would be damaged and the large paddles broken. Even as Carney worked to stop the turning wheel, Duane dashed outside to see if Winters had caught the boy.

At first no one realized what was happening. The sudden slowing of the great wheel brought about the stunning realization of the crisis which was unfolding. Duane dashed between wagons and swung around the wheel rim to sprint toward the back edge of the deck. He saw as Sammy neared the struggling boy and jumped from the deck's edge to land in the water with hand outstretched toward the child.

The man went under on impact, but managed to clasp the boy's wrist and hang on. As he bobbed to the surface, the two drifted against the Queen's side, pulled by her momentum toward the moving wheel. The sergeant pulled the boy close and hooked his arm around the naked waist, at the same time guiding their roll in the water's current to slide toward the rotating paddles feet first.

Duane ran to the end of the deck where the stern overhung the water beside the giant wheel. There was nothing he could do but watch. He felt alone and helpless, completely unaware that all aboard the Queen and along the dock had become witness to the unfolding drama. But the sergeant was in control. He planted his shoes against the edge of the paddle and pushed away as it slowly dipped into the water. It wasn't enough to break clear, but the slackened speed of the engine allowed time to prepare for the impact of the next paddle. Duane saw Winters say something to the boy, then hug him close against his chest as the broad paddle struck him from behind pushing both beneath the murky waters. A hush fell on the scene. A moment later the two bobbed to the surface in the foamy wash behind the vessel.

Loud cheers erupted when the boy and the man waved toward the boat and began their swim toward shore. Duane stood on the small piece of stern deck, holding the brace beam to the wheel for balance. Silent tears slid down his cheeks as he cried quietly, relieved that a tragedy had been avoided.

The Ozark Queen slid softly into place beside the wharf. Once more the air hummed with activity as the boy turned to walk toward the gangplank, leave the boat, and seek out his friend and the boy he had saved.

Captain Kearney paused in his descent from the pilot house deck to stand at the rail and watch as his cabin boy disappeared in the rush of activity on the wharf. Carney had reported on the speaking tube what had happened in the engine room. There goes one special boy, the man thought to himself. It was time to have a talk with Captain Masters. He would attend to that once they were underway. For now, there was work to do.

*   *   *

Early the following morning the steamboat set out to continue its journey southeast. A company of fifty-odd soldiers had joined the ship's roster along with a shipment of military stores. Included with rifles and munitions was a small collection of band instruments. The newly arrived soldiers had with them several musicians. As life aboard the Ozark Queen returned to its routine of monotony, some relief was to be enjoyed as musicians from both companies combined their talents and interests to render several spontaneous concerts.

On the second day out from Pine Bluff, the weather turned to a grey drizzle. The men huddled about in ponchos and coats, as far back under the overhead deck as possible. Even so, the wind-driven mist soaked their clothing and dripped from soggy hat brims. In the warmth of the pilot house, Duane enjoyed a good view of the river through droplet-coated glass, alive with squiggly chasings as moisture gathered enough weight to dash downward toward the sills. The river was broad at this point with a wide safe channel. The shorelines were often settled with farmlands and small towns. Under normal circumstances, the Queen would be making many stops each day. But this trip she carried men and munitions for the army and both required quick passage.

Captain Kearney called the boy's attention to the town of Napoleon along the shoreline to the south and to changing forces of river current evident in the rippling of the water's surface, and evident, too, in changes of the water's color and texture. Here the Arkansas River joined the great Mississippi. Slowly, as the riverboat entered upon the great waterway, moving further out from the shoreline, it became lost in the loneliness of water and drizzle.

In the ghostly grayness, the captain sounded the steamboat's whistle. It cut sharply through the thick weather, warning other vessels of the Queen's presence. Other whistles announced other vessels passing unseen. By late afternoon the weather was clear and the bustling traffic of the river highway was a sharp contrast to the lonely passage along the Arkansas.

As large as the Mississippi was, it twisted, backtracked, sidestepped, and turned so erratically that the journey was slower and of a more hazardous nature. The river was always changing, Kearney explained. New bends, islands, sand bars, and channels came and were lost from one trip to the next. Vicksburg was about a hundred miles south of Napoleon. But the river's wanderings nearly doubled the distance.

The last day dawned crisp and brilliant. In the early afternoon, Jamie Wyatt was at the wheel. Captain Kearney leaned over the chart table with Duane and pointed out their location on the map.

"We're comin round the point, now, Sir," Jamie announced. He spun the wheel hard to starboard and the Queen began a wide turn from a northeast heading, full-about to a heading of southwest.

Looking up at his pilot's comment, the captain pointed the stem of his pipe toward the distant shore outside the starboard window. "See off there ta the south?" he spoke.

Duane followed the outstretched arm, peering beyond the wisp of tobacco smoke to a series of land points barely visible in the afternoon sun.

"I think I see more channels," the boy stated "There's so many. How da ya know which way ta go?"

"It takes knowin the rive' real good. Thet's why ya start as a cub pilot an learn ta read the water 'n know the rive' fer ya eve' pilot yer own boat." Still pointing, the man explained the current landmark. "The clearin furthest ta right marks the side a the main channel. Thet's Milliken's Bend. Beyond there it's only one more set a bends round the mouth a the Yazoo River b'fer Vicksburg."

The boy watched the approaching landmark. For a few minutes nothing more was said. The vessel swung easily through the last arc of her turn until she was in line to follow the main channel. Milliken's Bend drifted off the starboard side, then slipped gently behind.

"Come on, Dee," Kearney instructed. "We've some thin's ta tend ta fer we reach port." He started toward the door. "Mr. Wyatt, ya hold yer course. I'll be back in a half hour."

"Yes, Sir, Mr. Kearney."

The boy followed the captain through to the deck.

"Ya go ta the main deck 'n bring Captain Masters ta my cabin," Kearney spoke as they reached the ladder. "I'll meet ya there."

Duane passed through the commotion of activity on the lower decks, passed the skipper's order to Captain Masters by way of Sergeant Reilly, and tarried to visit with Sammy Winters while the sergeant searched for the officer.

"Dee," Captain Masters called as he worked his way through the clutter of humanity lounging about the sun-shadowed deck, "Sergeant Reilly tells me yer lookin fer me."

"Yes, Sir. Captain Kearney wants ta see ya in his cabin." He spoke once more to Sergeant Winters before the captain arrived. "Soon's I kin, I'll be back down."

"I'll be here," the sergeant acknowledged. "Ya run 'long now."

Following protocol, which Captain Kearney had begun to teach the cabin boy, Duane led and the captain followed. "This way, Sir." They ascended to the quarters on the upper deck. There, Duane opened the door and announced the captain.

"Come in, both a ya," Kearney invited. "Dee, fergit the formalities 'n bring yerself a chair. Captain, take the rocker."

As the two made themselves comfortable, Kearney settled into the chair at his desk and drew quietly on his pipe while he awaited their attention.

"Dee," he began, "when we started this trip tagether I said I'd think on yer askin me fer help. An I've done a heap a thinkin. Captain," he paused to exhale a light cloud of aroma and to collect his thoughts, "yer familiar with the boy's story?"

"I've heard it," he glanced at Duane.

"Da ya know why he's on this boat?"

"I assumed he was workin fer ya."

"No Sir. He come ta me ta help him git ta the war so's he kin find his pa. I've bin givin it thought all 'long the way 'n I have a idea if yer willin ta help, too."

The boy sat forward with elbows on knees and chin on clasped hands, listening intently as the discussion unfolded. Kearney sucked gently on his pipe while the officer responded.

"How kin I help?" he asked.

There was a brief pause to lay the pipe aside and release a small cloud of tobacco smoke. It hung briefly in the air as it faded to a wisp of pleasant odor.

"Yer company's on its way fer assignment ta the army up north near Tennessee. We figure Dee's pa ta be up thet way. Ain't it so, Dee?"

"Yes, Sir," Duane confirmed. "His last letter says he's goin ta help git Grant at Fort Henry."

"We lost Fort Henry last month," Masters informed. "Ain't ya heard? Grant took Henry 'n Donelson, too."

The news came as a stunning blow. The boy was suddenly drained of all enthusiasm. It didn't matter any more. There was no reason left to go on. He cried within, but the tears did not come. A blank stare passed beyond the wall in front, focusing on nothingness.

"Dee," the captain continued, "thet don't mean yer pa's lost. A lot a our troops slipped away fer the end an only the garrison was taken prisoner. Even so, there's talk of a prisoner exchange."

Duane cheered up and listened while Captain Kearney continued. "Thet all bein what it is, I figger the captain's comp'ny could use a drummer boy 'n Dee here could go on with ya. When ya hitch up with the big army, ya could look up his pa 'n he could think on what ta do next."

There was a short silence while all three considered the skipper's proposal.

"Would thet help ya, Dee?" the officer inquired.

"Yes, Sir!" the boy beamed, breaking into a smile.

"We kin do it," Captain Masters agreed. "We'll check with our quartermaster 'n fit ya up with a uniform an see if the musicians from the Pine Bluff company have an extra drum. I'll have my lieutenant add ya ta the company roster. By the time we're arrived ta Vicksburg ya'll be an official drummer boy. Maybe we'll even find one who kin learn ya how ta play."

"Yer set, Dee," Kearney stated. "We'll git yer gear packed 'n see if yer sergeant friend kin find ya a have'sack fer ta put it in." He stood and extended his hand to the officer. "Captain, we sure thank ya fer yer help."

Masters rose from the rocker as the boy, too, stood. "Glad I could." He accepted the outstretched hand. "We best git ta puttin this in order. It won't be much longer." He turned to the boy. "Dee, ya come with me 'n we'll git ya outfitted. Then ya come back 'n pack yer thin's."

The three started for the door as the captain finished.

"Captain, I'll see ta the boy's needs at present 'n see ya later fer we go ashore."

"Thet'll be fine. I'll be busy fer a time until we tie up."

They left the cabin. The boy and the officer departed below. The skipper paused to watch them go and to knock the ashes from his pipe, then turned to climb back to the pilot house.

The Queen passed the mouth of the Yazoo and rounded the point to a heading northeast. Within the half hour the river rounded the point of land to the right, revealing high bluffs on the far bank and the city perched on its top.

During this time Captain Masters and Sergeant Winters had worked to transform Duane from a cabin boy to a drummer boy, and to equip him for his new lifestyle in the army. It wasn't much for a uniform. He wore his own trousers with an oversized brown shirt and grey forage cap. Now the captain was busy with the many details in preparation of landfall. Duane stood near the bow of the main deck, his arm around a deck support post against which he rested his weight. Sammy stood at his side with a protective arm across the boy's shoulders. They gazed in awe at the great city atop the bluffs – the biggest place either had seen in his lifetime. The river ahead was alive with motion. The great wharf had several riverboats at its side.

As the boat's whistle echoed off the surrounding hills, the boy thought back over the events of the past two weeks. Home seemed so far away and so long ago. He missed Pounder, Jaime, Mrs. Riggs, his ma, his home. God, how lonely he felt! A sharpness stung in his eyes and throat. His vision blurred as tears slipped quietly down his cheeks. Sergeant Winters sensed the boy's lonesome grief and squeezed the small shoulder gently to say he cared. Duane slipped both arms around the strong waist and buried his face in the folds of the man's shirt. He cried quietly as Sammy held him close. Momentarily the boy pulled away and wiped his face with the back of the sleeve on his new shirt.

"I'm okay," he announced.

"Thet's good," Winters acknowledged. "Cause we've a whole lot a work ta do ta git unloaded and move in ta the army camps. Here tell we won't stay here long, though. They got a railroad thet'll take us north in no time."

"I neve seen a railroad b'fer. But I heard of it," the boy stated.

"I ain't seen one neither," the sergeant added. "Guess it's a first time fer both of us."

Deckhands moved about to prepare the mooring lines, the gangplanks, derricks, and winch lines. Captain Masters called his subordinates together to assign work details for unloading wagons and horses and for reassembling wagon parts and harnessing up the teams.

"Where da we go from here?" Duane asked as the sergeant turned to go to the captain.

"As I hear it, the army's gatherin up north at a place called Corinth. The railroads go through there from all parts." He was gone toward the meeting which was held at the first wagon.

Commotion crescendoed about the boat. Passengers gathered at the upper rail. Soldiers from both companies set to work to free wagons and cargo from safety lines which had held them in place. The engines changed their rhythmic pounding as the vessel slowed for docking. The whistle shrieked. Foremen shouted orders. Duane found himself drawn in on a work detail preparing one of the wagons to be rolled down the rampway to the wharf. The din of noise closed in about him as the Ozark Queen slipped between two other riverboats and bumped gently against the timbers of the dock.

This was Vicksburg. It was the end of the trip. It was the beginning of a new journey.

Behind lay the boy's childhood.

Ahead lay war.

Duane Kinkade was a farm boy in the Ozark countryside. His dog was his close friend. His Pa was his best friend. That spring of 1861 was a season marred by the opening of war as a nation split in two. Disappearing into the fabric of a distant conflict was the father whose absence became increasingly unbearable to the son who loved him so much.

ON THE EVE OF CONFLICT is the story of that boy's experiences and eventual decision to go in search of his father. It is the beginning of a journey which will put him on the road to war and eventually carry him into the midst of the conflict.

ISBN 978-621-434-011-8

9 786214 340118

J. ARTHUR MOORE

UP FROM
Corinth

Book 2 of
JOURNEY INTO DARKNESS

JOURNEY INTO DARKNESS

a story in four parts

part 1

On the Eve of Conflict

part 2

Up From Corinth

part 3

Across the Valley to Darkness

part 4

Toward the End of the Search

book two of

JOURNEY INTO DARKNESS

written by
J. Arthur Moore

Dedication

Up From Corinth is dedicated in His love and in friendship to Charley French and David Rowland, each of whom has helped by becoming forever a part of the story through the photographic material, and to all who have enjoyed its telling and shared in the adventure of its creation.

Duane Kinkade

Johnny Applebee

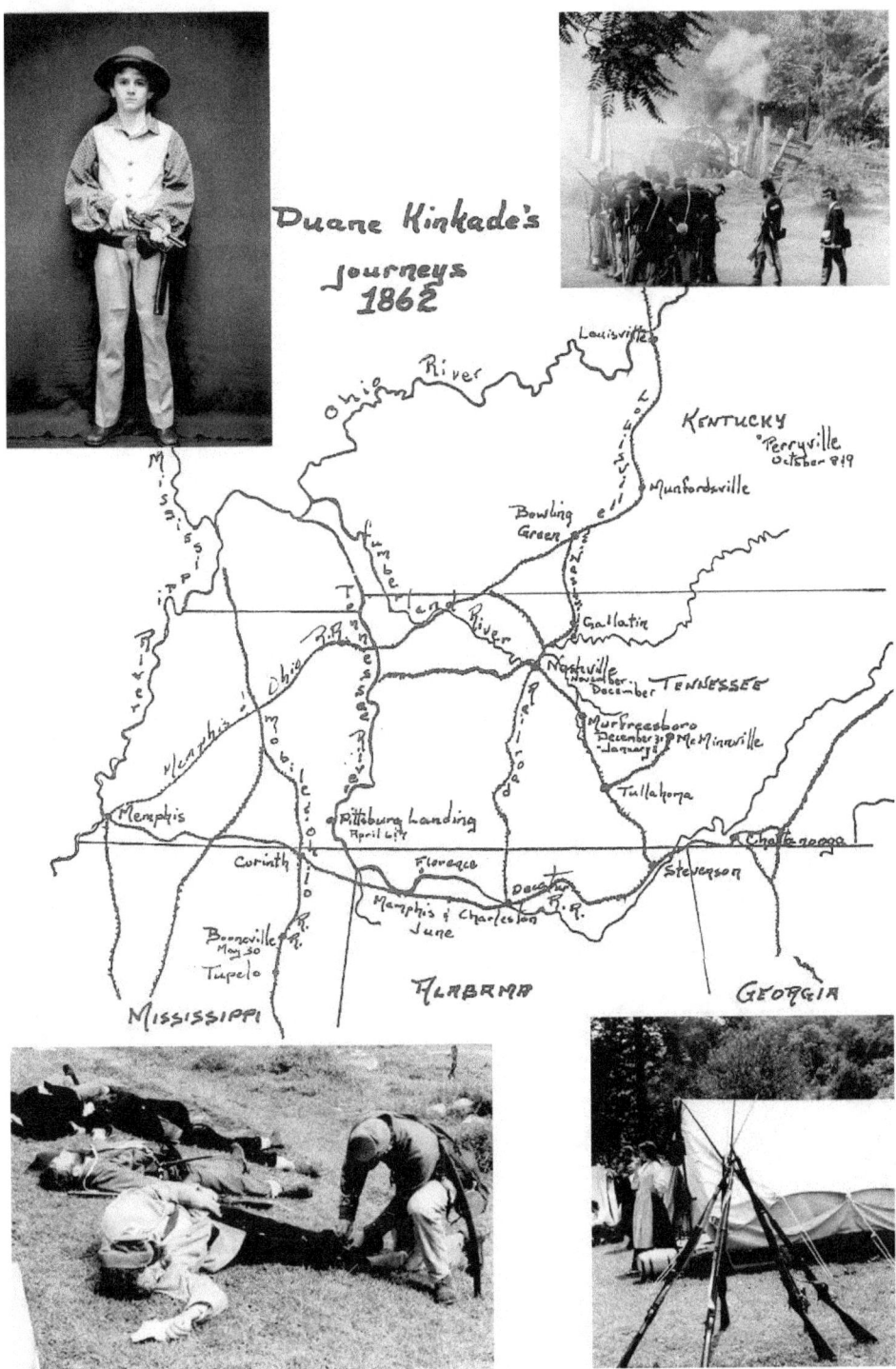

Duane Kinkade's Journeys 1862

In the coolness of the April night, firelight from General Breckinridge's troop camps flickered for miles along the Memphis and Charleston Railroad to the east of Corinth. A dampness hung on the air from scattered showers and storms over the preceding days. Roads were muddy and thick in places and scattered puddles reflected the dim light of the night sky. Wall tents and Selby tepees were lined in orderly fashion and most of the troops were gathered in small knots of conversation about their camp fires. Some had turned in and a few lounged about in front of their tents. Many had not yet seen battle, but had arrived with new units coming up from the south, gathering and drilling for battles yet to come.

Captain Masters stood to the side of his camp fire in quiet conversation with his lieutenants. At the next fire, Duane stood listening while Private Eagleson told how he would kill any Yank he might find. Sergeant Winters stood with a protective arm around the boy's shoulders.

"You city boys 'r all the same," the sergeant's gruff voice chided. "Why I'll bet Dee here could shoot the pants offin eny three a ya street bullies fer ya decided which end a yer gun was the business part."

The small gathering roared with laughter.

"Tell ya what, Sarg," Eagleson responded. "They give us guns in time, I'll bet a week's pay I kin shoot the buttons off yer shirt without even a scratch."

"Yeh 'n if ya miss I'll not live ta collect enyhow," Winters observed.

"Depends on how I choose ta miss."

"Mouthy little street bug, ain't ya."

"Hey, Sammy, let's not git riled, now. Why Brian here's too young ta know better. I swear he packs a razor so's he'll have it if 'n there's enythin ta use it on come summer." Sergeant Reilly chuckled at his own joke as he slapped the young private on the back with brotherly gentleness. He stepped toward the fire and hooked the handle of the coffee pot which sat near the flames, and lifted it aside with the toe of his boot. Dark steam rolled from the spout. "Looks real hot. Enyone else want a cup?"

Conversation ended briefly while several of the men took a cup from a nearby stump and held it under the spout as the sergeant poured. Duane seated himself on a stick of firewood in the heated dirt near the fire while his friend went for a cup of the hot brew. Returning, Winters stood beside the boy and sipped the steaming liquid, staring thoughtfully into the flames.

"Sarg?"

"Yeh, Boy?"

"We been here a week 'r so, now. Ya think we'll be fightin soon?" His brown eyes continued to focus on some point within the flames.

Winters squatted down beside the boy, his voice soft. "Don't know fer sher, Dee. But I spose we'll do somethin soon. I hear tell Ol Unconditional is movin in at Pittsburg Landing." He paused to sip from the tin cup. "That's not mor'n thirty miles north a here." All gruffness was gone from the sergeant's voice when he noticed a quiet tear slip down the boy's cheek. "Still no word on yer pa, is there."

"No," Duane rubbed at the offensive drop. "I really thought we'd find him here when Johnston's army was all in camp." He looked at his friend. "Ya think the captain'll find out enythin?"

"Don' know," Winters emptied the coffee from his cup and dumped the dregs on the fire. He stood and pulled the boy to his feet. "Come on, looks like he finished. Let's ask."

Captain Masters turned to the approaching pair. "Evenin, Dee, Sergeant."

"Howdy, Captain," Winters responded. "Did ya larn eny news on the boy's pa?"

The tall, clean-shaven officer shook his head sadly. "I'm really sorry, Dee. The general said yer pa had been reassigned to one of General Beauregard's corps before the loss of Fort Donelson. He's not sure if he made the transfer or was caught in the surrender at Donelson." He saw the hurt on the boy's face. "Look, Son, it's gonna be busy fer the next few days. Word has it we're goin after Grant tonight or tomorra. But when we settle agin, I'll see what I kin do."

"Thanks, Captain." Duane forced a smile.

The captain returned to his tent while the boy and the sergeant turned back toward the fire.

"I guess ya better be sher ya kin really play thet drum a yers." A large hand gently tousled the boy's hair. "Bein a drummer boy's gonna git real serious."

The man poured another cup of coffee, then set the nearly empty pot by the stump. The coffee was still warm, but no longer steaming. Few remained near the fire. Conversation had been replaced by the soft strands of harmonica music. Duane and his friend rejoined the group and listened quietly. Winters sipped from the cup.

"Sammy," the boy spoke softly. "Ya eve bin in a war b'fer?"

"No. Only a scrape 'r two with the Morton boys back home. Neve raised a weapon cept ma fists ta another." He paused, then remembering the boy's past, added, "Ya seen more serious fightin then I ever did when them raiders kilt yer ma."

"I fergot thet jest now," Duane said. "Somehow it all seems differnt now than thet was."

"Jest more people now," the sergeant responded. "They'll still be out ta kill ya."

Lieutenant Carson approached the fire. His uniform was wet with sweat from hurried travel about the camp. "You fellas git yer gear packed 'n turn in. We move out for mornin." He paused to catch his breath.

"What's up?" Sergeant Reilly asked from his seat near the fire.

"General Johnston is gonna attack Grant at Pittsburg. Breckinridge was called ta the telegraph office and received orders ta move up and join the rest of the army at Monterey."

"I guess this is it," Eagleson stated flatly.

The lieutenant moved on. The group about the fire sat silently; then, one by one, drifted back to their tents.

"I'm scart," Duane whispered to his friend as they walked toward their tent.

"Ta tell the honest truth, my insides is shakin some too, Boy." He placed his hand on the boy's shoulder and tightened gently. "You stay by me and I'll not let enythin happen to ya."

Duane smiled to himself, satisfied for the moment to be near a friend and secure in the belief that the sergeant could do anything he wished, including help an eleven-year-old boy stay alive and find his father.

*   *   *

The next morning the troops received orders to advance. Guns were issued along with one hundred rounds of ammunition and three day's cooked rations. Excitement erupted into a delirium of cheers and some firing of their guns as the mostly inexperienced soldiers celebrated the news of the forthcoming conflict. The army was to have been fully underway by three o'clock in the morning. But delays in preparing the orders meant that most of the army didn't get started until after sunup and some didn't even receive guns until the afternoon.

As General Breckinridge massed his forces at Burnsville to proceed to Monterey, Major-Generals Polk, Bragg, and Hardee prepared to move their corps out of Corinth. The soldiers were brought under arms by noon as troops, wagons, batteries of field cannon clogged all roads leading from the town. But due to confusion by General Polk's understanding of the orders, his corps did not move until late afternoon, thus blocking all progress since his corps was in front. It wasn't until the following day, Friday, that the corps were finally massed at Monterey.

The movement on Friday was hindered by rain, muddy roads, and travel through wooded and swampy countryside. Major-General Hardee's corps arrived within five miles of Pittsburg by day's end. As night settled in and the rain gave way to a drizzle, over 35,000 troops were spread across the countryside between Monterey and Pittsburg Landing, with nothing but the trees for protection and the open sky above.

Somewhere in the wooded landscape along the road from Monterey to Mickey's, Duane and his company waited for the order to attack. The command was massed in columns of brigades, poised for the decision to advance. His clothing soaked through, water dripped from the visor of his cap, plopping onto the skin head of his drum with a hollow echo. A continual dripping of moisture from the water-logged clumping of his hair caused an irritating streaming of droplets from under his collar down his spine, to saturate his shirt and drip into puddles at his feet. Pools of water puddled near the rim of the drumhead, cascading in minute falls through the rope holes. In whispered conversation, the news of the day was related between periods of silent gazing into the shadows ahead of the line.

"I heard tell the Yanks know we're here," a voice in the dark whispered.

"I'd not be so sher," Sergeant Reilly replied.

"Some of Bragg's troops engaged Federal soldiers this aftanoon," the voice continued. "Cannon were used. They couldn't miss thet."

"True," Lieutenant Reynolds acknowledged. "We'll jest hafta wait 'n see."

"When da we go?" Duane asked.

"S'posed ta be tanight," the lieutenant answered.

There was a long period of silence. Only the soft drizzle of the rain spread its soft but steady swish on the night air.

Duane leaned back against a tree and closed his eyes.

He could feel the fear welling up in a hollowness in the pit of his stomach. But exhaustion was heavier. The boy let his eyes fall closed, shivered in the cold wet, rested his head against the trunk behind him, and drifted into sleep.

The quiet was disturbed by a small group of ghostly figures riding horseback along the line. General Bowen and some of his officers were passing through, talking briefly with the company commanders before disappearing again into the mist. Duane was startled from his fitful sleep and listened to the conversation, muffled by the constant drizzle.

"The order to attack at 3 AM has been canceled. We are delayed too much by the rain, and all units have not been able to receive their orders from the adjutant general's office."

"What about the skirmish Bragg's corps encountered with the Federal troops?"

"According to information gathered from a major captured from his Ohio division, the Federal army has no idea we're here. They haven't even built any defenses."

"What now?"

"We'll go as planned. General Hardee will command the front line made up of the Third Corps and Gladden's Brigade. General Bragg will lead the second. We are the third, under Breckinridge, and will act as the reserve. We'll join Polk at Mickey's. He will move up the left side of Bark Road. We advance on the right side."

Silence fell as the riders moved on. Still the corps remained along the road. Duane and his comrades slept where they stood among more than six thousand soldiers with baggage wagons and cannon massed in full battle readiness. Shortly after midnight the weather turned worse as a violent storm swept through.

The boy woke with a start. He had never felt so deeply rotten and miserable as he did that night. Soaked and chilled to the bone, he shivered in the cold damp. Soon the tears of anger and frustration poured forth and mixed with the rain water streaming down his face. He cried quietly, any sound lost to the storm. Winters, who had dozed on the opposite side of the tree, sensed the boy's misery. Leaning his gun against the trunk, he moved around to his young friend, drew him into his arms and held the sobbing boy close to his own wet figure. The sergeant wasn't any drier, but there was some warmth and the security of knowing he cared. Time passed. Eventually Duane cried himself to sleep. The two passed the rest of the night together against the tree bark.

Saturday dawned with the passing of the storm. The weather began to clear. Any food consumed was taken from the packed rations in the soldier's haversack, as troops began to move into position for the forthcoming battle. The front line deployed across three miles from Owl Creek on the west to Lick Creek on the east. It was after 3 o'clock, Saturday afternoon before all the army had taken position behind Hardee's front, too late to begin the attack. About 800 yards separated the lines of battle.

At about four o'clock there was a meeting on the Pittsburg Road, just behind Hardee's line as Generals Johnston and Beauregard dismounted and gathered with their corps commanders. General Beauregard argued that delays, mistakes, and the noise of the army's movements must surely have alerted the enemy. Polk and Bragg disagreed. General Johnston listened quietly to the argument as well as to the reports on the conditions of the troops.

"Gentlemen," he spoke with finality, "we shall attack at daylight tomorrow." Turning to one of his staff officers he continued, "I would fight them if they were a million. They can present no greater front between these two creeks than we can, and the more men they crowd in there, the worse we can make it for them."

The meeting broke up. The generals returned to their various commands to make final preparations. They met again at General Johnston's tent in the evening. Saturday ended with a sunset in a cloudless sky. Night came calm, clear, and beautiful. The decision held firm. Full battle was only hours away.

*   *   *

Bowen's brigade began to move long before the morning light began to brighten the eastern horizon. Captain Masters spoke softly as he passed commands to his soldiers. Guns were loaded. Bayonets were fixed. Duane stuck his drumsticks in his belt and steadied the drum with both hands to keep it from banging against his leg as he hurried along. It felt good to be dry. He had slept much better, curled up in his blanket beside his drum. No one spoke except to relay orders. The boy sensed a tightness in his chest and a hollowness that almost hurt. Until these past hours, the war was always somewhere else. It wasn't real — only some distant story in which his father had been lost. Now it was over the next hill, through the next woodlot, across the next field, just beyond the little church of Shiloh.

The generals met once more on the hillside above Shiloh Church. The argument was repeated even as Hardee's troops advanced on the Union line, as yet totally unaware of the approaching storm on this clear Sunday morning. Sunrise was brilliant and beautiful in a cloudless deep- blue sky.

The eastern horizon had just begun to lighten on the tranquil rolling hills of the Tennessee countryside when the distant rattle of musket fire signaled the first contact of battle. Duane sensed an excitement in his comrades and his own determination to beat the cadence quick and lively. The soldiers that marched to his beat would be alert and vigorous. The enemy would suffer dearly. It was shortly after five o'clock in the morning. The battle had begun.

At the front, Hardee's skirmish line under the command of Major Hardcastle was attacked by the 21st Missouri regiment as it advanced up the Corinth Road. The struggle was brief as the Missourians were crushed and overrun by Hindman's whole division of Confederate troops. Following the ridge, the division drifted to the right and fell full force on the Union camp under General Prentiss. The attack was sudden and violent, catching the Union soldiers asleep or at breakfast.

Battle erupted with the blood-curdling yell from a thousand Rebel throats and a sudden wave of grey, butternut brown, thundering gunfire, and a cloud of blue smoke. Federal soldiers stumbled from their tents or jumped up from breakfast and grabbed for their guns. The din of battle closed swiftly around them and they were quickly cut down by the hundreds by the oncoming tide. Screams of pain and fear filled the air and mixed with the Rebel yells and the rattle of gunfire. Boys and men fell, bodies shattered by lead mini balls and slashed by bayonets. Blood flowed thick in the dry dirt, turning it to a red mud, slick and slippery underfoot. There was little defense, no time to fight back. The camp was carried before eight o'clock in the morning as the Federal front caved in and was pushed back toward Pittsburg Landing.

Battle exploded into full fury all along the three-mile front. Field batteries opened fire and Federal cannon were rolled into place to return the shower of death. A great cloud of smoke lifted from the fields and woods and rolling hills as the roar of cannon, the deafening clatter of musketry, the yells of attacking hoards, and the screams of pain and death mixed in brilliant April dawn.

Captain Masters' Arkansas company remained in reserve throughout the morning. As Breckinridge's corps followed the battle from behind, Bowen's Brigade found itself near the Eastern Corinth Road, cresting the rise above what had been Prentiss' camp of the early morning.

The bright sun and flawless blue sky spread its warmth over the landscape. Stark branches of trees had a soft glow of new buds and the color of fresh blossoms. The crisp green of new spring grass had been trampled across the rolling hills of the riverside farmlands. The road to Shiloh Church branched to the left. Woodland rose gently to the right, cut by a bubbling brook which joined Lick Creek and dumped into the Tennessee River less that a mile from the road.

Duane beat a steady and vigorous cadence. Eagleson was nearby with the company colors, drifting lazily in the still air as the brigade marched forward and limp with every stop. As the troops passed the road to the church, the road sloped downward through the Union camp. Bandsmen, teamsters, and other non-combatants were already at work helping the walking wounded wandering into the camp. Surgeons were busy with the wounded and dying from the first fighting when the camp itself was the battleground. Prisoners were being marched to the rear to be taken back to Corinth. Many of the dead had been laid out in rows. There were, at a glance, a couple hundred. Cries of pain and moans of the half-conscious drifted on the air. There was, too, the hint of the stench of death as bodies warmed by the midday sun, bloated and gave off the gases of decay, and the pile of amputated limbs strewn on the ground about the surgeon's table, began to rot.

The drum faltered slightly as the boy felt a sudden faintness in his head and a turning in his stomach. "Not now," the captain whispered. "You've a job ta do. Yer leadin an army now. Them boys is listenin ta yer beatin of the drum. Yer their heart. Yer their general." He moved away to the side of the troops as the boy picked up the drumbeat.

Following the road which forked right from the Corinth Road, the brigade moved along the rail fence of a newly turned field. The roar of battle was just ahead. Frightened boys could be seen cutting through the field. Others were slinking through the trees or retreating at a dead run, fleeing for their lives from the battle ahead. The air was thick with smoke, musket and cannon fire, screaming and yelling, the shout of orders. Suddenly the brigade was halted. The confusion of battle and the massing of troops were all around them. The line of battle stretched to both sides. Newly dead soldiers of both armies littered the ground. Among them lay the wounded; some being aided by friend or foe alike; others writhing in pain or attempting to crawl from the field. Gunfire continued steady to the front of the line, mixed with the cannon fire of Federal batteries located opposite the Confederate line.

A slight ridge marked the Confederate defenses. Beyond stretched a peach orchard after which there was a wooded hillside rising from the open field. General Prentiss had entrenched the remainder of his Union division along with artillery in a strong defensive position along the crest of the hill. For hours, heavy musket fire had rained across the field between.

General Bowen sent his staff officers up and down the line maneuvering the brigade into battle position. Another officer rode up from the battle smoke to the left of Duane's position. The boy was close enough to see. The officer, a man nearing sixty years, had greying long hair and a broom of a mustache. He sat tall in the saddle, very much at ease, enthusiastic, and commanding. Duane knew from his stature and the respect he was shown that this was the General-in-Chief of the whole army, General Albert Sidney Johnston himself. He listened as best he could. The Arkansas company was very near the general.

"They are offering stubborn resistance here," he shouted to his staff. "I shall have to put the bayonet to them."

Duane held his drumsticks ready for the command, whatever it might be. The general sent one of his staff officers to lead a Tennessee regiment. A brief conference was held with General Breckinridge. It was obvious the two cared very much for each other. Breckinridge addressed the troops, followed by his staff officers. Meanwhile, Johnston rode slowly down the line; hat off, sword in scabbard, a little tin cup in his right hand. He had acquired the cup earlier in the day, calling it his share of the day's spoils. His presence on his thoroughbred bay and his easy bearing were inspiring.

"Men!" his voice encouraged, "they are stubborn; we must use the bayonet." He reached the center of the line and turned. "I will lead you!" he cried and moved toward the enemy.

A chill of excitement ran down Duane's spine and he quivered with the thrill of battle. All fear was gone as he struck his drum with a vibrant, quick cadence and followed his general. A trembling thrill surged through every fiber of the two brigades, Statham's and Bowen's. With a mighty shout they charged forward to cross the field and drive the Federals from their hilltop defenses.

A sheet of flame and the roar of cannon erupted from along the crest of the hill. The din of noise was deafening and nearly dazed the boy's senses as soldiers dropped all along the line and cannon shot exploded in the ranks. The Confederate guns returned the fire in a clattering explosion of shot and fire and smoke. The Rebel yell, screams of pain, the smell of smoke mixed into one and wrapped the boy in a frenzied numbness. Something picked at his shirt sleeve. A flash of light exploded to his right. He saw one soldier's body fly apart and several others blown down like cornstalks in a hailstorm. His shirt was caught on something and the drum made a funny plop and rattle noise. Then he realized, those were bullets going through his clothes.

The charge advanced up the hill. The crest was reached. The Union forces fell back to form a new position in a natural hollow of the landscape. Volley after volley of rifle fire continued from both sides even as the Federal troops withdrew. Duane looked about to see if he could locate the general. He was nearby, still on his horse, continuing to direct the battle. As one of his staff officers approached the general, the boy noticed that Johnston's horse was bleeding from several wounds and the general's uniform, like his own, had several holes in it.

Enemy bullets continued to pick at the ground, kicking up puffs of dust, and to strike down soldiers nearby. The staff officer rode off to deliver a message to General Statham and return. Another rode up to whom the general shouted, "We must go to the left, where the firing is heaviest." He, too, was sent off with instructions.

The boy continued to beat the drum while his company regrouped and continued to fire upon the enemy. The captain was bleeding from a hole in his sleeve. Sergeant Winters had kept his word. He was unhurt and continued to stay near the boy. Duane had glanced away from his fascination with the general to see who was still nearby. Looking back, he noticed how pale the general seemed. The staff officer was calling to him.

"General, are you wounded?"

"Yes," the older man spoke emphatically, "and, I fear, seriously."

Several moved to offer aid. Tears came without warning and Duane felt them stinging in his eyes. He felt a deep sense of loss inside and was struck with the thought that this man was dying. He fought to keep from crying and put all his energy into his cadence. The company laid down a sudden burst of gun fire as to provide cover for the officers to guide their leader's horse to the nearby protection of a ravine. The boy followed and his troops with him. They continued the fight as the general was lifted from his horse and his officers searched for the wound. Duane glanced at the scene behind him. An officer held Johnston's head in his lap and spoke caringly to him. The general smiled weakly. He closed his eyes and was gone.

A rider was sent off toward Shiloh Church to inform General Beauregard of Johnston's death.

The battle continued to rage through the middle of the afternoon. But neither General Statham's brigade nor General Bowen's, made another charge. About an hour after Johnston's death, near three-thirty in the afternoon, Confederate batteries were placed in line to finish the assault on Prentiss' Federal position. As a heavy fire of field artillery exploded into an even greater thundering of killing fire, the whole Confederate line renewed its advance. The Federal army fell back to the road at Pittsburg Landing where it massed its troops and artillery. General Prentiss was trapped and finally surrendered with some two thousand troops.

Meanwhile, Duane found himself out of the combat, falling back with the rest of the two brigades toward a position in the overrun Union camps. Captain Masters was taken ahead to join the wounded in the makeshift field hospital. Sergeant Winters was somewhat pale, but unhurt. Many from the company did not return. Duane was constantly thirsty and drank repeatedly from his canteen. The two wandered slowly through the field of battle and became separated from the rest. The reality of what he had been through made the boy sick in his stomach as he looked about the landscape thickly carpeted with the dead and wounded. Finding the shade of a peach tree in the orchard between the battle line and the camp, he leaned back against its trunk and allowed his legs to give way as he slid to the ground. The drum was unstrapped and placed on the grass. Sammy strolled over, stared at the bullet hole in the wooden side, then rolled the drum with his toe.

"Ya okay?" the man asked.

"Yeh," the boy nodded.

Nothing more was said. The boy stared at a distant tree branch, swaying gently in the breeze. A single fragment of a pink blossom still clung gingerly to a twig. The blue sky was clouding over. The sun was in the west. The fragile pink blossoms carpeted the ground, trampled in the blood-red soil. A stillness hung on the orchard, the dead resting beneath the flower of the peach, cut down in the shower of bullets. Most of the walking wounded had gone from the killing ground. Others lay or sat about in a shocked daze, staring blankly at nothing. Nearby there came a moaning.

The sergeant had wandered off. The boy turned and saw a movement of blue. Rolling to his hands and knees, Duane pushed himself to his feet and walked toward the movement and sound. A Federal soldier, not yet twenty, was trying to get to his feet. The boy saw at a glance, it was hopeless. Pale from shock and loss of blood, the youth had been shot through the chest and suffered a shattered arm.

"Water," he whispered painfully.

"Hold on, I'll git help," Duane stated.

"No use, just... water." He sighed, exhausted from the effort.

Duane pulled a wooden canteen from a haversack, still worn by a nearby corpse. Kneeling by the dying soldier, he pulled the stopper and dripped the sun-warmed contents on the youth's parched lips. Painfully and slowly, the soldier licked the moisture. Duane continued, drop by drop, to relieve the young man's thirst. The youth smiled slightly. The body quivered as if he were chilled, then relaxed. Duane touched the bloodied hand and felt its warmth go cold. There were no tears, just that same sickness in the boy's stomach at the waste of life.

Sergeant Winters found the boy, still kneeling by the body. "We best git movin," the man suggested. "It seems a mite quiet. Could be the fightin's over." The man looked toward the western sky. "'Bout an hour a daylight yet," he observed. "There may be food fixin tanight. Thet Federal camp we come through earlier oughta be stocked right good of food 'n sech."

As they stood to move on, a new sound boomed in the distance and screeched overhead. The ground shook as a large shell exploded on a nearby hill.

"What was thet!" Duane exclaimed.

"A hell-of-a-big cannon!" Winters responded. "Let's git!"

The distant booming repeated and again a shell screamed overhead to crash in an open field.

"Where'd they come from?" the boy called on the run.

"Here tell them Yanks got gunboats in the river!" came the breathless reply from his fleeing companion.

Cresting a low rise, the two saw more of the soldiers from their reserve brigades gathering at the edge of a tree stand. A shell dropped with a blinding flash and a deafening roar. Duane felt himself forced to the ground. Rolling over, he glanced back. The sergeant lay crumpled against a tree.

"Nooo!" the boy screamed.

But his friend was dead.

"Boy! Over here!" a voice called.

Duane crawled toward his friend.

"Over here! Hurry!"

He ignored the voice. Suddenly there were firm hands picking him up by both arms, his drum dangling by its strap, the sticks still jammed in his belt. Two troopers from General Bowen's brigade had lifted the boy bodily from the ground and carried him toward their position, as the ground where he had lain, erupted in flame and shell fragment.

*   *   *

General Beauregard pulled his troops from combat during the shelling by the gunboats. They had been engaged in conflict for eleven harrowing hours, having lost nearly ten thousand killed, wounded and missing. The army remained under arms. Ammunition was resupplied to a few units. The troops were poised for the final assault to be carried out in the morning. They would sleep on their guns until daybreak.

It rained during the night and the Confederate divisions fell back to the shelter of the captured Union camps. Two Federal gunboats shelled the Southern positions at fifteen minute intervals throughout the night. Also in the course of the night, Federal reinforcements arrived. When the battle reopened early Monday morning, 23,000 fresh troops had arrived to strengthen the Federal Army.

The rainfall stopped during the darkness of the night. As Monday began to dawn, the Federal command launched its attack on the Confederate divisions. The battle raged fiercely back and forth during the morning and Duane eventually found himself once again in the fierce combat around the peach orchard. Artillery had been brought up on both fronts as Breckinridge's Division fiercely held its ground.

Captain Masters was back in the fight, along with Lieutenant Reynolds and more than half of the original company. Their position was reinforced by artillery. A Union assault had just started across the front. Muskets were loaded and leveled at the enemy awaiting the order to fire. Artillerymen were loading grape shot for close range. The drum held a steady roll.

"Fire!"

The cannon sent forth a roar of flame and smoke and shot as a sheet of fire burst forth from the line of muskets, searing bayonet metal with their heat. The Union line withered and stopped. The soldiers fell back, dragging some of their wounded with them. Federal artillery scored a hit putting a nearby cannon out of action and knocking down most of the gun's crew. Infantrymen filled the gap using the broken gun carriage for cover. The Union position continued a heavy fire. Duane was used to the grass and dirt being kicked up by the mini balls or the fine shower of lead dust when one shattered on tree or rock or nearby cannon. He was used to the screams, the yells, the blood, the silence of death. His drum gave off a loud splintering crack as pain seared his leg. He looked down and saw the shattered back of the drum where the mini ball, which had entered quietly from the front, exploded on its way out. A gash was torn through his trouser leg and was soaking red with his blood as it poured from his grazed flesh.

At first the boy felt fear. Then numbness covered the pain and he decided he wasn't hurt that bad. Men with worse were still in the line of battle. The din of battle continued all around. More men were falling and there were no reinforcements to bring up. Another Union assault was forced back.

A faintness dulled the boy's senses as the steady loss of blood took its toll. A caisson to his side took a direct hit and exploded as its powder charges ignited. Pieces of its wheel struck the boy's drum, shattering it, as the force of their impact and of the explosion, drove him bodily into the side of a nearby gun carriage. Pain crashed into his head. There was a loud ringing in his ears. Then silence.

*   *   *

Late in the afternoon Duane became aware of some heavy weight on his back, of the pain in his head, of his arms entangled in something, of his face pressed against a hard surface. It was quiet. He listened for the battle, but it seemed gone. Forcing his eyes open, the boy found himself staring at the spoke of a cannon's wheel. He focused beyond, looking under the gun carriage at the field of battle. The smoke was gone.

The day's light was fading. Soldiers quietly walked the carnage-littered, blood-soaked, killing ground. They wore blue. They were Federal troops. The boy watched as the soldiers searched to find the living. Litter- bearers were summoned by a soldier who knelt near a group of bodies. One was alive. Carefully it was eased onto the litter and carried off. The survivor wore Confederate grey. Yet they helped him anyway.

The boy realized he hurt all over; there was a stiffness in his muscles. He tried to move, to wiggle his fingers, and untangle himself from the spokes of the wheel and the pressure against his back. As he pulled his head from against the hardness of the wood spokes, there was a stickiness that pulled at his matted hair, and a throbbing pain. Sharp pain shot through his leg. He heard approaching footsteps.

"Hey, Dan!" a youthful voice called. "There's a live one over here!"

Duane felt the presence of someone behind him and was aware of another person approaching on the run. He felt the weight lifted from his back and the touch of gentle hands.

"Careful, Johnny," an older voice advised, "looks bad."

"He's just a kid!" Johnny exclaimed. Carefully he eased Duane's arms from the wheel and cradled the boy's head in his lap. "Easy, Boy. You'll be okay."

Duane moaned with the pain of movement, breathing rapidly to keep from crying out. Expert fingers inspected the bloody tangle of hair as the boy found himself in the care of a boy about three years his senior and a young lieutenant, both from the Union army. He forced a smile.

The older boy's blue eyes smiled back. Wispy blond hair stuck out from under a blue cap. "Name's Johnny," the boy introduced himself. "This here's Dan Marshalton. He's a lieutenant doctor. Just call him Dan."

The lieutenant's features were weathered from years of working out of doors. His face was lined from cheerfulness, but saddened with the worry of war. Dark hair was damp with sweat, yet shone with a reddish sheen. His uniform bore the dust of battle and the smell of sweat and gunpowder.

"I think you look worse than you really are," he commented, "I'd say your friend here saved your life."

Glancing to his side, Duane realized what had been so heavy, Private Eagleson's body lay beside him.

"What happened?" the boy asked. "How da ya mean?"

"My guess is he saw you go down," the lieutenant explained. "He came to help and was shot. Because he fell on top of you, several other bullets struck his body during the conflict. If he weren't there, they'd have hit you."

Duane struggled to get up, winced with pain and sudden faintness, and let himself ease back to the ground. "It hurts somethin fierce!"

"Like I said, you're lucky. But you ain't fit ta be up and about neither." The lieutenant took a look at the bloody leg. "What's your name, Boy?"

"Duane, Duane Kinkade. But most folks call me Dee fer short." Pushing himself up on his elbows, he watched the man's inspection of his wound.

"How bad's he look?" Johnny asked as he carefully lifted Duane back toward himself and supported him in a half sitting position.

Lieutenant Marshalton sat back on his heels and replied, "I don't find any broken bones. Bruises, a nasty bang on the head, and a flesh wound on your leg. You lost a bit of blood and will have to rest several days to heal and get your strength back. And you'll be hurtin some for a day or two." He stood and glanced about. "We'll brace you up against the wheel and Johnny'll stay here with you. You'll do fine. I'll be back when we've checked for any other wounded."

The two eased Duane into a more comfortable position.

"Johnny," Dan instructed, "find some water and rags and help Dee get cleaned up."

"Sure, Dan."

The doctor walked off to continue his work.

Duane gazed sadly at Eagleson. "Ya'll likely find whateve ya need in Brian's have'sack," he nodded toward the body.

"I'll look," Johnny acknowledged. Pulling the body to roll it over so that he could reach the pack, the older boy paused. Something wasn't right. A shattered wrist began to bleed. "He ain't dead, Dee! Least wise, I don't think so. Quick! your drum strap and a stick!"

Duane pulled the strap over his head and handed it to Johnny who wrapped it around Eagleson's arm. He then took the drumstick the younger boy offered, slipped it through the strap and twisted until the bleeding stopped. He tied it in place with the end of the strap. Duane watched, fascinated, as Johnny removed the haversack and straightened out the soldier's torn body. Leaning over him, he placed an ear to his chest and listened intently.

"Well?" the boy wondered expectantly.

"Just barely, but he's alive at the moment." Straightening up he continued, "But I really don't know if he'll make it." Pausing a moment, Johnny studied the situation. "Let's clean you up. Dan'll know what to do."

"No, I'll stay with Brian. Ya find the lieutenant." Duane started to move from the wheel which supported him and found himself too weak. "I cain't move," he groaned in frustration.

"Stay where you are," Johnny jumped to his feet. "I'll get help."

Duane watched the older boy dash off, then settled to watch the youth who had carried the company's flag. How ghostly white he looked – like death itself. There was no sign of movement. Dried blood caked the light brown shirt and the grey trousers. Beside the shattered hand, it was hard to see where he had been shot.

"God, don't let Brian die, too!" he whispered. Tears blurred his vision and he blinked them away. "Please," he begged quietly, "let him live."

*　　*　　*

As the sun dipped into the western horizon, a cold drizzle began to fall. Lieutenant Marshalton joined the two boys at the artillery piece. Private Eagleson had been removed to the improvised field hospital and, at last word, was gravely wounded, but still hanging on to life. Johnny had managed to clean up Duane's head wound and wrap a bandage around it. The lieutenant knelt beside the two boys.

"How you feeling, Dee?" the man asked.

"Better, I guess. But I got no strength." He rested his head against the wheel's rim. "I'm so tired, 'n this rain fallin is so cold."

"I'd expect that," Dan commented. "We best hurry and get you in before this storm really lets loose. Johnny can take your friend's things with him and I'll carry you in. Shouldn't be too bad – no broken bones to worry about." He took a last look at the leg wound. It was covered over by moist clotting, not yet dry. "But just to be safe, let's wrap this leg to keep out dirt. We'll clean it up in camp."

Blood-stained fabric had already stuck to the soft clotting around the wound. Johnny steadied the injured limb while the doctor wrapped a tight bandage to help prevent new bleeding.

The drizzle had quickened to a steady rain shower as Dan gently lifted Duane in his arms and Johnny gathered the things from the ground. They started on their way to the Federal encampment. A wind kicked up and the rain became mixed with a driving sleet as the three worked their way through the gathering darkness.

Once more, Duane found himself in Prentiss' camps near the Eastern Corinth Road. The Union army had recaptured all the ground it had occupied at the beginning of the battle on Sunday morning. The fighting had been broken off and the Federal Divisions were returning from their pursuit as the Confederate forces were in retreat toward Corinth. The camp was busy with the gathering of incoming troops and the fruitless efforts to seek comfort in the growing storm. Sleet and hail with stones as big as the boy's thumb were being driven by a merciless wind. The air was filled with the shout of orders, cries of pain, the rumble of wagons bringing in dead and wounded, the clatter of hail on wood or canvass, the panic of horses, the crunch of a white carpet underfoot.

Duane found himself settled in a field tent shared by Johnny and crates of supplies. A kerosene lamp lit the inside with its warm coziness as the storm pounded against the canvass overhead. Dan stayed long enough to lay out supplies and leave instructions so that the older boy could clean and dress the drummer boy's wounds and settle him in for the night. Then he left for the night-long work of tending wounded soldiers in the surgery tent on the edge of the camp.

The boys talked as Johnny worked, and told each other of their lives. Bandage material was gently removed from the leg wound and the trouser material was gingerly picked from the dried blood. Once loosened, the two boys carefully peeled off the torn grey trousers, stubborn in their dampness, leaving Duane in his long johns.

"Dan's pretty good with a needle 'n thread," Johnny informed. "We'll wash these out and he can mend them for you."

The bloody clothing was gathered in a soggy pile for cleaning. As the shirt was added, another cause for pain was discovered. A large bruised area spread its ugly color across the abdomen and lower ribs where the concussion from the exploding caisson had shattered the drum against his side. Johnny noticed the rough scarring of the old wound, yet, though curious, said nothing. It could wait for another time. Even so, he wondered, how could a kid so young have been hurt so much. Loosening the remaining fabric from the clotting, Johnny ripped away the leg portion of the long johns. He then cleaned the jagged gash in the younger boy's thigh, covered it with a fresh dressing, and wrapped it with a new bandage. New bleeding quickly soaked the dressing and was absorbed into the bandage spreading a bright red splotch on the clean white fabric. The older boy was shaken by the rapid blood flow.

"That sure is nasty," he observed nervously. "But it'll clean it out and help the healing." Johnny watched apprehensively until the expanding red slowed, then stopped. He exhaled a long sigh of relief.

Folding one blanket under his patient's head, he shook out another across him for warmth. Then he set to work rewrapping the head wound.

"How is it you come ta be with the lieutenant?" Duane asked.

"We're both from farm country near the Wabash up north in Illinois." He worked while he spoke. "Dan was old Doc Clancy's assistant. You see, Doc was plannin to retire. But the war came and the army needed a doctor. So Doc's still there and Dan's here." There was a pause while he bit his lip in concentration to carefully pick strands of dark hair from the caked blood around the wound. Satisfied with his work, he continued. "My folks died young. Pa knew he was going and he made Dan my legal family. They was good friends and he knew Dan could teach me doctoring and might even send me to school when I get older." He smiled at his next piece of information. "Never did tell you my family's name. It's Applebee. But don't be surprised when someone calls me Johnny Appleseed."

Duane laughed. "Ya really git called thet? Why'd enyone do thet?"

"Some old story about a guy who planted apple trees."

"Oh. Guess some'll call me Johnny, too – Johnny Reb."

"They probably will. Hold still while I clean this up better." Careful sponging with a damp cloth soaked the dried blood from the scalp around the wound. Duane winced at the pain. "Tell me. How is it a kid your age is in the middle of the battlefield?"

"It's kinda a long story."

"We got time. I'll rewrap this and listen while you're telling me."

So while the wound was rebandaged, Duane started to tell his story from the day he learned his father was going to war until he fell on the battlefield. But he never got beyond his decision to search for his father. Exhaustion and the steady clatter of sleet and hail on canvass took over and he fell asleep. Johnny finished the knot on the bandage, tucked the blanket in along the edge of the cot, and stood back to study his work and his patient. Lifting his cap, he pushed his hair back and reset it the same as it was. He rubbed his tired eyes with the backs of his hands and flopped down onto his own cot. A grumbling in his stomach reminded him how hungry he was. But the effort seemed too great. He lay back to rest a moment and soon fell fast asleep.

The storm finally blew itself out over three hours after it had begun. Some time in the early hours after midnight, Dan stepped in to check on his patient. Removing Johnny's shoes and setting them beside the cot, he pulled the blanket from under his feet, shook it open, and covered the sleeping figure. Then he removed the blue cap and placed it on a supply crate beside the grey cap, blew out the lamp and left to resume his night's work in the surgery tent.

The dim glow of starlight and a broken moon filtered through the white canvass. Quiet had settled over the camp. Crickets and tree toads filled the air with song. A cool breeze drifted in the April night. There was the scent of spring, a freshness, a peace.

*   *   *

The boy's consciousness exploded into pain pounding within his head, intruding on quiet dreams of a boy and his dog splashing in the shallows of a meadow's stream. A vision of his mother lying dead with the shotgun in her hands flashed within his mind.

"Nooo!" Duane screamed, waking himself with the sudden sound of his own voice.

The boy felt lost in the quiet black of the night. He stumbled through his mind in search of where he was and why he hurt. A faint movement nearby was followed by the touch of gentle hands and a sleepy voice that was familiar.

"Dee, it's okay," Johnny whispered. "I'm here. You're safe."

Then he remembered. "Johnny?" he asked.

"Yeh."

"It hurts sumthin fierce 'n I musta been dreamin."

The older boy knelt on the ground beside the cot and adjusted the blanket to be sure his friend was warm. "It's gonna hurt for several days til it starts ta heal up good."

"Yeh, it comes back ta ma mind. Fer jest a bit I fergot." Duane stirred as he raised his hand to touch the bandages on his head and traced them with his fingertips.

"Hungry?" Johnny asked as he sat back on his heels, resting an elbow on the edge of the cot.

"Yeh."

"Me, too. I think I got some hardtack left in my haversack." He crawled back and fumbled blindly under his cot. "Found it," Johnny announced as he returned and pressed some stale biscuit into Duane's palm.

The two chewed quietly for several minutes allowing the food to settle the grumblings in their stomachs. Darkness thinned to faint light as the first hint of dawn brushed the canvass of the tent roof. The army began to stir as the camp awoke. Whispered conversation, the snap of firewood, the crackle of flames renewed in nearby fires invaded the air. Footfalls approached from outside and the canvass was pushed aside as Lieutenant Marshalton entered.

"I see you boys are up already," the man greeted.

"Mornin, Sir," Duane added.

"Morning, Boys," the lieutenant acknowledged. "How's the patient?" He bent over the cot and gently checked the bandages feeling for tightness, moisture, dried seepage or clotting.

"Ow!" Duane cringed.

"I know it hurts," Dan consoled. "But it seems to be mending." He straightened up. "Figure you're both hungry. Dee, you try and rest some. Johnny an me will see to fixing something hot."

"Can't I come with ya?" Duane asked, pushing up onto his elbows.

"You're staying down for the next few days til you get your strength back."

"But what about the army movin?"

Johnny rose as the lieutenant turned to leave and crossed to his cot in search of his shoes. "This army ain't moving," he stated.

"He's right," the officer confirmed. "We've thousands of casualties to tend and word has it we've to wait on General Halleck for any real decisions are made. For now, I've more wounded to tend. But Johnny, here, is gonna find you some Yank clothes so's to keep you out of trouble."

"But he said ya kin fix my clothes," Duane objected.

"Sure. We'll get your things repaired an washed. But we'll pack them away until we get a chance to send you back to your people. Don't want to have to explain you or risk loosing you to a prison camp or such."

"Thanks," Duane offered.

Johnny finished tying the shoes, reached for his cap, then rose to join the doctor. "I'll see you shortly with something to eat."

"Yeh. I'm not goin nowhere."

The two left. Duane settled back and closed his eyes. Dawn had driven off the shadows, bringing with it the clamor of activity and the smells of fires and fresh-brewed coffee.

Tuesday drifted into Wednesday as the army maintained a settled routine. Word came back that the Confederate Army had withdrawn to Corinth, pursuit had been called off, and elements of the Union Army were returning to the camps around Pittsburg Landing. By the end of the week Duane was able to get out of bed and wander about the immediate area outside the storage tent. Activity increased during his first day out and as he lounged on some ammunition cases he noticed the soldiers in the nearby tents cleaning up their private belongings and straightening the appearance of their gear. The news was out. General Halleck had arrived to direct the operation to take the Confederate Army at Corinth.

Throughout the rest of the month Duane healed and grew strong. So did the Union Army as more and more troops were gathered and Halleck built up his strength to an army of a hundred thousand.

*   *   *

The sun stood high in a clear blue western sky causing blinding sparklings of light to flash on the water's lazy ripplings along the shallows of the river. Duane sat near the top of the low embankment, nestled comfortably in the wild thicket, and gazed out on the expanse of the Tennessee River. He had just settled down from wading in the back- eddies in search of crawfish or turtles or whatever might be of interest. His boots lay where he had tossed them, covered in part by his discarded shirt; and his rolled pants legs were soaked through. The water's coolness had felt refreshing in the afternoon warmth. But soon it would be time to turn back toward the camp.

At the moment, a river ferryboat rested near the landing to the north and the open water was empty and calm. It was good to get away from the mass of humanity packed into the army camps scattered about the countryside. The arrival of Pope's army toward the end of April had brought the overall strength in excess of a hundred thousand. The air about the camp stank of unwashed bodies and a thousand latrines.

Duane reached for his shirt and boots. After drawing them on, he stood, climbed through the thicket to the dirt lane, then followed out along the Purdy Road, cut past Bloody Pond, and wandered toward the peach orchard, gathering scraps of firewood as he headed back to camp. So many times he had walked the field of battle in the days since his bandages had been removed. His body had healed, but his mind would always carry the memories of battle and death and agony, and always that moment when the one friend he had was killed in a blinding flash, when this quiet countryside ran red with blood.

Duane paused near the hill where Prentiss' troops had fired upon Breckinridge's battle line, and gathered two tree branches which would provide good fuel for the cook fire. Something caught his eye – something metallic nearly buried in leaves and underbrush. Laying aside the firewood, he crawled into the thicket, pawed aside the leaves, grabbed the heavy object, and backed out into the sunlight to examine his find. It was an officer's revolver, lost during some point of battle.

Sitting back on his heals, he brushed off grass and dirt to examine the weapon. It had rusted quite a bit over the past three weeks, yet seemed generally to be in good condition. Two chambers had not been fired. The load was still in each and the caps remained on their nipples. For a brief moment Duane felt excited about his find and a temptation to see if it would fire. But caution ruled. Standing up, he jammed the pistol into the waist of his trousers, stuffed his shirt-tail in around the gun, and buttoned the lower buttons to keep it from falling out. Then he gathered up the branches of firewood and started for camp at a quick walk.

*   *   *

The flames danced merrily on the crackling cook fire as they licked the edges of the metal plates, balanced precariously on their rocks within the fire. Slabs of beef sizzled on the hot metal while the lieutenant and the two boys supervised their progress with judicious proddings of fork or stick. They resumed their conversation as they relaxed in the grass about their fire.

"You know, Dee, that gun you found is in real good shape. It does need cleaning up an greasing down. But that ain't too hard to do." Dan steadied his plate with a stick while he jabbed the meat with his fork and turned it over. It erupted into explosive splatterings before quieting to a pronounced sizzle.

"Dan," Johnny asked, "did you tell Dee about that captain fellow you went to find out about?"

"Not yet."

"What captain?" Duane questioned.

"The lieutenant, here, found out about an infantry captain who came in with General Halleck, but was with Curtis in Missouri." Johnny poked at his meat while he spoke.

"What about him?" Duane was puzzled.

Dan explained his reasoning. "It seemed that maybe he might be able to know who to ask about your pa. He's been on quartermaster duty and they sometimes get around more. Maybe your pa's been in Missouri all along. Could have been moved after he sent you that last letter."

"Guess he's worth a try," Duane agreed. "Maybe he could help me check out the gun I found."

"Maybe so," the man agreed. "I'll help you clean it up after supper. We'll go see him first chance we get. I need some medical supplies while we're at it."

"Think the taters are done?" Johnny changed the subject.

"Should be," Dan affirmed. "Meat's brown."

"I'll roll em out," Duane offered.

The boy took his stick which was forked at the end, and carefully nudged an oblong lump of baked clay from the coals. As it came to rest outside the circle of stones, he worked two more out of the coals. The three plates were carefully hooked with the tines of the forks and drawn from the fire to cool while the lumps of clay were broken open and steaming hot potatoes were taken from within.

Supper was ready.

* * *

Several days had passed and April had just slipped into May when the three finally found the time to journey toward Halleck's camp and look up the quartermaster captain. As they wandered through the various camps it was obvious the general routine was relaxed. Some of the thousand soldiers whose tents and company streets they passed were gathered in small groups to gossip, play at cards, make music, or slosh dirty laundry in a tub of soapy water. Others lounged about reading, writing a letter home, or dozing against tree or tent pole.

Wandering down yet another line of shelter halves, the trio approached a lone private, seated on his blanket roll absorbed in picking a tune on his guitar as he leaned against the tree branch that was the front pole of his small tent.

"Hey!" Johnny greeted. "How you doing?"

The young soldier, not much more than a boy himself, looked up at the sound of the voice. "What kin I do ya?"

"Looking for the quartermaster," the boy stated.

"Try up yonder where the flags is. There's some cannon limbers settin by." He rested his instrument on his lap, but made no move to stand.

"I see it," Marshalton acknowledged.

"Thanks," Duane added.

"Sure," the youth responded. Then he bent his ear to his instrument, ignoring the three before him as he continued to work out his melody.

The man and the boys moved on.

The quartermaster area drew their attention from all about them as it enfolded the three in its noise and activity. It was as a general store with a dozen clerks scurrying about to satisfy the requests of scores of customers. Dan caught the eye of a hassled sergeant and slipped close enough to ask his question.

"We're looking for Captain Sheridan. Can you tell us where to find him?" His voice was almost lost in the mix of conversation.

"Try the tent over yonder," the veteran soldier pointed.

"Much obliged," Dan stated as he gathered Duane and Johnny and directed them to follow.

"I neve seen so much goods 'n all!" the younger boy exclaimed. "Could we have a look?" His eyes pleaded his request and won assent.

"Let's see the captain first. Then we'll see what's here."

"Okay."

The captain's tent stood away from the activity of the large canopied expanse of equipment hanging from poles and lines and rails or spread on boards spanning wooden horses. The clustered tents were all larger than those in the many orderly rows of small conical tepees and button together shelter halves. These tents stood seven feet at the ridge with three-foot side walls and a breadth of eight feet from eaves to eaves. The front flaps were tied open on one revealing within an assortment of baggage and furnishings. It looked very similar to the inside of Lieutenant Marshalton's tent. Seated on a folding camp chair before a field desk mounted on wooden horses, was an officer of average stature, studiously reviewing a board full of papers. The captain looked up at the sound of approaching footsteps.

"Captain Sheridan?" the lieutenant inquired.

"That's right," the other responded as he stood and laid aside his work.

"My name's Dan Marshalton, surgeon with the Illinois 61st. Could we have a minute of your time?"

The two exchanged handshakes, then the older man took his hat and coat from the back of his chair. Placing hat on head, cocked slightly to the left, he slipped into the uniform coat and joined the three in front of his tent.

"It's a might warm and stuffy or I'd ask you in. But I think it might be a greater comfort if we met near that oak tree in the supply yard." He offered an area behind the tents where stacks of crates and barrels were arranged in orderly fashion, some protected by canvass covers. "Make yourselves at ease and tell me why you're here."

The captain picked a barrel where he could rest against a tree while the others settled among crevices or atop summits in the scattered containers of equipment and supplies.

"The boys here are Johnny and Dee," the lieutenant began. "Dee's the reason we've come."

He went on to explain Duane's search and how he hoped Captain Sheridan could be of help. After a quarter hour of reviewing the situation and all their known options, it became evident that Sheridan had had no opportunity to be aware of individuals from the Confederate Army or the activities of specific units from Arkansas.

"I can see why you'd hoped I could be of help," Sheridan stated. "I'm really sorry it doesn't work out that way." He stood, signaling the end of his time. "I will keep alert to any possibility of hearing information helpful to the boy. General Halleck is ready to begin his advance on Corinth, so maybe something will turn up. Be sure to leave your name and unit with my sergeant. If anything happens, I'll get in touch."

"Thanks," Dee said, saluting the captain.

"You're welcome, Son." He returned the salute. "Take care, Lieutenant."

The two shook hands. The captain walked off toward his tent as the boys stood to leave with the lieutenant.

"Come on," Dan invited. "Let's see what the quartermaster has of interest."

They worked their way through the crowd and managed access to the boards of equipment from one end of the canopied area. Working their way down the line they inspected or fingered for workmanship or texture, any number of items spread by the dozen across the rough planks. There were items of clothing, packs and haversacks, leather goods, camp kit, tools, and more. It appeared to be an open market, but in reality was not. Few of those present were taking much with them for personal use. Some individuals presented authorization papers to pick up specific items. Others presented requisitions for quantities of items which they would then load into a waiting wagon and take back to their company commander.

Lieutenant Marshalton watched for an opportunity. "Sergeant," he called when he saw the man had a moment. The sergeant was an older man, somewhere in his late forties. His uniform was neatly kept and neatly worn. In stark contrast to his captain, his hair was worn long though neatly trimmed just above the collar.

"Yes, sir, Lieutenant. What kin I do ya fer?" he approached.

"First, I'm to leave information with you so the captain can find me later. Next I have need for two requisitions to be supplied." He offered a set of papers to the sergeant.

Duane and Johnny followed along as the trooper picked the stock requested and the officer inspected it for quality. The soldier was good. The lieutenant found every choice to his satisfaction. Medical implements were first. A larger carrying case and greater quantity of implements were needed. While he had brought his own with him, this first major battle had seen loss and damage in the confusion and haste of field hospital operations. Replacements were needed. These he passed to Johnny to carry.

The second order was normal for a commissioned officer, but seemed strange to Duane because of its coincidence. It included a belt with cap box and holster for a revolver, a cartridge pouch, and two cylinders. All this was handed to the younger boy to carry.

"That it?" the sergeant asked.

"For now," Dan confirmed.

The paperwork was signed. The three turned to go.

"What's this stuff fer?" Duane asked as they left the quartermaster behind and started the return trek through the camps.

"A drummer boy doesn't carry a musket, Dee," the man explained. "But he can carry a side arm for protection in battle. As long as you have that revolver you might as well have all that goes with it."

"How did you get the requisition?" Johnny asked.

"Told the captain I needed it," Dan answered. "I already have what I need, but spare parts is a normal request. You have the revolver. The rest as I said, is a normal request."

They left the camp and continued along the deeply rutted road, passing wood lots, fields, and more camps as they returned to their own company's camp off the Eastern Corinth Road.

*   *   *

The following morning found the camp under orders to prepare to move on Corinth. An ever-cautious General Halleck was satisfied with the preparations of the previous three weeks and confident of victory with minimum loss of life. Most of the day was occupied with packing of equipment and supplies. Soldiers were involved in a variety of work parties assigned to everything from closing latrines to closing Division Headquarters. Duane and Johnny went with the doctor to help pack up the hospital at Sherman's 2nd Brigade encampment. All the wounded had been removed to their own camps or, if too serious to stay on, sent home. Confederate wounded had been exchanged. Private Eagleson had survived that far. Nothing further was ever found out.

Within the hospital tents, cots were folded down and bundled, blankets were folded and crated, implements were packed into the surgeon's personal lockers or boxed, supplies and utensils were crated, and stretchers were strapped into bundles. All was loaded into covered hospital wagons. Finally the tents were struck and loaded. Throughout the day, the road was busy with traffic as many companies of infantry began the move toward Corinth. By evening several batteries of artillery and companies of cavalry had also passed along the Hamburg Road. The dust of their passing hung on the air throughout the afternoon and settled onto everything as evening approached and a quiet settled over the countryside.

An exhausted Duane and friends wandered back along the tree-shaded road and across the low hills to their tents in what remained of the company camp. Much of the brigade had moved out. Patches of dead grass, circles of blackened rock filled with cold ash and charred wood, all in neat rows, marked the places where company streets had been.

That evening as the few remaining fires crackled about the smaller encampment and small knots of soldiers talked, played music or sang softly, or sat in silent reflections; many occupied their hands with preparation for battle. Johnny was busy with awl and heavy waxed thread repairing a seam in his pack. Dan was showing Duane how his new gear was assembled and worn. He had fitted the belt to the boy's waist, punching new holes so the buckle would close at the correct size. The shoulder strap had been pulled from the cartridge pouch and it, too, had been added to the belt. He knelt beside the youngster who stood in front and made final adjustments.

"How's it feel?" he asked as he sat back on his heels to survey the results of their effort.

"It feels good." Duane ran his hands around the belt, feeling the holster and cap box in their places at his left and the cartridge pack which hung on the right. "It sher seems stiff 'n hard."

"That's the newness," Dan explained. "It takes a time to soften and loosen up."

"Boy, you sure look smart with all that," Johnny observed, a touch of envy in his voice.

"You know, Johnny, I never thought till now, but you, too, should have something to defend yourself." He stood and walked to his tent.

"I'm sorry," Duane said as he turned toward his friend. "I neve' thought thet ya didn't have a gun thet's yer'n."

"Yeh," Johnny sighed. "I really shouldn't need it. But I guess I'm kinda jealous-feeling, you bein in battle and all. Maybe we find a drum some day and you can teach me how to play." He rested his work in his lap and gazed into the flames.

Duane settled beside him, sitting back on his heels and resting his hands on his legs. "Ya know, I neve really had much time ta lern maself. I'll lern ya what I know."

Dan returned to the fire and knelt on the ground beside Johnny. The boy's eyes lit up with surprise and excitement as he saw what the man carried.

"Found this right after the battle," he explained. "I've been waiting to see if anything was being said about scavenging. Since we're about to move on, I guess it won't matter. It's yours, Johnny."

He presented the boy with a full issue of musket with equipment including bayonet, belt, cap box, cartridge pouch, and canteen. It had already been thoroughly cleaned, but Johnny couldn't help rubbing the brass fittings with the sleeve of his shirt. He placed the equipment on the ground beside him and the musket across his lap.

"It's beautiful," the boy whispered. "How'd you get it?"

"Picked up the pieces about the orchard when we were bringing in the wounded. There was so much stuff laying about, you could outfit a whole company." He watched affectionately while the two boys fingered their treasures. A sad thought crossed his mind. Here were these two boys whom he loved as sons, and their greatest excitement was not for toys, but for tools of death, weapons of war.

"Thanks," Johnny said.

"Yeh, thanks," Duane added.

Dan pushed his ponderings from his mind as he suggested, "Since we're gonna be moving out, it might help to learn how to load these."

Leaning back on the ground, he stretched his arm toward the tent until his fingertips came in contact with the wooden handle on the closest case of ammunition. Slipping them behind the grip, he pulled the wooden box to his side.

During the next hour, the lieutenant showed each of the boys how to load and use his weapon. The case originally contained a thousand cartridges for rifled musket. Part of its contents had been replaced with 44-caliber cartridges for revolver. The powder was already measured out and the 58-caliber miniball or 44-caliber lead ball was packed with the measure – all wrapped tightly in a paper cartridge. These cartridges were carried in the cartridge pouch. The percussion caps were packed separately in tins. These, in turn, were carried in the cap box. To load, the contents of the cartridge were rammed down the musket barrel and a single cap was placed on a nipple under the musket's hammer. To fire, the hammer was pulled back. When the trigger was pulled, the hammer struck the cap which detonated into the barrel and fired the load.

Duane's revolver was similar. The cylinder had six chambers. Each was loaded separately, using the ram built into the revolver to tamp in the lead ball. It fit tightly and kept the charge from falling out. Once loaded, the caps were placed on the nipples, one for each chamber, and the weapon was ready to fire. After the cylinder in the gun was fully loaded and ready to fire, Dan showed Duane how to remove it; then replaced it with one of the spares they had picked up. Once all three were loaded, the man lit a beeswax candle and showed the boy how to drip the wax into the chambers and over the caps to seal the loads from moisture. Duane did as he was shown until all three cylinders had been prepared. Once finished, they were rubbed with a thin coating of axle grease to prevent rust; then two were wrapped in waxed paper and packed into the cartridge pouch with spare cartridges. The third was returned to the revolver. The cap was removed from one chamber which was then sealed with a drop of wax. This was rotated to a position under the hammer. A protective coating was applied to the weapon itself which was then placed in its holster.

The three had worked with very little comment. The only words spoken were matters of instruction and explanation.

"I sure hadn't planned to be teaching you this tonight," Dan broke the silence. "But now it's done and I hope you both learned real good. Chances are when you most need to know all this there won't be anyone free to teach you."

"It's pretty much like back home," Johnny stated. "Just a different gun."

"Yer right," Duane added. "It's a lot like my pa's shotgun. Sher, ther's differnces. But I kin do it."

"Then it's time we clean up here, and turn in." Dan stood and stretched cramped joints. "Put your gear by your beds. We pack first thing come morning. After breakfast we break camp and start south."

The boys gathered their new gear and carried it reverently toward their tent.

"Night, Dan," they chorused.

"Night, Boys," he responded.

When they had disappeared within the tent and a soft glow on the canvass signaled the lamp had been lit, the lieutenant squatted by the embers of the fire. He took his tin cup from its place beside the forked stick that helped support the coffee pot, and poured himself a lukewarm cup of coffee. Standing by the cartridge case, Dan sipped the warm contents of the cup as he watched the silhouettes on the tent canvass of the boys getting ready for bed. He allowed the sad thoughts from earlier in the evening to slip back into his consciousness and hoped the day would hurry when boys could play with toys instead of guns. The shadowy figures settled into their beds and the light went out.

Twilight faded to blackness as the embers on the ground crackled and glowed and a vast sparkling canopy glittered overhead. The air was brushed with the murmuring voices of others gathered about their fires and a distant chorus of bullfrogs in the backwaters of river and creek. The man drained his cup, placed it on a rock near the fire, then turned and walked to his tent.

*   *   *

For the next two weeks the Union Army advanced on Corinth. At each stop along the way, fortifications were thrown up in the form of breastworks and trenches. Finally, near mid-month, the army had arrived within four miles of the city. It stretched over five miles from the Mobile and Ohio Railroad on the northwest to beyond Farmington on the southeast. Breastworks were built. Trenches were dug.

Siege guns were mounted. Still another week passed without movement against the Confederates, except for a gradual closing of the distance between the lines.

Early in the week the routine was broken by a strange and almost humorous contest. Somewhere in a nearby camp, a Union band was breaking the monotony with an impromptu late afternoon concert. After the third number, the audience of bored soldiers, enjoying the musical reprieve, was surprised to hear a distant echoing of a Southern piece by a distant band of musicians, somewhere in the Confederate camps. So, for the next hour, the two bands took turns tooting their tunes to the rousing cheers of their own troops and some whistles and catcalls of the opposing troops. BONNIE BLUE FLAG traded with THE BATTLE CRY OF FREEDOM, LORENA with AURA LEA, and so forth into the evening. Finally there was an expectant pause and a hush fell over the camps. The rival bands joined in one final number – HOME SWEET HOME. The music echoed over silent camps as soldiers sat quietly and tears slipped unchecked, tracking on dust and sootcrusted cheek.

A few days later, with yet no sign of movement, Duane suggested that he could walk back to the Confederate camp and try to locate his old company. The lines in some places were less than a thousand yards apart, and so far, there had been no hostilities. Dan was uneasy with the idea. He had grown quite fond of the boy and really didn't want to see him leave. It had also been learned that there was a great deal of sickness in the Confederate camps. The risk seemed too great. Instead, the lieutenant would see if inquiries could be made as to the whereabouts of Sergeant Kinkade or the 13th Arkansas or of Captain Masters and his company. That afternoon Lieutenant Marshalton journeyed to a nearby stream to fill his canteen and called across to a Southern soldier on the opposite bank. The two conversed briefly and the Southerner agreed to ask about. He would meet the lieutenant at the same time and place the following day. Duane was excited when he heard of the incident and couldn't wait for the next day's report.

For three days, the afternoon meetings took place over the filling of canteens. It was learned that the Southern soldier was a corporal Jonathan Winthrop of a company from Missouri. He had been with Pierce in Missouri and had recently arrived in Corinth. In spite of several sources whom he felt very able and knowledgeable, Corporal Winthrop had learned nothing yet. But he was willing to keep trying. When the weekend passed and Monday afternoon rolled around, Jonathan didn't show up at the creek. The Confederate Army had begun to move. The contact was lost.

*   *   *

As the days slipped along, the Union Army made final preparations to attack. Two days following the last contact by the creek it was learned that the Confederate troops had been issued rations and moved forward into line for battle. Duane and his friends were in camp near the railroad to the northwest end of the Union line. Over a dozen companies were assembled in formation in the surrounding regimental camps. Rations and ammunition were being issued and equipment was being inspected. Some companies were reviewing drill procedures. In the headquarters area officers were meeting to review battle orders and surgeons were supervising preparations for equipping field hospitals. Duane and Johnny were with a work party unloading supplies from a medical wagon when a rider approached leading an extra mount.

By his uniform and insignia, he was a captain from a company of Michigan cavalry. He sat easy in the saddle. As he neared, it was evident he was of slender build, dark hair and dark complexion, clean-shaven except for a small, neatly trimmed mustache, and probably in his early thirties. The work party paused as he approached and reined his mount to a sliding halt. The second horse stopped beside the first.

"Afternoon, Captain," the two boys saluted as they paused in their work.

"Afternoon, Boys," he returned as he dismounted and tossed the reins of his horses to Duane who was nearest. "Can you direct me to Lieutenant Dan Marshalton?"

"Yes, Sir," Johnny answered. "Come with me."

The older boy took the captain to find the doctor while Duane found a tree and tied the horses. The rest of the group resumed their work.

"Wonder what he wants," one of the soldiers mused.

"Guess we'll know when Johnny gits back," Duane remarked as he pitched in once again to help with a case of supplies.

Several minutes passed. The wagon was emptied and the group of young soldiers dropped wherever they found comfort to rest and await the next chore. One had a canteen. He slipped it from his shoulder, took a swig of its sun-warmed contents, then passed it around to his friends.

Johnny wandered back and spoke to a young corporal. "Cyrus, the lieutenant says you can send the men back to their companies."

The soldiers were dismissed and wandered off toward their company camps. Several of the assembled groups drilling in the nearby fields, had returned to their tents. A few continued with their practice while the boys leaned on a wagon wheel to watch.

"What's the captain want?" Duane asked his friend.

"You," Johnny replied.

"What?!" the boy exclaimed as surprise distorted his face.

"Yeh, something about taking you behind the lines." Johnny turned to face his friend, leaning his weight against the iron rim of the wagon's wheel.

"Are ya sher?!" Joy lit the younger boy's face. "They found my pa! Oh, Johnny, they found my pa!" He hugged his friend in ecstatic excitement, as the older boy stumbled backwards to keep his balance.

A surprised Johnny held his young friend close to keep him from seeing the sadness he was sure showed on his own face. He was reluctant to say any more, but knew he must.

"Dee," he spoke softly. His hands sensed the tense reaction to his tone of voice. "Dee, you ain't let me finish."

"Ya mean it ain't so?" He stepped back, jamming his hands into his pockets. Tears welled up in his eyes, filling them to the edge of overflowing. He blinked and the moisture escaped through the dirt crusted on his cheeks.

Johnny put his hands on his friend's shoulders to comfort him. "You jumped on my words before I got to finish. The captain come to talk to Dan and see if you wanted to ride with the cavalry in case they found anyone who could help you. They's just talking. It ain't all worked out cause of you being a Reb and all."

"Oh," Duane looked away to watch the last of the company drill groups wandering off toward their camps.

"Come on, Dee," he released his friend. "Let's head in and see what they've decided."

"Okay. Don't fergit the horses."

The two boys, each with a horse in tow, wandered through the commotion of several company streets as they returned to their tent near regimental headquarters. All about them soldiers were busy building up their cook fires and digging out food and eating utensils. The smell of smoke was tainted by the smell of sweat in the hot afternoon air. There were several knots of activity or conversation in the headquarters complex. The two officers stood by the fire, each with a tin cup of coffee in hand, the captain listening to the lieutenant's reaction to his last comment. They looked up as the boys approached.

"Hi Johnny, Dee," the lieutenant greeted as the two approached. "This is Captain William Dawson of the 2nd Michigan Cavalry."

"Nice ta meet you boys." Dawson seemed curt, his voice cold and frank. He sipped from the cup as the lieutenant spoke.

"Dee, this Sunday past Captain Sheridan was made Colonel of the 2nd Michigan. They're moving come morning and will be operating behind enemy lines." Duane stood watching reactions from both men while Johnny took the horses to a nearby hitching post, as Dan continued to explain. "He figures your interest is in finding your pa and not in taking sides in this war. He's willing to take you on as a courier rider. You ride with Captain Dawson. You find your pa and you're free to do as you both decide. If not, you come back here when the operation's done."

"It don't figure ta be more than a scoutin look-see and maybe a raid on supply lines if the chance allows – not much chance of serious danger," the captain spoke up. "I wouldn't consent ta this otherwise."

Duane was stunned by the suddenness of the opportunity and wasn't sure he wanted to go. He had become very comfortable in the safety of the routine of the past two months. The war seemed so far away. Now his life was again on the threshold of tumult.

"What's wrong, Dee? You don't seem interested." Dan was concerned.

"No," Duane waved off the question with a slight gesture of his hands. "It's thet it's so sudden-like." He looked away and chewed on his lower lip as his mind flooded with confusion and he searched frantically for a response. "I gotta think," he stalled. "Yeh. Okay. What da I do?" Duane turned to face the captain.

"Ya can ride?" Dawson asked.

"Sher," Duane responded.

"Figured as much for a farm boy. Just bein sure." The captain bent to hang his cup on the fire rack which held the coffee pot. "I brought a mount for ya. Git yer gear, personals, and camp kit. We're ta leave immediately."

"It's all gathered on your cot," Dan stated. "Thought you might be going."

"Come on," Johnny called. "Let's get your stuff."

"Okay," came the dulled reply as Duane followed his friend to his tent. It was all so sudden. This was happening too fast.

In the tent, Duane fastened on his gun belt and slipped his canteen over a shoulder as Johnny passed each item in turn. It felt strange to be wearing all this gear.

"You look real fine, Dee." Johnny stood back to admire his friend. "I'm gonna miss you terrible if you don't come back." His eyes were moist as his emotion caught in his throat.

"I'm not real sher 'bout goin off like this. I do so wanta find my pa. But bein here with ya an Dan has come ta be so nat'ral like, it don't seem right ta go." He paused, wanting so much to hug Johnny, yet not. "But I gotta." His half smile seemed so sad and distant.

Suddenly the two boys reached for each other and embraced as brothers about to part for a long journey. Each held tightly, not wanting the parting to take place.

"Ya've been like a brother, Johnny."

"You, too, Dee."

They stood a moment longer before releasing their hold on each other.

"The captain's waiting," Johnny observed.

"Yeh, guess it's time."

Duane slung his haversack across his shoulder and picked up his pack and bedroll. After one last glance about the tent to be sure he had everything, the two left to join the others by the fire.

"You take care, Dee," Dan stated as he offered his hand.

But his eyes gave him away and the boy reached out with open arms.

Quickly the man scooped him off his feet as they gripped each other tightly.

"I love you like a son, Dee. So you take good care of yourself and know you've always friends here."

"Ya've been like my pa's brother, Dan. Only he ain't neve had one. An I love ya fer it."

"You take good care of my boy here, Captain," Dan called as he put Duane back on his feet.

"You can count on it, Lieutenant," the captain called back, already mounted and eager to depart.

Duane tied his blanket roll to the saddle, slung his pack onto his back, and mounted his brown mare.

"What's her name?" he asked.

"Don't know," Dawson answered. "Call her what ya like."

"Take care of yourself, Dee," Johnny waved.

"Thanks," Duane waved back. "Ya an Dan do likewise."

"Let's ride," Captain Dawson ordered as he swung his horse into a fast walk.

After one last wave, the boy guided his mount with expert hands, turning to follow the captain. The pair quickly left the camps behind as they cut cross country toward the railroad tracks.

"Where we off ta?" Duane asked as they neared the rail line.

"We'll join up with Colonel Elliot who's takin the brigade of cavalry south to interrupt the Confederate supply lines into Corinth."

They followed the tracks south for a mile before the captain signaled a halt.

"Listen carefully an tell me what ya hear."

The two riders sat motionless, the horses snorting their eagerness to move on. Duane strained to listen as he had been instructed. He sensed the distant presence of the camps in the soft rise and fall of a deep moaning as ten thousand conversations surged on the evening air. Then there was that other, distant sound. He remembered it from Vicksburg. It was the shrill cry of train whistles and the cheers of newly arrived soldiers eager for battle. It came as a faint whisper in the afternoon air.

"Yeh," Duane acknowledged. "I think I hear it – train whistles and cheerin troops."

"Ya got good ears, Boy." He slipped down from his horse and motioned for Duane to do the same. "Try this."

The captain knelt beside the track and put his ear to the rail.

"Ya do likewise, and listen fer a while," the man instructed.

For several minutes, the two listened and felt the distant vibrations in the iron rails. It took a while before Duane was able to sense anything in the metal, hot from the late afternoon sun. Gradually he was able to distinguish variances in sound and vibration. Finally the captain sat up and the boy did the same.

"Well?" the man asked sharply.

"Can't tell nothin," the boy responded.

"Ya'll lern." Captain Dawson rose to his feet. "Let's go."

Gathering up his grey's reins, he mounted. Duane, too, mounted and prepared to follow. They turned east and started to ride.

"All I can figure," the man explained as they began to pass more Union camps, "is that there's not a lot of activity. But there is some movin of trains."

The two riders were passing through a great series of regimental camps. Moving at an easy trot, Duane found the flop of his pack as it slapped against his back in rhythm with his horse, a painful annoyance. He tried to pull at the straps to make it tighter.

"Hold up," the captain raised his hand as he spoke.

The stop was a relief for the boy. The man eased his mount close to the boy's.

"Let me have that pack." He reached for a shoulder strap and slid it from Duane's back. Holding it in his lap, he continued. "See them saddle bags?"

Twisting in his saddle, the boy looked where he knew they should be. "Yeh?" he acknowledged.

"Let's stow your gear there."

The pack's contents were transferred accordingly and the pack tied in with the blanket roll. They were ready to move on.

"Before we go on, look to these camps," Dawson indicated with a sweep of his arm. Then he pointed to a spot in one cluster of company streets. "That flag yonder is headquarters for General Pope. Now, ya bein a country boy, yer most likely good at learnin your way by landmarks." He kicked the grey lightly and started on. The boy followed. "Ya lern yer way about. If yer ta be a courier, ya need ta be able ta deliver dispatches quick an safe."

"Yes, Sir," Duane responded.

The longer they traveled together, the more talkative the captain became. He was full of helpful tips and suggestions and constantly pointed out landmark references. The boy decided he was really friendlier and more caring than he first appeared to be.

Their journey took them east and south, past Farmington, and beyond the Federal lines. By evening they had joined up with Sheridan's regiment in Colonel Elliot's brigade encampment. It was really a great scattering of small cookfires about which the men of the various companies spread their bedrolls for the night. The following morning allowed time for a cup of coffee and hardtack, and a quick packing of bedrolls, pots, and cups, before saddling up and moving on as the sun began to clear the eastern horizon.

For two days the brigade moved south, foraging off the land and striking at supply sources or engaging in small skirmishes when the opportunity offered. Riding with Captain Dawson and traveling with the regimental command group, Duane saw little more than a few raids on small farms. They ate well in the evening, cooking the bounty of the day, then moved out quickly as morning dawned.

The third night out found the brigade far to the south of Corinth in the countryside near a town called Cross Ridge. Foraging had been good. Appetites had been satisfied. The thousand cavalrymen were gathered about their fires in low conversation, busy cleaning equipment used in the day's work or dreaming of home or the morrow's glory.

The small solitary figure strolled amidst the fires, hands in pockets, pausing to look out across camp or gaze at the stars above. The nightfall was strangely quiet. The crickets and tree toads chattered busily. Horses munched on grass or snorted sleepily where they stood along company tether rope lines. Nearby woodlands stood silhouetted in the dark. Walls and fence rows wandered across the landscape, mixed among the company groups of the encampment. Duane started back toward the fire near which his bedroll lay.

"Hey, Boy. Light a spell," a deep voice intruded on his thoughts.

"Me?" He stopped and found himself near a fire where a dozen or so cavalry troopers were busy cleaning and reloading their revolvers.

"Yeh," the soldier continued. "Ya look a might forlorn and lost wanderin about like that."

The voice belonged to a barrel-chested, round-faced sergeant, older than his pa and every bit as strong. Duane walked over to where the man sat cross-legged in the grass beside the fire.

"Kinda young, ain't ya?" another spoke up.

"I guess," Duane replied. "Don't much matter. Thet much lighter fer ta ride fast 'n carry the dispatch."

"Boy," a third cut in, "you do talk like a Johnny Reb. Where you from?"

"Up rive' in back country farm land," he avoided a direct answer.

"That must be it," the deep voice closed the question. "We're mostly city-bred men. Now, come set a spell and don't look so sad."

Duane knelt on the grass and sat back on his heels. "Ya all been in eny fightin taday?" he asked.

"Not really," the sergeant answered. "More like a barnyard shootout with some live-stock."

"What's your name, Boy?" another inquired, busy wiping a cylinder down with an old rag.

"Name's Dee." He noticed the moisture on the gun metal. "How'd yer piece git so wet?"

"Pass the coffee pot," the man responded.

"Huh?"

"Just pass the pot."

Duane reached out with a stick of firewood and lifted the pot from its hook to place it on the ground near the soldier's knee.

"Now look here."

Using the cloth to keep from getting burned, he lifted the lid and set it aside. Then he poked into the steaming contents of the pot with a long, slender stick. After some careful prodding, he withdrew the stick to display a cylinder suspended from its end by one of its empty chambers, steaming hot and dripping wet.

"What'd ya do thet fer?" the boy asked.

"It boils out the spent powder an cleans the metal up real good," the man explained. "You wipe it down good, load it, put some grease on, an it's ready to go."

"Purty slick," Duane observed. "Ya do yer gun the same?"

"Usually just the barrel. It ain't good to boil the wood grip."

"My name's Frank, short for Franklin," the sergeant introduced himself. "You wanta lend a hand?"

"Yeh. What fer ya want?"

Frank handed him a wet revolver, still wrapped in a cloth. "Wipe it down real dry."

Duane did as instructed.

"You know how ta load?" the sergeant asked.

"I lernt how, but ain't neve done it but once b'fer."

"Here, I'll watch."

He passed the boy a cylinder and placed the pouch of cartridges on the ground between them. As Duane worked with his hands, practicing what Dan had taught him and checking the results with the sergeant, he found comfort in the presence of strangers. The loneliness passed.

*　　*　　*

Duane awoke to the sound of voices in a nearby conversation. The last stars were fading in the western sky as the light preceding morning glowed in the east. He sat up, rubbing the sleep from his eyes as his blankets fell away to his side. Briskly rubbing shirt sleeves and trouser legs against his skin, the boy found warmth in the early predawn chill.

Colonel Elliot was meeting with his regimental officers by the fire. "Pope is attacking Corinth from the north. We will move in and take Booneville, cutting off and controlling the railroad, and in this way interrupting Beauregard's main source of support." The conversation went on as strategy was planned and instructions were prepared.

Duane pulled on his boots, then rolled his blankets. He gathered his gear near his saddle as the fireside conference broke up. Colonel Sheridan approached.

"Dee," he instructed, "you ride close by Captain Dawson. If there's any contact with enemy troops, he's to keep you out of the way. We'll see what we find. When all is done, you'll be carrying dispatches back to Pope and Halleck."

"Yes, Sir." Duane wanted to ask about looking for his pa, but decided this wasn't the time.

"Get ready ta go. We move in fifteen minutes."

The boy hurried to get his horse and to saddle up, as the camp came alive with preparations for the day's work. Dawn lightened into daylight as the sun peaked over the treetops casting its warmth in the morning air. By the time it cleared the horizon, the brigade was on the move.

Traveling the road in column, the cavalry neared the rail stop of Booneville. Distant train whistles shattered the morning quiet and locomotives could be heard chugging along the tracks, heading south toward the town. The advance stopped about a half mile from the outskirts of the community while Elliot scanned the area with his field glasses. Scouting reports indicated no sign of defenses or any troop movements in the area. There was an encampment of sick and wounded. A train waited on a siding. A number of stragglers could be seen along the roads. The decision was made to advance in force to prevent any chance of an organized resistance.

"Captain," Sheridan called as the brigade prepared to charge, "hold until we're past then follow behind."

"Yes, Sir." The response was lost in the crush of four thousand hooves breaking into a controlled gallop as the cavalry swept forward into Booneville.

"Let's go!" Dawson called as the last of the companies was passing.

The two urged their horses into a gallop and rode with the company toward the first houses of the town.

A scattering of shots rang out ahead as some of the Confederate stragglers fired on the advancing cavalry. The Federals fired back. But the enemy eluded them as they dashed behind fences or buildings, or disappeared down alleys. Resistance faded as most Confederate stragglers slipped into hiding and worked their way out of town to head south after a retreating army. A temporary center of command was set up at the railroad and a survey was made of the unfolding status of the operation.

After the brief interruption brought on by the arriving cavalry, the town's people resumed a routine of curiosity and apprehension. Two thousand Confederate sick were present in camp or temporary hospital. A large supply of muskets was found and destroyed. A few hundred stragglers from the army were found. Some were detained briefly. But all were allowed to continue on their way. No prisoners were taken.

Colonel Sheridan instructed Captain Dawson to take Duane and search for information about his father. They passed through every known tent or structure seeking information from all they met. Nothing was learned of Sergeant Kinkade or his Arkansas company. They did find out that the entire Confederate army had evacuated Corinth, the last trains having passed through that very morning.

By early afternoon the dispatches were ready to be taken north. A dejected boy mounted his horse and accepted the courier pouch handed to him by Colonel Sheridan.

"I'm sorry, Dee," the colonel stated. "We did what we could with the chance we had." He laid the bags across the saddle and tied them down. "You ride straight to General Pope with these reports. Once they're delivered you return to your lieutenant. And be careful. We understand there's still some Confederate cavalry that stayed behind."

"I'll take care, Colonel." He forced a smile of appreciation. "Thanks fer what ya done."

Duane turned his mount to the street as the officer slapped it loudly on the rump. It jumped into a run and the boy leaned forward into the rhythm of its movement. The colonel watched briefly as the horse and rider disappeared beyond a cloud of dust. Turning down a side street, the boy headed to the open country and the road north.

*　　*　　*

The road was lonely as it wound through woodlot and pastureland. Empty meadows and knee-high crops flanked the rutted roadway. Ahead a thicket of trees stood silent against the blue sky. Was it his imagination or did the shadows seem threatening.

Duane had spent the night sleeping in a stand of oak, hidden in the early summer undergrowth. The midday sun was hot and he had slowed to a walk. Corinth couldn't be more than a couple miles ahead. Soon the dispatches would be safe in General Pope's possession and Duane would be back in the tent he shared with Johnny. The boy ached all through from exhaustion and five days on horse. The mare was tired, too. The weight of the gunbelt on his waist was heavier with every clop of the mare's feet. For a moment, Duane allowed his eyes to fall shut and almost drifted into sleep. Just in time, he sensed himself slumping in the saddle, slipping toward the ground, and grabbed the front of the leather waking with a jolt and saving himself a spill in the trail's dirt.

The horse stopped as the reins slipped from the boy's hands, hanging free from the bridle. As Duane leaned forward, reaching with outstretched fingers to regain the lost leather lines, his eyes were distracted by movement in the woods ahead. Lunging for the lost reins, he caught them in his grip and yanked the mare to the side as several flashes of light were followed by the crackling of pistol fire. The horse pranced wildly and whinnied in panic as several bullets kicked up the dirt at her feet and one grazed her neck passing through the side of the boy's shirt.

Damn, a green mount, Duane thought as panic seized at him and knotted his stomach in painful tightness. Git hold a yerself, he thought. Ya been through worse.

"Yer okay, girl," he soothed softly, his voice calming himself as well. "Now we gotta git the hell outta here. Ya foller thet?"

More shots rang out as over a half dozen riders burst from the trees to chase the boy down. To the left, the meadow rose in a hill, laced by a variety of stone and rail fences. Open wheat fields to the right would be easier on the horse. The boy wheeled right in an instant breaking into a flat out run, riding low against the mare's neck, guiding her in a wide, zig-zag arc to make themselves a more difficult target. He knew the Southerners were good riders and the horses were most likely thoroughbred runners. His escape would depend on his wits. It would be impossible to outrun his pursuers.

More shots followed as he led a race, swishing cross country through the young wheat crop. Bullets went wild, striking ground, tree, or rock, or slicing through stalks of wheat. Occasionally he heard the whine of a ricochet.

"Come on, girl," he pleaded. "Ya kin do it."

A small stand of trees loomed ahead and a daring thought offered a plan of action. The trees were little more than a hedgerow. Passing through their shadows in an instant, Duane reined the horse hard to the right, riding the edge of the tree line toward the road. Calculating the time it would take his pursuers to reach the trees, he cut back through them and headed back the way he had come. It worked, giving him an extra lead. But three of the enemy caught on to what he had done.

Upon clearing the hedgerow and finding their quarry gone, the Confederate riders had divided their search. Three cavalrymen swung around the tree line where it ended at the road and spotted the boy as he galloped back through the wheat field toward the woodlands that had concealed them in the first place.

Again the pistols spoke. There was no way to outrun the three on the road. Perhaps he could use his temporary lead to make it up the hillside and lose them along the wooded ridge. It was worth a try. He reined his mount toward the slope.

"Come on, girl. Ya gotta clear them walls. We gotta lose them shootists fer they git us."

His heart sank as they crossed the dirt road and gained the slope of the hillside, and he felt the mare losing speed. They managed to clear a low wall, then a rotted tree trunk lying in the field. Shots kicked at the ground, plunked the fallen tree. The riders began to close on the boy. In rapid succession a bullet painfully grazed his neck and another imbedded in the flesh of the mare's rump. She screamed in pain and broke stride. A stone wall loomed up in front and he knew they couldn't clear it. He'd have to make a stand.

Shots sprayed stone chips along the wall as the mare cut to the left, throwing Duane off balance. He caught the saddle long enough to kick free of the stirrups before momentum flung him into a controlled fall. Dropping to the top of the wall, he rolled off to the ground behind, drawing his revolver as he struck the grass.

The horse wandered to the side and stopped to graze. The three cavalrymen approached rapidly, clearing with easy grace all obstacles in their path. Shaking violently in a sudden near state of panic, the boy rested the revolver on the wall. Gripping it with both hands, he pulled the hammer back with his thumbs and squeezed the trigger. The revolver spoke clearly, but the shot went wild. Three more times he fired as he felt the quaking within his own body.

Damn it, git hol a yerself 'r yer not gonna make it, Duane pleaded with himself. One more shot.

The approaching riders fired again as the boy ducked, pulling the hammer back behind the wall, then swung the barrel up and braced it with both hands on the stone surface. In another instant they would clear the stonework overtop of him. This time he took a moment to aim at the lead rider and squeeze off the shot. As the gun fired and kicked back in the boy's hands, the rider flew backwards as though struck from his horse by a tree branch.

Duane dropped behind the stonework as the approaching horses gathered their strength and pushed off to clear the wall. He threw himself to the side as the revolvers spoke again, kicking up dirt and stone chips. There would be a moment while the riders rode ahead and swung about to finish their work. Quickly Duane dove to the opposite side of the wall. Fumbling in his cartridge pouch, he drew out a spare cylinder, hastily broke open the revolver, and loaded the live cylinder. It was done in less than a minute.

Drawing back the hammer, the boy swung the barrel up and fired once as the two spurred their mounts into a charge.

"He's empty!" one shouted.

"He's dead!" the other added.

They're off their guard, Duane thought. Pulling back the hammer of his revolver, he swung it back to rest on the stone.

The approaching cavalrymen had holstered their pistols and drawn sabers. The boy waited for a close shot. With sabers held high to sweep down and slice as they passed, the two approached the jump. Duane fired. A killer flew backwards from his horse as surprise and fear registered on the other's face. The boy fell to the ground as the rider cleared the wall and swept downward with his blade. He heard his shirt rip and felt the sting of the steel as it slipped across his back. Rolling into a seated position, leaning against the stone, the boy braced his elbows on his knees and fired after the third rider. The man never turned, but rode straight down the hill and on across the field of wheat.

Suddenly all was silent. The boy relaxed, exhausted, allowing his legs to collapse and his arms to fall to his sides. Resting his head on the stone, he closed his eyes and let out a sigh of relief. A horse munched on the grass.

Others'll be comin. Gotta git outta here. Guess I ain't hurt bad. Don't feel bad. Maybe a bit sticky on ma back. Gotta git the dispatch ta the general.

Something moved. Duane opened his eyes to see the first soldier that had fallen was stirring.

"Ya hurt bad?" the boy called.

"Hell yeh! Ya damn near blew ma arm away!" The wounded cavalryman pushed himself up with his good arm. "Ow! What the hell'd ya do thet fer enyway?"

Duane stood, leaning his weight against the wall for balance. Suddenly he felt light-headed and an uneasiness in his stomach. He stared a moment at the figure on the ground before calling back. "I weren't wantin ta let ya all git me kilt. Jest wantin ta keep livin a piece longer."

"Where the hell ya from, Boy. Ya don't talk like a Yank 'r ride like one neither."

"Benton, Arkansas." He approached the fallen rider. "I can't stay ta pass words with ya. Yer friends'll be back."

He slipped the canteen from his shoulder and pulled the stopper. "Here's some water."

The man took it and drank. "If'n yer one a us, why fer ya wearin a Yank uniform?"

"Got shot at Pittsburg 'n a Yank doctor fixed me up. I ain't here takin sides. I'm lookin fer my pa. So if 'n ya sees a Sergeant Andrew Kinkade, 13th Arkansas, ya says his son, Dee, is okay, I figger. Look up Lieutenant Daniel Marshalton, surgeon, 61st Illinois."

"Stay with me, Boy. We'll help ya."

"Thanks, but we jest tried ta git each other kilt. I best git." He turned back toward his horse.

"I figger I kin folla yer thinkin. Looks as yer horse is hurtin. Take Stanton's. He ain't likely ta need it fer a piece."

"Okay. I hope he ain't dead. Ya tell him I sher ain't wantin ta hurt no one. I jest ain't fer gittin kilt neither."

A noise in the distance drifted on the air. Duane glanced across the valley and saw the rest of the riders returning at a gallop, kicking up a cloud of dust as they charged up the dirt road. Quickly, he picked up his revolver and the spent cylinder, returning them to holster or cartridge pouch. Then he transferred his gear and the dispatch pack to the brown thoroughbred stallion, grazing along the wall. Swinging into the saddle he glanced at the body crumpled against the wall. He was dead, his life blood having drained through a gaping hole in his chest, staining uniform and puddling on the ground.

Looking back at the other he called, "Yer friend's gone. What's the horse's name?"

"Called him Jeremiah from the Good Book."

Patting the horse on the neck, he leaned forward to speak softly in his ear. "Sorry fer yer friend, Jeremiah. But I'll treat ya real good. I ain't heavy. So let's git on up this ridge an lose them thet's followin behind."

Touching his heels to the stallion's flanks, they leaped into a run and disappeared into the forested slopes along the crest of the ridge.

*   *   *

The outskirts of Corinth were reached within the half hour. It took another hour of asking about before Duane was able to locate Pope's headquarters. The dispatches were delivered, then the search began to locate the camps of the 61st Illinois and the surgeon's quarters. From the time the boy rode into Corinth until he finally found his friends, there were raised eyebrows and many questions about the brown thoroughbred and the Confederate tack. The boy passed them off with, "I'm ridin fer General Pope" and continued on his way.

It was a relief to reach his destination and a celebration of joy for all three to be reunited. Shouts and wild waving greeted his arrival as Johnny ran to grab the horse's bridle and Duane slid wearily to the ground.

"Dan, look who's back!" Johnny called.

"Dee!" the man called as he stepped from his tent. "You're back! Thought surely we'd never see you again." Quickly he strode the distance to where the boy stood. "You look a mess! Come on," he put a hand on the boy's back, "sit down and…" He felt the stickiness and pulled his hand back to look at the red ooze. "What happened!?" he asked in alarm.

"Ain't mor'n a scratch." Duane tried to calm as the doctor turned him around to get a closer look.

"Where'd you get this horse?" Johnny asked, not yet aware of Dan's concern, "and the saddle has extra guns!"

"Ma innards is cryin fer ta be feedin," Duane stated. "Ya got sumthin fer thet need 'n I reckon ta be here a mite longer." He smiled and teased, "Could be I'll even stretch a story as ta ma wanderins an adventures an near chance ta dyin."

"Dying!" Johnny echoed.

"I'd say so," the lieutenant held up his bloodied hand for the older boy to see.

There was a scurrying and commotion as Johnny took the horse and tied it to a nearby tent's pole then returned with a folding camp stool for his friend, and Lieutenant Marshalton went to fetch a basin for water and his medical bag. The three then settled by the fire where Johnny cooked up some beef and beans, Dan worked at cleaning up the wound from the saber and the burn he found where the bullet had grazed the boy's neck, and Duane shared the story of his experiences since his departure five days earlier. Then while Duane ate, his friends told him of entering an abandoned Corinth, of how the Rebs had deceived the Federal command by removing their army by train with a great deal of commotion and cheering so that Generals Grant and Buell were rushed forward to reinforce Pope who believed he was about to be overwhelmed. The boy laughed at the thought that the deception had been so complete.

Lieutenant Marshalton finished tending Duane's wounds and settled into his own camp chair. Johnny settled on the ground, resting against the woodpile. Duane finished eating and set his camp kit on the grass beside his stool and rested his chin on his fists with his elbows propped on his knees. For a moment neither spoke. Jeremiah snorted impatiently, reminding them he needed attention.

"I plum fergot ya, Jeremiah," Duane spoke up. "Guess yer hungry, too."

"You get the rest of your gear, Dee," Dan said. "I'll take the horse to the stock pen and see he get's tended." He stood and started toward the horse as the boys followed. "I know you're tired and will need some sleep."

Duane untied the laces from the bedroll and saddle bags. He pulled them from the saddle and dropped them on the ground near the tent door flaps. The lieutenant turned an empty crate on its side and unsaddled the horse, placing the saddle and blanket on the crate. A rope was looped around the animal's muzzle as a makeshift halter, and the bridle was removed and draped across the saddle.

"What'll come a him?" Duane asked.

"For now he'll stay in the stock pens at the wagon camp. Then, I don't know."

The boy patted the muzzle affectionately and stroked the strong neck. Jeremiah responded with a gentle nibbling at his shirt collar.

"I think we kin be friends," he spoke softly. "Thanks fer gittin me here, Jeremiah. See ya agin."

"I'll be back shortly," Dan stated. "You two clean up from supper."

As the man led the horse away the boys returned to the fire. Duane filled the coffee pot from the water bucket, then hung it over the fire to heat. While Johnny put on more wood to build up the flames, the younger boy went to the tent to gather rags and a wax candle. As he returned to the stool, he brought the two saddle guns from their holsters and checked the water before setting his materials on the ground near his feet and settling himself on the seat.

"What you doing?" Johnny asked as his friend opened his own holster and cartridge pouch and removed the revolver and spare cylinder.

"Gotta clean this up," he explained.

"Can I help?"

"Sher. Jest a bit 'n I'll tell ya what I need."

Working together, the boys cleaned and reloaded the three guns, wiped down the leather, washed and wiped the plate and utensils, then packed up all Duane's gear. He suddenly felt the extent of his exhaustion. Gathering his gunbelt and haversack, Duane took his belongings to the tent and lay them on the bed. "Think I'll rest a spell."

Kicking off his boots, Duane settled back on the blanketed surface.

"I think you'll sleep real good," Johnny commented.

"Yeh," the other replied. He closed his eyes and was asleep.

*   *   *

The next few days drifted lazily by. An afternoon rain which soaked on through the night passed early in the week. Afterwards a hot sun beat down on the camps. A constant buzzing of tens of thousands of flies hung in the air. They were everywhere from the latrine trenches, to the garbage pits, to the white canvass stained by their passing and the passage of weather and time, to the food at mealtime, and always hovering around man and beast. An air of discontent hung about the camps as well. Soldiers were tired of soldiering. Many reported themselves sick to avoid drill and duty, or wandered off into the countryside to lose themselves for a few days. Others packed their gear and headed for home.

Early one afternoon Duane found himself lying bored on his cot, swatting at flies, while Johnny did the same on his cot. There was no conversation as each drifted in and out of a light sleep. The air was sultry still. Sweaty garments clung damp against the skin. A fly landed on the boy's forehead and hiked on down toward his nose. Absent-mindedly he brushed at ticklish footsteps and the pest buzzed off.

Outside, voices surged indistinct in the air like some faroff surf caressing a sandy beach. Then a voice cut through the doldrums.

"Hey, Dan. Some of us is getting up a ball game. Wanta join us?"

"Yeh, Willy," the lieutenant called from his tent. "Let me see if the boys wanta come along, too."

"We'll be out in front of the wagon park in the meadow there." From where he lay, Duane heard the voices and the footfalls as Captain Willy Tomlin moved on and Dan rolled from his cot to his feet.

"What's a ball game?" he asked.

Johnny swung his feet around and sat up on the edge of his bed. "Baseball," he stated.

"Huh?" he rolled over on his side to face his friend.

"Yeh," the older boy swatted at a fly. "You bang a hard leather ball with a stick and run to the bases before someone throws the ball there or tags you out."

"Neve' here'd of sech." Duane brushed an insect from his hair.

"I only played at it once myself," Johnny acknowledged. "It's real fun. Come on. Get your boots on."

The two slipped into shoes or boots and were out of the tent just as the lieutenant emerged from his.

"Guess you heard," Dan greeted.

"Sure did," Johnny returned. "But Dee, here, ain't never played before."

"Well let's go learn him."

The three headed out to join others of the regiment at the meadow near the wagon park. At first Duane watched from a fence rail with the hundreds of spectator infantrymen. The players were their officers and they filled the air with cheering and catcalls as they urged on their own or teased the opposition. As the game moved into a second inning, Dan took Duane to the sidelines and began to explain how it worked. He handed the boy a bat, placed his hands on the handle end and helped him to swing it. By mid-afternoon the boys had borrowed bat, ball, and an awkward-looking, fat-fingered glove to go off to another part of the field and practice hitting on their own. The hours passed lazily with the noise of the game always in the air as the two concentrated on their own play. From time to time the routine was broken as one or the other connected with a loud crack to watch the ball soar out over the grass and his friend go running after it. They finally wore themselves out and wandered back to the game. Dropping their gear among the scatterings in the grass behind an improvised team bench, the two searched out a shaded spot in the shadows of the spectators perched on a nearby fence rail. Beads of sweat streaked their faces and dripped from nose or chin. Each pulled off his shirt and wiped his face or toweled off arms and body before resting it in his lap. After watching the game for a minute, Duane shook his shirt open and spread it in the grass beside him. Then he lay on his side, resting his head in the crook of his arm. The noise about him seemed to fade into the distance as flies buzzed about his head and exhaustion drained him of energy. Silence.

Duane awoke with a start, realizing that he must have fallen asleep. The game was ending. The last play was run out as many of the spectators had already departed toward their camps. The boy stretched tired muscles as he sat up and the flies scattered.

"You boys hungry?" Dan called as he wandered toward them.

"Sure am," they chorused as they rose to their feet with shirt crumpled in arm or slung over a shoulder.

The crowd dispersed in small groups, several of which carried off the game equipment that had been shared by all. A half dozen friends joined the lieutenant and the boys on their return to camp. The boys hurried ahead to stir up the cook fire while the officers returned by way of the supply tents to pick up dinner rations.

The evening meal was prepared in leisure. During Duane's absence the mess had grown larger. Combining energies, the three were joined by two other officers, Captain Tomlin and Lieutenant Coates. With a larger assortment of cookware and a sharing of responsibilities, they boiled beans, fried up beef, set a pot of coffee, and mixed up biscuit dough which they wrapped around shaven sticks and roasted over hot coals.

Dinner conversation drifted from the events of the afternoon to the latest news on the war. The five ate ravenously as the food was transferred from cook pan to plate. The finished bread was broken apart from the cooking sticks and the pieces dipped in the beef drippings. Even as the five ate, they were constantly brushing aside the flies which hovered about their plates. Finally, with appetites satisfied, all set about the task of cleaning up, packed away their cook gear, and returned to lounge about on the grass or crate or camp chair, to smoke a pipe or sip a cup of coffee.

Another officer wandered over to join the group.

"Evening, Colonel," Captain Tomlin greeted.

"Evening, Captain," Colonel Etherington returned.

"Came to tell you the latest." The tall fair-skinned officer of blond beard and blue eyes settled on an empty flour barrel as Marshalton handed him a tin of coffee. "Thanks, Dan."

There was a brief quiet interrupted only by a crackling log or buzzing insect while the colonel sipped the coffee and the others settled to listen. He set the cup aside.

"There's been some reorganizing of units and reassignment of medical staff. We will be attached to the Army of the Ohio under General Buell. Halleck has ordered him to the front in pursuit of the Confederate Army. We move in the morning." He stood, finished the coffee, then set the cup on the barrel. "See that everything is ready tonight for an early departure in the morning."

"I'll take care of it," the captain confirmed.

"Good," the colonel turned to go. "I'll see the rest of the staff this evening. Then we'll meet for final instructions at my headquarters at nine tonight."

"Yes, Sir," Willy acknowledged.

"See you all later," Coates stated. "Time to get things packed."

The group broke up. Each officer headed to his own tent to pack his gear as company streets all around them became active with preparations for an evening muster and inspection in readiness for the next day's move toward the front.

As the sun hung low above the western horizon, dragging the day to a late dusk, an evening breeze drifted through the camp cleansing the stagnant air of odors and bringing a freshness with the evening songs of whippoorwill or sparrow. The boys prepared to settle in for the night. Twilight faded toward darkness. As Duane stripped to his johns and reclined on top of his bedcovers in the warm summery nightfall, he sensed a distant pain in the depths of his belly. It passed.

"Night, Dee," Johnny said as he lay back on his blanket.

"Night, Johnny," Duane returned.

He closed his eyes, thought briefly of the game, then lost all feeling to sleep.

* * *

Buell took his army south the following morning. Duane found himself astride Jeremiah and, a day later, in Booneville once again. There was no action this time. The army remained encamped for five days, then received new orders. The Army of the Ohio was to return to independent action in Tennessee and Kentucky, repairing the railroads in route.

For three weeks the army traveled, first north toward Corinth, then east along the Memphis and Charleston Railroad. It was slow progress repairing the railroad and suffering the harassment of attack along the way. At the same time, Buell sent orders ahead for the railroads to be repaired south from Nashville. Meanwhile, the army advanced eastward, suffering the effects of low water as lack of rainfall set the stage for a period of drought. Lack of rolling stock on the rail line and a bridge out to the east meant the army could not receive supplies by train, and low water on the river prevented supply shipments by boat. Thus every available wagon was pressed into service to feed the thirty thousand. Even so, there was barely enough even with foraging, to keep the men in partial rations, and nothing for the animals.

Finally, near the end of the last week of June, Buell's army arrived at Florence on the Tennessee River. There, three divisions were ferried across to board trains of the Nashville and Decatur Railroad and continue east through Athens to arrive in Huntsville by the end of the month. A fourth division took several days to ferry across at Decatur, arriving near the end of the first week in July. But the railroad north to Nashville remained in disrepair and the army was put on half rations as supplies continued to be brought in by wagon.

At Huntsville, the Army of the Ohio joined forces with General Mitchell's army which had been operating in the vicinity for several months. Though railroads were recognized as the key to control and movement, he had not accomplished the repairs required of him and had not secured control to the east and Chattanooga as an earlier raid by a group under a spy named Andrews had failed in its attempt to capture a train and destroy vital bridges. Buell's first order of business became the reopening of a railroad supply link to Nashville in the north.

Two divisions were sent east to Stevenson and Battle Creek to repair and defend the railroad and to rebuild a bridge across the Tennessee River. Two others were sent north to open the line to Nashville. Saw mills were set up in various locations to produce the lumber and timbers needed for the task and work was underway at a fever pitch.

Duane and his friends went north on the Nashville and Decatur line with General Nelson's division.

*　　*　　*

The late afternoon sun blazed hot on the expanse of railroad which hugged the shoulder of the hillside along the western edge of the wooded valley. More than 1400 men and boys, stripped to their waists in the hot July sun, worked along a mile stretch of the broken roadbed. Most were soldiers in Nelson's division with a few engineers from the 1st Michigan. Some were laborers, a few of whom were knowledgeable in railroad construction, including bridge and tunnel work. The soldiers' loaded muskets were racked in stands along the side of the right-of-way with cartridge pouches on the ground by the butt of each gun. Another six hundred remained under arms, scattered in company groups along the work area. Picket lines were thrown out a couple hundred yards to the east of the line to watch for Confederate cavalry, known to be operating in the area.

Duane, Johnny, and a sixteen-year-old private who had introduced himself as Daniel, were busy filling water buckets from the large wooden tanks of the water car. Warmed by the day's heat, the already foul water smelled particularly strong. Still, it was wet, and the sweating workmen would rather drink the fouled liquid than do without. Being the tallest of the three, Daniel leaned over the edge of the tank to dip each bucket until it filled, then passed each to one of the others to place along the edge of the flat car's wooden platform.

As the three boys prepared the water, the work progressed on the roadbed. Some crews shoveled debris from the right-of-way while others re-laid ties and rails or shoveled rock and ballast into place. Dust and noise were everywhere mingled with the summer heat and exhaustion.

The work, travel, and illness of several weeks had taken its toll. Diarrhea was still a part of daily routine. Duane found himself easily tired and Johnny was exhausted on the verge of collapse. The three boys worked without comment. The whole scene bore an eerie silence of conversation. Stripped to the waist, their shirts hung on the brake wheel.

Sweat glistened on their flesh, dripped from chin or plastered hair, and stained waist band and trouser leg. Flies were a constant bother.

Johnny received a bucket and turned to cross the deck when he stumbled and fell to his knees. The bucket landed with a loud bang on the car's floor, but did not spill.

"Ya okay?" Duane inquired.

"No," Johnny gasped. "My innards is going to pieces and the pain is something awful."

The younger boy moved to help his friend. "Yer burnin up!" he exclaimed as he grasped an arm. "Daniel, gimme a hand. Let's put him in a water tank. It might help ta cool him some."

"Sure," came the cracked reply from the other's parched throat.

Together they assisted Johnny to the tank, over its edge, and into its cooling contents. Once settled on the floor of the tank, he leaned his head against the dampened wood, closed his eyes, and slipped into unconsciousness. A fly paced, unmolested, across closed eyelids.

"How bad you think he is?" Daniel asked, leaning on the tank's edge, staring at the boy within.

Duane watched his friend a minute, seeing that his breathing was short and shallow. "It seems ta me thet Dan'll fix him up with sum a his blue pills 'r sech an see him ta bed fer maybe a week 'r so." After a pause, he turned from the tank. "Come on. We best git ar mounts an ride this water 'bout."

The two crossed to the edge of the car and dropped to the ground. Walking to the rear of the car, each untied his horse from a post loop, mounted, then rode back to the line of buckets. Dropping a tin cup into each of two buckets, Daniel took one in each hand and rode north along the track toward the furthest workers, guiding his mount with his knees. Duane, still riding his horse Jeremiah, did likewise.

With the day's track repairs completed, the men lay down their tools and paused for water before packing up for the return trip to the division's camp some five miles back south along the line. The boys each paused by a cluster of men while a bucket and cup made their rounds, then moved on as the soldiers gathered their weapons and tools and began to wander back toward the flat cars. A locomotive would be along shortly to pick up the carloads of men and would bring empty coaches for the extra infantry companies. Quiet conversation drifted on the air as work ceased and efforts were underway for water break and loading.

Soft thundering rumbled to the north.

All along the work area the men were gathering tools and weapons or had already begun the movement toward the waiting cars. There were pauses in the movement whenever one of the water boys stopped within a group. The companies of soldiers had also begun a piecemeal move toward the gathering at the string of flat cars.

The distant thunder crescendoed steadily without interruption and the moving mass of men became aware of its growing presence. Suddenly, one of the regimental officers called out.

"Form your companies in line of battle! That's cavalry coming, and fast!"

A drummer beat the call as the slow movement broke into pandemonium of shouting orders and general confusion. The uniformed soldiers created a first line of defense as they fell into line of battle across the right-ofway and into the vegetation on either side. A rider was dispatched to notify the picket line while the soldiers who had been working on the repairs took up positions on and around the work cars. Through the mass of movement, Duane urged Jeremiah on as he rushed back to the water car. There he tied his horse to the brake wheel as he drew the pistols from the saddle holsters and jumped from the saddle to the car's deck. Ignoring the preparations about the work site, the boy crossed to the water tank to scramble up its side and check on his friend.

Johnny lay as the two had left him, partly submerged in the water, covered by flies, resting unconscious against the wooden siding. Duane saw what he needed.

"Thank God he's still breathin," the boy thought to himself as he dropped down beside the tank to take notice of what was happening.

The first battle line was already in place about a half mile north of the flat cars. The workers were scattered between there and the cars as the first crews were forming a line using the cars for cover. There was a scrambling from behind as Daniel dashed to the younger boy's side. Then a blood-curdling yell erupted from a thousand throats to the north as a grey horde of riders charged into view. Flashes of flame burst from the advancing cloud of dust kicked up by the attackers. The battle line met the clatter of pistol fire with a sheet of flame and the explosion of uniform musket fire. The leading line of riders was broken as several horses went down and others lost their riders. Immediately, a second line of muskets fired while the first reloaded and fell back toward the underbrush along the track grade, to fire again while their comrades joined them.

The scene of battle became lost in smoke and confusion as the cavalrymen laid down a continuous fire from their revolvers and fell upon the line of infantry. Foot soldiers fled in panic as the Confederate forces divided and some pursued the fleeing while most continued to attack the work crews. The soldiers of the work crews had gathered in a second line of battle and had leveled their muskets, awaiting the command to fire. New gunfire opened from the east as the pickets joined their firepower in a broadside.

Duane had tucked himself between two water tanks while Daniel lay prone on the decking tucked around the end of the second tank.

"Fire!" a brigadier ordered.

The air erupted in flame, smoke, an explosion of gunfire; then the crashing, splintering, and screams of full battle. It roared by like a summer storm and within minutes there was an eerie silence, disturbed only by the fading thunder, the moaning wounded, a distant whistle of the approaching train, and the dainty splash of running water escaping through holes in the water tank.

Duane stared at the water as it splashed on the wooden deck in front of him, its murky stream stained red.

*   *   *

The camp was chaotic with commotion as the train arrived and began to unload its wounded. Runners alerted the surgeons. Others rushed to bring litters or assist the dazed victims who stumbled from the flat cars. As the tide of broken bodies surged into the camp, the operating theater was hastily thrown together. Boards were flopped across wooden horses, cases of surgical tools laid open, medicines and bandages set nearby in their boxes.

Amidst the confusion Duane was frantic in his efforts to find help for Johnny.

"Please!" he shouted above the noise as he tugged on the sleeve of a young corporal, "ya gotta he'p my friend. He's bin shot 'n lays in thet water tank."

The soldier motioned a friend to follow. "Lead on, Boy. We're with you."

Scrambling aboard the tank car, the boy led the way to the tank where one soldier climbed in and raised the unconscious patient to the waiting hands of his companion. Daniel approached having been busy helping other wounded.

"How bad is he?" the youth asked.

"Don't rightly know," the soldier replied. "Looks like one in the leg and another in the chest."

"Git on!" Duane challenged. "We gotta git ta the lieutenant."

The corporal and his assistant lifted Johnny from the tank and passed him to the boys to steady while they jumped to the ground. The boys then lowered him from the car and the four set out in search of the surgeons' hospital.

A few had been killed outright in the raid. Others would die of their wounds in the days ahead. Johnny was brought into a line where an assistant surgeon was determining the dead and sorting the wounded according to the seriousness of their injuries. The walking wounded had to sit by and wait while the unconscious or litter cases went to the surgeon's table. There they were lined up on the ground to await their turn.

A litter was found and Johnny was left in the row of wounded by an operating theater. Duane waited with him, kept busy brushing the flies from the bloody clothing. All around were cries of pain, moans of the unconscious, shouting of orders and instructions, the screams of agony and tearing of surgeons' saws, the buzzing of flies, the smell of blood.

The surgeons worked feverishly, elbow deep in blood and gore, their aprons soiled by the spillage of their industry. Assistants wandered among the waiting to stem the flow of blood while waiting further attention. For most, a tourniquet was used – a strap, a tie, a strip of fabric. For some scalp wounds a styptic of alum or the like was poured on a cloth and laid on the wound to help it clot.

Johnny's bleeding had already slowed on the leg wound and clotting had begun on the chest; thus, he was passed by for any further treatment before going to the table. Duane looked up and saw a familiar face inspecting some of the wounded.

"Lieutenant!" he called. "Over here!"

Dan saw the boy and worked his way in his direction. "It's Johnny," Duane announced.

The surgeon glanced down to confirm the boy's statement and to see if his friend was still alive.

"Here!" the man called to two orderlies. "This one's next."

"Kin I he'p?" Duane asked.

"Come on," Dan responded.

The boy followed to the table where Johnny was placed and watched while the man worked.

First the shirt was ripped open and the chest wound was probed with a finger. Without comment, the man took a long pair of tweezer-like probes and reached into the hole to pull out a round lead ball. This he dropped in the bucket of implements and blood-red liquid. Then he took a cloth, rung it out, and sponged the wound and surrounding flesh. The wound was sewn shut and attention turned to the leg wound.

Duane helped as needed by holding or passing implements upon request. He discovered the bucket was full of whiskey. It was quicker to grab a keg of the brew then to send for water; nevertheless, since the start of hospital operations, several buckets of water had been obtained and waited nearby as needed.

When the surgeon's work was finished, Dan moved on to others while Duane remained to help bandage the wounds before the older boy was carried off to his tent.

Once Johnny was settled in his cot, Duane returned to the operating theater to do what he could to help. By the end of the day he had learned new skills, assisting mostly in bandaging. He had comforted many of the wounded and exhausted his own energies.

It was late when the last implements were rinsed, wiped down, and returned to their cases. The sun had set and moonlight worked its way through broken clouds. The man and the boy left the temporary hospital to stroll exhausted, to a cook tent, still running coffee and leftover stew for medical staff. The two took their plates and cups and settled at a plank table with others already gathered in quiet conversation.

"Johnny was lucky," Dan stated. "The bullets that struck him had been slowed by passing through the wooden tank, but mostly because they were round lead balls."

"How's thet?" Duane inquired, shoveling a spoonful of stew into his mouth.

"Round balls do less damage as they are easily deflected. Some of those we saw today had been hit by mini-ball. They make big holes and tear up a body real fierce."

"I guess ya know a awful lot 'bout hurtin an fixin up an the like."

"Not true, Dee. There's a heap I wished I knew. This war's caused suffering no man knows how to heal. Yet even as I go, I learn new things."

They talked on for a short while and shared in conversations with other doctors as they told of what they'd seen and done that day. Duane also told the lieutenant of Johnny's illness only to learn there was nothing else to do but give him rest and time to heal. The conversation was brief. They were all tired. After a half hour had passed, the two rose from the bench and turned through the camp toward their quarters.

A quiet had settled. The army slept. The night creatures prowled and sang their songs. Clouds slipped across to cut off the moon's light. The man and the boy faded into the darkness.

*   *   *

In the days that followed, Johnny's wounds began the healing process with very little infection. But his illness and exhaustion kept him in a state of semi-consciousness. He would awake for a few moments to see his friend sitting nearby, but too weak to speak. A smile was all he could manage before drifting into sleep once more. Duane tried to keep his patient informed of what was happening, but doubted that Johnny understood much of what he said.

The line was finally opened from Nashville to Stevenson and the first train load of supplies was on its way. But it was not to get through. The very next day the Confederates struck again at Murfreesboro where they captured a newly formed Federal division and damaged the railroad. Two days later, Nelson was ordered to go by train to occupy Murfreesboro.

The days spent nursing Johnny allowed Duane some much needed rest and he began to regain his own strength and begin recovery from his own bout with diarrhea. Trips to the latrine trench were less frequent and whenever possible, he avoided going after dark. But evening muster in preparation for the move to Murfreesboro had interrupted the boy's normal schedule, and nightfall came.

The camp winked in its own myriad of firefly-like candle lanterns hung before the hundreds of tents which lined the company streets. The sky was dark as haze and clouds covered the heavens and the sparklings of starlight. Thus the trip to the trench was dim and lonely with only the light from the candle in the lantern to guide the way. Duane walked slowly along the familiar trail. He listened for the sounds of the night creatures as they scurried out of his way on their scavenging trips to the garbage piles. Candle light reflected in a pair of small round eyes which stared at him on the dirt path ahead. They blinked, then were gone in a scampering through the brush. His nose told him the trench was near. So, too, did the buzzing of ten thousand flies.

On the way back toward camp, a new odor caught the boy's attention. Preoccupied with thoughts about his father and wondering where he might be, Duane did not recognize the smell until a scampering and commotion at his feet alerted him too late that he had stumbled on a skunk with her young, in search of food. The squeals of the panicked kittens and the hissing stench, followed by the rustling retreat, were swiftly sudden and done before the boy realized what had happened.

"Damn it ta hell!" Duane exploded to himself. "Oh, God, it stinks." He nearly dropped the lantern as he stumbled to recover from his surprise. "This sher is a fine fix. I can't stand the smell," he thought to himself. "Maybe if I git outta these clothes."

Duane set the light on the ground and stripped off his clothing, abandoning it in a pile in the trail before continuing on to camp. Still, he could not rid himself of the stench.

As he neared the first tents, he was greeted by the taunts of men who wished him gone. "Damn, Boy, you keep your distance. We ain't wantin' to smell skunk this close up."

"May be ya need a washin," Duane taunted back. "Most skunks smell themselves fust."

Passing stark naked through the outskirts of the company camp, Duane approached the Lieutenant's tent.

"Dan!" he called.

"I smelled you a hundred yards off," Marshalton announced as he emerged from his tent. "Where's your clothes?"

"Left 'em on the trail," the boy returned as he stood in the candle light. "What fer kin I do ta rid me of this infernal stink?"

"Not much I know of." The man smiled as he wrinkled his nose against the odor. "Let's find a tub and scrub you down. Maybe I can find something to perfume the water and cut the smell. As for your clothes, they can be left as is since we're moving out at sunup."

A wooden tub was found and half filled with cold water. The boy shivered in the chill water as the lieutenant scrubbed him with a bar of store-bought soap from his personal kit. Three times he washed the boy's hair and lathered his body before the smell of skunk began to dwindle.

"Ow!" Duane cried from time to time as the rubbing burned his skin or the soap stung his eyes.

Finally the two agreed that they had done their best and managed to reduce the stench to a tolerable odor. Duane rubbed himself dry with a worn towel while Dan found an extra shirt of his for the boy to wear until morning.

"We'll find a new set of clothes come morning," he decided. "You need your sleep and can use my shirt til then."

Duane pulled the shirt on and buttoned the front while the man kicked over the tub of water and spread the towel across the overturned side of the container.

"Come on," the lieutenant put an affectionate hand on the boy's shoulder and turned him toward his tent. "Let's check on Johnny and get you to bed. You still stink. I'll bet it'll even wake Johnny and make him well just to keep his distance from you."

"Yeh," Duane smiled, "it'd be worth the smell if it worked thet way."

The two entered the tent where the man set a lantern on an upturned crate to check the older boy's condition. Duane sat on the edge of his bed to watch. Johnny stirred and opened his eyes.

"What's that stink?" he whispered only half awake.

"Dee, here, went romping with a skunk," Dan explained.

"Oh," Johnny acknowledged. "Just be sure he gets a bath."

"Yeh. First thing come morning."

"Night." He closed his eyes and was asleep.

"Wait til he wakes an larns I really stink." Duane smiled at the thought. "I'd give enythin he could smell me now an really fret." He lay back on the bed. "It's bin too long his bein sick 'n all."

"He's mending," Dan remarked as he brushed his hand across his patient's forehead. "The wounds are clean and his temperature's gone.

Won't be long now." He straightened and turned to the younger boy. "Dig out a change of clothes first light."

"Yes, Sir. Ya sher ya be wantin this shirt back?"

"Of course. The smell of it will always remind me of you. Now get some sleep." He blew out the candle.

"Night, Dan."

"Night, Dee."

The boy listened for the movement of the man's departure, then closed his eyes and allowed sleep to overtake smell.

*   *   *

It was sometime around five in the feeble glow before morning light when the first call was sounded. As Duane struggled to shake off sleep and prepare for muster, a voice surprised him.

"Hey, Dee." It was Johnny, alert and clear. "There must be a skunk nearby."

"Yeh, yer talkin ta him," the boy responded. "How ya feelin? Sher been a long time."

Duane threw back his covers and crossed to his friend's bed. Finding Johnny already sitting up in bed, he parked himself near the wooden bracing at the foot of the cot.

"I feel great!" the patient replied, "like I weren't even sick."

"Ya ain't knowin ya was shot?"

"I what?!"

"Yeh," he lifted Johnny's hand to touch the bandages under his shirt, "thet day we was workin the water car we was set on by Reb cavalry. Ya was shot up pretty bad. Dan ain't knowin fer sher jest how ya healed so good. But he swares it's the whiskey."

"The what?"

"Tell ya later."

A bugle interrupted with its call to muster.

"Gotta go," Duane stated. "I'll tell Dan yer up. Stay put. Back in a piece."

"What are you doing in that shirt?" Johnny asked as the dim first light through the tent flap illuminated his friend on his way out.

"The skunk. It got me fer sher 'n I ain't yet come ta find my own clothes. Ya kin hunt some while I'm out ta muster."

Duane disappeared into the dimness of the early morning camp and the troops gathering for first muster. Johnny paused a moment, laughing to himself at the recollection of the motley lineup he would miss once more, as the soldiers gathered in various stages of undress for the first attendance of the day. Then he pushed himself to his feet to test his endurance before continuing on to open a flap for light so that he could look through Duane's camp kit in search of a set of clothes.

Following muster, the encampment burst into motion as the division broke camp. A hasty meal was served through a series of company mess lines. Then most were loaded onto trains to begin the move to Murfreesboro.

It was the end of the mid week of July when Nelson and the first of his troops arrived at their destination. Even as they were establishing their camps, Confederates struck to the north and destroyed two bridges.

As July flowed into August, the cavalry harassment continued. By month's end supply lines were open once more, but a new threat had appeared. General Bragg had brought his Confederate army to Chattanooga by way of a series of railroads through four southern states. General Buell requested reinforcements from Halleck. By the second week of August, another break in the railroads occurred when the garrison was captured at Gallatin, Tennessee and the tunnel burned. This forced Buell to move to McMinnville.

In mid August, General Nelson was sent to Kentucky to help organize new units. For a few brief days Duane and his friends found Louisville a colorful and vibrant distraction from the routine of skirmishing along the railroad, and thoroughly enjoyed the change of pace. But it was short- lived. A Rebel army began to move toward Lexington at month's end and General Nelson was drawn southeastward into battle at Richmond. Defeated, he withdrew toward Louisville as a series of movements and skirmishes, maneuverings and small battles occupied the pieces of the two armies over a period of several weeks.

By the end of August, Bragg had moved his army across the Tennessee River at Chattanooga while other elements of his army were already moving toward Louisville. His army was well received by the Kentuckians and aided along the way, enabling an element of the army under General Kirby Smith to reach the outskirts of Louisville. Panic caused an evacuation to the north banks of the Ohio River and swelled the ranks of new units as volunteers hastened to join the Union army and defend their homeland. General Buell pushed his Federal forces to Murfreesboro, then Munfordville, and finally arrived at Louisville toward the end of September. Still, there was no major confrontation of the two armies. The organization of new units had continued in Louisville under the guidance of General Nelson. But four days after Buell's arrival, Nelson was murdered by a fellow officer causing General Gilbert to take over the III Corps.

Summer ended and early autumn had begun as General Buell started south with three army corps of three divisions each. The addition of new troops and the organization of their units meant some shuffling of personnel. General Sheridan was among those sent by Halleck and was attached to the III Corps. He ran into Marshalton during the course of reorganizing commands and had him transferred into his command.

It was a briskly brilliant fall morning at the start of October. A sharp blue sky arched overhead a countryside spotted with the crisp colors of wooded hillsides. Baggage wagons rattled noisily along the dusty ruts that were roadways, their harness chains jingling in rhythm with clopping hoofbeats. The air was filled with the noise and smell of the moving army as men, beasts, and vehicles clogged the road and overflowed along the surrounding countryside. Johnny rode the wagon seat. Dan was horseback to one side. Duane rode Jeremiah along the other. They were three veterans of a summer's campaign headed south on the road to Bardstown – south toward the Confederate army.

*   *   *

A sparkling sky with its brilliant moon cast an eerie glow on the dewless and parched landscape. The divisions of General Gilbert's III Corps moved ghostlike in great clouds of silty dust as it crawled eastward along the Springfield Pike towards Perryville in search of water and a place to rest the night. Every soldier, every beast, every vehicle wore a mantle of white dust. It had worked its way into every crack and crevice of equipment and tack, every fold of wagon canvass and clothing and skin. Duane rode his horse near the side of the wagon. He felt the gritty film in his hair, under his shirt, in the folds of his eyelids and the hairs of his nostrils. It was layered on his sweat and stuck inside his parched mouth. The extent of his misery was masked by the depths of his exhaustion having been on the march for a week of this extended drought.

Earlier in the late afternoon there had been the distant sound of a cavalry skirmish. Word had come that a Confederate presence was established at Perryville. But more important, there was water ahead. Darkness had fallen almost five hours ago, still the army moved. Suddenly the front of Sheridan's division came upon the puddled creek bed and found itself under attack from the ridge of land east of the creek. It was an hour before midnight. The night-lit terrain with its shadows and soft bright reflections was difficult to defend. As the division came to rest, an Indiana brigade was sent forward to seize the creek bed and scatter the Confederate defenders.

While elements of the division maneuvered for battle, an officer rode up to the supply wagon. "Lieutenant," he called to Marshalton, "get up there and see what you can do to help!"

"Yes, Sir, Captain!" he wheeled his horse around to the back of the wagon. "Johnny, pass me my field pack. Grab a supply pack for Dee." He turned to a quartermaster company nearby. "Sergeant, bring up litters and field supplies and follow! Johnny, bring the wagon as close as you can."

"Here!" Johnny called as he passed the requested gear. "I'll be along."

Orders were passed in the night confusion as the doctor, the boy, and two dozen soldiers moved toward the fighting to help the wounded. The brigade was repulsed and the walking wounded began to wander back from the field of battle. Midnight passed as the shooting ceased and the wounded were attended in the soft glow of starlight and the high, nearly full moon, wherever they met the surgeon and his party along the roadway from the creek. The lieutenant's party continued to work its way forward until they came upon the wounded who had fallen near the front of the assault. They lay along a ridge of land that paralleled the creek below. A small valley lay bathed in night light which reflected off the pools of water and caressed the bodies of fallen soldiers on the sloping ground stretching gently to the dry banks.

The boy could hardly swallow for the dryness in his throat. He stared longingly at the reflection of the water and felt a hand grasp his wrist as Dan read his thoughts and cautioned against a rash move. The two tied their horses to the branches of nearby shrubs, then joined the others as they turned their attention to the wounded. While the small groups worked quietly they could feel the enemy watching from the opposite ridge. They could sense their whispered conversations. There was a feeling of mutual truce. In that sense of safety, the boy worked his way down to the water. Then he lay in the damp dirt, pulling himself over to the pool to quench the dryness in his throat. The warm fluid felt comforting. Duane sat back on his knees and slipped his canteen from his shoulders, lay it in the water, and pushed it under to watch it fill. Returning to the wounded, he shared the precious liquid with the conscious.

Nearly two hours had passed in the first night of the new day. A few of the wounded had been removed from the slope. Suddenly the night was shattered by the approach of a new assault. Instinctively the boy dove for cover in a rocky flaw on the hillside as two new brigades from Sheridan's division moved down the slope, crossed the creek, and advanced up the far side.

The moonlit valley erupted in violent conflict as the Confederate line poured a devastating fire upon the advancing Federals. Relentlessly the Union troops pressed the attack in a deafening clatter of musket and rifle fire. The night was filled with screams of pain, the shout of orders, the Rebel yell, the smoke and din of battle, the whine of projectiles glancing off rocks. Duane kept low, not daring to look for fear a stray bullet would find its mark and strike him down. The assault stalled briefly, then pushed forward up the slope, forcing the Confederate defenders to fall back toward the town. The line was broken. The defenders continued a stubborn resistance as they withdrew. Sheridan's troops pursued the retreating forces and the fight faded noisily from the ridges of the eastern creek bank.

Duane and the others advanced cautiously as they moved to help the wounded. Before long the rest of the division began to move forward. More assistance arrived to help the wounded as the majority of the troops paused for water on their way up the slope to establish lines of battle along the ridge to the east of the creek before resting where they stood for what few hours remained of the night.

Johnny had arrived with the wagon and was on foot in the area of the recent fighting, when he called, "Dee! Come here quick!"

Duane sensed an urgency in the voice and dashed through the water and up the embankment. He found his friend kneeling beside a Confederate corpse.

"What fer'd ya call, Johnny?" He breathed hard to catch his breath.

"You might want to look close on that uniform," he pointed. "This regiment's from Arkansas."

Duane knelt to inspect the insignia in the moonlight. He glanced up to his friend. "Seventh Arkansas." His eyes were moist with a sudden surge of emotion. But any tears were forced back as he continued somewhat hoarsely, "We gotta find one thet's alive. I gotta know if 'n maybe some'n knows of my pa."

"You check along the top to see what you can find," Johnny suggested. "I'll continue to help along the slope here."

"Thanks," Duane accepted. "Jeremiah's still where I left him on the other ridge. Chance I don't see ya afte' a look about, I'll git him fi'st thin then follow on to where eve' ya head with the wagon."

"Be careful."

"I aim ta."

The two separated as Duane walked off through the noise and movement of newly arriving regiments in search of Confederate survivors. He paused a moment to scan the moonlit high ground. In the shadows beneath a stand of maples a little distant from the commotion of soldiers settling in for a few hours rest, there was a movement. Something metallic caught a stray beam of light and flashed in the darkness. The boy approached cautiously, unholstering his revolver as he neared the dark shadows, slowing his pace to allow his eyes to search for information. His heart pounded nervously as he wondered if danger lay ahead or someone who could help him or just a tree branch giving way.

An injured soldier leaned against a tree trunk. One arm hung bloodied and useless at his side. The other supported a musket with fixed bayonet, pointing directly at Duane. The boy dropped to his knees raising his revolver in one swift movement, but paused with his thumb on the hammer when he saw in the dim light that the soldier had not pulled back the hammer on his weapon.

"I ain't fixin ta be kilt," Duane spoke nervously. "But it ain't my wantin ta do no killin neither."

"Thet sets jest right with me, Boy." He lowered the weapon and Duane did likewise. "Wouldn't do no good nohow seein's it ain't loaded."

"Ya bad hurt?" Duane stepped closer as he slipped his weapon back into its holster and took the canteen from his shoulder.

"Don't figure ta be goin under fer it. Seems ma arm's busted up." He accepted the offered canteen and took a short drink from its contents. "Ain't ya the one thet went ta the water fer this last fightin?"

"Yeh." He took back the wooden container and shoved the cork back into the opening.

"Where ya from, Boy? Ya don't talk like no Yank I eve' heard."

"Benton, Arkansas." He looked at the shattered arm and saw it was still bleeding. "My pa's some'ere's in this war 'n I'm hopin ya'll be knowin somethin as kin he'p me fer ta find him." Dropping his pack on the ground, the boy pulled out some bandages and started to wrap the arm while he spoke. "I saw by one a yer dead as ya'll's from Arkansas, too."

"There's a heap a Arkansas regiments here. How's it ya come ta be a Yank 'n yer pa's a Reb?"

"Ain't no Yank. Jest picked up by 'em when I got shot to Shiloh." The boy concentrated on the job at hand, saying nothing. But he knew from what he had seen working with Johnny and the lieutenant, that a surgeon would take the arm off when this soldier's turn came on the table.

"Where'd ya larn whateve tis yer doin?" the man asked.

"Lieutenant Marshalton's a doctor. Seein as how he's lookin afta me, he's learnin me some, too."

As the moon dipped lower toward the close of night, its light brightened the shadows under the trees. Duane's eyes had grown used to the dim light and he studied the man he was helping. Green-grey eyes studied the boy, too. They were warm and kindly, a hint of a sad smile and the wish that war didn't exist. An agile body, firm in muscle tone, and calloused hands, suggested here was another farmer.

A sudden movement not twenty feet in front of them caught the man's attention and his eyes clouded with alarm. Duane felt a pressure from the shattered arm as the soldier spoke.

"Look out, Boy!" He raised his musket.

Duane dropped the ends of the fabric he was in the midst of tying. A gunshot shattered the night as he dove to the ground and grabbed for his revolver. The Arkansan fell back against the tree and slid to the ground as the boy raised his gun to the dark silhouette standing before him with smoking musket.

"Saved your life, Boy." the man sneered.

"Damn ya ta Hell! He wern't doin me no harm! It wern't even loaded!" The gun shook with the tense anger the boy felt as the senseless killing snuffed out the joy of hope in finding his father. "He was gonna he'p me find m' pa!"

The shadowy figure rested his gun on the ground as he reached for his cartridge box to begin to reload.

The sound of horses' hoofs became audible as several riders approached, as yet unnoticed by the shooter and the boy.

"Don't even think it, Mister." He pulled back the hammer. "But I'd sher thank ya fer good reason ta shoot ya dead."

"What's yer pa got to do with that Reb trash, Boy? The only good Reb is a dead one!" The man stared at the quaking gun and did not move.

Someone dismounted from the approaching group of riders.

"It's people wantin ta be killin like ya done here as makes this war! If 'n not, there'd be no war. My ma'd be alive taday 'n m' pa'n me'd be ta home takin in the crop."

The boy rose to his feet as he continued to shout at the still figure before him. "My pa's a Reb! I'm a Reb! But we ain't killers! We is farmers!"

Footsteps approached on the run at the sound of the gunshot and the boy's crazed voice.

"Boy, what's wrong?" a breathless officer asked.

"I was he'pin this here soldier," he indicated the body by the tree, "when this killer come on 'n murdered him."

The man came closer and knelt by the crumpled body to check for any sign of life. "He's dead for sure."

Duane thought he recognized the voice at the first question. Standing beside the kneeling figure he noticed the hat cocked slightly to the side and the short cropped hair. The stars on his insignia were those of a brigadier general.

The general rose to his feet. "Aren't you the boy I met at Corinth that day? You rode with us to Booneville? Dee?"

"Yes, Sir, General Sheridan." A sense of pride warmed him inside that the general would remember him.

"And this man was going to help you find your pa?" He reached a hand out to touch the barrel of the pistol still pointed at the soldier who was obviously distressed by the general's arrival and acquaintance with the boy.

"He's from Arkansas, Sir, an' was knowin there's a heap a regiments here from back home." He lowered his weapon, resting it in his other palm while he eased the hammer back down, then slipped the revolver into its holster.

"As soon as the business of war is settled, I'll see what can be arranged to inquire about your pa and, if he's with that army out there, see if we can get you two back together." He turned to address the nervous soldier, "Private..."

"I'm a corporal, Sir."

"Not any more," Sheridan returned. "I'll see to that personally. You're going to see to the burying. After that, this boy better never see you about again." The authority in the man's voice ended any thought of argument.

Nothing more was said as Duane and the general collected the dead man's belongings before the newly demoted soldier was instructed to pick up the body and carry it to a waiting wagon.

General Sheridan turned to his mounted staff officers, waiting quietly just to the back of where Duane stood.

"Captain," he instructed the closest officer who held the reins of the general's horse, "would you take care of things here. Make sure this man tends to burying the body and his commanding officer is informed of these events and his demotion. Take his name, write the order, and I'll sign it and leave the rest in your hands." He reached for the reins while the officer took out the order book, wrote the order, and handed it to the general to sign as he settled into his saddle. The order was signed and handed back to the captain.

"Dee," he turned his attention to the boy. "I'm sorry this turned out the way it did. Go back to your unit. My captain will take care of things here."

Night was nearing its end and dawn was creeping into the eastern sky as the general and his staff departed to continue to direct the establishment of his regiments in line of battle along the crest of the ridge running the eastern bank of the creek. Duane walked back toward the far bank of the creek while the captain took charge of the situation. The last of the casualties were attended and the soldiers moved into position with the rest of the division. The boy collected his horse from where he had left him and joined the lieutenant behind the lines as work was underway to set up a temporary field hospital in a nearby barn.

A few quiet hours passed as the armies rested where they had halted along the landscape. For some, there was relief from the long dry march as they gained water from wherever they found it in creek beds, shrunken ponds, puddles, or farmer's wells. Food had to come from whatever might be left in the haversack. The discomfort of the dust remained. To most, the foulness of the stale puddles was tolerated in the need to satisfy thirst. Yet when morning light revealed the carcasses of mules, livestock, or wild creatures, those who had drunk from those waters felt a repulsiveness that turned their stomachs. The hours slipped quietly by as the velvet black of the night sky faded in the growing light of the new dawn.

The sun rose on the new day, but a strange quiet hung on the air. The expected battle did not open. The armies did not engage. Periodic light skirmishing continued as small pockets of conflict contested water rights. Activity picked up in the early morning hours as General Sheridan prepared to move into Perryville. By mid-morning, one brigade was on the road and the remainder were forming up to follow when all were suddenly recalled. The defense of the ridge was quickly reestablished.

The ambulance train and medical baggage wagons were assembled in a field alongside the Springfield Pike. All was in readiness to move forward with the division and at the moment, no one near Johnny's wagon knew the cause of the delay. Several of the officers were gathered in a small group remarking on the weather, the water, the likelihood of an engagement. Teamsters and other personnel remained in relaxed formation exchanging opinions on the true strength and location of the enemy.

A corporal in his twenties slapped the dust from his cap with one hand as he briskly rubbed it from his dark matted hair with the other. "I truly think Bragg and his army are miles from here," he offered. "We've just come up on the rear end of one of his columns."

"Could be," another observed, leaning on his musket. "Could be, too, this is his meeting place and the whole of his army is just in front."

"Then why ain't they attacking?" the first asked.

Still another commented, "I'd wonder that, too. The sun's coming on to noon and nothing's happening."

Duane had dismounted and was leaning against the shadowed side of the wagon. Johnny had wrapped the reins around the brake handle and was sitting on the side of the wagon seat. The two followed with interest the conversation of the company gathered beside the wagon. But neither offered an opinion. Internal rumblings reminded Duane how hungry he was. He hoped the armies were miles apart and that they would remain here long enough to eat something. Even hard tack and coffee were better than nothing. But the information from the Arkansas soldier suggested otherwise – a heap of Arkansas regiments.

To the north, the midday quiet was shattered as artillery opened and began a bombardment in preparation for an attack.

"Something's happening," Johnny observed as he sat up to listen.

To the east another battery commenced firing.

"Sounds ta me we're in fer it," Duane added.

The artillery to the east concentrated its fire on the center of Sheridan's front. There was a sudden flurry of activity as Duane mounted his horse and Johnny unwrapped the reins. The company formed up quickly as the officers returned to their units to await further instructions.

A half hour passed as the Confederate artillery continued to fire upon the Union center. The units with the ambulance train could see the smoke rising from the landscape forward and to the right of their position. But the ground itself was just below their line of sight. Nonetheless, they heard the sustained clatter of musket fire and the Rebel yell and they knew the enemy was advancing rapidly in their direction. The quiet along the Union line was quickly shattered as Sheridan's regiments opened with musket and artillery fire.

The battle rolled onto the ridge like an early afternoon storm. The heavy musket fire poured out sheets of flame and a roiling cloud of smoke as bullets buzzed like hordes of bees tearing at the landscape, ripping at flesh, and shattering away bone. The Union line put down a heavy fire, tearing great gaps in the approaching Confederate lines. Yet still they came relentlessly onward, killing, maiming, wounding, threatening. As the roar and cry of battle rose upon the air, the walking and crawling wounded began to work their way toward the rear in search for help.

The men about the ambulance train quickly found themselves overwhelmed by the number of wounded. They were loaded into wagons and rushed to the nearby barnyard where the field hospital had been established. Others were attended on the spot and left to fend for themselves or lend a hand. Many collapsed in their efforts to seek help and remained where they fell as the battle raged about them.

Duane was kept busy helping those he could to hobble to an ambulance wagon or a gathering place where an assistant surgeon might help. He would locate the living lying about the area and call for help to move them. For some, all he could do was share a drop or two of water and a brief conversation while they died. The noise of battle wrapped the landscape in an awful envelope of deafening sound which cast such a spell on the boy's mind as to blot out fear with reflex reaction. He felt alone in a sea of combat which stretched about him like the sands of a desert.

He had knelt by a dying soldier, had given him water, had seen the picture of his family, had talked to him about the dry dust, had seen the breathing stop. As he stood to move on there came a tearing thump and a company's captain stumbled back against the boy. He broke the man's fall as he caught him in his arms, felt the blood, and saw that a cannon ball had torn away half his chest.

As the two fell back toward the ground, the boy caught his balance and broke their fall.

"Is it fatal?" the captain asked.

"Oh, I hope not," Duane replied. "But it sher does look bad." Yet to himself, the boy knew the wound was too severe to survive.

In an instant a corporal from the company was at their side.

"Help me git him ta a wagon," Duane ordered. The two moved the wounded officer to an ambulance which was nearly filled and was about to go bouncing off to the hospital.

Suddenly there was a commotion to the north side of the line. A Confederate advance was surging into a gap between the positions of General Sheridan and General McCook. There was a flurry of activity as batteries of cannon were rushed into position and set up to fire obliquely at the approaching enemy. Other artillery, already in position, was turned to block the attack. The guns opened fire with deadly results, cutting great holes in the Confederate brigades and forcing them to pull back.

Couriers were riding furiously up and down the two miles of battle from General McCook's division further north to General Sheridan's position in the center to General Crittenden's further south. Gradually the regiments along the center began to push forward. By mid-afternoon the attack was faltering and Sheridan's division was beginning to force the enemy back. By late afternoon the center had moved forward with one brigade entering the outskirts of the town itself before realizing it was dangerously overextended.

As darkness fell, the conflict dwindled to scattered firing between pockets of opposing troops in a mixed up battle line which saw units from both armies intermixed with each other.

As nightfall came a nearly full moon rose above the countryside. Scattered gunfire continued along the battle front. An eerie stillness hung on the carnage-littered landscape where the afternoon's fighting had been fiercest. Non-combatants roamed the blood-stained fields to find the living.

In the barnyard along the pike, surgeons and a corps of nursing personnel attempted to care for the wounded. The operating theater had been set up in one end of the barn while the rest was lined with rows of cots. As the ambulance wagons arrived, the living were brought in and laid out on the cots. The dead were laid out in neat rows in the barnyard. Even as the dead were unloaded from the wagons, others who had died in the hospital were being carried out to be added to the lineup. First care was given by nursing soldiers and a company of women nurses who traveled with the army. The surgeons were busy with amputations and suturing. They were fortunate to aid the suffering with chloroform which was used to saturate a cloth which was in turn placed over the victim's nose and mouth.

Duane knelt by a cot talking to a newly arrived soldier.

"Thanks," the man spoke as the boy helped him with a cup of water. "They took it off, didn't they." He tried to push up and look at the bandaged stump where his left foot once was.

"No sense ta movin much 'n gittin on the pain more," Duane placed a light hand on the man's chest. "It were a shattered mess an' weren't no way ta savin it. They's jest clor'formed ya out, saw'd off the mess, burned up the bleedin, 'n sew'd ya shut. Right smart work, too."

The man relaxed, then stiffened suddenly as pain shot up the leg. "Hurts like hell, Boy!" he squeezed through clenched teeth.

"Yes, Sir. I ain't no stranger ta bein shot up none. But ya bein the one thet's hurtin now, maybe I kin help some. Could be ya kin tell me yer name 'n unit so's we kin let som'on know as where yer at."

"Sure, Boy. But tell me where you got shot."

The two talked on while the activity of the hospital bustled about them. Duane wrote down the identity information requested of each wounded soldier, then excused himself and moved on to another.

As more wounded were brought in, a number of Confederate wounded were scattered about the makeshift ward. The level of commotion began to settle as night wore on and those who could, slept. Duane continued to move among the wounded. He heard a voice nearby.

"Boy," it whispered, "it ain't right." He motioned to the bandages around his abdomen. "It ain't stopped bleedin."

The boy paused, set down his bucket and dipper, then leaned over to inspect the bandages in the dim light. Crimson red had spread throughout and the saturated fabric was dripping blood onto the cot beneath.

"I'll fetch a surgeon," Duane said as he stood to go.

"Ain't much use ta thet, Boy. I figer it's pretty near blow'd away." Pain cut him off. Duane took out his pencil and paper and knelt by the head of the cot. "Boy," the youth whispered, "could ya git word ta ma folk 'n maybe git me shipped home?"

Duane waited while another wave of pain passed. He ain't much older 'n me, the boy thought. "What's yer name?" he asked aloud.

"Name's Avery, Avery Hill." He was so young. Long dark curls of hair wrapped around his ears and lay across his eyebrows. His face was so smooth. He couldn't be more than sixteen or seventeen. The dying youth continued, "Ma folks is good people. Pa couldn't fight none no more. He'd been with Price in Missouri an' was shot up bad. They sent him on home so's ta die. But he come 'round right good." The voice stopped. It was such a soft and gentle voice. How could one so gentle be involved in all this killing. He went on. "Now they run the dry goods store an I go off an die in this place. Please," pleading eyes, the color of emerald, focused on the boy's, "if'n ya kin, tell ma folks what happened 'n where I'm buried. They's Warden an Emma Hill in Bendton…"

"Arkansas!" Duane cut in.

"Yeh. How'd ya know?"

"I'm from north a there." Excitement knotted his insides as the boy asked, "Ya know my pa? He's Sergeant Andrew Kinkade."

The youth smiled. "Wish I'd time ta hear yer story." His voice grew faint as he barely whispered, "He ain't no more. He's a captain now." A smile creased the lips as they stilled with the last knowledge of having shared good news. The light left the eyes as the young body settled in the silence of death.

A painful lump caught in Duane's throat as he fought back his tears and reached out to close the sightless eyes.

*   *   *

A soft brilliance bathed the countryside as a nearly full moon shone in the crystal darkness twinkling with its infinite sparkling of stars. The land was littered with the wreckage of war. The dead, the dying, the wounded – beast and human; broken wagons, limbers, cannon, and caisson; abandoned packs, equipment, weapons, and personal belongings lay scattered about – debris in the aftermath of battle. Through this passed the road that was the Springfield Pike. A lone horseman rode slowly along the pike in the early hours of the new day. He paused to stare in disbelief at the vastness of the destruction.

Duane had left the bedside of the dead youth to return to the supply wagon, gather his belongings, scribble a hasty note to Johnny, saddle Jeremiah, and prepare to return to the Confederate Army and find his pa. He had ridden beyond the Union lines where most of the soldiers had wrapped themselves in their blankets and fallen asleep on the ground. The chill of autumn hung on the air, but no fires burned to show the enemy where to aim their cannons. As the boy passed through the fields and hills where the battle had raged a few hours earlier, he was astounded by the vastness of the devastation. For the first time in his life he saw the extent of the aftermath of full battle. He stopped and stared in disbelief at the eerie stillness, then moved on.

Duane approached the Confederate position with caution. He intended to be seen clearly in the moonlight and to be challenged by the soldiers on picket duty. Within he felt nervously excited. Someone should challenge him any second. But he was met by silence only. He stopped to search the landscape for some sign of the army. There was none, only empty silence. Suddenly he realized what no one in the Federal line even suspected – the Confederate army had retreated. The battle was over. Sadly the boy turned his horse about and headed back toward the Union line and the continuing task of attending the wounded.

It was week's end before the first unit of cavalry was dispatched in pursuit of the Confederate force. On Sunday the army began to follow and was totally underway by Monday. The pursuit was slow and arduous over rocky roads and rough terrain. After seven days, the order of movement was changed as General Buell ordered his army to Nashville. They had over-extended their supply lines and were unable to continue as an effective force. Three days later, President Lincoln ordered a change of commanding generals and Buell turned his army over to General William Rosecrans.

As October drifted to a close, rains began to bring an end to the drought with snow falling further east. General Rosecrans continued to move the army toward Nashville where it would be possible to stop and bring in new supplies in preparation for a new confrontation with Bragg's army. At the same time, the Confederate army had paused in Knoxville after two hundred miles of retreat over rough and muddy roads with 15,000 of its soldiers suffering extremely from exposure and illness; then had begun to move toward Murfreesboro by way of Chattanooga.

*　　*　　*

On Monday evening, October 20th, the various divisions of Buell's army were preparing for the long march to Nashville. The evening air was cool and damp. Soldiers huddled about their company campfires, more for warmth than food. There was little to eat other than what had been foraged during the day's travels. Duane and his companions had been sharing what they had with a mess group of nearly two dozen men and officers. This time it was a chicken with some ears of field corn which had been found in a broken corn crib, coffee, and some very infested and solid hardtack.

"That was nearly a feast," a young bewhiskered Sergeant Keller complimented.

A corporal pushed toward the fire with an iron pot of water. Placing it on the hot coals he instructed, "Throw in the bones, boys. We can boil up a pot of broth then throw in the crackers and cook out the weevils."

Laughter rippled through the group.

"How about a cup of coffee?" Marshalton asked as he held his cup toward Johnny, the closest to the pot.

"Sure thing," the boy replied as he poured the steaming brew.

Duane sat across from his friends on a stump of wood sucking the last morsels from a wing tip. Adding his contribution to the pot, he licked the tips of his fingers before wiping them on his trousers.

"Dee, you wanta share my coffee for some hardtack while we wait for the chicken pot?" the lieutenant offered.

"If'n yer fer doin the same, then's fit by me," the boy replied.

"Bring yours around and join me." He moved away from the nearest soldier to make room. "How about you, Johnny?"

"Coming."

The three squeezed together around the steaming cup. Each in turn dunked his biscuit and waited while it softened and the weevils it contained scrambled out in the hot coffee to escape the heat. They littered the surface of the liquid, wiggling frantically as they scalded to death and the lieutenant skimmed them off with his fingers, tossing them into the fire. When all three had thus cleansed their hardtack and consumed it, the officer checked for any remaining specks which he removed, then drank the coffee from the cup.

Others in the party waited for the chicken pot to come to a boil.

"Is this a good time?" Johnny spoke quietly to the lieutenant.

"Guess so. Fetch the package. And you best bring a lamp too." As he rose to his feet, the man set the tin cup on his camp stool and addressed the boy. "Dee, come on to the wagon a minute."

"Sher," Duane replied. "What ya plannin fer?"

"Just come along. You'll know real soon."

The two wandered over to the wagon carrying the lieutenant's quarters and medical supplies, where Johnny was waiting for them. Soft light from a candle lamp cast a circle of warmth in the darkness of evening. "I know how much you hurt when you didn't get to find your pa at Perryville and figured from what you said that your birthday's coming soon," Dan stated.

"Yeh, I'm ta twelve come Tuesday next."

"Well, we've been working on this for you since then and figure tonight's a good time, before we start a new trek come tomorrow," Johnny added as he held out the package. "Go ahead and open it."

Duane took the package which had been wrapped in the paper lining from a medicine supply crate. It was soft and rustled noisily in his hands.

"Well, open it," Dan encouraged.

The younger boy tore open the paper and found a set of clothes within. Laying the pieces across the edge of the wagon's tailgate, he found them to be a newly altered uniform – a grey uniform.

"How'd ya do this?" He fingered the fabric and found it was soft from wear. "Where from ya git the pieces?"

"Quite a few were killed back there," Johnny explained. "I know you can't see it too good in the night, but we found parts and insignia so that we could put together a whole uniform and hat and coat and everything in your size. Well, maybe a bit big. But you'll grow into it pretty fast."

"I know that's for sure," Dan added. "Twelve's a real growing year. When you can see it better, you'll see we found insignia to make it an Arkansas regiment and we made it the thirteenth."

For a moment no one spoke as Duane searched for the insignia and tried to turn it so the dim candle light would allow him to see it clearly. He would have to wait for daylight. "Thanks," he whispered.

"It shouldn't be too long before the armies lay in for the winter. Then you can put on your new uniform and ride off to join Bragg's army." Dan was confident his prediction would come true.

"I'll bet you and your pa will be together by the new year," Johnny added. "And maybe he'll get leave so you two can go home."

"I sher hope so," Duane stated. "Where kin we put this fer now?"

"I'll put it in my clothes chest till later," the lieutenant offered.

Duane handed the bundle to his friend. He stood awkwardly a moment, wanting to show how much he really cared, but not sure how. Then he reached his arms around the man's waist and the two embraced in a firm bear hug.

"Me, too?" Johnny asked.

They both reached out to include the older boy. The three stood holding one another for a brief but wonderfully warm moment.

"You two go back to the fire," Dan instructed. "I'll be right along."

When the three had gathered once more with the others at the fire, they found them busy removing the bones from the boiling pot.

"We're ready for the hardtack, now," the sergeant stated. "But pound it up first so's it can help to thicken the soup."

The group settled to the task of finishing preparations. First the crackers were pounded to powder on the ends of stumps using musket butts for hammers. As the crumbs were dumped into the pot, the vermin were skimmed off the surface and the soup was set aside to cool.

A harmonica came out and the soldiers passed the evening in song. Elsewhere across the landscape regimental bands began to play. The night was filled with music and song. The soup cooled. Finally one band began to play HOME SWEET HOME and was joined by all the rest. The gathering about the fire dipped their cups of soup and sipped silently as the bands concluded their melody.

While the last strands of music faded on the night, the empty cups were gathered in the empty pot and the tired men turned to settle in for the night. Most wrapped themselves in their coats and blankets and bedded down on the ground about the fire. The boys slept under the wagon, the lieutenant beside a wheel. Whispered conversations drifted to silence as burglers about the camps sounded TAPS.

*　　*　　*

The end of the first week of November saw the first of Rosecran's army arriving at Nashville. Encampments were established in and around the city as the veteran regiments settled in for a period of rest and the recruits found themselves in training. The river was still too low to navigate and the railroads continued to be interrupted by Confederate cavalry raids. The general, therefore, sent trains of wagons north to bring supplies for his army.

Meanwhile, General Bragg's army continued its march while the general arranged for supplies to be sent ahead to Murfreesboro, a town about forty miles from the city of Nashville. The vanguard units of the Confederate army began arriving in Murfreesboro near the end of the third week where it set its camp, rested, and was resupplied.

As November closed, the two armies were encamped and resting about forty miles apart from each other. While the armies rested and recovered from weeks of hardship, the Confederate cavalry continued to harass the Federal lines of supply. Rains turned to snow as the weather turned bitter cold. The ground became snowcovered and the rivers began to ice. Winter was setting in.

*   *   *

Duane buckled on his gunbelt and shifted the holster until it hung comfortably. "Well?" he asked, looking up at his friends seated before him on chair and stool within the lieutenant's tent.

"You sure look smart in that uniform," Dan commented. "How's it feel?"

"Real good," the boy replied. "May be it's a mite big, but it does feel real good. Yer right smart lookin, too, Johnny."

"Thanks, Dee." He stood and looked at the lieutenant. "Guess we're ready."

"The wagon's hitched and waiting outside," Dan stated as he pushed himself from his chair. "Bundle up warm. It's real cold." Grabbing an extra blue overcoat from the wooden tree beside his desk, he offered it to the younger boy. "You best wear this over your uniform. We wouldn't want to cause any trouble. There's some wouldn't care to see a grey uniform without putting you under arrest."

"Thanks." Duane accepted the coat and slipped it on over the new grey uniform.

"I'll drop you two on the edge of town, then head over to meet the rest of the supply train at the N and L depot. Soon as you're finished at the photographer's, you come over and meet me there."

The three finished bundling into overcoats, hats, scarves, and gloves. They left the comfort of the tent for overcast cold with its snow flurries drifting on windless air. The wagon team snorted its impatience to get underway. Pausing long enough to tie the tent flaps shut against the weather, the three climbed aboard the covered wagon. The boys huddled in the wagon bed behind the seat as the man took up the reins, released the brake, and cracked the team into motion.

Rumbling along the snow-covered roadway, the iron tires were muffled against the gravel camp lanes and main road. It was a half mile to the intersection where the boys disembarked. They found themselves traveling the side of a busy street which carried them through a small residential area on their way to the business district of small shops and storefronts. Companies of Federal soldiers marched the street on their way to duty assignments. Smaller groups patrolled the area on police duty. Residents of Nashville went about their business, but paused frequently to hurl insults at the troops. A gang of neighborhood boys marched along beside a company of soldiers, mimicking and insulting as they went. At one point an upstairs window flew open as a sharp-tongued woman cursed the soldiers and emptied a chamber pot in their direction. The contents fell harmlessly into the snow pile at the gutter.

Johnny and Duane observed the commotion casually as they continued at a quick pace along the opposite side of the street.

"How far ya reckon we gotta go?" Duane asked.

"Seems to me the shop's about three or four more streets yet," Johnny replied.

"'Tain't much of a friendly town," Duane continued. "Sher don't care ta be part a their funnin."

"Me neither," Johnny added. "This whole country side ain't at all hospitable. The Rebs burnt five riverboats the other day and also wrecked a train on the Nashville and Louisville up north of here."

As the two crossed the intersection, the company turned away from them and headed up a side street.

"I kin see why Dan's not asked about us headin out ta Murfreesboro," Duane observed.

"And with Mister Lincoln pushing Old Rosy to go after Bragg's army, it's still too likely we'll be into another battle before Christmas." Johnny trudged along with his hands jammed deep into his pockets. "But there's just as good a chance that winter'll mean we stay here until spring."

They had reached the walk on the other side of the intersection when a voice challenged from across the street.

"Hey, Frankie, look it yonder what I see walkin on Nashville streets!"

"Yeh, if it ain't a couple a Yanks. Let's go boys. No Yank refuse is allowed to foul our city."

There was general agreement as the gang of eight rushed across the busy street, dodging wagons and horses in their attempt to catch the two boys in blue overcoats.

"What ya think, Johnny. They seem much like a danger ta ya?"

"Bunch of loud mouths, Dee. We'll ignor them less they start to throw punches. I know it'll be hard to not answer them back, but it'll be harder on them if we don't say nothing."

The strategy was agreed to and the boys continued to walk as the local youth caught up with them and surrounded them. Duane and Johnny kept moving, forcing the boy in front to walk backwards in order to keep from getting pushed aside.

A freckle-faced red-head of about fifteen seemed to be in charge. "We got us a pair a jackasses."

"Sher does seem so, Frankie," a high-pitched ten-year-old squeaked. "They smells pretty bad, too. Like maybe they's rolled some in a cow pasture."

Another added, "We don't take ta sech dirt on ar walks. Best head these two ta the gutter where they b'long."

"We's talkin ta ya, Yank trash!" Frankie shouted. "Ya don't seem ta listen much good."

"Ya gotta git a ass's attention fust," a taller boy suggested as he shoved Duane off balance.

Duane said nothing as he staggered to regain his balance. Johnny grabbed his friend's arm to steady him as they continued without stopping. The two exchanged a quick glance and short smile in common acknowledgment that they were getting the best of their tormenters.

"We're talking ta ya!" Frankie snapped as he grabbed Duane by the shoulder and spun him around. The coat pulled open and the youth caught sight of the uniform underneath. "What the Hell ya doin in one a ar uniforms!"

"He's gotta gun, Frankie!" a black-haired youth exclaimed as another lunged for the weapon.

Duane grabbed the boy's wrist and squeezed tightly on the bones.

"Ow!" the boy cried.

As the commotion unfolded, pedestrian traffic detoured around the group, avoiding any interference, yet privately and smugly satisfied that their local youth were showing those two Yanks.

"Grab em!" Frankie ordered.

Johnny slammed his foot down on the toes of the first to approach him while Duane twisted his attacker's arm to force the boy to turn around, then shoved him hard into the next two youths.

"Ya all hold on jest as you is!" Duane ordered, pulling his coat closed to cover the revolver.

"You best do as he says to," Johnny added. "Now we ain't given you no cause for such unkindness. But just to set things a little straighter, only one of us is a Yank. That's me. Dee, here's a Reb. And a powerful more of a Reb than any of you poor excuses of humanity."

"What the Hell ya doin in a Yank coat if yer ain't no Yank?" Frankie asked.

"Ya git yer friends to be civil and kindly like 'n I'll think on givin a answer." Duane stood with his back against a tree while Johnny stayed close at his side.

"All right," the red-head raised his hand. "Hol' off boys 'n we hear what we got."

Before any more was said a voice was heard from the street. "Seize that pack of dogs," a lieutenant ordered.

Suddenly the boys were surrounded by a company of soldiers who grabbed Frankie and his companions and dragged them away toward the street. Duane and Johnny found themselves alone by the tree as they realized with surprise the unexpected change of events.

"Dare we save them?" Johnny asked his friend.

"Do seem like justice thet they was took so quick like," Duane smiled. "But I guess we might."

They turned from behind the tree to call to the lieutenant and were shocked by the spectacle before them. The soldiers were beating and kicking the boys who had been thrown to the ground where they writhed in pain crying for help. The torment continued and an angry crowd quickly gathered.

"Let them be!" Johnny shouted.

"No way, Boy!" the lieutenant replied. "They deserve what they're getting. It's time folks around here got back some of what they give out!" Angered, Duane drew his revolver and fired once into the air, then aimed it at the lieutenant. The loud report of the gunshot was followed by stunned silence.

"Lieutenant!" Duane called, "ya've done yer duty. Ya best git yer company an be goin."

A dozen soldiers leveled their muskets at the boy as angry observers stepped in front of Duane to block their line of sight and the boy drew back the hammer on his weapon.

"Order yer men ta put down. I ain't fer eny killin here."

"You're under arrest, Boy!" the lieutenant shouted. "Put your weapon down before someone gets hurt!"

"Yer the one 'll git hurt," a woman called from the gathering crowd.

"Come on, Ladies," another challenged. "This Yank garbage can't do no better than pick on children an womenfolk. We'll show 'em a fight!"

Angry jeers followed as the rest of the soldiers turned their attention from the boys on the street lying dazed in the bloodied snow to their muskets and the crowd before them.

"Aim low!" the lieutenant ordered as weapons were leveled.

"Hold on, Lieutenant," an authoritative voice interrupted from the side as an officer in blue uniform stepped forth from the crowd.

Duane heaved a sigh of relief as Johnny lay a nervous hand on his shoulder. "God, Dee, you've really caused one Hell of a mess."

"I figger'd sech. But damn it ta Hell, Johnny, what fer should I of done. They was gonna kill 'em. I seen it in ther eyes. They was fixin ta put all ther hate on them boys 'n no one show'd a sense ta knowin what was happenin even as they was lookin on."

The man that stepped forward was tall and slender. A beard of brown was even and full, and neatly trimmed. One sleeve of his overcoat hung empty.

"If you don't order your troopers to shoulder their weapons and stand to attention, that boy's going to blow a hole through you, Lieutenant. Are you sure you want to die today, Lieutenant?" The officer approached to a safe distance in case gunfire were to erupt.

"Do as the colonel says!" the lieutenant ordered nervously. "But that boy is my prisoner!"

Everyone present seemed to start breathing again at the same instant as the soldiers lowered their muskets, eased the hammers down, and did as ordered.

"Put your gun away, Lad," the colonel called to Duane. To the lieutenant he continued, "Not to be, Lieutenant. Those boys are attached to the medical staff of the First Brigade under General Sheridan. They're only following their instincts and trying to save lives. Besides, you'll be happy to note that the one who drew on you is known personally by the general."

The boy did as instructed, very much surprised at all the colonel said. Even so, he and Johnny remained where they were, keeping a safe distance from the lieutenant and his troops.

"Go ahead, Lieutenant," the officer ordered. "Take your company and clear out. Go about whatever business you're headed for. But get away from here. Now!"

The junior officer ordered his company into motion and within minutes was disappearing down the street. The crowd had grown to scores of citizens. Most began to disperse as several moved forward to attend the injured boys lying in the blood-splattered snow.

Duane and Johnny stood shaking in the realization of the intense danger that had just ended as the colonel approached them.

"How is it you know us?" Johnny asked.

"My name's Colonel Sherman of the 88th Illinois. I saw you boys in action at Perryville. That was a very foolish thing you did just now."

"I reckon so, Sir," Duane acknowledged. "But I couldn't come ta no other way ta stop them."

"How did you happen along?" Johnny asked as he glanced over at the boys being looked after by a dozen of the spectators.

"They'll be cared for by their people," Colonel Sherman advised. "We best move on." He turned the boys away from the scene of the incident and walked with them as he explained, "I pulled my shoulder the other day and was feeling need of a quiet walk." He indicated his other arm as he revealed it resting in a sling under his coat. "The snowfall was pretty so I decided on a walk to town. Might even have my picture took and send it back to the family."

"That's where we were headed before this all started," Johnny volunteered.

"I'll walk a ways with you, then, just to keep you out of trouble."

The trio continued along the walk and was soon lost from the scene of commotion as they blended with the pedestrian crowd and faded into the mist of falling flurries.

*   *   *

The large mess tent was noisy with the dinner conversations of some two hundred men from the companies of the 36th Illinois.

"I guess I was like everyone else in the crowd," Colonel Sherman was saying to the lieutenant seated beside him at a table of regimental officers. "We were shocked at the treatment the soldiers were giving the boys, but used to such harshness because of the war. Your boy was right; no one realized at first that they weren't going to stop until those boys were dead."

"Colonel, I say it again. I can't tell you how much I appreciate your stepping in when you did."

"You know, Lieutenant, that was a mighty foolish thing your boy did. Drawing on an officer is a punishable offense." He paused to drink form his cup of coffee. "But I must give him credit, he's a Hell-of-a brave lad. By the way, how did the pictures turn out."

"They're real nice. I have one of each of the boys. They each have one of the other. And we had a picture done for Dee's pa." Dan cut a piece of the salt pork while he spoke.

"By the way, where are those boys?" the colonel asked.

The lieutenant indicated a table with his fork as he finished chewing the piece of meat. Swallowing, he responded, "They're seated over there with Captain Willy Tomlin and his guests. Did I tell you he was up north this morning and ran into a couple of musicians off the river boats. Call themselves the Gum Tree Jug Band. The boat they were playing was burned in the raid the other day, so the captain figured we could use some entertainment in the camps. They're playing for the 36th after supper. Could be your boys can put them up tomorrow."

"Sounds good enough. But I'll hear them play first."

The evening drifted on in lazy comfort. Duane and Johnny entertained Captain Tomlin and the musicians, Alex Sladkin and Ethan French, with the adventure of the day. After the meal was cleared up, the trestle tables were taken down and the benches rearranged as more men and officers of the regiment gathered in the large tent for the entertainment. Colonel Nicholas Greusel, commander of the 36th, and several of his staff officers joined those already at the table with Marshalton and Sherman. Captain Tomlin and the boys helped the jug band set up.

The entertainment was great fun. Alex was tall and gangling looking while his counterpart, Ethan, was robust and broad-shouldered, but without the same height. Their songs were a combination of the currently popular minstrel music of Foster and a number of tunes the regimental bands played. CAMPTOWN RACES countered with WHEN JOHNNY COMES MARCHING HOME. And they did play on crock jugs, as well as a washboard, harmonica, banjo, wash tub base, saw, and motley variety of musical appliances. They had with them a trunk full of hats of all descriptions which they'd picked up in their travels and frequently paused to dress the band. After an hour and a half of entertaining, the jug band invited members of the audience to join them and continued for another hour with rotating membership. All present had an enjoyable evening with many laughs and many cups of coffee. The air was thick with pipe and cigar smoke and the smell of kerosene lamps and burning tobacco.

The jug band finished with HOME SWEET HOME as everyone present joined in the sing-along. Then the boys helped to pack up as the hundreds who made up the audience departed toward their tents.

"Well, Francis, what did you think?" Colonel Gruesel asked.

"Damn good, Nicholas. To answer your earlier question, Lieutenant, yes. We will host your guests tomorrow."

"With less than two weeks to Christmas, the least we can do is entertain the men," Gruesel stated. He rose to his feet and the rest of the table did likewise. "It would be so nice to allow the men some leave time for the holiday, but General Sill was informed that the Confederates are entertaining their President Davis at Murfreesboro."

"Where does that put us?" Marshalton inquired.

Several in the group had departed. The regimental commanders were buttoning their overcoats as they prepared to leave.

"General Rosecrans insists this army isn't quite ready yet," Colonel Sherman responded. "But Halleck and Lincoln keep pressuring him. We'll likely move on Bragg's army before another week is out." He put on his hat and wrapped a scarf around his neck. "Good night, Lieutenant." The colonel pulled on his gloves. "You look after those boys and see they stay out of trouble."

"Good night, Colonel. Thanks again."

The senior officers departed as Dan wandered over to check on the boys' progress. All had been packed and the five were standing about talking and laughing.

"Enjoyed your show," the lieutenant complimented.

"Come on, Boys. Time to turn in."

They exchanged farewells as the captain departed with his two guests and the lieutenant and the boys left for their quarters.

The tent was empty and dim as only a half dozen smoky lanterns remained lighted. Most of the others had come and gone with the members of the various companies. The remainder had consumed their fuel and gone out.

Quiet settled across the camps as the candle lamps were put out and campfires settled to glowing coals. A thin blanket of snow, churned up along the maze of company streets covered tents and wagons and woodpiles. The flurries had ended and a dark starry sky cast a feeble glow from a quarter moon across a sleeping army.

*   *   *

Christmas season advanced slowly for the soldiers in a routine of drills, musters, guard and picket duty. The weather turned wet and raw with an occasional day of sunshine. Time not spent on duties was needed to keep in a supply of firewood for stoves and fires, or to supplement meager rations through hunting and scavenging.

The day before Christmas was cold and blustery. Overcast skies dropped brief dustings of snow flurries to dance in the raw windy air.

Outside the lieutenant's quarters, Dan and the boys were gathering in preparation of a wood-gathering expedition.

"Did anyone bring the saw?" the man asked.

"I thought you had it," Johnny replied.

"No, it's in the back of the supply tent."

"I'll git it," Duane offered. "Here, Johnny, hold the ax."

In a few minutes, all was in readiness. Duane returned with a hefty tree saw which had a post at the end for a second person to help in operating. All were bundled in layers of clothes with scarves to tie down hat brims around the ears and gloves to keep hands warm. Others of the camp were departing to do some hunting.

Suddenly the commotion of activity was interrupted by a distant gunshot.

"Wher'd thet come from?" Duane asked.

"Sounds like the guard posted on the main road," the lieutenant answered.

"Only one shot," Johnny observed. "Probably trying to get some supper."

The others chuckled at the thought of some hapless rabbit or squirrel dashing for cover up a tree or into a hedgerow.

Activity continued as various parties departed on their errands. The trio shouldered their tools and started down the company street.

"Lieutenant!" an officer called from some fifty yards out of the camp. "This boy's looking for your boys!"

He indicated a youngster running in their direction, crying hysterically for them to stop.

"Oh God, ya gotta he'p me!" he sobbed. "They shot ma broth'r!"

"Who?" the lieutenant asked.

The boy ignored him. "The man said ya was fer savin lives. Ya gotta save ma broth'r!"

"What man?" Johnny asked. "Why us?"

"Ya was there! Ya sav'd me 'n ma friends from the sold'ers! Ya gotta save ma broth'r!"

"Thet day in Nashville," Duane figured. "Ya was one a thet gang."

"Never mind," Dan interrupted. "What's happened?"

Tears streamed down the face of the boy. "The guard shot Taylor right in the belly! We was jest out huntin. Now he's back there bleedin an dyin. Please save him!"

"Okay, let's see what we can do," the surgeon comforted. Turning toward the tents, he cupped his hands to his mouth and called, "Captain Tomlin!"

The man poked his head out the front flaps. "What's up?"

"Need your help! A boy's been shot!"

"Be right there!"

There was little time to get acquainted as Dan took charge and began giving directions on what to do.

Captain Tomlin and Duane were to go with the boy and bring in his brother. Johnny and the lieutenant would prepare the mess tent as a temporary surgical theater.

Several others nearby were sent to build up the fires in the stoves of the mess tent and to gather and prepare whatever lamps were handy. One was sent to a nearby pond for a bucket of ice.

"This way!" the boy urged. "Hurry!"

The three ran toward the guard post on the outer edge of the camp road. They quickly covered the quarter mile distance and observed a small crowd of curious as they approached.

Colonel Sherman had already arrived and knelt on the cold ground beside the boy. He had covered the still form with his overcoat and was gently caressing the long dark curls in the hope of getting a response.

A young corporal sat on a fence rail nearby and stared numbly at the small form lying silent on the ground. His lips trembled in uncontrolled shock. His hands were opening and closing in constant motion. Periodically he stated to no one in particular, "He had a gun. Was running at me with a gun."

Someone emerged from the crowd toward the lone soldier. It was obvious he was a friend as he tried to comfort the distressed youth.

The colonel stood as the captain and the boys arrived.

"Looks pretty bad, Captain. He's been gut-shot. Bleeding seems to have slowed. But he's slipping away fast."

"Can you help us get him back to the mess tent? Lieutenant Marshalton's setting up hospital there right now."

"We held this wagon which was headed out. You can take him back that way more quickly. But it'll be rough."

A freight wagon was waiting beside the road. The younger brother had dropped beside the unconscious Taylor and was pleading with him to talk. The fallen boy was perhaps a year older than Duane. He lay on his back as he had fallen from the impact of the bullet. Duane knelt with the younger brother and pulled the coat aside to get a look at the wound. Bright red blood had soaked the waistband of his trousers and the fabric of his shirt. It was fresh with a heavy wetness.

"Captain, we best git movin," Duane suggested.

"Colonel," Tomlin instructed, "pass him to me in the wagon and I'll see if I can soften the ride some."

"As you wish," Sherman acknowledged.

Carefully, the officer and an aide lifted the limp figure from the ground and placed him on a pad of blankets and canvass which the doctor had fashioned. The body hung limp like a freshly killed deer, as he was carried and laid in the wagon. Colonel Sherman lifted the younger brother over the side boards, then climbed up to the wagon seat with the driver. His aid passed up the boy's hunting shotgun, then stayed behind to attend to the aftermath of the incident.

The ride back was short. On the way the younger boy introduced himself as Leigh Brooks. He was the tall gangling ten-year-old from the incident with Frankie's gang. His brother had not been there that day because he had a clerking job at a feed store and had been working.

Upon arriving at the mess tent, the wounded boy was rushed inside where Lieutenant Marshalton had set up his surgery on a plank and trestle table surrounded by lanterns hanging from the ridge pole overhead or posts pounded into the hard dirt floor. The room was warmed comfortably by well-fed wood stoves. A clean cotton sheet covered the operating table. As Tomlin and Sherman carried Taylor in, Johnny and the lieutenant stripped off his boots and trousers, tossing them onto the floor out of the way. Leigh stood back and watched in awe at the swift activity which prepared his brother for the surgeon. As soon as he had been placed on the white surface, the rest of his clothing was stripped away except for his johns. These were cut down with a pair of scissors to bare the boy's abdomen for whatever might be done to save his life.

"Wash your hands in that basin," Dan instructed. The captain and Duane did as they were told.

"It's whiskey!" the captain exclaimed.

"It's all whiskey," the other pointed out as he indicated containers of implements and other basins with clean cloths alongside. "I don't know if it's coincidence or what, but working with whiskey seems to lessen infections."

Marshalton took charge of his surgical team which consisted of Doctor Tomlin and himself assisted by Johnny and Duane. The colonel stayed to watch and kept Leigh company as they sat at a nearby table. Others who had followed the incident stayed to await the outcome. They sat silently to the side as all attention was focused on the operation.

"I've never tried to repair this kind of damage before," the lieutenant observed. "I can only ask God's help and trust in Him to guide my hands. Use those extra sheets to cover the boy except where we're working and try to keep him warm."

Taylor's chest and arms were covered as were his legs and feet. The doctor began by rinsing clean cloths in a basin of brew and sponging the area around the wound. The bullet had entered the boy's abdomen above the right hip, tearing through flesh and muscle and intestine until it passed between two floating ribs on its way out his back.

"Drop the points of those ice picks through the stove plates into the fire so they can heat while we work," the surgeon instructed. "Then I want you to tie up cloths of ice from that bucket and pack them around the wound."

The boys moved to carry out the instructions while the two doctors inspected the wound. Removing a large rubber suction bulb from a container of liquid, the lieutenant squeezed it empty and passed it to the captain. While the one removed intestinal fluids from the wound, the other packed the ice cloths against the boy's side. Cloths were wrung damp and laid under the exit hole in the boy's back to absorb drainage from the abdominal cavity.

As the hours passed and the primitive surgical team attempted to work a miracle, word of the incident passed around the camp. Soldiers with nothing else to do gathered about outside or inside to wait or watch. A reverent quiet settled about the tent. Other medical personal arrived to watch.

The two doctors did things they had never thought of before for reasons beyond their understanding, improvising as they went with the tools they had at hand. Probes were bent and wrapped with bandages to use as hooks to hold open the wound as the two cut a larger incision to go in and repair the internal damage. Small blood vessels were cauterized with the hot ice picks to control bleeding. With tweezers, needles, and cat gut thread, the torn intestines were sewn back together. Slivers of bone from a rib splintered by the bullet, were carefully removed. As the two worked their way out, layers of muscle tissue were sewn closed; then, finally, the entry wound was closed. Carefully, Taylor was rolled on his side and the exit wound was repaired. Clean bandages were wrapped around the boy's abdomen to hold large pads of linen over the wounds.

Somehow Taylor survived the surgery and continued to cling to life.

"We've done all we can," the lieutenant stated. "I'm not sure I know what we did, Willy, but he's still alive."

"Yeh," the captain acknowledged. "I don't even remember half of what we did. It was almost like a dream and I had no control over what was happening."

"It seemed that way to me, too," Dan agreed. "You boys help the captain clean up while I see to the brother and talk to the colonel."

Johnny spread the sheets used to cover the boy's arms and legs, then added a blanket. Dan found a towel to wipe the blood and smell from his hands and turned to the table where Leigh and Colonel Sherman waited.

"Cup of coffee?" a corporal offered. He had just poured from a pot on one of the stoves.

"Thanks," the man accepted. Then to the two at the table, "Your brother's still alive, Leigh. But I honestly don't know how or why."

Tears overflowed as the boy tried to speak. "Thank ya, Sir," he choked. The colonel put a comforting arm around the boy and pulled him close. "Ya... were... right," the boy sobbed.

Whispered conversations broke the silence as some stepped outside and shouted, "He lives! The boy still lives!"

The tenseness of the waiting gave way to cheers and shouts of joy. There were tears, too, from men who were touched deeply by this miracle of life. The afternoon call to muster began to sound throughout the division camps. Slowly the gathering dispersed as the soldiers departed toward their gathering areas to prepare for the evening colors and pass in review.

"What are his chances, Lieutenant?" Sherman asked, still holding the younger boy close at his side.

"Colonel, I honestly don't know. He really shouldn't be with us now." He sipped from the cup of coffee. "We can put him in with the boys for tonight. If he makes it till morning, he should be moved to his home where he can get good nursing while he heals. Someone needs to get this one home and let his family know where he is."

"I'll see to this one and the family. You tend to things here." The colonel rose from his seat.

"Kin I see ma broth'r?" Leigh asked.

"Come on," the doctor invited.

The three walked across to the young patient lying on the temporary table. Leigh saw how pale his brother looked and how still he lay. The boy stared hard at the covers, searching for some movement of his brother's breathing. A very slight rise and fall gave evidence of slow and shallow breathing.

"Yer gonna make it, Taylor," he whispered. "I jest know it." A smile, a tear, and a sniffle showed the joy the younger boy felt as he looked up at the doctor. "Ya did it, Sir. Ya saved ma broth'r." He wiped another tear from his eye. "We gotta go, Colonel."

"I'll check back with you," the senior officer stated.

"Thank you, Sir," Dan returned.

A few remained after the colonel had departed. They helped move the boy to the supply tent using the table planks as a stretcher. There he was lifted by the sheets and placed on Johnny's cot for the night. Extra blankets were added for warmth as the trip through the windy cold had chilled everyone en route.

The mess tent was returned to service and the evening routine of the camp settled back to normal.

Night fell. A cold wind slapped at the tent canvass and sent a chilling draft across the floor. Duane and Johnny sat on Duane's cot playing checkers by the light of the kerosene lamp as they sat up with the young patient. He had not moved since his arrival. His breathing seemed to lessen. Periodic checks by the lieutenant and the captain found no new bleeding.

Throughout the camp soldiers celebrated Christmas eve by gathering about their campfires in song and music. Several bands entertained with a variety of popular songs and military marches.

Sometime in the last hour before midnight an expectant silence seemed to gather as the winds died away to stillness. Johnny stood from the bed and stretched cramped muscles. He glanced at Taylor and saw he was still breathing, then turned and walked to the door.

Pushing a flap aside with his hand, he gazed toward the sky.

"Dee," he whispered, "you should see the stars. It's clear as crystal and really beautiful."

The younger boy rose, stretched, and joined his friend at the door opening. Looking up, he smiled in appreciation of the sparkling brilliance in velvet blackness. Suddenly a shooting star streaked earthward from high above the great dipper, flaring into an intense brightness like a fourth of July rocket, then fading quickly to nothing. A moment passed. Far-off church bells began to ring in Christmas. A distant band erupted into HARK THE HERALD ANGELS SING. More joined in until music and bells filled the night air with celebration. There was a rustling from within the tent. "Am I in heaven?" a weak voice asked.

Johnny and Duane exchanged surprised joy.

"Lord, no!" Johnny exclaimed.

"Ya's here on earth an tis Christmas mornin," Duane added.

The two moved quickly to kneel at their patient's bed.

"Don't move," Johnny advised.

"Where am I? It seems I was shot, but I can't come ta mind if 'n I hurt 'r not." His voice seemed stronger.

The three began to talk at once, Taylor in search of an explanation and the others in their joy that he was getting stronger. Outside, the bands and bells fell silent and the jingle of trace chains echoed on the night. A wagon and riders approached. Stopping at the lieutenant's tent, there was the sound of soft conversation, then approaching footsteps. Duane rushed to the door to see who was coming and to share the news with Lieutenant Marshalton.

"He's awake," the boy called.

"He is!?"

"Hurry up!"

"Let's see!"

"Thank God!" a woman's voice cried.

Leigh and his parents, along with Colonel Sherman, rushed inside to see the boy as Duane remained to stand with the lieutenant and look on. Johnny stepped back, turned up the wick on the lamp, then went to join his friends at the door. Dan pulled the boys close as the three watched the joyous reunion. Tears slipped quietly down his cheeks as he touched his chin to the top of Johnny's head.

"Merry Christmas," he whispered.

"Merry Christmas," each whispered back.

*　　*　　*

Christmas day became a day of planning. During the early part of the day, attention was focused on preparations for Taylor's recovery. It would be many weeks before he would be up and about, yet each passing hour brought increasing strength in spirit and voice.

Evening saw a different sort of planning. General Rosecrans announced that he was ready to move on the Confederate Army. All were to be on the road by dawn the next morning. Heavy rain fell during the night. In the cold grey pre-dawn, the army began to move.

General Sheridan's division was underway before sunup, moving with those under Major-General McCook along the Nolensville Pike in route to Triune. Daylight had hardly come when the first encounter with the enemy occurred. At 7AM upon arriving at Nolensville, an attack was ordered against a detachment of Confederate Cavalry.

Throughout the weekend, the advance of Rosecran's army continued, but was slowed by encounters with the enemy.

In the early hours after midnight into Tuesday morning, General McCook's divisions arrived outside of Murfreesboro. Miserably drenched from hours of marching in the rain, the soldiers were maneuvered into position on the south side of the Wilkinson Turnpike. But the Confederates disputed the arrival. Skirmishing in the inky wet blackness of night pushed Rebel pickets back into their own battle lines as the Federals forced their way into position. Finally an uneasy quiet settled around four in the morning as the soldiers of both armies lay upon the wet ground for a few short hours of sleep.

No fires were permitted. No comfort from the cold wet was possible. Daylight came and there followed hours of troop movements while the generals kept their soldiers occupied as they set their battle lines in preparation for the forthcoming conflict. Skirmishes were a continuing harassment, yet no general battle evolved. A long day passed slowly. Evening fell to darkness. McCook was ordered to extend his right and to build many campfires in order to deceive the enemy and give the impression that his troops were greater in number and to cause the enemy to believe that his divisions would be the main thrust of attack.

Duane and his friends stood with a company of soldiers, warming themselves by one of the fires. The brigades had been placed in line along a wooded ridge overlooking an expanse of open ground widening from 200 to 500 yards toward a dense cedar thicket beyond. Fields of cotton and corn lay scattered about the open ground. The Union line stretched a mile further to the right with the brigades of two more divisions adding to those of Sheridan's – a total of nearly 7000 men. There was little talk. The dominant sound was the loud cracking of the fire.

It was nearly time for TATTOO when one of the regimental bands broke the mood of the evening. YANKEE DOODLE, HAIL COLUMBIA, and other tunes drifted on the night air. After a while the band fell silent as it yielded to a Confederate band playing DIXIE and a number of its own favorites. Other bands joined in the exchange which continued back and forth for more than half an hour. Finally a Federal band struck up HOME SWEET HOME and was instantly joined by a Confederate band. Soon one band after another joined the tune until every band from both armies was playing HOME SWEET HOME.

For a short time the music soothed aching hearts. Gradually the bands ceased to play as the refrain echoed in the frosty night, then died away to silence.

*   *   *

The men of the 36th Illinois slept on the ground in line of battle. Their muskets stood racked in rows along the line, loaded and ready. Horses remained under tack, tied near their riders or harnessed to wagons or artillery limbers. What rations and ammunition the soldiers carried were all they had. General McCook's supply train of 300 wagons had been threatened the previous day by a Confederate cavalry raid and forced to withdraw to safety.

Duane and his friends had settled in for the night at the base of a tree behind the lines. Captain Tomlin was with other senior surgeons of the division at a house a half mile to the north where a temporary hospital was to be set up. Lieutenant Marshalton and other assistant surgeons would set up first aid operations just behind the battle lines. Their horses and extra pack mules carried the barest of supplies, mostly bandages, splints, tourniquets, some stiptics.

The boy lay wrapped in overcoat and blanket, tucked in the ground pocket between tree roots. His head rested on his pack. Jeremiah was tethered nearby with the other horses and pack animals of the medical group. Duane slept lightly. Nervous tension kept him awake as an eerie stillness hung over the sleeping army. Others, he noticed, were likewise restless and might toss about uneasily or sit up to watch and listen. Some of the officers walked about, talked quietly, drank coffee, or leaned against a tree and gazed through the darkness toward the enemy.

Sometime around midnight, Duane drifted into a light sleep. About two hours later he was awakened by the sound of nearby whispered conversations. General Sill was talking to some of his officers as they looked intently toward the enemy lines.

"There's movement behind their fires," one whispered.

"It looks like whole brigades moving to our right," another agreed.

"I'll alert General Sheridan," Sill stated. He turned from the group and disappeared in the darkness.

A half hour passed. When the general finally returned, Sheridan was with him. For a moment the two studied the distant movements.

"I think you're right," Sheridan spoke. "Pass the word quietly for the men to rise, eat breakfast, and be ready. I'll alert the others."

General Sheridan moved on to his left to alert Roberts and Haughtaling to prepare their infantry and artillery while General Sill went about alerting his regimental commanders.

"Dan! Johnny!" Duane whispered as he shook the others to wake them, "it's time ta git to."

"What's happening?" Johnny yawned.

"The oth'r army's movin 'bout," Duane explained. "We're ta eat 'n be ready."

The hot embers of fires were used to boil coffee and cook breakfast. When finished, each wiped down his utensils with dirt and grass before returning them to their packs. Infantrymen took up their weapons, placed percussion caps, and checked their loads. To the right, Captain Bush of G Company 2nd Missouri checked his artillery and prepared his men. The horses were unhitched, taken to water, then returned to their limbers.

Sheridan's division was ready. Further to the right the other two divisions were following the same routine. But they had gotten a later start.

As the dark of night was about to yield to predawn light, distant sounds of battle rode the breezes from the far right. Rising like an incoming tide, it crept ever closer.

In the grey mist of the dawning day the Confederate Army came out of the cedars in front of Sheridan's division and began to assemble in lines of battle. They stretched over a distance of nearly two miles with a strength of more than 10,000 men in formation six lines deep. Silently the lines were formed. Silently they began a slow forward movement across the half mile of cotton and corn fields. Gradually they quickened the pace, then broke into a double-quick rush. Suddenly the morning tension was shattered by the blood-curdling Rebel yell as the picket lines fired and fell back. Sheets of flame cut the fading darkness as cannon and muskets roared into pitched battle.

The non-combatants with the surgeons lay low in the cover of trees and watched as the first defenders in blue fell. Bullets whined through tree limbs and rang off rocks. Their buzzing picked at the ground or thunked into wood or bodies of soldiers and beasts.

As Duane and others moved forward to aid the wounded, they gazed in momentary awe at the vast sea of humanity rushing toward their position. Cannon roared to the immediate right and the distant left as the batteries of the Second and First Brigades tore great gaps in the oncoming tide. The devastating crackle of Sill's infantry line firing in unison, combined with cannon shot to slow the Confederate charge. Artillery from the third battery in reserve behind the lines added to the first two. The enemy was being mowed down like acres of wheat, but still they came. The infantry reloaded. At fifty yards the soldiers of the four regiments fired in lines. Sheets of flame spit forth in repeated series along the Union front as soldiers fell by the score. The grey line held momentarily, then fell back to regroup.

Thousands more were thrown onto the field and again the Confederates attacked. They continued to fall in vast numbers before the deep shattering roar of artillery and higher-pitched clattering crush of musket fire. The new charge faltered as the line slowed.

"This is it, Men!" General Sill shouted. "We've broken their charge. Forward to drive them back to the river!"

The general fell dead as a bullet tore into his brain. Colonel Greusel took command.

"You heard the general, Lads! Forward!" he ordered.

The brigade charged from the woodline and broke the Confederate momentum. They, in turn, withdrew in good order to the cedars. Under continued firing from the protection of the cedars, the Union line fell back to its position on the wooded ridge.

Far to the right the Union line had collapsed and was in full retreat. As the full dawn broke and the morning light was nearly an hour old, the debris of broken brigades began to pass along the back side of Sheridan's position. The panicked ran by in their haste to find safety. Officers rode at full gallop to try and stop the retreat. Couriers rode to inform Rosecrans and his staff. Wagons rushed pell-mell, some without drivers, toward the rear. Riderless horses and runaway mules ran wildly amidst the confusion. The wounded who could, made their own way toward safety, their blood flowing fresh or caked on skin or clothing. Some needed help. Others ran out of strength and paused to rest at a tree or collapsed from exhaustion.

Through this mass of retreat, the Third Brigade was brought forward in the brief pause in the action, and placed on line in anticipation of another assault. Duane found himself with all he could do to help the wounded who could to get on their way toward one of the hospitals to the rear of the line. Those who couldn't travel on their own were assisted to safer positions behind the trees. Thousands lay dead or dying or wounded on the fields between the lines. Other hundreds lay along the wooded line of the Union positions.

The brigades of the far right continued to retreat as the Union line began to fold back on itself. Sheridan's division had been under fire for nearly three hours as the Confederates launched still another charge. Artillery was brought up within a hundred and fifty yards in front of Sill's brigade. Some of the brigades of Davis' division to the far right ran out of ammunition and were forced to retreat. They did so in orderly fashion, leaving Sheridan's division with little extra support.

The attack came. A furious explosion of shot and shell tore into the Union line. Men fell to bullet and mini ball. Some were torn apart with fragments from exploding shells. A company commander fell dead as a cannon ball tore away his head. Several soldiers were blown down by an exploding shell. The horses that pulled the artillery were shot dead in their traces. Many who were wounded fought on, the blood flowing from a wound or slowed by a makeshift bandage.

In the deafening din of battle, the non-combatants suffered, too. Johnny was grazed by a bullet. A bandsman bandaged him up and he was back to work. Clothing was riddled by bullets from many close calls and stained with the blood of the wounded. Some were killed trying to help their comrades, or wounded too badly to stay on.

Duane knelt by an older corporal who sat on the ground leaning against the backside of a tree. Expert fingers were wrapping a bandage around a rapidly bleeding scalp wound.

"Ya hold this here tight whilst I tie off at the back, here." He placed the man's hand where he wanted it, then tied a tight knot at the back of the bandage.

"Damn, Boy. You sure put a man's head to hurtin." The soldier winced in pain. "Is it stopped bleedin?"

"Ain't quite," Duane answered. "But 'tis a heap less flow."

"Thanks. You be careful. I'll be fine now."

The soldier picked his musket up from where it lay beside him while Duane moved off to help the next casualty he found.

General Sheridan rode up from the right. An artillery shell burst in front of the infantry and fragments clattered through the tree branches. Musket fire from the brigade clattered like a thousand giant woodpeckers while the guns from Captain Bush's battery roared in rapid succession like a hundred speeding locomotives. The din of battle was deafening.

"Private Kinkade!" the general called, barely audible in the crushing thunder of battle. "Your horse nearby?"

"Yes, Sir," the boy replied, shielding his face from a shower of tree bark.

"Then ride over to Captain Haughtaling at the artillery on our left and take a message." The general swung his horse as a miniball buzzed past his shoulder. "Tell him to look sharp. There's a build-up of infantry off by that brick kiln and it looks like he's in for it."

"I'm on the way, Sir!" Duane acknowledged as he dashed toward the supply mules.

Yanking the reins free of the hitching line, the boy swung into the saddle then turned the horse to open ground. As an afterthought he reached for a pack of medical gear from a pack mule and draped it across the front of his saddle. Then, kicking his heels into Jeremiah's flank, the two headed through the trees while cannon shells exploded about the battleground and bullets buzzed through the air. Without warning, the boy felt a back leg give way. His mount faltered, almost went down, caught his balance, and continued on. Tripped, the boy thought.

Passing quickly along the backside of the brigade, Duane approached an area of open ground between defensive positions. There was a brief moment when the air about him stopped vibrating from the constant concussion of gunfire. The boy approached the artillery position and once again was enveloped by the penetrating roar of battle.

"Captain!" Duane called closing on the officer and his lieutenants. "A message from the general."

Shells were falling every fifteen to twenty seconds. Their range was off. They tended to strike in front of the battery or in the open area across which Duane had just ridden.

"What is it, Boy?" the captain asked.

Duane reined his horse to a sliding halt near the officers. "General says ta look ta the brick kiln yonder," he pointed. "Ther's a heap a troops gatherin an he figgers yer in fer it."

"Thanks, Boy," Haughtaling acknowledged.

A shell burst nearby, throwing dirt and fragments. Jeremiah jumped as a fragment struck the saddle leather with enough force to imbed itself into the leather and send shock waves through the horse's ribs. Another ripped through the coat sleeve of one of the junior officers.

"Best get your horse to cover and yourself closer to the ground," the captain advised. "Don't know how bad he's hit, but…"

"Where?"

"Behind you, on his flank. Hurry and take cover. I see you're with the surgeons. You can help here. We're a bit short."

"Yes, Sir."

Duane glanced back to see where his mount was wounded and was surprised to see the track of blood caked with dirt, but still flowing. He guided Jeremiah into a thicket of cedar and underbrush. There he dismounted and tied his horse. Returning to the battle line, he found all six guns in rapid fire.

"Fire!" a corporal commanded.

One of the guns belched forth flame and smoke as it roared and jumped back. The crew quickly rolled it back into position and prepared to reload.

"Load!" the corporal commanded as he stepped into position behind the barrel to aim the gun.

A crewman swabbed the barrel with a large sponge as another stepped forward with the next round of ammunition, and yet another covered the vent hole to prevent any rush of air from setting off a spark within the hot barrel. The gun was ready to fire again within half a minute. With enemy shell-fire bursting around them, the gun crews returned fire with each field piece firing from six to ten rounds every five minutes. Their thunder was deafening. The artilleryman lifted his hand from the fuse hole and the primer was inserted, the lanyard pulled, and the gun fired – all within a matter of seconds.

The enemy's shells began to take their toll. Fragments flew forcefully from their explosive impacts. A private was leaning into the trail handspike, shifting his gun as the corporal sighted and called directions, when a shell fragment slammed through his arm, tearing it off above the elbow. There was an eruption of blood from his severed artery as he turned in shock and walked away from the cannon.

"Give me a hand!" a lieutenant called, rushing to help his gunner.

Duane rushed forward, pulling a splint from his pack. Another crew member took over the handspike as the lieutenant attempted to aid the wounded private. The man collapsed unconscious.

"Squeeze it tight!" the boy called. "Make the bleedin stop!"

The man did as he was told. Duane hurried to wrap the bleeding stump with a bandage. Slipping a splint under the bandage, he twisted the wrap tight until the bleeding stopped. Then he tied the stick so that it couldn't untwist itself. A driver rushed over from a limber to assist.

"Quick," the officer instructed, "get him back to cover as soon as you can."

As the man and the boy turned from their work, each wiped the blood from his face and hands on his shirt sleeves. The air continued to explode with battle. The lieutenant turned and moved back into the commotion.

"They're forming up!" the captain called. "Load canister!"

The artillerymen at the limbers quickly traded the shells in hand for canister loads and passed them to be loaded. In the field below, the Confederate infantry began to advance.

"Fire!"

"Load!"

Cannon roared. Enemy shells descended. Duane worked to help the wounded. The enemy infantry advanced. Great holes were torn in their ranks by the battery's canister shot. Federal infantry moved up to help protect the guns. A shell fragment shattered a gunner's face. A cannon ball took a foot from another. The infantry closed. Enemy artillery fire ceased as the infantry charged.

"Fire!"

"Fire!"

"Fire!"

Cannons belched forth flame, smoke, and a hail of shot. Screams of pain were heard as the roar of the cannon faded and the leading edge of the oncoming tide wavered and fell. The ranks of the enemy closed and the charge continued as gunners hastened to reload. A sheet of flame erupted all along the Confederate front. The air buzzed with a hail of bullets.

"I'm hit!" a young private screamed.

"Damn!" another shouted, and fell mortally wounded, his life blood pumping through a hole in his chest. A seasoned private fell by the wheel of the gun nearest Duane.

"Hurry!" he called. "Here's the pick, Boy! Punch the powder bag!"

Duane took the pick from the man's hand and passed it to the corporal. Jamming it through the vent hole in the breech of the cannon's barrel, he ripped open the powder charge within. The man beside him followed up by inserting the primer, then stepping back with lanyard in hand to await the command to fire. Meanwhile, the boy had knelt beside the soldier lying by the wheel.

"Yer leg's bin hit," he informed the wounded man. "Most likely broke. I'll wrap a splint fer now."

"You best just stop the bleedin. They're gonna hit hard and we're gonna be too busy fer bandagings."

"Here they come!" someone shouted.

"The captain's been hit bad!" another exclaimed. "Help me get him out of here!"

Several walking wounded and others rushed to help. The captain was carried to the rear, trailing blood across the rocky landscape.

"Hold the guns!" a lieutenant ordered.

"Charge!" the enemy officers ordered.

"Fire!" the corporal commanded.

The enemy charged across the last fifty yards, their blood-curdling yell joining with the rapid clatter of their musket fire, then folded into the thunder of cannon. Flame and smoke and death and agony erupted in an extended instant of insanity. Suddenly, the first of the attackers were on the gunners.

Artillerymen fought savagely with revolvers, sabers, and ramrods. The soldier Duane was assisting defended them both with his revolver. Many of the attackers had already been wounded but still they came like demons possessed. They fired their weapons and charged with bayonets. A ball splattered on the iron of the cannon and cut the boy through his shirt sleeve.

"Take cover, Boy!" the wounded man shouted as his revolver dropped a grey-clad soldier on top of them.

The bayonet of the falling enemy pierced Duane's boot and cut his ankle. "Ow!" he cried in surprised pain.

The wounded artilleryman caught the falling body with his good foot as he lay on his back beside the cannon's wheel, and shoved it to the side.

"Give me his musket," the man called. "Then get behind the gun carriage and help stop them!"

The wounded man pulled himself up beside the wheel and fought with the bayoneted musket while the boy crawled behind the gun and drew his revolver. Dozens more rebels seemed to appear from nowhere.

For a brief moment, Duane stared at the oncoming enemy and felt fear. His stomach knotted and he wanted to run. Then, as if from habit, he raised his revolver and fired. The shot dropped one soldier even as his musket fired. The bullet passed harmlessly through the boy's shirt. Fear passed for lack of time to dwell on it, replaced by the immediate need for action. The revolver spoke several times. Another attacker was wounded before being brought down by a saber.

"What's with yer gun?" Duane asked as he ducked to load a live cylinder.

"Empty," his wounded comrade replied, slamming aside an oncoming bayonet and knocking its bearer senseless with the butt of his musket.

"Same make's mine?" the boy spoke as he dropped the empty cylinder into his cartridge pouch.

"No."

The ring of steel on steel, the clatter of ramrod and empty musket, the shouts and screams of orders and agony, punctuated the confusion and chaos of fierce hand-to-hand combat. Some combatants resorted to fists or improvised clubs of handspikes, ramrods, or other tools.

On the far right, Schaefer's brigade was out of ammunition. Sheridan ordered them to hold with bayonets while the last brigade from Davis' division retreated for lack of ammunition. Sill's brigade continued to pour a heavy fire into the Confederate attack. Roberts' brigade had lost its general, killed in the action. Its men, too, were running low on ammunition.

Suddenly the fight for the artillery stopped. No more Rebels came to press the attack. The soldiers of Haughtaling's battery were momentarily stunned by the calm.

"We're pulling back!" a sergeant called. "The horses are down! Grab the prolongs and let's drag the guns out!"

But the terrain was too rough. The guns could not be moved fast enough. As the regiments of the brigade began to work back toward the Wilkinson Turnpike, it became necessary to abandon the guns in order for the men to save themselves and their wounded.

While preparations were being made for the withdrawal from the battle line, Duane took time to finish the work he had begun before the assault. Kneeling once more beside the wounded gunner who stood leaning against the wheel of the gun carriage, the boy retrieved wood pieces of the splint and tied them firmly to support the damaged leg.

"Thanks, Boy. I'm sure glad we both made it so's you could put that thing on."

"Ya wait here a bit," Duane instructed. "I'll git ma horse 'n ya kin lean on him ta be leavin this place."

The boy limped off to the underbrush behind the battle line and returned shortly with Jeremiah. The horse, too, limped slightly, favoring his hind quarter where the blood had caked from his earlier wound. Duane helped some of the wounded who could stand with assistance to join the injured gunner and hold on to either side of the horse's saddle.

As the divisions withdrew across the pike and passed behind the regiments to their right still heavily involved in holding their positions, a fresh division under General Rousseau moved forward to strengthen the right wing of the Union line from which Sheridan was forced to withdraw for lack of ammunition. The Federal troops to Duane's right were heavily involved in defending a stone wall as Duane guided his horse with its wounded toward relief. Many of the wounded became separated from the rest of the army as they were gathered at the hospital which had been set up at the Blanton house along the north side of the pike.

Duane assisted the wounded with his horse to find assistance at the hospital, then mounted and rode on to catch up with his retreating brigade. The sharp pain from the cut on his ankle, relieved from the weight of walking, became a dull throb as the foot relaxed in the stirrup. The boy became aware of a dizziness in his head and the warmth of his blood seeping into his boot. It had to be cared for as soon as possible.

An hour before noon the division was finally pulled out of combat to resupply cartridge boxes. Duane took the opportunity to attend to his wounded ankle and to reload his spent cylinders. They were back within the hour, just behind the front point of the Union center. General

Rosecrans had directed the artillery to the high ground behind the center and the infantry brigades to support the line to the right of center.

All along the new right line which, had been folded back at right angle to the center and in line with the Wilkinson Turnpike, the Confederate Army continued to press the attack. The Union Army had withdrawn from the roadway to the protection of dense cedar forest.

Near the corner where the center of the Federal front met the right wing, Duane found himself in heavy combat once more. Confederate reinforcements were brought up for a charge on the center. Federal cannon on the high ground and the line of infantry poured such a concentration of shot and shell into the attacking regiments as to tear them to shreds. More than half were cut down on the field without ever reaching the Union line.

At about one o'clock there was a lull in the battle while General Bragg maneuvered troops for yet another charge. General Rosecrans took the opportunity to mass all available cannon on the high point. A heavy Confederate fire from artillery was kept up through the lull in the fighting and the non-combatants were kept occupied in their attempts to aid the wounded.

By mid afternoon a quiet began to settle along the right. The field of battle was littered with piles of dead and wounded where charge after Confederate charge had fallen, one atop the other. The Union line stood ready, but the enemy was tired. All attention was on preparations to attack the Union center.

It was nearly four in the afternoon when the Confederate Army moved on the center. Attacking in two waves, they were torn apart first by the massed artillery, then broken and stopped by scathing infantry fire at close range.

Daylight faded. The conflict ended. The armies ceased hostilities.

*   *   *

Rations were short in the Federal Army. Most of the supply trains had been delayed. Soldiers ate what little they carried with them if they chose to eat at all. Many settled for coffee and perhaps some hardtack, dunked to soften.

For Duane, it was a lonely night. Hundreds had been lost from the brigade. His friends were among the missing. He huddled by a large fire where many from the regiment had gathered for warmth. In the gathering darkness a cold wind came up and it began to rain. The distant night was filled with the moans, the screams, the pleadings of the wounded and the dying. Some begged for help, for a warm fire, for water. Others called for their mothers, begged for God's mercy, pleaded for someone to end their suffering.

Inside, the boy ached with worry for Johnny and the lieutenant. He guessed they were busy with wounded, probably in one of the hospitals scattered across the field of battle. They could be hurt or dead, but that wasn't too likely. Pulling his overcoat up at the collar, he opened his blanket and draped it across his head and shoulders to help keep off the rain and keep in some warmth. The weight of the blanket folded the brim of his hat down around his ears. He huddled closer to the fire's heat. The movement reminded him of his aching ankle. Pain had been overcome for the most part by numbing cold. Yet, still, movement brought it back in a dull, subtle reminder.

The first hours after sundown had been quiet as the stunned soldiers of the army recovered from the shock of battle and their officers contemplated what to do next. A new kind of effort began behind the lines as supply wagons were loaded with the wounded and sent back to Nashville in long trains to deliver the casualties and return with food and other supplies. Preparations were begun to regroup the army and redeploy the lines to prepare for the expected attack from the Confederate Army on the following morning.

A figure approached the fire from the darkness, still wearing his bloodstained and muddy uniform from the day's events.

"It's the general," someone advised quietly.

The men stood respectfully.

"Who?" another asked.

"General Rosecrans."

The officer approached. "Good evening," he greeted.

"Evening, Sir," several replied.

"You're my men," the general began as he put his hand on the captain's shoulder, "and I don't want you hurt. But when the enemy sees a fire this big, he figures there must be a score or two gathered there. It's a good mark for a cannon shell. You should move away or make it smaller."

"Yes, Sir."

"That's my men." He stood a moment, quietly looking over the gathering of battle-weary soldiers, then turned to go. "Stay alert. We'll be moving about during the night to be ready for them come tomorrow."

"We will, Sir," the captain saluted.

The general returned the salute and was gone.

A moment passed as the men began to knock down the fire and gather their gear. The air hissed overhead as a shell fell nearby and exploded. No one was hurt.

Captain Olson had assumed command of the brigade. Colonel Greusel had commanded the brigade and had been replaced by Major Miller. But the major had been wounded and separated from them during the day's fighting, so command had passed to the captain.

"Come on, Men," the captain ordered. "Let's break this fire down into several smaller ones and scatter them a bit."

"Captain Olson," Duane asked, "have ya learned enythin 'bout Lieutenant Marshalton 'r eny a the doctorin people?"

"I'm sorry, Dee," he explained. "Our wounded and hospitals are scattered over three miles behind the enemy lines. I don't know any more than you do at present."

"Thanks." As he spoke, the boy worked on building a fire from burning fuel out of the first.

He remembered the general lay of the land across which they had retreated. There were two hospital locations of which he was aware – the one he'd passed and another a half mile west on along the road behind the original battle line. The waiting and the cries of the wounded were unnerving. As soon as he could, Duane slipped away to find Jeremiah, gather his gear, replenish his water, and check his medical supplies.

Duane left his comrades by the fire and started to work his way through the mass of men from the rest of the division. The horses were gathered with some of the wagons and artillery vehicles, where horse lines had been set on a treeline near a field. But as soon as he was away from the fire, the raw dampness cut through his blanket and clothing, chilling him to the bone. The boy changed his mind. He would go on foot. It would be much colder on horseback. Besides, on foot he was less likely to be seen.

Using the many fires as a guide, Duane followed the Union line to the edge of the clump of cedars. Once among the trees, he felt his way from trunk to trunk, listening to the cries of the wounded to guide him toward the field of combat. Several times he tangled in branches or brush and tripped over roots or stones. Nearing the edge of the cedar stand, he could see the fires of another troop line. It must be the other army.

The boy's foot caught on something and he fell. Landing with a thump on a cold hard mound, he felt the strange form beneath him. It was neither rock nor ground. His fingers detected frozen fabric. It was a corpse. No. It was a pile of dead, frozen together in their own blood. A sudden sickness surged through his gut and the boy vomited where he lay.

"Oh, God," he thought to himself, "I ain't never been sickened at seein soldiers hurt 'r kilt. But froze up in piles as this jest turned ma insides. I ain't feelin too good. Maybe ya could see yer way ta gittin me on ta findin Johnny an Dan. I sher would be oblidgin."

Wiping his mouth with his sleeve, Duane pulled himself back on his feet with the aid of a tree trunk, then carefully climbed across the pile of dead. He had to be nearing the earlier line of battle. Picking his way carefully so as to move away from the fires of the enemy line, the boy found his way through the stand of cedar, tree by tree. The dead were everywhere in the inky silence. Eventually Duane came out on an empty dirt road.

Listening carefully, he detected distant sounds of bivouacked troop lines and units in movement. Cautiously he proceeded down the open lane, always ready to dive into the cover of the underbrush. Judging from the earlier retreat and his initial direction to avoid the enemy, the hospital should be less than a half mile to the right.

Voices! Quickly Duane stepped into the underbrush and crouched by a rough-barked tree trunk.

"Easy, Justin," a deep voice spoke softly, "we's gonna make it. The docs'll git ya fixed."

"Jezes it hurts," a pained voice complained. "Ma head's gonna explode like as ta a cannon shell. Oh, God, jest let me die right here 'n take out this hurtin."

"Hey, Justin, we's got help ahead. Jest keep on 'n lean to ma shoulder. Yer gonna be fix'd right soon."

They were good friends, Duane thought to himself as he listened to their slow and painful passing. He had to find Dan and Johnny. They were his good friends. The voices faded into the distance. The boy returned to the road and continued on his way.

Continued rain and cold wind drove damp misery through the layers of blanket, coat, and clothing. And, oh, did that foot ache. But it was getting better. It was losing its feeling to numbness. The deepening dark of night grew gradually colder. A warm fire would be a welcome relief. Even better would be the dry inside of the hospital house or barn.

As he walked along, Duane became aware of the nearing noise of activity and talk in a large body of troops. Pausing, he searched the darkness for fires. He found them off to the right, about fifty yards in from the road's edge. A whole brigade or more, he thought. There were bound to be pickets and activity on the road.

Considering his options, the boy decided to cross to the corn fields on the opposite side of the road. He would work his way along the frozen furrows until he passed the line, then return to the road. The late-standing corn stalks would provide some cover. The troop line was soon behind him. But a quarter mile further, the road ended onto a crossing road. Judging from the new road's width and well-worn surface, it was a major pike of sorts.

Duane was confused. He had expected to find the hospital, not the end of the road. He was forced to make a hasty move as the sound of approaching horses signaled the rapid approach of many riders.

Crossing the pike, the boy found himself in another stand of forest. He paused in the cover of the trees to watch the passing of cavalry. It was a large Confederate unit riding up the pike in the same direction Duane was considering to travel. He would circle through the trees instead.

The silence of the trees was quietly disturbed by a strange and eerie noise from ahead. After a couple hundred yards, Duane found himself stumbling through an area of uniformly round boulders. They were slippery with a frozen rain-slicked crusting, yet soft as though moss-covered. Picking his way carefully across the uneven terrain, Duane made slow progress.

Suddenly he lost his footing and slipped on one of the rocks. Landing hard, he lay where he had fallen, waiting to catch his breath and listening to the eerie sounds which had grown louder and more distinct. They were the wounded. There must be hundreds, maybe thousands. It sounded as though they were scattered for miles. The boy moved to get up. His hands felt a freezing slush, too sticky to be frozen rainfall. Feeling about, he realized he wasn't on a rock. It was a pile of dead soldiers, frozen in their own blood and gore, bonded to the earth on which they had fallen. The woods were full of them.

The churning in his stomach came again. But this time he fought it and it passed. Regaining his feet, Duane realized he was hopelessly lost. He was also exceedingly tired from the events of two days with little sleep. The boy determined there was nothing else to do but make the best of the situation. At least he might be able to help some of the wounded.

It was a short distance to the edge of the trees. Duane crossed a rutted lane and found himself on the battlefield of the morning's conflict. There was much more activity then he had expected. Many moved among the wounded, offering water, comforting words, an extra blanket from the dead. Most of those offering assistance were themselves wounded. Army of origin made no difference. Federals and Rebels helped each other to try and survive the misery of the night.

Duane joined the efforts. In a protected hollow among the trees he built a fire. Others joined to help.

"Nice going, Boy," a corporal spoke. "Could ya help me move some of the wounded nearer?"

"I'd be likin thet fine," Duane replied.

Building up the fire first, he took his blanket from where he had dropped it and spread it across a tree limb near the blazing warmth. The boy then helped to move several wounded to the ground near the fire.

There was very little conversation among those offering aid. Each did what he could without instruction. Many fires had been built during the afternoon and evening since the fighting had shifted. Duane eventually recognized the area as the site of the morning's conflict. He was on the ridge where the Union lines had been located. The warravaged landscape was littered with broken pieces of artillery equipment and wagons, dead and wounded mules and horses, as well as the soldiers from both armies.

Wave after wave of charges had left layers of bodies on the openfields where they had crossed. The boy was helping a Confederate youth work through one of these piles toward a moaning from within. Prying with bayonet and musket stock, the two broke through the outer crust of frozen bodies and pulled away rigid corpses. Somehow, a pocket of air and the thawing of the wounded man's own breathing, had offered a protected cavity for survival. Buried within was a grizzled soldier in his late twenties. His leg had been shattered by a shell fragment in the first charge and others had fallen around him, killed by the same shell. Within minutes, continued slaughter had covered him with more dead and wounded. Another was found alive and unconscious. The right side of his head was bloodied and a wound in his chest was caked with dried blood.

"Yer God's own angels," the older man whispered.

"Jest hang on," the Confederate rescuer comforted. "We gonna move ya up ta a fire."

Others came to help and the two were moved to the warmth of the fire. Duane shook the water from his blanket and covered the unconscious man with it.

As the night wore on, temporary protection from the weather was improvised by moving a wrecked limber near the fire and resting the beam of the tongue on a stack of empty cartridge cases. A second beam from a broken wagon was added to extend the rail. Then a wagon canvass was spread across and staked to form a lean-to shelter. The more serious wounded were moved into the protection of the canvass.

Blankets were gathered from the packs of the dead to help protect the living. Bandages were created from whatever fabric could be found, usually torn from the clothing of the wounded or found in among the contents of the wounded man's haversack.

Duane felt a permanent chill creep into his body. As midnight approached, he began to shiver in the dampness of his clothes. A slight cough became more persistent. And a deep sense of exhaustion began to take control of his mind and to fog his understanding of what he was doing. There were moments when he felt momentarily dazed and slipped into a brief unconsciousness. Yet it passed and he went on with his work.

The firelight dimmed as the fuel was consumed. The boy went to a broken wagon which lay unsteady on its side, resting against a fallen tree limb. Some of the broken crates within would offer good material to use for the fire.

Duane was so tired and he couldn't stop shivering. He crawled under to pull out some broken wood, but paused a moment to rest. Shaking violently from the cold, he curled up against the furthest side of the wagon bed and fell asleep.

EPILOGUE

The night passed into a new year. As the first day of the new year dawned, the weary armies braced for combat. But the day passed quietly. Near evening there was a sudden explosion of artillery fire. However, it turned out to be a salute to the day's end.

The exhausted boy slept through the day, undisturbed by the activity around him as the wounded were removed to the hospitals of both armies. Only the evening salute penetrated to the subconscious. Gradually he awoke. When he finally crawled out, dazed from sleep and shaking with the cold, it was dark. The rain had stopped. The field was wrapped in a quiet stillness.

Disoriented from sleep and the effects of exposure to the cold and damp, Duane believed the night was ending and dawn was at hand. Looking about in the fading twilight he was surprised to find that only the dead and the debris of wreckage lay about him. The living had gone. Several of those he had helped remained among the dead. Staggering forth to the ashes of the fire, he found them cold and muddy. In the gathering darkness of the short winter twilight, the boy suddenly realized that night was coming, not giving way to dawn.

A day had passed. He was ravenously hungry. Perhaps there was a biscuit or some frozen scrap in one of the haversacks. Searching several of those scattered about or slung around a frozen corpse, the boy found some hardtack. It was too solid to eat. Shoving it into his haversack, he continued. The search turned up some coffee, dried beef, and one haversack with a full day's issue of flour, beans, coffee, and salt pork. Duane stowed all in his own haversack as he suddenly became aware of how easily he tired and how ill he felt. Feeling had gone from his ankle. His body felt no pain, only the numbing cold.

There was no way to know what had happened while he slept. It was likely the Union Army had pulled back still further. The best course of action was to find his way to Murfreesboro or an outlying farm and find a dry place to rest. The clouds were high and darkness was not as black. It was possible to see one's way through the open fields. Duane looked about for a blanket and found one still rolled in its rubber cover, tied to a field pack. He took the whole pack, slipped it on, and headed down the roll of the hillside across the fields of the Confederate charge.

Pausing in the open, the boy checked his revolver to see how wet it was, then his cap pouch and cartridge box. They were low. Wandering slowly among the Confederate dead, he searched for ammunition and another blanket. Stopping from time to time, shivering fingers probed haversacks and weapon gear. His search provided him with a full supply of ammunition, a second revolver with spare cylinder and holster, a rifle with bayonet, and a pair of woolen socks which he used as mittens to cover his frozen hands. It also occurred to Duane that he could find enough spare clothing to provide himself with a Confederate uniform. It was increasingly more likely that he would not be able to find his friends. Perhaps it was time to find the Confederate Army where he might even locate his pa.

The thoughts were encouraging and even helped give a lift to the boy's spirits. Wandering south along the field of battle, Duane found the wreckage of the Confederate charges stretched for more than a mile and a half. He had gathered all he needed and was moving quickly through the last fields, when the markings on one of the uniforms caught his attention. It was a regiment from Arkansas. He didn't want to search any further for evidence of the 13th Arkansas, but it would be best if the uniform he put together was from home. Wandering about in search of a haversack with a spare shirt, he found one near the body of a young corporal.

Just ahead lay a dirt road. Once on the road, Duane turned to his left in the direction he believed would lead to Murfreesboro. He followed the roadway for nearly a mile until he saw in the dark a structure to the side. It was a farmhouse. A small animal shed stood nearby. Finally, he thought, a dry place to rest.

Crawling into a stack of straw at one end of the shed, Duane buried all his gear between the straw and the wooden wall at the back of the shelter. He then unwrapped the dry blanket from its cover and lay the rubber, dry side up, on the straw. Covering himself with both blankets, he settled into the makeshift comfort and fell asleep.

*　　*　　*

The boy awoke to the sound of rain dancing on the wooden roof and dripping from the eaves. He sat up and looked out into a grey and misty dawn. A soft rustling sound approached from the straw above and he looked up to see a fat calico cat staring down at him. Its fur was matted with wet. "Hey, Kitty," Duane invited, "ya look kinda wet. Ya wanta friend?" He reached into the straw to find his haversack and searched by feel until he found a piece of hardtack. "Ya hungry?" he offered.

The cat purred contentedly as he descended toward the outstretched hand. Crouching into a resting stance, the cat gnawed noisily on the biscuit. Thus occupied, Duane was unaware of the door opening on the house. A woman wrapped in coat and shawl stepped out into the raw morning to fill her bucket at the well pump. As she glanced about the yard and worked the pump handle, she caught sight of the boy feeding the cat. The noise of the bucket clattering against the pump had startled Duane.

"Hey, Boy!" she called in a strong voice. "What ya doin there?"

"I ain't causin no harm, M'am," Duane stammered. "I jest come in outta the weather fer ta sleep some. The cat, it were hungry-like, so's I give it some biscuit here." He sat up and brushed the straw from his hair. "I'll be gittin right along. Don't fret none. Jest gimme a bit ta git ma thins 'n I'll be gone."

She had set the bucket on the back stoop and was crossing the yard to the barn. "Ya jest hold yer britches till I see what you is, Boy. There ain't no cause fer you ta up and head off in this weather." Entering the shelter of the shed, the woman stopped by the straw pile to stand with hands on hips and study the figure in her shed. "Why you ain't more than a young un! What ya doin all get up like a damn Yankee boy?"

"I was in the fightin a day 'r so back," he explained as he pushed off blankets and brushed off straw.

"Why I kin see that now. You're all covered with mud and yer clothes is stained in blood." The woman knelt in the straw. "Are ya hurt?"

"Not much," Duane replied, shivering involuntarily in the morning damp. "Least wise, not thet I kin feel eny more. I'm kinda numb all ov'r."

"Yer shiverin in the cold." She put a hand to his forehead. Its warmth felt like heaven. "And yer burnin with fever."

"I'll be fit 'nough."

"You ain't fit a tall," the woman objected. "You jest git yer thins and come on ta the house."

"But I gotta…"

"You ain't gotta nothin. Now come 'long with ya." The cat meowed softly. "You come, too, Cal. Yer milk's by the kitchen stove."

The cat watched while Duane dug his gear up from under the straw. The woman gathered up his bedding and slung it across her arm. Duane stood with his belongings and she steadied him as he lost his balance to dizziness. Pausing to get his bearings, the boy covered his head with his hat while the woman wrapped him in a blanket. As the two started across the yard toward the house, the cat ran ahead and waited for them at the door.

Inside, the first order of business was to get Duane into dry clothes and warmed up by the stove. Rooting through a trunk in another room, the woman had produced a dry set of clothes of about the right size. Duane was parked in a chair near the warmth of the stove and the clothes were stacked neatly on the table. A large copper pot was heating water with which to brew a cup of tea.

"Name's Katie Smith," the woman introduced. "I'm a wida woman. My children are gro'd an gone. Them's my Sammy's clothes we got here, when he was jest a young un. What's yer name?"

Mrs. Smith busied herself pouring a large pot of water and placing it on the hot stove plates.

"Name's Duane Kinkade. Most folk call me Dee."

"Tell me bout yerself, Dee." She turned from the stove to study her young guest.

She was a pretty woman, Duane observed, as he began to explain briefly who he was and how he ended up in her shed. Long auburn hair hung loose across her shoulders. Dark eyes sparkled with kindness of one used to mothering her children. She was a well-formed woman of moderate stature, used to hard work and tending her land.

The water began to sing as it heated against the metal of the pot and kettle. Mrs. Smith left the room briefly to return with a quilt and some towels.

"Ya git yerself out a them wet things, Dee, and wrap up in this quilt. We're gonna git you cleaned up and fixed up, and we're gonna make you healthy agin, too."

Duane stripped out of his clothing and slipped into a clean pair of johns supplied by the widow, then wrapped himself in the quilt to settle once more into the wooden arm chair by the heat of the stove. He continued to shake from fever and exhaustion. The wet clothing and gear was hung on a line, a wooden drying rack, and wall pegs behind the stove.

Katie poured some water into a pan and began helping Duane bathe away the caked mud and dirt and blood. To the boy, the cleansing felt soothingly warm. He had forgotten what it was like to be clean. Scratches, cuts, and wounds were washed and treated. Some redness marked the grazed flesh where the bullet fragment had cut his arm. The bayonet wound on the ankle was red from infection. Mrs. Smith treated it with a poultice brewed from her collection of herbs, hanging from the ceiling near a corner. Next came a warm cup of tea and some fresh biscuits which had been baking.

The two talked as the widow worked to mother the boy and attend to his needs. Cal lapped at his milk, then settled in a window sill to watch between naps. Outside, the rain became mixed with sleet. Inside, the warmth of the kitchen reminded Duane of home. It seemed so long ago. A melancholy mood overcame the boy as he thought of his family, his dog, his friends, of what it was like before the war. As the woman finished her ministerings, the boy settled back in the chair, curling comfortably into the quilt.

The day passed. The war was forgotten. The widow Smith and Duane enjoyed each other's company and shared the stories of their lives as though they were family come together after many years.

Late in the afternoon, in the last two hours before dark, there came the sound of distant thunder. It drifted in on the rain-swept breeze and hung faintly in the air for about an hour. The boy and the woman both knew it to be the last voice of battle, somewhere, miles to the north. A sadness filled their hearts. What a waste – this war, this battle, the wounding, the dying.

For two days the boy rested and regained his strength. There was a flurry of traffic on the road that passed the house as wagons traveled back and forth, carrying the dead from the field. The widow kept to herself, neither she nor Duane knowing how he might be treated if he were found at this time. He sorted his gear and clothing and gave Mrs. Smith his extra Yankee clothes. Packing his extra dry clothes, Duane set aside the grey uniform he had taken from the field. He cleaned and reloaded his weapons, and prepared to be on his way.

On Sunday, Mrs. Smith left Duane to keep the fires going while she rode in to church and to learn what she could of the outcome of the battle. Duane spent his time splitting firewood and filling the wood box. By noon he had split a half cord of wood and was putting the ax, mallet, and wedges away as the rig turned into the yard.

The two spent the afternoon preparing food and packing. The widow had learned that General Bragg had retreated to Tullahoma and that General Rosecrans was withdrawing once more to Nashville.

"Guess I'll be goin come sunup," Duane stated as he finished tying his pack together.

"You be careful, ya hear," Mrs. Smith admonished kindly. "Yer ankle's doin nicely 'n I sure don't want ya gittin sick out there."

"I figer ta be fine," Duane returned as he settled in a chair at the kitchen table. "Ya ben so kindly, I sher wish'd I could do real right fer ya, too."

"That new-cut wood is a real fine help. Don't you fret none." She worked at the table preparing potatoes to be boiled.

"Ya got pap'r 'n pencil?"

The woman paused to provide them from a cabinet shelf.

"I'm puttin down a letter fer Lieutenant Marshalton with General Sheridan in Rosecrans' army. If it happens ya git ta Nashville 'r they come by this way, ya gives it ta him an tell where I'm gone. He kin give ya some money from my pay as he has."

Duane folded the letter when he had finished and handed it to the woman.

"Thanks, Dee. I'll keep it near the flour bin so's I kin fetch it quick when the time comes."

She crossed to the cabinet to put the letter in its place, then returned to preparing supper.

*   *   *

Early Monday morning, the widow and the boy rose for their final meal together. Following a breakfast of eggs and grits, a fried slab of salt pork, and dark strong coffee, the boy gathered his things to go.

The two had become quite fond of each other and neither wanted to part. But each knew it had to be so.

Duane helped to clear the table and knelt to share the scraps on his plate with Cal. While the cat ate, he rubbed its ears. Cal's soft purring showed his contented appreciation.

Duane stood with the empty plate and watched while the cat rubbed against his boot. Satisfied, Call climbed to his window to lick his paws. The boy turned to the wash board.

"Kin I help clean up?" he asked.

"Not on yer life, Dee. I need to keep busy when ya leave so's I won't be settin an pinin my heart fer yer goin." She smiled kindly and a sadness creased her face. "Ya take good care a yerself." A tear slipped out and she caught it with her finger tip.

Duane buckled on his gunbelt and adjusted it for comfort. He slipped the bayonet into its sheath, then pulled on his coat. Next he hung his haversack and canteen across his shoulders. Mrs. Smith crossed the room to help him on with his pack. She hugged him and kissed his forehead. He reached around her waist and squeezed back, then kissed her softly on the cheek.

"Ya take care now, ya hear?" She stepped back. "I kinda love's ya like ya was my own."

"I will, M'am. I certainly aim ta."

Duane took his hat from the back of the chair and put it on his head, pulling the brim down over his ears. Mrs. Smith took a wool scarf from a peg behind the stove.

"Here, let me lend a hand."

She draped the scarf over the hat to hold it snugly in place and tied it under the boy's chin. Next she offered him a pair of woolen gloves.

"Thanks," he said.

"Good luck," she returned.

Duane crossed the room and picked up the musket from where it stood in the corner near the door.

"I best git on fer I git too hot in all these here clothes."

"Yeh," the widow opened the door.

Duane paused in the doorway. "Thanks," he smiled.

"God bless you," she tapped his chin with a gentle fist.

Katie Smith stood in the door and watched as Duane walked across the yard toward the rutted roadway. Cal watched from his windowsill.

The boy stopped to wave. The woman waved back. Cal purred softly and settled comfortable, his eyes only half open.

Duane glanced through the window glass at the cat, then at the chimney smoke rising in the brisk morning air.

"Bye," he shouted.

The sound of his own voice hung lonely in the morning quiet. The woman's hand was raised in a motionless final farewell.

Turning to the frozen ruts of the dirt road, the boy faced eastward and walked toward the rising sun.

Duane Kinkade's search for his father leads him to the Confederate Army at Corinth, Mississippi, and into battle near a church called Shiloh at a place called Pittsburg Landing. The circumstances of battle land him with the Union Army in the care of an army surgeon.

UP FROM CORINTH is the story of that battle and the months that follow through the summer and fall of 1862. Finally, in the winter of '62-'63, Duane is able to begin his trek back to the Confederate Army.

ISBN 978-621-434-008-8

9 786214 340088

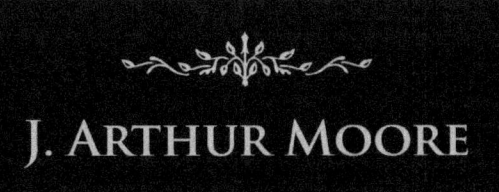

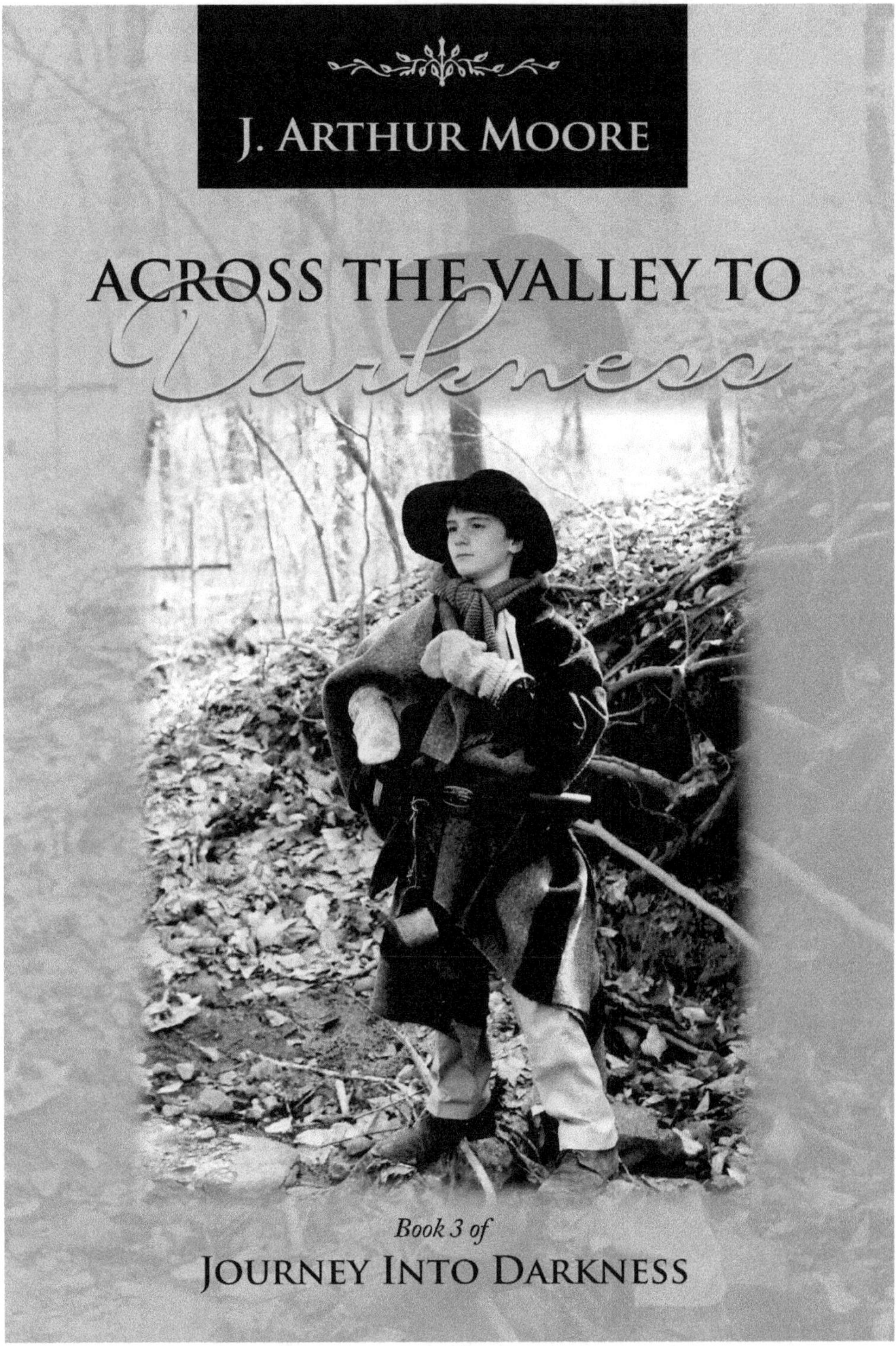
J. ARTHUR MOORE
ACROSS THE VALLEY TO
Darkness
Book 3 of
JOURNEY INTO DARKNESS

JOURNEY INTO DARKNESS

a story in four parts

part 1

On the Eve of Conflict

part 2

Up From Corinth

part 3

Across the Valley to Darkness

part 4

Toward the End of the Search

book three of

JOURNEY INTO DARKNESS

written by
J. Arthur   Moore

Dedication

Across the Valley to Darkness is dedicated in His love and in friendship to Charley French, Matthew Oswald, and David Rowland, each of whom has helped by becoming forever a part of the story through the photographic material, and to all who have enjoyed its telling and shared in the adventure of its creation.

Duane Kindade

Tod Gardner

Johnny Applebee

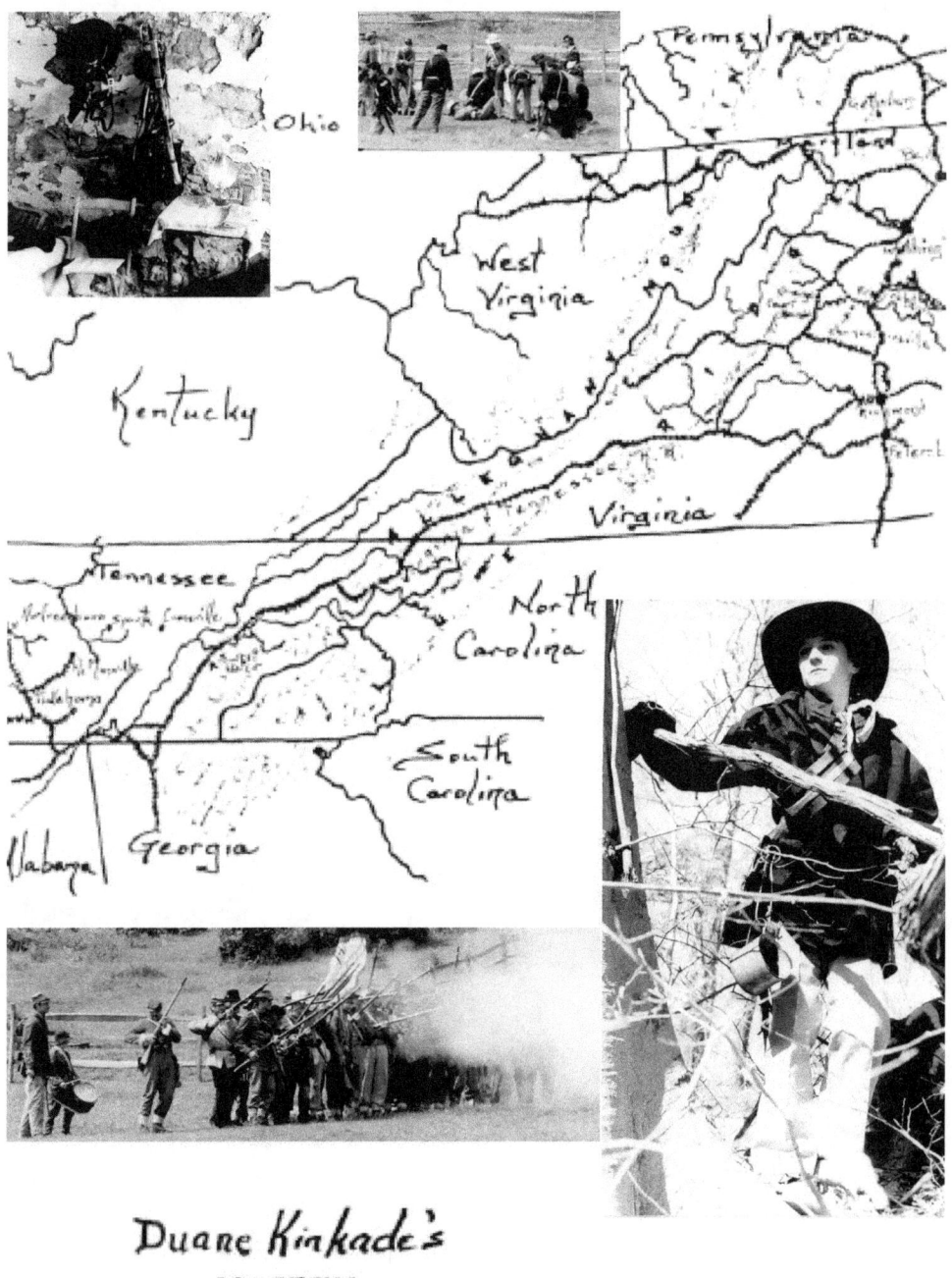

Duane Kinkade's
journeys
1863

A light snow swirled gently in the afternoon air, carpeting the countryside in new powder. The lone figure of the boy plodded along the empty dirt lane that was the main road, hardly visible in whirling whiteness. The chill air bit through his layers of clothing, and the confusing visibility made it impossible for him to keep his bearings. Duane paused to rewrap the scarf across his face as a new wind whipped about the back of his neck. Somewhere the road forked right toward Tullahoma. But it couldn't be seen. The boy listened to the snowy silence for some sound of life, then moved on.

Two years ago Duane was just another farm boy back in Arkansas. Then the war had come and his pa had left to fight for the Confederacy. During the months of summer his mother had been killed by raiders and he had been left for dead. Christmas came. It was lonely without his parents. Only his dog was left of the family he loved. Then, during the lonely months of winter, the letter had come. His pa was in Tennessee, but had no idea as to the events in his family's life.

Suddenly, the boy had to find his pa. Thus it was he left to become part of the fabric of war. As drummer boy in an Arkansas regiment, he fell at Shiloh to be found by a Union surgeon and his teenaged ward. The balance of the year was spent with the Union Army until the bloody battle at Murfreesboro. Alone on the battlefield, Duane had decided the time had come to go in search of the Confederate Army of which he had learned his pa's regiment was a part.

Duane had been alone on the road since morning when he'd left the outskirts of Murfreesboro behind to seek the Confederate Army encampment at Tullahoma. The Tennessee countryside was empty of activity this first full week of January, since most had settled in to ride out the first snows of the new year. The boy's thoughts drifted back to last week and the terrible battle that had snuffed out so many lives. He thought of the friends he'd left behind in the hope that in just a few days he would find the Confederate Army and be reunited with his father. Now he wasn't so sure he'd made the right decision. Every time he felt he was close, something happened to change the course of his plans.

A distant clatter intruded on his thoughts and the boy paused to listen. Quickly it approached from the road behind. Suddenly, ghostlike, it burst into view, materializing from the snowy atmosphere. A frenzied young driver pushed his panicked horse as though racing his flatbed wagon against the devil himself. Duane jumped out of the way, his sudden movement startling the wagoneer who hauled his beast up short.

"Git on quick!" the youngster shouted. "There's Yanks comin up fast!"

The foot-weary boy clambered aboard without pause as the driver slapped his horse into a run. Duane grabbed the seat mount as the vehicle lurched forward, nearly throwing him off the back.

"How many?" Duane asked, drawing himself up on the back of the seat board.

"Dunno really, but two fer sher." The younger boy, perhaps ten years old, was dressed warmly in an overcoat with his hat brim pulled down over his ears and held firmly in place with his scarf. Stretching forward with the reins held tightly between his fingers, the boy urged his horse to ever greater speed.

Duane managed to hug tightly the back of the seat as the force of the racing vehicle pulled at his grip. Snow stung his face. His gear slapped against his back or slipped awkwardly from his shoulder to his elbow.

"Why fer'd ya pick me up?" Duane shouted into the wind.

"Ya'r one a us, ain't ya?" the boy responded without turning his attention from his horse. "These Yanks ain't 'zactly friendly." Shifting his feet to brace himself, he continued, "Hang tight. We turn here."

With that, the young driver yanked the reins and the horse veered hard to the left, throwing the spinning wheels into a sideways slide. The beast was strong. He pulled the wagon out of its skid without breaking stride and disappeared into a snowy lane, nearly hidden by white-covered vegetation. Soft powder billowed about the moving mass, kicked up by the swirling motion, dusting the boys and their vehicle in white. A quarter mile along the lane, the horse was pulled from his wild run and allowed to trot briskly the remaining few hundred feet into a small farm yard.

"My name's Thomas," the boy introduced.

"Call me Dee," Duane acknowledged.

"Okay, Dee." He halted the rig. "Help me unhitch an run the wagon inta the shed. Then dust it with dirt 'n straw while I hide 'Ol Jake in the lean-to out back."

The two unhitched the harness for the wagon and rolled the rig backwards into the shed. Duane watched Thomas lead the horse out of sight behind the small frame house, then turned to do as he'd been asked. Several minutes passed. Duane finished, found a small bucket, and made a seat to await the other boy's return.

He studied the house, silent in the snow, its chimney smoke blending into the falling flakes. As he watched, Thomas appeared at the corner of the house, peering cautiously down the lane. The young boy motioned for Duane to look, then ducked out of sight. Duane glanced as directed and saw two mounted figures advancing slowly in the snowfall. Quickly, he slipped along the back wall of the shed to conceal himself in the dark shadows behind the strawpile, as a gust of wind whipped through the shed to dust over the footprints just left by the boys. There he hoped to watch in safety.

Cautiously the two entered the stillness of the farmyard. One grizzled cavalryman guided his mount along the front of the shed. He paused to study the wagon and glance about the shadows, then turned to join his stocky companion near the door to the farm house. As the bearded rider dismounted and approached the farm house, his fat companion reached for his rifle which hung on its swivel harness and brought it to bear on the house door.

The door opened to the knock and a tall homely woman stood there, surrounded by three small children. Duane couldn't hear the conversation, but he did hear the children's screams when the soldier slapped their mother and threw her to the ground. Angry voices made demands, but the woman remained seated in the snow.

The boy checked his musket, placed a cap on the nipple and cocked the hammer. His pistol was ready. Laying the weapon across the straw, he took aim on the mounted rider and waited.

Raised voices carried on the snowy breeze.

"We know that wagon just come in, M'am, and we aim to take the horse! There's no use to be stubborn, cause we can be stubborn, too!"

"Ya's git from here an leave be! We ain't left with no livestock cause ya'all's done made off with ever'thin we got."

The other rasped, "Woman, we either get that horse or we might take to burnin you out."

The woman moved to get up, but was pushed back to the snow by a muddy boot.

"Leave my ma be!" a small girl shrieked as she pommeled the soldier on his leg with her small fists.

"Ha!" he laughed as he pushed the child into the snow with the woman.

Suddenly a gunshot flashed through a window and Duane knew he had to act. He squeezed the trigger as the mounted soldier swung in the saddle to fire into the house. No one was hit, but the second soldier grabbed his rifle as the woman shooed her little ones into the house and quickly crawled after them. A shot ripped the door frame as they disappeared within and the soldiers fired in confusion. Duane fired wildly with his revolver, hoping to scare the two off. It worked. The thin one mounted hastily and the two rode anxiously down the lane.

After a moment of silence, Duane holstered his revolver, picked up his musket, and stepped from behind the straw pile. The door to the house opened and Thomas stepped out.

"Hey, Dee! Ya git yerself in here real fast-like!"

Duane dashed through the snowfall and disappeared into the house. The first thing the boy noticed within the dwelling was the warmth. It wrapped him in a comfort he hadn't felt since leaving the Widow Smith's. His vision grew accustomed to the dimness and he realized all eyes were on him. The little ones huddled in uncertainty behind their mother's skirt while their older brother stood with eyes dancing in hero-worship. Anger flashed in the woman's cutting glare as she sized up this stranger from head to foot.

"Ya had no cause fer sech unchristian-like behavin, Boy." Her hands caressed the small heads at her side.

"But, Ma!" Thomas defended. "Dee, here saved us from them Yanks."

Duane stood silently uncertain as the woman continued. "It ain't as how's I'm not appreciatin what ya done." She glanced at her older son. "It's how's I know they'd a done their meanness an gone on. Now as how they's riled up good, they's gonna git their friends an come back fer vengeance."

The boys knew she was right.

"We can beat them, Ma," Thomas beamed at Duane.

"Yer ma's right," the older boy spoke. "We kin take on two 'r three, an may be even four. But they'll come on, more 'n likely, with a scoutin patrol 'r could be a company lookin fer a bivouac."

"Come an set," the woman offered as she steered the youngsters toward the table and benches near the cook stove. "We'll meet yer friend, Thomas, an think on what needs doin."

"You a real soldier?"

"Did ya ever be in a fight?"

"Ya see any dead Yanks?"

The children lost their shyness and bubbled with curious questions. "I seen fightin," Duane responded. "There's lots a killin an hurtin. It ain't nice nohow."

Thomas laid his rifle across the table and sat on a bench across from his hero. "I was gonna fight, too. But Ma won't allow it."

"She's right, ya know."

"But I wanta help kill Yanks! Ain't that what it's all about? You kill any Yanks, Dee?"

"Yes, I've killed. But it's all wrong. They's people, too. Some is real fine folk." His voice broke at the thought of his lost friends. "Some as even saved ma life."

The small group talked on while the woman fixed some hot broth, flavored with some old bones left from a small rabbit eaten days ago. Eventually the conversation returned to the dilemma at hand.

Duane offered a suggestion. "If'n Thomas was ta hide his gun out back an I was ta head on out the lane, ya could say as how a lone Reb come on when the Yanks was here and started shootin. Ya show em ma tracks an may be they'd set off ta git me an leave ya's all be." He glanced at the woman.

"Well, Ma?" Thomas asked impatiently when she sat in silence.

"Could be, Dee. But what of you?" She stood near the table, absentmindedly wiping her hands on her apron.

"I'm fixin ta take the fork ta Tullahoma an ketch up ta Bragg's army."

"But that's west a here by mor'n a mile!" Thomas cut in.

"What?"

"Yeh, we's passed that on the run from the Yanks." No one spoke for a full minute.

"Thet does put thin's in a bit of a fix," the woman began. "But there's a rail stop on east at Manchester an I think it's open jest now ta git ta Tullahoma."

"I best git on then," Duane stated. "Ain't a whole lot a time fer some 'n heads in here."

"You go bye?" one of the girls asked.

"Guess thet be so," Duane acknowledged.

After a brief farewell, the lone boy found himself on his journey once more. He paused at the edge of the lane to turn and wave farewell to the family standing silhouetted in the open door of the farmhouse. Then, with the strengthening breeze whipping the snowdust across his face, he plodded along the lane toward the open road. Once beyond the protection of the shrub-lined path, Duane turned eastward and felt the force of the storm at his back.

*　*　*

Only a few minutes had passed when a rabbit darted from the underbrush. It paused in the middle of the road to stare in surprise at the boy who stood motionless so as not to frighten the creature. Duane watched admiringly as white fur moved on to blend into the snowfall. Suddenly, it occurred to the boy that something must have spooked the rabbit. He brought his musket from its resting place, butt up on his shoulder, to readiness in both hands, and reached his thumb to cock the hammer.

"Wouldn't do that, Boy," a tall bearded figure warned as he stepped from the bushes.

"Guess we told him, eh Bobby?" the fat man joined from across the roadway.

The Union troopers stepped forward from their hiding places. Each had his rifle leveled on their captive.

"Well looky here," the first continued. "If it ain't a little Johnny Reb." He reached out and removed the gun from the boy's grasp. "Wonder if he knows how we come to be shot at a while back?"

"Yeh," the raspy voice added. "Could be we should show him some respect for his elders."

Fear knotted in the pit of his stomach as Duane assumed they might decide to shoot him where he stood and let the snowfall bury him.

"Ya figger ta be real brave bein yer two agin me," his voice quavered. "Ya be..."

A rifle butt slammed against the side of his face, sending him spinning to the ground. He had seen it coming and stepped to avoid the blow, but wasn't fast enough. Still, it saved him from loosing any teeth, suffering instead, a bloody mouth. The boy lay motionless in the snow, conscious, but unwilling to let his captors know. He tasted the warm flow as his blood seeped from the cuts in his tongue and the inside of his cheek. Relaxing his jaw and letting his whole body lay limp, he permitted it to slip from his lips and pool on the white snow.

"Now look what you did!" the fat soldier called angrily. "You've gone and killed him. He ain't no use dead!"

Thank goodness for that, Duane thought.

"He ain't dead," the bearded man returned. "You get the horses. We'll heave him across my saddle and take him back for the captain. He'll probably want him for a trade along the way."

Duane shivered involuntarily as the cold stung his face. "See," the smaller man affirmed, "he's still alive."

The horses were retrieved from their place of concealment. Duane was laid across the saddle, gear and all. The troopers mounted, the lighter one riding the rump of his horse behind the saddle. They turned back the way they had come and rode westward, into the storm.

*   *   *

In the days ahead, Duane found himself captive of a small company of marauding Federal cavalry. Led by a puritanic contradiction of a captain, the company traveled steadily eastward on a scouting mission to gather information concerning Confederate strength in Eastern Tennessee, particularly around Knoxville.

Captain Terence Bartell was the model of Christian charity with his own men and people he knew. At the same time, he was just as quick to put strangers to the sword and property to the torch. A small man, only five foot seven, he walked and rode rigidly erect.

It was the heavy trooper with the deep rasping voice, Brandon Yardley, who first saved Duane's life. Upon their arrival in camp, Bobby wanted to do the killing and the captain was most agreeable. But Brandon, a corporal by rank, suggested the boy might come in handy as a trade-off in a tight spot, reminding his friend at the same time that the idea was originally his. Captain Bartell concurred and Duane become a prisoner of war.

For three days the small company of a score of men moved through the country roads, skirting Sparta and Crossville in route. Just east of Crossville, the company spied a wagon of Confederate wounded on the road. The captain called a halt.

After a brief meeting with his junior officers, he announced to his men, "We're gonna take them. The Lord has said an eye for an eye and a tooth for a tooth. So also is it a life for a life." There was a murmur of approval as he concluded. "There'll be no prisoners."

"I'll keep an eye on the boy," Brandon offered.

"Okay," the captain accepted. "But come up as soon as we're done."

"Yes, Sir."

The captain drew his saber, held it over his head, then silently lowered it forward. Breaking into an open run, the company charged the wagon. Duane watched the slaughter in helpless horror. Screams of agony rent the air. The boy noticed that Brandon, too, shuddered silently as he looked on. No shots were fired. The bloody work was done with saber.

"They needn't a done thet," Duane sobbed.

"I know," Brandon agreed. "But this war's made crazy men of them." The corporal led the boy to join the company, already at work scavenging the corpses and loading their booty into the wagon. Leaving the bodies in the blood-splattered snow, the troopers took the wagon and continued on their way.

Snowfall had ended the previous day. Grey weather had set in and darkness gathered early. The company left the road and made camp for the night in a small hollow, hidden in a forested hillside. A hot meal was prepared from the supplies found in the wagon, then all settled in for a cold night's sleep. Duane was tied to the wagon's wheel by a lead rope from his bound hands. Brandon found some extra clothing from the wagon for him to sleep on and covered him with an extra horse blanket. The boy slept fitfully, tossing and turning in his attempt to ease the discomfort in his wrists, and somehow passed a very painful night.

Shortly after dawn, all hell broke loose. Corporal Yardley had untied the boy and seen to his breakfast of cold biscuits and coffee. The two stood near the fire as the captain approached. He was about to pass when Duane spoke out.

"Ya shouldn't a kilt them wounded, Captain. It ain't being the Christian man ya calls yerself." It was simply a statement of his feelings, made in frustration. He was helpless to do any more.

"I'm beginning to take a liking to you, Boy." He stopped to face the boy, folding his arms across his chest in pious patience. "But you're kind of young to pass opinion. You ever shot a Yank?"

"Yes, Sir, Yank and Rebel both. I ain't fer bein kilt and I've shot many of a mind ta do me in."

Surprise registered on the captain's face. "You telling me you've been in battle?"

"With Breckinridge at Shiloh and Sheridan at Perryville and Murfreesboro."

"That can't be. One's of the Confederate Army and the other's of the Union!?" He shifted his stance placing his hands on his hips as he gazed into the boy's eyes to judge the truth of his statement.

Duane returned a steady look as their eyes met and the officer suddenly realized the boy was not lying.

"I ain't here takin sides in this fightin. It jest..."

A volley of gunfire erupted from the trees all around the clearing. The hail of lead sliced through the company like a storm through a wheat field. The captain grabbed the boy, spinning him by the arm, as he folded Duane in a protective hug and fell forward into the snow. The impact of a dozen bullets blew the corporal off his feet and threw him backwards onto the ground. The roar of continuous rifle and revolver firepower lasted for about three minutes as the Confederate force advanced from their cover to make sure there were no survivors.

"Don't move," the captain instructed as he fell on the boy, impressing his body into the foot-deep snow covering on the ground. His overcoat flew open as they went down and completely concealed the young figure beneath the man. "Wait till they've gone before you even stir a muscle or you're dead for sure."

The voice faltered as the dying man choked on his own blood, rushing forth from shattered lungs.

Duane endured the weight on top of him as a memory flashed through his mind of a distant battle and a friend who had shielded his body from death. He concentrated on remaining motionless and listened intently as the gunfire ended, hoping to hear the definite departure of the troops who had ambushed the company. All he heard was silence.

A single gunshot shattered the quiet. Someone was checking.

Silence.

Duane ached in his attempt to remain motionless. The cold damp of the melting snow soaked his clothing and chilled his body. He felt a sticky dampness seeping through the snow above his head and cramped hands. Still he lay unflinching. The silence stretched into an eternity. The boy became groggy and drifted into sleep.

An hour passed before he awoke with a start. His body was becoming numbed by the cold. He tried to move and found the weight on his back had stiffened with the cold and death.

It must be safe, now, Duane thought to himself. He pushed himself up and with some difficulty, rolled the captain's body aside. The impression in the snow where he had lain was pooled with blood. It was the blood he had sensed earlier. It was on his hands and in his hair, and covered the clothing on his back.

Duane shuddered at the litter of bloody bodies scattered about in the snow, shattered by a hundred bullets. He guessed the horses were spared. They were gone. Everything else remained.

Sensing a deep coldness within, the boy glanced toward the sky. Overcast had moved in. More snow was on the way. It was time to move on.

The captain's bullet-riddled coat was spared the blood bath, having remained spread across them both. Duane worked to remove it from the stiffening corpse, to have it for extra warmth on his journey. Gathering up his gear, he stripped off his own bloody coat and hat, wiping the blood from his hands and head on the inside surface of the garment before discarding it in the snow. Then he pulled on the great blue overcoat. Lifting his pack to his back, the boy headed off into the hills.

Duane had heard that the road ran east across the river to Kingston, then on to a railroad and connections to the army. He would cut through the hills and mountain country to avoid the possible danger of a run-in with renegade cavalry which could prove dangerous.

The boy wandered for two days in desolate mountain country, desperately aware that he had become lost. His provisions ran out to some cold hardtack and dried salt pork. The overcast had hung on with an occasional wet mist, but no storm developed. Night came, and Duane found shelter in a shallow cave. Dragging in a pile of dead branches, he broke them into kindling, lit a fire for warmth, ate the last of his food, and settled into a fitful sleep.

*   *   *

The coals glowed with a silent foreboding, disturbed occasionally by a flurry of cold snow born into the cave by the night breeze. A hiss of defiance greeted the flakes in their attempts to smother the warmth of the waning fire. A rustling movement intruded on the silent battle between heat and cold. The coals winked. Again the rustling movement. The damp black walls shivered. There echoed a splat as a drop of moisture fell from them onto a rock and slowly solidified into a slick solid. Fewer flakes were met with the haughty hiss. The embers were dying. The cold stealthily slipped in. Again the rustling movement, this time accompanied by a slow sigh of air. Silence. A splat. A hiss. Silence. Silence.

A startled movement shocked the stillness. Duane, shaking violently in the grip of the damp cold, sat up and dragged himself closer to the faint red glow. Shivering hands reached into the blackness in search of wood pieces. Placing the wood over the few remaining embers, he breathed with a halting steadiness on the red glow until a flickering of life appeared. Encouraged, he blew harder and the flames grew merrily to attack and to drive back the cold.

Dancing flames brightened the grim rock with prancing shadows and silhouettes. The boy rubbed his sleepy eyes with the heels of his hands and pushed back the dark tangle of hair. Stretching and shaking, he drew his blankets tightly about his wornly clothed, chilled self, and hunched close to the fire. The weight of constant travel pulled at his eyelids.

The morning breeze stung him on the face with a white flurry. Duane gazed beyond the fire. A sudden fear gripped him as he realized the need to find shelter, food, and warmth; or he would die. His food supply had just run out and he had wood for a few hours only. Now the snow made it necessary that he find a camp or a settlement, somebody, or else freeze to death.

As these thoughts ran through his consciousness, he reached for his gear. He pulled on the oversized blue overcoat and slung his pack over his shoulders. With the overcoat securely tied and the blankets folded and worn cloak-fashion, the boy left the glowing red warmth of the fire for the steady fury of the white cold and the deathly silent, smoothly blanketed world of snow.

He paused momentarily at the opening of the cave. Behind him burned the fire. In front lay a wilderness he'd never before seen, and the bludgeoning of a growing storm. Since the army lay in the east he would head in that direction. He stepped forward and melted into the snowy silence.

As Duane knew from the position of the last twilight the previous day that the cave faced to the southeast, he was able to take his bearings from it upon beginning the journey and head due east. But once away from it, he gradually lost all sense of direction. Everywhere there were trees and everywhere the trees were padded with white on the skyward surfaces. And all was encased in the silent swish of the white among the dark gnarled limbs, naked except for the padded surfaces.

The wilderness seemed to hold its breath and to watch in wonder as the boy pushed on, for not a breeze stirred; only the silent swish of the white prevailed. Traveling was not difficult at first; only a few inches of snow had fallen. But by full daylight, a hint of motion began to swirl in the air.

The boy did not know when the moment of daybreak had arrived or how much of the day had passed since that moment. He did not know how long he had been traveling or even if he were traveling in the right direction. He did realize that he was tiring, the snow was deepening and falling more thickly, and he could no longer see very far ahead before his gaze was lost in the white blaze. The boy stumbled and went down on his knees, but the reflex bracing of his arms and hands kept him from falling any further.

Duane suddenly realized that he must have dozed while walking, and the thought scared him. Washing his face with the cold white powder, he forced himself to his feet and moved on. The deafening silence swished about endlessly and the boy felt it squeeze him in its grip. A grumbling stomach growled for food. Aching muscles begged for rest. Burning eyes pulled for darkness. Visions of a soft bed by a fire danced on the weary mind. And snow stung the burning face.

Pausing, Duane brushed his coat sleeve-covered hand across his snow- wet face, then surveyed his surroundings. Where the branches forked on the trees, he could see foot-high drifts of white powdered dampness. The boy was caught in a sphere of white broken only by the dark undersides of tree branches. He moved on, but he could no longer sense any movement on his own part, only the motion of dark branches passing over his head. His ears roared with the swishing silence. He felt a tenseness surge through his body and a damp chill run up his back. He was afraid.

Suddenly he felt himself sliding swiftly downhill and momentarily everything became a blur. When all movement stopped and the boy felt the security of stillness, he looked about himself and discovered that he was sitting on ice. He moved to regain his feet and heard a resounding pop followed by the swishing stillness. He froze in mid motion. Trying once again, the silence was shattered by an ear-splitting explosion and Duane felt a foot fall away underneath him and felt a sensation of warmth as his foot plunged through ice and into icy water. Fighting panic, he carefully pulled the leg out of the water and back onto the ice. Then, with deliberately slow movements he inched his way to the banks of the river only to find that the embankments were too steep to climb. He saw where he had slid down and found his blankets in the snow at the edge of the ice. The boy was shaking with fear as he stood up and adjusted the blankets on his shoulders. The wind had been picking up for some time and was beginning to whip the snow into great clouds of white mist. Duane moved along the edge of the ice hoping to find a place to climb out onto the high ground. The soaked pant leg stiffened and froze solid and the boy was forced to limp along, unable to move the leg. A gust of wind buffeted him and he spun, staggering to hold his balance, then slipped and fell on the ice. He struggled to get up, slipped and fell again. The leg wouldn't obey. It couldn't. The boy screamed in fear, but the winds drowned out his cries. He thrashed wildly about like a deer felled, with a broken leg, trying vainly to accomplish what he knew he could not. Gradually he quieted down and sat there staring blankly at the steep slope. He slumped forward and lay limply on the ice. The wind wailed and the whipped snow drifted about the dark form on the ice.

* * *

Vaguely conscious of a warm dampness against his face, the boy opened his eyes briefly and perceived a dog licking at his near frozen flesh. There was a pair of moccasined feet beside the dog, and two hands reached down toward him. The boy felt a hazy sense of motion as though some almighty force were pulling him upward. He made no resistance, but slipped into the eternity of unconscious sleep.

A sweet sensation of warmth seeped in to embrace the boy's subconscious. He had no feeling of contact with anything, nor could he feel the presence of his own body. Deathlike numbness blanketed his mind. Gradually he became aware of a surrounding warmth, then the smell of smoke and of something which might be food. He sensed the crackling sound of a small fire and became aware of his own presence and of pressure on his body.

The boy, stripped of his wet clothing, lay on a bed of animal skins and was covered with a large, black, bear skin blanket. His clothing hung near the fire on a crude rack made of branches and rawhide. An occasional hiss mixed with the crackling of the fire as melting snow dropped from the clothing and onto the fire-heated rocks that corralled the flames. There was a temporary splash of running water as an Indian girl rung out a damp cloth and bent over the boy to bathe his frostbitten hands and face.

The fire's light illuminated the interior of an Indian dwelling built of branches and a mud plaster. Along one end wall stood some earthen jars and reed baskets along with the family's personal possessions. Animal skin beds on low frames of oak or ash wood splints lined the other end wall. A hide hung over the doorway to keep out the snow and weather. A small hole in the roof of the dwelling allowed the fire's smoke to escape. Beside the fire, a large earthen pot of broth simmered on the heated rocks.

Feeling a sudden coolness in the air, the Indian girl turned toward the door as the hide was pushed aside and a young man clad in a snow-blanketed, skin robe entered the lodge. A small mongrel dog following at his heels stopped just inside the doorway to shake off the fresh snow, revealing a well-brushed, dust-yellow coat. The man removed his robe, shook the snow from it, and hung it on a tripod beside the door opening. His long black hair glistened from melted snow. Sweat streaked the smooth brown skin of his face and bare arms. Outside the dwelling stood a fresh supply of wood which he had been gathering.

The woman quickly left the boy and filled a wooden bowl with broth which she served to the man standing there. Draining the contents of the bowl, he set it by the pot and went over to the boy. The dog had already settled on the furs at the boy's feet. Duane's face was turned toward the fire, and in the firelight it looked very pale. His arms lay limply on the furs at either side. No sign of motion was evident – not even a slight rise and fall of his chest. The man asked his wife if there had been any change. She shook her head.

Kneeling beside the bed, the Indian gently passed his hand over the boy's face and arms and found the flesh cold and dry. Leaving him momentarily, the man went over to a corner in the lodge and rummaged around until he found an old army blanket. With the help of his wife, he rolled Duane over, spread the blanket, then lay him back on it. Turning the bearskin down, the Indian began a long slow process of bathing the boy with slightly warmed water. After a while he heated the water until it was tepid and again bathed the body. For nearly an hour he continued, increasing the water temperature by slow steps, until the cold flesh began to take on some color and show some sign of life. He spoke to the woman and then walked over to the fire and warmed his hands. She dried Duane off, recovered him with the warm skin blanket, then went for some wood to build up the fire.

With new warmth in the air, the Indian returned to the bed, removed the wet blanket, and handed it to the girl who hung it near the fire to dry. Having wrapped the bear skin snugly about the child, he turned to his own bed and lay down for the night. The girl banked the fire, put a few things away, then she, too, turned in. The dog maintained his place at Duane's feet.

Even though he had been vaguely aware of all that had happened during the past hours, Duane had been unable to move or to think about moving any part of his body. He felt suspended in a void unable to react in any way to his surroundings. He couldn't even breathe, though the air seemed to flow in and out of his lungs without any effort on his part.

The night passed quietly and the following day dawned bright and sunny. Brilliant rays of sunlight streamed into the lodge illuminating the dust in the streaked pattern which they created. The girl was bustling about preparing a breakfast, but the Indian was already gone. It was mid-morning when he returned with two rabbits – skinned, cleaned, and ready for cooking. Hanging them on the outside of the lodge, he entered and hung his robe on the tripod. The dog entered at his heels, shook off the snow, and trotted over to check on the boy. The dog's whines brought the couple to the bedside. Leaning closer, the Indian saw that the boy was breathing more deeply.

Duane felt a damp nose on his face and stirred slightly to turn away from it. Next he felt a tongue licking at his cheek and reached up to find out what it was and to push it away. Suddenly he was aware of the close presence of people and of the noise of the fire and of the dog licking his face and of the sunlight streaming into the dwelling. He opened his eyes and winced at the brightness. He saw the brown-skinned faces and tried to relate them to his existence and could not figure out how they fit. Duane opened his mouth to speak, but nothing would come out. The pretty girl looking at him placed her finger to his lips as if to signal silence, so he ceased his effort to talk and smiled instead. The man smiled back and pointed to his stomach to ask if Duane was hungry. The boy nodded weakly and the girl dipped out a bowl of broth.

As he ate, a youth entered the lodge and spoke quietly to the older man. Duane guessed him to be a year or two older, but wasn't sure. His clothing was a mix of crude home-spun fabric and a factory-loomed cloth. He stood a few inches taller than Duane and was of a slender build with long black hair hanging freely across his shoulders. The youth approached the patient and sat on the dirt floor next to the bedding.

"Hello," he greeted.

"Ya kin talk?" Duane returned.

"Some," he replied in a strong voice. "I am called Eqwani Stetsi, or River Child, because I was born in a boat while my mother traveled the river."

"I'm Dee," Duane introduced.

Eqwani Stetsi introduced his uncle Inali, or Black Fox, and his aunt Nunda Dayi, or Moon Beaver. "You are from the great war across the land?" he continued. "You wear the clothing of a soldier."

"I'm lookin fer the army of the Confederacy," Duane confirmed.

"If you talk of the army with clothes the color of yours, you wear both. Which one do you seek, the coat or the shirt?"

"The shirt."

"Your army is many days journey toward the morning sun. But horse of the iron trail goes there."

"Who ar you, Ak... a... ni?"

"Eqwani Stetsi," he helped. "We are of the Cherokee Nation. We hide in these mountains where your people can't find us to follow the trail of tears."

"Then why fer ya he'pin me?"

"My uncle saw you needed help." The reply was simple, and accompanied by nodded agreement from the man and the girl who stood nearby, watching with interest the conversation of the two boys of different worlds. "He was on a hunt," the Indian boy continued, "when the storm struck. On the way back to the village his dog found you on the river ice."

"I sher am obligin to ya," Duane said. "Ya jest set me fer thet iron trail an I'll not be sayin nothin 'bout eve' seein ya."

The older boy and his family spoke briefly. Then Eqwani Stetsi continued, "I will guide you through the mountains when you are strong enough to travel. My uncle says to wait three days. Now eat and get strong."

* * *

The days passed quickly. In part, they were an adventure in learning of a people very new to him. In part they were a time of rest from the tenseness of the war. The peace of the mountains was a medicine all its own. It helped to heal a wounded spirit deep within the boy in affirming that there was a part of the world where beauty and peace and goodness really existed. Gladly would he have stayed in the mountains if his father were there with him.

But he wasn't. He continued to be lost in the war which was now so far away. Even as he walked the snowy beauty of the winter forest and watched the living creatures in their daily wanderings, he knew he had to go.

The third day found the boy fully healed as Inali had said he would be. Duane gathered together his gear and packed to leave. Nunda Dayi prepared some extra dried venison and fried bread for the journey. In appreciation, Duane offered his rifle and all its ammunition to Inali. He figured that he had the revolver which would serve him well. The gift was accepted with honored pride and carefully placed on the far wall of the dwelling.

Duane left the warmth of the lodge for the journey through the mountains with Eqwani Stetsi. The man and his woman stood before their home with all their relatives to wave the boys off on a safe journey.

The sun was bright. The air was crisp and clear. The boy was refreshed and enthusiastic as the two left the home place and headed into the wilderness.

Were the two able to travel in a straight line toward the rail line, the journey would have been about twenty-five miles. As it was, the mountainous terrain stretched the distance to about thirty-six rugged miles. To make matters worse, the weather shifted quickly as fog settled in about dusk of the first day, only to give way to rain. Torrential rains hampered travel throughout the second day. Finally, late in the afternoon of the second day, the two were able to gaze from the wooded slopes to view a narrow valley and its fragile ribbon of railroad, barely visible through the soaking mist during a brief letup in the stormy weather.

"Here I say good-bye," the Cherokee youth stated as he stood, drenched by the day's travel. "You will have a safe journey. I cannot go further with you and be safe."

"Are ya safe ta git back home?" Duane asked. He shook the water from his hat and returned it to his rain-soaked head.

"I know this country well," Eqwani Stetsi replied. "Many days to the east, many of my people live on lands a good white man bought for them. There are also many of my people still hiding in these mountains. I will journey first to a place I know near here. There I can rest by a warm dry fire. Then I'll go home. You see where the valley grows narrow toward the south?" he pointed and Duane nodded an acknowledgment. "There you will find a place called Sweet Water. Your people there can help you find your army and maybe a dry place for the night."

"I sher do thank ya. An I hope yer people do okay." Duane extended his hand.

The older youth accepted the hand in friendship. Quietly they shook, smiled at each other, then parted. As Duane began to work his way toward the valley floor, his guide watched briefly his progress. But after a hundred yards of travel, the boy looked back and his friend was gone.

*   *   *

Sweet Water proved a welcome stop. A young storekeeper and his sister gave Duane a place to sleep the night and spend a dry day. The boy learned the main army, which was under the leadership of General Robert E. Lee, lay encamped nearly five hundred miles to the northeast. Duane wondered if he might work his way back toward Tullahoma. To this idea, the storekeeper explained that such a trip was very dangerous and not likely to succeed due to Union Cavalry activity throughout eastern Tennessee. The safe, sure way to get to the army was to join Lee in northern Virginia.

So it was that Duane began his journey into Virginia the following morning. The storekeeper secured passage on the Virginia and Tennessee Railroad most of the way. Due to the rainy weather and war conditions, the trip could take several days and require changes in route. Duane didn't care. He was happy to be dry and warm, and to know he would soon be on his way again.

The journey from Sweet Water began with two more days of rain. After five days of travel and delay, the boy arrived at Orange Court House in northern Virginia. By the time he arrived there, the weather had turned once more to snow.

From Orange Court House, the boy took the road east toward Fredericksburg and the encampments of the Army of Northern Virginia.

*   *   *

The morning of the second day was beautifully sunny. Duane had traveled constantly from the rail stop, so that he could cover the thirty miles as quickly as possible. It was slow going in the deep snow, so he stayed to the road as much as possible. Traffic was light, a local youngster afoot or someone riding horseback on an errand. Once, a horse-drawn sleigh went past, but it was headed in the wrong direction.

Somewhere in the distance, the air reverberated with the Rebel yell. Hundreds of soldiers were charging an enemy. The boy stopped to listen. Air currents must be playing tricks, he thought. He couldn't hear the sound of battle. The musket, rifle, and cannon fire were missing. Duane hurried on, walking briskly, too tired to run.

New sounds drifted on the air – the long roll beat of the drum and the call of bugles assembling their troops. They weren't that far away.

The smell of the smoke of hundreds of cook fires drifted strong on the morning breeze. Yet still the sound of battle was absent.

Cresting the rise in the road, Duane gazed down more than a mile of open valley, flanked along both sides with thousands of tents and rough-cut log cabins, gathered about a maze of company streets. At a glance, the valley appeared to hold the better part of a division's camp. The hills bore acres of tree stumps from which the logs had been cut for winter quarters. Further back were thick stands of red oak and pine woodland.

There it was that the battle was unfolding. A mass of many hundreds of troops in line of battle with flags and banners flying in the breeze, was in hot pursuit of another, smaller, troop line in slow retreat. Wild yelling from a thousand throats echoed about the valley as the soldiers fired upon one another with volley upon volley of snowballs.

Duane watched in disbelief. It was a scene of madness, so inviting in its humor and great fun. But he was too exhausted to rush forth into the fray, and chose instead to find a snow-covered rock outcrop which would serve as a vantage point for spectating.

As the rampage moved sluggishly up the valley, fresh troops joined the action. A line of reinforcements, nearly a mile long, all in orderly companies with banners slapping in the breeze, arranged itself along the nearer hills and began to advance. In the distant camp, more regiments prepared to enter in support of their retreating comrades. Duane stared in awe as the conflict swelled to nearly ten thousand soldiers, all letting loose a barrage of snowballs or rushing to seize members of the opposition as prisoners. The reinforcements clashed in one great mass of humanity and flying snow.

Unexpectedly, a flash of white fabric was hoisted high on a fence rail, and the entire conflict gradually ceased as many companies, believing a surrender to have occurred, began to drift back to their camps. The great snowball battle ended. The valley lay littered with hats, torn clothing, discarded packs, and a few wounded soldiers, scattered about the torn-up snowscape.

As Duane prepared to enter the army's camps, he became aware of another who had been watching nearby. A Negro youth approached the boy.

"Mass'r, yuz don wanna go in ther," he warned. "They's a bunch a crazy men from Texas an' Georgia." He shifted the weight of a sack slung over his shoulders. "Ya come with me, Mass'r, 'n I'll put ya up with real fightin soldiers from Alabama."

"An how fer might thet be?" Duane asked.

"No mor'n three miles south an east a here," the young slave replied.

"Why fer ya so fer out?" the boy inquired.

"When yuz gonna pick up sum extra vittles, ya's not wantin ta take from yer closer neighbors." He pointed to the sack.

"Oh," Duane acknowledged. "Who are ya eny ways?"

"Call me Willis. I'm Willis Rogers on account as I'm Captain Zachery Rogers' personal boy."

"Call me Dee."

Duane rose from his seat and stretched tired muscles as he studied the young servant. He seemed in his late teens. His black hair was in tight curls, close to his scalp. His skin was a rich brown in color, where it showed through the bundle of thread-bare clothing.

As the two started on their way, Duane noticed the tracks in the snow. Willis had followed him to his vantage point having come across the open fields from a distant farm, then turned up from a swale in the snowscape that seemed to indicate a buried roadway. The two returned to the roadway which the black youth seemed to know well, then journeyed across country to the camp of which he'd spoken.

Conversation along the way provided an opportunity for introductions between the two and news of the war from their differing experiences. The boy learned they were almost two miles south of Fredericksburg with Confederate troop camps in a semicircle from the riverbank on the north to the riverbank on the south. The Union Army was encamped across the river. It was half again as large as Lee's. Yet the two armies had fought to a standstill some seven weeks back, with heavy losses on both sides. The battle had unfolded in and around the city of Fredericksburg from which the Federal troops had withdrawn to the opposite banks of the Rappahannock River. The two armies were now in winter camp. A mutual truce had settled throughout the region as the common soldiers had declared a temporary end to hostilities and were busily engaged in commerce through whatever means the imagination could devise.

Willis explained that Company K was from a small town called Bell's Tavern, in the northern wilds of Alabama. The nearest place of any size was Elyton, about 20 miles due east. Company K was part of the 13th Alabama under Colonel Birkett D. Fry. Their camp lay to the south of the Texans by two miles or more. Along the way, Duane realized that he and his companion were skirting the outer camps of an immense army. More than 60,000 troops sprawled about the stretch of camps of the various divisions of the Army of Northern Virginia.

Having already passed through a number of camps along the way, the two finally entered the area inhabited by the regiments of General Archer's brigade. The area was quite open with many acres of orderly company streets, lined with rows of tents and crude log structures by varying degrees. Many log walls were roofed with canvass. A very few had wooden roofs. Some structures, log and canvass tent, had chimneys added at one end, created from long saplings stood upright and packed with mud. The camps were packed close to one another so that a single acre might hold close to three hundred soldiers or the better part of a regiment.

The air was thick with the noise of an active outdoor community of thousands of men and beasts. It was thick, too, with the odors of such a gathering from fire smoke, to coffee, to food, to unwashed bodies and clothing, to refuse, to latrine trenches, to rotting straw. Duane felt the thickness close in on him as he traveled the camps and arrived at his temporary destination. In spite of the camp's desperate appearance, it was fairly clean and orderly. Some of the infantrymen were busy washing their laundry in large wooden tubs. Others had shared the tubs earlier. Their wash hung across lines which had been strung between tents.

"Whar's Cap'n Rogers, Mass'r Foley?" Willis asked a 19-year-old private, busy at his wash tub.

"If'n I was a bettin man, which ya know's I ain't, I'd say as ya'd find him with Lieutenant Guthries, Willis." The young private paused to wring out a wet pair of socks, then lay them across the wooden rim while he searched the sudsy water for his johns. "Ya know how fond they are of cards. They kin smell the promise enywhere's in camp."

"Ol' Sarg about?" Willis substituted.

"In his house."

The private bent back to his work.

"Come on, Mass'r Dee. I'll lead ya on ta meet Ol' Sarg Raymond. He's 'bout the oldest man in the company."

The company's quarters were a line of canvass tents with side walls about three feet high. At the officers' end were some stranger quarters with log walls. One even had a door frame, complete with solid oak door, built into the front end and a stove pipe protruding from the back.

Smoke drifted from the chimney pipe and the front door stood ajar. It looked dark inside as Duane and Willis approached the dwelling.

The black youth tapped on the door frame.

"Mass'r Sarg. Mine's if I's come in?"

"Come on, Willis," a firm voice answered. "Ya know it's open."

The two entered to find the man stretched on his bed, reading a volume of Mark Twain. Shifting to a sitting position, he lay the book on the makeshift table created from a cracker crate stood on end.

"Who's yer friend?" the sergeant asked.

"This here's Mass'r Dee," Willis introduced. "I picked him up near ta Hood's camp. We was watchin them blame fool Texans a sno-fightin them Georgia fools."

The sergeant seemed friendly enough. He was strict-looking with his dark eyes and deep brown hair. His full beard with its two stripes of white added to his firmness, and was enough to remind people of a skunk. Duane smiled to himself, but made sure his face gave no hint of the humor he'd observed.

"Fetch us up some vittles, Willis," Raymond ordered. "Dee here must surely stand in need of nourishin."

"Yes, Mass'r Sarg, Sir." The slave turned and left.

"Sit down, Dee," the sergeant continued. "There's a rations box by my trunk ya kin pull up."

Duane pulled out the box and settled in the middle of the floor. Dropping his gear on the packed dirt floor at his side, he peeled off the overcoat and enjoyed the warm feeling of the heat radiating from the small coal stove. The two visited for almost an hour. Willis brought a plate of beans with some scraps of salt beef. They were still warm from the fire. Sergeant Raymond poured two tins of coffee from the pot on his stove. Duane learned the stove had been taken from a wrecked railroad coach back in the fall and packed in with the company's camp wagon. The boy shared his description of the snow battle and they both laughed at the thought of whole regiments firing snowballs back and forth. The man explained that there had been a number of smaller such engagements, but this was, by far, the grandest about which he had heard.

Duane learned some of the company's history and its membership. Many of the men were relations. Its youngest member, Tod Gardner, was its fourteen-year-old drummer boy. He had lost his older brother, Jason, in the battle in December. A cousin had been wounded and sent home earlier in the fall campaign. Three uncles were still with the company. The Jenkins family and relations had at one time made up about a sixth of the company. Tod was part of that family.

Sergeant Raymond decided that Duane's medical training and battlefield experience would make him a valuable orderly. Tod could use his company to help distract him from his grief and make him responsible for showing the new boy around. Tod's uncles, Foley and Kim, would be pleased to see him out of their tent and occupied with responsibility. So it was decided that Tod's tent would be set up where the wood yard presently stood between the officers' country and the rest of the company's quarters.

*   *   *

The days passed slowly as Duane became acquainted with his new outfit. Tod was tolerant of the new tentmate and quarters situation, but remained cool toward the outsider who had caused him to be removed from his uncles' tent. The company's routine began with morning muster, followed by breakfast, followed by drill, followed by free time, followed by noon muster, and so on throughout the day. On some afternoons, the whole regiment would drill together. Regimental muster took place each evening and was usually reviewed by the balding Colonel Birkett D. Fry.

Duane felt a growing sense of loneliness. His only friendly acquaintance was the houseboy, Willis. The black youth had become quite protective of the company's newest and youngest member, and sought to help him out of his sadness.

Early one morning during the first week after Duane's arrival, he and Tod were awakened by Willis in his usual duty to rouse the drummer for muster. As the two sat in their cots, rubbing sleep from their eyes, the older youngster decided to sleep in.

"Hear'd tell ya was a drummer," he began sleepily.

"Thet be true."

"Thet bein the case, may be ya'd spell me jest now and I'd git back ta dreamin." Tod dropped back on his bed and pulled the blankets up over his head as he shivered in the freezing cold.

"I'd be pleased ta stand in fer ya." Duane pushed off the covers, shaking uncontrollably in the cold air, then moved quickly to pull on his clothing which he had taken to bed. It was still warm from being slept upon. "Ya sure, Tod, ya be wantin me ta do fer ya?" He reached for his blue overcoat and his scarf.

"Yeh fer certain. Too cold fer drummin," the muffled voice confirmed.

Duane pulled on his cold boots, jammed his hat on his rumpled head, secured the drum strap over his coat, then reached for the drum and sticks.

Sliding the sticks under the strap, he tightened the drum with its leather pull tabs, hooked it to the strap, and left the tent.

Outside in the early dimness of the new dawn, Duane positioned himself and beat the mustering roll. It had been a long time and he was really out of practice. The drum roll was embarrassingly rough.

Kim and Foley Jenkins were among the first to gather.

"Whar's my nephew this fine hour?" Kim asked, his voice hoarse with a winter cough.

"In bed, I'll wager," his cousin, Foley, commented.

"Thet so?" Kim looked to Duane.

"Thet's so," Duane replied.

"Well, Cuz, let's roust him out," Kim suggested, a mischievous smile wrinkling his face.

The two disappeared into the tent which immediately erupted into loud cries of protest.

"No! No! It's too cold! Oww!"

A triumphant pair emerged from the tent bearing a struggling nephew, clad in his johns.

"No one gits ta miss fu'st muster. Right, Cuz?" Kim smiled.

"Right, Cuz," Foley grinned in agreement.

As the company gathered, the Jenkins cousins plopped their nephew in line between them for safe-keeping. The sight of the blanketed boy brought laughter to the gathering and humor to the day's beginning.

Lieutenant Damien Jenkins, Kim's older brother, checked out the company for attendance.

"Soldier," he mocked at the shivering blankets, "yer out a uniform."

"Lay off, Uncle Damien!" the angered boy returned.

"My, my, what harsh words ta yer superior officer," the lieutenant chided.

"I ain't voted fer ya. Jest leave me be!" The boy's voice broke as tears of anger and embarrassment slid down his cheeks.

"Thet's 'nough teasin, Boys," Captain Rogers interrupted as he approached the company for roll call and inspection.

The company came to order as the captain checked his troops and completed the mustering routine. At thirty-two, he was of sturdy build. His black beard was trimmed close to follow the curve of his jaw. He looked official and was neatly dressed in a well-worn uniform, complete with grey great coat.

Throughout the nearby camps, companies were lining up and the new day was officially underway. The musters were completed and the noisy routine of breakfast was begun. Willis traveled the camp issuing the morning rations to each mess group. Tod glared at Duane as the two worked on the fire they shared with three other tents in their mess group.

As far as he was concerned, the embarrassment he'd suffered was all Duane's doing. How rotten his luck at being saddled with such a lousy tentmate.

"Mass'r Dee," Willis interrupted as he returned from issuing rations, "Ya come's ta Cap'n Rogers' quarters afta this mornin's drillin."

"What fer ya askin?" the boy questioned.

"Ya's jest be there."

"Sure, Willis, I'll be."

Tod remained sullen throughout the morning. He said little during breakfast and did his job silently during drill. As soon as the company was dismissed, he deposited his drum in the tent and wandered off into the regimental encampment. Duane reported to the captain's tent as instructed. Willis was waiting for him and led him aside to the storage tent.

"What ya say we does some tradin?" he offered.

"Whereve' is there a place fer tradin?" the boy asked in surprise. "An what fer we got ta be traded?"

"Neve' ya mine's, Mass'r Dee." He picked up a tied flour sack from beside a pork barrel. "Yuz jest come 'long with Ol Willis an we's goin ta the rive'."

"Huh?"

"Jes' come's on. Yuz'll see."

The morning air had warmed with the rising sun. Duane and Willis journeyed through the bustling camps as they wandered just under two miles to the banks of the river. Selecting a secluded cut amidst the vegetation, the youth motioned the boy to settle on a drift log. A short time later, the two were joined by Sergeant Raymond and Corporal Cameron Doherty.

"Ya bring yer supplies?" the sergeant asked. "Right here," Willis indicated the bag.

"What's happenin?" Duane inquired.

"We's what ya might call, one of the company's tradin partners," the sergeant explained.

"We gathers supplies from home an around an brings em here ta trade with the Yank's tradin' partners." Corporal Doherty described the weekly meetings that had been arranged the previous month. He had run into a couple of Yanks while exploring down river. They were out fishing. Together they had worked an agreement to put a trading raft across the river. The Yanks could get supplies of coffee and Cameron had access to tobacco.

As he spoke, he uncovered a cord line, buried under the dirt, and tied to a sapling. The line disappeared from where it stretched across the ground to where it passed beneath the surface of the water's edge.

Sergeant Raymond pulled a watch from his pocket and checked the time. "We're early," he observed.

The small group waited quietly for several minutes. Suddenly, the cord began to rise and fall in the water as some unseen force tugged slowly in the distance.

"Easy," Willis said as Cameron began to pull slowly on the line. After ten minutes, a small raft came into view. It was about three feet square, constructed with small tree limbs and store-bought heavy cord string. A sheet of paper was tacked to its middle. The sergeant read the note.

"They've five pounds of coffee, a new razor, and a pair of shoes. What do we have to offer?" The older man looked about the group.

"I has two pounds a tobacca, give 'r take a portion." Willis set the bag by the raft.

"Here's another." The corporal produced a small cloth bundle, tied up by the corners.

"I brought two pieces a chaw an a new cob pipe." The sergeant added his booty to the pile. "Shall we see if they's wantin this trade?"

Willis and Cameron nodded in agreement. Sergeant Raymond drew a pencil from his pocket and jotted their offer on the paper.

"This being so secret-like, why fer'd ya bring me along?" Duane asked while the raft made its journey.

The sergeant explained. "Willis thought ya bein' new and experienced, ya'd be good at he'pin find tradin goods. Enyway, thar warn't nothin else fer ya ta be doin. An he's takin a likin to ya."

"Fine by me," Duane accepted.

The trade was agreed upon and the goods exchanged. Date and time were set for the next meeting. The raft line was buried and the area swept of tracks. Finally, the group broke up to make their return to camp.

As Duane and his companion walked the countryside, he noticed the terrible destruction from the battle. Some buildings had been pock-marked with shot or heavily damaged in part or gutted by fire. The scattered debris of battle remained about the landscape, softened by its covering of snow. Clusters of cracker box wood slabs marked the graves of hundreds who had perished. Everywhere were the camps of the living – a noisy contrast to the silent slabs with their penciled names and notes about the dead.

"Ya seen much fightin?" Duane asked as the two passed a cluster of markers alongside a broken farm house.

"The company came on afta the summer crops was put in," Willis answered. "This here's bin ar fu'st real battle. It put me in mind of the devil's own hellfire. Neve seen sech killin. Cain't find no words ta tells of it."

"I know," Duane sighed. "It conjures up my rememberins of the fightin at Murfreesboro. It's God-awful 'n ther's no sense ta it."

The two continued on in quiet thought before Duane asked, "Why is it ya all's do yer tradin so secret?"

"Ya see's, Mass'r Dee, we knows we kin trade wi d' enemy, but we daresn't git seen at it. Is okay, so long's d' officers don't sees ya doin it.

Then they's gotta punish ya. 'N they's don wanna. Ya's knowin' my meanin?"

"I knows yer meanin," Duane smiled. "Ya'll divy this stuff up?"

"It's only fer 'bouts ten a us. They's nigh ta half a dozen tradin groups as use the landin. The timin's careful so's not ta set up too much traffic ta once."

The two hurried on, returning to camp in time for noon muster. Tod was not talking yet. He remained angry for the rest of the day. The coffee was divided after muster, each bringing a small tin can in which to store his share.

*   *   *

Days of winter drifted quietly by. Duane's friendship with Willis grew as the two shared in each day's events. It was part of the house boy's duties to pick up supplies from the regimental commissary and to run errands to the quartermaster. He was also good at scavenging the countryside for an occasional chicken or sack of corn. The boy became quite familiar with the lay of the land as they wandered about the camps of the Confederate army.

One wintry evening was particularly memorable. It had been learned that a number of regimental bands of the Federal army were gathering at the river that night. Troops from all around Fredericksburg headed for the river to hear them play. Most of the Union army was gathered as well, seating themselves on the steep hillsides overlooking the river. A hundred yards away, on the plains along the opposite banks, the Confederate soldiers gathered.

Massing themselves as one, the bands began a performance of well- known Yankee war songs. There were JOHN BROWN'S BODY and RALLY 'ROUND THE FLAG and more. Bravado gave way to sentiment and finally finished with TENTING TONIGHT.

Duane and Willis and the rest of the company had listened along with the rest of the multitude. The boy felt a pang of excitement mixed with deep sentiment and loneliness. The music had been a grand sound and a sad sound. It tore at his emotions as thoughts of home mixed with memories of war.

Somewhere in the quiet after the last piece, a Southern soldier shouted across the stillness of the river, "Now play sum a ars."

Night was approaching. Blackness edged the eastern horizon. The 150,000 soldiers of the two armies remained seated and listened as the massed bands opened with DIXIE and went on with a second repertoire of Southern favorites. MY MARYLAND, THE BONNIE BLUE FLAG, and all the rest filled the air to mix with the smell of smoke from a thousand flickering fires.

Dusk deepened to darkness. The music ended. The soldiers stood to return to their camps. Then, as if an afterthought, the bands gave forth with one final song, HOME SWEET HOME. At first the gathered soldiers tried to sing along. Their voices joined with the music from the bands into one grand reverberation of song. But the voices faltered, choked off by a great sadness while tears ran unchecked down the cheeks of a hundred thousand men and boys. Buglers throughout the Union camps began their final call of the day. TAPS mingled with the last strands of HOME SWEET HOME, stirring visions of the finality of the death of war to mix with memories of home and all that had been left behind.

The song ended. The mass of humanity began to disperse as the 150,000 separated into smaller groups, going their diverse ways as they returned to their camps.

Darkness deepened. Flickering firelight danced with the stars on black ripplings of the river's surface. Silence blanketed the countryside. The armies settled to sad and pensive ponderings, and then to sleep.

*   *   *

The weeks of winter had advanced routinely toward spring. February's final week was finishing with a misty damp drizzle of several days duration. The troops had been confined to quarters. Drill had been cancelled and musters had been cut back to mid-morning and evening only.

Earlier in the week, Duane had found a treasure as he wandered an abandoned portion of the battlefield from December. Buried in the rubble of a shattered dwelling on the southern edge of the city, he had uncovered a pantry cupboard, still stocked with staples. Stuffing the pockets of his great coat, he had brought back to Willis a supply of coffee, sugar, flour, salt, and beans. The two had then returned with empty sacks to cart off more of the same along with a broken crock of butter and stale baked goods, preserved by the cold weather. Much had already been scavenged by the rodents; but, again, the winter cold had kept it to a minimum and the two human scavengers simply cut away what they felt they must. Out of this bounty had come a plan.

Duane and Tod were on speaking terms, so Duane asked if he thought his Uncle Damien might want to have some fun with the gamblers of the company. Tod liked the plan and shared it with his uncle. He, in turn, was thoroughly taken by the plan and went ahead with the arrangements. Duane secured his entire stash of coffee from Willis and gave it to Tod to give to his uncle.

Most of the Jenkins relations had gathered in the lieutenant's tent. It had a well-fueled stove and plenty of room. Damien was the oldest. His brother Kimberton, Kim for short, was eleven years his junior and two years younger than cousin Folsom, known to all as Foley. Their nephew, Tod, was the youngest of the clan and half the age of the lieutenant. Damien's friend, Lieutenant Travis Guthries and the company's Captain Zachery Rogers had gained quite a reputation as gamblers. Cards was their favorite, but they were known to bet on anything, even such trivial and mundane affairs as how many weevils could be boiled from a stale biscuit.

The lieutenant's tent was crowded. All interest was focused on the four gathered about the makeshift table engrossed in a serious game of draw poker. The captain and Lieutenant Guthries were teamed against Lieutenant Jenkins and his cousin Foley. Private Matthew Guthries had come to watch his older brother play. All the Jenkins clan plus Willis and Duane were on hand to watch. The players sat around a large overturned wooden tub. The spectators perched on footlocker, camp chair, bed and boxes, or stood behind. The company gamblers had plenty of cash money and Confederate promise from weeks of card games. The Jenkins team had four pounds of coffee, a valuable rarity at the time. Coffee matched cash, thimbleful per dollar.

The quiet rain danced on canvass roof as warm flames crackled in the stove. Silent concentration filled the air, marred only by the clatter of a stove plate as an occasional chunk of wood was added to the fire, the slap of a card against the wood, or brief conversations whenever the deck was shuffled and redealt.

The game tottered back and forth for nearly two hours before falling in definite favor of the experienced duo. Finally the captain and the younger Jenkins dropped out to let the two lieutenants battle it out. Jenkins was down to his last half pound of coffee. There was a pause to shuffle the deck.

Foley excused himself. "I'm feelin a bit poorly," he stated. "My innards is creepin some. I best go lay down a bit."

The youth left. The cards were dealt. Lieutenant Jenkins slipped off his boots as his opponent passed the cards.

"My toes are cramped," he complained as he rubbed his feet, pulled up his socks, then resettled himself. Reaching beside the table for his boots, he felt for a sewing needle he knew lay nearby, passed it through his sock, and slipped it into a knot before retrieving the boots and setting them aside.

The game continued. Behind the tent, Foley peered through a small hole in the back canvass and watched the cards Lieutenant Guthries placed in his hands. With a string in hand which ran to the knot in the socks, he telegraphed the contents of Travis's hand to his older cousin by way of a predetermined code of pulls.

Over the next hour, the game turned. Lieutenant Jenkins began to win again. Eventually, he regained all his coffee and a good deal of cash. The boys began to snicker. The joke was too good. Afraid they would give it away, Kim reprimanded them.

"Quit yer noise!" he demanded. "Ya tell yer private jokes another time an don't be botherin the game."

"I cain't help it," Duane apologized.

"It's jest too funny."

"Ya best leave, then," Kim suggested sharply.

"Ain't needed," Captain Rogers interjected. "Seems our luck's gone sour. It's a good time ta give it a rest."

"How 'bout one more?" Jenkins offered. "I'll lay up all the cash winnin's against equal value."

"Since yer holdin close to four thousand a my cash money, I kin only match ya with promise mixed in," Guthries remarked.

The boys watched in anticipation, trying hard to contain their laughter. Kim moved toward them to send them on their way and caught the heel of his shoe on the string. It ripped the knot from his brother's sock.

"Ow!" Damien exclaimed.

"What's wrong?" Travis asked.

Thinking quickly, the other replied, "I knocked my toe against the tub. Guess yer right. Time's come ta give it a rest."

"Well, now," Travis reconsidered. "With yer concentration broke, it jest may be a good time fer thet one last bet."

Tod noticed the needle and sock fabric where it lay on the floor. Trying to be casual he stood to stretch and moved to stand on the metal and fabric until the guests had left.

"Another time?" Jenkins hoped.

Lieutenant Guthries offered his hand to his opponent. "I surely didn't know ya was sech a poker player 'r I wouldn't a been so reckless. We'll do this agin tamorra 'n I'll git back my money."

Jenkins accepted the handshake. "Thet'll do fine so long's this weather's so bad. Next good day 'n I'll hafta fetch more firewood."

While the game was busy breaking up, Foley sneaked back to his own tent to change into a dry set of clothes. Once the gamblers, the younger Guthries, and Willis had gone, the line was hurriedly wrapped on a stick and stowed in the trunk.

"I cain't b'lieve it! We done pulled it off!" Duane exclaimed in a checked voice.

"Keep it down," the lieutenant warned. "Jest hope fer good weather tamorra. I ain't wantin ta go through this agin. It's too strainin ta the nerves. Ya all best head off ta fixin supper."

"What ya gonna do with all thet money?" Tod asked.

"Put it away fer now. They's sure ta figger they's bin had 'n I'll wanta be able ta give it back. If the truth ne'er be learned, we'll split it when the war's ended."

"Good by me," Kim stated. "Yeh," the boys agreed.

Duane and Tod returned with Kim to his tent. Since it had a fire with chimney, the four had been cooking supper there during the days of foul weather.

Willis brought around the evening rations and the company settled to fixing supper. Throughout the company, the game was the topic of conversation. But only five truly knew how it had been played. And they weren't telling.

*   *   *

Six weeks had passed since Duane's arrival in Company K. Winter had slipped into March. The weather had begun to warm. Foraging expeditions for food supplies and firewood required extended travel. Newly arrived sutlers were setting up camp near the various army camps to sell whatever they could in food and comforts. Others had a long-standing business, but were short on everything, causing prices to rise sharply. Many of their customers had little in the way of money, only notes which promised pay. Trade between the armies was dwindling as soldiers and their officers became more cautious toward disciplinary measures. The Union Army had been reorganized by General Hooker, appointed to replace General Burnside about the time Duane was journeying toward Fredericksburg. The Confederate Army was running short on everything to the point where General Longstreet had left in February with Pickett's and Hood's divisions to forage for provisions in southern Virginia and along North Carolina's coast.

Duane, Tod, and Willis had left in search of the daily supplement of sassafras buds, wild onions, lambs quarter, and poke sprouts. These were required to help replace the lack of vegetables in the company's food supply. Meat and sugar were also in short supply. As the trio walked the countryside, passing others on their daily search, they were reminded how short they were of other things as well. The blue overcoat which Duane wore was a rare treasure. His boots were badly worn, but they still served their purpose. There were many who had no shoes at all, only improvised wrappings of crate board and rags.

Tod's uncle had given him $50 from his bankroll in case they should find a sutler or some citizen, willing to part with anything needed by members of the company. The truth of the game had never come out, nor had a follow-up game taken place. Duties had conveniently put it off and the company's gamblers had found other interests. The winnings were used as needed for the benefit of various members of the company.

Willis had been busy traveling the camps in search of whatever. The boys had often gone along. In the process, they had become more friendly toward each other, yet an obvious resentment was occasionally evident in Tod's behavior toward Duane. Willis had explained that it was due in part to jealousy of the younger boy's experience and the hurt of his brother's death. For his part, Duane had not yet told of his personal life, especially his family. All that was known within the company was that he had no family and had gone off to war as a drummer boy from Arkansas.

The three scavengers had journeyed toward the southwest corner of the city. Along the way they had gathered enough wild onion and lambs quarter to meet their needs. Now they looked to find anything of interest in the debris from war in a broken city. Many of the homes and outbuildings had been damaged or destroyed during the fighting. Several were abandoned. Some were under repair. Some were inhabited. Activity abounded in the good weather of late winter as soldiers and citizens went about their business.

"Did ya see this part a the fightin?" Duane asked as they turned onto the dirt thoroughfare called Hanover Street.

"We was further south, Mass'r Dee," Willis answered.

Tod added, "Here was some a the bloodiest killin. See thet hill yonder?" He pointed to the high ground which rose beyond the street's end.

"Uh huh," Duane acknowledged.

"Them's Maryes Heights. Ther's a road 'cross its face, hidden b'hind thet stone wall. General Cobb's brigade held off at least six Yank charges 'cross these fields 'n yards. Back ta the rive', there was a pontoon bridge 'n the Yank army jest kept on comin ov'r from t'other side. But we jest kept cuttin 'em down on thet hillside. It was like mowin' the wheat at harvest." As the three continued along the road, they noticed the shell-torn buildings and one barn that had been reduced to scattered debris covered by its collapsed roof structure. Rows of small mounds along the base of the slope marked the final resting places of several dozen soldiers.

"Ever' man kilt an' buried 'round the battlefield went under in his johns," Willis stated matter-of-factly.

"What fer?" Duane questioned.

"Both armies is short a clothes, 'specially shoes. 'N theys sure weren't needin 'em eny more." Willis paused to shade his eyes with his hand and scan the hillside.

"Ya don't 'spose they's missed a few?" he wondered aloud.

"We could take a look," Tod offered.

"Look out!" a nearby pedestrian shouted.

A commotion spread through the motion of people as they scattered from the road ahead to get out of the way of a runaway wagon. The frightened horses tore down the roadway, stirring up a wild cloud of dust as they dragged behind an empty freight wagon with its petrified driver clinging to the seatboard. The three just barely missed being run down as they dove to the side of the road. The swirl of dust was accompanied by a child's shrieks and the pain-filled yelping of a dog. Again the motion of people flowed, this time to gather in a knot a short distance from where Duane and his friends rose to their feet and brushed the dirt from their clothes.

"Let's see what's happen'd," Tod called as he rushed toward the crowd.

The others followed close behind.

"Ya see thet!" someone exclaimed.

"Yeh," another agreed. "Thet dog could a kilt the child if the wagon hadn't a struck it down."

"He weren't doin me harm," a young girl sobbed as she knelt in the dirt by the wounded animal. "Please, somebody help my Beauty!"

No one moved.

The girl bent over a large, bloodied head. "Oh, Beauty, dear Beauty, please don't die," she whispered as tears streamed down her cheeks and choked her words. "I love ya, Beauty."

A vision of the past stole across Duane's memory. He pictured Pounder, laying bloody in the snow, having taken a bullet met for his master. The boy stared dumbly at the scene before him as tears came without warning and a tightness in his throat prevented him from speaking. He moved forward and stood beside the girl, then leaned over the dog to check its injuries.

"May be as I kin he'p some." Duane's voice was hoarse as he wiped aside his own tears. "Easy, Beauty," he whispered softly. "Let's see what's hurtin."

The dog was a well-bred hunter. Good care and the girl's love were evident in its grooming. This girl was also of good family. Though worn, her petticoats and dress were of quality fabric. She was ten or eleven years of age. Delicate features and long brown ringlets made the boy wonder why she was alone. She looked up at the boy's approach, her eyes wet with tears and pleading for help. Quiet apprehension settled on the crowd as Tod and Willis moved closer to watch. Cautiously, Duane lowered himself beside the dog, his soothing voice seeking to calm the animal.

"Whar's yer people, Missy?" Willis asked.

"Papa's on business," was all she said, her attention focused on the boy and her dog.

Duane stroked Beauty's head in light, gentle touches. The dog shook convulsively in fits of pain and shock. Blood flowed from her mouth and from cuts on her head and side. A leg lay grotesquely out of place, broken below the knee.

Gradually the boy's hand stroked and searched as he explored for injuries. Finally he moved to the broken leg. Suddenly, the animal cried out in pain and snapped at Duane's wrist, completely closing on it with her large, sharp teeth. Duane froze in motionless anticipation of a shattering pain which did not come. Beauty never bit down, but only touched the boy's skin lightly with her teeth. She immediately released him as a great sigh of relief escaped from the spectating crowd. The large head eased back onto the ground.

"Yer a good girl, Beauty," Duane whispered. "'N I think ya kin be fixed up good 's new."

"Annie!" a man's voice called in panic from the far side of the crowd.

"Here, Papa!" the girl responded, standing at the sound of her father's voice. "Beauty's bin hurt!"

As the girl's father worked his way through the crowd, Tod and Willis knelt in whispered conversation, asking Duane what he would do.

"How bad's it look?" Tod inquired.

"Broken leg fer certain," Duane replied. "'N I think her jaw could be broke, too. I think we kin help her."

The girl's father was a handsome man in his late thirties. She clutched at him as soon as he approached, and sobbed into his silken shirt and vest as she described the events of the past ten minutes. He listened quietly while Duane and his friends watched respectfully, and considered how to help the animal. Annie calmed down as her father assured her he would take care of things.

"I'm Mr. Hasslett," he introduced. "Thank ya fer stoppin ta look. I'll take it from here."

"'Scuse me, Sir," Duane offered. "But Beauty here ain't needin ta die. She kin be he'ped 'n made better."

"It's none a yer affair, Boy. Ya jest..."

"Please, Papa. Hear him out." Pleading eyes won her father's consent.

Now that the excitement had passed, the crowd dispersed as people went about their business and left those concerned to do what they would.

Duane explained the dog's injuries and suggested treatment. "She may always walk 'n run with a limp, but if she's truly loved, it shouldn't make no difference."

"How is it ya come by all this larnin? An' who's ta say it'd work if I was ta okay it?" Mr. Hasslett was skeptical.

"He sher knows his doins," Willis offered at risk of reprimand for speaking out of place.

"Thet's a certain," Tod broke in, sensing the black youth's reckless situation. "He's from the fightin an's bin learned real good on doctorin."

"Ain't the same," the man persisted.

"But, Papa..."

"Okay!" he threw up his arms in surrender. "We try."

The man brought around his buggy and all helped gently to lift Beauty onto a horse blanket in the wagon bed. Annie spread the blanket, then carefully folded it across her beloved pet.

"Climb in," Mr. Hasslett invited. "We'll drive over to the house and see what ya kin do."

The Hasslett home was once a grand plantation manor to the north of the city. Much of the help had been sold off and a few house servants and older field hands remained. They were evident about the property fixing fences and tending gardens and household chores. Mrs. Hasslett greeted the party from the door as the buggy entered the yard. She was accompanied by two younger children, a boy of about eight and a girl about seven.

Annie told of older brothers who were off fighting in the war. She also explained that her family had been prosperous in cotton and tobacco, but much of their wealth had gone to the war effort. Her Papa was very proud of his heritage and believed completely in the strength and purity of the Confederacy.

"Matthew, what's happened?" Mrs. Hasslett called at the site of strangers and of the dog in the blanket.

Reining the team to a stop, he explained, "Beauty's bin run down by a wagon 'n this boy says he kin save her." He pointed to Duane.

"What's yer name, Boy?" the woman asked.

"Duane Kinkade, M'am," he replied.

"Well ya jest tell me how I kin help ya 'n we'll see ta Beauty straight off." She smiled and Duane knew Annie's mother would see her dog got the best of care.

The porch became the operating theater as the leg was set and splinted. The jaw was checked and found to be okay except for some broken teeth. Then the cuts and scratches were bathed and covered with salves. It took an hour of slow work in an effort to keep Beauty from being upset. She seemed to sense everyone's caring and allowed herself to be treated.

"She'll need lot's a time 'n rest," Duane said when they had finished. "Bones take weeks ta mend. She may be hurtin inside an' thet'll take time fer healin, too."

"I don't know how we kin thank ya," Mrs. Hasslett stated, "but we kin certainly offer some lemonade an' sweet cake."

"Yes, M'am!" Tod accepted.

"Shoes, Mass'r Dee," Willis whispered.

"Mrs. Hasslett," Duane spoke up, "if ya has some shoes 'r coats 'r blankets, our company could sher use 'em. We got some money ta pay fer it with."

"Some sugar 'r fresh meat 'd sher be nice, too, M'am," Tod added.

There was an awkward moment as the boys wondered if they'd asked too much and the Hassletts were taken by complete surprise at the nature of their requests.

"Matt?" the woman wondered aloud.

"We kin help some," the man agreed. "How much money ya got?"

"Fifty dollars, Sir," Willis produced the money. Then he worried if he had been too quick.

"Come on in an' we'll see what kin be arranged," Mr. Hasslett invited. "I'll join ya after I see ta puttin Beauty in the kitchen. Yer nigger kin help carry the dog an' I'll see he gits fed somethin, too."

*   *   *

Mid-afternoon brought a chill in the air as the wagon bounced along the road leading south toward the camp. Matthew Hasslett and one of his colored had loaded it with a variety of provisions from the outbuildings and from some friends' businesses along the way. There was a barrel of salt pork, some cases of staple goods, a dozen blankets, three coats, a half dozen pairs of shoes, and an assortment of used clothes. The fifty dollars was accepted as payment in full. Should Tod's uncle wish to advance another fifty, the man had offered to bring a second wagon load within three weeks.

Passing through the various camps, the wagon finally approached Company K's tent lines. Corporal Cameron Doherty looked up from the fire he was building. The noise of the approaching wagon had caught his attention.

"Hey, Tod!" Doherty waved as he stood and approached the vehicle, "where ya'all been?"

Others came from their tents or afternoon chores to investigate the odd manner of the boys' return.

"What ya got there, Tod?" Damien asked as he stepped from his tent.

The door to Sergeant Raymond's house opened as curiosity drew him from its comfort. Eventually, half the company gathered about the wagon. While Tod stepped aside to converse with his uncle about the offer for a second supply run, Willis and the Hasslett colored unloaded the wagon. The sergeant directed that all materials be placed in front of his house until the captain decided on their distribution.

"Dee," Mr. Hasslett called him aside. "This here's fer you." He handed the boy a brown paper package.

"But, Sir..."

"Jest open it. Ain't a great deal, but figger'd it'd be handy."

Duane slipped the string off and opened the paper. Tod and his uncle had come up to talk business and paused to watch. The package revealed a bar of store-bought soap, a pound sack of coffee, and a new shirt.

"The shirt was my Lance's. He's only fifteen, so's should fit ya." He smiled proudly at the thought of sharing something from his family.

"I dunno what fer ya done all this. It weren't nothin what I did. But I sher thanks ya, Mr. Hasslett." He set the soap and coffee aside to open up the shirt and hold it up for size. It was large and would hang very loose. "It'll fit right finely, Sir."

"Ya take care, now," the man said. "I'll be back by ta let ya know how Beauty heals."

"Could Annie come long, too?" Duane asked.

"We'll see."

"Mr. Hasslett," Tod spoke up. "This here's my uncle, Lieutenant Jenkins."

The two men greeted each other as Tod asked Duane to show him what he'd gotten. Wandering to their tent, the boys found something warmer to wear against the evening chill. Duane found an empty sugar sack and divided the coffee, giving half to Tod. Meanwhile, the two men discussed and agreed upon a second supply purchase. As the wagon departed the camp and the officers looked over their unexpected good fortune, the various mess groups began to build their cook fires and to prepare for dinner. This meal would include extra rations from the newly arrived stores.

*   *   *

The scent and sizzle of salt pork hung with the heavy odor of wood smoke as dinner was prepared. There were flour for baking stick bread and coffee for brewing. The smells of dinner were a bouquet of fragrance.

As the group about the fire prepared dinner, Tod related the tale of the day's adventures. It was evident in his voice that he felt a sense of pride in Duane's actions. Having completed the story, he returned to a point which had puzzled him at the time.

"Dee," Tod asked, "why was ya cryin when ya first saw the dog layin there?"

Finishing the last of his dinner, Duane paused to gulp down some coffee. Setting the cup at his side, he looked straight at the other boy.

"Ya know how it was savin Annie thet got her dog hurt?"

"Yeh."

"Well, I've a dog, too. His name's Pounder. Last I saw him he was mendin from being shot ta save ma life. I ain't seen him since 'r eny a my family. Ya see, Ma was kilt afta Pa went ta the war. I left ta find him. Got close some, but ain't found him yet." He stopped, sensing a sudden silence in the gathering.

"We're real sorry," Foley broke the silence.

"But I ain't wantin fer pity," Duane returned. "It's a friend I'm wantin, like Willis been ta me."

"Guess thet's why fer ya neve' spoke a this afer?" Kim asked.

"I figger ya really ain't needin ta know. Ya's had yer own losses 'n hurts," Duane replied.

Tod said nothing. Pretending exhaustion, he rubbed his eyes and stretched, to catch the tears before they got loose to slide down his cheeks and give him away. Guilt brought a pain within and he wasn't sure how to handle it. He hoped it would go away.

Perhaps he could change the subject. "Eny one fer a song? First good meal in a while an' it ain't too bad a night."

"Good idea," Foley agreed. "I'll git Cameron ta bring his harmonica Let's git cleaned up 'n put some wood on the fire."

The dishes and utensils were cleaned and put up and the evening was spent in song. Sergeant Raymond, Willis, and several others joined the group to add their voices, too. The day's events were retold and news was shared by others as well. Lieutenant Jenkins brought word of the captain's decision to distribute the new clothing supplies following morning muster, and orders for company drill during the next day.

Darkness crept over the countryside. Candle lanterns were lit. The encampment winked with its thousand scattered fireflies. Tattoo called the troops to their tents, and taps settled them in their blankets.

*　　*　　*

Winter passed into Spring. As the weather warmed, the drill schedule increased. Companies drilled in the morning. Regiments drilled some afternoons and gathered for evening muster and review. Mr. Hasslett was as good as his word and delivered a wagon load of food supplies, a few used shoes, and an assortment of clothing. Beauty continued to mend as she thrived under the loving attention of Annie and the other youngsters of the family. It was as though she sensed she had to stay off her leg and was content to lie around as the center of attention.

Duane asked if he might visit later to see Beauty when she was back on her feet. What he really wanted was to get away from army life. There was a feeling of family warmth which lingered in his memory from the day he'd been there to help save the dog. He liked Annie. He liked a strange inner warmth that had been touched by the joy she had shown when he helped her Beauty. Mr. Hasslett got the captain's permission to have the boys out when the time came.

Tod had a new-found respect for his tentmate. He had someone to talk to who could understand his inner aching for his brother. He talked of Jason, remembering the things they'd done together and opinions shared and lessons learned. For the first time since he'd left home, Duane spoke of his mother in great detail, her likes and dislikes, reprimands for his foolishness such as the time he fed the livestock in mid-morning because they looked hungry, moments of warmth like the day the storm flooded the dam he and Jamie had built. The two boys developed a closer friendship and were frequently seen together in their travels about the camps. One day as the two paused to watch one of the Virginia artillery batteries at drill, they were surprised to observe a spunky youngster about Duane's age on one of the gun crews. When drill was finished, they stayed on to visit and to learn all about artillery warfare from a proud expert.

Near mid-March, word came of a great fight of cavalry at Kelly's Ford, nearly twenty-five miles northwest of Fredericksburg. The Federal cavalry force was unexpectedly well organized and proficient. It cost the Confederates dearly as they lost twice as many to casualties as did the Federals. A noted officer from Alabama, Major John Pelham, was killed in the engagement. He was well known to the men of Company K and much respected by his fellow officers right up to General Lee himself.

Early April brought an invitation to the Hasslett estate. Beauty had recovered enough to begin exercising her leg. Annie rode into the camp with her father to pick up Duane and Tod. She sure looked pretty, the younger boy thought. Both boys had bathed in the wooden washtub the night before. They wore their best clothes for the day's visit.

The beautifully mild day passed quickly as Duane and Tod roamed the farm property, enjoyed a picnic lunch with the other children, played with Beauty, and visited with the Hasslett family. Annie was the perfect hostess– polite and formal femininity as required, and the playful tomboy when permitted. All too soon, the boys were once again riding the wagon. As they returned to camp, chattering along the way, Duane suddenly realized there was little chance they'd get away from the camp again. It had been such a perfect day. He stared at Annie as she answered some question his friend had asked. She sure was beautiful.

He'd really miss her. He wished he could hold her. What were these strange feelings? He must be falling in love.

Annie caught him staring. She never broke her train of conversation, but she smiled. Duane felt himself blush and his face get hot.

Suddenly they were stopping. The wagon had reached the camp. A short time later it was gone again and Duane was standing alone, waving, and watching it disappear into the distance. Tod had already gone to build the fire for cooking supper.

*　　*　　*

In mid-April, the rains came. For over a week they continued to turn the countryside into a muddy quagmire. Finally, over the last weekend of the month, the skies cleared and brisk winds dried the mud. Within two days word came that Jeb Stuart's cavalry had reported Federal troops moving north along the river.

*　　*　　*

Wednesday's predawn light was just beginning to brighten the canvass when Willis burst frantically into the boys' tent.

"Hurry, Mass'rs!" he called. "Ya's gotta drum up the camp Mass'r Tod and the captain wants Mass'r Dee right quick. The Yanks is crossin the rive'."

"Damnation!" Tod exclaimed. "Sure a hell of a way ta be gittin a day goin!"

"Thet's fer sher!" Duane agreed. "Tell the captain as we's movin," he spoke to Willis.

The two boys dressed on the run as the drums began the long roll throughout the division. A hazy fog covered the riverlands, giving a ghostly cast to the camps. Tod took his position near the captain's tent and began his drum roll, the last of his clothes on the ground at his side. Duane suddenly realized he had left his gear behind out of everyday habit, and wasn't yet equipped for battle. Rushing back to the tent, he buckled on his gunbelt and grabbed the rest of his equipment, then hurried toward the captain's tent. Throughout the camp the men were stumbling forth in dazed and sleepy confusion.

"What's up, Tod?" Foley asked as he rushed up, still tucking in his shirt tail.

"Yanks comin," his nephew replied.

"But I ain't even brought ma gun!" Kim exclaimed as he overheard the conversation.

"Dee," Captain Rogers called from within his tent. "See Willis fer a mount, then git ta Colonel Fry's courier staff."

"Yes, Sir!" the boy acknowledged.

"Folla me, Mass'r Dee." Willis instructed.

Meanwhile, Lieutenants Guthries and Jenkins instructed the company to prepare immediately for an expected attack. The sergeants quickly issued ammunition and checked to be sure each man had gun, cartridge box, and gear. Loud and orderly confusion reigned throughout the regiment as companies of men were brought under arms and officers scurried about to learn the state of affairs.

Duane secured a frisky young stallion, roan in color, and rode off to regimental headquarters only to be sent on to General A. P. Hill's division headquarters. There it was learned that Federal troops had crossed on pontoon bridges and were entrenching in line along the river road under cover of Union batteries on the river's north bank. One of Lee's divisions had already deployed along the railroad embankment near the Old Richmond Road and another was in motion to reinforce it. General Hill was to bring his division into line along the crest of the ridge to the right. Duane carried the news back to Colonel Fry, then back to Captain Rogers. The troops were rushed into position. Poised for the attack, the armies faced each other expectantly. Nothing happened.

For Duane, there was little time for boredom as he kept busy relaying information. Messages from scouting reports came in through General Lee's staff to be relayed by the couriers to the various division and regimental commanders. During the afternoon, word came from General Stuart that Union troops had moved in force to cross the Rappahannock northwest of Fredericksburg and were gathering at Chancellorsville. That night, a division was sent west to protect the Confederate left.

Thursday dawned with the Union army still entrenched at their river crossing. More reports came of Federal troops to the west. Finally, orders were given to leave one division facing the inactive Union bridgehead and march the rest of General Jackson's corps westward at dawn the following morning.

The day was spent packing field packs in preparation for the move. During a brief moment after delivering a message to Captain Rogers, Duane gathered his personal gear to be grabbed at the last minute. That night, all was in readiness for midnight muster.

As midnight passed in brilliant moonlight, the company struck camp and the corps prepared to move out. General Early's division remained in place along the railroad while the rest of the corps departed by the Old Mine Road, out of sight of the unsuspecting Federal force. When night slipped to a dense misty dawn the first day of May, Fredericksburg had been left miles behind as Jackson's troops advanced to join up with the divisions sent ahead the previous day.

For a while, Duane rode with General Hill's courier staff. He learned that two divisions were already engaging the enemy at the Tabernacle Church, about four miles east of Chancellorsville. Jackson was advancing to join them with four more divisions and more than a hundred and fifty pieces of field artillery. The boy sensed a growing excitement as he moved ever closer to certain battle.

An hour before noon, the elements of the Confederate Army came together. Brisk skirmishing began as Generals Lee and Jackson ordered their troops to advance and pressure the Yanks. Musket fire rattled along a two-mile front, mixed with Rebel yells. By nightfall, the Union pickets and skirmishers were forced back to their army encampments.

The boy was exhausted. He had been on the road relaying dispatches since before dawn. Duane spent the night in a forest glade beside the road. The division slept under arms, their heads pillowed on their packs. The officers conferred as plans were made to circle around and strike the Federal forces from behind their right flank. By dawn of the next morning, the troops were on the move. Silently they proceeded as the air echoed with the rhythmic clicking of bouncing canteens.

The ten-mile march took most of the day. For fifty minutes of every hour, the column advanced. After a ten-minute rest, it marched another fifty minutes. Duane heard gunfire to the rear of the column during the late morning and learned of a Federal attack which had been checked by remaining troops under General Lee. Word came around mid-afternoon that the troops of the Federal right were unaware of the Confederate move as they relaxed in the sun or slaughtered local beef cattle. Their weapons were all stacked. General Jackson also learned that the enemy lines extended beyond the road he had intended to use to outflank them. Thus it was late in the afternoon before his corps was in position to attack.

General Hill's division was third in line of march. The two front divisions had cleared the last dirt lane onto the turnpike to the west of the Federal defenses. Duane found himself with others of the courier staff crowded off the dirt roadway to allow the troops to pass. They slipped into a break between brigades and rode out to the turnpike where there was room to get off onto an open field.

A short distance up the roadway, General Jackson sat astride his Little Sorrel. With his watch in hand, he supervised the disposition of the troops as they arrived on the field. As quiet as 26,000 men can move, the brigades advanced from the wooded lane onto the turnpike and into position.

Duane saw that beyond the general, the front division was spread across the roadway to disappear almost a mile to either side. Thick woodland lay between the armies, preventing the enemy from viewing the massing for the attack. The boy watched as General Hill's division moved slowly into place. There was no sign of his regiment since it was advancing far off to the right of the turnpike. Glancing toward the sun, far to the west, yet still well up in the warm afternoon sky, he judged it to be between five and six o'clock. All was in readiness.

The front line began to advance into the thick woodland. Suddenly the woods echoed with the crackle of musketry as Union picket lines opened fire on the leading regiments. Immediately, Confederate buglers carried the call to charge and were joined all along the line by the blood- curdling Rebel yell. Ten thousand human voices shattered the evening quiet with such a fearful commotion as to stir up every living forest creature and drive it before the advancing onslaught. Rabbit, fox, and deer rushed in terror before the Confederate charge to race across the Union defenses and through the camps, busy with preparations for the evening meal.

Jackson and his generals followed in the thick of movement along the pike. Staff officers and courier riders kept nearby. The artillery was divided. Much was parked in a field on the right while some batteries advanced in column along the road.

Captain James Power Smith, assistant Adjutant-General, was the designated center of communication. Riding a black charger, he gathered his staff of couriers to maintain the flow of information from the point at which the charge had begun.

Ahead, the roar of artillery joined the thunderclaps of the leading ranks of rifle fire ripping into the first companies of Federal infantry. A few volleys of murderous musket fire seemed to check the advance briefly. Then the advance was swift and quickly outdistanced Duane and his comrades as the Union Army collapsed and fell back. Before the half hour was out, the sound of orderly gunfire had disintegrated into scattered pockets of fighting as the heavy underbrush and woodlands tore at the bodies of the men rushing through them, and fragmented regimental and company organization.

Duane listened to the distant sound of battle and thought of his friends in Company K. He wondered where they might be and was lost in thoughts for their welfare while all about him, officers and messengers came and went. His ponderings were rudely interrupted by one of Smith's aides.

"Private!" a young lieutenant called, "ride ahead to the farm house about a quarter mile on the right and see if General Hill is there. Tell him that artillery will be following."

"Yes, Sir," the boy responded as he dug his heels into his stallion's flanks and leaped into a run.

On the way, Duane crossed the first lines of battle where a fierce slaughter had taken place. Several hundred dead and wounded lay along the breastworks of earthen defenses that stretched across the road. A number of their comrades were attempting to help the wounded until ambulance wagons could arrive and carry them to the hospitals. At the farm house the battle was quickly advancing eastward as artillery was letting fly a terrible storm of shot and shell and the infantry continued to fire and advance on the enemy. Union troops were in a general route as they fled in panic before the deadly storm. The quick lightning of hundreds of rifles dealt death and damage from a dozen different directions.

Duane located one of the brigadier generals. "I've a message for General Hill," he hollered above the storm.

"He's moving toward the tavern yonder!" the general pointed.

The boy gazed at the panorama of war as far as the eye could see. Ten thousand men surged eastward as the Confederate brigades poured forth a murderous fire in a thousand flashes of riflery, and a wave of blue fell and ebbed in retreat or rallied briefly around some point to pause and fire back. Duane started forward to find the general when suddenly a line of Federal resistance took form at right angle to the road near the tavern. Artillery and rifle fire began to erupt in deadly explosions of canister and gunfire. Yet as each eruption mowed the road clear of advancing Confederates, a new wave replaced the one cut down.

Unexpectedly, Duane found himself in the midst of the violent fury with bullets picking at his clothing and shell fragments tearing at men as they screamed and fell nearby. Quickly he reined his horse to follow in the midst of regiments charging down a country lane to the right. Within minutes the mass of Rebel regiments was struck head on by a charge of Union cavalry. The roar of battle was deafening as a volley of Confederate rifle fire slammed into the advancing cavalry and stopped it dead in its tracks. In seconds more than two dozen cavalrymen and three times as many horses, lay dead or dying or wounded.

Muskets clattered and rifles shattered the countryside with violent death and destruction. Screams of men and animals rent the air as cannon shells crashed into massed humanity. Confusion and horror reigned as riderless horses panicked and cavalrymen on foot ran to catch a mount or seek cover. Men and animals ran into each other in their fearful dash for safety. Confederate infantry fired in volley at fleeing Union cavalry troopers caught afoot. Pack mules from the cavalry ran wild, tied in pairs and carrying their burdens of extra ammunition. Cannon shells exploded in the trees as rifle fire ripped along the ground. A panicked pair of mules being chased by a cavalryman in search of a mount, became tangled in a tree. A shell exploded in the tree, setting off the packs of ammunition and disintegrating the animals. As the murderous fire from the grey-clad soldiers cut down great numbers of men in blue, those who could, fled as fast as beast or foot would carry them. Weapons and packs were cast aside in their haste to get away.

Duane was unable to move. Caught in the pack of humanity, he was forced to the side of the road. Eventually the boy managed to move into a thicket, dense enough to force the tide of advancing Confederates to split and flow around it.

As the battle surged ever eastward, Union artillery was gathered on high ground about a mile from the tavern. Soon it sent forth a shower of death which slowed the Confederate front and gave the shattered Federals a chance to rally and establish a new line of defense.

Duane retreated, unable to find the general and deliver his message. Too much had happened and it seemed too late to make a difference. The Federals were quickly organizing a line of defense and more artillery was being brought to bear. The attack slowed as daylight faded and the boy worked his way back toward the main road.

Captain Smith was gathering together his staff and proceeding to join General Jackson when Duane came into view. All about the battle field, the Confederate units were trying to reorganize as they brought together the scattered companies and officers gathered their men.

"Hurry, Boy!" the captain called.

Duane rode to catch up.

The couriers were gathered. The captain and his staff continued to seek the general. Twilight fell, and with it a silence. The party rode through groups of prisoners under guard, regiments trying to regroup, and wounded waiting under trees by the turnpike. Finally the captain's party approached an open field in which there were horsemen near a cabin.

Captain Smith recognized the officer in charge. "General Rodes?" he called.

"General Jackson's ahead on the road, Captain," the general responded. "Tell him I will be here at this cabin if I am wanted."

"I'll do that," Smith replied.

As the group moved on, a pair of shots was heard. Then a company volley from the right was followed by a volley from the left. An officer whom Duane recognized from General Hill's staff, rode up in a panic.

"Generals Jackson and Hill are wounded and some with them are dead!" he called.

The group rushed forward at a gallop to lend assistance. They found Jackson in General Hill's arms, lying on the ground. Smith quickly dismounted to check the general's wounds. Cutting the senior officer's coat sleeve its full length, he took a handkerchief to tie off the flow of blood from a shattered arm. Duane and others were sent off in search of Doctor Hunter McGuire, corps surgeon and friend to the general, and for an ambulance. In the time it took to secure an ambulance, Captain Smith brought the general by litter within friendly lines, under a hazardous fire from the enemy. The boy returned with the ambulance and stayed with the staff as they left from the front.

"I must pull my men back and reorganize!" Brigadier-General Pender, commander of the troops in the immediate area, told the general.

"You must hold at all costs," General Jackson ordered his brigadier.

"What now?" an aide asked.

"Find Jeb Stuart," one of General Hill's aides instructed. "Pass the word we're moving forward."

As riders were sent out, the ambulance carrying the general proceeded to the tavern where a rest stop would be made.

"Private," Captain Smith turned to the boy, "I understand you're from General Archer's brigade of Hill's division."

"Thet's right, Sir."

"Earlier they were off to the right." The captain paused to check on the general. Continuing, he instructed, "We've pushed the line far enough that the road is open behind the lines."

"Which road?" Duane asked, worried about becoming lost in the dark of night.

"Hold a minute," the captain held his horse as the ambulance continued on. Turning to face a farm house they had just passed, he pointed out a road to the south. "See the road that cuts south behind the farm?" Duane nodded. "Follow it to where it forks, then keep south. The right of the line should be about a mile or two south from there."

"Thank ya, Sir," his voice quavered slightly from exhaustion and concern.

"The sky's night light and the broken moon'll see ya through. Go quickly and get some rest b'fore dawn. Tell General Archer ta go with first light."

"Yes, Sir. I'm on ma way."

The two parted and Duane pushed his stallion into an easy canter.

Traveling the country lane was easier than he had expected. It was alive with regiments from two of General Hill's brigades, as they shifted into position to renew the attack. Brigadier-General James Archer was with his brigade about a half mile from the fork in the road. Duane found him sitting by a tree with some of his staff. He rode up and dismounted.

"One a yer couriers, General," an aide observed.

"What news have you, Private?" the general asked.

"Generals Jackson and Hill was wounded, Sir, 'n General Stuart is in command," the boy reported.

"What!"

"Yes, Sir. Not mor'n fifty minutes back," Duane continued. "Captain Smith says fer me ta say fer the general as yer ta go with first light." Out of breath with exhaustion he added, "Will ya be needin me fer a bit?"

"No, Private. Where's yer company?"

"Company K of Colonel Fry's regiment, Sir."

"They're across the road in the woods behind the Virginia artillery. Get some sleep."

Duane walked in search of the company, leading his stallion by the reins.

The soldiers of the brigade lay in company formation in the woods and thickets straddling the road. Sleeping on the ground or against the trees, many rested with their weapons at their side or across their body. Captain Rogers and his lieutenants were standing near a small fire on which they'd brewed a pot of coffee. They looked up at the approaching shadows of horse and boy.

"Who's there?" the captain asked.

"Private Kinkade, Sir."

"Ya look like hell," Lieutenant Jenkins observed. "Ya okay?"

"Yes, Sir. Jest wore out 'n a bit messed from the fightin." He tied the horse to a tree.

"Here," Lieutenant Guthries offered a cup of lukewarm coffee.

"Thanks." The boy took the cup and drank slowly.

The men studied the boy while he drank. They had not yet been in the immediate conflict. He obviously had. His clothing was torn by bullets and fragments of shellfire, and his face and hands were blackened from gunsmoke and dirt, and streaked from sweat. Duane glanced along the lines of sleeping soldiers, searching for Tod and his drum. He found his tentmate about thirty yards off and was satisfied. Then he noticed some bandages among the men.

"Ya see much fightin?" the boy asked.

"Yeste'day it was a might fierce," Damien answered. "We was at the back end a the march 'n a Yank division hit b'hind. But General Lee brought up some brigades as were with him and took on the Yanks so as we could git along. There was others further back as got the worst of it."

"Ya git some sleep," Rogers ordered. "Tamorra ya take General Archer's report ta Hill."

"Hill ain't runnin thin's. He 'n Jackson was wounded."

"Hell, no!"

"Yes, Sir. General Heth has the division an Jeb Stuart's doin fer Jackson."

Duane described briefly the action he had seen and the wounding of the generals. Afterwards he settled by the tree to which his horse was tied. Resting his head on a rise in the root structure, he was soon fast asleep.

*   *   *

It was still dark when Willis shook Duane by the shoulder to awaken him.

"Here, Mass'r Dee," he offered. "Have a biscuit."

"Thank ya, Willis," he said. "What time is it?"

"Stars is fadin ta day," the youth answered.

All about them, the men were eating from the provisions they carried if they were hungry. The fire had been put out and the coffee pot packed. Duane untied his horse and stood by, ready to mount. Weapons were checked and the company was formed in line of battle. Orders were passed in whispers. The brigade was ready.

On the high ground in front, called Hazel Grove, the Federals had a strong position of artillery and infantry, capable of devastating the Confederate wing of Jackson's corps as well as the troops of General Lee's left about a mile to the east.

Confederate skirmishers were sent ahead to drive back the Federal pickets and to feel out the enemy's strength. As the light of dawn began to lighten the forest landscape, the sharp crackle of musketry opened to the front. Word came back that the Union force was withdrawing. Quickly the advance was ordered and the brigade charged the slope onto the hilltop. As the infantry moved forward, Colonel Alexander put his artillery batteries into motion. The guns, already hooked to their limbers, were rushed forth to be placed into position on the hill.

General Archer, easily spotted for his slight build and long beard, followed the movement closely. Duane mounted and rode over to join the general's staff and observe the action. Riding toward the fighting, they entered the smoke of battle and observed the excitement of success as the Confederate troops rounded up some hundred prisoners and added a handful of captured artillery pieces to the lineup.

Searching for signs of the Alabama 13th, Duane's attention was distracted by the artillery as he caught sight of the youngster he'd met previously, enthusiastically helping to prepare his gun. After several minutes, the batteries began to open against the Federal position to the east. The boy worked the lanyard to his gun. Duane smiled as he watched him pull the lanyard to fire the charge, roll about on the ground in clownish glee, then jump to his feet and grab the lanyard to fire again.

Meanwhile, General Archer wrote out a brief description of the action to be sent ahead to General Stuart.

"Private," he called to Duane, "take this pouch to Stuart and add any information ya learn along the way."

"Yes, Sir. On the way." He slung the bags across the saddle in front of him and started back toward the road.

Duane listened to the orderly thunder of the guns in Hazel Grove as he worked his way through the regiments which had not yet engaged. Once clear of the brigade and its support wagons, he leaned into a gallop to race north toward the turnpike.

The boy courier had just begun his race along the road when the guns to the north opened on the enemy. Shells shrieked through the air and the ground beneath him trembled as the cannon roared forth a hellish rain of death and destruction all along the line. Clouds of smoke rose through the trees. Within minutes, the charge was sounded and the infantry attacked with ferocious firepower.

Riding the road in the earliest light of day, Duane entered the reserve lines of General Rode's corps. There he was directed to the farm house on the turnpike where he was relieved of the courier pouch and sent forth to gather information on Brigadier-General McGowan's brigade, advancing on Archer's left.

McGowan's brigade was heavily engaged in the woods less then six hundred yards beyond the house and just south of the road. Duane rushed forward into an explosive hellfire of searing musketry and tree-splitting cannon shell. At the moment, the Confederates were advancing. Fierce fighting surrounded the young rider as he debated pushing further to find the general. Shells exploded in the trees overhead, splintering branches and sending large limbs smashing to the ground below. Shrapnel from exploding shell fragments ripped through the tree-tops and tore through the movement of advancing infantry. A new sound was evident in the smoke-filled forest – the crackle of fire. In several places, the woods and underbrush had burst into flame.

Suddenly a sheet of rifle fire roared into the ranks on the right, cutting down grey-clad soldiers in waves. The stallion rose up on its hind legs, screaming in pain as a swarm of bullets ripped through the screaming, yelling mass of troops around the boy. He felt pain as a bullet burned across the back of his hand. A tree limb came crashing down on a company to the left, felling a dozen unsuspecting soldiers. Flames spread noisily in the underbrush, engulfing the wounded caught in its path. Union soldiers advancing on the right pushed the Confederates back. Wounded of both armies clung to trees, frantically pushing away the brush and leaves at their feet in hope of staying the flames. Still they came.

All about the boy on the screaming horse, the woods were full of cries, gunfire, and crackling flames. Trying to stay with the crazed stallion, Duane found himself on the verge of panic. Still on its hind legs, the horse staggered to the side. Duane heard the impact of a half dozen bullets ripping into his mount's chest and belly and cringed with the expectation of bullets striking his own body. Instead, he found himself falling as the stallion toppled backwards and pinned the boy under its corpse.

The brigade fell back in retreat, taking along whomever of the wounded that could be gathered up. Not far to the left another Confederate brigade was being swept back. Pinned beneath his dead horse, Duane struggled to free himself. Grabbing the saddle, he pulled himself up and saw the horror as several dozen dazed survivors milling about in confusion, were mowed down at point-blank range by advancing Federals. Screams of pain, the crashing roar of infantry fire, and the crackling conflagration of burning forest made a living, breathing, crying, fear-filled hell. The boy pushed frantically with his free foot in terrified attempts to break free. Inch by inch he drew himself from beneath the weight of the animal as movement of men in battle surged through the surrounding woodland.

New gunfire erupted behind the Confederate front. Fresh brigades were entering the battlefield, rushing through the ranks of the retreating. As the Union troops fired into the collapsing brigade, the new arrivals flung themselves on the ground and began firing over the heads of their retiring comrades. Duane hugged the ground close to the stallion's back, hoping to stay low enough to remain safe. Circulation in the pinned leg had been restricted by the pressure of weight and the boy felt a loss of feeling as the leg went numb.

Some of the retreating were wounded by their own rescuers. The rest dropped and froze in place. The advancing Confederates did the same. Their officers could do nothing to budge them as fear took command.

Caught in the middle, Duane looked to the front where Federal forces were massing for a counter attack. Two more Confederate brigades came to the rescue and poured a devastating fire into the Federal line, pushing it back. Shortly after they began to push forward, Union infantry returned such an exploding hail of lead as to decimate the leading edge of grey, mortally wounding both commanding generals.

Again the position was in danger of being overrun by men in blue. The rescuing Southern brigades fell back, exhausted. They included the Stonewall Brigade which had been involved in so much of the action because of its strength and experience. They were worn out. Yet once again they advanced, this time under the personal encouragement of General Stuart.

For Duane, time had been an eternity. Now the tide was turned and the Federals were driven back upon their own artillery, about a half mile back. A passing soldier helped Duane free himself from his horse, then moved on. The storm of battle continued to tear its way through the wooded wilderness. The fires burned in patches about the forest and underbrush. The boy dragged himself toward a broken tree. There he sat and rubbed his leg to regain circulation and feeling. Prickling needles of pain gave way to weakness. Eventually Duane was able to stand tentatively before hobbling aimlessly toward a company of survivors, debating their next course of action.

Deciding there was little left for him to do, Duane joined the efforts to help the wounded. He found himself unhurt, but bloodied from his horse's wounds and from the bloodied forest floor. The scene was one of horror. Dead and wounded carpeted the blood-soaked ground as far as one could see in all directions. Charred corpses hugged the trees where the fire had caught the wounded. Others littered the charred thickets where they had fallen and died. Cries and pleadings of the wounded added a mournful wail to the sound of battle strong in the distant fighting and artillery fire.

The battle ebbed by mid-morning as the Union Army pulled back and prepared to retreat. Duane busied himself throughout the morning in the efforts to save the wounded. He found it hard to believe that some he found were still alive. Ripping fabric from whatever was at hand, the boy worked quickly to stem the flow of bleeding and to keep the battlefield wounded alive for the surgeon's table. Working his way across the battlefield, he found his way to the edge of the tree line opening onto Hazel Grove. By noon he found his way back to his own company in his own brigade.

The guns were quiet on Hazel Grove. General Lee and his staff had gone ahead to the Chancellor House where the Union command had been. Many of the batteries of artillery from early morning had been moved farther to the front. The field was scattered with fragments of the brigade, still recovering or regrouping from the morning's fighting. Wounded were being attended and the dead were being gathered for burial. Company K was gathered with others of the regiment. Duane was overjoyed to find his companions. He approached at a very tired walk and noticed the men of the company had dropped in disorderly exhaustion wherever they had been when the fighting had stopped.

"Where's the captain, Sergeant?" the boy asked the first person he found.

"Where's yer horse?" Sergeant Matthewson asked upon recognizing the courier on foot.

"Shot out from under me," Duane explained.

"The captain's hurt bad, Dee. They took him off early this mornin," the sergeant answered. "Lieutenant Jenkins is in charge 'n he's talkin ta Willis an' Sergeant Raymond on supplies."

The man pointed to the trio in conversation near a supply wagon about twenty yards off.

Approaching the conference, Duane waited respectfully to be noticed.

"Our wanderin' boy has returned," the sergeant acknowledged.

"Dee," the lieutenant asked, "could ya see ta Tod? He ain't lookin' much good an ain't sayin' much neither."

"Yes, Sir," the boy replied. "How's Captain Rogers an' when d' I git duty?"

"Dunno 'bout the captain. Lots a officers is hurt an' the general's doin' fer General Heth an' the colonel's doin' fer the general. We stay put till orders is passed."

"Yes, Sir. I'll look ta Tod, now."

"Thanks, Dee. He's layin' yonder where's Kim an' Foley kin keep watch on him."

Duane found his friend very pale and only half conscious.

"What happened?" the younger boy asked.

"Don't rightly know," Foley answered from where he knelt beside his nephew. "He was near the end a the company by the captain when a enemy shell exploded in the air. Near 'bout a dozen went down from our company an' the next. Four was killed outright 'n Captain Rogers tore up bad. But Tod got up 'n looked okay."

"Thet you, Dee?" a feeble voice asked. "Ya look real bad hurt."

Duane dropped by the older boy's feet. "Yeah, Tod, it's me. But I ain't hurt. What's wrong?"

"Ain't knowin' fer sher." He winced from sharp pain. "Is ma legs both there? I cain't feel two, but cain't say as what's missin'." He paused, tired from the effort to talk. "God, it hurts!" he whispered.

"Kim," Duane instructed the youth beside whom the drum lay, "I need Tod's drumsticks and strap."

"What fer?"

"Jest hurry." There was a panic in the voice that ended any question.

Duane slipped the strap under both legs and lay the sticks between.

"Hold his shoulders," the boy instructed as he grabbed a boot by its heel and toe. His eye caught sight of a flaw – a hole through the upper leather. Releasing his grip, he tied the strap around the leg, just above the boot top, and slipped a drumstick into the knot.

"What fer ya doin thet?" Kim asked.

"Jest hold him an ya'll see."

Once more he gripped the boot and eased it off.

"Oh, God!" Kim gasped. The boot spilled forth a puddle of blood as it revealed sock and pant leg saturated and dripping with blood.

Quickly Duane tightened his tourniquet.

"What happened?" Foley asked.

Duane held the boot so they could see the hole. "Seems a fragment a thet shell shot through 'n inta his leg. Lucky he ain't bled ta death.

But still we could be too late. Kin ya find some bandages? Ya best fix ta git him ta the hospital, too."

As Kim went to see his brother for bandages and transportation, the boy sent Foley for a bottle or keg of whiskey. Corporal Robert DiPhilippo and Private Matthew Guthries, who were nearby, came to offer their help. Others became aware of what was happening and turned to watch. Sergeant Raymond joined them as soon as he learned from Kim that Tod's condition was discovered.

Duane found a knife and carefully cut open the bloody trouser leg, then peeled off the saturated sock.

"What fer ya'd do thet?" Tod asked faintly.

"Yer shot through the leg," his friend answered. "We gotta git ya fixed up."

Satisfied his friend knew what he was doing, the wounded boy relaxed and drifted into unconsciousness. Robert and Matthew helped expose the wound and offered their canteens to wash away the blood. Duane examined the wound along with the sergeant.

"Don't look broke," the man announced. "But thet piece a shell's still in there. Ain't no second hole."

Duane agreed. Foley returned with a half bottle of whiskey which the boy took and opened. Kim returned with some bandages while half the whiskey was being poured over the wound. The wound was wrapped and the fabric soaked with the rest of the brew.

"Keeps it from festerin bad," the boy explained in answer to the quizzical looks from those around.

A wagon arrived and Tod was sent on to the hospital.

"Ya best go with him, Foley," the sergeant instructed. "Be sure ta bring back thet drumstick an' strap. The new drummer boy'll need em."

"Who's thet?" Duane asked.

"You, of course," Sergeant Raymond replied. "Ya've done afer. Ya kin do it now. We need you, Boy," he cocked his head and cracked a smile. "Yer too valuable ta be off doin courier."

*   *   *

As Sunday ended and nightfall darkened the countryside, the armies rested quietly. Their soldiers were tired. Those on picket duty settled in quickly with no interest in harassing each other. General Archer's brigade, now under the command of Colonel Fry, had been moved forward to press the attack against the retreating Federals. But word had come of a new threat from the Union forces back in Fredericksburg. The divisions at Chancellorsville settled in along the turnpike while General Lee turned his attention to the potential danger from behind. The troops slept where they lay, having taken their leisure to cook a supper of salt beef, beans, fried bread, and coffee.

Foley had returned to report that Tod was very critical. He had lost so much blood, and only time would tell if he could hang on to recover or take sick and die. The youth had brought back the bloodied strap and stick as the sergeant had instructed, and Duane had collected together all that remained of his friend's gear to keep with his own.

Monday saw little change in the brigade's situation. It remained in its position across from the Union center. As the day passed, another division was sent toward Fredericksburg to check the new Federal offensive. At Chancellorsville, the divisions remained poised but inactive. Tod's relations took advantage of the calm and went to visit him. Duane sent his tentmate's gear along, knowing he would probably be sent on to a proper hospital as he got stronger.

Throughout the day a fierce battle was fought miles away, while quiet reigned along the turnpike. By evening it was evident that Tod was hanging on. Word came, too, that Captain Rogers had lost an arm, but was expected to recover.

The night was spent in the open as soldiers slept in line of battle. Tuesday brought word that the distant fighting had ended when the enemy retreated across the river. Rain came early in the day and soaked the countryside all day long. Some companies set tentlines alongside the roadway. Many just stood around in wet misery with an oilcloth raincoat draped across their shoulders, if they owned one. Duane sat on the drum which he had turned on its side, and draped the great blue overcoat across his shoulders. His brimmed hat offered some protection at first. But eventually everything was saturated with rainwater and there was nothing to do but sit amongst the thousands and wait in misery for the storm to pass.

As another day dawned, the weather cleared and it was learned that the whole Union Army had pulled back across the river and was retreating to its camps at Fredericksburg. The Confederate Army did the same. Three days later, Duane found himself and his comrades back in the camp they'd left the previous week.

* * *

May passed into June. At mid-month General Lee had gone to meet with President Davis in Richmond to discuss his plans for the next campaign. After his return, he had reorganized the army into three corps. General Jackson had died of his wounds on Sunday the tenth and was sorely missed as new leadership was selected. General Longstreet's command continued in the I Corps. Jackson's II Corps would be commanded by Lieutenant- General Richard S. Ewell. General Archer's brigade became part of the new III Corps under the command of Lieutenant-General Ambrose Powell Hill. The passing weeks had been spent in a routine of drill and foraging.

There had been visits to the hospital in Fredericksburg to which the wounded from Chancellorsville had been brought. Some who hadn't seemed so badly wounded had died from blood poison. Others went through a rough time of pain and infection before healing. Captain Rogers was among them. Tod was one of the lucky ones who began their recovery early and continued to do well.

The first day of June saw great excitement as the soldiers shared their opinions on the new organization and leadership which had been announced the day before. There was also an air of high expectation and enthusiasm as the general's plans to invade the north became the talk of the newspapers and the driving energy for the soldiers.

A warm sun played peek-a-boo with white banks of clouds as Willis and Duane plodded along the River Road on their way back to camp. Fishing had been profitable, and each carried a string of bass and some trout in one hand and a fishing line rolled on a stick of wood in the other. "Sher were a good ketch, Mass'r Dee," Willis commented. "Supper'll be a good change from salt pork as is gittin strong."

"Ya mean rottin spoilt-like," the boy added. "It does smell some when it cooks an' could twist yer innards good 'cept fer some sugar ta he'p the taste."

The air was vibrant with the movement of wagons and equipment and the activity of men and companies busy at drill, foraging, camp chores; or relaxed about their camps. The smell of the army blended with its sights and sounds to invade the senses with the aromas of latrines, animals, fire smoke, and unclean bodies. Across the river, the Union Army kept active in its camps.

The boy and his black companion paused to watch a couple of rowdy young infantrymen stir up a whirl of dust as each attempted to wrestle the other to the ground. Scores of cheering comrades encouraged the combatants as they wagered everything from cash money to coffee to boots on the outcome of the fray.

"Who ya think's gonna win?" Duane asked.

"Whatcha say fer the big guy?" Willis offered.

"May be," the boy responded, unconvinced.

"Not too sure?"

"No."

"Ya seein somethin in the other soldier?"

"He does 'pear ta be fast," Duane smiled.

"Sher does." A grin of agreement revealed Willis's teeth.

They waited a few more minutes, watching expectantly for the match to end. Suddenly, the smaller man saw an opening, dove for his opponent's knees, and drove him backwards to the ground.

The air erupted with wild cheers and yells as Duane and Willis turned to continue on their way. The sound of an approaching horse caused them to look ahead. A grey horse with black mane and tail walked toward them bearing a regal rider.

"Aftanoon, Mass'r Robert," the boy greeted. "How's Traveler taday?"

"He's just fine, Soldier," the general replied, easing his horse to a stop.

"Mighty fine string of fish you have there. Your company will be mighty pleased to see you."

"Thank ya, Sir," Duane returned. "When da we git ta movin north? Here tell we's gittin ta some good foragin in Maryland and Pennsylvania."

"All in good time, Son," Lee replied. "You see your friends eat well and are ready when the time comes."

"Yes, Sir, Mass'r Robert."

The two waved as they continued on their way and the general acknowledged before he rode on.

Arriving in camp, the youth and the boy went about giving away their fish to those present who wished to clean and cook them. Keeping a couple each, Willis returned to headquarters and Duane looked up Kim and Foley. Along the way, he passed Corporals Robert DiPhilippo and Howard Griffin.

"Too bad yer not the company's drummer no more," Robert teased as he set a sock of coffee grounds into the pot of water.

"Yeh," Howard added while adding kindling to the newly lit cook fire. "We was jest gittin use ta ya."

Duane stopped, hurt by the news. "Why fer? Ain't I doin good by ya all?"

"Sher ya are," Howard agreed.

"But we come by this real neat feller as we's wantin real bad inta the company." Robert paused as he set the coffee pot onto the fire. "Ya has ta see Kim and Foley. Theys'll set ya straight an gives ya sompin else ta do."

The two men smiled as if all was a joke. A disheartened boy wandered to the cousins' tent.

Kim and Foley were seated in front of their tent, busy preparing beans and coffee for dinner.

"Brought us some fish," Duane offered as he approached.

"Thanks," Foley reached for the offering. "Ya gonna he'p clean em?"

"Sher." Duane drew out a knife and settled beside the fire where he found a tin plate on which to work.

"Why so gloomy?" Kim asked.

"Robert an' Howard said as I wasn't needed no more fer ta do the drummin."

"They say why?"

"Jest as ya's got some real neat fella as is wanted in the company."

"Thet sure was mighty nice a them ta care so," a third voice joined from behind.

Duane turned as he recognized it. "Tod! Sher as tarnation is!" He jumped to his feet.

The two stood staring at each other.

"Go ahead," Foley encouraged. "Ya kin hug each other. Yer same as family an' we's already done ar share."

The two embraced in the joy of finding themselves together once more.

"Doc says as ya saved ma life," Tod said, somewhat subdued with emotion.

"Oh, God, I'm so glad yer okay 'n back. Thet tent sher is mighty lonely." The younger boy stepped back to study his friend. "Damn, you look good."

"Yer a fine sight, too," Todd declared. "But I do detect the definite smell a fish. What ya say I lend a hand an' we fix em up fer fryin."

"Good idea."

The four settled to fixing dinner. Throughout the camp, others of the company were doing the same and the air about took on a fine aroma of fish frying in several iron skillets.

As evening settled, several arrived to share the news gathered from the day's travels and to learn what news Tod might have gathered in the hospital. The drummer boy had heard of plans to advance north and shared a number of combat stories he had heard. The captain, he added, was healing slowly and had been sent to Richmond for a time. He would return by end of summer. Some who had been foraging had found little or done some hunting instead. All shared that the common talk was of the planned invasion. Duane and Willis told of their passing General Lee on the River Road and his confirmation of the intended movement.

The talk passed. A harmonica and a fiddle were brought out by Cameron Doherty and a friend from the other platoon, and the group turned its attention to song. DIXIE led off, followed by BONNIE BLUE FLAG , and a number of other favorites. Lively songs gave way to love ballads, then the sadder songs of lost friends, mother, and home. Candle lamps were lit as the last light settled in the west and sparkling blackness reached up out of the east. Throughout the camps the smell of smoke and the smell of coffee blended with the sounds of insects and of the frogs along the river to mix with the quiet murmur of ten thousand quiet conversations. The countryside flickered with the firelight of a myriad tiny lanterns and the June bugs. Across the river another army shared the same routine.

*   *   *

The move north began midweek. Two divisions of the I Corps were sent to a meeting place called Culpeper. The II Corps followed the next day. General Hill was to hold his III Corps in its camps on a regular routine to keep the enemy occupied. The order was passed to send personal trunks to the rear and to pack light for the operation to come.

Those in Company K who had anything to ship, sent those items to be held in Richmond, care of Captain Rogers. He was convalescing with relatives there and would take care of anything his men sent.

Over the next week and a half, the III Corps did as it was instructed and the Union Army remained in place across the river. Meanwhile, news came of a heavy cavalry engagement in the early part of the week and of combat at Winchester in the Shenandoah Valley.

On Monday of the following week, the III Corps followed the same route as the II Corps before it. By midweek it was at Culpeper. There the men were instructed to cook three days rations and pack them in their haversacks. Rations for another three days were carried in the regimental wagon. Still more were carried in the corps' supply train.

The end of the week found the corps at Chester Gap crossing the Blue Ridge Mountains into the valley of the Shenandoah. From there it was north toward the Potomac River at Shepherdstown. By this time, advance divisions from General Longstreet's corps were already in Pennsylvania.

The second week of the march began. Company K was in the midst of the long stretch of advancing infantrymen. The road was crowded as the officers pushed their men to keep the ranks closed. The day was hot as the soldiers bumped elbows and tripped over each others' feet in order to maintain the pace. A great whirling cloud of dust rose up along the miles of moving troops, choking the men and burning their eyes. The lush beauty of the Shenandoah farmland was lost to the men as they concentrated on moving ever forward. It was just as well; there was nothing left of its bounty. The Shenandoah had already been stripped as earlier campaigns saw first one army and then the other living off the land. At night, the troops bivouacked where they stopped, sleeping in the fields or woodlands alongside the road, only to rise the next morning to continue their march.

Word was passed down through the divisions to the regiments and their companies that General Lee had issued general order number 72 which gave strict instructions to officers and their men as to how they could procure supplies and carry out foraging expeditions while in the enemy's countryside, towns, and cities. All must be acquired in a civil manner. Nothing was to be taken or destroyed. No one was to be hurt. The Confederate soldier did not war on women and children.

Duane and his companions crossed into Union territory on Wednesday as the corps crossed the Potomac River at Shepherdstown and entered the state of Maryland. On the following day, they entered Pennsylvania to pass north through Greencastle and to follow General Ewell's corps through Chambersburg. There Hill headed east to end the week in camp at Fayetteville, where the divisions set their camps during the day. Fires were lit to cook dinner and companies put up their tents for the night.

A footweary bunch of filthy and ragged soldiers settled to a cooked meal from the spoils collected on the passage through town. The men of Company K reflected on the day's events over dinner. The local militia had fled at the sight of the advancing army. Just as well, Tod had observed, as someone could have been hurt. The local citizens had lined the streets in a quiet sullen humor to watch the army pass. Confederate soldiers had been placed to guard the homes of wealthy and prominent citizens according to general order 72, to prevent looting by members of the army. The town had been ordered to turn over specified goods and produce, some of which it had; thus allowing for the soldiers to live off the land without destroying property or harming the citizenry.

One soldier had been overheard to address a small crowd of frightened women, "You have nothing to fear from this dust-covered army of ragged- looking soldiers. We are at heart Christian and knightly men and protectors of children and womanhood."

Sunday dawned with first muster after daybreak. Breakfast was cooked, then the camps were struck in preparation for whatever orders might come. Once preparations for the march had been completed, the brigades rested along the roadside in line of march, or gathered in a field with their chaplain for Sunday services.

Tod sat with his drum at his side. Duane returned from helping Willis pack provisions in a wagon for the company. The wagon had gone off to join the division's supply train and the boy had joined his friend for the march.

"What ya think a company quartermaster type duty?" Tod asked.

"It's toler'ble," Duane replied. "Bein 'round the officer talk ya git ta hear what's happenin'."

"Eny news?" Tod drummed his sticks on the side of his drum in boredom.

"General Early sent word thar's a shoe fact'ry ahead in Gettysburg. Thet's a town 'bout twenty miles from here. General Ewell's marchin on the capital at Harrisburg. So far, there's no word on the Yank army, an' all the towns 'long the way is surrenderin."

"Sounds easy," Matthew Guthries added from nearby. He was carrying the company banner for the march.

"Jest so's they keep feedin us well," Tod said.

"I could git use ta this kind a northern hospitality," Sergeant Raymond stated as he approached. "Jest now, we's got orders. So on yer feet."

"Whar to?" Guthries asked.

"Ta jine the march on Harrisburg," the sergeant replied.

But the march did not begin. It was past noon before the corps was ready to move. They moved east along the pike. Cashtown lay about ten miles down the road. From there they would turn north to join General Ewell's corps and attack the capital. That night the corps bivouacked around Cashtown. During the early hours after midnight, new orders came. The Confederate Army was to gather at Cashtown. The Yanks were on the move. General Hill was to stay where he was and wait.

The III Corps was spread out along the pike. General Heth's Division was in the front. Elements of the I Corps were also in the line of march. As the army corps began to gather, the lead divisions settled along the pike, just east of Cashtown, about ten miles from Gettysburg. They were settled in and waiting by the last day of the month, with little to do but rest until the remaining divisions were gathered.

A quiet morning drifted lazily beyond breakfast. Men occupied their time in cards or gambling, or gazing at the rich farmlands that stretched to the gentle hills and distant ridges. Many of the platoon's dozen lay along the berm of the road – their muskets stacked, their eyes closed, their minds dreaming of home. The crunch of moving troops brought them quickly to their senses as a brigade headed on down the packed surface of the pike.

"Where they headed to, Lieutenant?" Cameron asked as he sat up and observed the company's officers standing nearby.

"Rememb'r thet shoe factory we heard 'bout?" Lieutenant Jenkins answered as he watched the units disappearing down the road.

"Yes, Sir."

"They's bin sent on ta git us a supply a shoes while we sits and waits on the rest a the army."

The wait continued. Duane and Tod spent the midday in small talk and their own projections as to what events lay ahead. By mid-afternoon, Brigadier General Pettigrew returned from Gettysburg with most of his brigade and staff. Some had remained on the road ahead on picket duty.

"Somethin musta happened," Tod observed. "Wonder where the rest of the brigade is?"

"Dunno," Duane responded. "Think I'll wander over ta see if Lieutenant Jenkins needs a runner."

The boy reported to the lieutenant to see if he were needed for courier staff and was sent on to Colonel Fry who sent him on to division headquarters. Several on courier detail milled around division staff as they waited for further instructions. They remained quiet in order to overhear the conversation between General Heth and General Pettigrew. Lieutenant- General A. P. Hill rode up in the midst of the discussion.

"As I stood on the ridge and surveyed the town through my field glasses, I observed a large column of Federal cavalry approaching fast on the road from Emmitsburg," Pettigrew reported. "In as much as we were after shoes and not a fight, I've withdrawn along the Chambersburg Pike to a point four miles from the town."

"That's very unlikely," Hill put in. "The enemy are still at Middleburg and have not yet struck their tents."

"Then if there is no objection, General, I will take my division tomorrow and get those shoes," Heth offered.

"None in the world," Hill replied.

Duane carried the report back that the division was preparing to move out and would advance to join Pettigrew's pickets. From there they would move on Gettysburg at dawn in order to get those shoes. The enemy, however, was present, and a fight was expected.

As night fell, a feeling of apprehension grew in the boy's stomach. He lay alongside his older friend in the edge of a meadow, his head pillowed on his pack, gazing at an overcast sky.

"Looks like rain," Tod stated.

"Kinda does," Duane agreed. "Ya skart?" he glanced toward his friend.

"Yeh," Tod answered. "I git real tight hurtin inside 'fer every battle when I knows as there's gonna be one."

"Tod," Duane whispered, "I fears it'll be bad tamorra. If I go down, could ya send a letter ta my home town and say as where I'm buried? Could be my pa'll git home an' wanta know."

"Ya ain't gonna die, Dee," Tod whispered back. "Enyway, I'll do fer you if'n ya's promise the same fer me."

"It's a promise." The two reached instinctively for each other's hand and shook on it.

They lay there for a while longer listening to the quiet breeze of a thousand soldiers sighing in the night as their thoughts dwelt on tomorrow. The insects were loud in their night songs. Cattle lowed softly in distant pastures. Dogs barked in distant farm yards. The night deepened and the army slept.

*　　*　　*

Tod, Duane, and many in the company awoke in the dark hours before dawn to the discomfort of an early morning drizzle. The whole division was roused before five as preparations began for the march on Gettysburg. A cold breakfast was taken from the provisions in the haversack which Willis had passed out the previous evening.

"Hurry up," Lieutenant Guthries whispered. "Git in line with yer platoon. We's pullin' out eny minute now."

"Mass'r Dee," Willis approached with some cumbersome collection in his arms. "Mass'r Jenkins said as you's ta have this musket 'n gear. Even if ya does git ta run messenger some, he wants ya ready ta fight if needs be."

"Thank ya, Willis." The boy accepted the equipment. "I'll do what needs doin'."

The black youth helped the boy with his belt and cartridge pouch, then left for other duties.

"It'll be good ta know yer nearby," Tod said, strapping on his drum and tightening the heads.

"Let's move out," a voice in the dark commanded.

By five in the morning, General Heth had his division on the road. Advancing ghostlike in the drizzly dawn, the column moved without comment along the pike. The sound of shoes in unison, crunching on the hard-packed surface, and of canteens clicking against cartridge belts, blended softly with the rainfall. It was nearly 5:30 as the first brigade approached a stone bridge across a small creek, nearly hidden by bottomland mists hanging over the water. A regiment of General Pettigrew's brigade had spent the night on picket, encamped on the west side of the bridge. As the column approached, they gathered in order, prepared to join their brigade. General Archer, riding at the head of the column, guided his horse to the side of the road to let his brigade pass.

Suddenly, a single rifle shot rang out; then silence.

"Skirmishers to the front!" The word was whispered down the ranks. The skirmishers from Archer's brigade moved quickly to cross the bridge and spread out to the right of the road. The brigade followed to take the right of the road in line for battle. General Davis's brigade followed onto the left of the road. In the distant mist, the sounds of retreating horsemen could be heard falling back to a ridge just ahead. Cautiously the Confederates advanced. There was a burst of musketry as the Union cavalrymen engaged the line of skirmishers then fell back. A squadron of Federal cavalry continued a slow retreat, keeping up a continuous rifle fire. The cavalrymen dismounted and engaged the advancing brigade for a few minutes, then mounted to fall back and repeat the deployment.

After two miles of slow skirmishing and forward march, the infantrymen felt the terrain rise in front as it lifted across a ridge. The two leading brigades of the division paused on the crest near a building on the left of the pike identified as Herr's Tavern. As eight o'clock neared, the drizzle and rising mists had given way to a clear sun, and the panorama of fields, farms, woodlots, and gentle rolling ridges could be seen clearly in the quiet countryside surrounding the distant town of Gettysburg.

A thin line of Federal horsemen was evident in the lowland along a creek that crossed at the bottom of the ridge. At their right and straddling the road, was a battery of horse artillery.

Beyond was another ridge with a farm where the road crossed its crest, flanked by fields with woodlot rising from the stream at the middle of the valley toward the crest of the ridge. The brigades advanced to the attack.

General Davis's brigade moved forward along the left of the road. General Archer led his troops past the crest of the ridge on the right, across from the farm and its woodlands. The regiments, formed in line of battle, stretched about a half mile along the top of the ridge. Nearly a thousand men made up the five regiments of Alabama and Tennessee infantrymen, with the 13th Alabama just right of center. The division's batteries of field artillery were strategically located across the pike at the height of the ridge.

Regimental flags and company banners hung on the morning air as the Federal line kept up a continuous fire. The soldiers stood poised with weapons loaded. Tod held his sticks over the drum head. Duane waited at his side. The order was passed along the lines.

"Advance," the lieutenant stated.

Tod struck the cadence as other company drummers did the same. The line of grey and butternut brown began to flow down the slope of the ridge toward the stream below with regimental flags to the front and companies dressed smartly on the colors. The morning sun glinted off the ranks of gun metal as orders rang out and muskets were brought to ready. Advancing first, the skirmishers continued to draw fire all along the stream's course.

"Fire!"

"Fire!"

The order carried along the slope as the regiments fired in ranks, sending a deadly volley of lead into the underbrush below. Union cavalrymen returned the fire in rapid succession, faster than the attacking Rebels could reload.

"What the hell they usin'!" Sergeant Henson exclaimed.

"Here tell there's a new repeatin' rifle!" Lieutenant Guthries called above the noise of battle. "Stay low! And keep firing!"

The soldiers reloaded and fired at will while moving across open pastureland, then a small wheat field, in route to the thickets along the stream. Using whatever cover they could find to keep from getting hit, the advancing regiments pressed the Union line to give ground. Bullets rang against rocks, splintered branches and vegetation, kicked up the dirt, and whined through the air. All along the valley, a cloud of gunsmoke began to gather in the air as the smell of burnt powder grew pungent. There were the cries from the wounded and the shouts of orders. The Union battery of artillery opened fire and shells screamed through the air and exploded along the sloping ground. For nearly an hour, the fighting was a standoff. Then, gradually, the Union forces began to pull back up the western face of their ridge, giving as little ground as possible. The brigade advanced to a fence line parallel to the stream, then to the thickets along the stream. So far, casualties were light.

"Keep it up, lads!" Colonel Fry encouraged. "We're wearin' 'em down."

The battle wore on as the brigade continued its slow advance. Word was passed to prepare for a charge. It was only Union cavalry in front. General Pettigrew had said that yesterday and, so far, that's what had been seen. Moreover, they were withdrawing.

At mid-morning the order was given to charge. The bugles sounded, the drums rolled, the men yelled their wild challenge which struck fear into the hearts of their enemies. The thousand surged forward, across the run and up the slopes of the facing ridge.

A sudden volley ripped into the right flank from the acres of woodland behind the farm and in the center of the face of the ridge.

"They ain't cavalry!" someone shouted as they caught sight of the adversary. "It's them damned black-hatted fellows!"

"It ain't militia!" another shouted. "It's the Army of the Potomac!"

The regiment at the right fell back and soon the Union troops broke from the woods and began to flank the brigade and move across its back. Fighting became fierce as Archer's troops turned to retreat. As the right pushed into the center of the line and more companies broke and ran, the soldiers pushed against each other, tripping over their comrades in their haste to get away.

Screams of panic and pain were drowned in the clatter of musketry as the Union infantry poured a devastating fire into the retreating Confederates. Sergeant Matthewson went down. A bullet had smashed his knee. Private Guthries was caught in the line of musket fire, and disappeared from the retreating tide. Breaking toward the rear, Tod tripped over a private from the next company who fell dead in front of him. Glancing over his shoulder, Duane saw a burly Union trooper grab up General Archer as others encircled and captured several dozen more. The enemy leveled their weapons and fired into the retreating mass.

"I'm hit!" Griffin screamed as he fell against Duane, knocking them both to the ground.

"Hurry!" Colonel Fry called. "Fall back across the stream!"

"Give em cover!" Lieutenant Jenkins ordered. "Load and fire on the run!"

A handful of Company K's troopers raised their muskets and fired on the advancing enemy. Crawling to his feet, Duane picked up his musket and found it empty as a Federal soldier charged with bayonet. Grabbing his weapon by the muzzle, he swung the butt against the gleaming blade. The attacker lost his grip as the musket fell from his grasp. Duane took advantage of his brief reprieve to help Tod to his feet.

"Here, take my musket an hold em if ya kin!" Duane shoved the weapon into his friend's hands and stooped to help Howard.

Tod jammed the drumsticks into his belt and slung the drum around behind his back as he knelt to reload the gun. In the surge of action, the men of the regiment broke into a wild route as the enemy continued their heavy fire and began to round up prisoners. Howard was bleeding from a head wound and temporarily disoriented in the roar of battle. "Look out!" Tod warned.

Pushing his wounded comrade toward the drummer boy, Duane drew his revolver. "Hurry, Tod! Help Howard!"

Tod grabbed the corporal as the boy and his enemy fired at each other, and the random firing about the battlefield continued to take its toll. Neither of the two was hit. Duane fired again to stop the oncoming bayonet. His bullet tore through the arm of the attacking trooper, its force spinning him off his feet. The boy kept his revolver ready as he hurried to help Tod to assist their wounded friend toward the rear. The first soldier had recovered his weapon and was once again on the offensive. Before the boy could react, a shell exploded behind the enemy soldier and ripped him to pieces. Fragments of the shell whizzed through the underbrush as one ripped through Tod's shirt, cutting a gash in his side.

"Damn!" the drummer boy cried. He dropped the musket, fell to his knees, and pressed his hands to the wound.

The blood flowed fast and soaked between his fingers as the corporal tumbled into the grass and Duane hurried to his aid.

"Ya bad hurt?" Duane asked as he glanced first at the flow of blood and then toward the action around them.

"Ain't knowin," Tod's voice quavered. "Cain't feel no pain yet."

Gunfire continued all around the slope and men continued to retreat in the rush of the oncoming Federal infantrymen.

"We gotta git 'r we's gonna be taken," Duane advised.

"Ya gotta git without me," Howard instructed. "I cain't see right 'r move straight an'll only slow ya down."

"We gotta try enyhow," Duane replied.

"Dee's right," Tod agreed. "I'm okay. Ya jest hang on the two a us."

The boys helped the youthful corporal to his feet and the three moved away, keeping low to the ground. The air was filled with the pulsating sound and motion of the murderous conflict. Caught up in the midst of retreating infantrymen, the three soon found themselves splashing through the creek toward a small stand of trees in a bend in the water's course. Suddenly Tod collapsed bringing the others stumbling to the ground.

"Sorry," the boy apologized. "My legs give out."

Duane saw the bleeding had soaked through a large area of the drummer boy's shirt and waistband.

"We ain't goin no fu'th'r," he stated. "Ya needs tendin' an this tree stand's as good cover as we kin git."

"Ya look like death," Howard observed. "How bad's it look, Dee?"

"Better 'n the last time he was hit. Jest needs bandagin' fer the present an safe passage ta friendly territory fer some rest."

The three were not alone in their piece of woodlot. Several other dead and wounded lay about the underbrush. Some moaned for water or wept at their fate or the loss of a friend. Some lay conscious in the last moments before death would take them. One mumbled to himself in a state of shock while another sat against a tree gazing at the bloodied ground.

Outside the relative quiet of the trees, the battle was subsiding. Elements of the Confederate brigade had established a skirmish line along the fence on the west side of the meandering run. The Federals were herding their prisoners up the slope to the back of the ridge. More troops and artillery were forming along the ridge as the cavalry was relieved. The remnants of Archer's brigade had retreated to the opposite ridge where a new Confederate offensive was being prepared.

Over the next hour, Duane tended first to Tod and Howard, then, with Griffin's help, did what he could to comfort others nearby. Fabric for bandages and a flask of brandy were rummaged from the victims scattered about the ground. Dressings were fashioned from a linen shirt found in a haversack, soaked with the brandy, then secured in place by fabric strips ripped from another spare shirt. Water was shared from canteens taken from the dead or carried by the living.

The noise of activity from the Federal lines and from the skirmishers, firing along the fence, served to mask any noise or movement from Duane and his comrades. Their position was near the edge of a no-man's land, and no one seemed interested in their small piece of territory.

Once settled medically, Duane and Howard turned their attention to securing weapons and ammunition and to seeing to Tod's safety. A slightly wounded sergeant was helped to a safer position as well. Both were tucked as comfortably as possible alongside a fallen and partially rotted tree trunk, where it was hoped they would be protected from shell fragments and bullets. The drum, unhooked from its strap, was likewise set along the fallen trunk. There was nothing more to do but wait and watch. For the corporal, time was its own medicine. The longer they waited, the better he felt.

The skirmishers sniped at the Union regiments taking position about four hundred yards beyond the creek and up the slope. But their activity was brought to an abrupt end when the Federals sent out their own companies of skirmishers to charge down the slope and force the Rebels to beat a hasty retreat to Herr's Ridge.

Duane and his comrades could see their own brigades forming in the open fields near the tavern. In a short time, they moved out of enemy fire and into a thin line of trees that edged the top of the slope, starting a quarter mile back from the road. As the three watched, two brigades of General Hill's corps spread out amongst the trees, the first in a fairly straight line of regiments shoulder to shoulder and the second in echelon – stepped by regiments with each off the front right corner of the other.

The Federal forces were moving into three lines of battle with the first along the thickets bordering the stream, the second part way up the slope, and the third near the crest. They spread from the road, through the wood lot in the middle, to the fields beyond the woods. A battery of artillery was added to the middle of the Union left.

In the valley between the ridges there was a brick farm house and a barn with a wheat field out behind. The fugitives watched as the grand action during the midday lull consisted of Federal sharpshooters occupying the farm to snipe at the Confederates, and a Confederate company's sweep to drive off the sharpshooters. Otherwise, the day was marked by some long-range artillery exchanges to feel out each other's positions.

"Ya think ther'll be eny action?" Tod whispered.

"Should be," Griffin responded. "The lines keep buildin' so somethin's gotta happen. We jest gotta lay low so's them Yanks don't come at us."

A crashing was heard in the underbrush and voices approached.

"Play dead," the wounded sergeant instructed. "They's too busy gittin' ready fer an attack ta give eny notice ta dead 'r wounded layin' 'bout."

Duane and Howard had both loaded their weapons and were prepared for battle should it come to them. They quietly eased themselves to the ground, stretching prone alongside a rock and the root structure of a tree. Duane covered his revolver with leaves and rested his hand overtop of it. Howard lay his musket snugly along the edge of a fallen tree limb. The voices came closer. A small group of Federal skirmishers walked past the wounded toward the edge of the tree stand near the wheat field. There they took position using the trees for cover, and awaited the inevitable attack. Numbering a half dozen, they were well-disciplined, for once in place, they settled quietly with only soft whispers between them. Duane and his companions remained silent. Each knew he must not make a sound or a move.

Waiting seemed forever. The day had become hot and sultry, though the midday heat was blessedly relieved by the shade of the trees.

At noon, the waiting was interrupted by the distant booming of artillery. A moment later, shells could be heard screaming over the road near the farmhouse on the ridge, and crashing about the fields. A new Confederate position about a mile to the north had begun to bombard the Federals.

It should be soon, Duane thought. But the waiting continued.

The distant artillery fired for over an hour. It was followed by distant sounds of a growing battle. Still nothing had happened in the immediate area except for the shouting of orders amidst exploding shells up near the farmhouse, and the rearranging of Federal brigades along the road.

Another hour passed.

"They're getting ready," a Union skirmisher told his comrades.

Duane looked toward the ridge. The regiments were dressing on their flags and preparing to attack. Federal musketry and cannon opened the instant the Confederate line stepped from the trees, but their aim was high and ineffective. What a grand sight, the boy thought as he watched the elements of his corps step off and advance down the hill.

There was a quarter mile to cover. Once on the move, the Rebel brigades opened fire on the skirmishers and the underbrush along the stream. Bullets ripped through the thickets, tearing at the trees and shrubs. Some dug up the ground in small puffs of dust. Duane prayed that a merciful God would protect them from a stray bullet. Within minutes, the Confederate regiments had swung into a single line of battle and were sweeping across the bottom land through meadow and wheat field as they approached the underbrush along the run.

The skirmishers pulled back toward the stream, joined by dozens more who had moved into their positions from either side, unseen by the Confederate refugees remaining motionless on the ground. The air suddenly erupted with the scream of demons as the attacking regiments advanced in order through the thickets along the waterway and reformed on the far side. Caught up in the surge of advancing troops, Duane and Howard found themselves swept forward in the disciplined ranks of a North Carolina regiment. They went with the knowledge that neither the sergeant nor Tod was critical and would be safe in each other's care.

Erupting in full fury, the battle was joined at about twenty yards with each army pouring a continuous withering fire into the other. The Carolinians fought with disciplined determination as their ranks were pounded by artillery on the right and were wickedly cut down by a raking musketry to the front. Bullets filled the air with their deadly buzzing and whined off rocks and trees. As the front line of Confederate infantrymen was shattered, those still standing formed immediately on their silken banner and continued to press the attack.

The color bearer fell dead and another rushed forward to lift the flag. He, too, was immediately shot. In seconds a third was killed instantly. Still the regiment reformed and held its center. The right end of the brigade advanced in the fields along the back side of the woodlot while the rest worked its way through the trees. Artillery fire had taken out an entire company on the right leaving but two or three of its members in the fight. Duane and Howard moved through the woods, firing from trees where they could. Muskets and rifles scythed down ranks of attacking troops as they fired in line. Splinters filled the air from trees and rifle butts to tear through flesh and clothing. Shrieks of agony mixed with the whine of bullets and the thunderclaps of exploding shells. Smoke-filled air stung the eyes and burned the lungs. The elements of the two armies continued to clash at short range— standing, shooting, falling, dying, reloading, and shooting again. Another color bearer went down and a young colonel took the flag. A soldier rushed to relieve his colonel of the bloodied banner and both went down in the hail of lead. All about the surge of movement shifted in constant motion. A lieutenant colonel knelt beside his regimental commander for a moment, then pulled the blood-soaked silk from beneath the officer and waved it high. A lieutenant tried to stop him.

"Twenty-sixth, follow me!" he called, then collapsed from a bullet through his head.

A severe slaughter had covered the wooded landscape in the space of forty minutes with a carpet of over a thousand dead and wounded. The men of the North Carolina regiment filled the air with their wild yelling and a fresh hail of lead, and their enemy fled. They surged forward and the fight advanced halfway up the wooded hill.

Wrapped in the concussion of battle, pounding at every nerve and smothering the senses and the brain in a dull blanket of reflex action, Duane advanced with the tide. His clothing had been torn by flying debris, and soiled from the dust and dirt of battle, the sweat of his own body and the life-blood spewed from those struck down at close range. The boy had emptied his revolver in the early minutes of the battle and holstered it for a rifle off the ground. Kneeling beside a wounded soldier, he leveled the weapon at a figure in blue. Squeezing the trigger, he saw through the smoke, the impact of his bullet as the man fell back, grabbing at his shattered leg.

Still the air hummed with flying lead and roared with the explosive musketry. There was a sudden impact in his side and a surge of pain as he fell back and was struck by the heel of a passing soldier's shoe. A short distance away in the movement of grey, Howard went down as a bullet tore through his chest and erupted in red.

The second line of battle gave way and the attack moved to the crest of the wooded slope. The boy and his companion found themselves near one another as the din of battle moved forward.

"Ya hurt bad?" Duane asked.

"Yeah," his friend answered. "Tell em as I died facin' the enemy." He was gone.

Duane looked to see where he'd been hit and found the bullet had passed through his cartridge pouch and lodged in the leather of his belt. The boy found another musket and ammunition and moved forward to join the battle. The thought never entered his mind that he could stay where he was and no one would care.

The conflict had moved to the crest of the ridge, but few remained of the original combatants from either army. For more than an hour, the fight had been fought as the brigades of two armies had destroyed each other. Fresh troops charged across the little valley and roared up the ridge in a new wave of grey. The enemy broke and fled to another ridge, a short distance beyond where a school building stood. The remaining men of the North Carolina regiment were out of ammunition. They paused to resupply themselves from the dead and wounded as fresh brigades took up the fight, then hurried to follow with them.

Duane glanced about him as he stood with his own new supply of cartridges, and saw that the rest of the exhausted remnants of the leading brigades had been relieved of further combat. He went no further, deciding instead to retrace his journey and check on Tod and the sergeant.

*   *   *

Cool evening breezes drifted up the slopes of the ridge, wafting off the waters of Willoughby Run. Duane, Tod, and others from the company worked their way through the thickets along the run to begin the grim task of gathering the dead and to help the remaining wounded as best they could. It was three hours since the Union line had broken from the top of the ridge. The distant sounds of battle continued along the heights on the far side of town. Here in these fields and woods the cries and moans of the wounded begged for water or help or the peace of death. Some called to God. Some called for their mothers. Thousands of broken and bloodied men and boys lay scattered on the battle-torn and blood-reddened landscape. The slaughter of the afternoon had been beyond belief. Nearly three quarters of all who had fought on the wooded acres had fallen.

"Oh, God!" Lieutenant Jenkins whispered. "If only those who sit in capitols of countries would walk this field an see their families slaughtered as these are."

"I really don't figger they'd do no differ'nt," Sergeant Raymond commented. "Let's do as we kin fer these poor souls."

Bearing litters from the ambulance wagons, the small company began to work their way up the slope.

"The battlefield robbers've already bin here," Tod observed. "Shoes 'n gear is already gone."

"Yeh," Duane agreed. "Seein' as I picked up thin's fer us an others musta done the same."

"Water," a whisper of a voice begged.

"Right here," Private Matthewson responded.

Fifteen-year-old Jamie Matthewson knelt by a wounded soldier to offer his canteen. Sergeant Raymond joined him to help place the ragged soldier onto a stretcher. The others moved on. By two's and three's they dropped aside to help the wounded or to gather the dead from the company.

The wounded were the first order of business except for those dead whose friends had come to gather the remains. Across the acres of McPherson's farm, the bandsmen, survivors, and capable wounded worked among the fallen.

Duane and Tod had decided that their first effort would be to locate Matthew Guthries. They knew he had fallen in the morning retreat, but had no idea as to how badly he'd been hurt.

"Over here!" Corporal Doherty called. "It's Matthew an he's alive!"

They rushed to a spot in the open field where the corporal knelt.

"Sher am glad ta see ya all," Matthew smiled weakly. "It's bin a hell of a day, lyin round an wond'rin if someone would git me fer the fight could end."

"How'd ya make it?" Duane asked.

"God's own luck, Dee. This poor Yankee boy weren't thet bad off. A stray bullet caught him in the back. He knew he was goin an told me 'bout his mama. It were damned pitiful as he couldn't go quick, but lingered with his back broke fer more'n an hour."

"Where ya hit?" Cameron asked.

"First one got ma foot. Then I took one in the hand, another in the leg, an a few scratches 'bout. The real devil is ma arm. I think it's pretty much tore up by a shell piece."

"Ain't at all pretty," a bandsman commented as he approached bearing a litter. "Ya kin load him on an me 'n Theo, here'll take him ta the hospital."

"Thanks," Corporal Dougherty acknowledged.

The wounded teenager was eased onto the stretcher to begin his journey back to health. The corporal and the boys moved on.

"I wanna git Howard," Duane stated. "Somewhere's in them woods. I think he's dead."

"Ya take us ther," Tod said.

Stepping carefully among the carpet of corpses and wounded, the three walked to the woods in the center of the ridge's slope. Blackened by powder smoke and dirt, the shattered bodies made footing difficult as they lay so thick about the grassy landscape made slippery from its coat of blood.

McPherson's woods was a horror all its own. Trees and vegetation had been splintered and shredded by artillery and rifle shot. Their debris blended with such a compressed volume of casualties that the mix of blue and grey fabric with green and brown vegetation splashed everywhere with red and gore caused even the stoutest of men and boys to sicken at the sight.

Duane had been there before with the frozen dead at Murfreesboro. Tod was seeing it for the first time. His stomach retched and convulsed as he became sick without warning and began to cough and vomit. His head began to swim in dizzy confusion. Badly shaken, he collapsed to his hands and knees. The smell of gore and death was as a great cloud that completely enveloped the senses and twisted the boy's insides beyond description. The corporal was also paralyzed with illness as Duane, too, fought to keep from losing control.

Finally, the boy and the young man were able to help the drummer boy up to lean against a scarred tree.

"Oh, God, Dee," he spit the vomit from his mouth and wiped his face with his sleeve, as his voice shook with sobs and his body convulsed with uncontrolled emotion. The violent racking tore open his wound and he grabbed suddenly at his side as pain seared his mind. "No!" he screamed. His blood seeped through the bandage and clothing to escape between his fingers.

"Hurry!" Cameron reached to steady the boy as he lost consciousness and slipped to the ground. "Git some one ta help Tod!"

"We're comin!" It was Foley. He and Kim had followed into the woods when the sergeant had informed them that he had seen Tod headed in that direction with the others.

"What happened?" Kim asked, choking in the stench.

"The sight a this place made him so sick he hurt his self," Cameron explained.

"Why'd ya come in here?" Foley asked. Anger tinged his voice.

"Dee was takin us ta git Griffin's body," the corporal explained.

"Ya stay with Tod," the youth ordered. "We'll go with Dee."

Corporal Howard Griffin's body was located near the middle of the woodlot. The stiffness of death had begun to set in as it was lifted onto a stretcher for removal from the battleground.

"Dee, we'll take the body," Kim said, his voice edged in anger. "Ya help Cameron git Tod back ta the camp an tend ta gittin him fixed proper ta healin. An ya stay's there, hear! I ain't wantin either a ya out on this death place no more!"

"I'll do as ya says, Kim. But don't ya be takin it out on me." Duane's voice broke as deep hurt and emotion tightened in his throat. "We're all in this war of the same army. He's hurtin cause we're soldiers in the fightin. It ain't my doin!"

Foley reached for the sobbing boy and pulled him into his arms. "I'm sorry, Dee. God, I'm sorry," he cried. The older youth's tears rolled off his cheeks and fell wet in the boy's hair.

The two stood for a moment, locked in a caring and hurt-filled embrace, their tears damp on each other's body. The three wept quietly as Kim wrapped his arms around the first two. For a long moment neither spoke.

All about the woods, the living worked to care for the fallen as the cousins sent Duane to take care of their nephew while they took their burden to be buried.

* * *

General Heth's division had gone into camp on the back side of Herr's Ridge. The survivors of the day's fighting were exhausted as they lounged about their camp. Many remained out on the other side of the run, on the slopes of McPherson's Ridge, helping the bandsmen and other non- combatants to bring in the dead and wounded. Hospitals had been set up in nearby buildings or in tents at the edge of the camp. The cries and moans of the wounded in the field were joined by the screams of pain and the pleadings of those on the surgeons' tables. It was a night of pain, of sadness, of mourning. The stench of death rankled the air as beasts, slaughtered in the battle, rotted on the fields or roads. Burning cookfires scented the air, lanterns cast their faint circles of light, soft conversation carried on the breeze. The rattle of wagons and artillery, the march of infantry, passed along the pike and other distant roads, as the elements of the Army of Northern Virginia continued to gather from points north and west.

General Lee had moved ahead to the ridge closer to the town and stretching south from the seminary school that Duane had seen from the edge of the woods wherein he had fought. General Longstreet had joined him there and located parts of his corps along that ridge. Others from General Ewell's corps were camped to the north of the town. The Union Army had taken position on the far side of Gettysburg along the cemetery heights. The day's fighting ended after nightfall with sounds of battle far distant from the slaughter in farmer McPherson's fields and woodlot.

Duane had returned to the encampment with Tod and Cameron. Tod's wound had been cleaned and redressed and he had been settled in his tent to rest. Kim and Foley had gone on to a field across the pike where several of the dead had been buried. Corporal Griffin was laid to rest in an unmarked grave twenty paces due north of a sycamore tree. Foley had made a map of the grave's location in case his family would want to move the remains home after the war.

Daylight had gone as night crept on with a clear sky and a brilliant sparkle of starlight. Duane sat by the fire with Kim and Foley. Tod lay on his blankets under his shelter tent, chin resting atop his clasped hands. His drum lay back near his feet. The coffee pot contained boiling water and the cylinders from the revolver. In addition, Duane had brought back, with the help of Tod and the wounded sergeant, another revolver and full gear along with two rifled muskets, cartridges, and caps.

"This how it's done?" Foley asked as he worked to clean a spare cylinder.

"Thet's the hang of it," the boy affirmed, busy wiping down the revolver.

"Yer sher gonna be in good shape, Tod," Kim stated. "Dee here's seen ta it ya kin carry a gun jest in case ya cain't git em with yer sticks 'n drum."

The four chuckled at the thought.

"Sher do thank ya fer gittin me back in one piece," Tod commented. "Sorry I went sick on ya in the woods."

"Cain't think a not havin a tent partner," Duane replied. "'Sides, if ya weren't here I'd have ta drum an it'd be certain as I'd be shot fer messin up the beat."

Another bit of laughter rippled from the gathering.

Others of the company were gathered in quiet groups, reliving the events of the day, sharing stories or news they'd gathered along the way, and telling of the horrors they had witnessed while helping the wounded. As the night deepened and some of the exhausted slept, others lay awake, conversed with friends, or continued to help in the field. Activity of the litter brigades and the burial parties continued through the night. There were some who settled by a fire in the wee hours of the morning to write a letter to the family of a friend who had been killed.

Duane and his friends finished cleaning the guns and reloading the cylinders. The weapons were set aside, the coffee pot rinsed out, and a pot of coffee brewed. As it cooked along, Foley worked in the dimness of the firelight to write a letter home to the Griffin family. The night wore on to midnight. The four stayed near each other, shared hot cups of coffee, wrapped their blankets across their shoulders, and lay down by the fire. Drifting in and out of sleep, they listened to the insects of the night, the distant dogs, the lowing cattle. Somewhere a cock crowed, disoriented by the day's events.

Eventually, the weight of exhaustion took over and soft snoring drifted on the night air.

* * *

Thursday dawned quietly. Roosters crowed in the predawn glow. Black crows cawed raucously at the intruders who inhabited the countryside. The soldiers were called to muster as the camps came awake. Their ranks had been drastically thinned by the losses of the previous day's fighting. Fires were rekindled and breakfast of biscuit and salted meat was cooked. Those who had it, boiled coffee.

The morning wore on quietly. Some of the regiments were entertained by their bands who attempted to raise their spirits with music.

General Heth had been wounded during the afternoon assault in which so many had perished, and General Pettigrew had assumed command. General Hill had sent his division under General Anderson to the front. Pettigrew's brigades would be held in reserve for the day. But the day continued to pass quietly as the temperature climbed into the 80s and the weary soldiers sought relief from the sultry heat in the shade of their tents. But even the tents were like ovens as the sun radiated through the canvass.

In the late afternoon, the battle erupted to the south with the thunder of artillery. As the batteries of Hill's corps added their firepower to the storm, the air shook and the ground trembled. For the men on Herr's Ridge, the fight was far away. They hoped their comrades would succeed in beating the enemy, but they knew it would not happen.

The men of Company K gathered for evening muster. They felt the loss of their thinned ranks as the role was called and they looked about where friends and comrades had been. The company broke for supper. The evening wore dark, and the bugler called the soldiers to their beds.

Duane awoke sometime after midnight, restless in anticipation of more battle yet to come. A brilliant moon, just past full, illuminated the sleeping camps. Unable to sleep, the boy crawled from his bed and wandered to the crest of the ridge. There he stood and gazed about the softly lit landscape. Shattered buildings and the shell-torn woods and fields lay bathed in quiet brilliance. Gettysburg's silhouette stood crisp in the distance. The town clock struck three in the morning. As the boy turned to go back to his bed he heard the creak of wagons. As a farm boy it sounded like hay rigs off to an early start. As a soldier he knew it to be artillery being set in place for the coming day's work.

Duane wandered back to the tent. Glancing once more along the line, he gazed for a moment at his comrades, asleep in their field tents, bathed gently by soft moonlight. The boy lowered himself to the ground, crawled beneath the canvass roof, and wrapped himself in his blanket. Pillowing his head on his outstretched arm, he soon drifted back to sleep.

*   *   *

The moon had passed far toward the western horizon, casting long shadows in the soft light edged with dawn. It caressed the dark tangles of hair of drummer boy and tentmate. The two stirred. Tod lifted his head to gaze out in the predawn light as Duane rolled over and opened his eyes. The older boy propped his chin in the palms of his hands. There was movement in the camp as officers were about, talking in small knots, then moving on.

"Hi," Duane greeted.

"Cain't sleep," Tod returned.

The two lay awake, listening to the morning sounds of distant farms and nearby birds. An incessant chatter in the treetops greeted an approaching dawn as robins and sparrows flitted about and blue jays called to each other.

"They sher sounds perty," Tod stated.

"Wished I was in ma bed back home an this war 'd never come," Duane added. "This sounds like ar farm back home, so full a peace 'n perty bird song."

Suddenly a deep booming erupted in the distance as artillery fired on the heights beyond the town. The boys both shook as the unexpected concussion startled them. The air quickly exploded into a continuous thunder of cannon as the first fighting of the day got underway.

"They's sher as hell got a early start," Tod commented.

"Reckon we best git to," Duane suggested. "Muster cain't be far off." The boys sat up and pulled their shoes on, then packed their blankets.

Before they finished, Willis was by to pass the word for muster.

"How's the bandage doin?" Duane asked as the older boy slipped the drum strap over his head.

"Still holdin," Tod replied. "Feels a bit wet from seepin'. But I think it's started ta scab ov'r."

The two stepped out and Tod hooked the drum to its strap. Duane glanced at his friend's shirt to be sure there was no significant bleeding.

He sure must be running on nerves and energy, Duane thought. The blood he'd lost should have put him out of action.

The two proceeded to Lieutenant Jenkin's tent and sounded the muster roll.

Once the company had gathered, the lieutenant gave the men their instructions. "Cook yer breakfast 'n pack yer gear. Fill yer canteens. We move in an hour."

"What's happenin', Lieutenant?" Corporal DiPhilippo asked.

"We're movin up ta the Seminary ridge inta the line a battle ta wait further orders."

The men were dismissed to eat and strike their camp. Throughout the early hours of sunrise and camp activity, the distant fighting continued. Artillery was mixed with rifle fire. The shout of orders and the yelling of charging brigades, drifted on the quiet air. As the sun rose on the new day, so also did the temperature and the humidity. It would be another sultry July day.

"Think we'll be seein' action?" Jamie asked as he passed Duane and Tod in route from filling canteens at the stream.

"We has ta," Tod answered, rolling his tent half to tie into his field pack. "We rested yestaday an' ever'one else was fightin'."

"May be as the fightin' goin' now'll end it all," Duane put in hopefully.

"Ya know's it ain't ta be," Tod said flatly.

"Yeh."

"I ain't sher I kin go inta 'nother fight," Jamie whispered staring at the ground. "It ain't thet I's a coward," he looked at the two boys, not much younger then himself. "It's jest as I'm all a quiverin' inside 'n ain't got maself t'gether yet from the fightin' day b'fer."

"Jamie, ya ain't gotta tell us. We was ther 'n as feels much the same," Tod comforted.

Sergeant Henson approached the three boys. "Call the muster, Tod." he instructed.

"Let's go," the boy stated.

The three walked together to where the company's headquarters had been. There Tod sounded the roll and the men began to gather.

Across the open ground of the ridge, the camps had been struck and the companies were assembling. As elsewhere, their commanding officers were giving out instructions for the next movement.

"We're gonna be part of a major offensive on the center of the enemy's line," Jenkins was saying. "Ev'ry able man is goin' with us. Thet includes wounded who kin fight and camp staff, too. So, Willis, ya be sher ya has a gun fer with ta shoot those people."

"I sherly will, Mass'r Jenkins."

"We move inta place quiet-like an out a the enemy's sight," the lieutenant continued. "Thet means no cherrin' and no drum, Tod."

"Yes, Sir, Lieutenant," the boy acknowledged.

It was early morning, yet, when the division started down the road, then across the fields to the back side of Seminary Ridge. All along the crest of the high ground, the troops saw the lines of artillery. Duane counted over four dozen varying pieces as the brigade moved quietly to its position. Across the shallow valley, a little more than a mile away, the fighting continued. From their position below the line of sight, the moving soldiers could not see the panoramic view, only the high thick cloud of smoke which hung above the battle.

Colonel Fry took his regiments to the back side of a wooded line. There they moved into the shade of the trees and were ordered to lie down, keep quiet – no cheers, and keep low. General Pettigrew checked the positioning of the troops in the division. He had assumed command in the absence of the wounded Heth. His brigade, in turn, was commanded by Colonel Marshall and placed in line to the left of Colonel Fry's brigade. About a quarter mile through the woods, to the right was the left of General Pickett's division, just arrived on the battlefield. Thus, Company K was near the edge of a large gap between two lines of assault which would later unite to become the center of the advancing charge.

General Lee and Lieutenant-General Longstreet rode by to inspect the preparations. Knowing they could not cheer their general, the men raised their hats instead. He acknowledged them as he moved along, conversing with various division commanders along the way.

"Many of these poor boys should go to the rear," he was overheard to say. "They are not fit for duty."

Duane glanced about from where he sat beside Tod. There were a lot of men and boys with filthy wrappings of bandages to cover wounds of varying severity. Some of the men sat in small groups to talk. Others stretched out and slept. Some quenched their thirst or munched on a biscuit. A few stood, too nervous to remain in one place. And a couple here and there wandered toward the front to gaze through the trees at the lay of the land and the enemy lines.

"I'm goin up ta take a look," Duane told his friend.

"I think I'll stay put," Tod said. "Tell me what ya see."

"I'll go with ya," Foley offered.

The two walked through the mass of troops to the front edge of the trees. There they stood to gaze about the gentle roll of farm and fields and the battle line beyond. From their vantage point they saw where the woods extended to a point at their right and a fence line continued beyond. A road traversed the center open ground running across at an angle from left to right. Smoke continued to roll up from a distant hill to the left and the cannon flashes could be seen near the ground. The spang from the smooth-bore guns was distinctly different from the slap of the rifled guns as the sound carried in distorted delay over the distance between flash and concussion.

"Look!" Foley pointed to a barn near the road in front of where they stood.

An advancing wave of blue charged across from a stone fence and attacked the barn. There was an exchange of musketry, clearly distinct on the morning air, as the white puffs of discharge popped out from the wooden wall of the barn and the rifles of the soldiers in blue. A new sound erupted suddenly from the woods to the left as a battery of guns fired on the Union attackers. The exchange was brief. In a few short minutes, Confederate sharpshooters were retreating to their battle line while the troops in blue streamed back toward their fence, leaving the barn ablaze and of no further use to anyone.

Colonel Fry approached from the side. For a moment he watched quietly with the boy and the youth from his command. The sound of distant battle continued to rise and fall as the tide of the sea.

"See that clump a trees," he finally spoke. "The one near the angle in that stone wall." He pointed to a spot in the center of the Union line where the ridge was low and almost indistinct and the fields rose in a broad and gentle sweep. The two nodded. "That's where we're headed," the colonel explained. "Just now I'm on my way ta see General Pickett ta be sure that we meet out there before we get to the enemy."

"Would be a good idea," Foley grinned. "It'll be hell ta go it alone."

The colonel agreed, then continued on his way as Duane and Foley took one last look before returning to their company. There, along the fence at the point of woods, they saw a lone figure sitting and gazing sadly across the farm lands. It was General Longstreet.

As the sun climbed toward noon, the distant fighting ended suddenly. A quiet hung over the battlefield. Hardly a breeze stirred. The fields outside the woods radiated waves of heat as the temperature soared through the eighties. The woods offered little relief. There was little movement or breeze to cut away the stuffy staleness in the air. The soldiers had consumed their water and lay in extreme discomfort.

During the hours of waiting, the generals continued to ride the line and inspect the disposition of infantry and artillery. Maximum supplies of ammunition were placed by the guns. The generals met with their division commanders who met with their brigade commanders who met with their regimental commanders who met with their company commanders who met with their men. Every detail of the intended charge was explained to the men. There would be an artillery bombardment first to soften the enemy line and to destroy their artillery or drive it from the field. Then the charge would follow. There would be no Rebel yell or quickstep until the very last moment. They would advance in perfect order until they reached the enemy line of fire. The men knew what was expected. It was time to send out the skirmishers to clear the way and to break down the fence lines.

Quiet continued through the middle of the day. The skirmishers went forward to prepare the way. Among the members of Company K on skirmisher assignment, was Corporal Doherty. The wait continued. The artillery was to begin its work at 1:30 sharp. The men checked with a friend who had a watch, and waited.

"Everybody down," Sergeant Raymond finally ordered.

There was an anxious moment of silence. Then to the far right, a cannon fired. A moment later, a second gun fired. Suddenly, a crescendo erupted in steadily increasing intensity sweeping from right to left as a hundred and forty guns exploded into action. A great cloud of smoke rolled up about the batteries and drifted into the woods. The roar of cannon continued as the ground shook and the air vibrated from the constant concussion of sound. It rose and fell in waves as batteries paused here and there to reload and fire in salvo.

Duane held his hands to his ears as he flattened himself as low to the ground as his empty stomach would allow. At the first sound of the guns, a rabbit had scurried from the underbrush as flocks of birds took flight from the treetops. Tod had called after the rabbit.

"Git along ya little rabbit. I'd be gittin, too, if'n I was a rabbit like ya!"

Then he, too, had flattened out with his hands over his ears.

Roaring cannons shook the ground and the air with a violence greater than an erupting volcano. A vicious rain of death and destruction poured forth against the Federal lines. All about had become one constant and continuous explosion of sound with such intensity as to press against the nerves and bodies of the thousands lying in readiness along the woods, like some great weight from heaven above. The concussion of cannon continued unchanged for fifteen minutes.

Suddenly there was a horrendous crashing through the trees above joined by the whir and whine of enemy shells raining through the woods. Shells exploded in the air and amidst the massed troops on the ground. As tree limbs and shrapnel rained down from above, blankets, packs, and human flesh erupted in flashes of flames from the ground. Cries of "We have wounded!" mixed with the screams and moans of injured and dying infantrymen. Chaos broke lose as officers warned "Keep down!" and tried to calm their troops. Duane could hear the rip of flying shell fragments and the whump of solid shot as the rain of death and destruction continued all about.

A shell exploded nearby killing Corporal DiPhilippo and two others as it wounded a half dozen more. Colonel Fry was struck in the shoulder by a fragment of shell. Another hit close and Duane could hear it clearly as it sliced through fabric and flesh.

"Ahhh!" Tod screamed in pain.

The younger boy turned quickly to see what he could do. Tod lay on the ground, shaking violently in shock and pain as blood pooled beneath his leg. A portion of flesh had been ripped away from the calf of his leg along with the fabric of his trousers. A ragged hole of shredded tissue and muscle poured forth its flow of blood.

"Ya ain't dyin'!" Duane screamed at his friend. "Gimme a shirt from yer pack!"

While the air about rained its deadly storm of destruction and the ground continued to quake with the cannonade, Duane worked to wrap Tod's wound to hold until he could get to a surgeon. The drummer boy calmed as fear was replaced by pain.

"I cain't be there," he sobbed. "The company won't have a drum beat fer the march."

"I kin do fer ya," Duane assured. "Let me have the drum."

The drum's skin head hummed in the intensity of noise and vibration of air as the artillery fire continued for an hour and a half. When it finally ended, and the guns were quiet, it felt as though such a weight had been lifted that Duane sensed a light-headedness and a feeling of floating in air. Tod lay where he had been when struck by the piece of shell. The wound had been wrapped with a shirt. Duane sat beside him. The drum was strapped in place. He was ready to beat the cadence for his friend.

"Here," Tod offered his revolver. "Ya'll need this mor'n me, now."

"I'll do fine with jest mine," Duane smiled. "I's seen where we're ta go. It ain't likely I'll come back."

"Oh, God, no!" Tod gasped. But he saw in his friend's eyes that he believed it to be so. "Ya gotta come back," the wounded boy said. "Ya jest gotta."

"Form up," Lieutenant Jenkins ordered.

"Ya take care," Duane said as he stood to leave.

"Ya do the same," Tod waved.

As the troops formed in ranks and prepared to move out, there remained in their shell-torn waiting area more than three hundred dead and wounded who could not go along.

Tod watched the company take its place with the regiment. The regimental flag moved to its place in front as the companies dressed on their banner and straightened their ranks. Company K set its two files with Duane and Lieutenant Jenkins on the front right corner. The remaining officers followed behind to keep the files closed and to discourage any who might prefer to flee.

"Forward. Guide Center. March!"

The cadence was struck. The brigade advanced into the sunlight.

Tears streamed down Tod's cheeks as he watched his friend go forth to an uncertain fate. Duane's face, too, was moist with tears as he thought of the friend whose drum he beat and the possibility that this could be the last event in his life. He pushed these thoughts from his mind, straightened erect, and felt a surge of pride as he glanced along the line of men and flags.

*   *   *

The 13th Alabama regiment advanced to the right of center. The 1st Tennessee held the right end of the line. The remaining three regiments stretched to the left. Duane saw only one other brigade clear the woods with Fry's. It was Pettigrew's. General Pettigrew appeared concerned that the remaining brigades on the left were not advancing. Finally they appeared and the whole line was dressed and in straight order as it neared the end of the point of wood to the right.

Duane continued to keep the cadence – a hundred and ten steps per minute for a forward rate of just under a hundred yards per minute. Looking ahead the boy saw clearly in the distance, beneath the rising smoke from the cannonade, the lines of blue defenders along walls and fences, and the clusters of artillery whose crews were busy preparing their guns. It certainly didn't appear that the artillery had done its job.

On either side of the road in front, were the thin lines of skirmishers, bobbing in wheat fields as they prepared to open fire on each other. They had been the safest during the artillery duel. The shells had simply traveled overhead.

The advancing line cleared the last trees and the boy could see the men of Pickett's division in the field a little ahead and far to the right. If he weren't so twisted in his gut by a deep-set fear, Duane might have seen something grand in the mile-wide front of brigades in dressed formation. But the distant puffs of smoke on the hilltops beyond the right and left were followed by the booming of artillery.

Still the line advanced. Artillery opened on both flanks and in places along the front. Shells screamed through the hot mid-afternoon air and exploded in the ranks. Pieces of bodies and gear blew into the air as the missiles of death took their toll. Great holes appeared in the ranks as ten men or more were taken out by a single shell. So far, the center of the line was relatively safe.

Pickett's division reached a stretch of low ground, out of the line of fire. There it paused to redress its lines. Moving forward once again, it came under a sudden and destructive fire. Then, on command, the whole division shifted to a left oblique and marched at a 45 degree angle. This slowed down the forward movement as it brought the entire division to the left to link with the end of Fry's line. The far left of Pettigrew's line collapsed under a flanking attack and began to fall back in disorderly retreat. The remaining brigades approached the road.

Because of the road's angle, the center of the line would strike it first. Colonel Fry's brigade was about two hundred and fifty yards from the Union line when the enemy fired in line by brigades and regiments. The impact of flying lead slammed into the front lines with devastating results. The flags went down, were picked back up, and continued forward. Scores of men fell wounded, some dead. Duane felt a sting of pain from a bullet that buzzed the side of his left leg. But it failed to slow him as another ripped through the wood of the drum. Artillery from several batteries opened with canister. All that the boy could see of the Federal front was a roiling cloud of smoke specked with flashes of fire in a long line.

"Forward!" Lieutenant Jenkins cried and waved his sword.

The companies advanced in bunches. Coming up against a board fence, the men of the brigade tried to break it down with their rifle butts. It would not give. The skirmishers before them had not been able to break down this section of fence. Here they waited and joined the line of attack. It would be necessary to go over the top.

As the first file crossed the top boards, sharpshooters opened fire. Foley was hit in the wrist but continued to advance. Duane heard a bullet whiz by his head and another strike the rim of the drum. Many slammed into the wooden planks and posts. Sergeant Henson was seriously wounded as a bullet passed through his neck and shoulder. He toppled into the ditch beside the roadway. Private Wilson was killed.

The line paused briefly in the safety of the roadway which ran below the grade of the field. The men lay down to rest a minute before going over the second fence on the opposite side of the road.

"I ain't wantin ta do this!" Jamie called to Duane over the roar of the battle.

"We're this far!" Duane called back. "Let's go finish it!"

They were on their feet again. Jamie slipped his rifle between the fence boards. Clambering over the planks as quickly as possible, they dropped to the ground on the other side amidst a hail of bullets, then rolled to their feet to go on.

Once past the fence, the lines redressed, linked up with Pickett's division, and moved forward as one solid front.

Enemy artillery and infantry continued heavy all along the front as the Confederate line closed and began its own destructive fire. The air was thick with cries of pain, the shout of orders, the whir and whine ,of lead. Great empty spaces continued to be blown in the Confederate ranks as artillery took out large numbers. The artillery back on Seminary Ridge continued to wreck havoc as its shells fell along the Union line and disabled men and cannon.

Officers were falling in great numbers as bullets and shell fragments found their marks. But still the colors remained upright and the remaining troops continued to close on them.

A slight grade remained before the Union fences. Colonel Fry led the charge as his little brigades swept furiously up the gentle slope. Firing and yelling, they flew forward. The colonel fell with a bullet in the thigh.

"Go on!" he called. "It will not last five minutes longer!"

To the right, the men from Pickett's left were with them. A lieutenant in a Virginia regiment clasped hands with a captain of the 1st Tennessee shouting, "Virginia and Tennessee will stand together on these works today!"

Both flanks of the Confederate line were being turned in. Duane felt the push of troops as they closed in on the center. Regimental colors were crowding into bunches as the men swarmed toward them. The low stone walls were only a few yards away. Now, for the first time since the lines stepped from the trees some twenty minutes back, the attackers let lose their blood-curdling Rebel yell and swept across the walls. Tennessians, Alabamians, and Virginians moved together.

Masses of blue ebbed about, trying to stay the attack. A few remaining artillerymen frantically loaded canister shot. Duane jammed his sticks into his belt and drew his revolver. A gun crew was loading to the right. He fired on one who went down. Others ran. The gun was turned. The boy fired again. In front, the Federals gave way in full retreat. The cannon fired its charge of canister into the flank of the Rebel mass. Screams of pain, cannon fire, muskets and rifles, the Rebel yell, shouts of orders, exploding shells pressed against the senses. The boy also felt a cutting pain as a shard from a shattered stone sliced across his ribs.

A blue line of infantry paused on the higher ground in front, to fire on the Rebel infantry at the angle in the wall. But it would not advance.

"Look!" Jamie shouted. "They's perfect targets on the sky!"

The boy fired along with several in the closing companies and the Federal soldiers fell in bunches. But their line held and their return fire was deadly.

One of Pickett's generals crossed the wall where the Union gunners had been driven from their battery and the guns stood silent.

"Come on, Boys, give them the cold steel! Who will follow me?"

He went forward with hat held high on the point of his sword. A rush of men and colors followed him over the wall. Fierce hand-to-hand combat surged about the wall. Infantrymen and artillerymen fought back with rifle butts, hand spikes, and rocks. Men on both sides fired and loaded and fired again. One battery of cannon continued to operate with double loads of canister. But its crew was being thinned at a rapid rate.

As the tide of grey and blue surged and ebbed and mingled in mortal combat, and the air filled with smoke and noise, debris and blood, the few who remained in Company K continued to load and fire on the men in blue. They fought without order. The lieutenant had fallen. Standing, kneeling, pushing through the massed humanity, they did their work.

A flying stone caught Jamie on the head and he went down, blood streaming from a scalp wound. Duane had felt the pull of bullets passing through his clothing, felt the warm dampness of his blood running down his leg and pooling in his shirt, and had heard the missiles of death singing through the air. He knelt to check on Jamie and to load a fresh cylinder into his revolver. The drum sang out as a bullet ripped its head. His companion would be okay. Rising to his feet, he dropped the empty cylinder into his pouch and felt pain seer through his left arm. A bullet had passed through the muscle below his elbow. Blood quickly soaked through his shirt.

There wasn't time for this. The boy moved toward the silent guns for cover. The general who had crossed the wall was gone. Duane saw the general where he lay wounded near the wall. Lead sprayed and burned his cheek as a bullet struck the gun barrel. The blood dripped from the finger tips of his wounded arm as he rested the revolver in his good hand on the gun carriage and fired into the chaotic mass of Federal troops in the trees to the right.

The fragments from the remaining Confederate regiments were falling fast. Some of the colors lay on the ground or were propped against the stonework. Union reinforcements rushed to the scene, but had not yet advanced. Fear held them back. Pain struck Duane's ankle as a sliver of metal cut through his sock. Beyond the trees there was a fierce volley of artillery fire as smoke billowed down the slope and across the stone wall to erase an entire Confederate charge. An eerie silence fell ahead.

Union fire into the mass of grey, mingling leaderless near the angle in the wall, intensified.

"Help me with this gun!" Duane called as he noticed a charge of canister on the ground behind the gun.

Bullets ricocheted from stone and field piece. Suddenly, the powder charge attached to the canister load erupted in flame and smoke. The explosion wrapped around the gun and slammed debris through the drum and the boy's flesh. He felt the heat of the fire and the sting of flying metal.

The concussion of explosion wrapped him in pain and the smell of smoke.

Blackness invaded the boy's senses with one grand roaring crescendo and sudden pain.

Then silence. Darkness. Nothing.

*   *   *

Rain fell in sheets. It cascaded from stone walls, gun carriages, and the hat brims of the soldiers wandering the field of carnage. Twenty-four hours before, the sky had unleashed a storm of shot and shell. Now it washed the blood from the grass. Across the landscape the dead and wounded lay where they had fallen or had been able to crawl. Some had tucked themselves into the rocks and crevices of the land, beneath trees and bushes, up against the walls, or underneath the wagons or nearby buildings. The stench of death that had hung about the land was cleansed somewhat by the storm. Still the air was thick with currents of foul odors where the dead lay thickest and the battle had been heaviest. Cries of the wounded had gone silent. Many had passed into eternity. Others had simply become too weak to continue their pleadings. The wreckage of war lay everywhere. Discarded packs and equipment littered the ground. Weapons were scattered about. Exploded artillery chests, unlimbered cannon, wrecked gun carriages, bloated carcasses of horses and mules – all marked the passage of the conflict.

Small groups of men, soaked by the torrential rainfall, searched the muddied landscape for the living. Burial parties gathered the dead in wagons. Some local citizens attempted what they could to help. Scavengers searched the battlefield for souvenirs.

The bodies along the low stone wall near the angle by the clump of trees, were bathed and cleansed by the downpour. Small streams flowed around quiet forms scattered about the landscape. Rivulets trickled along the creases and dips in the fabric which clothed them, to fall with gentle ripplings in the puddles at their sides. In the midst of the blue and grey-clad men and boys who carpeted the ground bordered by the angled wall, lay the fallen of Company K. A few had gone back with the retreating survivors. Some had regained strength or consciousness long after the guns fell silent, and waited for darkness in a cloud-banked night sky where the moon lit the hell-scape, then crawled away to hide from the horror.

Lieutenant Damien Jenkins lay among the dead. The bullets had crossed through his lungs, and he had bled to death, his sword still in his hand. Not far away, amidst the layered dead, his cousin Foley had died. A bullet through the heart had made his passing swift. Sergeant Raymond lay outside the wall. His body had been violently torn by the cannon shot. The trail of the dead stretched back to the road and its fences – a carpet of shabby grey and butternut brown in lush green pastures and fertile fields trampled beneath the passing of twelve thousand men.

Beneath the gun, the torrent of rain had puddled about the bodies. The clothing soaked on the still forms, the abundant moisture dripped its washed-out drops of red from edge of collar or coat sleeve, from crumpled hair matted against pale white skin, from fingertips so still. The revolver lay, half submerged, in the red-tinged puddle, not far from the hand that had held it. The boy lay in sodden silence, caressed by trickling falls of water, dripping softly from the gun carriage. One small and intermittent fall played out a steady tapping on the wooden shell of the broken drum which rested in the mud beneath the hub of the wheel.

About this stillness the splash of feet traveled in search of the living and in search of relics. Someone stopped, bent down, and picked the revolver from the water. He moved on, jamming the gun into his waistband and searching for something else of interest. Another paused to take the sword from a dead captain's hand. In awed silence, the footsteps passed on the sodden ground. Some paused to look. Some wept.

The rush of heavy rain wrapped the land in a hushed blanket as the skies wept over the fallen.

Another stopped, as many before him, to look at the sad scene. A boy so young, his shattered drum nearby, lay in the mud not far from the stilled cannon. For some unknowing urgency to caress the child so young, the man knelt down to stroke the soddened locks of brown and matted blood. He was dressed in the long black coat of a reverend. His broad flat-brimmed hat shed the rain in streams. A long charcoal beard dripped water from its carefully groomed point. The long fingers of the shepherd's hands gently pushed the tangled ringlets from the soft cheek.

"Dear, Father," he whispered hoarsely, "why must Your children hurt so? Why must this child die so young?"

The man wept. His tears fell abundantly to mix in the muddied red pool in which he knelt. Again he stroked the cheek, so soft, so cold – his fingers so light against the flesh, so gentle, so caring. The reverend's heart ached with its grief. Oh how he wanted to lift this child's lifeless body from the mud, to hold it, to breathe life back into it. Perhaps if he took it with him he could care for the remains and see that they were buried in the local churchyard. Perhaps he could find out who this boy was and find his family.

Slipping a hand beneath an arm, he froze in astonishment. Why hadn't it occurred to him when he touched the face? It was soft. The arm lay limp. He was alive. The stiffness of death was absent!

"Dearest Father!" the tears flowed in joyous anticipation, "let him live! Let me be your instrument of life!"

Carefully he removed the drum strap, passed it through a rope stay on the drum, then slung the wooden remains across his back. Gently, the coat-sleeved arms slid beneath the mud, beneath the still body, and lifted the boy from the rain-swept ground beside the silent gun.

Duane hung unconscious in the reverend's arms, his limp form lightened by the long weeks of march. The man carried his burden over the rise in the ground behind the wall to a barn on the back of the ridge where a field hospital was in noisy turmoil. Once inside, the falling rain no longer washed the two, but danced instead in thunderous constancy on the roof overhead.

The interior of the structure was a maze of cots attended by an army of women vivandieres and male nurses, aids, and orderlies. Outside, the bodies of the dead lay in rows, waiting for the burial parties to take them to the cemetery ground for burying. As the reverend entered through the large open door, two men passed on their way out with another who had died on the surgeon's table. Moans and cries of pain blended with dozens of conversations about the cots to mix with the smell of death, excrement, rotting limbs in tubs near the surgeons' tables, smoke, and medicines. For some the barn meant life; for others a pause on the journey to death or the cause of death itself.

A short motherly woman approached the reverend.

"What have you this time, Reverend Smythe?" she asked, wiping her hands on an apron.

"He's just a boy, Mrs. Dowd," he paused for the woman to see. "He's just so pitiful-looking. Truly, I thought he was dead, but the Lord seems to have given a chance for one of His miracles."

"Bring him over here, Reverend." Mrs. Dowd led the way to an empty cot beside the wall. "Just a minute," she said, spreading a blanket across the canvass. "Now put him down." The woman reached across the cot. "Here, let me help."

The two lay Duane on top of the blanket and placed the drum near the head of the spindly frame.

"Let me see if Doc Hurlbut is free to come and look him over." Mrs. Dowd stood and cast a sympathetic smile on the filthy wet figure lying battered and bloody on the bed. "You get his wet things off and gathered in a pile. We'll tend to them later."

The woman hurried off, skirts rustling in her haste, to find a doctor. The man busied himself removing the boy's gear and clothing. Both he and the boy were dripping water from their clothing. The man could not contain the mud and water as he prepared to strip the boy and gather his soaked belongings in a pile. The bed was soaked and dripping through its bottom canvass. The packed dirt floor was puddled about the pile and about the man who worked to help the patient.

Thelma Dowd returned with a basin of water and a bucket of bandages and wash rags.

"He looks so absolutely filthy and smells so. I don't suppose he's had a bath in a month." She emptied the bucket's contents on the floor and settled beside the cot on its overturned bottom.

"It ain't likely, as they've marched all the way from Virginia since the first of last month." He carefully peeled the shirt to reveal the bullet hole in the arm, the shallow gash across the ribs, and sundry other marks and bruises of battle. "Where's Doc?"

"Busy."

Working together, the two did their best to cleanse the weeks of travel and the dirt of battle from the wounded boy. His face was seared and his hair singed from the powder blast. The scalp was bloodied where pieces of the charge had torn through his hat. When finished, Duane was wrapped in a clean dry sheet and moved to a dry cot. Doctor Carl Hurlbut, a local practitioner, joined the effort.

"What do you think is wrong, Doc?" Reverend Smythe inquired. "Why doesn't he respond?"

"He's been burned by a powder blast," the graying physician responded as he carefully examined the wounds about the head through wire-rimmed spectacles. "Could be that he was hit by shell fragments in the head and his hat saved his life. I think his skull is broke or at least banged up pretty bad."

"Serious?" Mrs. Dowd asked.

"Only time will tell." The doctor finished his examination. "Put a salve on the burns, be careful around his eyes, and a poultice on the bullet wounds. Wrap them up and keep them clean. Plenty of rest. Feed him broth or tea until he's fully conscious and can eat." He stood to go. "He's in God's hands, Reverend. All you can do is wait and watch over him."

The doctor packed his bag, smiled a melancholy half smile, then left to continue his work somewhere else in the bustle of the hospital. Duane's treatment was carried out by nurse and reverend. The bandages were wrapped, with extra padding where they crossed his eyes. His belongings were piled beneath the cot. Finally the boy was covered with a light blanket and left to rest. The man and the woman left to care for others while time and God were left to care for the boy.

*   *   *

Reverend Leighton Smythe stood just under six feet tall. He was of slender build, stood erect, and generally looked much sterner than he really was. He had been in Gettysburg to visit an aunt when the battle developed. It had not been expected. Neither general had intended to pass through Gettysburg or to occupy the town. It had just happened. Reverend Smythe had gone to the battlefield first out of curiosity, but remained out of a deep feeling of compassion for the men and boys who fell there. Since then, he'd devoted all his waking hours to serving the wounded in the fields and in the hospital.

It had been early afternoon when the reverend walked the battlefield near the angle. Later he had returned to find more who had survived and to help some others to die. Night had fallen. The rain had ended by the time he returned to check on the boy and the other wounded in the hospital barn.

The boy had stirred. Thelma Dowd had checked on him when another reported he was waking. He had moved, but not become conscious. Reverend Smythe stopped to sit a while and to spoon some broth between his lips. Again the boy stirred.

"Thank you, Father," the man prayed quietly. "Stay with him and bring him back."

*   *   *

Duane regained consciousness during the night. He woke to the sounds of moaning in the dark. Discovering himself in bandages, he was confused. But perhaps it was a dream. He went back to sleep to worry about it later.

The early hours of the new day found Mrs. Dowd making her rounds. The boy heard the rustling of her skirts and ventured a question.

"M'am, where am I?" he asked.

The woman stopped, startled by the unexpected voice. It was surprisingly strong. "What?" her voice faltered, tripped by joyful emotion.

"What's happened? Where am I?" He pushed himself up to sit in the middle of the cot. Suddenly aware of his nakedness, he pulled the blanket around himself, then explored with the tips of his fingers to feel the bandages across his eyes.

"Yer in Spangler's barn hospital." The skirts rustled again as she hurried to the side of the bed. There was a milking stool nearby which she brought and placed as a seat. "You were hurt in the great charge. Doc says that your hat saved your life."

"What charge?" Duane asked. "Who are ya?"

"Why, I'm Mrs. Dowd. I'm a seamstress here in Gettysburg. What's your name?"

"I'm...," he couldn't remember. "I'm... not sure. I cain't git it in ma mind ta say it. But I know's fer sher it's ther. Jest call me Dee. The rest'll come later." He continued to check out the bandages. "Musta bin a mite bad, huh? Sher am wrapped plum up like as some package. Ya use some whiskey 'r brandy? Doc says as it stops the festerin. Gettysburg where?"

"Who says?"

"Cain't rememb'r zactly." A quizzical expression wrinkled around his cheeks. "Ya know, Mrs. Dowd, I cain't seem as ta rememb'r a whole lot."

"You don't remember the war and the fighting? Not even the big battle across the fields the other day?" She put her hand to her chin.

"No, M'am. Seems as ther's somethin' I might a dreamed on, but as all gone fuzzy."

"Well, Dee, I guess we'll just have to get you healed up real fine then see what we can do for your memory later."

"I ain't likin' not knowin', Mrs. Dowd."

"I know, Dee. We'll do as fast as we can."

Reverend Smythe approached on his first visit of the morning. He had just arrived to visit among the patients and was overjoyed to see the boy awake and talking to Mrs. Dowd.

"Good morning, young man," he greeted. "I thank our Father in heaven to see you regaining your strength."

"Mornin', Sir." He turned his head in the direction of the voice.

"We have some work, Reverend," the woman smiled. "This here is Dee, but he's lost his memory for now and can't say that's surely his given name. Dee," she introduced, "this is the Reverend Smythe. He carried you in from the battlefield yesterday."

"Thank ya, Reverend. But I ain't knowin' no battlefield. When kin I gits off these bandagin's an see ya folks? Ya sounds real nice like."

"Thank you, Dee." The nurse went on to explain, "The doc says you were burned in some explosion. We'll wait until he approves, then take them off."

"I have to go back to search for more," the reverend excused himself. "Do you need anything?"

"Yes, Sir," Duane spoke up. "It's real nice yer doin fer me 'n all. But I needs ta git up now 'n agin' an don't feel right, naked as I is. Could ya git me some clothes?"

"I surely can, Son. For now, though, Mrs. Dowd can find you something from about the barn, here."

The man left for his mission on the battlefield. The woman excused herself to her work within the hospital. Nurses were already at work, changing bandages, feeding breakfast of sorts, and visiting with some they had come to know. Nurse Dowd returned later with a clean shirt, then helped Duane to make a needed trip to the privy outside.

It was a slow day for the boy. There was little to do but lie around and wait and listen to the activity of the hospital. When evening arrived, Reverend Smythe returned with a basket for dinner which his aunt had prepared and a clean set of clothes.

First order of business was to get dressed. Then Duane sat on the side of the cot to share dinner of fried chicken, corn, and biscuits. It was heavenly food. He couldn't remember when he'd eaten such food last. Only his mother... but she was dead? Why? He pushed the thought from his mind until he could remember what had happened to him and who he was. "Tell yer aunt as she's a real fine cook. I ain't et so nice since I don't know fer sher."

"You just get your health back. When the bandages come off we'll take you to stay with my aunt until we find your folks and send you home." Reverend Smythe smiled at the boy's good spirits.

"Thank ya, Sir." Duane turned to the woman. "Where's ma thin's? Ya said as I was in a battle?"

"They were a mess," the nurse explained. "I threw them out."

"Could be they'd a he'ped me rememb'r," he suggested.

"True," she agreed. "I'll fetch them home and get them cleaned up for when you're better."

"Thank ya, M'am."

Dinner was finished. The basket was repacked. The boy was free to wander about and to stretch his legs. He was cautious, but glad to be up and out of bed.

*   *   *

The days passed. Duane felt his way around and got so he could help with some simple chores to break the monotony. Finally it was time to remove the bandages.

Doctor Hurlbut had changed dressings several times to keep the wounds clean. Now it was his last time to unwrap the boy's head and to let him see again. Mrs. Dowd and Reverend Smythe sat nearby in expectation of seeing their patient without his wrappings. The fabric was removed. The dressing came off the eyes.

"How much longer?" Duane asked, blinking his eyes at the absence of pressure.

"It's done," the doctor said.

"But I cain't see yet?" concern edged his voice.

"I was afraid of that," Doctor Hurlbut stated. "The blast has damaged the eyes. I'm just not sure how bad yet."

"I'm blind?!" the boy cried. "Will I see agin?" His voice became hysterical.

"I really don't know," the doctor said, shaking his head solemnly.

"No!" Duane cried, wringing his hands then rubbing his eyes.

He sat silently, his mouth quivering with fear. The tears came quietly to stream down his cheeks as he shook with inward sobbing.

"I'm sorry," Doc said as he stood to go.

The woman sat down on the bed beside the boy and pulled him into her arms. He broke down and cried violently, burying his tears in her embrace. They both cried.

"Come on," the reverend said softly. "I think it's time you left here, Dee. There's nothing else that my aunt can't do. Let's go home."

"Yes, Sir, Reverend," his voice quavered. "I don't know what fer ta do now. I cain't see. Oh, God, I hope it ain't forev'r." He wiped the tears with his sleeves, then stood beside the cot. "We kin go now?"

"We can go now," Mrs. Dowd assured.

The three stood testily to be sure the boy had his balance. Cautiously they worked their way to the large open door. A friend on either arm guided Duane's footsteps across the hay-strewn floor. Stepping into the mid- morning sunlight, the boy sensed its warmth on his face.

"I kin feel the sun." A smile lit his tear-streaked face.

"That's God's way of saying that there's hope," Reverend Smythe offered.

The trio turned their footsteps towards the town and the home of the reverend's aunt.

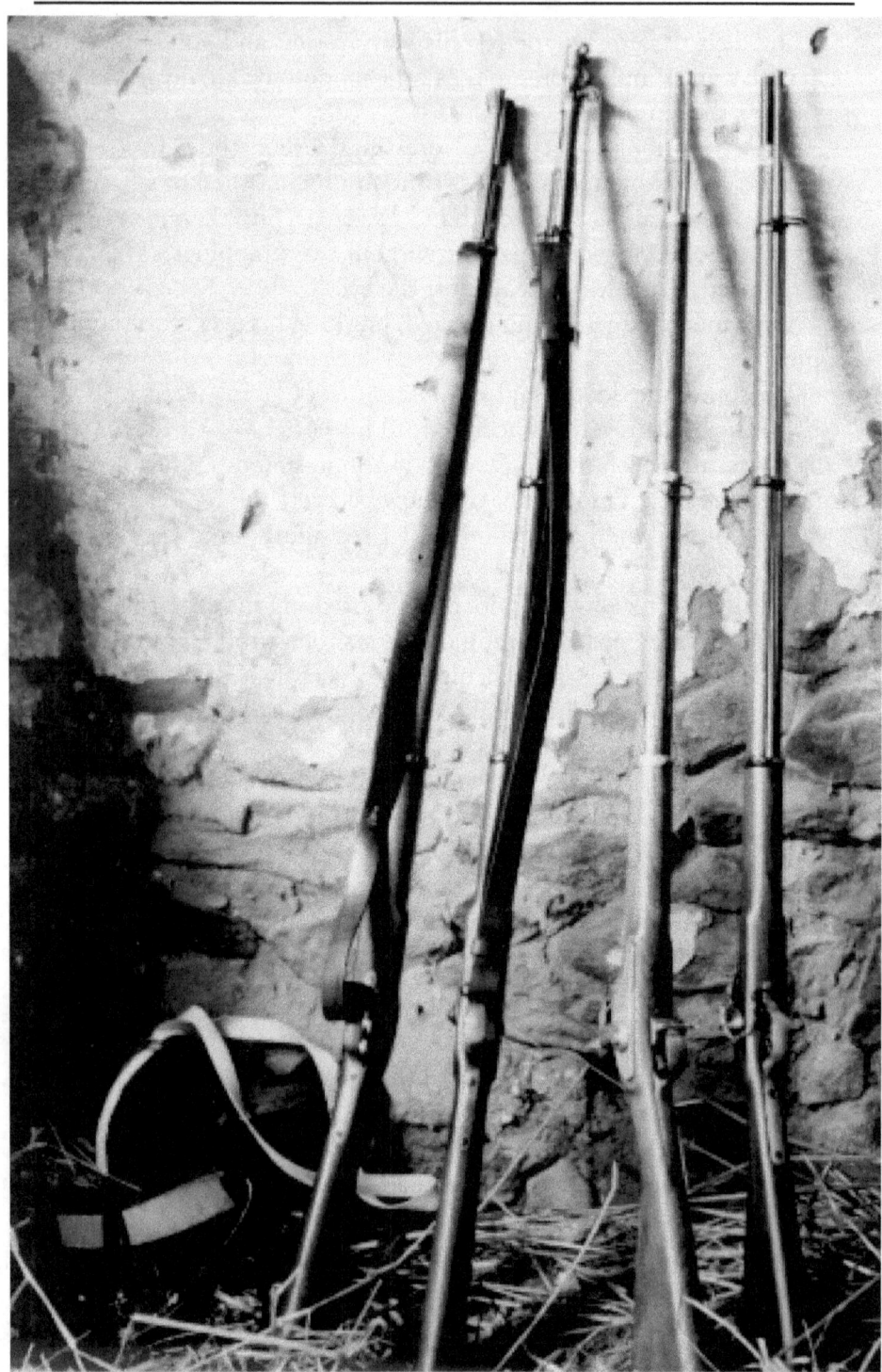

EPILOGUE

Crisp brown leaves danced about the white picket fence that edged the dirt walk in front of the grey, wood-frame house. Broad yellow leaves carpeted the neatly trimmed yard behind the fence where the silver maple tree had shed its summer coat. The raw steel-blue sky of autumn hung over the town with an overcast chill to the air. The summer harvest had been taken in. November was at its mid-point. The war had long since left the country town of Gettysburg and traveled to distant places. Duane Kinkade had not.

Aunt Jennifer Morrison's plain wood-frame house had been home for the boy since the day he left the hospital barn. Here in this tuscan-trimmed, grey clapboard house with its white lace curtains and heavy draped windows, he had learned to cope with blindness and had healed from his wounds. But in the four and a half months he had spent with the Reverend Smythe, he had not found his identity. His past remained a locked secret. Only the brief present held meaning and understanding.

The reverend and his aunt were kind enough. Mrs. Dowd stayed in touch and had taken the boy to spend days with her as she ran errands or worked about her home. The three had helped him learn how to survive the daily routine without the benefit of sight. He became more attuned to his remaining senses as he memorized rooms and frequently traveled locations, and developed an ability to feel the presence of people and objects. Aunt Jennifer had put him in a spare bedroom in the front of the house because it faced east and he could feel the sun rise each new day. Duane had become independent in caring for his personal needs and in small household chores such as maintaining his room and helping with meals.

The front door opened. Reverend Smythe and Duane stepped out into the brisk mid-morning air and walked down the flagstone walk toward the rose arbor gate. They proceeded slowly while the boy felt his way with a thin cane stick. Once through the gate, they paused momentarily to listen for passing traffic. One carriage rattled along the empty street.

"Ain't much movin' this time a day," Duane observed.

"I reckon most traffic is staying to the main pikes," the man responded. "But there are greater numbers of curious arriving every day."

Turning right, the duo headed toward the downtown business district beyond the stream which passed under the bridge a block away, and the railroad beyond the bridge.

"What fer we goin' ta Forrester's taday?"

Duane knew the route quite well and moved easily with his hand against the man's elbow.

"I understand he has put up a display of battlefield photographs to draw extra business. People who are coming early for Mr. Lincoln's visit and the cemetery dedication will want to see them."

"Are they all his own pictures?"

"Mostly. Right now he's teaching himself how to use photographic equipment because he plans to sell it. He believes in knowing about the things he sells. He also has a collection of things he's gathered from the battlefield. May be that if you handle some of it, your memory could be helped."

There was a slight arch to the bridge, so Duane knew when they crossed the stream. Just ahead, he heard the bell ringing on the locomotive of a slowing train, preparing to discharge a new and ever noisy gathering of curious sight-seers.

"Same ol' crowd?" the boy asked.

"Not all of them," Smythe answered. "Looks like quite a few soldiers, too. I figure there'll be a number from the troops being transferred from the west who have heard about this battle and the dedication."

They approached the crowded station overflow. Duane stopped as he sensed several people walking in their direction. The man paused with him.

"It's a big crowd, Dee. I don't blame you for waiting." After standing several minutes in the crowd he added, "Let's sit on this wall for a while, until the mob has passed."

"Good by me," Duane agreed as he turned toward the low stone wall he knew bordered the roadway.

A half hour passed before the two could continue on toward the storefront blocks between the Chambersburg and the York turnpikes. Passersby tipped their hats to the stern-looking reverend with the blind boy, but otherwise ignored them. Dressed in dark woolen trousers with a warm coat and hat over a store-bought shirt, Duane bore no sign of his experience as a soldier. He had become, in fact and even in his own mind, a blind orphan without a background.

The two arrived at Samuel Forrester's Mercantile Store. It's proprietor was one of the many local residents who scavenged the battlefields, even before the armies had gone. He had converted a corner of his storefront into a mini-museum of sorts with weapons and personal items he'd gathered about the countryside, and photographic prints on tin-types which he'd taken throughout the battle.

"Morning, Mr. Forrester," the reverend greeted.

"Hello, Reverend Smythe," the storekeeper approached. "What brings you two in today? You were just here last week."

"We's come ta see yer battle thin's," Duane said cheerfully.

The store was crowded with a noisy invasion of curious visitors. Most had come to see the collection. Most decided to buy something they had not thought to seek, but saw while wandering in the store.

"It's kind of crowded." Mr. Forrester warned. "But you're welcome to stay as long as you like, Dee. May be you'll see or feel something you remember."

"Thanks, Samuel," Leighton smiled. "This was a good idea. Business must be booming."

"That it is – especially in little things like sewing items, soap, buttons, pencils, and the like. I just finished hanging the photographs day before yesterday. Well, got to get back to work."

The storekeeper returned to his counter to be sure the clerks were encouraging sales and to answer visitors' questions about the battle. Duane and the reverend worked the back of the crowd near the special display, allowing themselves to ease toward the front with the flow of moving people. Everyone seemed to be talking at once, commenting on an object or picture, or calling to a wandering child or friend. Duane kept a tight grip on Reverend Smythe's elbow to avoid being separated by the force of the human tide.

"What's it like, Reverend?" the boy asked as he shuffled along beside the man.

"It's a very fine collection, Dee. I surely hope we can get close enough for you to feel some of the pieces of equipment or clothing." The stern countenance of the figure enabled him to ease closer, drawing the boy along, as others gave way in awkward uncertainty. "His tin-types are quite remarkable."

There was an absence of conversation as Reverend Smythe studied the pictures and the boy clung at his side, uncomfortable with the press of people.

The man caught his breath, startled by something. "God have mercy," he whispered. "You're in this picture, Dee."

"Cain't be. I don't even rememb'r eny a this. Though I gotta say as somethin's right there in ma head, jest not clear yet."

"It's you, all right – just like I found you, only early, before it rained."

"Mama!" a small boy at Duane's side called. "Mama, this dead boy's alive. He's right beside me with a preacher-man!"

"Silas," an embarrassed woman reprimanded, "don't be so impolite." She looked at Duane and at the picture. "My heavens, you're right." There was confusion in her tone of voice.

"It's all right, M'am," the man assured. "It is the same boy, but he wasn't killed."

"You're blind!" she exclaimed.

"Yes, M'am," Duane acknowledged.

"Oh, my! Come along, Silas." They moved away.

"I wish I knew what as happened," Duane said. "I wish a knew who I is."

"Let's get a copy of this picture," Reverend Smythe decided. "It may be a help."

They brushed up against an object leaning against the wall which started to move. The boy reached in hope of catching it, but it was moving away from his hand and clattered onto the floor. A short-tempered visitor took notice.

"What's your problem, Boy, clumsy?" a flat-nosed, well-dressed gentleman asked.

"Sher do wish I was, Sir. Truth is I's blind."

"You don't say," the man continued with a sneer.

"You might take a look at this picture," Reverend Smythe pointed. "That's this boy out on the battlefield."

The man stared hard as surprise and embarrassment registered in flush pink on his cheeks. "Oh," he said quietly, then turned and walked away.

"Everything okay?" Mr. Forrester asked, hurrying across at the appearance of commotion.

"Yes, Sir," the boy said, "if I didn't break nothin'."

"It was a pole of some sort," he retrieved the object. "Here, nothing broken." The storekeeper took the boy's hand and put the object into it.

The reverend watched hopefully as the boy ran his fingers along the slender shape. "It's a trail handspike fer movin' a cannon ta aim it."

"Well I'll be," his guardian smiled. "I do believe your mind is going to let you know yourself." The boy's smile of pride was mixed with tears of grateful hope. "Mr. Forrester," the man continued, "I'd like a copy of this photograph. It's Dee, here, from the battlefield."

The storekeeper-photographer took a serious look at his photograph. "Why it surely is." There was surprise in his voice. "I'll make a copy this evening and you can pick it up tomorrow."

"Thank you," the reverend stated. "I think we'll stay a while longer to see what else is familiar. Then we'll go our way and I'll be back tomorrow."

The two stayed and explored the exhibit while the storekeeper returned to his business. There was a new excitement as the boy recognized much of what he touched and felt a sense of joyful expectation that soon he might remember who he really was.

*   *   *

The small, white-haired Aunt Jennifer washed the dishes in the porcelain basin and set them carefully on the towel-covered drain board. One by one, Duane searched out each piece, dried it, and placed it toward the back of the surface in a safe pile. Leighton Smythe was seated at the table preparing a letter to a church in Richmond requesting help in identifying the boy in the picture to be enclosed.

Outside, the broken moon was rising in the east as the last twilight of the day was fading in the west. A chill air was gathering in the evening. Somewhere a cat yowled. Otherwise the neighborhood on the northeast corner of town was quiet.

There was a warmth of companionship in the kitchen as each worked in the other's presence and Duane and Aunt Jennifer's nephew shared the story of the day's discoveries. The fire crackled cheerily in the kitchen range, its snapping to blend with the dripping wash water cascading from the woman's hands to play a symphony of sound in the boy's mind which, deprived of sight, cherished the rich blend of noise. An unexpected rapping on the front door interrupted the routine of harmony. The boy heard it first and stopped in the middle of his statement.

"Afta we was done with the rifle, the reverend put… thar's a knockin' on the door, Sir."

Everyone paused mid-motion. The ticking of the parlor clock was being joined by a series of rappings on the door.

"I'll see who it is," the man said as he stood from the table. "You two go on."

But curiosity had the better of boy and woman who paused in their work as they tried to listen. They could hear a murmur of conversation as the man opened the door and stepped out to talk to the visitor.

"God be praised!" they heard him exclaim.

"Who do you suppose it could be, Dee," Aunt Jennifer asked.

"Cain't hear em much. Don't rightly know," he answered.

Footsteps approached the kitchen.

"Wait here a minute," the reverend stated before entering the room. "Duane Kinkade, I know who you are!" The thrill of ecstatic triumph filled his voice. He was almost crying.

"What!" the woman gasped.

"Thet sher sounds right, but where'd ya hear?"

"I told him, Dee," the officer stepped into the room.

"The voice!" Duane nearly cheered. "I know ya!" he exclaimed. "Lieutenant! Lieutenant Dan Marshalton! Oh, God! Oh, God! Ya cain't know how happy I is!" The boy broke into tears as he stumbled against the chair in his eagerness to reach the man.

Another entered the room quietly and stood in respectful silence as the boy and the officer embraced. Both had given way to tears and hugs. Then Duane froze.

"It's Johnny!" He could say no more, only reach toward the presence he felt so close.

Johnny stood transfixed at the sight of his blinded friend, but moved at a nod from Reverend Smythe. He held his hand to touch Duane's outstretched fingers. They met and the younger boy pulled at his friend. The three embraced each other as the reverend went to stand with his aunt. She was bawling into her apron. Her nephew stood with the tears cascading silently down his cheeks. The boy and his friends held onto each other as if afraid to let go and sobbed uncontrollably for several minutes.

When all had finally regained their composure, the lieutenant was the first to speak.

"I believe this is yours, Reverend Smythe." He offered a large flat paper envelop. "Mr. Forrester said I could bring it over since I was coming."

"Thank you, Captain Marshalton."

"Captain?" the boy asked.

"Yes, Dee, I finally got a promotion."

"But, Captain," Leighton continued, "I won't be needing this now and can get another if I wish. You keep it for Dee."

"Would you all like to set in the parlor?" Aunt Jennifer offered. "I'll put on a pot of coffee and you can share the making of this miracle."

She wiped her eyes on her apron, then reached down a coffee tin in which she kept her ground coffee. As the reverend shepherded the boy and his friends toward the parlor, his aunt pumped a pot of water from the kitchen sink and prepared the pot to be placed on the hot kitchen range. Then she, too, moved to join the others and satisfy her curiosity as to the identity of the boy she had kept these past four months.

Captain Marshalton had taken the velvet green gentleman's chair, offered by his host. Johnny and Duane had settled on the elegantly upholstered settee. Reverend Smythe was comfortable in a platform rocker. Aunt Jennifer joined them in her high-backed Boston rocker.

The captain had already begun, "...and decided to see what he had. It was Johnny who saw the picture. He asked me to look at it and say what I thought. I knew from the expression on his face that he was very upset. As soon as I saw him I knew inside it was Dee, even though this doubt kept poking at my mind. You can't imagine the awful agony we felt, believing he was dead, or the sudden joy when we asked Mr. Forrester about the picture and he told us he was alive. He was shocked as were we at the coincidence of our meeting and was obviously proud to be able to tell us all he knew. Then he gave me the copy you had ordered and told us how to get here."

"I cain't b'lieve it," Duane said. "I ain't been knowin' who I was all this time, but jest as soon as I heard yer voice, ever'thin' come back. Ever'thin' that is but ma eyes."

"Do you have any idea about them?" Johnny asked.

The boy replied, "The doctor says as he thinks I'll neve' see agin. But then I guess I's still lucky. I should a been kilt by them pieces a canister shot."

"God works his miracles," Leighton praised.

"That he does," the captain agreed. There was a moment of quiet before he continued. "I know you two want to learn more about Dee and I'm going to let him tell it. But now we must decide his future."

"I want ta go with ya, wherever' yer headin'," Duane stated. "I know it ain't no place fer a blind boy, but if there's some way ya kin git me ta the Confederate Army an find ma pa, I wanna go, no matter how long it takes."

"There's a relatively recent serious move in establishing what's called the Invalid Corps." Captain Marshalton leaned forward in the chair with his elbows on his knees. "It allows for wounded or ineligible soldiers to work in non combat areas like supply or hospitals or prison camps. I don't know as there're any blind soldiers in such a position, but I will certainly try to do what I can."

"Would it help if you were the boy's legal guardian?" the reverend asked.

"It has had its advantages with Johnny."

"I have some friends over at the courthouse. I'll see to the paperwork."

"Captain," Mrs. Morrison joined in, "would you and Johnny care to stay here while you're in Gettysburg? I've yet another room and you're welcome to it."

"That would be wonderful, Mrs. Morrison. We certainly would."

"I smell coffee," Johnny interrupted.

"Coming right up." The woman rose from her rocker and went to get the coffee.

"We'll help," Duane offered.

"Sure," Johnny added.

The two hurried to join her.

"He does get along well," Dan observed, watching Duane maneuver about the house.

As the evening passed, arrangements were made for Duane's immediate future and for the captain and Johnny to settle in for the next several days. They had come to witness the dedication of the new cemetery as they were transferring commands from the army in

Tennessee to the Army of the Potomac. The war in the west was nearly won.

The new effort was to stop General Lee's Army of Northern Virginia. Once business was concluded, the gathering settled to coffee with cookies and Duane's tale to the reverend and his aunt as to who he was and where he had been in the war. Dan and Johnny were also very interested in all he had done since the last battle in Tennessee. Widow Smith had informed them that he had headed off to Bragg's army and they had assumed that he had made it. Yet, they had hoped to hear for sure and became concerned as time passed that something had gone wrong.

The visit lasted late into the night. Mrs. Morrison added some wood to the parlor stove to keep off the autumn chill as the boys helped return the dirty dishes to the drain board. The parlor clock struck the hour at eleven. Dan and Johnny would bring their things from their boarding house in the morning. They would spend this night in their new guest accommodations. The stoves were banked. Candles were lit for the trip up to bed. The lamps were put out. All retired to their rooms, still chattering in exhausted excitement and the wonder of the reunion. The boy said good night to Dan and Johnny. They were shown to their room and he went on to his.

As Duane changed into his night shirt, he listened to the sounds of the rest of the household settling in for the night. How good it was to be with his friends once again. But more than that, how thankful he felt to have come out of the darkness of his lost memory and to rediscover who he was. Feeling his way to the bed, the boy pulled the covers down and crawled in. The house quieted. But Duane lay awake, listening to the house's noises as he thought of what had been and what might yet be. His mind relaxed. He drifted into a restful sleep and dreams of hope.

Duane's decision to set out on his own to join Bragg's army at Tullahoma proves to be a mistake. A rapid chain of events carries him from capture along a snowy road by a renegade band of Union cavalry, to near death in a blizzard in the mountains of eastern Tennessee, to Lee's Army of Northern Virginia in its winter camp around Fredericksburg. Late winter is a time of reprieve from war as the boy joins a company from Alabama. The beginning of spring sees the reopening of warfare in the battle at Chancellorsville.

ACROSS THE VALLEY TO DARKNESS follows Duane as 1863 stretches into summer, the army moves north into Pennsylvania, and the boy finds himself crossing the valley at Gettysburg in a great charge against the Union center on Cemetery Ridge.

ISBN 978-621-434-014-9

 OMNIBOOK Co.

9 786214 340149

J. ARTHUR MOORE

TOWARD THE END OF THE
Search

The Conclusion of the Story
Book 4 of JOURNEY INTO DARKNESS

JOURNEY INTO DARKNESS

a story in four parts

part 1

On the Eve of Conflict

part 2

Up From Corinth

part 3

Across the Valley to Darkness

part 4

Toward the End of the Search

the conclusion of the story
JOURNEY INTO DARKNESS

written by
J. Arthur Moore

Dedication

Toward the End of the Search is dedicated in His love and in friendship to Charley French, David Rowland, Christopher Oswald, and Richie Christman, each of whom has helped by becoming forever a part of the story through the photographic material, and to all who have enjoyed its telling and shared in the adventure of its creation.

Duane Kinkade

Johnny Applebee

Jonah Christopher

Jamie Fowler

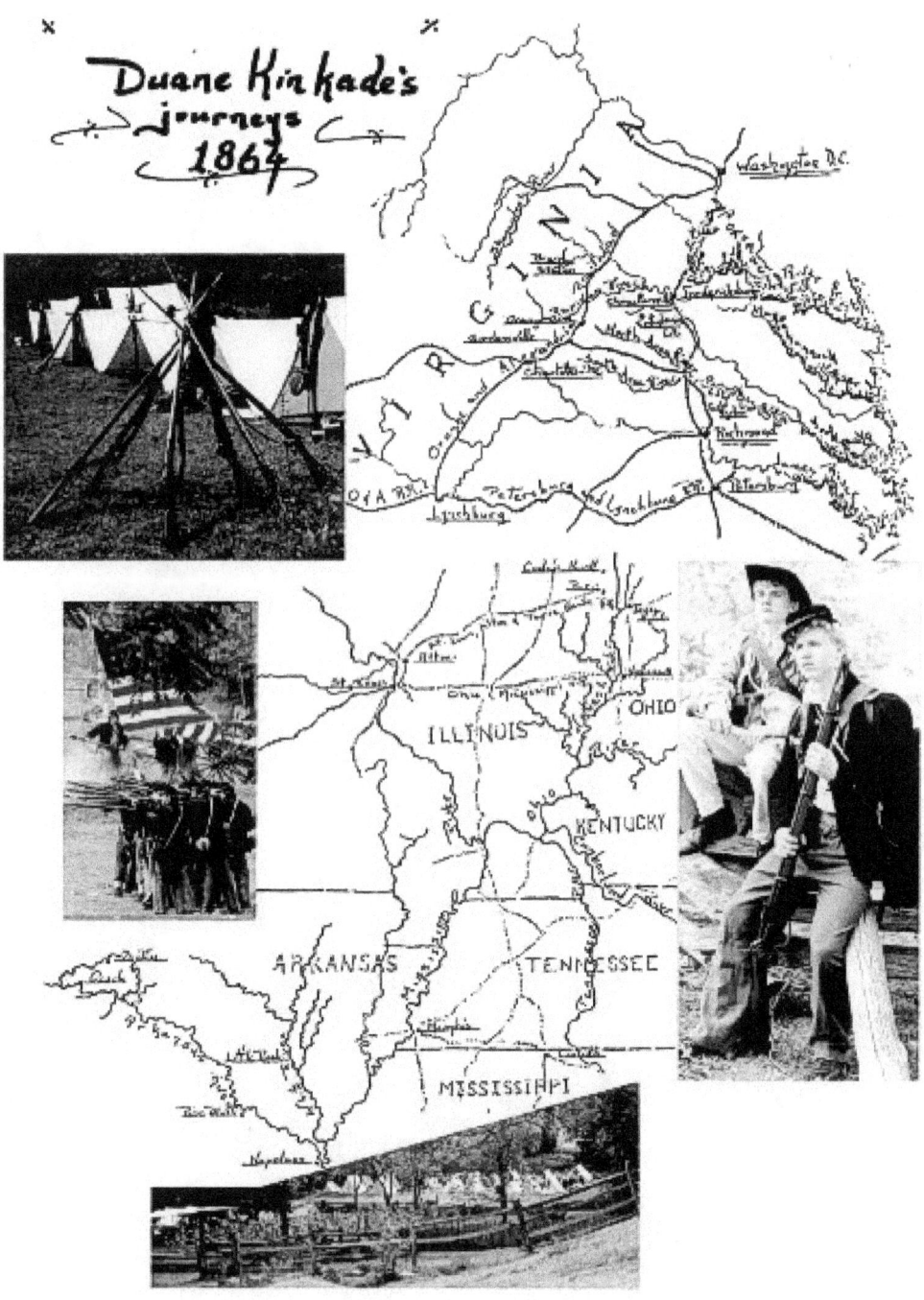

Practiced fingers followed the leather harness strap across the brown mare's rump, in search of the trace chain hanging off her hind quarter. Taking up the chain link with one hand and the end of the whipple tree in the other, the young teenager quickly looped the chain over its catch hook to finish attaching the mare to the ambulance wagon.

"You done on your side?" an older companion asked from the opposite side of the team.

"She's hitched proper-like," the first responded. "Where's Captain Marshalton?" he went on to ask as he turned and reached blindly for the rim of the front wheel.

"He's been called to a staff meeting." The older boy climbed his wheel to the wagon's seat. "I have the papers for the stationmaster. We're to go without him."

The younger boy felt his way to the wheel, then reached for the metal seat rail and pulled himself up the wheel and into the wagon.

"How do you do that, Dee?"

"What, Johnny?"

"How do you get around so good bein blind?"

Duane settled onto the seat board before responding, and pulled his coat around himself to ward off the chill of early spring. "Ya hafta rememb'r, I ain't always bin blinded, Johnny. I's learnin maself ta use pictures in ma head ta the way ever'thin is an' kin judge as how fer ta reach an' move about."

Johnny unwrapped the reins from the brake lever, kicked it free, then slapped the team into motion. Trace chains jingled as the whippletrees swung taut and the team pulled the vehicle into motion.

Both boys were dressed in worn blue uniforms of the II Corps of the Federal Army of the Potomac. They had been in winter camp around Brandy Station, north of the Rapidan River in northern Virginia, since the two armies had ceased hostilities in early December 1863. The elements of General Lee's Army of Northern Virginia were scattered for miles throughout the country to the south of the river. The Union Army's camps covered nearly ten square miles in the general vicinity of the Brandy Station stop of the Orange and Alexandria Railroad, which served as the army's supply center and shipping link from Washington.

In the months since Gettysburg, Duane had passed his thirteenth birthday, been reunited with his friends, Johnny Applebee and Daniel

Marshalton, and journeyed with them to join the 20th Indiana before the closing activity of General Meade's move against Lee's army at the end of November. The last three and a half months had been spent in the extremities of boredom of winter camp. For some, the encampment had been a time for festivity, balls, horse races, and whatever competitions or methods of gambling the imagination could devise. For most it had been exceedingly boring, broken only by the routine of drill.

During the months of winter, many enlistments ran out and newly drafted companies arrived. The ranks of new arrivals were swelled with a number of professional bounty jumpers who filled in for draftees for a price, then disappeared during their first picket duty to find another who would pay. Thus, several Fridays saw hangings or firing squads as deserters were caught and executed to discourage others from trying to leave.

In mid-March, General Ulysses S. Grant was put in charge of all the Union armies and came from the west to be near General Meade and the activity of his army. Just Wednesday of this week nearly ended, General Meade had reorganized the Army of the Potomac into three corps of which the 20th Indiana was part of the Third Division of the II Corps. General Hancock, who had been seriously wounded at Gettysburg, had just returned to duty and was given charge over the corps.

It was a raw final Friday in March of 1864 as the ambulance wagon made its way north through the Federal encampment toward the expansive stacks of supplies along the sidings at Brandy Station. Duane's brown eyes saw nothing, but his ears bore witness to the activity about the moving wagon. Johnny chattered away sharing a running account of all he saw. Three years Duane's senior, Johnny had continued to serve as a medical aid and was now actively assisting Captain Marshalton in routine sick call duties. Duane had pushed himself to learn everything he could to assist as inconspicuously as possible. Blind soldiers were unheard of and there were many who frowned on Duane's presence. More than once, a court decree naming the captain as his legal guardian was all that kept the boy in the army.

"I smells horses an hears 'em too," the blind youth observed. "Could be thet cava'ry camp agin?"

"Sure is," his friend confirmed. "They've made wooden floors on top the mud for their horses to keep their hoofs dry. The troopers are standing about with nothing better to do than stare at us going by."

Duane turned his face toward the smell and feel of the camp, smiled, and waved. Some waved back.

"You did it again," Johnny stated. "It sure keeps them guessing."

"Sher does," Duane smiled to himself as he faced ahead once more. The wagon continued its journey through the vast sea of camps.

Thousands of tents and log cabins were laid out in streets, rows, or neat clusters. There were quartermaster camps with rows of wagons for ferrying men and supplies from place to place. There were wagon parks where wagons waited by the hundreds for the spring campaign. Everywhere there were wooden walkways to help the men keep out of the mud as they traveled afoot about the camps. In various parts of the encampment, craftsmen plied their trade. Carpenters were building pontoon boats for the army engineers to use in bridging the rivers for the spring advance. Wheelwrights, carpenters, and harness makers were busy building or repairing wagons in their field shops about the camps while blacksmiths and farriers worked from mobile forges and wagon-based shops.

Nearly an hour had passed before the boys approached the cluster of buildings that was Brandy Station. The air hummed with activity as work crews unloaded rows of box cars lining the sidings, to stack and arrange crates and barrels for distribution to the quartermaster camps of the various army corps. Another train, newly arrived, stood on the main track while its crew prepared to switch the loaded cars for empties from one of the side tracks.

Johnny guided the wagon to the station office before halting it and setting the brakes. "Wait here," he instructed his friend as he took his paperwork and climbed down the side.

Waiting on the wagon seat, Duane listened carefully to the surrounding noises to develop a sense of activity and to orient himself to the setting. The shout of orders, the grating of crates on wagon beds, the jingle of chain and harness from impatient horses, the rumble of steam from the locomotive – all filled the air with the discordant sound of purposeful activity. Alert ears picked up a quiet sound of furtive feet and hands sliding along the wagon's side boards.

"What is it ya be wantin?" the boy asked, turning to face the invisible stranger.

There was a moment of silence. The approaching colonel paused.

"Say yer piece," the boy stated calmly.

"Well I'll be damned," a tenor voice responded. "You are blind."

"What if I is?"

"You ain't fit to wear that uniform. Simple as that. This army doesn't allow for blind soldiers." The voice was frank. There was no tone of hostility or threat, just a plainly spoken stating of fact.

"I'm called Dee," the boy introduced. "How might I call you?" He offered his hand where it should be right by the sound of the voice.

The man took the offered hand. "I am Colonel Russell of General Haye's staff. I see by the clover on your cap that you're also with the II Corps."

"Yes, Sir. I'm assigned to Captain Marshalton, assistant surgeon for the 20th Indiana." The boy's voice was firm as he controlled the pain of fear that was growing within.

"Your courtesy is noted, Corporal. But you have no business in the army and I shall personally see to it that you are sent home. Good day, Corporal."

"Yes sir, Colonel."

The man went on his way and was soon lost in the activity around the station. Johnny returned from within the station and climbed back up to the wagon seat.

"What's wrong, Dee?" he asked, taking up the reins and releasing the brake. "You look like you've seen a ghost."

The wagon began to move as the youth guided the team to the left.

"There was a Colonel Russell from General Haye's staff as said he was gonna git me sent home cause a my bein blind and not fit ta be in the army."

"He can't do that!" Johnny exclaimed.

"I do hope ya's right," Duane said.

"There are others who've tried before. None of them got their way."

"Guess yer right."

The two rode quietly as Johnny drove the team to a designated area stacked with incoming medical supplies. All about were the voices and clatter of intense activity as dozens of wagons came and went with their assigned movement of materials.

"There goes the U.S. Mail," Johnny observed as the square-looking, canvas-covered rig rattled past, drawn by a team of dappled greys.

"Thet's gotta be the most movin wagon in the camp," Duane added.

"Here we are," Johnny changed the subject. "Let's get loaded and out of here."

The older youth handed the papers to a supply agent as the man turned from a customer just finished, then climbed down to start loading. Duane climbed around the seat into the wagon bed where he rolled and tied the canvass side and carefully positioned himself to stack the load. He'd done this before and had become very proficient at the task. Johnny simply identified each item as he lifted it to the side boards and Duane knew how to grab it and place it in the wagon. The loading began.

"Bandages."

The crate hit the board edge and the boy lifted it in, sliding it against the far side.

"Bandages."

Again the crate was placed.

"Morphine."

The case was loaded.

After a half hour of working throughout the yard's various stacks of materials, the job was completed and the wagon cover lowered into place. Duane hopped down from the tail-gate, felt his way around the vehicle, then climbed back up to his seat. Johnny made a final check to be sure the wagon was secure, then he, too, climbed back up to the seat. Taking up the reins for the last time, he released the brake and turned the team south for the trip back to camp.

$$* \quad * \quad *$$

A fire crackled in the rough stone and log fireplace with its barrel chimney on the outside. The end of the wall tent had been set snugly against the fireplace construction like many others along the company streets of the regiment's camps. This section of the camp housed hospital personnel, bandsmen, and teamsters. Nearby was Colonel Taylor's headquarters. The colonel commanded the 20th Indiana. Captain Marshalton was next door. Once again, Duane and Johnny shared quarters with the medical supplies. They also had a makeshift table and pair of chairs which had been fashioned from empty crates during the first month of winter camp.

Duane sat on his cot, slowly sewing a separated seam in a shirt. Johnny perched on a chair near the fire reading a medical book he had borrowed from the captain.

"How am I doin?" the younger boy asked, holding his work for his friend to see.

Johnny laid his book aside and went to inspect the job. After careful study, he replied, "Won't be quite so drafty, but sure is awful looking. There's still a piece to go."

"Jest so's it's bein done," Duane said. "Don't 'spect I'll be too good fer a long time, yet."

Johnny returned to his reading, but sat instead and stared at his friend. Finally he raised a question that had bothered him a long time.

"Dee, remember us passing the corps' mail wagon?"

"Yeah."

"How come you've never written your pa a letter?"

The needle paused mid-stitch as the question caught the boy by surprise. He thought to find the answer.

"I reckon it neve' come ta mind ta try," he finally replied. "Ain't neve' writ ta no one regular-like b'fer. They's no relations ta home an I neve' figger'd fer mail goin ta the enemy." He thought a minute. "Ya really think a letter could go ta the enemy side?"

"Why not? There's lots of Union men with family in the South."

"Would ya put ma words ta paper fer me, Johnny?"

"Sure thing. Let me find a pencil and sheet of paper."

Laying his sewing aside, Duane hugged his legs and rested his chin on his knees. The warmth of the flames flickered on his face. Rummaging through a box of requisition paperwork, Johnny found a pencil and a sheet of blank paper. Resting it on his book, he announced he was ready.

"Dear Pa," Duane began. "I hope this letter gits ta ya so's ya knows as I is alive. I ain't thought ta write b'fer 'cause it neve' come ta mind it'd eve' find ya. If this here letter does git ta ya, I's in Virginia with..."

"Not so fast," Johnny interrupted. "I ain't the army's fastest writer."

Together the two continued to establish Duane's location and to explain how he had gotten there. The writing was finished and addressed to Captain Andrew Kinkade in the 13th Arkansas with the Confederate Army in Tennessee.

"We'll put it in tomorrow's mail and see what happens," Johnny stated.

"I cain't wait!" Duane exclaimed. "How long ya think it'll take ta git there?"

"Don't really know. Maybe a couple of weeks."

Johnny stuck the letter in the cover of the book and let it protrude so he wouldn't loose it.

Outside, footsteps approached the tent. The door flap was pushed aside as the captain entered.

"Evenin, Boys," he greeted.

"Evenin, Dan," they chorused.

The man approached the fire and settled on a chair.

"Eny news from yer meetin?" Duane inquired.

Warming his hands in the heat of the flames, the man answered, "General Grant's still in Washington, but due to arrive here tomorrow. I figure it won't be too long before the spring campaign begins. The officers have been told to send their families home tomorrow."

"That would sure seem to mean we're to move before long," Johnny agreed. "Any more from that Colonel Russell?"

"Not yet," Dan replied. "Nevertheless, Dee must continue to do all he can to be as useful as possible so no one can complain that he's a liability to the army."

"We wrote a letter ta my pa," Duane beamed.

"Good idea, Dee. I wonder why we never thought of it before?" the captain stated.

"Jest ain't give it no thought," Duane answered. "But how will it git ta the other side in this war?"

"It should go, shouldn't it?" Johnny added.

"I'll tell you what might help," Dan offered. "I have to see the chaplain for some testaments that's been asked for. I'll give him your letter and he can send it through the churches."

"Thanks, Dan," Duane said.

"Here's the letter." Johnny pulled the folded paper from the book on the table and handed it to the captain.

"By the way," the man added as he stood to go. "Your little sutler friend, Jonah, was around selling some maple sugar fresh from Pennsylvania. I bought you a bar so you could sweeten your salt pork. Said he'd be by again to see if you had any odd jobs for hire."

"Eny idea when he'll be back?" Johnny asked.

"Reckon to see him near sun-up tomorrow." The captain crossed to the door flap. "Keep warm."

"Yes, Sir," the boys chorused.

As the door flap fell shut behind Captain Marshalton, the mellow tone of a bugle cut the night air with TATTOO. It was immediately picked up and joined by regimental buglers throughout the camp, as they signaled it was time to settle in for the night.

Duane concentrated on finishing his sewing while Johnny opened the book to complete the page he had started.

After fifteen minutes, the older youth closed the book and laid it quietly on the table, then turned to watch his friend. Duane was carefully examining his work with finger and thumb tips, running gently along the stitching to see that it was closed. Satisfied the job was done, he patiently guided the needle point under the last stitch to tie off the thread.

"Does it look ta be done?" Duane held the work up to be examined.

"It'll do," Johnny answered. "Time to turn in."

The shirt was laid across a barrel end at the head of the cot. Both kicked their shoes under their beds and stripped to their johns. As Duane climbed in, Johnny blew out the lamp before he, too, climbed under his blankets. After some squirming, both settled into comfortable positions.

"What's yer thinkin fer tamorra'?" Duane asked.

"If Jonah shows up," Johnny suggested, "we could use him for you to practice some nursing chores like bandaging, giving water, and writing information. You got to be real good to help at the field hospital. We can also practice folding blankets and cots, and packing things for the wagon."

"Sounds ta be a real dull day." Duane shifted onto his side. "You know what Captain Marshalton says."

"Yeh, gotta prove maself ta be a' use."

The two lay quietly for a moment. Outside, the night was momentarily filled with the soft strands of TAPS as the last call echoed through the countryside.

"Night, Dee."

"Night, Johnny."

Hot coals crackled in the fireplace. Quiet settled over the encampment. As the two teenagers drifted off to sleep, so too did the nearby quarter of a million souls of the opposing armies, scattered across the landscape.

*　　*　　*

"You sure you know what you're doin?" ten-year-old Jonah asked. He lay on Johnny's cot, partially wrapped in white bandaging with loose ends hanging in every direction.

"Guess it ain't too good," Duane stated. Frustration edged his voice as he knelt by the cot with an end of rolled fabric in one hand, trying to feel for its position with the other.

"I suppose a wounded soldier wouldn't be too happy. He might even get worried," Johnny observed. "But you've gotta admit, it should give his companions a good laugh."

"Yer sher?"

"Definitely!" Jonah snickered.

Suddenly, the three burst into hilarious laughter. Duane placed the rest of the bandage in Jonah's hand and sat back on his heels, laughing quietly to himself and shaking his head in wonder that he should try such impossible things.

"I think we need to get out of camp for a while," the eldest suggested. "It's too nice outside to stay cooped up in here. Besides, with officers packing out their families today, there's little around here that needs doing."

"Ya think Sergeant Baker will let us take two horses?" Duane asked.

"Sure. Let's go." Johnny stepped to the bed to help Jonah free himself of the wrappings.

Duane felt his way back to his bed, then rummaged for his coat and hat. Freed of fabric wrappings, Jonah sat up and reached for his coat while Johnny banked the fire.

It was mid-morning as the three boys left the tent, gathered Jonah's horse, then wandered over to the open stabling area for the division's supply train livestock.

Jonah Christopher came from Pennsylvania. His father was a sutler who had come into the Federal camps in January. He was assigned to a Pennsylvania regiment where he built a cabin roofed with canvass and went into business selling soldiers and officers anything from tobacco, candy, and canned goods to stationery, some clothing, and cards. Officers could buy whiskey. Some of the enlisted would con it on occasion by impersonating an officer. But prices were twice what they should be and Mr. Christopher quickly became as disliked as most of his lot.

The boy wanted to be a soldier. He was afraid the war would pass before he got his chance to fight. Of slight build, he looked lost in the oversized Union coat and forage cap he wore. One day in late January, the captain and his boys had stopped at the Christopher store to purchase some candy. The boys met at the counter and took to each other at once. Since then, Jonah had frequently ridden the three miles to the camp of the 20th Indiana to visit, and the two teenagers have enjoyed his presence and his constant chatter of news from about the camps.

As the trio approached the open stables, they knew they were near from the sound of a hundred thousand flies buzzing about a mountain range of manure. The smell was awful, perfumed slightly by the mountains of hay and bags of feed. The sergeant allowed them two horses which they saddled quickly for a fast departure from the odoriferous valley.

"Where to?" Duane asked.

"How about southeast to the river and spy on the Rebs!" Jonah suggested enthusiastically.

"Southeast it is," Johnny stated.

As usual, Johnny looped a long lead line from the bridle of Duane's horse over the horn of his saddle. One thing the loss of sight affected unexpectedly was the ability to ride. Unable to see what lay ahead, Duane could no longer anticipate the horse's moves. Still, he could sit his saddle well and Johnny saw to it that there were no surprises.

The three riders struck off toward the course of the Rapidan River near the Germanna Ford to the southeast.

They rode through acres of tent cities and log communities spread over rolling hills and open fields. Stands of oak and cedar were scattered about the landscape as were acres of stumps where trees had been felled to provide for structures, walkways, roads, and firewood.

Along the way the riders observed some regiments at morning drill and paused to watch. Stopping near a Rhode Island company, the trio was distracted by a raucous cheering. Turning toward the camp, they saw a large number of men gathered in a cluster. On closer investigation, Jonah pointed out a crated cock bird and they figured there were more in the center of the crowd. Dismounting, the three moved close to the edge of the crowd to watch the excitement. Duane used a thin cane when walking to help "see" where he was going. When riding, it hung from the saddle horn on its own leather loop.

The boys stayed on for a half hour to watch the cock fights and the betting, and to cheer for their favorite bird. When their interest faded, they mounted and continued on their way. The ride was leisurely, allowing for frequent stops to rest the horses or their riders. The sun was high toward noon as the trio crossed the open ground approaching the river.

Duane reined his mount to a stop and the others did likewise. "Tell me as it looks," he requested.

"There's what's left of a broken-up barn just ahead," Jonah described. "There's a house about a half mile to our left."

"Looks like a broken bridge of sorts off right," Johnny added. "The countryside's pretty open and rolls down to the river's edge."

"Anyone hungry?" Jonah asked. "I packed us some candy."

"Dismount!" Johnny mocked. "There's a fence rail here to tie your horse on, Dee."

As the three settled on the grassy roadside, Jonah handed each a small bag of hard candy. Duane selected a piece, smelled it, and placed it in his mouth. Stuffing the bag in a pocket, he lay back with his hands under his head to rest and to roll the candy about with his tongue as he sucked on its sweetness. His companions did the same.

A distant sound caught the thirteen-year-old's attention. "I hear som'thin ta the rive'," he whispered.

The others looked hard to see what might be there.

"I can't see no one," Johnny whispered from where he stood by the fence, shading his eyes with his hand as he scanned the country along the riverbank.

"What's that?" Jonah pointed toward the embankment near the bridge structure.

The oldest youth studied the spot indicated before he replied. "Looks like a patrol on picket duty settling to make a fire."

Duane sat up, rattling his candy into his cheek before he spoke. "Which army?"

"Yanks," Johnny replied.

For a quiet moment the two studied the distant activity. Suddenly a voice called from across the river.

"Hallo the Yank Patrol!"

"It's Reb cavalry," Johnny discerned.

"Hallo yourself," a Federal soldier replied.

The boys listened to the distant exchange.

"We got tobacco! Ya all got some coffee to spare?" the cavalryman inquired.

"Pound for pound," the reply was called.

"Mind if I cross over?"

"Come on along. Save me from gettin wet."

As the boys watched, a grey-clad rider forded the river with his sack of tobacco to meet with the blue-clad infantrymen and work out a trade. A few minutes later, they exchanged goods and the rider rode back across the river. Once safe on the opposite bank, the soldiers from both units waved farewell and the cavalry patrol rode off.

"Did I tell you about the company I heard of on picket duty in a old cabin?" Jonah asked as he watched the riders depart.

"Don't remember as you did," Johnny replied as he turned his attention to his candy and settled on the ground with his back against a fence post.

"There was this company on picket duty that stayed in an empty cabin each day outside their lines and returned to their camp each night." The youngster sat down on the grass to explore his candy selection while he shared his story. "One morning as they arrived at the cabin, they saw it was taken by Reb cavalry and was about to have a shootout when someone had a idea. The Rebs used the place at night and the Yanks at day. So they figured each could go on havin his turn and agreed to leave a warm fire goin for each other."

"Sher is a heap better 'n shootin each other," Duane observed. "Thet would be sech a waste as no one would git no good of it."

"You two want to go on down to the river?" Johnny asked.

"Don't reckon as it'd be too good a idea," Duane thought. "Could be they'd fret we might a seen 'em tradin an wanta be sher as we couldn't say nothin."

"Yeah," Jonah agreed. "And me and my pa ain't exactly popular with a lot of fellers."

"Think they'll see us?" Duane asked.

"We're pretty easy for them to see," Johnny stated. "But they're probably too busy fixing something to eat." He rose to his feet. "Just the same, it wouldn't be a bad idea to head back. I'd hate to have to leave in a hurry."

Jonah selected a candy and popped it in his mouth, then stood and stuffed his bag into his coat pocket. Johnny guided Duane to his horse. They all mounted, then turned away from the river to start back toward camp.

* * *

March drifted into April. Pay day passed and with it came new stock at the many sutler tents. Jonah was kept busy by his father and had not been around in recent days. With the onset of the new month came an increase in drilling and the realization it wouldn't be long before the neighboring armies would march against each other.

The Federal soldiers were well rested and well supplied. Sickness had taken its toll. Even so, the troops were ready, though some were still determined to cut and run.

Duane and Johnny stood shoulder to shoulder in company formation along with musicians, teamsters, and others from the surgeon's staff. The regiment was gathered along with everyone else of Major-General Birney's Third Division. Before the troops, some fifty yards distant, stood Jason Trible and Thomas Kirkland. The two men, in their late twenties, had taken money to fill in for draftees, then had run out while on their first guard duty assignment. Behind each man lay his coffin beside an open grave. In front stood a company of riflemen and their captain. The regimental chaplain was addressing Trible and Kirkland.

"What's happenin now, Johnny?" Duane whispered.

"Their chaplain's talking to them," came the soft reply.

"Cain't hear nothin."

"Me neither."

The two stood fidgeting uneasily along with the other thousands in the division. "I hate this. It's such a waste," Johnny stated.

There was the clatter of rifles coming off the ground at the command of "Make ready!"

"Take aim!" Hammers clicked back and fingers rested on triggers.

"Fire!" Two dozen rifles clattered in volley, spitting fire and a rolling billow of smoke.

The air reverberated with gunfire, then was caught up in a collective breath of surprise.

"Damn!" one of the bandsmen exclaimed softly.

"What?" Duane wondered.

"They only shot one of them!" Johnny explained. "The other's just standing there."

"Reload!" the captain ordered.

Again the commands were given. Again the volley was fired. Again the man remained standing, after staggering back from a bullet in his arm.

"Run, damn you!" another intoned quietly.

"Why ain't he runnin?" the boy asked. "Ya think they'd shoot him in the back?"

"I don't know, Dee," the bandsman replied, glancing at the boy.

Again the company fired. This time the man fell dead.

"Oh, God," Johnny whispered. "That other fellow ain't dead neither. He's getting up."

"And the one they just shot's still movin," another observed.

"Ain't it been enough?" Duane asked. "Why ain't they callin it even an quit this. It's jest a plain murderin waste."

"The captain's taking his pistol and going to finish them off," Johnny whispered.

There was a very distinct click as the revolver misfired. The man was shaking terribly as the two condemned men twisted about on the ground in agony. Again the captain fired and the gun roared as the shot slammed through the man's chest and blew him dead against the ground. The other awaited his fate in agonizing distress. Once more the revolver spoke. But the shot was not fatal. Finally, the officer put the barrel to the condemned man's head and fired.

The final gunshot echoed and reechoed about the landscape and within the minds of the witnessing division, numbed by the horror they had just watched. It was one thing to shoot the enemy in battle or to die an agonizing death from the wounds of battle or from disease. But this! These were two of their own.

The burial detail placed the bodies in their boxes and lowered them into the ground. The dirt was shoveled in and the graves closed over. Nothing was placed to mark the graves. Deserters were not permitted grave markers. Jason Trible and Thomas Kirkland were gone forever, except in the minds of those who witnessed their passing. There they would be remembered until each soldier's dying day.

Following the execution, the regiments returned to their drill fields to practice the rest of the morning. The bandsmen gathered for a practice of their own. Duane, Johnny, and other non-combatants gathered to watch and listen.

Hours slipped by.

During the afternoon Joshua Bacton, a nineteen-year-old drummer from upstate New York, continued in another teaching session with Duane and Johnny.

"Here's a cadence we used in our community band back home." He played a catchy rhythm, part on the drum head and part on the wooden rim. "Now you try it, Dee."

Duane had his old drum strapped on. It had been repaired with new skin heads and replacements of damaged rope and leather tabs. He caught the cadence to perfection and didn't miss a beat.

"How's thet fer doin as yer done."

"You're real good. You've a great ear for music. Maybe you can play with us sometime when we do a sit-down for the regiment." Joshua's interest in music was far greater than any political interest in the war. He didn't believe in the fighting, but was willing to help musically and when his turn came in the litter brigade to bring the wounded in to the hospitals.

"Johnny," he turned to the older teen, "do you think you're ready to try a drum roll?"

"Show me how," the youth requested.

Duane slipped his drum from his shoulder and passed it to his friend, adjusting the strap for greater length.

"Hold your sticks like this," Joshua instructed.

Duane took his friend's hands and worked the fingers into the correct position.

"Now watch what I do and count each tap."

It was awkward. Yet he managed a fair copy of the tappings.

Captain Marshalton approached the trio. The war had aged him. He looked like a man in his forties. His dark hair had grown down over his collar and was ragged at the edges. The man paused to watch the lesson before interrupting with his own concerns.

"Not bad, Johnny," Captain Marshalton complimented. "But I'd rather you take up the harmonica. This army does not need another drummer boy."

"No need for worry, Dan. I've seen enough damage to keep from volunteering," the boy assured. Jamming the sticks into his belt, he found a barrel for a seat to await the captain's news.

The other two paused and turned their attention to the doctor.

"What's everyone looking at me for?" Dan asked.

"Jest waitin ta hears what fer ya come by," Duane answered.

"It's not good news, I'm afraid." The man propped his foot on a box and leaned on his knee. "Remember that colonel you ran into last week, Dee?"

"Sher, Colonel Russell of General Hayes' staff."

"Well, he's taken his objection to General Hayes who has come to General Ward. The general wants to see you, now." There was concern in the voice as the captain stood to depart.

"Will ya be with me, Sir?" Duane stood.

"I will, Dee. I have the court papers. Let's go."

"I'll put the drum back," Johnny stated. "Good luck with the general."

"Thanks, Johnny." Duane reached for his guide stick which lay on the ground at his side, then stood to go.

Turning to the captain from the last sound of his voice, he approached to where he felt the man's presence at his left elbow.

"See you boys later," Marshalton stated.

Duane placed his hand on the man's wrist and the two departed for the brigadier-general's headquarters.

*   *   *

Brigadier-General John H. H. Ward was seated in a camp rocker at a table under the canvass canopy which projected from the front of his wall tent. Long hair curtained the perimeter of a balding head, ending with a slight curl just above his collar. A walrus mustache added to the dark gaze and a full face to give an authoritatively stern appearance. He was a large man and amply filled his chair. With his concentration focused on a game of chess with his staff secretary, the general was unaware of the approaching youth and surgeon.

Some who were watching the game looked up. The captain and the blind corporal paused respectfully to wait and be recognized. Some with the general exchanged whispered remarks. Thus aware of some new presence, the general glanced up to see the cause of the whisperings.

"One moment, Captain," he acknowledged, then returned to his game.

The moment stretched into fifteen minutes. The game progressed slowly.

"Won't you be seated," a staff officer offered pointing to an empty chair and a stump.

"Thank you, Lieutenant," Marshalton replied. To Duane he whispered, "We're going oblique right. Chair is left of stump. The lieutenant is close to the right."

The boy used his stick to check the way for objects and kept a sense of closeness to the captain at his left. The two proceeded slowly, Duane reaching out cautiously with his sense of feel for any awareness of air pressure change in his distance from the captain and approaching figures. The general glanced up from his game to observe as the boy paused near the lieutenant.

"I ask yer pardon, Lieutenant, but I ain't wantin ta step on yer shoes 'r knock inta ya."

The man stepped aside. The boy and the doctor continued to their seats. Duane searched out the stump with his stick. When his toes found it, he checked its surface with his hand, then turned and settled on it.

"You do very well, Corporal," the general spoke.

Duane jumped to his feet.

"Relax," General Ward stated. "You may be seated."

Duane lowered himself cautiously. Captain Marshalton settled in the chair.

Leaning back in his rocker, the general opened the conversation. "Corporal Duane Kinkade, is that correct?" "Yes, Sir."

"Tell me, Corporal, how does a blind boy get into this army?"

"I weren't blind, Sir. I've bin in this war since Shiloh an did good service the whole time since, 'cept when I bin laid up some from sickness 'r woundin." He sat straight on the stump, resting his walking stick across his lap.

"How did you lose your sight, then?" General Ward rested his hands on the arms of his chair.

"I was in the fightin at Gettysburg when a powder charge blew up in ma face. It were a long while fer I was healed up ta travelin. Now as I's fit agin, I kin do a bunch a thin's ta he'p out fer the doctorin."

"Why don't you go home, Corporal? There's many a lad stuck a toe out to a cannon shot and lost his foot just so he could go home. Why are you still here?"

There was a moment of quiet as Duane tried to seek the answer to the question from within himself.

"I's scairt," he whispered. "There ain't none a ma family left an I know's how it is here. I ain't knowin what I'd find at home an' I'm plumb fine as I is."

"Where is your family?"

"Ma was kilt by raiders an Pa went ta fight in the war. I left ta find him an ain't yet."

General Ward leaned forward in his chair, resting his elbows on his knees. "Haven't you written him."

"At first, Sir, but the letter neve' got ta him."

The general stood and paced to the side to stare out over the camp. He turned, with hands clasped behind his back, and faced the captain. "Captain Marshalton."

"Yes, General."

"Why is this boy with you?"

"He's my legal ward until we find his father."

"What steps are being taken toward that end?"

"He has written to his father through our chaplain who has routed the letter through the church in hopes of getting directly to his father's unit."

"Why should that be necessary? Just send the letter through the regular mail."

"The boy's father is in General Bragg's army, Sir."

There was a moment of stunned silence. "But that's the Confederate Army, Captain," the general finally stated, leaning his hands on his table near the chess board.

"Yes, General," Marshalton confirmed. "Corporal Kinkade is from Arkansas."

There was an exchange of shocked stares from the officers who had been listening to the conversation.

"What in God's sake is a Rebel cripple doing in my brigade!" the general exploded.

"With all due respect, General Ward, he has proven himself on the battlefield and off in bravery and in trust."

"In whose army, Captain!" The general had risen to his full stature and moved to the front of the table facing Duane with his hands placed authoritatively on his hips.

"General Sheridan's command, Sir," Duane stood. "General Ward, Sir, I ain't wantin ta cause ya no kind a embarrassment an' I ain't wantin fer yer staff here ta be upset none. I ain't in this war ta kill Yanks 'r Rebs, either one. I only want ta find my pa. I done my part he'pin those as was wounded an' I done a share in the killin – both Yank 'n Reb alike. I do feel a heap prideful fer the fi'st an' damnation fer the killin. But I ain't wantin ta let no one put me und'r if'n I kin he'p it. Fer this present, I only want ta do what I kin ta he'p the captain till he kin see me ta findin my pa."

The statement was firmly made without the rise of emotion or anger. The general stood a moment, then glanced around at his officers to study briefly the reactions on their faces. It ran from strong disapproval to respectful acceptance.

"You may be seated, Corporal," the general stated as he stood a moment longer to study the sightless youth.

Duane resumed his seat on the stump as the general dropped his hands to his side and wandered back to his chair. Standing behind it, he rested his hands on its back.

"Captain Marshalton."

"Yes, General."

"Does General Sheridan know this boy?"

"Since he rode with Sheridan after Shiloh."

There was a restlessness among the staff officers who had been listening throughout the discussion. Some shifted to a more comfortable stance or found a place to sit or lean.

"In light of all that's been learned, and I know there's much more should I ask for detailed accounting, I will allow things to remain at their current status while I review this with my staff. I'll be in touch early next week." The general remained behind his chair as he waited for the two visitors to stand and depart.

Rising from his chair, Captain Marshalton tapped Duane's elbow to signal it was time to go. Then he spoke once more to General Ward. "Would it be appropriate, General, to inquire of General Sheridan in pursuit of a letter of recognition or support on behalf of the corporal?"

"You have my permission, Captain. Such a letter would make my decision much simpler," the general responded. "Good day to you, Captain Marshalton and to you, Corporal Kinkade."

"Good day, General," each returned.

The two departed as General Ward rounded his chair to resume his seat and continue his game. The boy took the doctor's arm and they moved quickly to disappear from the curious stares of the staff officers as they lost themselves in the commotion and movement of the surrounding camps.

Back at regimental camp, Duane returned to his friends and their practicing while Dan retired to his quarters to write a letter to General Sheridan.

* * *

As the days slipped by and a new week reached its midpoint, Jonah returned. Duane lounged sleepily in a canvass camp chair while Joshua and Johnny lingered in drum lessons on the ground beneath a large oak tree some forty yards distant. An older bandsman, a horn player named Zachary Bennett, had joined them in their musical endeavors.

"Hi," Jonah greeted as he approached the napping boy.

"Hi, yerself," Duane acknowledged quietly, having heard the other's approaching footfalls.

"You heard me comin?" the ten-year-old asked.

"Yeh," was the reply. "Somethin gnawin at ya?" Duane inquired.

"How'd ya know?"

"Yer voice. It sounds as like ya's havin yer troubles."

"You can say as I have." Jonah knelt on the ground beside the chair and took his friend's hand to touch its fingers against a black-and-blue knot on his head.

"What's bin done ta ya?" Duane asked. He ran his fingers lightly across the face in search of other signs of brutality.

"A bunch a soldiers got mad at my pa as the canned meats they'd bought was putrefied. They got themselves all liquored up an' come tore up the business. Pa's broke up bad and the doctor put him to hospital with a cracked head, broken arm, and stove ribs. I fixed up the store best I could and closed it up taday." A tear or worry slipped free. "Dee, what am I gonna do?!"

"I reckon as ya kin stay here tonight an Johnny 'n me'll go back ta he'p ya best we kin. Besides, I ain't so sher as ta what'll come a' me. General Ward's likely ta have me shipped out fer being blind." He put a comforting hand on the younger boy's shoulder. "Could be as you 'n me'll both be cut loose ta fend fer arselfs."

"It ain't right," Jonah stated indignantly. He stood to find a seat for himself and stopped motionless as he saw, in the distance, a small group of riders headed along the tent street in their direction. "There's a general and his staff ridin this way," Jonah whispered.

"I figer'd as he'd send a orderly to the captain with a letter," Duane mused aloud.

"They's not from here," Jonah added. "And I think they's cavalry, cause there's yellow on their uniforms."

The boy found a barrel and moved it beside Duane's chair as a seat. The two waited in quiet expectation as the others continued with their music, unaware of the approaching visitors.

The officer and his staff rode slowly, glancing about the camp at the soldiers in their routine, obviously in search of someone. Eventually he paused in front of the boys. Sensing the presence and hearing the impatient snort of the horses, Duane stood respectfully. Jonah followed his friend's example.

"You aren't Corporal Kinkade, are you?" the officer asked.

"Yes, Sir, General – Sheridan?" Duane wondered.

"Yes, Corporal," he answered, swinging down from his horse as Jonah stepped forward and took the reins.

"But how...?"

"Captain Marshalton's letter." He removed his gloves and tucked them into his belt. "How are you, soldier?" he offered his hand.

The general's staff looked on in mild surprise at a conversation, so personal, between the general and this mere boy.

"I'm doin okay, General," Duane offered his hand and met the general's. "Would ya like ta set a spell? Jonah here might have a candy with him as his pa's a sutler."

"I'll accept a piece if you're offering," the man took the chair while Jonah searched his pockets for his bag of hard candies.

Duane held the horse during the candy search. The bag was retrieved from a deep coat pocket and offered to the general who made his selection. Duane then settled on the barrel while Jonah made himself comfortable standing with the horse and stroking his neck.

Returning the bag, General Sheridan explained, "I was in Washington on my way here when the letter reached me. Since I was coming down to meet with General Grant and his cavalry commanders, I decided a stop at your camp would help me respond to the captain's concerns. How did you lose your sight?"

"A powder charge blew on the ground near ma feet," Duane answered briefly.

"I haven't seen you since that day at Stone's River. Have you had any luck in finding your pa?"

"I come close. But bad luck had it I was headin the wrong way and neve' did git ta Bragg's army."

"Could be I don't want to hear the particulars of your travels, but it does surprise me that you haven't found your way back to your own people. I must agree with the concern that you really don't belong here. Blindness is a tremendous disadvantage. I recognize you are a good soldier and have done your duty. Knowing what I do of you and of the army's immediate needs for the coming campaign, and of your relationship with Captain Marshalton, I know you will make a contribution to your regiment. I think as soon as your captain can be spared, he should personally see that you are reunited with your own people and sent home."

There was a moment of silence. "General Sheridan?"

"What is it, Corporal?"

"I know as how yer right. I 'spect as how it got easier ta stay on with thin's as I knew they was then ta try ta git home not knowin how thet would be. I's scairt a not knowin what may be if 'n I was ta go."

"I understand, Corporal. I will recommend that you stay on until such time as Captain Marshalton can be given leave to personally see to your affairs." The general stood to leave.

"Thank ya, General Sheridan." The boy stood.

"You're a good soldier, Corporal Kinkade. My recommendations are based on my personal knowledge of that fact. I wish you well." He took the reins from Jonah. "Thank you for the candy, Jonah." Mounting gracefully, the general waved. "Take care, both of you. And give my regards to the captain."

As Sheridan and his staff moved away, the general turned to his staff officer and instructed, "Captain, please take down this letter, then I'll tell you where to deliver it."

The general's party faded into the landscape of company camps.

The two boys stood as the general's staff faded out of sight. Johnny and the two bandsmen approached as they suddenly realized someone had stopped and was gone again.

"Who was here?" Joshua asked.

"It was General Sheridan!" Jonah exclaimed.

"Seriously, Jonah, you expect me to believe such foolishness?" the youth mocked.

"It were so," Duane confirmed.

"What did he say?" Johnny asked.

"Do you believe this, Johnny?" Joshua persisted.

"It's true. We know the general."

"Let's go see Dan," Duane answered his friend. "I'll tell ya then." "What happened to Jonah?" Johnny exclaimed noticing the bruised lump on his head.

"Tell ya 'bout thet, too."

"I have to go now, Joshua," Johnny excused. "I'll talk to you about playing again this evening."

The bandsmen watched as the boys headed off to the captain's tent. Then they, too, went their way to gather with the rest of the company for afternoon drill.

* * *

The following day the sutlers were ordered out from all the army's camps. Jonah bade his friends farewell and said he'd find a way to pack his pa's business and have it ready for his pa when he got out of the hospital.

General Ward sent instructions to the effect that Duane would stay until Captain Marshalton could be sent on leave to put the boy's affairs in order. General Sheridan's reaction was evident as much was in accordance with his comments to Duane during the previous day's visit.

Serious preparations were set in motion to get ready for the spring campaign which was expected to finish Lee's army and to bring the war to a close. April passed slowly. Finally in the last week, General Meade was notified to advance. The baggage wagons were loaded as the supply trains prepared to get underway. General Grant had been back and forth to Washington on weekly visits as he coordinated the plans of all the Federal armies. Corps commanders increased drill schedules and set about putting their commands into battle trim. General Sheridan stayed on to assume command of the combined cavalry forces which were to operate as an independent force.

The Army of the Potomac was well supplied by way of the railroad connection to Washington. The men were equipped with everything a soldier could want, were well fed, were in their best health, and were in good spirits.

May had begun before the immense wagon trains were ready to roll. Their six thousand wagons would stretch for sixty miles. The roads would have to be clear and the moving army would have to be able to protect them.

Wednesday, May 4th, was a glorious spring day. Wild flowers danced in all their splendor, caressed by a gentle warm breeze. The last of the camps were packed. The three army corps were gathered in ranks. At five o'clock in the morning, the advance was finally underway.

*   *   *

The fragrance of pine scented the air. The blossoms of dogwood splashed the woodscape with patches of white. The thickets of the wilderness crowded alongside the roadway reaching to snag the thousands who passed in their journey toward Chancellorsville. As the army's corps advanced southward, the II Corps moved further to the east to cross the Rapidan River at Ely's Ford. From there it followed the narrow wilderness road toward Chancellorsville. It was mid day when the divisions of General Hancock's corps began arriving at the crossroads where the charred remains of the Chancellor House stood silent against the blue sky, rising above the cloud of dust kicked up by the gathering army.

Dispersing across the open landscape about the ruined mansion, the corps' divisions set their bivouacs for the day. Johnny and Duane pulled their medical supply wagon into line with the others in the brigade's train. The horses were unhitched to be tethered at the horse lines. There the boys left them to graze on the grass at their feet. Returning to the wagon, each took his gear to join the others of their company to make a bedding area for the night and to share a fire for their dinner. Next they headed toward the edge of the woodlands in search of firewood.

As the two wandered the underbrush that skirted the field, someone shouted, "Hey, look what I found!"

"What is it?" another called.

"A skeleton," the first replied.

Several rushed to examine the find when still another announced, "There's one here, too. No. A couple of them!"

"Johnny, where's the house from where we stand?" Duane asked.

"Off behind us a ways," the youth answered as he added another branch to his friend's load. "No, what direction?"

Johnny glanced toward the sun then responded, "I guess it's north and east of us. Why?"

"I was here at the fightin last year. I was in these woods when they was burnin an' men was dyin. Yank guns was in these fields. My friend, Tod, was wounded here. It were a true Hell with the shootin 'n screamin 'n fires burnin all 'round 'n smoke burnin yer eyes 'n lungs." Duane stood remembering, his mind wandering the battlefield of another year.

"I guess there's a lot of dead that got left behind," Johnny thought aloud.

His friend didn't hear him. Johnny paused to study the landscape and to visualize what most of the men present had experienced.

"What did ya say, Johnny?" Duane suddenly came back.

"Nothing," the sixteen-year-old replied. "Let's get our firewood and get back."

Reaching into the thicket he grabbed a smooth stick and picked it up.

"Oh, God," he whispered.

"What's frettin ya?"

"It's a bone!"

"Yank 'r Reb?"

"Dee!" He dropped the white remnant, then pushed aside the vegetation to see what remained of the body."Blue uniform scraps, must have been a Yank. It's charred, too. Musta been burned in the fire."

"Sher hope he was gone fer the fire got ta him."

"Yeah," Johnny agreed quietly.

A small group of infantrymen passed the boys in their own search for firewood and paused to look at the remains.

Before moving on, an older sergeant remarked, "That's what we're comin to tomorrow."

No one said any more. Some nodded in agreement, then they continued on.

The boys finished gathering their wood and returned to their fire site. Activity continued throughout the countryside as more of the corps' wagon train continued to arrive and other brigades settled in for the day. Fires were made and the air was scented with their smoke and with the aroma of brewing coffee. Many of the companies broke out their shelter halves and two-man dog tents soon lined acres of company streets.

As the afternoon wore on, activity quieted. The soldiers settled by their fires to cook dinner from provisions in their haversacks. Following dinner, the men amused themselves with gambling, song, gossip from the latest news, and quiet talk and reflections. Joshua, Zachary, and Thomas Siddle shared the fire with Duane and Johnny. Captain Marshalton also sat a spell. Thomas had a guitar with him and was a very proficient player. Joshua also played a harmonica. The five sang some ballads and love songs and one of which Duane had become very fond – **JUST BEFORE THE BATTLE, MOTHER.**

> Just before the battle, Mother
> I am thinking most of you,
> While upon the field we're watching,
> With the enemy in view.
> Comrades brave are round me lying,

Filled with thoughts of home and God;
For well they know that on the morrow,
Some will sleep beneath the sod.

Farewell, Mother, you may never
Press me to your heart again;
But O, you'll not forget me, Mother,
If I'm numbered with the slain.

Hark! I hear the bugles sounding,
'Tis the signal for the fight;
Now may God protect us, Mother,
As he ever does the right.
Hear the "Battle Cry of Freedom,"
How it swells upon the air;
Oh, yes, we'll rally round the standard,
Or we'll perish nobly there.

The song brought warm memories of his mother and Duane liked to imagine her standing on the porch back home waving to him as he returned, welcoming him back. But the reflection always ended with the image of her headstone in the churchyard with heaps of wild flowers lying at its base and the boy and his dog sitting by the grave to spend time with her.

As the gathering finished the last chorus, the boy lost his voice to an emotional tightness in his throat and simply mouthed the last words. But this was nothing new to those about the fire and they simply paused a moment in silence while each poured a cup of lukewarm coffee.

"Guess we'll be startin early in the morning," Zachary stated.

"Any idea where to?" Thomas asked.

"Captain says we're headed south through a place called Todd's Tavern and beyond," Johnny offered.

"Do you really think we'll get by Lee's army without a fight?" Thomas wondered.

"He ain't like ta give us no more time 'n we's already had," Duane mused.

"I agree," Joshua put in. "We won't see a quiet sunset tomorrow."

Nothing more was said. As each finished his coffee, he wiped the cup to tie it once more onto his pack.

Twilight faded to night.

"Good night," each said in turn.

The fire had dwindled to quiet coals, winking in the gathering darkness. Tree toads and crickets sang their night songs. A billion bits of light danced in the blackness overhead. A soft hum of ten thousand subdued conversations drifted on the night.

"It's gonna be real bad tamorro'," Duane stated as he lay on his back facing the stars.

Johnny rested his head on an outstretched arm as he lay on his side facing his friend and wondering how he would handle the fighting. What would he be able to do being blind? It was one thing in winter camp. But an army on the move and in combat would be something very different.

"I'm guessing you're right, Dee," the older teen responded. "I think it will be the worst yet."

"Night, Johnny."

"Night, Dee."

The two drifted into a restless sleep.

*　　*　　*

The new day began early. It was still dark as Duane and Johnny hitched the team to their supply wagon and moved it into the line of march. General Hancock had his corps on the move by the time the first faint glow of dawn began to light the eastern horizon. All around the moving column of infantry, the wilderness rang with the cheerful babble of the sparrows and robins and the raucous cawing of the crows. More than an hour after the sun had risen, about seven o'clock in the morning, Johnny and Duane were rattling along in silence when a distant thundering became audible to the northwest.

"It's begun," Johnny stated.

"I know," Duane agreed.

The column continued its advance another mile and a half before it halted. General Birney's division was first in line, so it wasn't long before Captain Marshalton rode up with information. He paused on Johnny's side of the wagon.

"There's a fight developing to the north," the captain stated. "We're to hold here at Todd's Tavern crossroads until decisions are made. You two okay?"

"What fer am I ta do if we goes in ta the fightin?" Duane asked.

"You stay with me helping the wounded behind the lines," Dan replied. "You know how the field pack is arranged and will stay at my side or Johnny's. Okay?"

"Yes, Sir. I'll do ma best," the youngster replied.

"I'll be nearby," Johnny added. "We'll do all right."

For nearly an hour, the troops waited as the activity to the north intensified. Finally orders were received and the division started north on a narrow dirt lane called Brock Road.

As the lead division advanced, the mass of wagons and artillery and manpower quickly clogged the roadway which was hemmed in on both sides by the jungle-like entanglement of the wilderness landscape. Nearing the intersection of the Orange Plank Road, the crescendo of full battle just ahead brought a sudden urgency for action.

It was nearly two o'clock as the division under General Birney was thrown forward to support another Union division that had been in the fighting for three solid hours and was nearly out of ammunition. As the brigades advanced into the conflict, their first order was to throw up breastworks of log and earth from which to advance on the enemy. The air rang with the riflery of engaged troops to the front, which ranged along the left of the road running north and south, and the ring of axes and shovels in the immediate vicinity. Amidst this frantic activity, Captain Marshalton took his company of medical and non-combatants to set up a field station behind the second line of earth works near the crossroads. They quickly found themselves overrun with wounded as men from General Getty's division, in combat since the morning, overburdened their own surgeons in search of help. The sounds of battle subsided for a while, replaced by the sounds of intense preparation for a combined assault of several divisions.

In the meantime, Duane found himself with all he could handle trying to do a competent job of assisting the wounded.

"Bandages!" someone called.

Reaching in the pack where bandaging materials had been placed, the boy grabbed a roll of cloth and held it toward the sound of the voice. It was taken from his hand.

"Alum!"

Duane withdrew the stiptic and passed it.

"Bandages!"

"Tourniquet!"

"Bandages!"

The chaotic press for materials drained the supply quickly. "Empty!" Duane called.

Joshua rushed forward a fresh pack as he moved back and forth with those transferring materials from the medical supply wagons.

Others assigned to the litter brigade rushed wounded from the front who were within reach of friendly lines. A mile behind the lines a clearing was found and a field hospital was set up as a gathering place for those who could be evacuated by ambulance. The captain had set up an operating table with planks straddling wooden horses, just off the side of the roadway near the entangling undergrowth of the woodland.

After two hours of preparation and maneuvering, the attack began. Federal forces advanced through the dense tangle of brambles and vines on either side of the Orange Plank Road. Several pieces of artillery had been placed on the road itself, but they were of little use in the thickets of the Wilderness. After covering about four hundred yards, the Union front was struck furiously by a withering fire from the waiting Rebel lines. Hell exploded with searing fury and the screams of pain, the shriek of the high- pitched Rebel Yell, the clattering and ear-splitting waves of riflery firing in line, the shouts of orders, the beating of drums, the frantic whinny of horses, and finally – the crackle of flames. A thick smoke from gunpowder and the burning woodland began to roll up through the wilderness to burn the eyes, nose, and throat; to seer the lungs.

The fury of the battle spread over a half-mile front, constantly widening as more troops were pushed into the conflict. The field medical operation worked at a feverish pace to keep up with the incoming wounded. Brigade first aid operations were scattered all along the backside of the fighting. But their numbers were insufficient to handle the flood of casualties.

The wounded came on their own if they could walk. Some were assisted by others less seriously hurt. Some were carried in blankets by their comrades or on litters by members of the litter brigade.

Duane held his own at first, working from memory out of the field packs of supplies. Then the pace became frantic and he froze in a panic.

"Dee! What's wrong!" Zachary called, seeing the boy sitting motionless.

"I cain't do it! I ain't no good!" the boy shouted back.

"Here, be useful," the musician responded. "Help me hold a tourniquet on this guy's leg."

Zachary dragged Duane to the side of a wounded soldier, then grabbed the boy's hands and placed one on the bloody remains of a shattered leg and the other on the stick in the bandage.

"Is he dead?" the boy asked.

"No," the horn-player answered. "But he's unconscious. He will be dead if you let go. I'm going to tie down the tourniquet while you keep it in place."

The conversation was shouted over the din of battle and the confusion of activity behind the lines.

The battle wore on into the evening before the action subsided. Throughout the action, the line remained stalled. No ground was gained or lost. The casualties continued to flood the temporary aid stations. The seriously wounded went to the surgeons' tables as fast as possible. Minor injuries received little or no attention due to lack of time. The dying were left to die. If someone had time, they might get some water or a last friendly word. When possible, the chaplain wandered among them and sought to give some solace or to write down their names for later identification.

Lamps were lit as darkness fell, and the aid stations continued their work through the night. The soldiers on the line slept under arms if they could, or sat up, waiting for the new day's fighting. Some crawled through the entangled thickets in search of water only to find themselves in the enemy's lines. Their search for water became a search for safe refuge.

As Duane continued his work, he became acutely aware of his limitations and struggled to adapt to whatever chores he could carry out successfully. But the situation kept demanding the impossible and he was forced to improvise and to stretch the fine tuning of his senses.

"Oh God, help me!" a voice begged.

"How?" the boy asked, crawling on hands and knees in the direction of the voice.

"My leg, it hurts like hell!" the man moaned between clenched teeth.

"I cain't see ta do nothin," Duane stated.

"Damn it, Boy! Get someone who can!"

"Ya kin see, Sir?" He dragged a medical pack around to a convenient location at his side.

"Don't play games, Boy!" The pain-filled voice was tight.

"Jest tell me what yer leg is like 'n I'll do as I kin." The boy's voice was steady and authoritative. To the wounded soldier there was a confidence, comforting enough to let the boy try.

Pushing himself up on his elbows, the man described a shattered knee, laid open to the side. Gingerly feeling his way with gentle fingertips, Duane folded the torn flesh, chips of kneecap bone, and shredded pants leg fabric back across the top of the knee. Then he wrapped it carefully to hold until the surgeon would get to it, and splinted the leg.

"I ain't got nothin much fer the pain but a sip a' brandy," the boy apologized.

"That'll do fine," the man stated. "You're okay, Boy. Thanks." The words came slowly with painful difficulty.

The man took a sip of the brandy. Duane moved on at another's request to help with others of the wounded.

Night wore on past midnight. Though the line of battle was generally quiet, preparations behind the breastworks went on as ammunition wagons were brought up, generals checked their lines, and the wounded were returned to duty or loaded into ambulances to be moved further to the rear. Finally, around two in the morning, Duane and the others found some time to collapse and rest.

Johnny found his friend lying among the wounded.

"You okay?" he asked.

"Yeh. Jest a heap wore out," Duane answered. "Eny news 'bout the fightin?"

Johnny settled on the ground beside his tired friend. "It seems part of Lee's army is in front of us about a mile down the road, and another part is facing V Corps and VI Corps up on another road. This wilderness makes it real hard to get any place. But General Hancock is preparing for a really early start in just a couple hours." He paused to study his friend, covered with dirt and blood from the long day's work. "You sure you're doing okay?" he asked again.

"I do hope so," the boy responded. "I ain't so sher as I's bein a' much use ta no one. 'Tain't much I kin do 'cept as some'ne is doin with me. I gotta make the wounded ta he'p if there ain't no one else 'bout, jest so's I kin git him fixed up fer ta hold him ov'r a spell fer the doc."

"I'll try to work with you for a while, Dee," Johnny offered.

"Sher would be a comfert," Duane accepted.

"Let's get some rest," the older youth suggested.

He stretched out on the ground between his friend and one of the wounded. Both were asleep in an instant.

*   *   *

The time for sleep was short. Predawn glow had just begun to redden the eastern horizon when gunfire erupted to the northwest. It was 5 AM as the battle was renewed. Within minutes, a clattering of musketry announced the advance of skirmishers as General Birney's division moved to the offensive. More than 20,000 Federal troops advanced against General Lee as the noise of conflict awoke Duane and Johnny. Suddenly the woods exploded with the roar of violence as the mile-wide wave of battle surged relentlessly forward.

During the next two hours the Federal line continued to push forward. At first, the two youths worked together as the ebb tide of wounded stumbled to the rear in search of help. Along the Brock Road from the north of the aid station, troops and artillery flowed southward into the battle. The immediate crossroads hung thick with the rolling dust of their passage and the noise of the moving masses and their vehicles, spurred on by the shouts and commands of their officers.

Word came that the battle line was nearly a mile to the front of the breastworks.

"Dee," Johnny shouted over the din of activity, "you stay here with Joshua and Micah. I have to go forward with the brigade!"

With that, Johnny was gone. Wagons of ammunition and medical supplies rumbled down the road. Duane heard all this feverish movement of battle and worried in the back of his mind that Johnny would be killed. He was sure something terrible would happen. Nevertheless, he continued to help dispense materials from supply packs and to follow the guidance of the two bandsmen as he assisted them in whatever way they needed.

The roaring tide of battle continued in the distance for most of the morning. For a time, numbers of Confederate wounded and prisoners were brought in as the Union line had collapsed the Rebel line and forced it back upon itself. Then, as the sun neared its high point at noon, there came a distinct crescendo in the fighting. The tide was turning and the Confederates were pushing the Federals hard toward their own breastworks. A great rush of activity spilled from the woods as retreating infantrymen dashed to the rear and a vast horde of wounded was brought in.

Shortly after noon, the retreat was complete as the Federal forces returned to their breastworks and Johnny rejoined his friend. The smell of burnt powder became strong in the air as it blended with the smell of blood. The ground about the aid station was littered with the mix of wounded, both Union and Confederate.

"The surgeons are having a real rough time of it," Johnny observed as he helped Duane distribute stiptics, bandages, and splints. "Just as fast as one poor fellow is cut and moved another is on the table. The blood is so deep, the ground at their feet is a red slime. The bloody pieces of bodies are stacked in piles knee high."

"Damn it ta Hell, Johnny, but this be one time I's glad I cain't see 'n I really ain't needin fer ya ta say as how bad it is. The pain an' screamin 'r bad 'nough. Ma nose an' ma ears is tellin a real heap a horrifyin sufferin. I reckon too, as I hears Reb voices in the wounded likewise."

Hundreds were occupied with the task of treating the wounded. The fighting continued along the first line of breastworks as the brigades of General Birney's division continued to withdraw to the line of defenses. The momentum slowed and the battle line settled in a stalemate just a few hundred yards from the field medical activity. By mid afternoon there was a welcomed lull in the fighting during which General Hancock directed a rearrangement of troops for greater strength and in preparation of a concerted charge to be mounted in the late afternoon.

As fast as they could, the non-combatants at the aid station loaded the wounded who could travel onto ambulances to be transported off to Fredericksburg.

"Hey, Dee," Johnny called. "What was your brigade at Gettysburg?"

"Thirteenth Alabama. Why?" He tied off a bandage knot, then stood to face the voice.

"There's a wounded Reb here from the 13th, a kid named Matthewson."

"Jamie!" Duane shouted. "Is he bad hurt?"

Johnny moved to guide the boy to the lanky youth who lay among the wounded. "Looks bad."

"Dee, is't really thet yer alive?" the faint voice called weakly.

"I is fer sher," he knelt beside the sixteen-year-old.

"Ya got back from the fightin thet day?"

"Yeh," pain cut him short.

Duane remained beside his Confederate comrade while Johnny left to continue his work.

The youth went on, "I come to near evenin an saw as they was takin in wounded. I made like I was dead an waited fer night ta git back ta the company. I sher did think as ya'd met yer maker when I last saw ya layin in yer blood." A fit of coughing overcame the wounded youth.

The younger teen sought his friend's face with his fingers and explored gently to see how bad he was hurt.

"Hey," Jamie whispered, "it tickles. What ya doin?"

"I cain't see, Jamie. Lost ma sight thet day when a powder charge blew in ma face." He felt the sweat and dirt of battle and the long curls of dusty hair, but no indication of a wound. Wait. There was a trickle of blood at the corner of his lips. "How bad hurt is ya?"

"There's one as burned ma arm. Another grazed a shoulder. Wu'st one's in ma gut – broke a rib an' got ma innards. Weren't so bad fi'st off. But the Yanks had already gone by an' the only way out an' not bein shot agin, was ta the Yank side. I started ta walk 'n only went a few yards an' had ta crawl. Some with a litter carried me out."

"What's this?" Duane asked, wiping blood from his friend's mouth. "Banged inta a tree branch durin the fightin. Kinda dumb, I s'pose." Duane slipped his hand to the bloodied shirt around Jamie's abdomen. Ripping it open, he gently explored the wound, first where the bullet entered; then, by sliding his hand around the older boy's side, the exit hole on his back.

"Oh God! Thet hurts!" Jamie gasped in sudden pain.

"I'm gonna put some bandagin ta hold ya tageth'r, Jamie," Duane explained as he searched his pack for more fabric.

"It ain't wo'th yer tryin, Dee. I know I ain't got much time left. Jest stay with me an' talk some." The wounded youth fought hard to control his voice and to keep the pain from taking over.

"Sher, Jamie," Duane agreed as he gently withdrew his hand from the pooling blood beneath his friend and laid the front of the shirt back across the broken body. "But I ain't wantin fer ya ta die." His voice cracked.

"I ain't a'fear'd none, Dee. I ain't wantin it neith'r, but I knows it's a certain." His voice quivered and a tear slipped free to course its way through the powder which blackened his face. "Jest stay with me a piece."

As the two continued to talk and Duane learned the fate of some he'd known, the hour slipped away. Suddenly, at four o'clock, the air was rent with gunfire as a fierce Rebel charge burst toward the first line of breastworks. The Union line exploded in destructive volleys of riflery and thunderclaps of artillery fire.

The two teenagers shook at the sudden explosion of activity. They were quickly enveloped in the smoke of battle as a breeze blew the sulphurous cloud in their direction.

"Kin ya see how fer the fightin is?" Duane asked.

"'Bout two hundred yards," Jamie answered.

As the battle erupted all along the Brock Road defenses, the woodland once more burst into flames. The wind blew them toward the Union defenses and soon Jamie reported to Duane that the Federal breastworks had caught fire.

"The Yanks is fallin back an' ar people 'r comin through the fire ta the wall!" Jamie described while the bullets whined overhead. "The two armies ain't twelve paces apart shootin each other through the flames," he continued.

Shouts of orders, the roar of cannons, the rattle of frantic wheels, the whinny of horses, the raking volleys of musket fire, screams of pain and panic, rose to a numbing intensity.

"Get down!" Johnny shouted as he rushed to Duane's position. "We're holding them!"

The leading edge of attacking Confederates mounted the breastworks, but the fighters were cut down as fast as they came. Finally, the men of General Birney's division were rapidly reinforced as new troops were brought into the conflict. The line held. Frantic activity behind the line kept everyone busy who was able to help as the new flood of casualties fell in the immediate front. Eventually, the fighting subsided as the sun sank low in the west and twilight dimmed the woodlands. A crackling red glow moved eerily through the wilderness. As the fighting ceased and the moans of the wounded rose on the air, fires raced about the underbrush. Moans turned to screams. Scattered gunfire popped about the wilderness as pockets in the clothes on the dead and wounded, filled with rifle cartridges, ignited, and the charges exploded.

The troops settled warily as the wagons raced about to re-supply ammunition and caissons were brought in with fresh munitions chests for the artillery. The work among the wounded was constant. Hundreds had gathered and lay about the area waiting to be attended. Once more, the nurses and non-combatants worked into the night.

Duane took a break around midnight and asked Joshua to guide him back to where Jamie lay.

"Sorry I bin so busy, Jamie," he spoke as he knelt. "Want some water?"

There was no response.

Duane reached out to be sure his friend was there. His hand touched a shoulder. But it was hard as rock. His fingers searched for the face.

"This ain't the right one, Joshua," Duane stated, as he felt the cold hard flesh and the soft curls of hair. "Damn this war!" he exclaimed quietly to himself. "Damn it all ta Hell!"

*   *   *

The fighting in the Wilderness had ended. The following day, Saturday, saw only sporadic activity. A fog hung over the battlefield, mixed with smoke and the stench of burned and decaying bodies. The dead were buried. Ambulance trains clogged the roads to Fredericksburg.

Joshua helped Duane to find a quiet glade alongside the Orange Plank Road where the fighting hadn't cut down the trees or burned the landscape, where a small brook bubbled along, where wild flowers danced in the spring breeze to splash the green grass with their color. There the two dug a clean three-foot-deep grave in the soft soil, taking care to save the sod from its top. Jamie's body, carefully folded in a blanket and wrapped in a tent half, was lovingly placed in the ground. The dirt was laid back in and the sod neatly placed on the top.

"Could ya make a small map ta tell where he lays, Joshua?" Duane asked, after the work was completed.

"Sure, Dee. You hold the shovels for me."

Joshua took a piece of paper and a pencil from his pocket and made a quick sketch of the glade. He paced the grave's location from the edge of the road and from a cluster of dogwood saplings. The measures were marked on the sketch and the date was added, May 7, 1864. He gave the paper to Duane who carefully folded it and slipped it into his pocket. He would put it with the one possession of Jamie's which he had kept, his cap box.

The two took their tools and returned to the crossroads.

That night, the army completed preparations to begin its move southeast toward Spotsylvania Court House.

*   *   *

Guiding his work with his left hand, Duane carefully dusted the sergeant's bleeding scalp with alum. It would help the blood to clot and allow the man to be sent on in an ambulance before further treatment was administered. All about the smoldering line, the troops had settled to sleep by the road. The day had been spent gathering the wounded and burying the dead. Blue or grey, it made no difference. All were equal in their need for attention. At one point in the smoking embers of the wilderness, five hundred from a single charge were buried in line where they had fallen. Yet, as night fell, hundreds of wounded remained in the field.

The boy finished administering to the sergeant as he wrapped a temporary bandage around the bloodied head. Others were at hand to direct the wounded man to a waiting ambulance.

"It's time to pack up," Johnny stated as he joined his companion.

"Ya got ar gear?" Duane asked.

"It's in a supply wagon with Dan's gear."

It was nearly 8:30. The last light of day was fading to night. As the two moved toward the wagon, others were clearing the area of all remaining wounded.

"Give way to the right," a voice called on the road.

Advancing from the north was a large column of troops, headed south on the Brock Road. A small group of men was passing to the front along the right side.

"It's General Grant," Johnny stated. "We're moving towards Richmond. He's not going to retreat." There was surprise in the youth's voice.

A great burst of cheering filled the air as the general was recognized and the soldiers along the line realized these past days of fighting had not been in vain. The army would not retreat.

Grant was obviously not pleased at the noise as he spurred his horse, Cincinnati, and rode swiftly by in stony silence.

"What corps is this?" someone asked.

"General Warren's V Corps," came the reply.

Orders were passed for General Hancock to hold his position until the rest of the army had passed behind his lines, then prepare to follow the march southward. The two boys leaned against the side of their wagon to watch and listen while the corps marched past. It was hours before the road was clear and II Corps was to form up and move out.

"Make ready," Johnny instructed.

The two climbed to the wagon seat and prepared to move with their brigade.

As the corps moved south toward Todd's Tavern, the distant night echoed with three high-pitched yells from ten thousand throats. Lee's army was also on the move.

*   *   *

Thick dust and slow-moving troops delayed the movement south. Periodically, the wagon would be forced to halt. Nearing Todd's Tavern, the entire column was stopped by two divisions of Union cavalry, asleep in the road. As Duane and Johnny sat waiting on the wagon's seat, they were overcome by sheer exhaustion and fell asleep where they sat. It was six in the morning before the leading corps was able to resume the march. Distant gunfire, barely audible on the morning air, signaled the beginning of new fighting.

It was nearly 9 AM when Hancock's corps managed to arrive at Todd's Tavern, having been the last to leave its line of defense in the Wilderness and the last in the line of march on the Brock Road. There, most of the corps waited while the distant conflict unfolded and some divisions were sent on separate missions. Birney's division finally moved early on the following morning when General Hancock sent it and two others to cross the Po River to the south and attack the flank of the Confederate left. At 6 AM three pontoon bridges over fifty feet long each were set in the water. The troops and artillery crossed over. It was evening before the division was in position to attack, and it was too late. Recalled during the night, the division withdrew the following day. On the way back, it was attacked by a division of the Confederate Army. The Confederates were repulsed with the Union suffering heavy casualties and the loss of one field piece which became jammed between two trees. Once more the woodland burst into flame and many of the wounded perished in fires. Duane remembered their screams, the smell of smoke, the crackle of the fire, the currents of hot air, the stench of burning flesh, as they rode the wagon in retreat.

The II Corps was returned to position on the Union right by late afternoon. At seven in the evening, General Birney's division was sent with part of the V Corps to attack the Confederate defenses. The attack faltered.

Three days had passed since the night march south along the Brock Road. The heat had been oppressive. The division had been continuously on the move. The medical resources had been strained to their limits as more than twenty thousand soldiers had been killed or wounded in the six days of fighting since crossing the Rapidan River at Ely's Ford the previous week.

*   *   *

Heavy rain mixed with hail pelted the boys about the head and shoulders as they worked to hitch the horses to the wagon. Protected by rubber ponchos and cap covers, the two finished hooking the harness chains. Movement was hampered by the darkness of night and the severity of the weather. The night was raw as the temperatures took a sudden drop during the evening hours.

The storm had come up during the afternoon of a relatively calm day. After the heavy fighting of the previous day, most of Wednesday had been spent planning and moving. Once again it was time to move as General Hancock prepared to take advantage of the stormy weather to move his corps around to the center of the Federal line in preparation for an assault on a salient of the Confederate center.

"You would think these generals had learned their lesson by now," Johnny muttered as he settled on the seat and unwrapped the reins from the brake lever.

"How da ya mean?" Duane asked, grabbing the seat while the wagon rattled into motion to join the others in line.

"They keep giving Lee time to set his line and Lee keeps doing just that – building defensive works and trenches. They're lined up right with artillery put right and our generals keep sending charges against them only to get everyone blown to Hell!" Johnny's voice bore a strain of emotional frustration and anger.

It was 10 PM as the corps moved around the back of the Union line. Johnny guided the wagon into its position of march and the rest became routine. The rain and hail poured down on the moving troops as others in place along the way huddled by drowning fires with rubber ponchos or gum blankets draped across their shoulders. Some wore their tent halves as capes. Others tried to pitch their tents and crawl under the folds of canvass which served only to puddle the run-off in the mud where their occupants sat. It was a pitiful sight as the tens of thousands endured the wretched weather.

"Sher do hope this storm ends come mornin," Duane wished.

"I don't think it will," his friend returned. "The air's turned downright cold and raw and it seems like it means to stay that way."

"I 'spose thet means tamorra's work'll be put off?" The rain rolled off the rubber folds across the boy's shoes and into puddles in the wagon bed.

"No chance," Johnny stated. "This General Grant means to fight no matter."

The two rode on in silence as the rainfall continued in torrents and the raw cold crept through their clothing. With the movement of troops and vehicles, the road turned to a thick mud and sucked at feet and wagon wheels. Progress was increasingly more miserable. Finally, in the early hours of Thursday morning, the corps was in position and all was in readiness.

General Hancock established his headquarters in a convenient farmhouse. The troops were placed in line of battle in the woods opposite a creek which ran in front of the house. The Rebel defenses lay less than a half mile to the front. As the rain continued to fall and a thick ground fog gathered, Captain Marshalton and his company prepared to set up field medical facilities as close to the front as they would be able to get. A full field hospital was already in operation a little over a mile west at the Alsop barn and house on the Brock Road.

Now there was the waiting. No one slept. Nerves were on edge. The work about to begin was expected to be very heavy. Dan had agreed with the boys. This practice of assaulting entrenched enemy positions was predestined to fail in the end leaving only the high cost in human lives.

The rain continued to fall. The fog and mist thickened so that it was impossible to see one's own feet. The appointed hour came and went as the thousands waited in massive formation, fifty ranks deep. The general determined that visibility was too limited. From where he sat on his horse, he could not see the bottom half of the men around him. All was lost in the swirling mists.

Duane and Johnny watched the silent mass, perched quietly on their wagon seat. Captain Marshalton waited on foot, standing beside the wagon with the non-combatants gathered in ranks nearby or on other wagons and ambulances. The divisions were poised – bayonets fixed, no caps on their rifles – waiting the signal to advance. Finally, at 4:30 AM, the brigades moved forward.

The enemy fortifications which lay ahead began with an abatis made up of limbs and branches woven into one another along a line of pointed pine and pin-oak pikes, in front of which was a ditch. Behind this line were the trenches, banked in front with earth over a wall of fence rails and logs creating a height of about four feet on the back side. Along the top was placed a head log, one that was raised above the rest just high enough to allow a musket to be inserted in the space between it and the rest of the wall.

General Birney's division advanced along with General Barlow's. The men moved swiftly and quietly. They emerged from the woods, crossed a stretch of open ground, and swarmed into the enemy works. Using their rifles as clubs, and fighting with pistols, swords, and bayonets, the Federal troops battled fiercely and were soon in possession of the trenches. Caught by surprise, the Confederates retreated or surrendered. Three thousand were taken prisoner.

"Damn that was fast," Johnny commented from a vantage point near the edge of the trees, as the enemy prisoners were passing to the rear.

"Ain't a whole lot a shootin," Duane observed as he stood beside the older youth with a supply pack in hand.

The captain approached – a ghostly apparition in the misty torrents. "Were we wrong," he asked, "when we concluded this was a lost cause?"

"I figure they'll get us back," Zachary suggested standing with his arms around a folded litter.

The distant conflict was little more than far-off shooting and indistinct shadows in a swirling fog cut by the slanted torrents of rain. It was soon lost as the attacking troops continued to advance beyond the first earthworks to the inner line of defense. Suddenly an intense thunder of riflery exploded on the air. It spread and grew louder. Word came back that a Rebel countercharge was driving the two divisions back to the outer trenches. The divisions of the VI Corps which were waiting in reserve were ordered forward.

The action was an hour old as the walking wounded began swarming to the rear. Duane went to work at the captain's side as he passed the materials for the surgeon to do his work. The table had been prepared under a canvass canopy and was quickly occupied by a large corporal in his thirties who had taken a bullet in the face. It had shattered his jaw and passed through his shoulder. Marshalton began his task to salvage what he could while Duane passed materials as requested.

"I need a sewing needle and thread." The man spoke loudly to be heard above the pounding rain bouncing on the canvass overhead.

Duane fished them out of the surgical case.

"I have 'em," he announced.

Within minutes the sergeant was gone and a young lieutenant was in his place. The man was pale from loss of blood, and shaking with fear. His left arm had been shattered by a mini-ball and the splintered bone protruded just above his wrist.

"Amputation," Dan announced as he directed the litter bearers to stand by.

Duane ran his fingers along the edge of the table of implements until he found the familiar shapes of the amputation knife and saw and a tourniquet. Another put a cloth over the wounded man's mouth and nose and soaked it with chloroform. Captain Marshalton took the tourniquet which the boy held up and quickly tied it above the wound to cut off all bleeding. Next he took the knife, slipped it through the flesh and against the bone beneath the muscle tissue. With a flick of the wrist he deftly cut through from the bone outward, laying the open tissue clear of the bone. Trading tools, he applied the saw and, in a few quick strokes, completed the separation. The artery was tied shut by knotting a string around it and the tissue of the stump was pulled over with needle and thread. All was finished in less than three minutes and the patient was returned to the litter bearers.

While work progressed at the table, the wounded lined the area. The advancing VI Corps had to push its way around the returning tide to clear the wooded area and move toward the front. It was nearing 6 AM as the second assault made its way forward to a marsh of long grasses where the men fell to the ground to await further orders. After being swept by a murderous enemy fire, they rose up with a loud cheering and moved on.

The noise of the conflict swept across the stormy terrain and hung in the ears of those at the aid stations. Chaos reigned as the wounded returned, reinforcements went forward, and artillery and ammunition advanced to support the attack.

Tens of thousands of Confederate and Union troops fought over an area the front of which would hold a single brigade. As the mass of troops fired volley after volley into one another, the men in the fronts fell by the score. The combatants fought in ankle-deep mud, their faces layered and crusted with powder from biting open the paper charges to load their guns. Barrels became so hot that ram rods were fired as powder ignited spontaneously. The bodies fell so thick in the trenches that the dead and wounded had to be pulled out to make way for the fight to continue. The bottoms of the trenches ran red with blood. The mud on the slopes shed sheets of red water. The intensity of the gunfire shredded the head logs as a partial battery of artillery was brought up by the Union attackers. Double loads of cannister mowed down the front of the Rebel line and tore through the oak trees behind them. The cannons continued their work until every horse was slaughtered and every artilleryman cut down.

Throughout the day, the battle roared and the slaughter continued. Ammunition cases were carried forward by pack mule where they were dropped along the line. The company officers broke them open and distributed the rounds to their men. Those who survived to carry the fight fired over four hundred rounds apiece. So intense was the shower of lead that the carcasses of the dead animals and the bodies of dead soldiers were stripped of their flesh and their bones were shattered by the fury. Sometime during the middle of the afternoon, the oak trees fell with a thunderous crash, cut down by the torrent of gunfire.

As evening approached, more troops from II Corps moved up to relieve those who had been fighting throughout the day, allowing them time to reorganize and to take time to eat something. Darkness came; the storm and the fighting wore on. Captain Marshalton was exhausted and bloodied from hours of surgery. Stripped to the waste, he had had time only between patients to wipe his implements on his apron, then begin again. Duane had stayed at his side and survived the ordeal only with the assistance of Johnny and others who had kept the supplies coming and had stepped in when blindness interfered. The ground was covered with bits and pieces of amputated body parts. At times it had been necessary to shovel them aside to make room to continue working. The air stank of blood and gore. It stank of burnt powder and vomit and death. The moans and screams of the wounded rose on the torrents of rain and the constant thunder of the battle just ahead. An eerie glow lit the landscape from the lanterns hung about the surgical areas and from the flashes of gunfire, like lightning on the horizon. A constant motion ebbed about the landscape as wounded came in, relieved troops returned, supplies went forward, and ambulances were loaded and sent off into the night.

Finally, near midnight, General Lee began to pull his troops back to a newly built line of defense. A quiet began to settle. Still, one segment of the line remained in conflict for another two hours. Then it, too, ceased. The dominating sound of uniform constancy was the rain. It continued to slash through the trees and drench the mass of humanity. The work of the surgeons slowed. Men could take so much horror before they became numbed and eventually collapsed from the strain. Some stopped to rest while others tried to continue the work.

A new sound wore on the night. Somewhere in the Confederate line, a band played THE DEAD MARCH.

"Come on!" Zachary called. "Our band is forming up."

As the strains of the march faded into the rainfall, the immediate air reverberated with NEARER MY GOD TO THEE. The two bands continued to alternate with THE BONNIE BLUE FLAG followed by THE STAR-SPANGLED BANNER followed by DIXIELAND. Finally, the Federal band closed with HOME SWEET HOME.

Duane lost track of his work as the music played on his mind. He hadn't cried in months other than to mourn Jamie's death, his emotions somewhat numbed by the carnage. But as he listened and remembered people of long ago, a tear slipped free and tracked through the dirt on his face.

The last strains of music faded into the constant splash of the rainfall.

Duane staggered from the surgeon's table as he was relieved, in search of a place to drop.

"Come with me," someone offered.

The boy took a friendly hand which led him to a nearby wagon.

"Thank ya," Duane said as his guide disappeared.

Running his hands down the rim of a wheel for reference, the boy eased himself to the ground. He tripped over the edge of his poncho as he walked on it with his knees, crawling beneath the wagon bed, then collapsed in the sheltered mud. Struggling for a moment to find a comfortable position in which his rain gear didn't pull at him, Duane eased himself across the rubber garment, then lay his head on his arm to slip into the peace of sleep.

A quiet settled across the countryside. Fields and woodlands were lit by dim circles of light which glowed softly in the continuing rainfall. There, the medical teams worked their miracles or lost their individual struggles to the ravages of warfare. The moans of the wounded were drowned by the constant rush of rain. An occasional scream of pain pierced the night as a surgeon's patient cried out. The exhausted soldiers slept where their work for the day had ended. All around lay the dead, their grotesque forms frozen by death's stiffness. Along the line of battle, their hands had been cupped by the living to form a holder for cartridges in death. In the trenches they lay in heaps, as many as eight or ten in a pile. In the sleep of death or exhaustion, the human forms which carpeted the battlefield were bathed by the constant rain as they rested peacefully in the quiet of the night.

*   *   *

Four more days passed before the rain ended. Except for General Birney's division, much of the time was spent in move and countermove as troops and equipment trudged through knee-deep mud. For the time, however, there was no major engagement. The mud and weather made it impossible.

Monday afternoon saw sunny weather and rapid drying of mud and rain puddles. General Birney's brigade had remained out of action since the assault on the Bloody Angle of Thursday last. The troops had set a temporary camp and generally found time to rest. Duane sat by his fire, carefully feeding the fuel by sensing the fire's position from the sound of its crackling flames and the feel of its heat. Twenty-five-year-old Corporal Siddle was breaking up firewood at his side. Johnny and others were out collecting more. Light footsteps approached.

"Hi, Dee," the young voice greeted. "Can I cook supper on your fire?"

"Jonah!" Duane exclaimed. "How is it yer here?" He lost track of the fire. "Ouch!" The youth quickly drew back his hand and dropped the stick of wood.

"I'll get it," Thomas volunteered.

"Thank ya," Duane acknowledged. He stood and addressed the sutler's boy. "Ya was sent out two weeks back. Why fer ya here now?"

The boy stood awkwardly, a guilt-ridden half smile tugging at his mouth. "You see," he began, "I started to leave when some officer came by and thought I was lost from the II Corps because my cap has a II Corps clover pin on it, and he asked if I was lost and I said yes, and he showed me where to go, and I ended up in the army's supply train. Some one complained I was too young, but they kept me on anyway." The youngster shifted his stance nervously. "Can I sit with you?"

"Sher," Duane stated. "But I ain't got no extra rations."

"I got food. See?" He dug into the pockets of the coat he wore and brought out candy and canned meats. "I'll even trade you some."

"I ain't got but biscuits and salt bacon, and some coffee beans ta brew."

"Okay." Jonah approached his friend and reached out for a hand. "Here." He pressed a tin of meat into the ash-dusted palm.

"Thanks," Duane took the offering. "Walk me ta ma tent ta git ma thin's. Johnny an' the others'll be back in a few minutes."

"Don't get lost," Thomas called as the two went off to get Duane's haversack.

All about the field and wooded area, the company camps of the division were active with preparations for supper. Coffee beans were being ground between rifle butt and rock, firewood was being gathered, salt bacon was being sliced, and fires were being fed. Johnny, Joshua, and Zachary returned with their arms full of firewood.

Dumping his load on the ground, Zachary stated, "That should hold us through breakfast."

"How will it do for an extra plate to cook?" Thomas asked, a mischievous smile pulling the corners of his mouth. "You won't believe who showed up."

"Hi!" Jonah greeted, returning from the tent with Duane at his elbow.

"What in Sam Hill are you doing here!" Joshua exclaimed.

"You'd been sent out," Johnny added.

"What about your pa?" Zachary asked.

"An officer made a mistake an he he'ped 'im," Duane answered. "See thet clover pin on his hat?" The others acknowledged. "Some'n come ta figger Jonah fer a wagon'r a' the II Corps 'n he went 'long with it."

"But what about your pa?" Johnny asked once more.

The blind boy paused when a whiff of smoke blew into his face and he suddenly remembered the fire. His young friend guided him to a place to sit, and the two settled beside the fire.

A sadness crept into Jonah's eyes as he sat and stared through the flames. "When I went to see him at the hospital, he didn't know me. The doctor said he was hit on the head and it addled his brains. I ain't got a pa no more."

The other four joined them as Jonah swung his haversack into his lap to draw out his eating utensils.

The youngster proceeded to tell his story while the mess group started on the food. Joshua ground the coffee and set the prepared pot on the coals to brew. Johnny sliced the slab of bacon and passed the pieces to Zachary and Thomas to start cooking on their plates. Duane opened the cracker box and started to pass out the biscuits. Jonah shared a bag of hard candies while he told of weeks with the supply train, the days it took to catch up with the army, and his search for the 20th Indiana.

As the food cooked and the meal was consumed, the boys told each other of the events they'd experienced in the campaign so far. After all had eaten and the utensils had been cleaned and returned to their haversacks, Captain Marshalton brought his camp chair and joined the gathering at the fire.

"There better be a good explanation, Jonah," the surgeon admonished when he saw the boy with the group.

"There is," Johnny stated as he went on to explain briefly.

"I'm gonna be a drummer boy," Jonah announced enthusiastically, when Johnny had finished.

"I'll teach you," Joshua volunteered. "But only if you stay with the band. I'll not see you going off to get killed."

"I won't get hurt," the boy said in all confidence.

"You're both missing the point, here," Dan intervened. "Jonah already has his job. He's a teamster for the supply train and has a wagon and team to care for. There won't be any heroics."

"This ain't no game," Duane added. "Men really do die out there on the battlefield. Boys die, too."

"Then why were you able to be a drummer boy when you weren't much older than me!" Jonah cried.

For a moment no one spoke. Duane fumbled for a stick of wood and cautiously added it to the fire. Johnny took a moment to inspect his haversack. The captain poured a cup of coffee. Joshua lay back in the grass to await Duane's response. Thomas and Zachary joined the captain in another cup of coffee. Finally Duane tucked his knees under his chin with his arms wrapped around his ankles, and sat remembering the events of two years back.

"Jonah," he began, "I ain't come inta this war fer ta be killin no one. It weren't even real ta me. I jest knew as it was where my pa was 'n if I could be drummer fer a company, I could git ta the war an' find him. I ain't so sher as eny a' us really knew nothin real 'bout war 'til we was in battle at Shiloh. I remembe' the fi'st time I walked in ta thet Union camp an' the docs was cuttin an' the dead was layin in the sun. I was real sick inside an' the captain said as I weren't allowed ta feel bad as I had a job ta do. My beatin a' the drum was real important ta if the men would live. Then we was in the real battle fer the fi'st time. It were a sight ta shake ya good inside, but ya git so worked up an' busy in all thet's doin thet ya stop thinkin.

"I saw a lot a men hurt 'n dyin. But it didn't really git ta me 'til I saw General Johnston git kilt. 'Til he was hit, it weren't real. Next day I was wounded pretty hard an' finally Johnny an' Dan here found me an' got me fixed up good."

The boy paused as his mind raced through the years. "I saw my ma kilt by raiders an' was nigh ta kilt maself, but it didn't seem the same then. I knows better now." Again his mind wandered. "I r'member the fi'st time I shot another soldier, an' he were a Reb. I ain't even thought a'fer it. I jest did it cause he were gonna shoot me."

The small group around the fire watched the youth in wrapped attention as he searched his soul and tried to impress on Jonah the reality of war. Duane released his grip to fold his feet Indian-fashion and to rest his hands in his lap.

"War does thin's ta ya." He faced the direction where he sensed the boy to be seated. "Ya ain't yer real self. It makes ya kill when ya really ain't wantin naturely ta do it. It's a horror ya cain't b'lieve really happens. When we fought at Stone River in the winter an the dead was all 'round in piles, froze in ther own blood 'n gore, my innards up an' I was sick all ov'r the place. This here fightin a' last week was so fierce as men was shootin each other with pistols stuck up so as ta touch each other, an the shootin tore the flesh from the dead an' cut down trees.

"Jonah, war is a 'xcuse fer people ta stop feelin an go fer glory by killin other people. An ya know what they does when they're kilt? They sends messages ta tell ther family as they died facin the enemy 'r they died a glorious death. How kin men be so lost a' ther senses?"

"But ain't this war to make people free?" Jonah asked. "Ain't we fighting to end slavery?"

"I really ain't thinkin so, Jonah," Duane answered. "I think it's more fer power n' glory. These generals ain't all got slaves an' some as don't believe in it. Some are wantin ta become governors an' sech. The leaders in the Confederacy want ther own power separ't from the leaders in Washington."

"But it's all so exciting," Jonah pursued.

"Da ya wanna kill me?" Duane asked adjusting toward the sound of his friend's voice.

"No. You're my friend," the boy answered.

"But I'm from Arkansas an one a' the enemy."

"No! You're my friend!"

"In a war, people ain't real no more. But yer right, Jonah. Yer ma friend, too. I's seen friends die. Jonah, war ain't no playin! It's a Hell on earth! People, real people, are kilt! I ain't wantin it ta be yer kilt too!"

"Jonah," Captain Marshalton spoke softly, "there are many in this war that are here to save lives. I'm a doctor. I want to be a good doctor. If I hadn't offered to transfer when my sister state was seeking medical people, I'd not be here with Dee today, and there's a whole lot of new information I wouldn't have learned. But I want to learn, and have learned a lot from trying to help the wounded. These men are musicians. They offer their talents to try to take men's minds off the war. Dee's right. The fighting makes men do terrible things and things not natural to them. Some do extraordinarily brave things. Some are exceedingly kind. Give up your search for adventure on the battlefield. Find adventure in helping save lives or just enjoying being alive."

"How about some music," Zachary offered. "The band is planning to play for the regiment this evening and the others are beginning to gather."

"Yeah," Jonah jumped to his feet and stretched cramped muscles. "That sounds real good."

"Give me a hand, Jonah. Ma feet is lost ther feelins." Duane reached his hand out as he stretched his ankles and wiggled his toes in his shoes.

Johnny joined the boy and the two pulled their friend to his feet. Pausing a moment to gain his balance, then retrieve his haversack, Duane started slowly to the tent to put his gear away. The others did the same. The fire was down to hot coals as other members of the band were emerging from their tents to gather with their comrades.

Jonah took Duane's hand to serve as his guide and they started on their way.

"You going to play with us, Johnny?" Joshua asked.

"Okay!" the youth answered. "Can I use your drum, Dee?" he asked.

"Sher by me," Duane replied.

"Be right back." Johnny dashed to the tent to get the instrument.

As soon as he returned, the three continued on to join the stream of men headed toward an open field for an evening of musical entertainment.

*   *   *

Two days later an attack was ordered on the center of the Confederate line in the belief that the movements of the previous days had left it weakened. As the division advanced, an early morning slaughter commenced from a well-fortified Confederate position and the action was called off. The following day, General Lee's army committed the same error and was repulsed. That action lasted most of the day.

The days that followed saw the II Corps moving south in the hope of drawing out the Confederate Army. But it didn't work. General Lee relocated on a whole new front, some twenty-four miles to the southeast, using the North Anna River for his line.

Jonah had returned to the supply train the morning following the band's concert. The week of activity that followed had kept him busy and out of touch with Duane's brigade. The beginning of the fourth week of May found General Birney's division engaged amidst a pelting rain, as the Federal assault attempted to drive across a bridge on the North Anna River. Following three days of action in heavy rain storms, the conflict paused for a day. At week's end the armies moved again.

As May neared its end, there was fighting further south when the armies met just north of Richmond on the Totopotomoy Creek. The Generals sidestepped from there to a tavern crossroads called Cold Harbor, and clashed once more on the final afternoon of the month.

June 1st found Hancock's Corps on the move once more. The day was oppressively hot with temperatures nearing 100 degrees. Duane and Johnny rode the wagon seat in the column of march with dust rolling all about them. Their clothes were soaked through as the sweat poured from their bodies. Its moisture attracting the dust from the air, the two were thickly covered in a sweat-splotched layer of brown.

"How much longer ya reckon this fight'll go?" the younger boy called above the grinding rattle of the wagon's wheels along the country lane.

"It seems like forever," Johnny called back. "I have never seen such continuous action."

"It sher does seem as it ain't neve' gonna end," Duane complained.

"We're coming to a creek," Johnny warned. "Hang on while I run the team through."

Duane grabbed his seat tightly while his companion hollered and whipped the horses to keep them from stopping to drink the water.

"They's dyin in this heat!" Duane shouted.

"I know," Johnny agreed, "but we're ordered to keep on the move."

The column continued on across the countryside, cutting in a southeasterly direction toward the fighting which had already begun at Cold Harbor. The last to arrive, the corps finally stopped some four miles to the north of the crossroads, at the far end of the Union line. The men were quickly put to work digging fortifications. Near the end of the day, new orders came: March around the rear of the Union position to the opposite end of the line under cover of night, and be ready to attack at dawn.

Again the division moved. The oppressive heat, the dark of night, the thick dust, and a wrong turn, resulted in a slow journey which ended with exhausted troops arriving in position at about 6:30 in the morning. The attack was postponed for twenty-four hours.

Johnny pulled his wagon into position behind the brigade's segment of the defenses currently under construction. The two boys climbed into the back of the wagon bed and went to work lining up materials at the tailgate.

"They did it again," Johnny stated while he worked at the back stacking the packs and other materials as Duane felt for and passed each item.

"What's thet?" the other asked as he extended a requested item toward the voice.

"Gave Lee time to build fortifications. We won't be able to get through."

Footsteps were heard from outside as Captain Marshalton approached through the activity of the troops.

"Dee," he called, "I've a letter from your pa's company."

"Where?" the boy called excitedly, tripping over the equipment in his haste to get out of the wagon.

"The chaplain gave it to me just now. He said he's had it several days, but forgot it in all the confusion." He took the boy's hand and helped him over the tailgate and onto his feet.

"Hurry up an' read it, Dan!" The boy stood leaning against the back of the wagon.

Johnny settled on a box of medicines near the back of the wagon bed to listen to the reading of the letter. The doctor tore the end of the envelope and drew out the letter from within.

"Dear Captain," he read. "We were most excited to receive your letter and learn that Captain Kinkade's son is still alive. The captain, however, is not here. He was badly wounded in this last fighting and sent to hospital to recover. From there he is expected to be sent home. The captain believes his son is dead and I have forwarded your letter to him. Sorry I cannot give much in particulars, but I don't know where this letter may go or who may read it. I suggest, if possible, that Duane be sent home and seek his father there. Good luck, James E. Murray, Colonel, 13th Arkansas."

There was a moment of stunned silence.

"Are there any markings on the cover?" Johnny asked.

The man carefully examined the paper. "Nothing," he reported. "Only my name and unit."

"Pa's alive," Duane whispered joyously. "He's goin home!"

"When do we leave, Dan?" Johnny wondered.

"This is not the time to ask," the captain stated. "The summer campaign is just beginning. Let me see if I can think of a way to work it out. Here, Dee, put this letter in your haversack." He pushed the paper into the boy's pocket. "I'm fixing to set a pot of coffee and have a biscuit. Want to join me?"

"Yes, Sir," the boys chorused.

The three walked along the construction sites where the troops were busy digging trenches and cutting trees for their earthworks. In an open space behind an angle in the breastworks, the captain had established a temporary operating area with trestle table covered by a canvas fly. Supplies had already been placed at hand and a fire lit for coffee.

As the day wore on, the clouds thickened and the sky darkened. In the distance, there was the sound of skirmishing mixed with thunder and flashes of lightning. By late afternoon, the storm broke with heavy rain. That turned to hail and settled to a drizzle which lasted into the night.

The boys took refuge in the wagon as the soldiers along the five-mile line broke out tent halves, ponchos, or rubber gum blankets. Huddling in whatever shelter they could manage, the men passed the day reading and rereading old letters, sitting in pensive silence, or talking quietly among themselves. As night came on, some took off their coats and got out sewing kits. Each wrote his name and homeplace on a piece of paper and pinned it to his coat so that when the fight was over and his body found, his family could be told where he had died.

Night fell, but there was little sleep. Duane sat in the wagon with his friend and listened to the soft drizzle on the canvass and the quiet moaning of nearby conversations. After a while, the sounds lulled him to a drowsiness. The boy slumped against the wooden wagon bed and into dreams of reunion with his father.

*   *   *

The Confederate line extended over seven miles from the Totopotomoy Creek on the north to the Chickahominy River on the south. It consisted of a lacework of carefully constructed trenches skillfully blended into the terrain's low ridges. There was a maze of works within works, designed with a zig-zag pattern that allowed lines of fire from the side and from head on to sweep opposing lines in simultaneous action with infantry and artillery. None of this was obvious from the Union front. It had been hidden in the contours of the landscape in a countryside of field and forest and swampland. Duane and Johnny were awakened shortly after midnight by activity along the line. Crawling from the wagon, they found the rainfall had dwindled to a thick mist and the men were busy packing their blankets and rain gear.

"Jonah's here," Johnny announced.

"What's he up ta?" Duane asked.

"He's helping to issue rations," the older youth explained.

"What da we do?" Duane wondered.

"I'm taking you to work with Dan. I'll work along the back of the line with the fellas from the band."

Johnny took his blind friend by the arm and the two worked their way along the back of the regiment. Activity was subdued as the soldiers packed their haversacks with hardtack, coffee, and sugar to last them two days, lifted their gear to their backs, and checked their weapons. A morning chill cut through the damp clothing and the swamp odors hung in the air.

"Want a cup of coffee?" the captain offered as the two arrived at his fire.

"Sher." Duane searched for his cup.

"Sounds good." Johnny untied his from its thong and held it to the spout.

"Where do you want this water, Captain?" a soldier asked, arriving with two slopping buckets.

"Put it by the tent pole," the officer directed.

The activity continued as officers talked to their companies and formed them into line of battle.

"I've got to go," Johnny said. "See you two later."

"What does it look like out there, Dan?" Duane asked as his friend departed.

"Looks quite empty, Dee," the man answered. "There's a long line of low flat hills in the distance and an empty plain between here and there."

"But ain't the other army out there?"

"Can't see them through this mist."

The misting rain ended. It was nearly time for predawn light to cut the night sky on the eastern horizon. General Birney's brigades were restless as they waited for the signal to go. All along the two-mile line occupied by Hancock's corps and two more to its right, some 50,000 infantrymen waited, poised for battle. A thin fog swirled across the fields and swamps.

"What time is it?" Duane asked.

The captain pulled his watch from its pocket. "Nearly 4:30," he replied.

Suddenly the air echoed with the lonely notes of bugles sounding the advance. The soldiers climbed from their defenses and were arranged into lines of battle, two dozen deep in places. The attack began. As two divisions of the corps stepped off, General Birney's paused to follow in support.

Duane stood by the captain, the man's hand on his shoulder, as the two listened to and watched the initial movement. Suddenly the air exploded with a concussion of sound more violent than anything the boy had experienced in all the war. Artillery thundered with volcano-like tremors far greater than the cannonade at Gettysburg. Riflery roared in scathing sheets of flame, shattering the air with a crashing fury that crushed upon the ears.

The wall of led and fire slammed into the Union front, reeling the line on impact as it spun the bodies, dead before they fell, into those of their comrades, who in turn were struck down, so that it appeared like dominoes falling, one against the other, so rapid was the slaughter. As they leaned into the fury of the hailstorm of lead, the advancing mass was so dense that there was no way for those in front to retreat, and for many behind to even fire their weapons.

The Confederate line appeared as a long cloud of smoke with flashes of artillery and musketry writhing and dancing like lightning in a storm. The roar of gunfire crescendoed across the line as the men in blue fell like cordwood, piling up all along the battle front.

Some advanced to the very edge of the Confederate works, only to be cut down by such heavy gunfire as to shred their bodies beyond recognition. The fire became so intense that every discharge of shot and shell blew apart a score of advancing soldiers sending gear and guns, and broken pieces of arms and legs and bodies exploding into the air. Within fifteen minutes, three thousand in the corps had fallen and the rest of the leading brigades were burrowing into the ground wherever they were, digging in frantically with bayonets, plates, cups, spoons, and their bare hands. At the end of an hour, the entire Union assault line was dug in.

The thunderous wave of vibration began to recede as the firepower slowed and the fiery glow along the western landscape gave way to the light of dawn in the east. An intense ringing filled the boy's ears and a creeping numbness crawled across his skin as the violent shaking of earth and air began to still.

"Is it ove'?" he asked, his own voice humming in his head.

"I'm not sure, Dee," the captain's voice was fuzzy. "It seems to be quieting, but the troops aren't returning. Even the wounded are only trickling in, a few at a time."

For the moment, the surgeon was idle. Activity in the area was slow. "Over there!" someone directed.

Two battle-weary infantrymen assisted a wounded comrade toward the table.

"Where to, Doc?" one asked.

"Lay him here," the captain instructed.

The bloodied veteran was placed atop the table. "How bad?" Duane asked.

"Just a minute," Dan responded as he examined the bloodied shreds of clothing and the body within.

The man was conscious, but in shock. His wide eyes peered in white contrast to the blackened face, covered with powder, smoke, and mud. Blood soaked the fabric of one trouser leg and ran from a half dozen other holes in the clothing. The two who had brought him waited momentarily for word on his condition.

"This foot is shattered and will have to come off," the doctor announced. "I won't know for a while just how serious his other wounds are. But most appear to be treatable."

"Thank you, Sir," a private said. "Take good care of him for us." They left.

"Chloroform," Dan ordered. "I'll also need the amputation knife and saw, and two of you to steady his leg."

It was over in less than three minutes. The severed foot was tossed aside. Two men then placed the wounded man on a litter and set him aside to await an ambulance while the captain rinsed his surgical saw in a bucket of murky red water.

Throughout the morning orders were received from the commanding general for General Hancock and the other corps commanders to press the attack. The men in the field responded by pouring rapid volleys of riflery toward the enemy trenches, but none rose up to advance. There were periodic barrages of enemy artillery and riflery. The divisions in forward positions were pinned down and could neither attack nor retreat in safety. The wounded could not be reached. Enemy fire struck down any who tried. The dead could not be buried. No one was willing to call a truce to permit it.

As the sun made its journey to its zenith, the severity of the damage was gradually realized. By noon the horrifying truth was known. Nearly 7,000 Union soldiers had become casualties, most during the first fifteen minutes of devastating horror. Work at the aid stations became steady as wounded who could, crawled toward the Union works and others were brought in by some who dared to go after the fallen who seemed within their reach.

The small figure of the boy danced its way toward the operating table as Jonah weaved among the wounded who carpeted the ground and dodged the nurses and litter bearers moving among them.

"Captain Marshalton!" he cried. "Hurry! Johnny's hurt!"

"What?" the man called over the noise of commotion in the area, startled in his work by the calling of his name.

The boy worked his way to the doctor's side, ignoring the hands, wrist-deep in blood, trying to probe a man's abdomen for a bullet.

"Johnny's shot! He's needing help!" the boy cried.

"How bad?" the man asked without stopping.

"I don't know. He's trapped on the battlefield." Glistening dark eyes pleaded for help.

"I can't go!" Dan shouted in frustration and anger. "Take Dee!" His hand trembled with sudden emotion. "Oh, God!" he whispered, "bring him in safe." Turning to the boys he shouted, "Take bandages and a tourniquet!"

Jonah grabbed Duane by the shirt sleeve and began to drag him off. "Here!" one of the nurses called and passed a pack, quickly stuffed with bandages, some stiptics, and splints.

"I cain't go fast," Duane called as he tripped over an unseen litter and fell to his knees.

"I'm sorry," Jonah cried. "I'll be more careful."

The youngster pulled his teenaged companion along the back of the Union defenses to a point where the brigade had been. Joshua met them as they arrived.

"Dee!" he exclaimed, "Zachary went out with Sammy Ellison. They're trying to crawl far enough to grab a hold of Johnny and drag him in."

"What happened?" Duane asked, worry edging his voice.

"Johnny was working with several who were helping the wounded get back to safety. They were hit by a volley of fire from the right. We know Tim Adams is dead. But others are still alive."

"They're coming in!" someone exclaimed.

A half dozen rescuers crawled back behind the defenses with four wounded in tow. They were quickly surrounded by a dozen friends who sought to render assistance.

Zachary assisted Johnny to a spot of shade under a tulip tree. Jonah dragged Duane along and the two helped settle their friend on the ground.

"Ya okay?" Duane asked as he knelt by Johnny's head.

"No," came the exhausted reply accompanied by a fit of coughing.

"You don't look bad," Jonah countered.

There was no response as the wounded youth breathed heavily, fighting for air.

"Zachary! What kin ya see?" Duane asked in a panic.

"Move aside, Jonah, and let me have a look," the man instructed.

The boy scampered backwards on his hands and feet, dragging himself to Duane's side.

"Here," Duane handed him the pack. "Hand us what we need."

The younger teen waited anxiously while the bandsman opened his friend's shirt and sought to learn his condition.

"He's shot in the lower chest," Zachary stated. "Give me your hand."

He took Duane's hand and placed it on the wound. The boy's fingers sensed the ribs and the sticky blood below the right lung. His ears picked up a soft bubbling sound as blood seeped inconsistently from the wound. The body quivered from pain and shock. Across the chest, the heart pounded frantically and Duane could feel its vibrations.

"Is he hurt enywhere else?" the youth asked.

"Grazed to the head and a hole in the flesh of his thigh," Zachary described.

"Dee," Johnny whispered. "It hurts like Hell."

"We'll git ya fixed up proper," Duane assured. "Hang in ther."

The blind teen closed his eyes in a moment of prayer and an attempt to decide what to do.

"Git a blanket," he ordered. Then to Zachary he asked, "Is the bullet still in?"

"I think not in the leg. But the one in his chest is still there."

Duane slipped his hand under his friend's back to confirm there was no exit hole. Jonah returned with the blanket.

"Thank ya, Jonah," Duane acknowledged as he used the blanket to pillow his friend's head. "He'p me ta do the bandagin, Zachary?"

"Sure," the man said.

Jonah held the pack convenient for materials while Duane gave instructions and the bandsman helped with the work. Thomas stopped by and was sent to find a litter. A stiptic was used to control the bleeding from the head wound. The leg was wrapped. After debating whether or not to probe for the bullet, it was decided to wait and the chest wound was covered. Johnny said little. His eyes pleaded for relief and he attempted at one point to help hold a bandage with his left hand. Weakness grew on the older youth and he seemed to fade in and out of sleep. Pain was obvious, but he withheld his cries and clenched his teeth on occasion.

All along the battle line, fighting continued to flare in pockets of exchanging gunfire. Supply wagons and ambulances were in continual motion. Generals, too, passed along the line to determine troop positions and levels of success.

A litter was brought and Johnny was carefully lifted onto it. The bandsmen left to carry out what assistance they could for others. Duane and Jonah remained with their wounded friend, offering him sips of water when he asked. The afternoon wore on. Jonah built a fire, found a coffee pot, and helped Duane prepare a pot of coffee. He sweetened it with some sugar from his haversack and offered sips to the wounded youth. Johnny smiled weakly in appreciation. The two young sentinels munched on hardtack to settle the grumblings in their own stomachs and shared a tin of meat from Jonah's supply.

Several of the bandsmen came and went to check on their friend's progress. Finally, as the sun was settling toward the distant horizon, Dan was able to get away. He knelt beside the boy who was like a son to him, and examined the wounds.

"Will he be okay?" Jonah asked.

Duane sat back against the tree to be out of the way. He, too, listened for the answer.

"No," the man said, emotion catching in his throat.

"Why?" Duane asked, barely audible for the tightness in his own throat. "The bullet's still in there," he spoke with effort. "But worst, it's around his lung. He's bleeding inside and it's filling the lining around his lungs. After a while they'll collapse and he won't be able to breathe."

"Dan," Johnny tried to talk. Light coughing cut him off.

"Try to rest, Johnny," the man instructed.

"No time," the youth forced. He rested a moment before continuing. "Please... get... Dee... home."

"Please, Son, don't give up," the man pleaded.

"Promise... me," Johnny pleaded in return.

"Yes, I promise," Dan said.

"I'm not... quitting... yet." There was a moment of quiet when Johnny closed his eyes and seemed to drift away. He worked his fingers so the man knew he was still alive while he rested and caught his breath. He swallowed hard.

"Coffee?" Jonah asked.

"Yeh," the youth sighed.

The boy lifted the cooled cup of sweetened liquid to the quivering lips. Johnny sipped slowly as some leaked out and ran down the corners of his mouth. Duane crawled from the tree to get by his friend's side.

"I ain't goin home ta yer better, Johnny," he said as he felt for his friend's hand.

Their fingers met and their grip tightened.

"You've got to," Johnny said. "I'm... dying."

"No!" Duane shouted, then calmed himself. "Ya cain't!" he pleaded.

"I can't... stop... it," he paused, exhausted.

No one spoke for a moment. Tears slipped down Duane's cheeks. He let them go. Dan saw the grief on the boy's face and felt the inner pain of his own grief. He blinked rapidly as the moisture rose up in his own eyes and a tight pain stuck in this throat. He stood and turned away, his body shaking with silent sobbing. Jonah was lost as to what to do. At first he didn't realize it, but he, too, was crying. He wiped the tears from his eyes and sat looking on in disbelief. Death had never come this close to him before. His mother had died in childbirth and he'd never known her. He had never been really close to his father. Sure, he loved him, but it was different. It hadn't hurt to leave his father behind in a hospital, not knowing if he would ever see him again, and not caring much either. Here was a friend who was dying and he wasn't sure what that should feel like, but he did know that it would mean they could never see each other again.

"Dan," Johnny whispered, "I want... to go... home... to be... with my... folks."

"Oh, God, I hate this war!" the man cried. "I don't know how I can take you." The tears flowed and his voice choked. His mouth quivered with grief and his eyes searched hopelessly for an answer.

"Johnny, I love ya," Duane whispered. "Please don't die. Yer the only one I eve' had as like a brother."

Johnny's hand tightened in response. With a great effort, he lifted his left hand to place it on his younger friend's head and pulled it toward his shoulder so he could hug the sobbing boy. Duane bent beside the youth and the two embraced for a long moment.

"I love you... too... Dee." He swallowed hard and shook slightly with shallow coughing.

The embrace lost its strength and Duane gently eased his friend's arms back to his side.

"Captain Marshalton," Jonah spoke, barely audible as he worked to force his voice from an uncomfortable pain in the throat, which he'd never known before.

"What, Jonah," the man answered.

"I can take Johnny home. Me and Dee can ride with him to his folks place, then I can go with Dee to his home, too." The offer was innocently simple. There was a sense of expectation in the voice, an excitement of possible adventure.

The man smiled. "I don't think you understand, Jonah."

"Yes, I do, Sir. Johnny's going to go to sleep and he won't wake up again. But you won't have to put him in the ground. He can go with me and I'll see he gets to his own home."

Johnny smiled at the unknowing sincerity. Duane and the captain couldn't help but to laugh.

"What's wrong?" the boy asked.

"It's okay," Dan said. "You just don't quite understand what's happening here."

"Jonah... you're all... right," Johnny said. "You can... take me... home... anytime."

"Sher, why not," Duane asked. "We kin do it, Dan. Me an' Jonah kin do it."

"Okay by you, Johnny?" the man asked.

"Sure thing," Johnny answered. The coughing came again. "God, it hurts," he cried, the tears of pain slipping free.

Darkness came as the four had talked.

"Let's find some place more comfortable," Dan suggested.

"There's no hurry," Johnny said. "I'm okay... here."

Duane sent Jonah to get blankets from the wagon. He covered his friend and made his own bed beside the litter. Jonah curled up by the fire. Captain Marshalton draped his blanket over his shoulders and found an empty ammunition box to use as a seat for the night. As the boys settled to sleep, he prepared another pot of coffee, refueled the fire, and settled to keep a vigil through the night.

In the fields to the west, the wounded begged for water. Those of the living who could, slept. Others were haunted by the moaning and lay awake agonizing in their helplessness to render assistance. The sky overhead sparkled with its glittering of stars. The frogs of the river banks and swamplands filled the night with their song. The lonely man poured a cup of coffee, then sat on the box, huddled beneath his blanket, to keep watch over the dying youth. As he put the cup to his lips, a curl of steam wafted into the night air and a gentle breeze carried from the battlefield.

The smell of death was in the air.

*　　*　　*

In the hour before midnight a shadowy figure approached. The captain had drifted into a light slumber, but heard the footsteps and lifted his head.

"Captain Marshalton," the man spoke.

"What is it, Sergeant?" Dan responded.

"There's wounded coming in, Sir. Can you come and help?" The man stood waiting by the fire.

"Certainly. I'll be with you in just a minute." He stood, letting the blanket fall from his shoulders, and leaned over the youth on the litter.

Johnny's breathing was very shallow. Each breath was forced.

"Hang in there, Johnny," Dan whispered, as he gently stroked the bandaged head.

Stepping back for one last look, the captain left to attend the incoming wounded.

As dawn brightened the eastern horizon, Captain Marshalton returned to find coffee brewing and bacon sizzling. Jonah was doing the cooking under Duane's supervision. Johnny was awake and had turned his head to watch. Several of the bandsmen had come and gone. Joshua occupied the seat on the ammunition box.

"Hi," Dan greeted gently.

"Morning," the boys at the fire chorused.

Johnny forced a weak smile, but said nothing.

"He can't talk," Joshua explained as the doctor knelt by the boy's side. "There's too much pain."

"Coffee's done," Duane announced, as he carefully poured a cup for the captain.

With the cup resting on the ground, the boy hung his finger over the side and waited for it to sense the rising level of hot liquid. The coffee reached the fingertip and Duane set the pot on the ground for Jonah to take and reset in the coals of the fire.

"Here, Dan," Duane offered, holding the cup toward the captain.

"Thanks, Dee." He took the coffee, sipped some, then handed it to Joshua. "Set this on the box, please."

Unbuttoning Johnny's blood-wet shirt, Dan commented, "Let's take a look and see what's happening."

The bandage was soaked with blood which continued to seep from the wound. It bubbled up and down with every effort to breathe.

"Joshua," the captain instructed, some alarm in his tone, "pass more bandages from that pack."

The bloodied material was left in place as more was placed overtop. Once the new wrap was secured in place, the man listened carefully with his stethoscope to determine what was happening inside.

"It won't be long, Johnny," Dan stated. His voice cracked.

The youth nodded in agreement.

To the west, volleys of gunfire reminded everyone of the battle, but didn't last long.

"What's that awful stink?" Jonah asked. "They didn't kill that many horses. Did they?"

"That's the dead you're smelling, Jonah," Joshua explained. "There's acres and acres of them out there."

"People?" Jonah asked in surprise.

"Dead soldiers, rotting in the heat and sun since early yesterday." Joshua passed the cup of coffee back to the captain who had just finished closing Johnny's shirt.

"Oh." A sudden truth was realized as Jonah continued, "That's why Kyle Baker and his friends were funnin me so much every time I complained how bad the air was smelling this summer." He turned the bacon slices over on the plate, then stared at Johnny. "Do people die like animals and their bodies rot, too?"

"Thet's fer truth," Duane put in.

"Will Johnny?"

"Yes," the captain affirmed.

The boy turned his head to gaze, disbelieving, about the camp. This new reality was very upsetting.

"Jonah," Duane began, "I know's how ya feels in yer gut." The younger boy stared at the young teenager with a new respect. "It's part a' thet reality I said a'fer thet is war."

"Dee, I feel sick," Jonah cried.

"It's natural," Dan said. "It will go away."

"How's Johnny?" Joshua asked.

"The lung's give out," Dan answered. "The other one's going, too. There's a great deal of pain."

Jonah pulled the plate of bacon from the fire and set it on the ground. He wasn't hungry. Instead, he stood and walked to the captain's side to stare at Johnny. The youth forced a painful smile, then started to cough again. Blood spewed from his mouth and sprayed his clothing. Jonah turned away, confused by his feelings.

"Dee!" Johnny called hoarsely.

Duane reached toward the voice and Dan took the hand to guide him to his friend's side. The sutler's son started toward the tree, but stopped a short distance from the litter and stood watching, struck by a horrifying realization that he was witnessing death, close-up, for the first time in his life. The captain placed the blind boy's hand on that of his friend. Johnny sought to grasp the hand and affirm his friendship.

"Dan," he rasped, "give Dee my... things."

"I will." The tears began to flow.

Johnny began to choke and cough as blood seeped into his throat. He reached for Dan who gathered him into his embrace and held him close while the coughing continued to rack the body. Duane reached around them both and felt their last embrace, the tremors of grief, and the lost fight with death. He felt the coughing subside and the body go still. He felt the man quaking as his sobbing knew no limits and his soul was wretched to its core. Duane's tears and the pain that ripped within reached for an eternity. Suddenly the war had ended as the knowledge was born within that it was the people who had kept him from going home. Now, the one person who had been so close, was gone.

There was nothing left to live for.

But his pa was going home. Now, he too, would go home.

"Wer goin home, Johnny," he whispered. "The war's ended 'n wer goin home."

EPILOGUE

The shrill shriek of the train's whistle rent the night and intruded on the boy's dreams. A warm June breeze whipped through the open coach window, blowing across the soot-streaked face. Duane opened his sightless eyes, as he turned his head to better hear the soft snoring of his young companion, stretched across the opposite seat.

Jonah was there and he was okay.

Duane turned to let his feet slide from his bench to the floor and sat closer to the window to allow the draft to blow full upon his face, whipping his hair about his ears and stinging his forehead and cheeks with sharp twinges of pelting pinpricks. There was a fresh smell in the air of the moisture of night dew. There was a comfortable rhythm through the floorboards, through his body, of the train's clattering along the steel rails, of the engine's chugging to pull its load, of speed and motion through the countryside.

The dream had seemed so real, yet even as he lived it through his slumber, the youth kept telling himself it was only a dream. Johnny's presence at his side as he arrived in his home town of Bendton could never happen. He was dead. The box in the baggage room at the front of the coach was where he lay now.

Once more, Duane relived that last day, so long ago, and the course of events that had followed. Once more he heard Johnny's last words and shared that last embrace and felt the stillness of death. A tear slipped free as he mourned the loss of a best friend and a piece of his life. The war was only a memory. Yet it had been a way of life with some very special people for whom he cared so much. It was people who had lived and touched his life – people who were real, but were lost forever. The fighting, the battlefield, was only a detail. The people were what mattered.

"Oh, God," he thought. "They're gone – all gone." And the faces passed in his mind – Sammy Winters, the widow Katie Smith, Tod Gardner, Willis, Sergeant Raymond, Colonel Fry, Lieutenant Damien Jenkins, Jamie Wilkinson, Reverend Smyth, Thelma Dowd, Annie Hasslett, Johnny Applebee, Daniel Marshalton – the living whose lives would go on their separate ways to never meet again and the dead who could never again be more than a distant memory.

After Johnny's death, while the battlefield continued to echo with cannonades and rifle volleys, Dan had taken the body to his surgery table. There, with Duane's assistance, he had cut an artery in the leg and pumped a chemical solution through the corpse, forcing out the body's blood. It was called embalming, the captain had explained. It preserved the body so that it wouldn't decay. A casket was fashioned from the boards of a damaged out-building.

Johnny's body was bathed and dressed in his own uniform, then gently laid in the box which had been lined with a blanket spread over a bed of straw. Before the lid was nailed in place, Dan and Duane bade their friend farewell. Sitting by the open window of the railway coach racing through the night, the boy brushed his fingertip across his lips as he remembered again the last kiss. He had felt the stilled face with his hands and had bent over the simple wooden edge of the casket to kiss the forehead. Its smooth solid coldness that was like polished marble was impressed forever in Duane's memory, along with the sound, a moment later, of the pounding hammer as Dan drove the nails into the wooden box.

For two more days the volleys and cannonades had roared back and forth between the armies. It was Tuesday before the first burial parties could set about to attend the dead. By then, only two of the thousands who had fallen remained alive to receive care for their wounds. The rest of the week had been quiet as the two armies set about the grim task of burying the corpses. The remains had decomposed badly in the heat of the June sun. None were more than rotted flesh clinging to partially exposed bones and grinning teeth where lips had been, bound together by ragged uniforms. They were heaped upon wheelbarrows and wagons to be carted to large excavations for common graves. There, these nameless thousands were dumped and covered over with the dirt of the battlefield. Some found a final resting place in a shell hole, others in a trench which was closed over them where they lay.

It was during these days of quiet that Duane had begun his journey homeward. The captain had arranged for the use of an ambulance to transport Duane, Jonah, and Johnny to the Virginia Central Railroad near Hanover Court House. There he had seen them safely onto the train and had given last instructions on how to transfer trains as they worked their way west from railroad to railroad. All had been written out on paper and given to Jonah, along with all Duane's army pay which the captain had saved over the years, to keep in his pocket for reference and to pay expenses along the way. Duane knew then that he'd never see Captain Marshalton again. The two said their good-byes, Duane speaking to his friend through the open window of the coach as the train eased out of the station.

It had been a long and lonely trip, first to Gordonville where the small party transferred trains to the Orange and Alexandria Railroad, then on into eastern Tennessee and points north. Jonah was good company and very clever when the need arose, to talk his way through uncertainty or seek information or get the best price on food or refreshment. He was dependable as he made it his business to be sure Johnny's casket was carefully moved from car to car as they transferred trains, and that a trunk, carrying their combined belongings, passed with the wooden box. Jonah kept his rifle with him, tied in a blanket to avoid questions. Duane kept his drum, with its strap attached, to rest at his feet or be carried slung over a shoulder.

Somewhere in the middle of farm country, the train slowed as it approached a small station where a single lantern cast a feeble glow across a wooden platform occupied by a solitary figure. The engine's whistle announced its arrival and its bell clanged mournfully in the night as the brakes screeched, steel against steel, in a gathering chorus of brakemen on the various cars turning down their wheels to check the forward movement and assist the engine's efforts to halt the train. Finally, the entire consist came to a clattering stop and a quiet of sorts settled about the air as Duane listened to the hissing steam in the locomotive's piston chambers and the quiet conversation of the engineer and the station agent. Their voices were clear on the night air as information was passed of an eastbound freight train, due to pass within the half hour. To either end of the train, switches were thrown, their metallic slap, swift and sudden. The passing track was open. For now, it was a time of waiting and stilled silence.

An eerie quiet enveloped the scene as the absence of noise and motion allowed for a moment of peace. Jonah stirred, but did not waken. Duane opened his grey jacket as the stilled air grew warm, then settled comfortably to drift back to sleep.

Suddenly, a distant whistle cut the night. It wailed in gathering intensity, racing eastward, ever closer in the night. It quickly crescendoed, was upon the pass track with a sudden whoosh of air pressure clattering noisily by in thunderous smoke and soot, then passing behind and beyond to fade as quickly back into the night. Once more the switches clapped as they were realigned.

"Board!" a single voice called from the station platform. There were two short blasts on the whistle. A surge of steam accompanied the squealing turning of the brake wheels. The train strained and clattered into motion. The station slipped slowly out of view.

An hour later, Duane felt the warmth of the new day's sunrise as the first strong beams of sunlight struck out across the land and caressed his face through the open window. In his mind he saw the light playing in the soft blond curls of Johnny's hair as he lay silently on the litter that last morning of his life. He saw Jamie on his litter in the wilderness as they spoke of the friends from another year. He felt a song he'd sung with his companions in Company K. Quietly the words stole into his mind. Softly he sang them in the privacy of his imagination, the words barely audible in the early light of morning amidst the clatter of the coach's wheels.

> Into the ward of the clean white-wash'd halls,
> Where the dead slept and the dying lay;
> Wounded by bayonets, sabres, and balls,
> Somebody's darling was borne one day.
> Somebody's darling, so young and so brave,
> Wearing still on his sweet, yet pale face—
> Soon to be hid in the dust of the grave,
> The lingering light of his boyhood's grace.
> Somebody's darling, somebody's pride,
> Who'll tell his mother where her boy died?
>
> Give him a kiss but for somebody's sake,
> Murmur a prayer for him soft and low;
> One little curl from its golden mates take,
> Somebody's pride it was once you know;
> Somebody's warm hand has oft rested there,
> Was it a mother's, so soft and white?

Or have the lips of a sister so fair,
Ever been bathed in their waves of light?
Somebody's darling, somebody's pride,
Who'll tell his mother where her boy died?

The song drifted off and a feeling of melancholy held the boy in his reverie of sad memories.

"Dee," Jonah's voice startled him from his thoughts. "Will Johnny go to heaven? Will he be with God?"

The voice and the question caught the youth completely by surprise.

"I ain't knowin fer sher, Jonah." Duane pulled himself from his dreams and reflections. "He sher oughtta."

Jonah had been wakened by his companion's song and had listened without moving until it was over. Now he stretched, sat up, and moved to the window to gaze at the passing countryside, washed in the radiant glow of the dawning day.

"Is God really there?" he asked without turning from the window.

"He has ta be, Jonah." Duane faced the small voice. "We ain't no accident. The flowers 'n trees 'n living creatures ya's lookin at ain't no accident neither."

"How'd you know what I was seein?"

"What else would ya be seein?"

The two smiled at each other.

"Is Johnny with God?" Jonah asked.

"He sher is, Jonah," Duane replied. "An' he's with us, too. As long as we ain't fergittin ar time tageth'r, he ain't neve' goin from us."

"What about the box?"

"He's ther, too. But he's in thet trunk as has his thin's. An when his box is in the ground, his thin's 'll still be with me, an' so will he."

Somewhere else in the car a child whined. A voice soothed. Others in the car awakened to the new day as the quiet was gradually invaded by renewed conversations, arguments, card games, and the telling of wonderments. Some stood to stretch or pace the aisle. Duane and Jonah paused to listen. The car door from the baggage room opened and the conductor entered.

"Vincennes, next stop," he announced. "We stop for breakfast and connections north and south." He strode through the car to pass his announcements to the passengers on the cars behind.

"That's a blessing," Jonah stated.

"What is?" Duane asked.

"I'm starvin!" the boy smiled.

"Yeh, me too," Duane agreed. "What da we do here fer changin trains?"

Jonah took the information packet from his pocket. "Here we get a train for Terre Haute. But we gotta wait a couple hours and they serve breakfast."

"Sounds fine by me." Duane stretched and resettled himself in his seat.

The engine's whistle announced the approaching stop and the train began to slow.

*　　*　　*

At Vincennes, Jonah supervised the transfer of the wooden casket and the trunk to a baggage cart for loading on the northbound train to Terre Haute. Once in place by the tracks of the Evansville and Crawfordsville Railroad, the boys left the train of the Ohio and Mississippi Railroad to enjoy breakfast while the locomotive's crew went about the business of taking on wood and water. After a brief flurry of activity following a one- hour breakfast layover, the train continued on its way. The two boys settled on a station bench to await their next train.

By mid-morning they were on their way again. At Terre Haute, Indiana, they stayed the night to change trains again as the pair continued west the following morning on the St. Louis, Alton, and Terre Haute Railroad. By noon they had crossed into Illinois and arrived at their final stop in Paris. There, an elderly Doctor Jamison Clancy met them at the station, loaded the trunk and Johnny's casket onto a buckboard, and took the two on the final leg of Johnny's journey, north to the farming town of Cedar Knoll.

*　　*　　*

The flatbed wagon, drawn by a pair of chestnut mares, bounced along the lonely dirt lane that was the road north. The flat landscape of grasslands and fields stretched away from the roadway across the monotony of the Central Plains toward distant horizons. The air was warm and quiet, yet blended with the sounds of insects, chattering in hordes so as to sound as one constant wave of noise, rising and falling across the open country. Duane rode on the bouncing spring-board bench, to the right of the veteran doctor. Jonah sat behind, perched on the front edge of the casket, with his hands gripping tightly on the iron rail seatback, to maintain his balance for the rough ride.

Doc Clancy was a paunchy sixty-seven years of hard, country experience. His white hair flowed in thick waves which hung just above his collar and was kept neatly trimmed. Clean-shaven, his face was lined with comfortable crinkles which reflected wisdom, humor, and a firmness that was not to be questioned. His ever-present brown leather medical bag rode securely on the floor, just beneath the seat. Firm hands held the reins. Yet there was a gentleness in their pull so that the horses were not in pain from the bit of the bridle, though they were never in question as to their driver's intentions.

The loneliness of the ride from the station had been filled with conversation along the way and an occasional greeting from a close-by farmhouse.

"You'd have really liked the Applebees," Doc was saying. "They were a good, God-fearing couple who were filled with love for their neighbors as well as their son. It was truly unfortunate that sickness took them both. Before the war, Mr. Marshalton had become so well-known as a caring and compassionate doctor that the community was most happy when he took Johnny as his adopted son. We knew we were in for three generations of really good doctorin. Now the war has ended that. Johnny is dead and Doctor Marshalton is gone. We hope he'll return when the fightin's done. And we can't wait for it to end."

"Yer people ta holdin strong feelin's 'gainst us Rebs?" Duane asked.

"I'm afraid there's some as will give you a darn hard time, Dee. But there's others that have a way of letting a body make his own way of his own merits." The man glanced at the youth beside him and smiled with the satisfaction that he had rightfully judged the teenager as a young man of fine character.

"Do they kill Rebs in Cedar Knoll?" Jonah asked. "'Cause Dee's my friend and I'll hurt anyone who hurts him. I got a musket and Dee can still use a gun real good." The boy's voice was resolute with loyalty and a firm belief in his and Duane's ability to fend for each other.

"I ain't knowin I kin still shoot good," Duane declared. "And I ain't neve' know'd ya ta hurt a fly, Jonah. Please don't say nothin thet'll git ya hurt none."

"I really don't think there's anything that serious about to happen in Cedar Knoll," Doc Clancy assured. "We're going to put you up with Charlotte Ross. She's the president of the Ladies' Auxiliary of the church and will see to your needs while you're with us. She's also a sort of matriarch for the town, being its oldest citizen at ninety-four years, and still very spry and alert. Her hearing's gone some and she's blind without her glasses. But trust me, she's a very able lady and you will have the best she and our community can offer."

"Why fer da ya say thet?" Duane asked.

"Johnny's our darling. And you being such a friend of his makes you very special, too."

"But ya all ain't knowin much a me an' Johnny's life tageth'r. We's been off ta the war an all."

"Daniel Marshalton sent us a telegram while you've been journeying across the country to bring our Johnny home. He said a lot of real proud things about you and told us some of Jonah, too."

"What did he say about me?" the boy asked.

"He said most how you were Duane's eyes and were responsible for taking care of all the information for you both as you traveled."

"Oh," Jonah smiled. "Does that mean I'm important?"

"Very important," Doc affirmed.

"Ya sher is," Duane agreed.

"You want to hear about me and the war?" Jonah asked.

"I'd be honored," the man said.

For the next half hour the older two listened while Jonah entertained them with the story of his life as a sutler's boy. His ramblings were surely not boring and often quite humorous. Eventually, the outlying farms around Cedar Knoll appeared and the journey neared its end.

Duane sensed the town's nearness. There was a change in the air as a noise level of activity and the presence of people invaded the quiet that had been, and the clatter of the wagon was echoed off nearby structures. A dog's bark and the cackle of chickens busily pecking about a farmyard gave evidence to an approaching community.

"Is this Cedar Knoll?" Duane asked, when Jonah paused in his account.

"Sure is," the doctor confirmed. "There's a small business district of shops, bank, sheriff, cafe, hotel, feed store, and the like. A school house and church are on the northeast edge of this district. The side streets are mostly homes and some trades such as the shoemaker and cabinetmaker. The cemetery is north of town about a quarter mile out."

As the wagon's clatter blended with the traffic on Main Street, its passengers were absorbed into the routine of activity. Few acknowledged its arrival, yet many took note of the newly-arrived visitors, caked with the dust of the road, accumulated over the miles of travel from the rail stop at Paris.

"Where d' we go fi'st?" Duane asked.

"We'll stop at my house where you can get cleaned up. Then we'll go to the hotel for dinner and on to Mrs. Ross's place." The man guided his team across the opposite lane of the dusty street and onto a side street, somewhat smaller, but just as dusty.

"What about Johnny?" Jonah asked.

"We're cutting down Murray's Alley, here, to the back of the undertaker's shop. Mr. Bernard knows we're stopping and will take good care of Johnny until the burial this Saturday."

A tall thin, sad-faced man in his fifties, Jethro Bernard helped unload the wooden casket and carry it into the workroom in the back of his shop. There it was placed on two wooden horses to await his further attention. He bade the trio good-bye and closed the door without any further visiting.

The wagon continued to the end of the alley where it turned away from the center of town and crossed over to a tree-lined lane named Fox Street. A wooden walk followed either side and was edged with clean wooden houses with roofed porches across their fronts and gingerbread trim along their roof-lines and eves. The vehicle turned in at a light tan dwelling trimmed in a burnt orange color.

"This is it," Clancy announced.

Stopping at a small side porch, the trunk was unloaded by the path to the step, then the team and wagon put into the carriage barn. Water was drawn from the pump by the back door and grain was dipped from a feed bag into the mangers. The horses were content. The man led the boys back to the house where they could bathe in the backyard tub and put on a clean change of clothes.

*　　*　　*

The two days before the funeral passed quietly. Charlotte Ross proved to be a woman with a golden heart. But first appearance had raised serious doubts. She was a spindly old grey-haired lady, wrinkled as a prune, with legs like broom sticks and long bony fingers which looked fragile as egg shell. The boys quickly learned she had a gritty strength as she took them shopping for new clothes and managed to move from store to store and around within each, with such ease and speed as to leave them both exhausted.

In the afternoon she took them to help with chores as she fed the chickens, gathered eggs, worked her garden, and milked her cow. They helped prepare and clear the meals. In the evening they sat with her on the porch, in one of the four red wooden rocking chairs that graced the house, and shared their stories about Johnny and Dan. They were well known to her and she craved every detail of their lives in the war. Duane soon learned there was a part of each he'd never before known as the grand old lady spun tales of life around Cedar Knoll and some of the childhood pranks each had played. It was hard to think of them as boys of ten or twelve, but Charlotte Ross had known them then, and the things each had done were embarrassing, daring, and endearing in turn.

Friday evening after the supper dishes had been put away, Duane and Jonah joined Mrs. Ross on the back porch where each in turn perched upon a high stool while she painstakingly trimmed his hair. The late sunlight of the June evening was helpful to her failing eyesight and cooler with the evening breeze. While the sun's lengthening rays continued to stray through the bedroom windows on the southwest side of the house, the three adjourned to the room the boys shared to sort through the freshly laundered clothes which the woman had laid across the bed earlier in the afternoon. She had already inspected and repaired those items which had been worn through or torn. Now, Jonah picked out his Union uniform clothing while Duane advised Mrs. Ross in the selection of his uniform items. They looked very neat all washed and sewn. The woman felt proud as she envisioned the boys, dressed smartly in their clean clothes.

Duane asked that his field gear be taken from the trunk so he could be sure that it was clean and polished. Jonah wanted his gear, too. Pack, blankets, rain gear, mess gear, tent half – all these items were carefully returned to the trunk. Belt, canteen, cap box, cartridge pouch, revolver, bayonet, rifle, haversack – all were to be clean to be worn for the funeral. Drum and sticks would also be worn. For Johnny there would be one last long roll.

Everything was in readiness. The trunk lid was closed and the uniforms laid neatly across its rounded top. The drum and accoutrements were gathered neatly on the floor beside it. Satisfied that all was in proper readiness, the old lady and her charges went out on the front porch to watch the sun go down and the June bugs flicker in the gathering darkness.

* * *

The early morning sun shown brightly outside. A warmth flooded the bedroom, but was absent of the strong rays of the rising sun since the room's windows were on the shadow side of the house. Still, Duane could sense the light as the crowing cock and twittering sparrows invaded his subconsciousness and brought him fully awake. The sizzling aroma of pan- fried ham blessed his nose and aroused an appetite. The smell of coffee and baking biscuits added to the delicious smell of morning.

"Jonah," Duane called softly, "ya 'wake?"

There was no answer.

"Jonah?"

Duane flung his arm out to waken the youngster who slept at his side. But the covers were empty.

"Thet little sneak," he thought. "He's already at the food."

Throwing the covers aside, the boy sat up and crawled to the foot of his bed and searched for his trousers on the top of the trunk. Finding the piled clothing, he quickly dressed, added his socks and shoes, then stood to orient himself. Carefully Duane worked his way around the bed and across to the door. Trusting in part a mental image of the lay of the house, he found his way from the bedroom to the kitchen. He paused in the kitchen doorway.

"Mornin, Dee," Jonah greeted.

"Good morning," Charlotte's cracked high voice joined. "Are you hungry?" she asked.

"I sher is, Ma'am," the youth stated. "An the fixin's sher do smell handsome."

"Come on," Jonah encouraged. "I'm standin at your chair and it's clear from where you stand."

Guided by the voice, Duane approached the table, felt for the chair, and eased himself onto the seat.

"Put a cup of coffee for Dee. Would you please, Jonah?" the aged voice quavered.

"Yes, Ma'am," Jonah responded.

"Breakfast 'll be along shortly," the woman stated.

Duane sipped the coffee while he waited, listening all the while to the bustle of the kitchen activity and savoring its perfumed air of wood smoke and food.

"It sher ain't been natural these couple weeks," the youth remarked. "The war's so fer off an' ain't likely ta eve' be near agin. Yet it's bin sech a reg'lar part a ma days."

"Our lives change," Mrs. Ross comforted. "Chapters end and are closed forever as new ones begin and take their place. But they stay forever a part of us, tucked away in our memories. Like a dream, they drift with our past, and with them sometimes go some very important people who touched our lives, will last with those memories forever, but will never cross our lives again."

She paused to gaze about the kitchen, her own mind flooded with the memories of nearly a century past. Her hands held a plate of eggs and ham which began to quiver as it was forgotten with reflections on another time.

"Do you want me to put that on the table?" Jonah asked.

"Wha? Oh, sure, Jonah. Thank you." She handed the plate to the boy who set it in the middle of the table.

"The war's like thet," Duane thought aloud. "An' when I git home, it'll mean ta start a differ'nt life. I ain't knowin fer sher as it'll be. But ain't nothin, nohow, gonna eve' be the same agin. It's like ma whole life is gone an' now it's all... it's all... jest differ'nt."

"I really do know how you feel, Dee," Charlotte assured as she brought a plate of biscuits to the table. "My life has stretched a very long time. I was born before this land was ever settled. I was just a child when General Washington fought the British and have seen this country grow from its very beginning." She sat in her chair at the end of the table and motioned for Jonah to be seated, too. "My life has seen many chapters open and close. It is very hard. But we do it. And the past falls away so fast that it seems it never happened, but truly was just a dream."

The aged voice of wisdom had scratched unstable on the boy's ear, but the message had penetrated to his soul and he felt it deeply for the truth he knew it was.

Breakfast was consumed in a short time with little conversation. The boys did the dishes as the elderly matriarch inspected their work and put each piece in its proper place.

Returning to the bedroom at Jonah's hand, Duane put on his gunbelt and the rest of his gear as Jonah did the same. The revolver had been Johnny's. The captain had acquired it to replace the musket long before they'd transferred to the east. It was loaded and ready for use, yet Duane had never known his friend to need it. Spare cylinders were in the cartridge pouch, ready should the need arise. Johnny's haversack and personal things were left in the trunk. As Duane slipped his own over his head and adjusted it at his side, he slipped his hand inside and wrapped his fingers around Jamie's cap box. It was reassuring to feel its presence and to know the map was folded within. After a moment's reflection on the war he'd left behind, the youth quickly finished preparations as he reached for his hat, and finally, his drum.

Jonah had his own gear, including the rifle which rested against the trunk. His belt held a bayonet as well as cap box and cartridge box. He flopped his forage cap with its II Corps clover pin upon his head, took up the rifle, and was ready to go.

"Ya ready?" Duane asked.

"Yeh. Are you,?" Jonah replied.

"I'm ready," Duane confirmed.

"Here's your stick," Jonah offered, taking it from where it rested across a chair. "Give me your arm and I'll guide you to the door. You can help hitch the widow's rig and we can go."

"Lead on," Duane instructed as he reached out his hand. "But ya best be careful as I ain't fer runnin inta thin's."

"Okay," the youngster smiled.

They headed for the bedroom door.

*　　*　　*

The two and a half days that Duane had spent at the Ross farmhouse had not prepared him for the event that unfolded Saturday morning. He never dreamed that anyone other than he had grieved over Johnny's death. Three hundred and seventeen people gathered for the funeral – the entire community. Old Doc Clancy had seen to it ahead of time that no one would visit at Charlotte's farm until after the services.

Johnny's casket had been placed on a black-draped frame in the front of the church. It had been there since the night before, covered with the flag that usually hung at the schoolhouse. The people had come to pay their respects, filing past the box since the previous night. Some of his boyhood friends had spent the night in the church pews, to sit with him one last time.

There were the regular church-goers of the congregation and those who had never attended. The building was packed with people crowded into its pews and standing all about the walls and in the aisles. More than a hundred who couldn't fit inside, stood outside the open doors.

When Charlotte Ross's rig pulled up, a quiet settled on the crowd.

"Oh, God!" Jonah whispered under his breath.

"What?" Duane asked.

"There's hundreds of folks here, Dee. Is this right, Mrs. Ross?" A very humble Jonah turned sheepishly to the woman.

"It's right, Jonah," she whispered, loud enough for both boys to hear. "Everyone who knew Johnny has come to say good-bye. Some have even brought their young-uns who have no idea what this is about."

The three stepped down from the buggy to be met by old Doc Clancy in his finest white shirt and dark suit. He escorted the party into the church and down the aisle to the front. The doctor walked with Mrs. Ross and Duane with Jonah. The people pushed aside just enough to let them pass, then closed upon the open space as soon as the four had moved ahead. The boys suddenly felt self-conscious with the drum and rifle in tow. But there was nothing else to do but carry them along.

A hushed gathering watched, their sniffling and stifled sobs intruding intermittently upon the quiet. The four approached the sanctuary. Duane reached out to touch the box, to be sure it was the same, and found its feel to be the wood that had been taken from the field of battle.

"It has a flag," Jonah whispered. Then, as everyone watched, he laid the rifle across the top.

Duane sensed that something had happened because he felt the movement when Jonah let go of his hand.

"What?" he asked.

"I put the gun on the casket," the boy explained.

Duane knew what to do with the drum. He set it on the floor in front of the black fabric. As a sudden afterthought, he reached into his haversack. His fingers touched the cap box, but slipped aside in search of a roll of bandaging cloth which he carried of habit. Withdrawing his hand, he placed the roll beside the rifle. Doc Clancy struggled to keep from crying out loud. He knew the meaning of the fabric. He guided his party to four chairs which had been placed for them beside the casket.

The service went on with prayers and words and music from the town's band and the church's choir. To Duane it was but a confusion of noise which wandered in his head, as he sat suffering the heat and the close stuffy air that smelled of sweaty bodies packed tightly inside the small church. He was a stranger in this company. He just wanted to be alone with Johnny. Couldn't anyone understand?

A group of local youths carried the wooden box from the church the quarter mile to the graveyard. Jonah recovered his rifle and Duane his drum and bandage roll. The flag was folded and left behind to be returned to the schoolmaster later.

The procession was a surging wave of humanity as the gathering walked to the open grave site. There, Duane bid a final farewell as he played the long roll one final time. Some words were said. Many tears were shed. The box was lowered by rope into the open hole and the dirt shoveled in echoing with a hollow sound as the first clumps bounced off the wood. A thin slab of oak had already been carved:

John Davidson Applebee
born February 23, 1848
died June 4, 1864

There was no more. Beside him were the graves of his parents. Here the family slept together, gathered in eternity.

Returning home with Mrs. Ross, Duane and Jonah found themselves swamped with visitors throughout the balance of the day. Most came out of curiosity. A few stopped out of genuine concern, knowing Johnny as they did and realizing the friendship he must have shared with Duane.

The boys were drained emotionally. For Jonah it was another look at the reality of life and the finality of death. He was emotionally numbed.

Duane and Jonah slept soundly that night, passed a quiet Sunday, then departed with the doctor on Monday to ride south again to Paris where they would take the train once more to continue the journey to Duane's home in Bendton, Arkansas. Once aboard the train, Duane felt the final passing of that part of his life that had been the war. There was no box aboard this train. It was left behind, secure in the ground; its occupant asleep beneath the sod, covered by the dust of the grave. The chapter was closed, forever.

*   *   *

The afternoon sun beat hot on the wooden decking of the wharf. Overhead a blue, cloudless sky was busy with crows and pigeons who scavenged noisily for any refuse or food, abandoned on land or water. Black laborers unloaded wagons and muscled bales of cotton and other cargoes to align them for loading on riverboat or barge. Napoleon, Arkansas, was a busy port of junction where the Arkansas River emptied into the wide open expanse of the great Mississippi.

It was July as Duane and Jonah wandered out onto the busy decking to await the arrival of the Queen. Their journey had taken them by rail to St. Louis, then by riverboat to Napoleon, a distance of more than 600 miles. It had taken eight days and an extra two of waiting in Napoleon. Ozark Queen was the next boat scheduled to stop at Napoleon on its way up the Arkansas River.

Walking slowly to allow Duane to guide on his younger friend's voice, the two carried their trunk between them. Jonah also carried the rifle, wrapped and tied in its blanket; and Duane carried his drum which hung from the strap across his shoulder. Each wore the lightest elements of his uniform. Jackets and vests were in the trunk along with all else except haversack and canteen.

"Stop!" Jonah whispered loudly. "They're movin cotton bales."

The pair paused until Jonah gave the all clear, then continued on until Jonah figured they were in a good location.

"Let's put it here," he suggested.

The trunk was lowered to the flooring and both settled comfortably on its lid. The drum hung low enough to rest on the plank decking.

"What time ya reckon it is?" Duane asked.

Jonah scanned the sky. "I'd guess about three o'clock," he answered. "The man ta the ticket winda' said as it was due near ta four. Should be hearin her soon." The thirteen-year-old turned so the smell of the water suggested he was facing the river. "How much money we got yet, Jonah?" he asked.

"After the tickets, about sixty-three dollars."

The noise of activity played on Duane's mind and he tried to remember how it looked. He asked Jonah to describe what was happening and the younger boy was eager to respond. Eventually his chatter was interrupted by the distant sounds of a steam whistle.

"Thet's her," Duane announced. "I r'memb'r the tone of her whistle."

"I can see her smoke," Jonah stated.

"When she puts in, Jonah, I'll wait here an ya go find the captain. His name is Kearny."

"Okay," the boy agreed. He stood and leaned the rifle against the trunk. "I want to look around."

"Jest don't git lost," Duane advised.

"I won't," the other promised.

As the minutes passed, activity picked up with the approach of the boat. So, too, did a sense of excitement in the air. The wild screams of local boys signaled the challenge of races to the incoming vessel. Duane heard the splashes as several dove into the river to swim out toward the Queen.

"Look's like fun," Jonah said, returning from a short exploration of the activity in the area.

"Ya ain't even thinkin a goin with 'em," Duane commanded.

"Don't know as I can swim that far," Jonah assured. "Besides, I thought you might like this. I got it from a farmer over a ways in the crowd."

"What is it?" He held out his hand for the offering.

"It's a honey comb and a loaf of bread."

The treasures were placed in the open hands.

"Wrap 'em an' stow 'em in yer have'sack. Captain Kearney'll have some coffee an we kin eat this tanight."

"Sure. That sounds like a good idea."

The bread and honey were put away for later. A surge of commotion and the sound of smoke rolling from the stacks as the Queen's wheel slowed against the water, confirmed that the riverboat was on the verge of tying up. Winches squeaked, orders were shouted above the noise of massed passenger conversations. The boat bumped against the edge of the wharf as the linesmen tossed the ropes to waiting hands which quickly wrapped them on the heavy cleats to hold the vessel fast against the wooden platform. The gangways were lowered. A sudden surge of movement burst forth as people rushed to disembark and laborers began to move freight, cargo, and luggage.

"Kin ya see the ship's captain?" Duane asked.

"He's at the upper railing shouting at people on the deck."

"Try ta git ta him an tell him I'm here."

"You think he'll remember you?"

"He did a time back. I'm sher he will now."

"Okay. I'll be back in a bit."

Jonah danced his way through the crowd, cavorting to one side or the other of a burdened worker or departing passenger. At one point, a pile of luggage was in his way and he vaulted across. Bouncing onward against the tide of movement, he soon worked his way to the gangway and across its edge to the vessel's deck. Dashing up the broad risers of the grand staircase, he was soon climbing the side stairs to the upper deck near the wheelhouse.

"Hey, Boy!" an angered captain barked. "Stop where ya are. Ya ain't allowed up here!"

"Are you Captain Kearny?" Jonah asked.

"Who be wantin ta know?" the blue-clad man shot back.

"Dee, I mean Duane Kinkade. He sent me to find the captain."

"Who!" the man exclaimed. "Dee's alive!?" He turned to meet the boy on the steps. "Is he here?"

"Yes, Sir," Jonah pointed. "He's sittin out there on the trunk with the drum beside him."

"He's changed," the man stated as he saw the youth in the distance. "There's a strange look ta him."

"He's blind, Captain Kearny. I came with him to be his eyes."

The man suddenly paused to study the dark-haired youngster he had bellowed at a moment before. A spirited bit of a boy, he thought, then smiled. "You'll do all right, Boy. What's yer name?"

"Jonah Christopher, Sir." He looked the captain over from head to toe, sizing him up and deciding he could be trusted. A tenseness slipped away and the boy felt relaxed within.

"Well, Jonah. Ya kin see as I'm busy. Ya git thet friend a yers on board quick an bring him ta the wheelhouse. Ya kin leave yer thin's ta the top a' the grand staircase."

"Yes, Sir, Captain."

The boy disappeared as quickly as he had come and William Kearny watched as he bounced off toward his friend, then gently helped him to gather their gear and walk toward the boat. The slender figure in the tailored blue captain's uniform reached into a pocket for his pipe and tobacco. As he watched the activity below, he knocked the ash from the bowl into his palm, dumped it on the breeze, and proceeded to refill it from the pouch. By the time the bowl was packed and the match was struck for the light, he heard the footsteps on the stair treads. He turned to meet the boys.

"Howdy, Dee," he greeted as the two reached the top of the step.

"Hi," Duane returned, extending his hand.

Jonah stepped aside, placing his friend's hand on the railing for reference.

"It sher is good ta see as yer alive," the man said.

"Is my pa alive?" Duane asked. "Da ya know if'n he's headed ta home?"

"Yes, Dee. He's gone home." The man released his grip of Duane's hand and put both hands on the youth's shoulders. "Let me look ya ov'r." He studied the figure before him. "Ya sher have done a heap a growin. I kin see, too, it's bin a hard couple a years."

"Yes, Sir," Duane responded. "I sher am glad ta see ya, Captain. I cain't wait ta be back home."

"Ya hungry?"

"Sher is."

"Well ya both come with me. You, too, Jonah," he repeated as the boy hesitated. "We'll put ya in a fi'st class cabin where ya kin leave yer gear an' head on down to the dinin saloon an git a fi'st class meal."

He reached for Jonah's shoulder to motion him by to guide Duane back down to the passenger deck. As the two boys descended the steps, Kearny paused to draw on his pipe and to observe the care with which

Jonah guided his blind friend, yet tried to hold back and allow Duane his own lead whenever possible.

The boys were settled in a very comfortable cabin. Their gear moved in, they went with the captain to dine at his table in the nearly empty saloon. The evening was spent settled in deck chairs outside the captain's cabin, deep in conversation while each shared his news of the war and told of his experiences. Coffee was brought from the galley and the bread and honey shared around. Finally all retired for the night.

Ozark Queen laid over until morning while laborers worked to stack the wood racks full of fuel and to pile extra on the deck outside the engine room so that the sternwheeler would be ready for a straight run up-river.

The journey was expected to take four days if the weather cooperated and stops went as planned and were kept brief.

In the days that followed, the boys took their ease, lounging on deck chairs, watching the activity in the grand saloon, visiting the wheelhouse, leaning on the rail to watch the landscape slide by. It was a lazy time, a comfortable time, a time where everything beyond the world of the vessel itself was temporarily forgotten. The boat was in and out of several ports of call along the way. Otherwise, the rhythm of the engine, its great piston rods and drive bars, the swoosh of the billowing smoke, the continuous splash of the wheel – all ran constant, day and night, their all-present motion surging through every fiber of the riverboat. One last time the boys sat together on the grand staircase as the river went to night with the last glow of day fading to velvet black on the western rim of the water.

Finally, in the early morning of the fifth day, as the sun hung low casting long shadows across the water, the river town of Ozark came into view. In the midst of the gathered passengers and their varied conversations, Jonah stood with Duane at the forward railing of the passenger deck and described the approach. Captain Kearny joined the two for just a moment to assure them he would see them ashore and help secure transportation to Bendton. Then he was gone to attend the business of bringing his vessel into port.

The dawning day continued to brighten as the sun climbed higher in the east. Within his mind and body, Duane sensed another dawn – of excited anticipation. Before this day was ended, he would be home. A tingling ran his spine and his body trembled with the sensation. Jonah sensed the excitement in the hand that gripped the railing beside his. He saw the white in the knuckles and the slight tremor in the wrists.

For Jonah the feeling was different. Deep inside a sense of apprehension was born. What would become of him once Duane was home? No longer would there be a need for the younger companion who had been his eyes, his caring guide who navigated the journey over 1800 miles. As a tingling of anticipation rose within the thirteen-year-old youth, a tear escaped to slip down the cheek of the ten-year-old sutler's boy.

The Queen's whistle sang on the morning air to announce her arrival. As the wharf slipped closer, linesmen prepared to tie her in and deck hands stood by to lower the gangways. The rhythm of the engines slowed. Activity stilled, awaiting the moment of contact. Gliding gently on the water, the vessel bumped against the pilings. A sudden burst of commotion followed as people and goods moved between the riverboat and the wharf.

*   *   *

Following breakfast aboard the sternwheeler, Captain Kearny had the boy's belongings moved to the Kolstee Freight Company's offices while he took Duane and Jonah to arrange for their passage to Bendton on the morning freight run. Nathaniel Kolstee saw to it that their gear was added to the day's shipment and the boys were put in the care of the driver to ride with him on his delivery run to the freight house at Bendton. By eight o'clock in the morning, they were on their way once again.

There was a flurry of conversation at the start of the trip as the driver answered some questions about changes in the past two years. But he seemed a tight-lipped and reserved man in his thirties, allowing them to know him only as Jake. The miles passed in silence as the boys retreated into themselves and their mixed emotions rambled in their thoughts, and the miles of country rolled by.

It was early afternoon when the wagon pulled in at the warehouse in Bendton. The office agent emerged to the front walk at the sound of the wagon's approach. He and Jake saw to the unloading of the boys' luggage first, then went about their business as the horses shook their traces, impatient to be rid of them. The boys grabbed their trunk, rifle, and drum to go as far as the town's main street before gaining their bearings to move on.

"Jest git us ta the corner an we'll think from ther," Duane puffed as they moved awkwardly down the dusty side street.

"Swing around left," Jonah instructed. "There's a walkway about two paces, then a step up."

With one hand gripping the trunk's leather handle and the drum slung over his shoulder, Duane felt his way with his guide stick in his free hand. Cautiously the two mounted the wooden walk, then set their burden down.

"Let's set a spell whilst I fix in ma mind where we is," the older boy instructed.

The two presented a strange sight as they sat on the corner in the middle of the sidewalk, forcing pedestrian traffic to move around them. People stared at these young strangers – a rather peculiar pair. One was a Yankee, too young to be a real soldier, and the other was a blind youth in a Rebel uniform.

"Where do we go from here?" Jonah asked.

"I figg'r the best place ta begin is Marshall Fowler's office," Duane considered.

"Where is that from here?"

"Gimme a minute." The boy searched his memory for the lay of the street. "Face ta the east down the street."

"All right," the younger boy turned.

"Da ya see the hotel?"

"Yeh."

"The marshall's office should be 'cross from it an' down a piece."

"Okay. I think I see it. But I don't know how we'll get this trunk down there in all the traffic."

"Yer right," Duane agreed.

Jonah glanced about.

"Wait here," he instructed, then was gone.

Duane sat, self-conscious of the stares he knew were on the faces of each whose footfalls passed beside him. A light rig rattled to a stop beside the walk and a light-weight figure bounced down from its seat.

"This here's Mrs. Parsons," Jonah's voice announced. "She was just coming out from the millinery store and said she would leave our trunk at the marshall's office after she finished picking up some things at the general store."

"Thank ya, Ma'am. Yer mighty kind," Duane said.

"Here, give me a hand." Jonah reached for one strap as Duane stood and took the other.

The woman helped give instructions as to where to place the trunk on the back of her vehicle, then bade the two farewell.

"I'll meet ya ta the marshall's in a half hour," she informed. "Gee up," she slapped the reins.

The light wheels of the one-horse buggy crunched softly in the dust as Mrs. Parsons pulled away to cross the street to the store.

"Come on," Jonah instructed. "Give me your arm and we can move faster."

The office was just over three blocks off. Most people gave the boys clear passage, yet twice Duane felt his friend deliberately knocked against him by someone who disliked his uniform. No words were exchanged, but he heard the mutterings of the culprits after they had walked on behind.

No one extended any kindness. Perhaps it was because of Jonah's presence. They seemed to frown their disapproval at these two strangers in their midst because they were a pair from opposite sides. What true Southerner would have a Yankee for a friend.

Suddenly, opposite the street from the marshall's there was a wild commotion as a large dog raised its head from where it lay at the office door, then sprang to its feet barking in a loud frenzy, and charged excitedly across the street.

"Stop!" a panicked youth called as he burst from the office door to see what was wrong.

Traffic hauled up short to avoid striking the animal that darted into the street toward the boys.

"Git 'em, dog!" someone shouted in anticipation of a blood bath soon to follow. "Good riddance ta Yankee trash an' turn-coats!"

"Look out!" Jonah screamed as the great canine leaped into the air onto Duane.

Forewarned, Duane turned to face the attack and put an instinctive arm across his throat. The impact threw him back against Jonah who fell beneath him as the three went crashing to the wooden walk. Women screamed and those nearby ran away in fear. Some shouted encouragement to the dog as a thirteen-year-old youth ran from the marshall's office to call off the animal.

Duane felt a large tongue bathe his face in ecstatic joy.

"It's okay, Jonah!" he cried with joyful recognition. "It's my dog! He reached his arm about the great furry neck and hugged it tightly. "Pounder!" he cried, the tears pouring down his face. "Oh, Pounder, ya knows me! I missed ya so! God, I love ya!"

Jonah crawled on his back, pushing himself free of the frenzied reunion to sit against the wall of the storefront. Duane slipped free of the drum and rolled on the ground with his dog, hugging and kissing the bulky beast which in turn bathed him in a profusion of wet kisses as well. The boy who approached from the office stopped dead in his tracks as he stared at the sight before him and exchanged quizzical glances at Jonah. In a moment he realized what was happening when he heard the boy call the dog's name. "Dee!" Joy lit his face as he watched the two rolling in the dirt. "God, it's really you!"

"Hi, Jamie!" Duane called from beneath his dog. "Okay! Okay! It's me, Boy! Kin I git up?"

The dog stepped back, prancing with excitement, to allow his master to push himself to his hands and knees and brush away the dirt.

"You know each other?" Jonah asked, working his own way to his feet and picking up the blanketed rifle as he stood.

"Sher do," Duane said. "Jonah, this here's Jamie Fowler."

"Howdy," Jamie greeted. He turned to study his friend. "But..."

"I knows. I'm blind." It was a frank statement.

Pounder continued to prance and whine while Duane regained his feet and Jamie bent to retrieve the drum. Jonah found the walking stick and pressed it into Duane's hand.

"How's Pa?" Duane asked.

The boys and the dog started across the street to the office as disappointed spectators turned to go about their own business.

"Yer pa's okay," Jamie began. "Boy, is he gonna be glad ta see ya! Ya ain't knowin the hurt he's felt thinkin at fi'st ya was dead, then gittin yer letter an wonderin if'n ya'd come back safe."

"Where kin I find him?"

They were at the steps, climbing to the front porch.

"He's out ta the farm. Bin workin hard ta fixin it up agin."

The four entered the office, Pounder staying close to his master, his nose busy smelling his clothing.

"Here, have a seat." Jamie cleared a bench near the front door and motioned for both to be seated. He left the drum at the end of the bench, out of the way.

The dog lay at their feet, resting his muzzle on the toe of Duane's shoe.

"Pa's gone on his rounds," Jamie explained. "He sher 'll be su'pris'd when he gits back!" Parking himself in his father's chair, the boy continued, "I sher neve' 'spected ta see ya 'gin."

"It's bin a long time," Duane responded. "Is the office like it use ta be?"

"Pretty much so, I guess." Jamie stared at his friend. "What were it like?" he asked.

Duane reached down to scratch Pounder's ears. "I guess it were adventure at fi'st," he reflected. "Some I was lonely. Some I were scairt. When I's bin ta home fer a bit I'll come in an tell ya all 'bout it." Sensing the quiet figure at his side, he added, "Jonah here's bin 'bout the most important friend these past weeks. He's bin ma eyes so fer ta git me home."

"Hi," Jonah spoke, a lost loneliness in his voice.

"When Pa gits back we kin ride out ta yer place an' find yer pa," Jamie offered. "He's sher ta be 'bout the happiest man in the county this day." Jamie rocked back in the chair, the spring squeaking as it complained of the pressure. "We went ta see him one day afta yer letter come. He took us ta the fishin hole in the meada an' said as how he'd made a promise ther jest a'fer leavin ta the war. Somethin ta do with you, Dee."

"Yeh," the boy responded as he thought back to the night he had first known his pa would be leaving. "We walked down ther the night he said as he was goin. Pa said thet when the war was ov'r, we'd go down ther ta git the big'un."

For a moment, no more was said. Jonah was becoming increasingly uncomfortable as he felt more and more like an outsider. He began to wiggle his feet and glance about the office. Pounder seemed to sense this and to sense as well an importance in the younger boy's relation to his master. The fingers were still that had scratched his ears, as the hand rested quietly on his head. Carefully, the dog slipped away, crawling to the next figure on the bench. Then, sitting close at his feet, the dog pushed his muzzle beneath Jonah's hands and was rewarded with a vigorous rubbing of his neck and a kiss on his nose.

"You're a good friend, Pounder," he whispered.

"What will be done for Jonah?" Jamie asked, suddenly remembering the boy's presence.

"It's fer sher my pa 'n yers kin he'p us ta do right fer him," Duane replied. "Ya ain't got no worry, Jonah," he assured. "We's gonna see ta the best. Yer ma friend an my pa'll let ya stay with us fer now. I jest knows he will."

"Thanks," Jonah said. For the first time since early morning, he began to feel he wasn't to be forgotten.

"Mind if I tries yer drum?" Jamie asked.

"No, go ahead. The sticks are here in the strap." Duane felt for the strap, running his hand around the rim of the instrument near his feet, then stood to take it toward his friend's voice.

"I'll get it," Jonah volunteered, his old enthusiasm back in his voice once again.

The boy slipped the strap from Duane's hand as he stood, stepped around Pounder, and strode across the office. Jamie stood to put it over his head, then walked to the front of the desk to lean against the corner while he tapped at the drumhead with an awkward lack of beat.

Jonah wandered about, exploring the office while Duane tried to explain to Jamie just how to hold the sticks. Pounder returned to Duane's side and sat with his head on the youth's knee. An air of contentment settled in the room as the boys passed the time, awaiting the marshall's return.

*　　*　　*

Marshall Jonathan Fowler was overwhelmed with the joyful discovery of Duane's return. After the trunk was delivered through the kindness of Mrs. Parsons, the man gathered the boys together, locked up the office, and walked everyone around to the Fowler home. There was a brief reunion with the Fowler family over milk and fresh-baked cookies while the marshall and his son hitched the team to the wagon. Then the boys and their gear were loaded with Pounder taking his traditional post, behind and to the center of the seat bench. A great deal of excitement and barking accompanied the departure of the wagon as it pulled out toward the Kinkade farm. Mrs. Fowler and her daughters waved the menfolk on their way, then returned to the house to prepare a late dinner for when the marshall returned. It had been agreed that the Kinkades and Jonah were to spend the night with them so that all could share in the celebration of Duane's return from the war.

Just as the wagon was leaving town, Duane asked for a brief stop along the way. Pausing at the cemetery, he asked Jonah to guide him to his mother's grave.

"It seems it was ta the northeast corner," the older boy directed.

"I think I see it," Jonah said. "Your dog has gone ahead and is waiting there."

When the two caught up to Pounder, the boy confirmed that he had guessed right. The dog sat quietly. Duane knelt down to touch the coarse grass and to run his fingers over the lettering of the headstone. Satisfied, he sat back on his heels.

"I'm home, Ma," he said. "Me 'n Pounder is here an Pa's back, too. I reckon Pa's bin by ta see ya. I want ya ta know a friend a mine from the war. His name is Jonah. He got me home.

"I sherly do miss ya, Ma. We're goin on ta see Pa. Then I'll be back ta bring ya some flowers from the meada."

Duane stood. Tears glistened in his eyes. He paused a moment to regain control of his feelings before returning to the wagon.

"Come on, Pounder," he called softly. "It's time ta go home." Reaching in search of his friend he added, "We kin go back now, Jonah."

Duane returned to the wagon with his dog and his friend to finish his journey homeward.

It was late in the afternoon as the wagon neared the farm. The end was near. Duane felt the excitement mount within as it rattled along through the afternoon's warmth. Hurry! he thought inside. The tingling ran within once more. Finally he felt the wagon turn into the lane and heard its wheels rumble across the wooden planks of the little bridge.

"Whoa," Marshall Fowler drew on the reins. The wagon came to rest in the farmyard.

"Pa!" Duane called. But there was no answer, only an open silence.

"He might be down ta the meada, Dee," Jonathan suggested.

"Jonah, would ya take me ther?"

"Sure."

"Jest folla the lane from where the barn once was," Jamie instructed. "Ya cain't miss it."

"Thanks," Jonah acknowledged as the marshall helped Duane from the wagon and passed him his walking stick.

Pounder jumped down and pranced in circles, eager to go. "We'll be here when ya git back," the man called after them.

Duane put a hand on Jonah's shoulder and followed close at his side. "Stay close, Pounder," he called.

The dog had run ahead to the beginning of the lane. He stopped and stood panting, waiting for the two to catch up. Jamie Fowler and his father watched from the wagon as Duane and his young guide moved on down the lane, growing smaller in the distance.

The fragrance of the cultivated fields and the approaching woodland caressed the boy's nose as he thought back for a moment to the last time he had walked along this path with his pa. The two continued beyond the rows of young corn to pass under the canopy of pines that arched overhead. Soon they arrived where the path opened from the woods into the meadow with its scattered coloring of wild flowers. Beyond, the stream coursed its way to ripple across the rocks into the pool beneath the overhanging oak.

Andrew Kinkade was standing there, silently watching the ever-widening rings where a catfish had broken the water's surface.

"Is he ther?" Duane asked, breathless for an answer.

"Yes, he's there," Jonah stated.

Suddenly it was over. The years of conflict and wandering in far-away places and the loss of people so important in those times past, had fallen away into a distant memory. The search had ended.

Duane turned to his young friend with tears flooding his eyes, and grabbed him in an emotional embrace. "I'm home, Jonah! I cain't b'lieve it's really ov'r!"

The boy felt warmed yet embarrassed, too, as dampness soaked through his shirt and his own eyes welled up with his own feelings of emptiness over his father's absence. Standing free once again, the older youth brushed the tears from his face with a sweep of his sleeve.

"Jest point me in the right direction, Jonah, an' hold ma stick fer now." The boy did as he was asked. While tears coursed down his cheeks unseen by the older youth, Jonah took Duane's arm to face him toward the figure beneath the tree.

"He's right in front of you, under the tree," Jonah explained, attempting to control his voice and to keep his own pain hidden.

The boy let go and stood quietly aside as Duane stepped forward, into the sunlight.

With Pounder at his side, allowing his master's hand to rest on his head for guidance, the two started slowly across the meadow.

The man sensed the movement off in the grass, turned his head, and saw the boy and the dog walking toward him.

Puzzled at first, he wondered who the stranger was that walked beside his son's dog. Turning for a better view, he shaded his eyes to study the pair. Suddenly, he knew! It was his own son, grown in years, taller, very different from the little boy he'd left behind. Excitement raced through his mind. Yes, it really was his son! He was alive! He had come home! He was walking toward him in the meadow! Oh, God! It's really him!

Andrew Kinkade had broken into a run as his emotions erupted from deep within. Pounder was barking excitedly.

"Dee!" the man called, a flood of tears nearly blinding him as he ran.

"Pa! Pa! I'm home!" Duane called, his joy echoing across the fields and bouncing from the trees.

The boy and his father reached each other, pulling together in a tear-filled embrace. The man swept his son off his feet. The dog circled the two, barking ecstatically, dancing joyously.

In the quiet of the tree-shadowed path, Jonah watched, and cried.

POST SCRIPTS

Through the combined efforts of Duane's father and Marshall Fowler, Jonah was reunited with his father in Pennsylvania in September of 1864. It was learned that the sutler had fully recovered from the injuries that had hospitalized him.

Nine months after Duane's return home, on April 9, 1865, General Lee surrendered his army at Appomattox Court House in Virginia. The Civil War was ended.

Reunited with Captain Marshalton and Johnny Applebee following the battle at Gettysburg, Duane journeys with them to become part of General David Birney's division of the Army of the Potomac. As the army prepares to begin the spring campaign, Duane is told he must leave the army due to his blindness. But the spring campaigns begin and a decision is put on hold.

TOWARD THE END OF THE SEARCH follows Duane's experience through the horrible slaughter during the weeks from The Wilderness, to Spotsylvania Court House, to Cold Harbor. There events and a letter about his pa send him from the war to return homeward in the company of Jonah Christopher, the young son of a Yankee sutler.

ISBN 978-621-434-017-0

9 786214 340170

BACK ALBUM

REFERENCE

Army of Northern Virginia
or Army of the Patomac or etc.

[commanded by a general]
3-6 army corps

Corp
[commanded by a lieutenant-general]
average of 3 divisions plus a unit of artillery

Division
[commanded by a major-general]
about 5 brigades plus a battalion [5 batteries] of artillery
note:- a battery of artillery included about 6 cannons with
caissons of ammunition, limbers for each, horses, men, and officers

Brigade
[commanded by a brigadeer-general]
about 5 regiments

Regiment
[commanded by a colonel]
up to 10 companies

Company
[commanded by a captain]
2-4 platoons, about 50 men plus officers

Platoon
[commanded by a lieutenant]
about 12-20 men and officers
note: When armies were at full strength, companies tended to have
100 soldiers and officers, later in the war some might be down to less than 36.

read more about it

The books below will help provide a greater depth of understanding about the Civil War – its conflict, the lives of the men and boys and women who were an integral part of life on the battlefield and in the camps, the times in which the war took place, and individuals whose lives were molded by the experience. This is only a sample list, those books from which JOURNEY INTO DARKNESS was developed. Some of these titles will be particularly helpful in offering a more detailed description of some of the events that were part of Duane Kinkade's experience.

Bauer, K. Jack, ed., <u>Soldiering - The Civil War Diary of Rice C. Bull</u>, Presidia Press, San Rafael, California, 1977

Clark, Champ and Time-Life editors, <u>Gettysburg: The Confederate High Tide</u>, Tlme-Llfe Books, Alexandria, Virginia, 1985

Davis, Archie K., <u>Boy Colonel of the Confederacy: The Life and Times of Henry King Burgwyn, Jr.</u>, University of North Carolina Press, 1985

Donald, David Herbert, ed., <u>Gone for a Soldier: The Civil War Memoirs of Private Alfred Bellard</u>, Little, Brown and Company, Boston,1975

Edwards, William B., <u>Civil War Guns</u>, Stackpole Company, Harrisburg, Pennsylvania, 1962

Esposito, Brigadier General Vincent J., chief ed., <u>The West Point Atlas of American Wars</u>, Vol. 1, Praeger Publishers, New York, 1978

Folmar, John Kent, ed., <u>From that Terrible Field, Civil War Letters of James M. Williams</u>, Unlverslty of Alabama Press, 1981

Giles, Val C., <u>Rags and Hope, The Recollections of Val C. Giles</u>, Coward- McCann Inc, New York, 1961

Goolrick, William K. andTime-Life editors, <u>Rebels Resurgent: Fredricksburg to Chancellorsville</u>, Time-Life Books, Alexandria, Virginia 1985

Gordon, General John B. of the Confederate Army, <u>Reminiscences of the Civil War</u>, Charles Scribners Sons, New York, 1913

Jaynes, Gregory and Time-Life editors, <u>The Killing Ground, Wilderness to Cold Harbor</u>, Time-Life Books, Alexandria, Virginia 1986

Jordan, Robert Paul, sr. ed., <u>The Civil War</u>, National Geographic Society Washington, D.C., 1969

Miller, Francis Trevelyan, ed. in chief, <u>The Armies and the Leaders, The Photographic History of the Civil War</u>, part 10, Castle Books, York York, 1957

Nevin, David and Time-Life editors, <u>The Road to Shiloh, Early Battles in the West</u>, Time-Life Books, Alexandria, Virginia, 1983

Robertson, James I., Jr., <u>General A. P. Hill, The Story of a Confederate Warrior</u>, Random House, New York, 1987

Robertson , James I., Jr . and Time-Life editors, <u>Tenting Tonight, The Soldier's Life</u>, Time-Life Books, Alexandria, Virginia, 1984

Stackpole, Edward J., <u>They Met at Gettysburg</u>, Stackpole Co., Harrisburg, Pennsylvania, 1982

Stewart, George R., <u>Pickett's Charge</u>, Houghton Mifflln Co., Boston, 1959 Street, James, Jr. and Time-Life editors, <u>The Struggle for Tennessee, Tupelo to Stones River</u>, Time-Life Books, Alexandria, Virginia, 1985

Wiley, Beil Irvin, <u>The Common Soldier in the Civil War</u>, Grosset & Dunlap, New York, 1952

The History Behind Journey Into Darkness

Journey Into Darkness takes place during the American Civil War from 1861 to 1864. It is the story of Duane Kinkade's journey through the war in search of his father. The war is very real and the events of the war as seen through Duane's story are very real. The central event in the first book of the series was the raid on the Kinkade farm. Raiders from the north were active throughout western Missouri, Arkansas, and the nearby Indian Territories. Mail was also an issue when Duane's letters to his pa were lost in transit. The Confederacy had its own Post Office Department established in February 1861. Not all mail crossing into northern territory and going from civilian to military carrier made it, while mail sent by soldiers was generally more secure and safe in its passage. Descriptions of Duane's journey by riverboat were taken in part from period maps and *Life on the Mississippi* by Mark Twain.

Throughout the series, information about the weather during historic events was taken from soldiers' diaries as well as the researched information gathered about the events. The rain prior to Shiloh, the day after Gettysburg, at Spotsylvania Court House did happen. The freezing conditions at Stones River and the 90 degree drought at Perryville are all part of history. Each battle in which Duane finds himself is described from the point of action of the soldier on the ground at given points within the event. There is no overview of troop movements or the actions of generals. The regiments, their officers, their participation are all according to history by way of research. Duane entered Shiloh with Bowen's brigade and was in the fighting opposing the Hornet's Nest. With Sheridan at Perryville, he experienced the opening of the conflict along Doctor's Creek during the wee hours after midnight. At Stones River, again with Sheridan, he witnessed the piles of dead frozen together in their own blood and gore as temperatures fell below freezing and drizzle and rain fell during the battle.

With General Archer's brigade at Chancellorsville, Duane was assigned courier duty assigned to General Hill's staff. His view of that battle varied according to his assignment. At Gettysburg the boy was once again on the battle line in Archer's brigade entering the fight at Herr's Ridge and Willoughby Creek on the first day with A.P. Hill's division and in combat at McPherson's farm. He entered the woods with a North Carolina regiment witnessing the slaughter of that first afternoon; then found himself under Colonel Fry attacking the Union center on the third day. In the Wilderness Campaign with General Birney's division, Duane witnessed the battle from the breastworks on Brock Road where the battlefield went up in flames, which engulfed the wooden works, through which the enemy attacked and was driven back. He was at the Bloody Angle in the pouring rain during Spotsylvania Court House and the opening assault at Cold Harbor where three thousand fell in fifteen minutes and the dead lay in the hot sun for three days because neither general would call a truce.

The history isn't limited to the battles. The description of an incident wherein the pickets from both armies shared a cabin and kept a fire going, one side during the day and the other at night, was based on recorded fact. Battlefield incidents where the bands from both armies played in exchange did happen. The execution of two deserters as described in the fourth book, did happen. Those who read *Journey Into Darkness* will not only share the journey with Duane, but also experience the history of the war as it actually happened.

Duane's history is also based on fact.

In the series Journey Into Darkness, Duane Kinkade found himself on both sides during the war. He not only served as a drummer, but also as a courier and assistant in the medical corps.
Historically: Eleven-year-old Harvey Buffington of Circleville, Kansas, ran away from home and served as messenger [courier] in both armies. [Jay S. Hoar, *Montana's Last Civil War Veterans* (Temple, Maine: Bo-Ink-um Press, 2010) 12.]

While in camp at Shiloh, following the battle, Duane found a revolver on the battlefield which he cleaned up and kept as a personal side arm. Historically: Fifteen-year-old musician Julian Scott wrote in a letter to his father, "I had my revolver cocked, and ready to take him if he meant to get away." as he described the capture of a Confederate soldier by him and another soldier.

At the Battle of Chancellorsville in book three, Duane observed a twelve- year-old on an artillery crew pulling the lanyard to fire the cannon and rolling on the ground gleefully after it fired.

Historically: "In one battery, a boy not more than 12 years old was pulling the lanyard on a gun. Every time he yanked it to fire the cannon, he rolled on the ground with joy, to the delight of his older comrades." [William K. Goolrick and the Editors of Time-Life Books, *The Civil War: Rebels Resurgent, Fredericksburg to Chancellorsvile* (Alexandria, Virginia: Time-Life Books, 1984) 147. This battery was part of the Parker Company, a company of mostly boys whose history is recorded by Royal W. Figg, *"Where Men Only Dare to Go!" or the Story of a Boy Company C.S.A.* (Richmond, Virginia: Whittet & Shepperson, 1885).

At the end of the third book, Duane was seriously injured resulting in the loss of his sight. In the final book of the series he had become a thirteen- year-old blind drummer boy, serving with his friends in the medical corps.

Historically: Thomas Ranson, the youngest officer in the 52nd Virginia Infantry, wrote to his cousin, "I was the youngest officer in the fifty-second Infantry, and the youngest man except one – our little blind drummer, Maurice." He was thirteen years old at the time of the incident about which Ransom wrote, referenced in the letter as "not yet fourteen." [Susan R. Hull, collated by, *Boy Soldiers of the Confederacy,* (New York: Neale Publishing Company, 1905), reprinted (Austin, Texas: Eakin Press, 1998), 150.]

The Research Behind Gettysburg and Shoes on the First Day

The following excerpt from **Across the Valley to Darkness**, book three of **Journey Into Darkness**, refers to a very controversial element surrounding the events leading up to the start of the battle at Gettysburg. Some have challenged the validity of this history in **Journey Into Darkness**. Herein the story builds on the research that suggests the move into Gettysburg by General Heth was to get shoes. Today's historians point out that there was no shoe factory in Gettysburg and the movement had nothing to do with shoes. Nevertheless, this interpretation of the events on July 1, 1863, is built on research.

The Research

Clark, Champ and Time-Life editors, <u>Gettysburg: The Confederate High Tide</u> , Tlme- Llfe Books, Alexandria, Virginia, 1985, page 35, "That force – under Brigadier General James Johnston Pettigrew of Henry Heth's division in A. P. Hill's corps – had come looking for shoes." This from the second column of that page begins a 2-paragraph description of the circumstances and conversation surrounding that decision. Pettigrew's statement below is crafted from that description and the words spoken and highlighted below are taken directly from the quotes in that description.

Johnson, Robert Underwood and Clarence Clough Buel, editors, <u>Retreat From Gettysburg, Battles and Leaders of the Civil War</u>, volume III, Thomas Yoseloff, New York, 1956, page 271 "Next day Heth sent Pettigrew's brigade on to Gettysburg, nine miles, to procure a supply of shoes."

Robertson, Jr., James I., <u>General A. P. Hill, The Story of a Confederate Warrior</u>, Vintage Books, a division of Random House, New York, 1992, page 205 "Two educational institutions and a shoe factory were there [Gettysburg]," and, a quote from Hill, "the enemy are still at Middleburg, and have not yet struck their tents"; on page 206 "Heth said, "If there is no objection, then I will take my division tomorrow and go to Gettysburg and get those shoes." "None in the world," Hill replied without hesitation."

Stackpole, General Edward J., <u>They Met at Gettysburg</u>, Stackpole Books, Harrisburg, Pennsylvania, 1969, page 122 "Heth had sent Pettigrew to capture some stocks of shoes thought to be at Gettysburg."

....

--- excerpt ---

**Reports of Maj. Gen. Henry Heth, C. S. Army, commanding division
JUNE 3-AUGUST 1, 1863.--The Gettysburg Campaign.
O.R.-- SERIES I--VOLUME XXVII/2 [S# 44]**

HEADQUARTERS HETH'S DIVISION,
Camp near Orange Court-House, September 13, 1863.

Capt. W. N. STARKE,
Asst. Adjt. Gen., Third Corps, Army of Northern Virginia.

On the morning of June 30, I ordered Brigadier-General Pettigrew to take his brigade to Gettysburg, search the town for army supplies (shoes especially), and return the same day. On reaching the suburbs of Gettysburg, General Pettigrew found a large force of cavalry near the town, supported by an infantry force. Under these circumstances, he did not deem it advisable to enter the town, and returned, as directed, to Cashtown. The result of General Pettigrew's observations was reported to Lieutenant-General Hill, who reached Cashtown on the evening of the 30th.

On July 1, my division, accompanied by Pegram's battalion of artillery, was ordered to move at 5 a.m. in the direction of Gettysburg. On nearing Gettysburg, it was evident that the enemy was in the vicinity of the town in some force.

I am, very respectfully, your obedient servant,
H. HETH,
Major-General.

Excerpt from Journey Into Darkness, a story in four
parts, 2nd edition written by J. Arthur Moore, page 305

The boy reported to the lieutenant to see if he were needed for courier
staff and was sent on to Colonel Fry who sent him on to division headquarters.
Several on courier detail milled around division staff as they waited for further
instructions. They remained quiet in order to overhear the conversation
between General Heth and General Pettigrew. Lieutenant-General A. P. Hill
rode up in the midst of the discussion.

"As I stood on the ridge and surveyed the town through my field glasses,
I observed a large column of Federal cavalry approaching fast on the road
from Emmitsburg," Pettigrew reported. "In as much as we were after shoes
and not a fight, I've withdrawn along the Chambersburg Pike to a point four
miles from the town."

"That's very unlikely," Hill put in. "The enemy are still at Middleburg
and have not yet struck their tents."

"Then if there is no objection, General, I will take my division tomorrow
and get those shoes," Heth offered.

"None in the world," Hill replied.

Duane carried the report back that the division was preparing to move
out and would advance to join Pettigrew's pickets. From there they would
move on Gettysburg at dawn in order to get those shoes. The enemy, however,
was present, and a fight was expected.

MAPS

NOTE: The historic maps reproduced in this section of references were found through the Civil War Trust, www.civilwar.org. The Civil War Trust is the largest and most effective non-profit organization devoted to the preservation of America's hallowed battlegrounds. Although primarily focused on the preservation of Civil War battlefields, the Trust also seeks to save the battlefields connected to the Revolutionary War and War of 1812. Through educational programs and heritage tourism initiatives, the Trust seeks to inform the public about the vital role these battlefields played in determining the course of our nation's history.

Use the link provided above to join them in their mission.

The troop movement maps that accompany each historic map are from the Time-Life Civil War book series. Each of these books is identified in the bibliography section "read more about It." The maps are used with permission from Time, Inc. You can locate the various units within **Journey Into Darkness** by referring to these maps. These regiments are real, and so is their history within Duane's story.

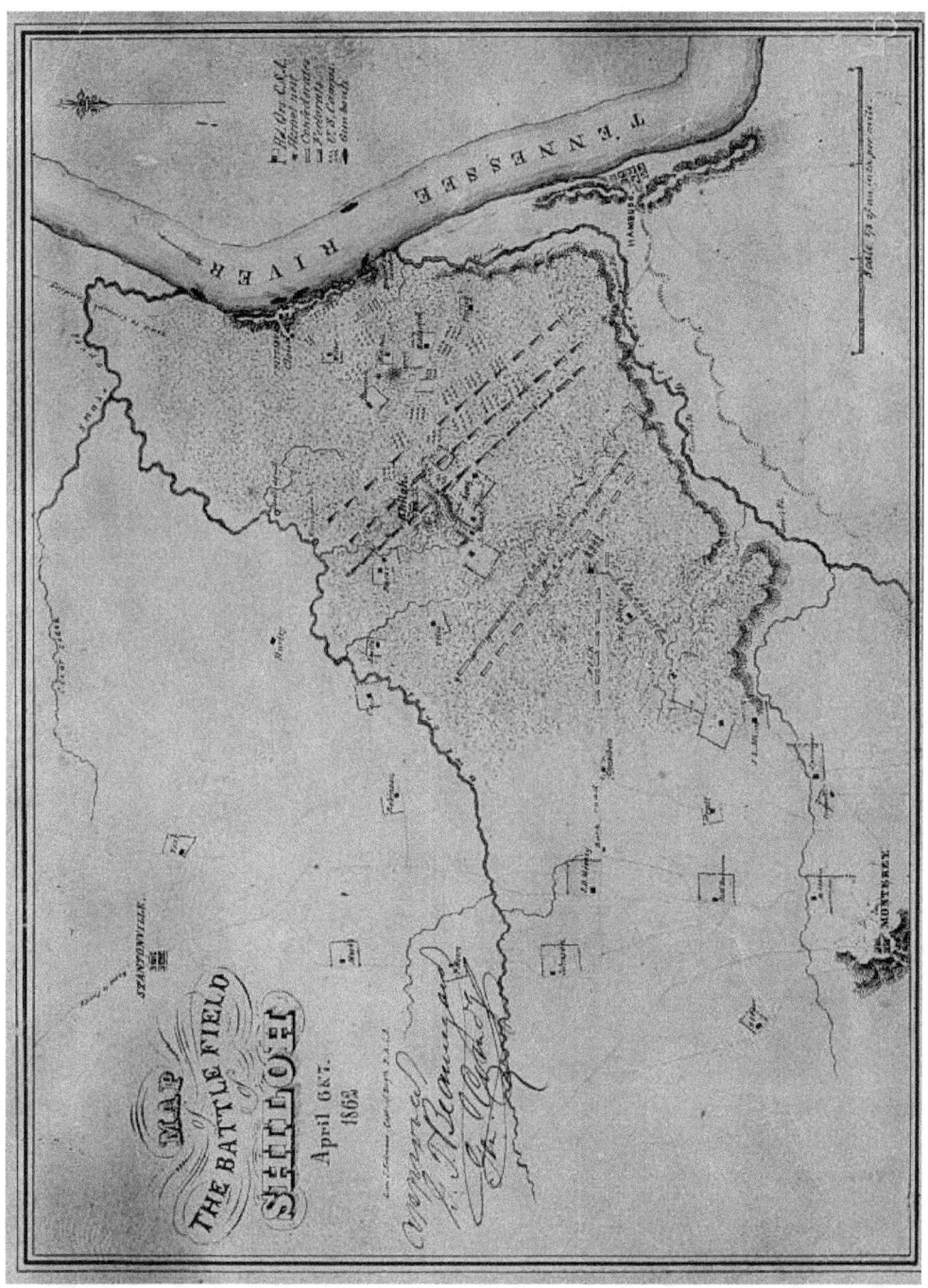

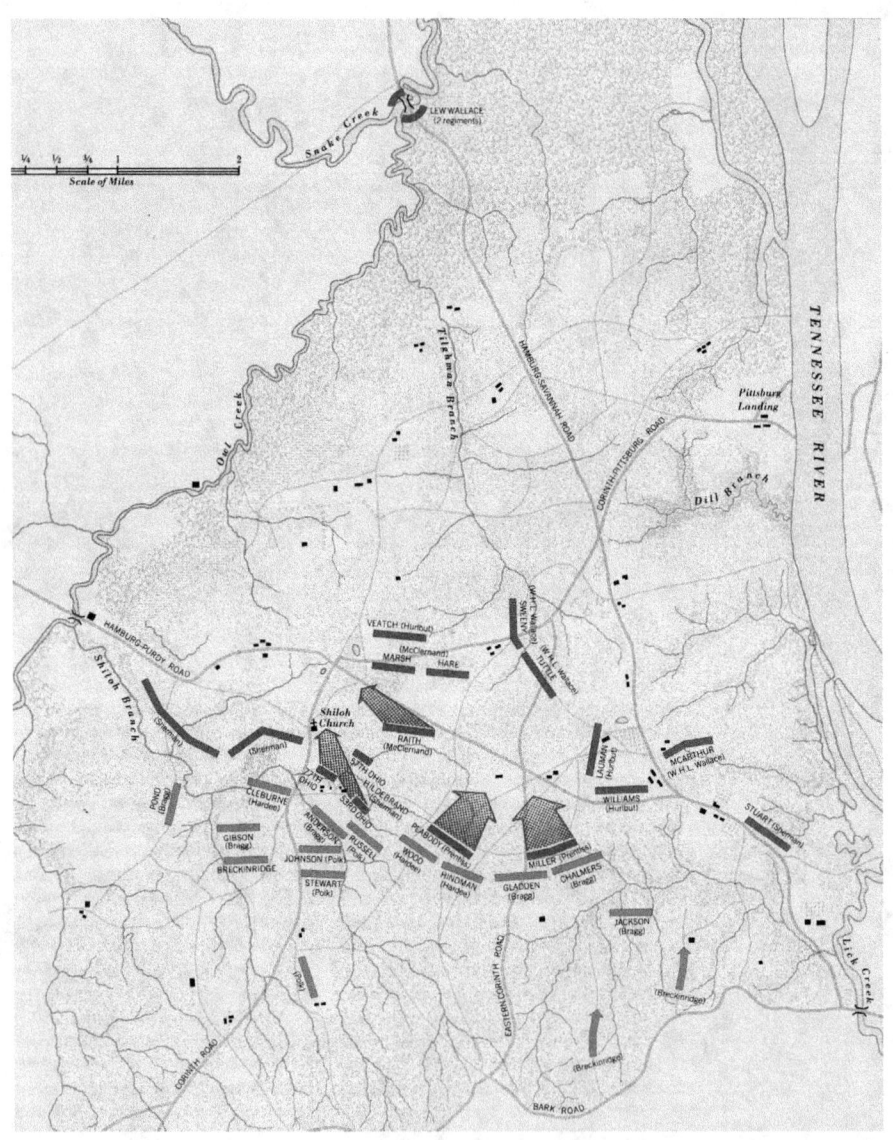

**Battle at Shiloh
April 6-7, 1862**

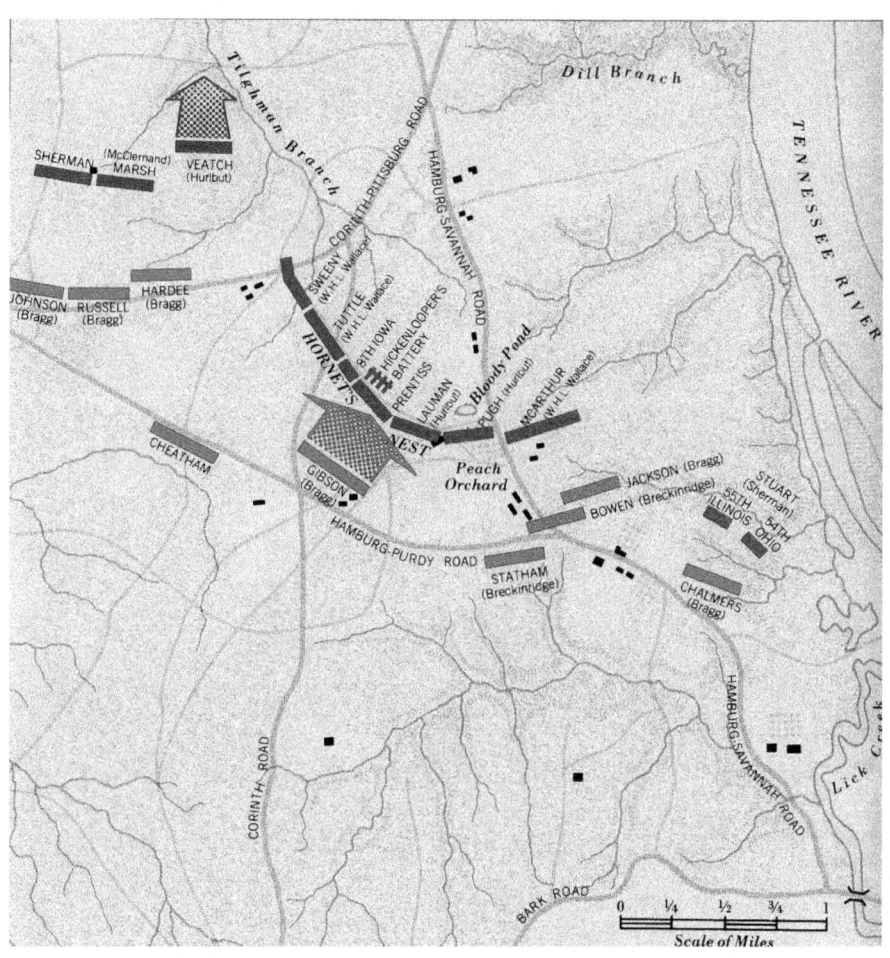

Shiloh, April 6, 1862, 12:30 pm

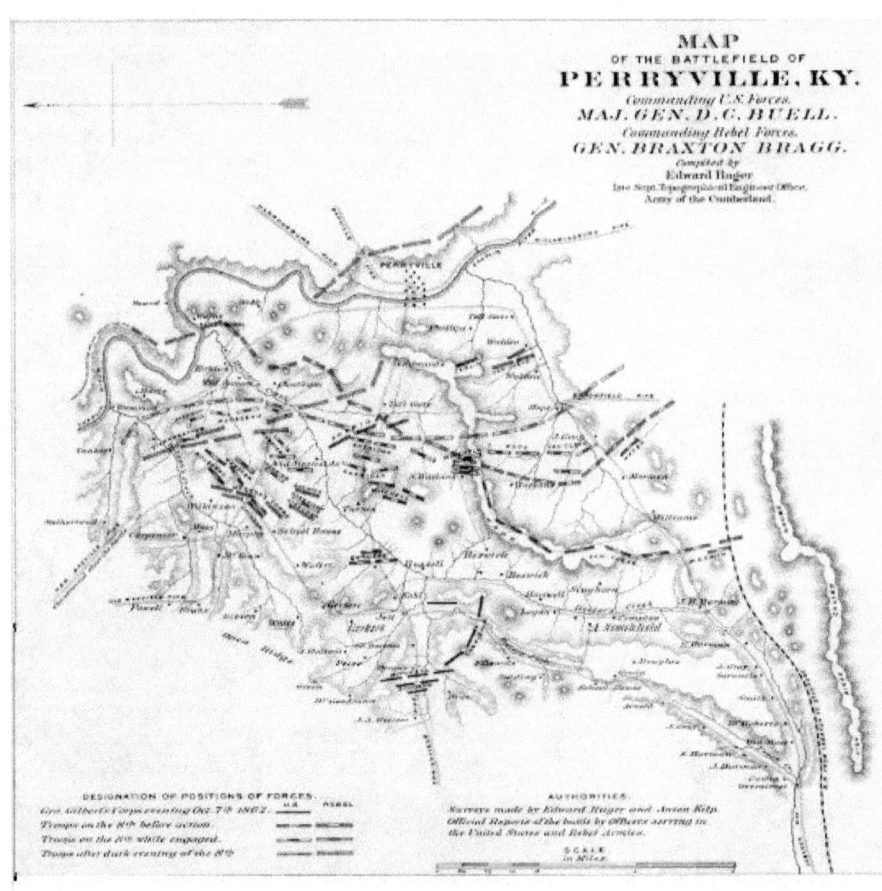

Maps of Perryville, Kentucky (1862)
BATTLE OF PERRYVILLE - OCTOBER 8, 1862

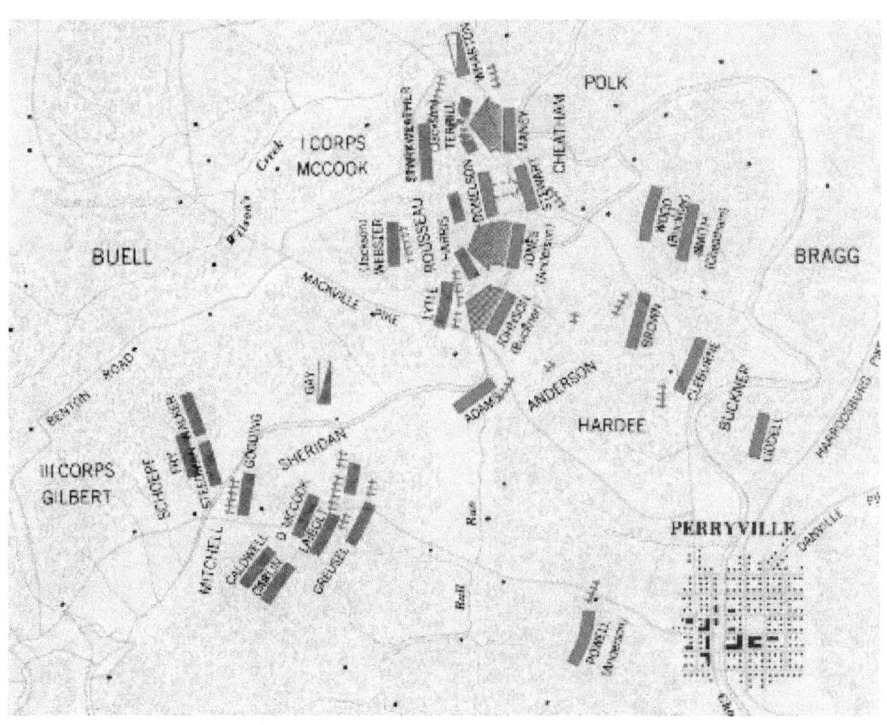

Kentucky Campaign of 1862

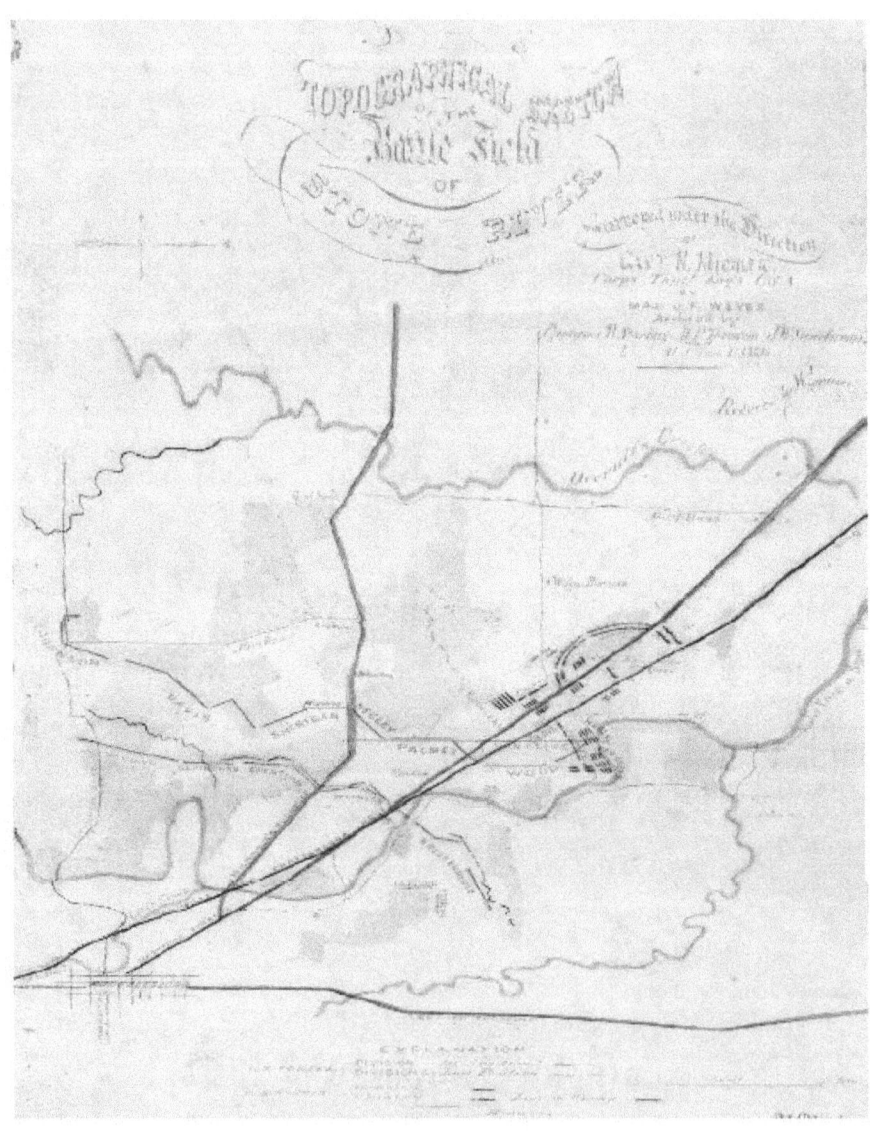

Perryville, October 8, 1862

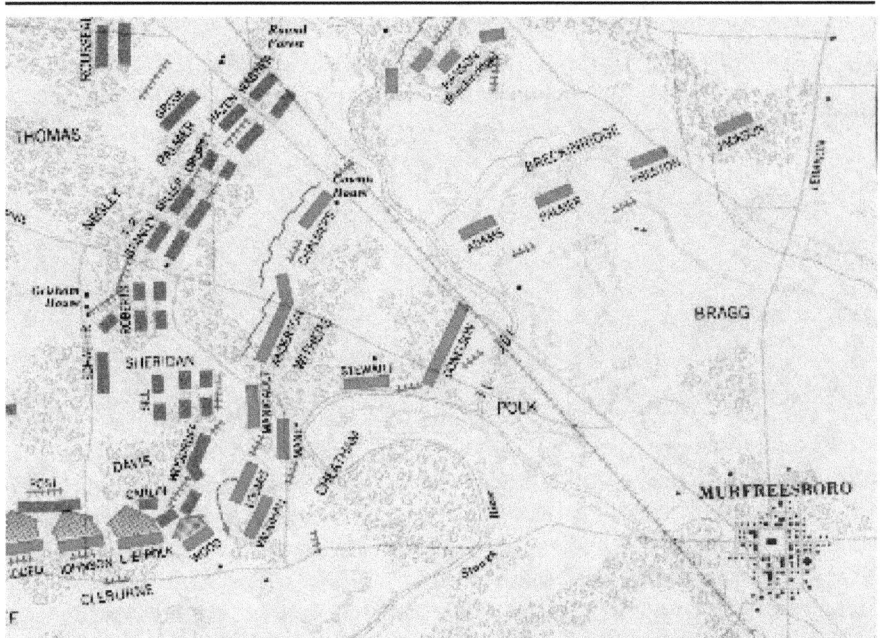

Murfreesboro, morning of December 31, 1862

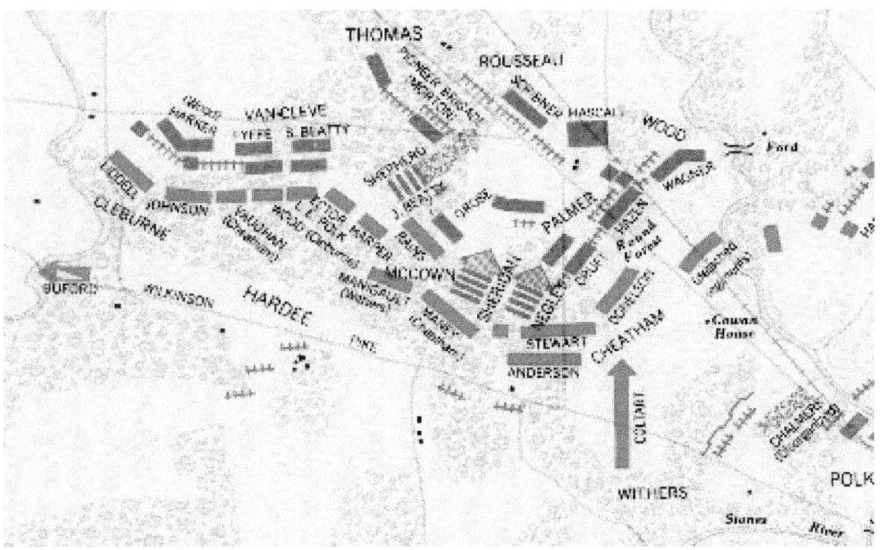

Murfreesboro, afternoon of December 31, 1862

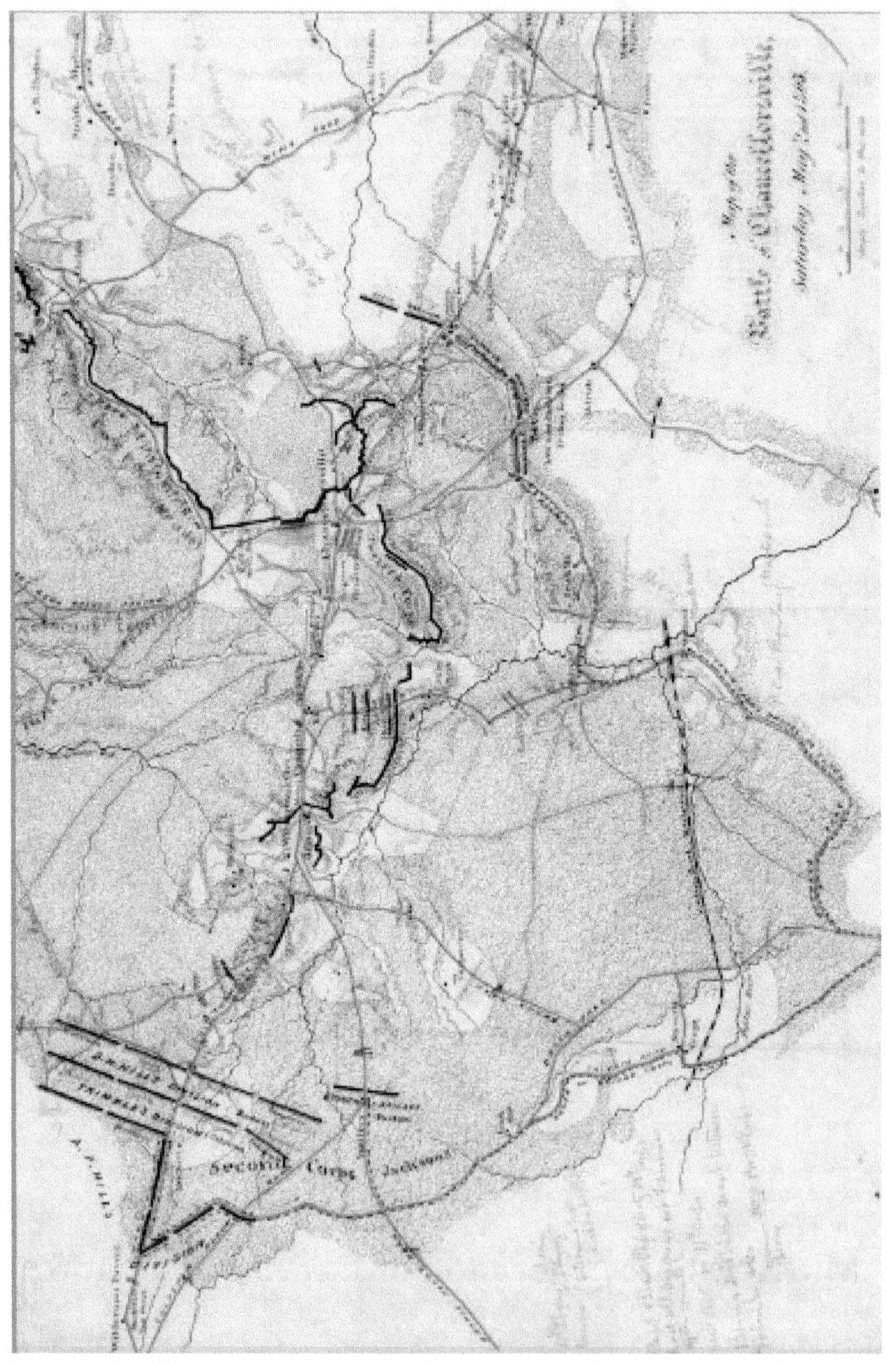

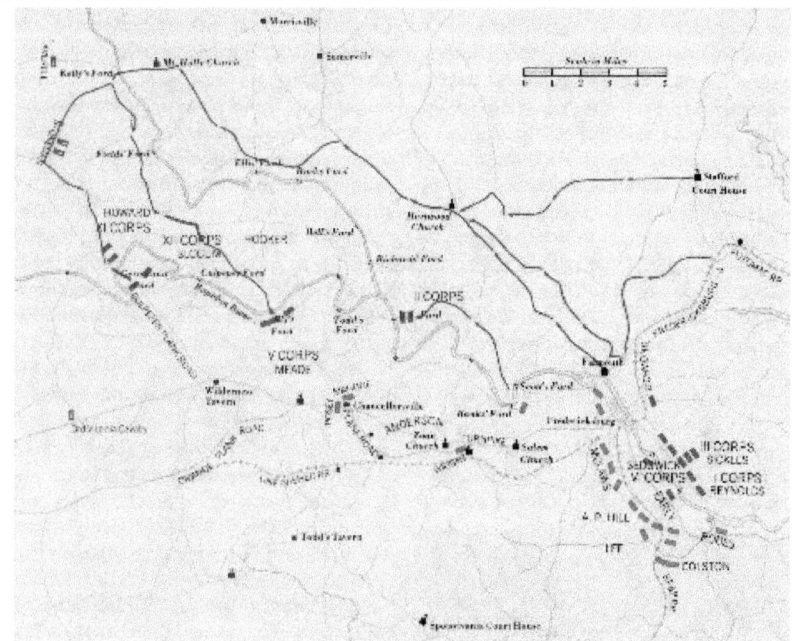

Chancellorsville, April 29, 1863

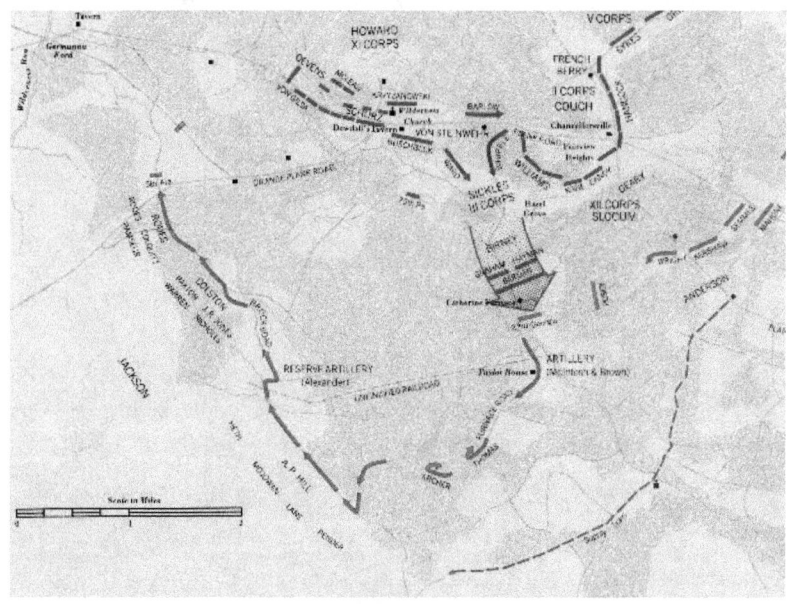

Chancellorsville, May 2, 1863

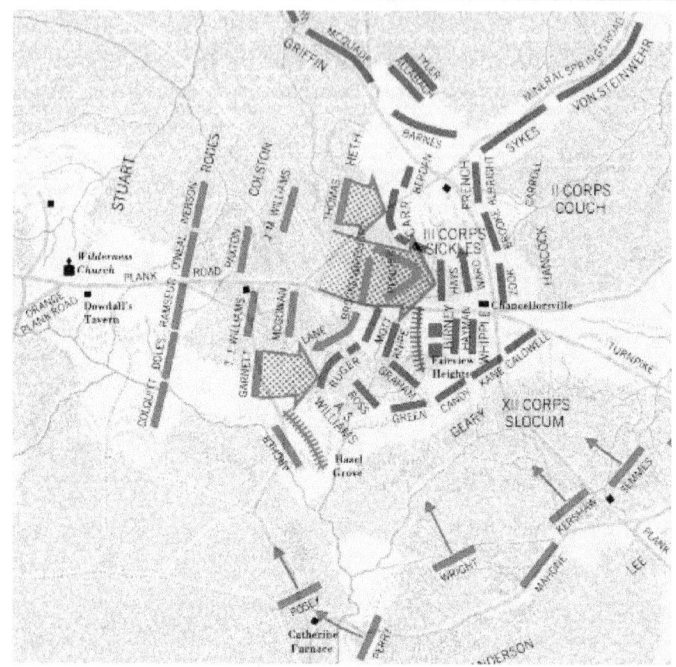

Chancellorsville, Morning of May 3, 1863

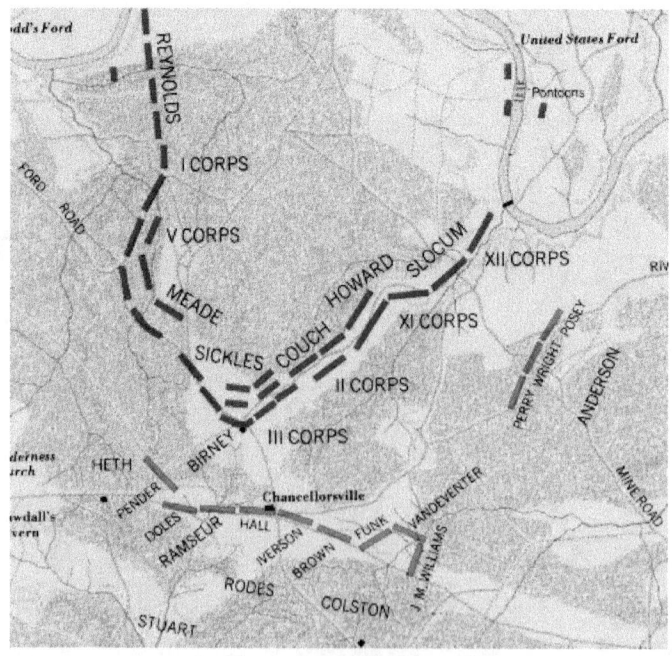

Chancellorsville, Afternoon of May 3, 1863

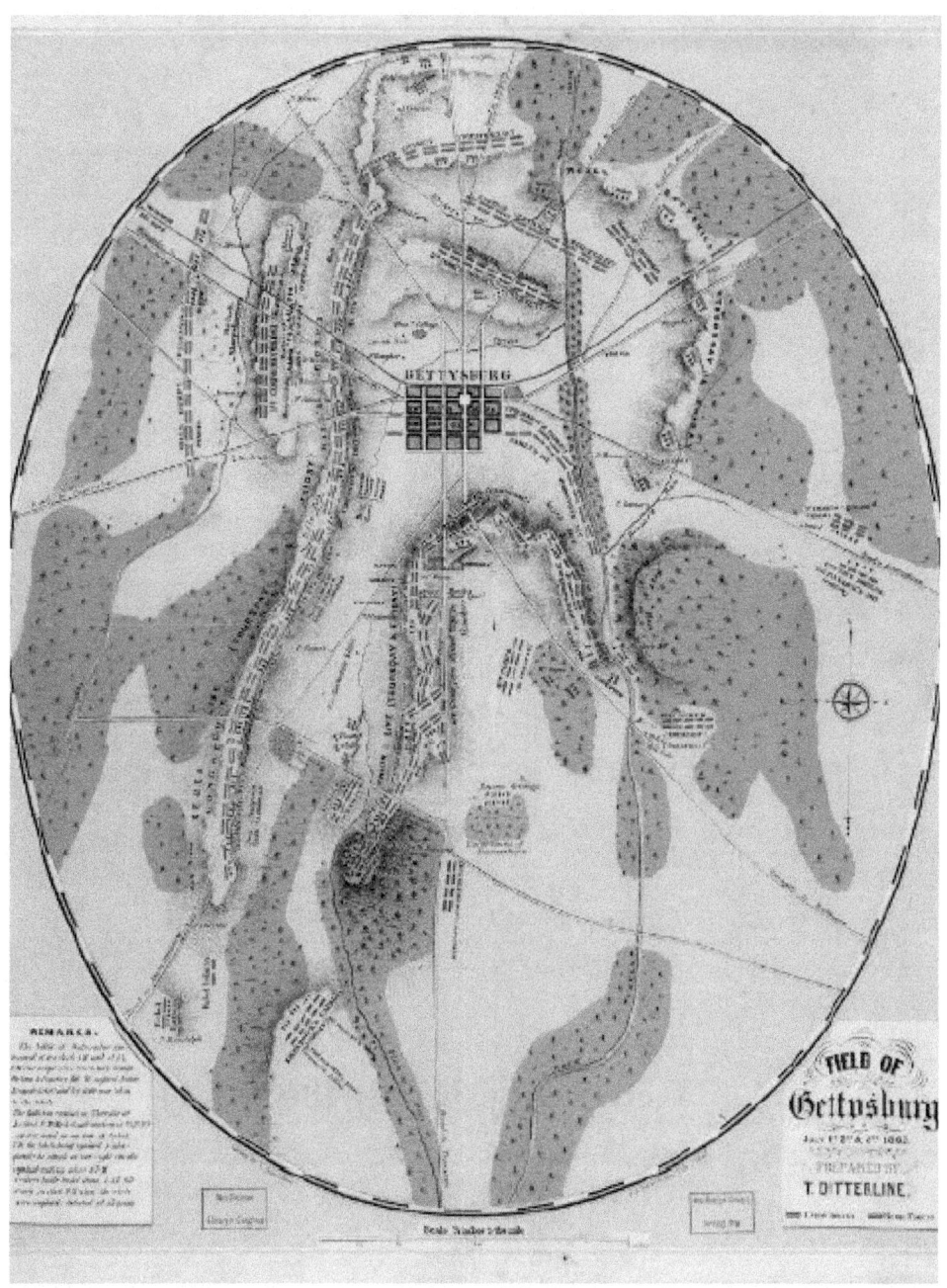

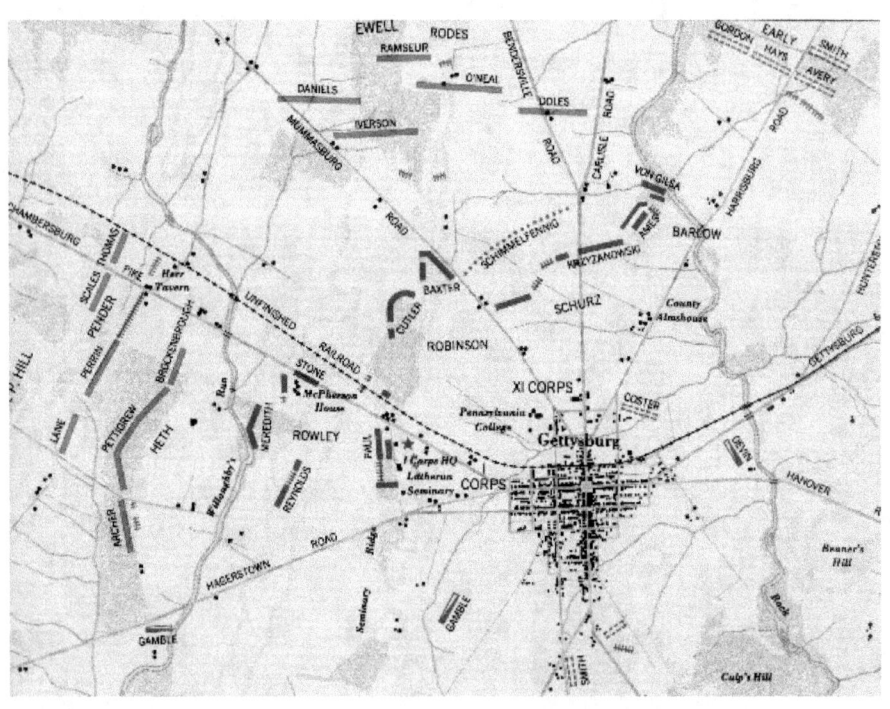

Gettysburg, July 1, 1863

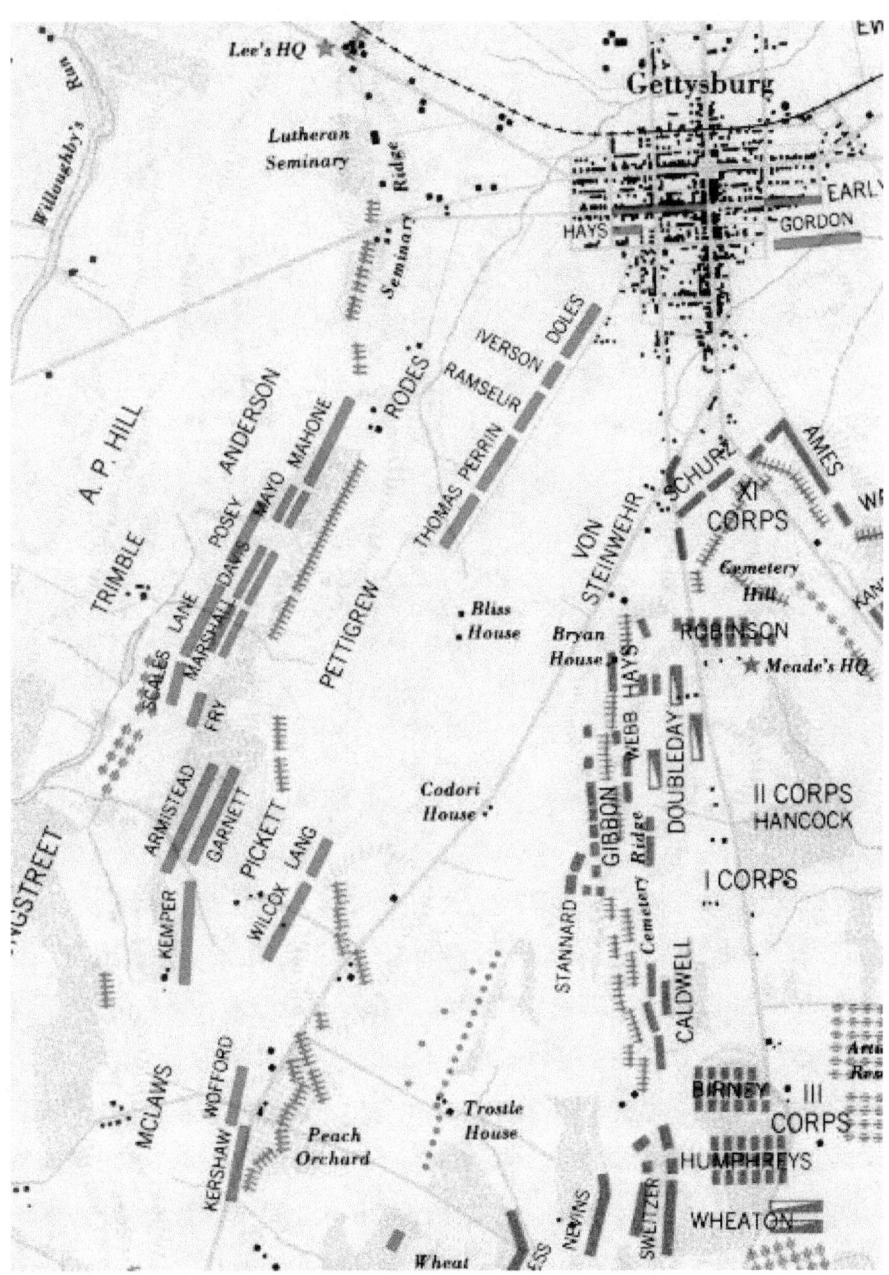

Gettysburg, July 3, 1863

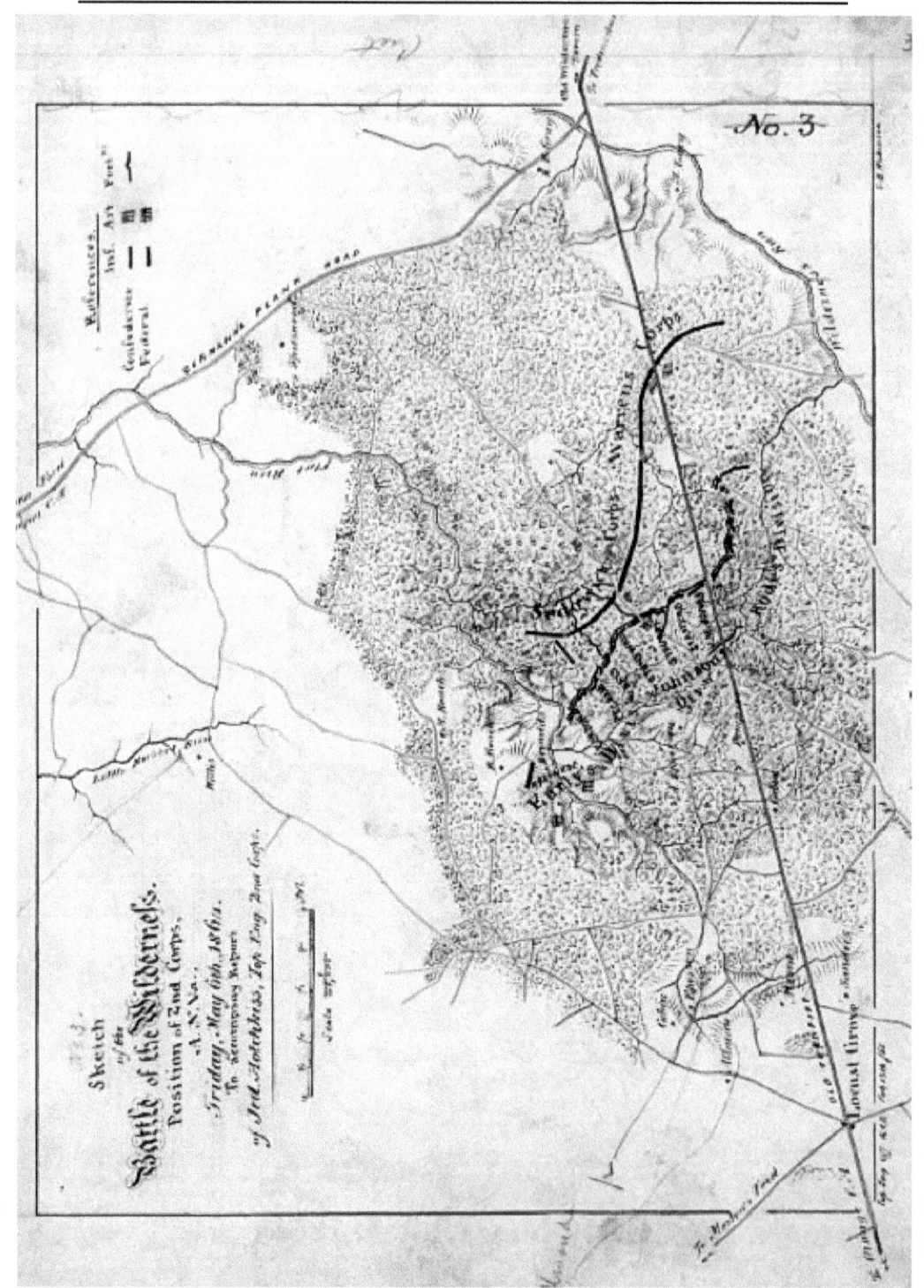

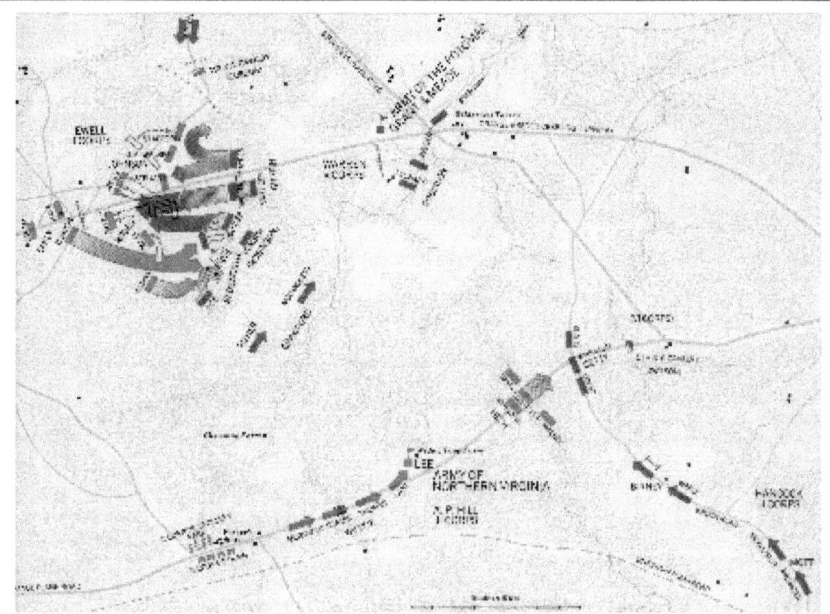

Wilderness, May 5, 1864, Afternoon-full battle

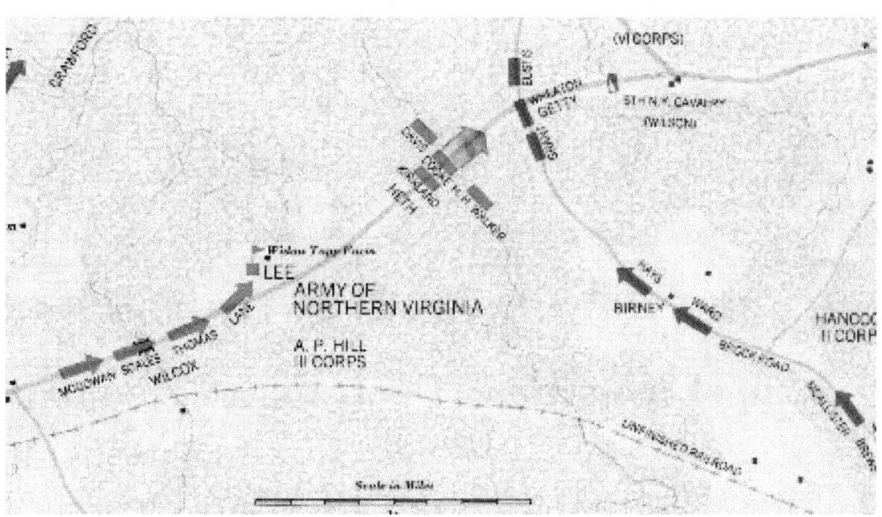

Wilderness, May 5, 1864, afternoon-Brock Road & Orange Plank Road

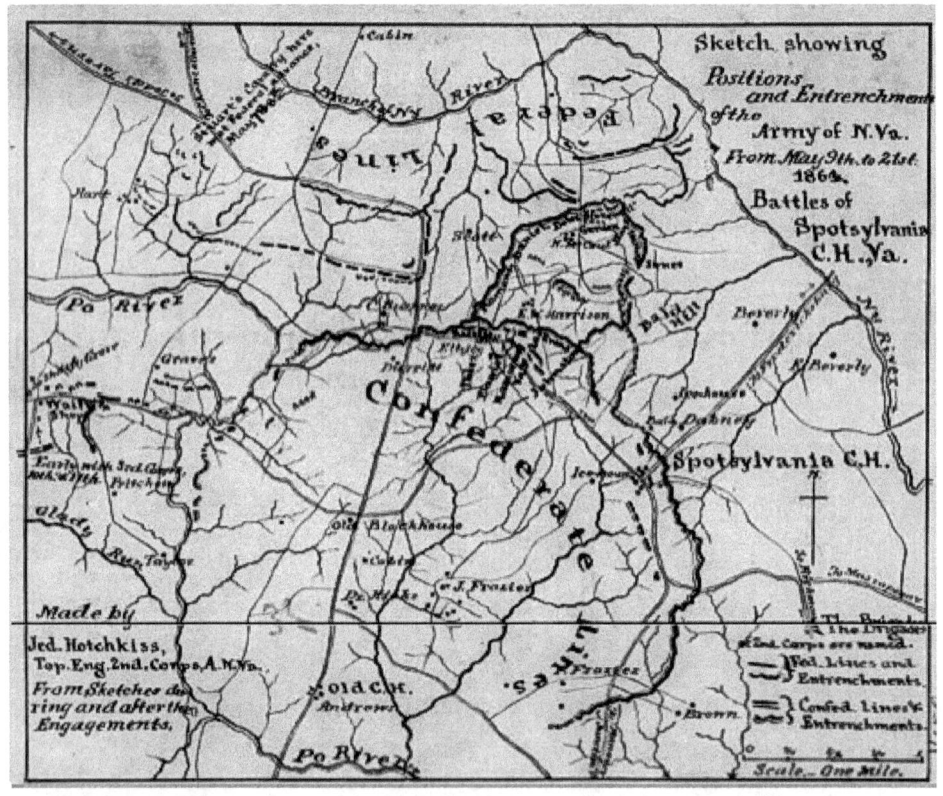

Maps of Spotsylvania Court House, Virginia (1864)

SKETCH SHOWING POSITIONS AND ENTRENCHMENTS OF THE
ARMY OF N. VA. FROM MAY 9th TO 21st 1964,
BATTLES OF SPOTSYLVANIA C.H., VA.

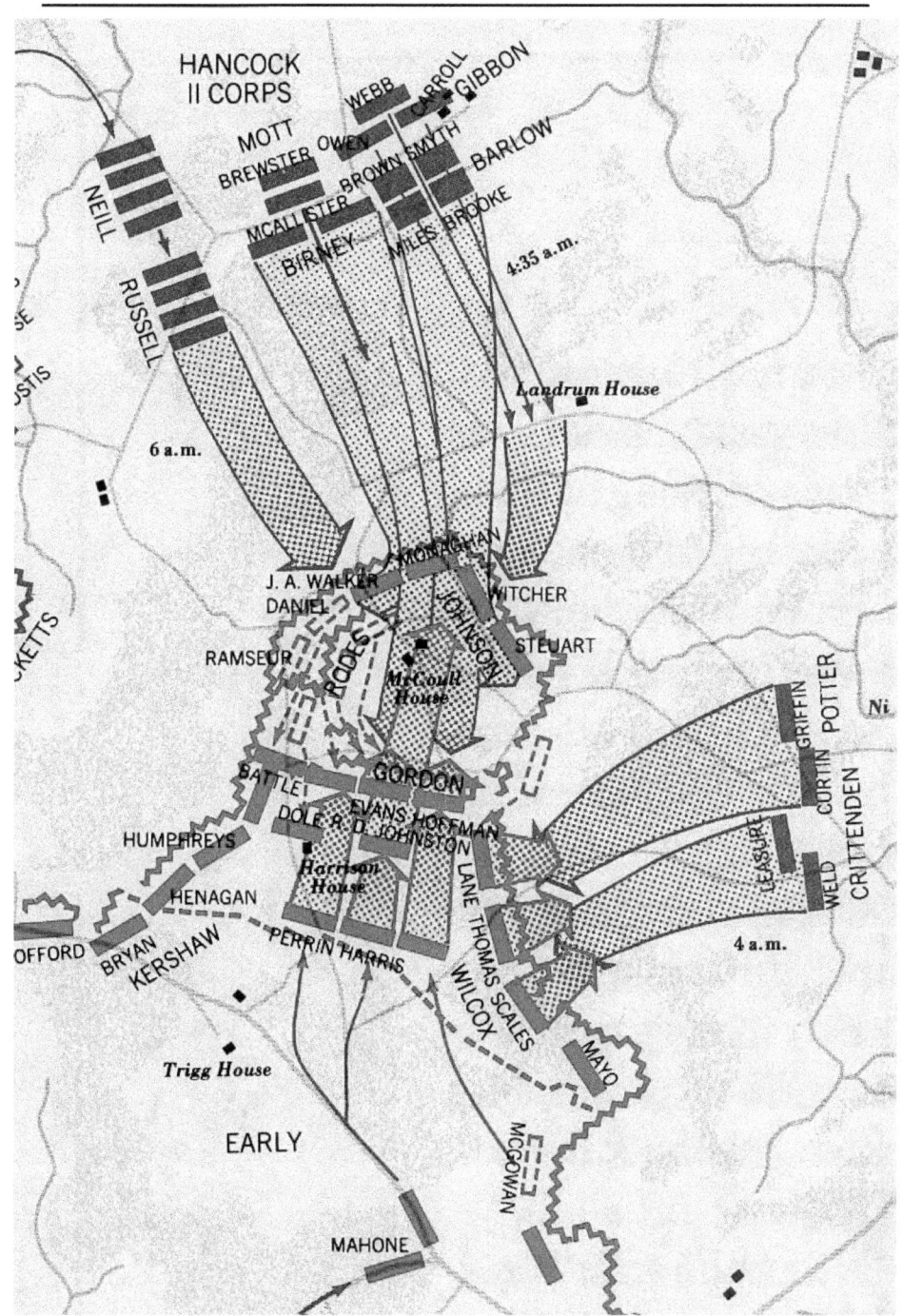

Spotsylvania Court House, May 12, 1864

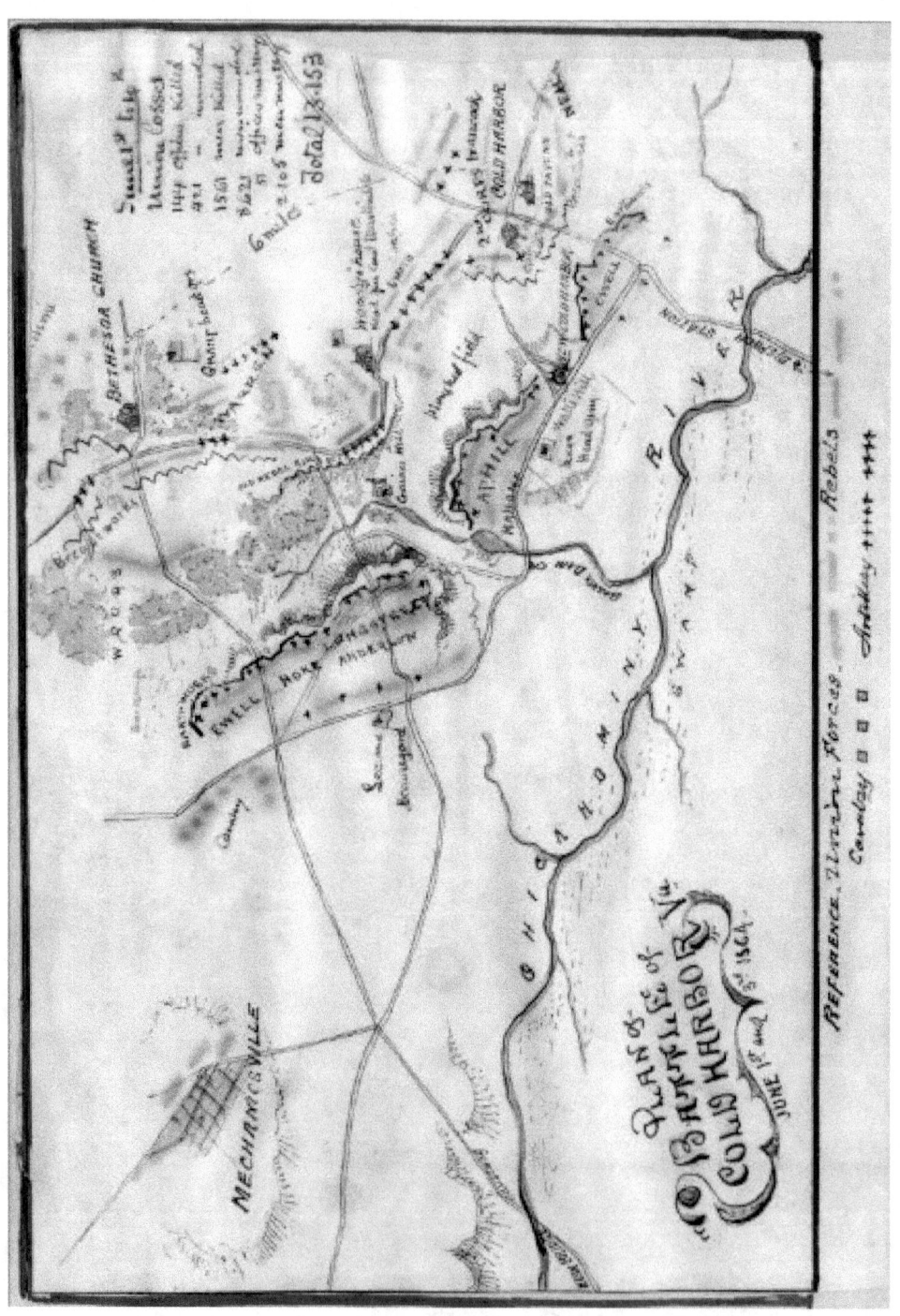

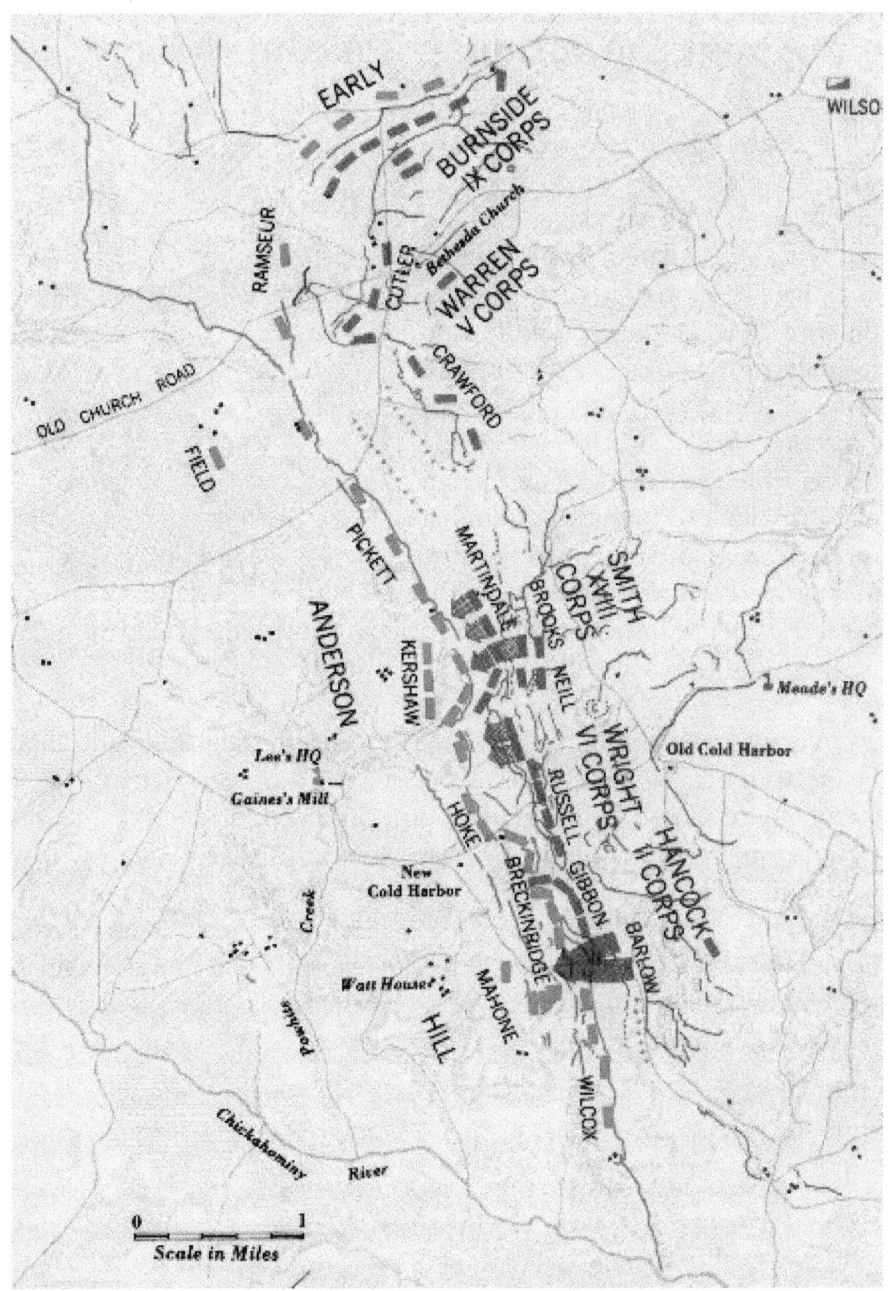

Cold Harbor, June 3, 1864

About the author—J. Arthur Moore

J. Arthur Moore is an educator with 42 years experience in public, private, and independent settings. He is also an amateur photographer and has illustrated his works with his own photographs. In addition to Journey into Darkness, Mr. Moore has written Blake's Story, Revenge and Forgiveness, a Civil War historic fiction set in the Kentucky Campaign of 1862; "Heir to Balmawr", a drama for his fifth grade students; a number of short pieces and short stories. His latest release, just prior to Blake's Story, is an earlier novel titled Summer of Two Worlds, set in Montana Territory in the summer of 1882.

A graduate of Jenkintown High School, just outside of Philadelphia, Pennsylvania, he attended West Chester State College, currently West Chester University. Upon graduation, he joined the Navy and was stationed in Norfolk, Virginia, where he met his wife to be, a widow with four children. Once discharged from the service, he moved to Coatesville, Pennsylvania, began his teaching career, married and brought his new family to live in a 300-year-old farm house in which the children grew up and married, went their own ways, raised their families to become grandparents themselves.

Retiring after a 42-year career, Mr. Moore has moved to the farming country in Lancaster County, Pennsylvania, where he plans to enjoy the generations of family, time with his model railroad, and time to guide his writings into a new life through publication. It also allows for the opportunity to participate in a local model railroad club as well as time for traveling to Civil War events and presenting at various organizations and events about the boys who were part of that war. He also shares the process of writing and readings from his work, and does book signings at a variety of locations.

Mr. Moore can be reached through the contact page of the website for his books at www.jarthurmoore.com with links to his Facebook and Twitter pages; and and a boys page focusing on the stories of the boys who served in the Civil War.

Comments from Readers and Reviewers

"It is with great pleasure to announce that you have been selected as a Book Excellence Award Winner for the following book and category: Book Title: Journey Into Darkness; Category: New Fiction (only published in 2016/2017) There were hundreds of entries from around the world and your book was selected for its high quality writing, design and market appeal." Book Excellence Awards

"I highly recommend this series of four historical novels. I believe that books such as these are an important way of preserving our national heritage and bringing it to life for the students in our schools. They can relate to the experiences and perspective of Duane Kinkade as he lives through the central event in our national history, the American Civil War." Paul Sanborn, historian, Freedoms Foundation, nominated for the Freedoms Foundation Award

"Congratulations! Freedoms Foundation at Valley Forge is pleased to inform you that you have been nominated and selected to receive Freedoms Foundation's National Award – The George Washington Honor Medal. Your book, "Journey Into Darkness," exemplifies the essence of the National Awards: promotion of an understanding and appreciation for our country's rich heritage, principles and unique freedoms." David Harmer, President and Chief Executive Officer, The Freedoms Foundation

"I have to tell you, I read the 4 books in 1 – Journey Into Darkness. I loved it! I'm not a history person at all and I could not put this book down! It is written really well and I loved learning about the Civil War from a child's perspective. As a mom I was crying learning and in my mind visualizing through your words what these young boys and men went through. It is just unbelievable. I'm actively looking now for similar books to read to learn more. Great job." Rachel Wetzel, Office Manager, Steam Into History

"One boy's experiences during the time of war from age 10 through 13 are told with the turn of each page. Experiencing sadness, grief, heartbreak, friendship, loneliness, value, worth, and pride, a boy journeys through one of the toughest times America has had to endure, in search of his father who had gone to war. He finds himself on both sides at times, Confederate and Union, not taking either side, just trying not to perish with so many others." Readers' Favorite 5-star review, Michelle Robertson, reviewer

Dear Mr. Moore, Journey Into Darkness is beautifully written and extremely moving. I rate this alongside Trinity and A Tale of Two Cities. Thank you for the sheer enjoyment of your story. Best wishes always, Katherine C. Lewis, reader

"I think you've done a magnificent work. Now that I see the books all together, I appreciate it even more. I'm enormously impressed. It's a moving, large scale and splendid story, and those remarkable photos really add a special dimension." Lloyd Alexander, author

"I found the series to be very interesting. I enjoyed the excitement and suspense and couldn't put it down. I just finished studying about the Civil War and found these books to be an excellent supplement to my studies. They were very historically accurate down to the smallest details. These books showed the harsh reality of the Civil War. They also showed the great sacrifices made by our countrymen so that we may enjoy the freedom we have today. I would really recommend this story to kids my age and to anyone who likes adventure and is interested in learning more about the Civil War." Isaac Sassa, age 14

"The second thing that grabs me is the attention to the five senses - it's an interesting way to write. Gives it more of a "you are there" feel than say a strict narrative history. Congratulations on a fine work." Matt Atkinson, National Battlefield Parks speaker

"Throughout Duane's quest the reader sees obstacles overcome, friendships forged, loyalties challenged, and life lessons learned, while at the same time a vivid history lesson is unfolding before your eyes. Not only is this story a startlingly detailed time line of major and minor events of the Civil War, but also a diary of a boy's commitment to find his father and who, in the process, finds himself." Charmaine Ball, reviewer

"This book does have a place in schools, I think it would be the perfect adjunct to a Civil War class. It also has a place in everyone's home library." Simon Barrett, Blog News Network

"Mr. Moore writes clearly, cleanly, and correctly, describing the conditions of the time and bringing his characters to life, characters who, with the exception of a band of vicious, lawless raiders, are admirable and likable. Parents and teachers who want students exposed to well-written, highly informed historical fiction can safely start them on this series." Douglas Winslow Cooper, PhD, reviewer

"Across the Valley to Darkness by J. Arthur Moore is a great book. It makes you feel like you are there, suffering in the snow as the boy crosses the mountains, and then hearing and feeling all the battle of Gettysburg. This is a really good book for youths and also for adults." Shirley Willard/Amazon reviewer

"a great book to read and learn about history at the same time. since it's one of my favorite subjects i enjoyed every second of reading this, it will draw you in and make you feel like you're living it. it's well written and very entertaining i recommend it." Ivy, reader/Amazon reviewer

"Gifted it to my dad because he loves books like these about and he says he loved it. I began by giving him the first book and he kept asking for the other ones, and now it's all he reads. So I would say Thank you J. Arthur for creating such an interesting and amazing book that keeps you drawn to the stories." Nessa, reader/Amason reviewer

"A really good read for anyone of any age. Many soldiers in the Civil War were only boys. This book lets the reader see the war through the eyes of one young soldier." Maraposa, reader/Amazon reviewer

"Foremost, I found Dee's adventures during the North/South conflict to be most engaging and must admit that although I am not one to be overly emotional about stories of young people's escapades in general and those about a bygone era in particular, more than once you managed to hook this 81-year old to the point of tears. Secondarily, I found your clever use of characterizations and vernacular of the time interwoven with your impressive knowledge of Civil War geography and chronology to keep the story line topical and relevant." Stan Stubb, reader